John Knox Laughton, Henry Reeve

Memoirs of the Life and Correspondence of Henry Reeve

by John Knox Laughton

John Knox Laughton, Henry Reeve

Memoirs of the Life and Correspondence of Henry Reeve
by John Knox Laughton

ISBN/EAN: 9783337094744

Printed in Europe, USA, Canada, Australia, Japan

Cover: Foto ©Raphael Reischuk / pixelio.de

More available books at **www.hansebooks.com**

MEMOIRS

OF THE

LIFE AND CORRESPONDENCE

OF

HENRY REEVE, C.B., D.C.L.

BY

JOHN KNOX LAUGHTON, M.A.

HONORARY FELLOW OF GONVILLE AND CAIUS COLLEGE, CAMBRIDGE
PROFESSOR OF MODERN HISTORY IN KING'S COLLEGE, LONDON

IN TWO VOLUMES

VOL. I.

LONGMANS, GREEN, AND CO.
39 PATERNOSTER ROW, LONDON
NEW YORK AND BOMBAY
1898

PREFACE

THE life of every man who attains distinction almost necessarily resolves itself into two divisions—the preparation and the fulfilment. In the biography of a man of action the interest lies mainly in the fulfilment; in the detailed examination of the methods by which success has been won, of the care, the prevision by which it has been secured; in the description of the success itself, whether in the contests of war or peace—in the broad battle-field of life. In the case of a man of letters it is different. Here the biography has comparatively little to do with the fulfilment, the record of which lies in the author's published works, whether they have appeared in the columns of a newspaper, the pages of a magazine, or between the boards of a volume. To repeat it would be to set forth a more or less complete edition of the man's writings. The biographer's task is rather to trace the origins of these writings—the sources from which they sprang, the fancies by which they were inspired, the conditions by which they were directed, the methods by which they were elaborated; the labour, the toil by which they have been produced; in a word, the preparation. More especially does this seem to be the case with a subject such as Henry Reeve, whose biography is here attempted; a man of most fertile and fecund pen, whose writings exercised a profound influence on social and political life, whose judgement and whose counsels had a large but unreported share in the decisions of Cabinets; a man who for upwards of sixty years, as Clerk of Appeals, Registrar of the Privy Council, as critic, leader-writer on the 'Times,' editor of the 'Edinburgh Review,' literary adviser of a great publishing firm, lived—if I may use the expression—with his fingers on the keys of public opinion, directing it, leading it, guiding it with a power which was none the less real because few recognised it or knew of it; none the less vast because he himself was not fully aware of it. To me, at least, the Life of Henry Reeve has the peculiar charm of opening out a clue to the solution of many vexed problems both in politics and in literature, and of throwing a light, often unexpected, on the history of the recent past. The intimate association of Reeve with the undercurrents of that history, though guessed at by many, was known by very few, was perhaps fully known by none.

On considering this, the inquiry into the way in which this man was prepared for the position he was to hold, the work he was to accomplish, seemed to me most interesting; and it was clear that, irrespective of the natural bent of his genius, the secret of it lay in the story of his education and early life. I had already given form to this idea, and had outlined the plan of the present work, when my attention was specially called to a few lines in his own short study of the life of one of the great pioneers of the revival of Western learning—Petrarch—where he says: 'The most pleasing form of biography is that in which a man retraces the events of his own life and the incidents that have formed his character, more especially in his earlier years, of which no other record might exist.' I had read this long before, and though I had no conscious recollection of it, it is still very possible that I had been guided by it. At any rate, I felt my hands strengthened by the assurance that the plan I had sketched out was one that Reeve himself would have approved of. It is thus that I have dwelt—or, more strictly speaking, have permitted him to dwell—at some length on the peculiar, or at least unusual, form of his education; on

his early associates and associations, on his life and intimacies in Paris, at a time when Parisian society still
retained much of its old brilliance and its old courtesies ;
when the world of intellect and art, of politics and of
fashion, still met on equal and familiar terms ; before
fashion was dominated by vulgar wealth, and politics were
sunk in the abyss of democracy ; when, as Disraeli recorded,
'throughout every circle of Parisian society there is a
sincere homage to intellect, and this without any maudlin
sentiment. None sooner than the Parisians can draw the
line between factitious notoriety and honest fame, or sooner
distinguish between the counterfeit celebrity and the standard reputation.'

To Reeve, young, clever, and aspiring, nothing could be
more wholesome than the freedom of this society ; and the
influence of his early initiation in the world of Paris is
strongly marked throughout his whole career. When afterwards settled in London as a Government servant and a
knight of the pen, his youthful training, his intimacy with
the leaders of Parisian thought and Parisian manners, and
his perfect knowledge of the language, all tended to push
him into an exceptional position, both socially and politically, while his acquaintance with many out-of-the-way
subjects of study—Bohemian and Polish history, for instance
—left him in readiness to take advantage of any exceptional
opportunity. It was thus that his services came to be used
by premiers and presidents of the Council in unofficial
embassies, with the idea, perhaps, that the soft answer
which turneth away wrath could sometimes be better conveyed, in the first instance, by a personal friend who was
known to be in the confidence of ministers, and yet without
any *locus standi*. This is what I have endeavoured to bring
into prominence in the following pages, the form of which
has necessarily been shaped by the nature of the materials
with which I had to work.

The record of the second quarter of the present century,

as set forth in ' The Greville Memoirs,' came as a revelation, perhaps even an unpleasant revelation, to many. Reeve, who, from his long intimacy with Greville, his social position, his manner of life, literary habit, and special training, was peculiarly fitted to be the editor of that very remarkable work, attempted nothing of the sort for himself. He was through all his life an exceedingly busy, hard-working man, who, though he found time to get through an enormous amount of work, to carry on a gigantic correspondence, and to mix freely and constantly in society, had no leisure for the keeping up of anything like a full journal. Had this been in his power, with equal opportunities and superior industry, he might have left a work equal in interest to that of Greville, however much it would have differed from it in the details of its construction. On that, however, it is useless to speculate. Long before he knew of the existence of Greville's ' Memoirs,' he himself recorded his opinion ' that to write a journal of any value a man must do nothing else ; ' and thus, with few exceptions, his own notes of occurrences were limited to scanty entries in a ' Letts's Diary '—entries which to himself would recall memories of events or conversations, but of themselves have now little meaning to anyone else. A few years before his death he amused himself, in dallying with the memories of the past, with transcribing some of these notes—adding occasional short comments—into a manuscript book which he entitled ' Chronology of My Life,' and this he continued almost to the end. Most commonly, the notes in this are the very barest indications of what he was doing, the places he visited, the people he saw, conversed with or dined with—all named in the curtest manner, the mere suggestion of a thought. It is only as giving such indications that they can be used ; interesting as showing the secret springs of his knowledge of passing events, but making—as a rule—no mention of ' the feast of reason and flow of soul ; ' of the conversations which he held, the anecdotes he heard, the opinions he discussed. The elucidation of these has to be sought elsewhere; and, with the exception of one more serious but abortive attempt to keep a journal (vol. i. p. 267)—such as an idle man with his opportunities might have kept—the 'elsewhere' is in the boxes filled with the letters which he received from his numerous friends and acquaintances. A very marked feature of these letters is their extremely confidential nature. Scarcely a name prominent in politics, literature, or society, in England or in France, is unrepresented in this voluminous correspondence, much of which, of a nature essentially private, it would be improper or unbecoming to give to the public. But the bulk of it is also prohibitive, and many letters of the greatest political or historical interest—letters, for instance, from Circourt, Rémusat, Geffcken, Guizot, Bunsen, Lord Stanmore, Meadows Taylor—have been necessarily omitted in deference to the exigencies of space. Similarly, I have been obliged to omit the long letters which he received, in great numbers, from Mrs. Grote, Lady Stanley of Alderley, Lady Dartrey, and others; chatty letters, charming in themselves, but which—after all—have little relation to the subject of the present work.

Of the other side of this correspondence—letters from Reeve to his friends—there is comparatively little. His letters to his mother and to Edwin Handley, the friend of his youth, are purely biographical, in the sense already referred to as laid down by Reeve himself in the short extract from his 'Petrarch.' So, also, are many of those to his wife. His letters to the Longmans range over a period of forty years—from the date of his becoming editor of the 'Edinburgh Review'—but are for the most part on matters of business, or of an extremely confidential character. For many years Reeve acted as adviser to the firm, and his formal reports were very frequently accompanied by a private note, in which the opinion was explained with an unguarded frankness which could not now be specified (vol. ii. p. 382).

It will be seen that his friendship with William, and more especially with Thomas, Longman dated back to the time when they were young men together at Hampstead (vol. i. p. 34), and that his intimacy with the family is one of Mr. Thomas Norton Longman's earliest recollections.

The letters to Tocqueville, extending over twenty-four years, were sent back to Reeve by Mme. de Tocqueville after her husband's death (vol. ii. p. 75). Several of them, however, as well as of those from Tocqueville to Reeve —who lent them for the purpose—were published in Gustave de Beaumont's ' Œuvres et Correspondance inédites d'Alexis de Tocqueville ' (1861), and it seemed unnecessary to repeat them, more especially as an English edition of the work was published at the same time under the supervision of Tocqueville's—and Reeve's—friend, Nassau Senior (vol. ii. p. 69), whose own correspondence with Tocqueville was published ten years later. A few semi-official letters to his early patron, the Marquis of Lansdowne, have been put at my disposal by the present marquis ; and some, of a more personal character, to Lord Brougham, by the present lord, Brougham's nephew. Lady Granville has most kindly lent me a few to her husband ; Miss Charlotte Dempster, those to her uncle ; Mr. Capel Cure, those to Mr. Edward Cheney ; and Lord Stanmore, one or two to himself, as well as privately printed copies of several to his father, Lord Aberdeen, written from Paris in January 1846 (vol. i. p. 177), in reference, for the most part, to the state of opinion there on the Oregon boundary dispute, then active between England and the United States. The sum of all these is, however, very small in comparison with the many thousands which must have been written, but have not been preserved or are not accessible. There are, doubtless, many which the owners would have been perfectly willing to lend had they been aware of the need for them. It is only since these pages have been in print that I have had from Captain Xavier Raymond the obliging offer of a considerable number of letters to his father, and have been under the painful necessity of declining it, as coming too late. I shall probably, before long, feel a like regret on hearing of other and similar collections.

Few as they are, however, these letters of Reeve's are the most interesting contributions to the biography, considered strictly as such. The later ones—to Brougham, Cheney, or Dempster—speak for themselves; the earlier, to his mother and to Handley, are the more purely personal; and it is to them that we must look for the presentation of the developement of mind and character. We have in them the opinions of a very young man, often incorrect, often the evident repetition of what he heard, but delivered with the unhesitating conviction of one-and-twenty. In his judgements of men and things there is no uncertainty. M. Thiers, for instance, joins 'excessive arrogance' to 'excessive versatility,' and wins high position in the State by want of principle and by perfidy (vol. i. p. 64). It does not appear that when he thus wrote he had ever seen Thiers, or had any knowledge of him except the current gossip of his associates; in later life, his personal relations with Thiers were cordial, though with Thiers's politics he never agreed. Similarly, Victor Hugo is described (vol. i. p. 36) as 'so mad, so childish, and so blackguard that all his acquaintance have cut him.' It is the mere repetition of hearsay. 'I saw him,' he wrote, 'at the Bibliothèque du Roi, but did not care to renew our acquaintance.' Whether he ever did renew it is doubtful. I am inclined to think that he did not; but he certainly would not have described the poet and politician in this manner fifteen or twenty years later, when Hugo's eccentricities of character were more fully developed. So, again, as to his remarks, at the age of nineteen, on Germany and the Germans (vol. i. p. 29). He has conceived, he says, a positive dislike for Germany, ' because it is the only country where one does not find the vulgar virtues which oil the wheels of life. It is the land which has in it the least noble and generous feeling, and perhaps the least truth, in all Europe.'   And the people—'the Germans are the most uninteresting nation in the world . . . their ideas lie bed-ridden in their brains, and when they come out in words they stumble about most clumsily.'   Forgetting the writer's age, this might be thought splenetic : remembering it and the conditions under which these sentences were written, we understand them as the manifestation of home-sickness and the expression of ' his erroneous opinions on things of which he knew but little ' (vol. i. p. 21).

It is well to call attention to this, or the crude, though positive, assertions of youth might be repeated as the sober judgements of maturity.   The quickness with which his intellectual powers reached their maturity is, however, very remarkable, and is admirably brought out by his familiar letters.   Unquestionably a leading factor in this rapid developement was the distinguished society into which he was early thrown.   Of the singularity of this he was himself well aware.   It will be noticed that in his letters to his mother he frequently refers to it, as, for instance (vol. i. p. 109)—' It is strange that at twenty-six I should find myself on terms of acquaintance with the whole Cabinet, except Lord Melbourne and Baring.'   But all this appears in the correspondence itself—in words, in hints, in allusions, or concealed ' between the lines ; ' and is emphasised by the mention of the people of rank—the social, professional, or intellectual aristocracy—with whom he was familiarly associating.   This is to me, as I think it will be to others, the meaning of the bald entries, in the ' Chronology,' of dinner parties or receptions, some of which I have reproduced in the crude, unconventional words of the original. It would have been easy to quote the names with the titles to which society is accustomed, or to expand the notes in the manner of a journalist dealing with a telegram from India or Australia ; but this would have conveyed a very false impression of the extreme ruggedness of the material. To Reeve, when, at the age of seventy-five or more, he transcribed these notes, they no doubt called up many memories of the past. To us they can but indicate the framework which supported and rendered possible a very remarkable, a very exceptional individuality.

As has been said, the place of the conversations, the actual intercourse, the experiences which in life filled in this framework, is here supplied by the letters of the men who spoke; letters which have thus a direct biographical interest, independent of the very great interest which they have as comments on the events of the day, now passed into history. These letters now printed are merely a small selection, in making which I have been mainly guided by a desire to elucidate the character and career of my subject, though also, in a great, if secondary degree, by the intrinsic interest of the letters themselves. When Clarendon discourses of the state of Ireland in 1848, or of Europe in 1853-4; when Guizot or St.-Hilaire, or the Comte de Paris, discusses the politics of France at any time during the last half-century, the letters have an interest far beyond that attaching to the career of any one man, however eminent.

A word must be said as to the language of the letters. Reeve's correspondents for the most part wrote to him in their own language, English, French, or German. His Polish and Russian friends wrote in French. Circourt alone, of Frenchmen; Bunsen, Geffcken, and Vitzthum, of Germans, wrote in English. Guizot, Tocqueville, St.-Hilaire, the Duc d'Aumale, the Comte de Paris and others, who certainly spoke English fluently, all habitually wrote in French, though some of them—more especially Guizot—were fond of larding their letters with English words or phrases, in the same way that Lord Clarendon and others of Reeve's English correspondents, and indeed Reeve himself, in his youth, larded theirs with French. The Queen of Holland, at one time a frequent correspondent of Reeve's, wrote in

English or French, as the humour seized her. These letters are now for the most part translated. It would, of course, have been easier, and, from some points of view, preferable to give them in the original French; but, on full consideration, I thought it better that the text of an English book should be mainly in English. The exceptions I have made are where the subject is purely social, and the interest of the letter lies in its manner rather than in its matter; and, again, as to some of the letters from the Comte de Paris, where I felt that it was more prudent and infinitely more interesting to quote the *ipsissima verba* of the original.

All the letters now printed are published with the consent of the several writers or their representatives, to whom my best thanks are due for a permission that it would, sometimes at least, have been easier to refuse. More especially is this the case with the letters of the Comte de Paris, which have all been submitted to the consideration of his son, the Duc d'Orléans, and with the numerous letters of the Earl of Clarendon, which have been examined by the present Earl and his brother, the Hon. Francis Villiers, to whom I am further indebted for valuable assistance in clearing up doubtful allusions. Sir Thomas Sanderson has similarly assisted me in editing the letters of the Earl of Derby, and the Hon. Mrs. Nash with those of her father, Lord Westbury, some of which, already published in the 'Life of Lord Westbury,' I am now permitted to reprint. To all others who have encouraged or assisted me with permission or advice, whose numbers render nominal mention impossible, I tender my sincere thanks. But most especially am I indebted to Mrs. Ogilvie and Mrs. Reeve, to whose neverfailing kindness and assistance any merit that the editorial work may be thought to have is almost entirely due.

J. K. L.

September, 1898.

CONTENTS

OF

THE FIRST VOLUME

LIFE AND CORRESPONDENCE

OF

HENRY REEVE

CHAPTER I

BOYHOOD

IT has often been remarked that literary talent is more commonly inherited from the mother than from the father. To this rule the subject of the present memoir was no exception; for, though his father had shown some ability as a writer, before his professional duties prevented its further cultivation and an early death put an abrupt end to it, he stood absolutely alone among his kinsfolk, whose energies do not seem to have led them beyond the limits of their everyday occupations. The family had been settled for many generations in Essex, and especially in the neighbourhood of Maldon, where, in the end of last century, Abraham Reeve owned some corn mills, and in the course of an industrious life amassed a considerable fortune, estimated at not less than 100,000*l*. During the latter part of his life he lived at Hadleigh, in Suffolk, where he died at the age of 86, in 1826. In or about 1776 he married Elizabeth, daughter of the Rev. Job Wallace, D.D., rector of Messing, and had by her five sons—Charles Abraham, Henry, George, who died young, Edward, who served for some time in the West Suffolk Militia, and Thomas, rector of Raydon. Mrs. Abraham Reeve was of the same age as her husband, and died in less than a fortnight after him.

Henry, the second son, was born in 1780, and having shown some fondness for study as a schoolboy, was, according to the traditions of both his father's and mother's families, destined for the medical profession. At the age of sixteen he was sent to Norwich, and placed under the care of

Mr. Philip Meadows Martineau, then well known in the
eastern counties as a skilful surgeon and physician. Having
served with Mr. Martineau for four years, he went to the
University of Edinburgh, where, in 1803, he graduated as
M.D. He was thus, at this early period, thrown into a
particularly brilliant set of young men, including Francis
Horner, Henry Brougham, Sydney Smith, Charles and
Robert Grant, Jeffrey, Cockburn, and several others, whose
names were afterwards familiarly known in the world of
literature or politics. Naturally, then, he drifted towards
literature, and was one of the early contributors to the
'Edinburgh Review.' The article on Pinel's 'Treatment of
the Insane,' in the third number, is specifically mentioned as
his; but whether it was his first or not is not stated. On
professional subjects he wrote frequently in the 'Edinburgh
Medical Journal,' and for his degree wrote a thesis in Latin,
'De animalibus in hyeme sopitis,' which he afterwards ex-
panded into an essay, published in 1809, on the Torpidity of
Animals. On taking his degree he went to London to
continue his studies, and in the spring of 1805 set out for
Switzerland, in company with a young Genevese, Dr. de
Roches, who had been his fellow-student and most intimate
friend at Edinburgh. At Neuchâtel he remained for several
months perfecting himself in French; afterwards he went
on to Vienna, where he studied medicine, watched the course
of public events, and kept a Journal, which was published by
his son some seventy years later.[1] On his return to England
he settled down at Norwich to practise as a physician, and
in September 1807 married Susanna Taylor, a relation of
Martineau's, with whose family he had been intimate from
his first coming to Norwich in 1796.

The Taylors' was one of those families which, in the end
of the eighteenth and the beginning of the nineteenth
century, gave Norwich a distinct reputation as one of the
most intellectual of our provincial towns. Originally
belonging to Lancashire, Dr. John Taylor, a Presbyterian
minister, had, in 1733, accepted a call to Norwich, where his
son Richard married Margaret, daughter of Philip Meadows,
Mayor of Norwich in 1734, and had a large family. John,
Richard's second son, married Susanna Cook, a very
remarkable woman, who combined highly cultivated tastes
with a sound practical capacity—' a handsome and gifted
woman, whose energetic character and liberal opinions,

---

[1] *Journal of a Residence at Vienna and Berlin in the eventful Winter of
1805-6.* By the late Henry Reeve, M.D. 8vo. 1877.

joined with great kindness of heart, made her a centre of the circle of remarkable people who frequented the provincial Athens.' She is described as 'darning her boys' grey worsted stockings while holding her own with Southey, Brougham or Mackintosh.'[1]

Her younger daughter, Sarah, married John Austin, known as a writer on jurisprudence, and was herself afterwards well known by her literary work. The elder daughter, Susanna, who was born in 1788, married Dr. Henry Reeve, and made him the father of three children : Susan, who died at the age of five, in April 1814; Wallace, who died, aged four, in April 1815; and Henry, born on September 9th, 1813. Dr. Reeve appears to have been constitutionally delicate, and to have been already in failing health, when the death of his children gave him a shock which proved fatal. He died at Hadleigh on September 27th, 1815, and was buried there in the family vault in the chancel of the church. The widow, having thus lost her husband and two children in one year, was left, at the age of twenty-seven, with one delicate little boy—the subject of the present memoir—and an income of about 500*l.* a year, 100*l.* of which was derived from the rent of the house at All Saints' Green, in which her married life had been passed ; she, with her boy, now moving to a smaller house in St. Martin's Street, with a garden nearly adjoining that of the Bishop, who showed them 'the greatest kindness.' The incidents of the boy's early life may best be told in the language of the Journal.

1817.—The first event of which I have a clear recollection is the death of the Princess Charlotte, on November 4th, 1817. We were staying with a cousin of my mother's, Mrs. de Pontigny, on Tower Hill. Mrs. John Martineau came in, pale, to announce the calamity, and the great bell of St. Paul's tolled.

We afterwards went to stay at Stoke Newington, with Mrs. Barbauld, who had a particular regard for my mother. I remember her slight graceful figure, and Dr. Aikin's scratch-wig ; also the winter flowers in the garden. Mrs. Barbauld said, 'Can this child read?' and, as in fact I could read very little, she used to read stories to me, to give me, she said, the love of reading. 'Atalanta,' 'Midas,'

---

[1] *Three Generations of English Women.* By Janet Ross.

and other tales were read to me from the MS., and I think written for me. I still recall the whisper, like the whisper in the bulrushes, in which she said, ' Midas has ass's ears.'

1818.—I was very much petted by my grandfather Taylor and my aunt Sally Taylor, afterwards Mrs. Austin; but I was not an amiable child—excessively passionate, and extremely averse to the spelling book and the Latin grammar. The summer, or part of it, was spent at Cromer, where I began to ride a donkey. In the autumn I was sent to a small day school, where Mr. Drummond, an old Unitarian minister, taught a few boys, and I began Latin in earnest.

1819.—I continued at Mr. Drummond's school.

The chief event of the year, to me, was Mrs. Austin's marriage, for she had always been my kindest and dearest friend. My other friends were John and Kate Taylor, children of my uncle Edward Taylor, somewhat older than myself; and Enfield and Eliza Barron, who lived opposite to our house in St. Martin's Street, Norwich.

1820.—A journey to Switzerland in 1820 for a lady and a child was a serious undertaking, and great were the consultations that preceded it. My mother took with her no maid, but a sort of companion or *bonne* to look after me. The object of the journey was to visit M. and Mme. de Roches. He had been my father's friend at Edinburgh, and between his wife and my mother a correspondence had sprung up. My mother had never seen either of them.

We started in June, crossing from Dover to Calais in three hours in a sailing packet—there were as yet no steamers—and we proceeded in the cabriolet of the diligence to Paris, in forty-eight hours, by Abbeville and Beauvais. I well remember the unpleasantness of that journey. At Paris we lodged at the Grand Hôtel de Charlemagne, Place Royale, in the Marais, to be near Mrs. de Pontigny, who was now living there, over the archway into the old Place.

From that archway I saw the procession of the Fête Dieu, and the Reposoir in the square. The three Duchesses of Angoulême, Berri, and Orleans walked in the procession. It was remarked that they were dressed respectively in red, white, and blue. Women brought infants to the Reposoir to have their hands touched with the Pyx. We went to Mass at the chapel of the Tuileries to see the king. He did not appear, but 'Monsieur' (afterwards Charles X.) did. Louis XVIII. reviewed the troops in the Carrousel from the central balcony. He was dressed in black velvet, with the blue cordon of the Saint Esprit.

The Jardin des Plantes delighted me, and I remember some of the pictures in the Louvre.

We drove from Paris to Geneva in a berline with three horses, same all the way. Edward St. Aubyn and a young brother and a doctor had the other seats. I think we were nine days on the road, sleeping at Fontainebleau, Sens, Auxerre, Joigny, Dijon, Poligny, &c. How well I remember these sleeping places, and the French country inns; and Antoine the driver, who was a fierce Bonapartist, and rather won my mother's heart; and the first view of the Lake of Geneva from the Jura! We drove safe at last into the courtyard of Malagnou.

We stayed at Geneva three months till the first snow had touched the mountains. Went the *tour du lac* and called at Coppet. Mme. de Staël was not there; but we found Miss Randall, whom my mother knew in Norfolk. My mother went to Chamonix. I did not. She was a good and bold rider and did great part of this tour on horseback. The St. Aubyns were living at Plongeon, and there, for the first time in my life, I went out to dinner.

My portrait was painted at Geneva by M. Massot, and is still in my possession.

We returned in October or November by way of Lyons, and I remember meeting Miss Edgeworth at the table d'hôte. The journey of seventy hours in a diligence from Lyons to Paris was excessively tedious. I remember that, in coming home, the packet was a whole day crossing from Calais to Dover.

During our stay in Paris, Mme. André and M. Pictet, a banker, were kind to us, and I was taken to the Français to see Talma and the Duchesnois in Ducis' 'Marie Stuart.'

It was my first play; and I have still before my eyes Leicester in his brown velvet cloak, and the dignified adieux of Marie. By this time I could speak French pretty well, and when I got home I was fond of reciting passages from ' Marie Stuart,' to the great amusement of my kinsfolk.

1821.—In this year I went to the Norwich School, Rev. Edward Valpy master; an accomplished scholar and gentleman, full of enthusiasm for the classics, which he had taught all his life. I was rather a favourite with him; but my boyhood was not a happy part of my life. I disliked the drudgery of school and cared nothing for its rewards. I took no part in the games of the school. My own amusements were riding my grandfather's pony, boating, and chemical experiments. This relates, however, to a somewhat later period.

In the summer of this year Lucy Austin, afterwards Lady Duff Gordon, was born.[1] They lived in Queen's Square, Westminster, hard by Mr. Bentham's garden and James Mill's house. My mother went there to be near her sister in her confinement, and I contracted an intimacy with our neighbours, the young Mills. We had been out of England during the Queen's trial in the preceding year; but I remember seeing Caroline drive past Hyde Park Corner, in a pink bonnet, with Alderman Wood by her side. John Mill[2] was with me at the time.

Living in Westminster, we were in the midst of the preparations for the coronation of George IV. I was taken to a gallery to see the procession pass from the Abbey to the Hall, and a very magnificent spectacle it was. The king wore his crown.

Later in the year the Austins came into Norfolk, and I was with them at Cromer. Whilst there, I read the ' Arabian Nights ' with great delight.

1822.—It must have been this year that I spent the summer holiday with the Austins at Yarmouth and Cromer. They had John Mill with them. He and I went to collect seaweeds, dry them, and Mill knew their names.

---

[1] Cf. Mrs. Ross's *Three Generations of English Women*.

[2] John Stuart Mill, born in 1806, was a boy of fifteen, and must have seemed quite grown up to a child not yet eight.

1823.—My grandmother, Mrs. John Taylor, died—a very remarkable woman ; as energetic as Mme. Roland, whom in some respects she resembled.

1824.—My mother and Emily Taylor went to Ireland. I declined to go, and spent the summer at Coltishall, in Norfolk, with my old nurse, Esther Fuller, who had married a baker there.

1825.—My mother had a serious illness in the early part of the year, and was sent to Cheltenham in March to take the waters, which cured her. Meanwhile—that is, from March to June—I was sent to board at Valpy's. In the holidays I joined my mother and Emily Taylor at Cheltenham. We went down the Wye from Ross to Monmouth and Chepstow, and thence to stay with the Philip Taylors at Aberdare in North Wales. Then posted by Ludlow and Shrewsbury to Coed Ddu (John Taylor's)[1] in North Wales. Then to Liverpool, to stay with Mr. Roscoe.

1826.—My grandfather, Abraham Reeve, died about the close of this year. After his death two farms at Copdock and Washbrook, in Suffolk, came to me under the will of Jordan Harris Lisle. They were worth about 140l. a year. The sum of 6,000l., settled on my father at his marriage, was paid over to the trustees and invested in the New Three per Cents., where it remained till 1876.

A letter from Henry Reeve to his mother, dated January 1st, 1827, giving an account of the funeral at Hadleigh, is noteworthy for the excellence of the handwriting, the straightness of the lines—which, however, may have been guided—and especially for the manly tone so little to be expected from a boy only just turned thirteen, but partly explained by his account of his reading during the following year.

1827.—I was near the top of the Norwich School, when my mother judged it right to take me away and place me to read with the Rev. Frank Howes,[2] as a tutor. Edmund Nelson Rolfe read with me ; Philip Wodehouse, afterwards Governor of the Cape and Bombay, was there too. Howes

---

[1] Mrs. Reeve's eldest brother.
[2] He graduated at Cambridge as eleventh wrangler, in 1798. In 1815 he was appointed to a minor canonry at Norwich, where he died in 1844.

was a most accurate scholar and deserved more success in life than he obtained. He published an excellent translation of Persius. I read with him Porson's four Greek plays and some others—a good deal of Cicero and Horace.

I had access to two good public libraries in Norwich, and from an early age read largely—much more than I remembered; but I had an insatiable appetite for books. I remember reading about this time Mitford's 'Greece,' a good deal of Gibbon, the 'Edinburgh Review' constantly, Scott, Byron, Cowper, Cook's 'Voyages,' Shakespeare, Hume, Lingard, Thomson's 'Chemistry.' The little I know of physical science was acquired at this time. We were fond of chemical experiments, and constructed an electrical machine, with which I remember we gave some lectures on electricity to our young friends.

I conceived at this age a decided preference for the services of the Church of England, and attended them, whenever I could, in preference to the Octagon Chapel [Unitarian].

1828.—The plan of my education was that I should spend two or three years in Geneva, begin the study of medicine there, and then go to Edinburgh to follow in my father's steps. The medical scheme entirely failed, as I felt no confidence in that profession. But to Geneva I went.

We left Norwich in the spring, selling or packing up books and furniture, and crossed from London to Havre; drove along the Seine to Paris; stayed there in the Rue de l'Échiquier, to be near my uncle Philip Taylor; saw and knew Jean-Baptiste Say, and reached Geneva in the autumn. An apartment was hired in the Grand Mezel, overlooking the Corraterie, and furnished by us.

In November I was entered at the Auditoire as a student in Belles Lettres. The range of classics was much below what I was used to in England; but I learned French by taking notes, and especially by the admirable private lessons I had from M. F. Roget, who gave me a taste for the French language and literature. I had no talent at all for mathematics, but Professor Pascalis did for me all that it was possible to do for so hopeless a subject.

A letter from Mrs. Reeve to her cousin Mary Taylor, written about a fortnight after her arrival in Geneva, is interesting, not only as showing the manner of life she proposed to lead, and the course of education and instruction she was outlining for her boy, but, and perhaps still more, for the glimpses which it gives of her own character, and of the influences under which the child had grown into a boy, and the boy was to grow into a man. It is very long; but much of it is mere friendly chit-chat, for at that time the postage of a single letter from Geneva to England was 2*s.* 3*d.*, and a thrifty housewife made it a point of conscience to send as much as possible for the money. It is dated vaguely 'September 1828;' with a supplementary note 'Finished September 30th.' It would appear to have taken about a week in the writing.

MY DEAR COUSIN,— . . . As to the affair of hiring house and servants, and procuring furniture, my task is far advanced, and will soon be completed, more advantageously than I hoped. But the great anxiety is to come. The examinations do not take place so early as I had expected . . . Henry is rather frightened at finding that his repugnance to mathematics stands much in his way. But for that, I think he would not feel such a strong disinclination to enter the college as *étudiant*. If he enters as *auditeur*, he will not be able to attain any honours, and he will not be esteemed as he might be; but it certainly does require prodigious resolution and perseverance to go through the course as prescribed, seeing that many of the most zealous students have half killed themselves. The examinations are very severe, and there is a great emulation among the students; so much so, that the stories we have heard of York are nothing to what they tell us here. . . . You may conceive I am not a little anxious till this is settled. . . .

Dr. de Roches sees Henry's character at once, and I believe he does me justice as to the views I have taken, and do take, with regard to the moral part of education. I cannot but feel my own insufficiency to cure the tendencies I disapprove. What must I do then? I am arrived at a point where two roads present themselves. The one a continuation of our old road, full of temptations, lax discipline, indulgence; the other, strict, laborious, disgusting, but safe, honourable, and proper to give a complete moral and intellectual education. I expect Henry has much to suffer. His self-love will often be severely wounded. If he sets himself up, he will be taken down, and perhaps in a way to do him harm. My good friend, whose knowledge of human nature is more complete than we usually find, sees all the different dangers for Henry. His nice perception makes him alive to everything, and his warning voice, if attended to, may prevent many evils. . . .

Poor Henry is, to-day, wearing less the air of a victim. He begins to look as if Dr. de Roches' kind efforts to procure him masters would not be thrown away upon him, though one of them is to screw him down to mathematics. The other, M. Roget, appears from description to be the very man I should have compounded, if such an art existed, to suit and benefit Henry. He undertakes to give him lessons in French composition; but being a great scholar, and particularly a Grecian, he will be respected accordingly, especially as his conversation is very interesting and agreeable from the variety of information he possesses. This is all very good; and when I hear that he is not merely a minister, and therefore religious, but also a fine preacher, I confess I cannot help building much upon such an acquaintance, and shall try to make him our friend. Add to all this, M. Roget is Professor of Philosophy, and therefore will, by-and-by, have more to do with Henry. It will be a great thing to secure his friendship, and I hope my poor boy will find a compensation in his lessons for the less attractive ones of M. Pascalis in mathematics. The subject alone is the cause, if the latter gentleman is less a favourite. He is extremely kind and amiable in his manners, and quite the head of his department. Both these gentlemen are so much occupied, that it is a great favour to obtain their assistance, and we must take care to treat them accordingly. Henry's attendance on Mr. Howes has been of use in this respect. . . .

Henry is now gone with Dr. de Roches to be introduced to M. Roget. I hope to tell you in the corner of my letter that he feels more encouraged and in good spirits. It is well we are here so early, for he will now have a month's preparation before the college opens; and as for me, I have full occupation, so that we shall but just be quietly settled before our thoughts are required for more important subjects. I speak in the plural number, because, without my entire sympathy, Henry may find his heart sometimes sink within him; . . . but I hope the worst is over, and that he will not long be without a friend. The two young men, or rather

lads, of this family (De Roches) are amiable and kind, but
no more fit for Henry than his fellow-student Rolfe. . . .

Your obedient Cousin,

S. REEVE.

To continue the Journal:—

1829.—At Geneva, owing to our intimacy with the
De Roches, we lived entirely in Genevese society, then very
brilliant. I became a sort of member of a *société* of lads
a little older than myself, Lombard, Jean Binet, Duchesne,
Huber, De Luc, most of whom remained life-long friends.
My greatest intimacy, however, was with Count Sigismond
Krasinski, afterwards celebrated as the 'Anonymous Poet'
of Poland. We were both in the poetic age—fond of writing,
and enthusiasts in all things.

The literary society of Geneva at this time comprised
M. de Sismondi, M. Simond (the traveller), M. Bonstetten,
M. Dumont, M. de Candolle the botanist, M. Necker de
Saussure, M. Chévénix, M. Rossi, Auguste de la Rive, old
De Luc, Mrs. Marcet, the Romillys.

I attended the lectures of M. Davillard on Latin literature
(Tacitus) ; Choisy on moral philosophy ; De la Rive on
physics and chemistry ; De Candolle on zoology and botany.
I had a boat built for the lake, and spent a great deal of
time on it. I also went a great deal into society—to the
Bals de la Redoute, and all sorts of parties. I remember a
dinner with M. Dumont, the friend of Mirabeau, at which
William and Edward Romilly were present ; it was very
interesting. Dumont died at Milan in the following year.
Sir Humphry Davy died at Geneva this summer. I attended
his funeral ; and afterwards went a walking tour in Switzerland with his late secretary, John Tobin.

1830.—After the academic term, which I passed pretty
well, having been moved from Belles Lettres to Philosophies,
we spent July at Montreux. The two Mosses used to row in
my boat, the 'Ariel.' On July 25th we ascended the Rochers
de Naye. That was the first of the 'glorious days.' On August
1st there was a ball at the Sauthers' at Burtigny ; and on
the following morning I started with Krasinski for Chamonix.
We went to the Jardin, the Brevent, and back by the Tête
Noire. Meanwhile, the Revolution had taken place which

changed the face of Europe. An officer of the Swiss Guard, whom we knew, had defended the Caserne de Babylon. He wrote an account of it, or rather Krasinski and I wrote it for him. That was almost the first time I had seen myself in print.

Adam Mickiewicz was with us as Geneva. I translated his ' Faris.' It was published in the ' Metropolitan Magazine ' and afterwards separately. But it was the Polish Revolution that excited me most. Auguste Zamoyski started to join the army. Krasinski was held back by his father, who took the Russian side. He afterwards went to Rome. In the course of the autumn the Genevese contingent was sent to guard the Simplon. Duchesne and I went to Brieg to see them there.

1831.—During this winter I followed a private course of lectures by Professor Rossi on Constitutional Law. Albert Pourtalès (afterwards Prussian ambassador in France) and Baron von Ende were my co-disciples. These lessons contributed to form my political opinions, and to give me a taste for international law. Rossi wrote a kind note to my mother about me.

My intimacy with the Poles made me take a deep interest in their cause. I knew Count Walewski, Napoleon's son, who was their agent in London ; Prince Adam Czartoryski, when he came ; old Niemiewicz, and, more particularly, Ladislas Zamoyski.

We left Geneva in June and posted to Paris ; then returned to London, where I felt myself a stranger. I shot at Copdock and in Norfolk, and afterwards went to Coed Ddu, the John Taylors' house in North Wales.

One of my first friends in London was old Edward Sterling of the ' Times.' John and Anthony Sterling were his sons. I called on old William Godwin and made the acquaintance of Carlyle. I was also introduced to Arthur Martineau's Cambridge friends, John M. Kemble, Thackeray ; and at Mr. Austin's house I met Hayward, the Bullers, Roebuck, the Grotes, and many others.

I was also entered at the Middle Temple and began to keep terms, having entirely relinquished the idea of following the medical profession. I longed to return to the Continent,

and gladly availed myself of a suggestion of John Austin's
that I should go to Germany to read Roman Law. We
spent the winter at Dimond's Hotel, Great Ormond
Street.

1832.—My mother resolved to take a house at Hampstead (3 Well Walk), where she continued to reside for ten
years. I started early in the year for Paris, and thus, at
little more than eighteen, I began the world in an independent position.

I arrived in Paris on February 4th. D'Eichthal introduced me to Mendelssohn. We went together to see Taglioni.
He said her dancing was *Glieder Musik*. Prévost introduced
me to Lerminier, V. Cousin, Ballanche, and Victor Hugo.
I met Lord Clarendon, then Mr. Villiers, at a dinner at
A. d'Eichthal's ; but I was not *lancé* at Paris till my next visit.
The cholera broke out with great violence and I left, posting
to Geneva, where I found Krasinski, with whom, a few
weeks later, I started for Italy : Turin, Milan, and Venice.
Venice in May was delightful. We had the grand apartment at the Leone Bianco on the Grand Canal, till the ex-
Empress Maria Louisa turned us out of it. She was on her
way to Vienna to see the Duc de Reichstadt, who was
dying. Sir Walter Scott was also in the hotel. I saw him
at the Academia. My dog Trevor jumped into his gondola,
which amused him ; but he was paralysed and a mere
wreck.

During his absence at this time, young Reeve wrote to his
mother at least every week, and his letters give a detailed
account of his travels and experiences, of which, however,
the short notes in the diary are now sufficient. They
are remarkable not only for their length—three quarto
pages of small, close, very neat handwriting, which at this
early age was already shaping itself into that which he
preserved to the last—but, and still more, for the maturity
of the thought and style. They are, of course, abundantly
charged with the mannerisms and affectations of youth,
though we may suppose that these would have been in a
great measure avoided, had the letters been addressed to
anyone but his mother. As it is, they appear to be written
currente calamo, the frank outpourings of a youthful heart.
Some extracts are here given rather as illustrating the

developement of his intellect and the formation of his
character than as intrinsically important.

To Mrs. Reeve

Paris, February 8th.—When I returned to Norwich
Mrs. Beecroft stuck me up against her parlour closet door to
measure my physical growth during three years of absence,
and thus it is with me now that I meet again my friends of
eight months ago. I can precisely estimate what I have
gained, and what I have lost. I feel that I have grown
by more than inches. In the meantime, I have, I believe,
'found out my task.' If I have not formed opinions, I have
learnt what opinions are to be formed. I have tried, and
perchance not in vain, to seize and handle the instruments
of future goodness and greatness ; and I have learnt the
great lesson—to believe. Do you think that I exaggerate ?
It may be so—but at least I do it not wilfully. So now let
me tell you what I have seen. . . . I have already seen
several very agreeable people. Adolphe d'Eichthal is delightful. I have been received at his house quite *sans façon*,
and they are constantly finding engagements and occupation of the most agreeable kind. Prévost is indeed *lancé* in
the best learned society. He is about to present me to
Victor Hugo, Lerminier the jurist, &c. D'Eichthal has
already introduced me to Felix Mendelssohn, who, without
being an angel of harmony or of grace, is a very pleasant
little Frenchified German ; in fact, the Teutonic part of him
seems well-nigh extinct. I was last night at a ball at
M. Cotlier's, the partner of M. André. I met Eugène de
la Rive. . . . Of womankind I know none, save only the
loud-voiced, fat Madame André la jeune, and the small and
bustling Madame André la vieille, who invited me to an
immense ball on Saturday, and said, ' Nous y causerons de
madame votre mère, dont le souvenir me fait tant de plaisir.'
Idée française, par exemple, que cette causerie-là.

February 10th.—The row in Paris was got up by the
police, just as the Cato Street one was by Lord Sidmouth.
I was too late for it, and, indeed, there was not much to see.
Everyone groans for bleeding France, and no one can hope
for a remedy. The general opinion is that this Ministry

will fall when ours does. Trafford is at this moment the talk of all Paris, and the butt of all the journals. He gave a ball last week to the *vieille cour*—that is to say, the *Henri-Quinquistes*—whereat the health of ʼle petit montagnard exiléʼ was drunk with enthusiasm. It was reported that he was ordered· to leave Paris in consequence, but that is contradicted. The ball cost him 40,000 francs, and in the course of the winter he has given –5,000 [1] to the poor. So I will not vouch for the fulness even of his coffers this week.

The other day the editor of ʼLa Caricature ʼ was prosecuted for a derisory likeness of Louis Philippe. His defence was this. He brought into court a large sheet of paper containing four diminishing likenesses of Louis Philippe, the first being the one for which he was prosecuted, and the last a pear. Now, says he, if you condemn the first you must condemn the second, because it is like the first, and the third because it is like the second, and the fourth—*i.e.* the pear—because it is like the third. *Ergo*, Louis Philippe is a pear. They did, however, condemn the innocent fruit to please the guilty king.

Paris, February 16*th.*—Prévost has been unremitting in his attentions and civilities. He has presented me to M. Lerminier, one of the law professors in the Collège de France, a frothy French rhetorician to be sure, but nevertheless a man who will be heard among the noisiest, and consequently among the leaders of the *enfants de Paris*. I am now reading his book, which serves as a good introduction enough to the biography of jurisprudence, if one may use the term. . . .

February 17*th.*—From Lerminier we went to Cousin. You know what I thought of his lectures when I was reading them some twelve months ago ; they have influenced in no slight degree the opinions and conceptions I have formed in the last year ; and now I came to see—*familiariter versari* with this man, this philosopher. How anything so cynical in ordinary life can co-exist with a soul and a faith so platonical and so refined is, and ever will be, to me a subject of great

---

[1] The first figure has been torn away with the seal.

wonder. If he speaks like the sage of Academus in the walls of the Sorbonne, he growls like Diogenes when entubbed in his easy-chair. His *Nos!* and *Has!* his gesticulations, his wit, his vanity, his malice, and his philosophy are all—I mean no disrespect to Mr. Emmanuel Kant—transcendental. I did not hear him say a kind nor, certainly, a foolish thing. We talked a great deal on all subjects, but especially on the St.-Simonians. He thinks with me (that is to say, as I have long thought) that they will accomplish to the full their strange destiny in this strange era, and that they will especially flourish in England, by reason of the eminently sectarian spirit of our nation, and by reason of the strange sceptical speculations which have laid hold of the minds of some property-holders and of all property-seekers. I have been to hear them hold forth. They talk to us a great deal about Attractive Sociability, and Cosmogonies, and Kata-clysms, and Mastodons, and Fishes; and I came away as wise as I went, impressed with the alarming folly of their doctrines, for folly is alarming, and no less alarming than the confederacy of fools is vast. . . . .

M. de Ballanche is of another school, whom, unknown, I called upon, again with the indefatigable Prévost. He is the author of the 'Palingénésie,' which may some time or other fall into your hands. Lost from time to time in the luxuriancy of his imaginative philosophy, but ever chained, for the internal, to the solid basis of his faith; and, for the external, by the brilliant and positive nature of his style, he will always move, though he may not always persuade; always lead to the Absolute and the True, through avenues other than the greater part of the philosophers of the nine-teenth century have deemed it fitting to follow. To each his path—perhaps to each his goal.

Geneva, February 27th.—Paris cost me a terrible deal of money, but I am living here, with Sigismond, for 130 francs a month, so I shall have two months of grand economy which will make my accounts square. Rossi is as he ever was. There be none at Paris like unto him; as, indeed, they all feel and say. I meant to have written you an account of my presentation to Victor Hugo, but other and better things have happened since. Upon the whole, I was disappointed in the external man, and more especially in his powers of conversation.

Geneva, March 5th.—The extreme gaiety of the *haut ton* during this first week of my stay has prevented my making as many calls as I could have wished, but I have on the other hand seen almost everyone in the crowded drawing-rooms and ball-rooms. The six first days of my stay I went to five balls and three parties. . . . I have called, *comme de raison*, at Malagnou. Mme. Lombard has been poorly, and I still found her somewhat pale ; she no longer goes out of the house, yet I hope the summer will not belie the promise of this early springtide, and that it will set her on her legs again. Mademoiselle is just as usual. M. Lombard, le père, s'adonne tout entier à la philosophie indienne, thereby fructifying his literary ease. But it is ill talking of such old people except for the sake of affectionate remembrance, inasmuch as that between seventy and eighty there rarely remains more than one change to be made. . . .

In the midst of our gaieties and joy at meeting again we have received news the most fatal to our happiness that the post could bring, saving only bad news from you—namely, the recall of Sigismond to Poland. I had long expected this or something as bad. The restless scythe of that imperial devastator may not and will not leave one flower to bloom within his reach, and so to Poland returns my friend. God only knows what may happen. We hope that by avoiding Warsaw he may spend his time quietly enough in the country till he be allowed to go forth again. August 15th is the day on which he is to re-enter the halls of his fathers ; it is the *fête de Napoléon*, which the General K. always celebrates with great pomp. We are now in March, and we know not what five months may or may not bring forth. But, *en attendant*, it is the first part of their plan which more especially concerns you and me. They—Sigismond and his chamberlain—are to leave Geneva in the end of April and go to Turin ; thence through Milan and Verona to Venice, across the Adriatic to Trieste, and through Klagenfurt to Vienna. Now just take out your map. They propose to me to go with them some part of the way, and as my immediate object is Munich, I should leave them either at Verona, and pass up through Trent and Innsbruck, or go as far as Klagenfurt, and see Salzburg in my way thither. This tour would take me about three weeks more than the ordinary route, which I should subtract from my stay at Dresden in the autumn, and the increase of expense will be nothing at all, as we should go five in Sigismond's carriage, Count Zaluski [1] being of the party. *Enfin, ma chère mère, c'est à toi à décider.* Such an opportunity for seeing Styria, Carniola, and the Tyrol may not again present itself. I will not argue for my wishes—that would be unfair; but if you are in doubt pray ask John's or Richard's opinion. They made an immense circuit to see these identical places. Prévost will not be at Munich before June. We wait your decision.

March 15th.—I am glad that you are going to take a house now, because, in the first place, I shall find you in a real home when I return ; and because, secondly, neither you nor I are very easy to live with impertinent inferiors. All I have to say is that, if you really find a house you like, I should be well pleased if you were to buy it. For which purpose you would sell out the 600*l.* or 700*l.* you lately invested in the Three and a half per Cents. You know my horror of funded property, *par le temps qui court*, and if the price came within your means, I am sure that a house in Hampstead must be a good investment. *Enfin*, my dear mother, what I have most chiefly to regret is that I am so unable to help you in your *embarras*. 'Tis shameful for us youngsters to be scampering over Europe while those we ought to attend on are in such straits. . . . . .

I am, as I told you in my last, completely *lancé*, and since my arrival I have never spent an evening at home. The Moultous and Favres have given us dinner parties ; also we have dined at the De Roches, and notwithstanding the *finis* of the Bal des Étrangers, we have on hand a large appendix of balls and a copious body of supplementary parties. M. de Roches—*qui est très bien avec moi à l'heure qu'il est—* declares that Prévost and I shall generalise over much in this life, and generalise away the best part of our career.

[1] In a later letter Reeve describes Zaluski as a cousin of Sigismond's and a delightful companion ; a man of about thirty-nine, an old soldier under Napoleon and 'one of the principal and most successful diplomatic agents of the late Polish Government.'

Il me fait beaucoup d'honneur en m'attelant avec Prévost ;
but I doubt if all his prophecies come true. His telescope
embraces but a speck in the horizon, and he will not use his
free sight ; Prévost and I shall seek and perhaps find a wider
sphere than the Grande Rue, or the little Senate House of a
Swiss Canton ; and when we are there the wheel is not too
crowded for us not to find our place, nor, I imagine, so hard
to turn as to render our labours vain. The bloom is wearing
away from me, the exquisite æsthetical sense of early youth
is in its decay, for the spring destroys as well as the autumn ;
but it destroys only to bring forth the better fruits of the
summer. Our age will not be without its fifteenth-century
men—its Columbus, its Faust, its builders, its creators ; and
it is from amongst our generation that they will be chosen.

March 21st.—Your letter was punctually received
yesterday, and I may now consider it as pretty certain that
in a very few weeks we shall cross the Mont Cenis, and be
travelling through the north of Italy. If it were not from
Geneva that we go, my delight would be unmixed and
unqualified ; but after all it must end. By a most singular
and unexpected case and lot, I have returned to the place of
my youth while all its freshness was upon it, not a face
changed, not a heart estranged ; but now at this second
parting, it seems that all is indeed past, the circle broken
up, its members dispersed, and the waters of the coming
tide washing away the little wall of sand which we had
built in the serious nothingness of early youth. The men,
now that they are men, will live a stronger life, and bear
burdens, and seek perils, and brave difficulty ; the women—
for such is the imperious necessity of the time and place—
will narrow yet more their fairyland of innocent love, and
cultivate above all things the steady virtues of the nursery.
And be it so. My first act is, or will be, complete, and I am
no stickler for dramatic unity. The next may begin anywhere, since it must begin somewhere. . . .

I like your tirade about 'dolls,' and do not doubt that
Anna Enfield merits all you choose to say about her. If
ever a ' doll ' has exercised any influence over me, and it is
not impossible that such has been the case, I beg you to
recollect that a young head has a whole'wardrobe of fancy

dresses—a rich garb of imaginative *gros de Naples*—in the which all successive Chloes, Lauras, and Sophonisbas have been dressed, and by which they have certainly been set off to the best possible advantage. But, finally, there are in the world stronger things than these. We must all leave our isles of Calypso to brave the dangers of a stormy archipelago; the way to our Ithaca is dangerous and long. . . .

April 1st.—C'était à une soirée de noces chez Mme. Gaussen-Huber qu'une jeune personne rayonnante de joie me dit: ' Quand vous écrirez à Mme. Reeve vous lui communiquerez mes grandes nouvelles, et direz que si elle avait été un peu plus près, je lui aurais envoyé une communication.' Bref, la jeune fille avec sa guirlande de fiancée au front voulait que je vous disse que Mme. Diego de Combes ne vous sera pas moins attachée que ne l'est Constance Sauther. Such is the change which is about to take place. In a month or six weeks the damsel will espouse Diego de Combes, the brother of her sister's husband. A goodly case of matrimony, in truth; a man endowed with a soul, a mind, and a body; and a lady ' réunissant l'esprit à la beauté,' as the man says in the vaudeville. And few marriages have caused more sensation. The young ladies have, of course, been thrown into a delicate confusion by this early *enlèvement* of one of their virginal band; *puis, de l'autre côté,* the cohort of male admirers in dire dismay and disappointment; pale lovers gliding like ghosts with skulls in their hands, and others flushed with wrath, breathing fury and revenge. I, for my part, at the above-mentioned soirée, made my congratulatory bow with all due gallantry; but in my own room I have felt that a very vain bubble, when it bursts, leaves almost as great a chasm in a man's spirit as if a mountain rose from its foundations and became air. *J'ai senti l'impossible;* why should I hide my head in the sand, and deem myself unseen? Such a reality, coming in all its truth before me, has done away more illusions than five years of most reasonable thought. . . .

Sigismond's eyes are somewhat better. We shall start on May 4th at latest. He is much annoyed, and I much amused, at the necessity of his being presented to his dear cousin, Charles Albert, by the grace of God King of

Sardinia and Jerusalem. His father particularly desires it.
I shall grin on seeing him return from an interview with
the man who betrayed Santa Rosa, and sought to hang
Prandi & Co.[1] Much good such cousinship cannot do him;
but it is no new discovery that he is the best of his family.
His father is put at the head of the Polish Government,
with the father of Zamoyski and two others. . . .

April 30*th*.—You seem to find that the letter, to which
your letter of the 18th replies, was written in somewhat too
ferocious a mood. Perhaps so. I know not what it was
about. When the wind is strong, it makes the harp sing
loud; and Heaven knows that this is a crisis for us young
ones, all—all simultaneously—torn from our habits and our
haunts, all going forth like labourers with tools upon their
shoulders—going forth, but not to return like labourers at
the close of the day. I shall soon be able to vent myself in
the novelty and beauty of a material world, which will
amuse you better, and interest you more than my erroneous
opinions on things of which I know but little.

Turin, May 9*th*.—It cannot enter into the heart of man
to conceive an Italian springtide; it must be felt. To feel
Thought living upon air, an air which brings back all the
sweetness one has ever felt, and marries it to all Hope
can tell us of Heaven; to lose oneself in exquisite listlessness,
as if one had already passed the cave of the Wonderful
Lamp, and was sleeping under the diamond trees in the
magical garden to dream of bright things for ever. . . .

Tout cela est bel et bon pour un voyage d'un mois. But
after one has felt the air they breathe, one readily allows that
the Italians can never be strong or sane, and one's memory
turns proudly to our own North, with its smoke, and its
fires, and its strength. Here all nature is in a fever; there
man goes forth like a hale and hearty peasant on a frosty
morning. Truth to tell, I have been but twenty-four hours

---

[1] In the revolutionary government of Piedmont in 1821, of which Charles
Albert was the head. Santa Rosa was minister at war. When the prince
deserted or betrayed the cause, his associates had to look out for themselves.
Prandi got to England and stayed there; Santa Rosa had also escaped, but,
though absent, was condemned to death. He was afterwards reconciled to
Charles Albert, and died in 1848. There is a curious account of his death in
the *Edinburgh Review*, vol. xciii. (Jan. 1851). pp. 175–8.

in Italy, so my impressions are rather hasty; mais en dix coups de poumons on est furieusement lazaronisé.

A longer experience taught the young traveller that even in Italy, in May, the weather could sometimes be wet, cold, and disagreeable, reminding him more of the winters of the north than the summers of the south. But bursts of youthful enthusiasm over the scenery, the landscapes, the Duomo of Milan, the memories of history and literature, fill his letters.

Verona, May 17th.—To-morrow we go to Vicenza, and sleep at Padua; the day afterward we shall get to Venice. At every step on which I go in this wonderful Italy, I feel more and more admiration possess me. Art and the Beautiful come so seasonably after the Science and the Strength of England. We are treading ground of immortal remembrances. Did we meet neither Proteus nor Valentine on their way to Milan? Shall we not find Bellario, the learned jurist, in the halls of Padua? . . . Has not history written her story on the face of these towns, more legibly than in the books of the wise?

Venice, May 22nd.—Venice is not to me so sad a town as Verona. The eternal motion of the water, and the fresh breezes of the Adriatic, have in themselves something more cheerful than the cold deserted pavement of the latter place. I know of no description which gives one a physical idea of Venice. One thinks of it as a place of a thousand remembrances; as the throne of Dandolo, and the scaffold of Faliero; but when one is in one's gondola, the luxurious present hushes the sad voice of the past, and one is wrapt in perfect enjoyment.

Venice, May 26th.—I am almost surprised to find how fully my own prophecies come true—in the political world, I mean. I have never for an instant doubted that we should come to the breakers at last, and I think we are fairly arrived there at the present time. The knell of the triple constitutional power of England has rung; the spirit of the age has broken the balance, and it is absurd now to talk of Kings, Lords, and Commons, when all exist in error or madness, or rather do not exist at all. I beg your pardon for invading you, in my turn, with a little bit of a political lucubration, for you must be thoroughly drugged with that article; but

I would only humbly exhort you, if I thought such exhortation necessary, to pay the king's taxes like an English subject and a loyal one. I dare say you are not sorry, upon the whole, that I am out of the way of all this toil and trouble, and that I content myself with reading Galignani in my gondola, instead of waging a war of words at the corner of every street in London. For my part, I cannot sufficiently rejoice at being out of word-shot of the two fierce parties which I abhor and regard as equally destructive of the national welfare and happiness. Happiness—good God! what a word for us to write! Perchance in thirty years from the present time, peace and love may shine over the cradles of our grandchildren; but till then we may e'en say 'Good-bye' to anything like tranquillity in the old island of England. I repeat, and will always repeat, my dear mother, what I said in my last letter—namely, that I am here as one waiting for a summons to return to you; let it come to-day or to-morrow, but let it not come too late. What do you wish me to do if war breaks out on the Continent? There is to be—as I have said already—no peace at home or abroad; therefore, where stand we? I hate this paltry martyrdom for opinions of a day, for laws which are but scrolls to be burnt or effaced in blood; and I believe that the spirit of Revolution has never walked in our days by the side of true religion. I would that I knew how to walk steadier than walks our world. Our faith lives by suffering, and not by crime; and all we can hope is, that the prayers of those who suffer will be stronger than the curses of those who persecute.

Surely, this is a very remarkable letter for a lad still four months short of nineteen, who neither belonged to a political family nor had been thrown by circumstances into the clash of political factions. The bitterness and the cocksureness of youth are indeed there, but the formulation of opinion is no less noteworthy than the correctness of the diction or the neatness of the handwriting. And having relieved his soul of the 'political lucubration,' he continued in a more personal narrative.

The Lido is an island about six miles long, which forms a part of the circlet of islands which serve as so many

breakwaters to the town of Venice. On the side opposite
the city lies the burial-ground of the Jews ; and oftentimes,
seated on some Hebrew tomb, my friend and I have watched
the sun setting over the towers and churches of Venice, till
it is hid behind the faint line of the Alps in the distant
horizon ; or we walk along the beach on the other side,
whence one discovers nothing but the blue surface of the
Adriatic, speckled with the white lateen sails of the vessels
from the Greek islands, or here and there the broad white
canvas of some larger ship. . . . . Every evening we visit
some new island in the neighbourhood of the city. Thus
we have seen the island of the Cemetery, to which the coffins
of all those who die in the Republic are brought; the
Armenian convent, at about four miles from the city, with
its bright red church and walls ; the arsenal which sent
forth the armament of Lepanto, and a thousand others.
. . . . Last night we spent some hours in the botanical
garden, which is more like a pleasure garden than a stiff
place of classified plants. There was nobody there, for there
is nobody anywhere at Venice except on the Place St. Mark.
We were accompanied by an old gardener, who showed us,
with delight, his cacti and his pelargoniums di Inghilterra,
and his roses of Italy in full bloom. He gave us each a
nosegay of his best flowers, and took us to the sweetest
nooks you can imagine ; to an arbour, for instance, where
the tomb of some old abbot served for a table—for the
garden is on the site of an abolished monastery—and whence
we looked over the calm lagunes to the mountains of the
Tyrol, hiding their summits of snow in the mist of light
which haunts the horizon of the north of Italy.

Venice, May 30th.—You will, no doubt, be delighted to
hear that I have given up all poetical scribbling, journalising,
and writing in general, which is a vast economy in stationery.
Nevertheless, when I am under the wings of Schelling, I
will try to pen something worthy of the 'Foreign Quarterly.'
I intend to write notes on the men I see in Germany, which
may serve to amuse you when we meet, and which I may,
at some later period, work up into a form analogous to
Mme. de Staël's book, the which is now completely aged ;
for since her day religion has become philosophy, and

philosophy religion. The tree planted by Kant has borne its fruits and flowers; and in England people remain all the while in marvellous ignorance of the land which sent forth Luther, the printing-press, and gunpowder, and which will, in my opinion, be the mother of the great revolutions which the signs of our own times announce.

His movements on leaving Venice are told, in a few words, in the Journal:—

At Innsbruck, Sigismond and I parted—he for Vienna, I for Munich; and though we continued to correspond, I never lived in his intimacy again.

I was charmed with Munich, and took lodgings in the Frühlings Strasse. Schelling, to whom I had letters, received me kindly, and I resolved to follow his lectures. I wrote poetry in abundance and with great facility, some of which is not absolutely worthless.

A fuller idea of his manner of life is given in his letters to his mother.

Munich, June 23rd.—Here the king governs his people by poetry and painting; he invites them to walk in his palaces and to feast upon the canvas of Italy and the marble of Greece. He meets them nightly in the beautiful theatre, where one hears none of the dramatic ribaldry of the nineteenth century, but the pure and noble and grand poetry of Goethe and Schiller and Körner, which alternates with the music of Weber, or from time to time of Rossini. I know not what it may be for the natives, but for a stranger it is the best and politest Government I ever lived under, inasmuch as it studies the art of giving pleasure, which is rare enough in our days. . . . . .

From seven till ten I am engaged with my German; then till twelve I write letters or read. At twelve I go out to read the papers, to call on Schelling or Lord Erskine,[1] or to the picture gallery or the statue gallery. At two I dine at the table d'hôte of the best inn for 2 fr. 10 sous (with wine), and mix a little with my fellow-creatures. The dinner lasts two hours. From four to half-past six I walk with

---

[1] The English Minister.

my beloved Trevor [1] in the English gardens. At half-past
six I go to the theatre, which ends at nine ; and from nine
to eleven I prepare my German lesson for the following
day. My time, you see, is divided as regularly as Alfred's,
and nothing happens in this peaceful city to disturb the easy
current of the life I lead.

Gradually, as he made acquaintances, the young student
modified the rigour of this routine ; but he continued working hard at German, of which, by the end of August, he
had gained a fairly adequate knowledge. According to the
Journal :—

In the autumn I went a tour to Dresden and
Frankfort. Spent some days with the Beckers at Offenbach
and on the Rhine. At Dresden I called on the old poet
Tiedge, and I also made the acquaintance of Tieck, and
heard him read 'Romeo and Juliet' in German, for which he
was celebrated ; but he read excessively fast and without
much effect. The Dresden and Munich galleries were my
schools of art, and gave me that strong taste for pictures
which has been one of the great pleasures of my life.
Goethe was dead [2] when I reached Weimar. Carlyle had
given me a letter to him. But I saw Mme. Ottilie v. Goethe, [3]
who received me very cordially.

Reboul and Prévost came to see me on my return to
Munich ; here I made the acquaintance of Edwin Hill
Handley, and he fell in love with Delphine v. Schauroth.
Count Max Taufkirchen took a fancy to me and presented
me to the Court society—Mme. de Cetto's, Mme. de
Rechberg's, &c.—and took me to the great winter *chasse* of
Prince Max zu Baiern. The winter was very gay. I was
très lié with Michael Beer, [4] author of 'Struensee,' and he
introduced me to the artists, &c. I worked pretty hard,
however ; read and translated Mackeldey's 'Roman Law ; '
attended Schelling's lectures ; learned German well ; and
wrote a great article (my first attempt) against the Reform

---

[1] His dog. See *ante*, p. 13, and *post*, p. 30.
[2] He died March 22nd, 1832.
[3] Widow of Goethe's only son, who died October 28th, 1830.
[4] A younger brother of Meyerbeer, at this time 32 years old, of some
repute as a poet, and wealthy.

Bill, which I sent to the 'Quarterly Review.' It was not published; but Lockhart approved it, and old John Murray called on me at Hampstead in consequence.

The flesh of this skeleton is supplied by the letters to Mrs. Reeve :—

Munich, November 3rd.—I have made a new and very remarkable acquaintance. This is a Mr. Handley, well known to Arthur Martineau, Kemble, the Bullers, and fifty other of our friends. You may imagine the pleasure with which I met in this wide and lonely heaven a star wandering, like myself, from the constellation to which he belongs; but my pleasure amounted to delight when I discovered in this Mr. Handley the marks of deep and original thought, considerable acquirements, and, above all, a vast sympathy in my present and future tastes. If Sigismond is the type of my past, I feel convinced that this individual, in principle if not in person, is the representative of my future. He is a feature in the countenance of England which I must learn to know if I am to learn to live. We are at issue on innumerable points, and so much the more united on those on which we agree. He is republican and *un homme de mouvement*. Above all, the point which strikes me at the present moment as the one of the greatest practical utility to me, is the essentially communicable or catching ardour which he displays in working out his knowledge. He is the man who is necessary to me, and I feel him to be, in one sense, my Messias, believing as I do that all men are sent to their tasks, and brought to the field of action where their free will displays itself. I am not in the habit of *engouéing* myself to people. My friends have all been made by slow stages, and I stand in the power of none of them, not even of the dearest. My sudden attachment to this man is merely an exemplification of our old Bonstetten's very sensible remark : 'J'ai vu les amitiés les plus profondes naître presque instantanément; c'est que le cœur a son tact pour le sentiment profond comme le génie a le sien pour les conceptions profondes.' This *liaison*, however, is but an acquaintance at present—an intimate one to be sure, and which lacks nothing but confidence to make it a friendship;

but I never give confidence; I sell it on grand occasions only. I never, to tell the truth, remember to have confided in any human being except yourself. I am, of course, very curious to know what you will be able to learn as to this man; he may be an intellectual sharper, but, if he is, he is a very clever one. . . . Handley is neither richer nor poorer than myself; older and wiser he is, and from those best of fortunes I am free largely to borrow, as my Aunt and Uncle Philip are with you.

Munich, December 27th.—I have been meditating for the last few days a proposition which will no doubt astonish you; it is, to speak without further preface, to ask leave of you to return to England in March instead of in September. My reasons are manifold. In the first place, the great object of my tour in Germany is accomplished. I have acquired the language sufficiently for all purposes of study, and by the time I mention I shall have accomplished a succinct but general view of the whole body of Roman Law. I shall have heard the first metaphysician of the age enough to see that I differ from him on many points, and that there are no metaphysics in the world worth anything except the readings of a man's own heart, except the work and fruit of self-inspection. I have seen much of art, and have arrived at some understanding of it; and, above all, I have caught a glimpse of my future which has co-ordinated the developement of such activity and capacity as I possess. But my reasons for returning to England are, that I am convinced that the system of German study is essentially vague, and not practical; that there is little intimate connexion between thought and action; that the lore of their schools is over-dusty, and the language of the wise men over-dogmatical; that, in short, the speculative has overgrown and overtopped the real. I therefore question whether the advantages I can gain in Germany are worth the sacrifice of half your income, and whether it would not be far more advantageous to me to keep my terms now, and to leave myself a little space of time three years hence, after the terms are kept, to be employed in travelling or as circumstances may dictate. If I return, I shall spend the summer and autumn with you at Hampstead, and go into chambers and a special pleader's office at the beginning of winter.

Munich, January 14th, 1833.—I am still anxiously waiting for your answer about my returning home. . . . I confess I look forward with great hope and longing to the time of my leaving Germany, to which I am very ready to bid a long adieu. . . . The Germans are the most uninteresting nation in the world. One gives them credit for erudition because one rarely hears any foolishness in their mouths ; but their ideas lie bedridden in their brains, and when they come out in words they stumble about most clumsily. The Germans are the owls who only come out in the night, ' wherein no man shall work.' To-night, however, I am going to see the Teutons—the Suabian swains—in a new scene. Handley and I are going to a masked ball at the opera, as Faust and Mephistopheles, to play off our pranks with the rest. Thus much must be said for the Germans, that their kings, princes, and beer-drinkers of lowest degree are always ready to mingle together where beer is to be had. For me, however, who am no beer-drinker and not a great masker, this carnival brings little besides that word which I hope other years and other carnivals will bring me also : I mean the word ' study.'

Munich, January 23rd.—Beer and I are actually beginning to talk about trunks and post-horses. . . . . We intend to start somewhere between February 25th and March 1st. We shall go through Paris, stay there about a week, and be with you the 10th or 15th of March. . . . It is with true pleasure indeed that I shall quit this strange outlandish *vie de garçon*, and with deep joy that I shall again find myself beside you. . . . . Germany is the only country for which I have at any time conceived, by experience, a positive dislike, because it is the only country where one does not find the vulgar virtues which oil the wheels of life. . . . It is the land which has in it the least noble and generous feeling, and perhaps the least truth in all Europe. I have read Mrs. Trollope's tour in America ; but Mrs. Trollope may yet reserve herself for Germany, where she will find a rich appendix to her former volumes.

Returning to the Journal for a few lines :—

Towards the end of the carnival, the King gave a masked ball in lieu of Prince Max, and as I was going to the one I went to the other. I had not been presented at Court because I was a student.

I went in Madame de Taufkirchen's quadrille, *en Bohème*, and my lady was Baroness Ritter. Michael Beer was to have been of this quadrille, but the king said he could not receive a Jew, whereupon Beer took a fever and died [March 22nd]. I nursed him to the last. Handley, meanwhile, engaged himself to Delphine v. Schauroth.

Many circumstances, and especially the death of his friend Beer, concurred in delaying Reeve's departure from Munich till March 29th, and the correspondence with his mother ended, for the time, with a letter giving an affecting account of Beer's death, announcing his probable arrival in London on April 10th, and continuing—

Nuremberg, March 30th.—It has cost me much to quit a place where all, from the King to my washerwoman, have striven which shall oblige and befriend me most. Whatever may be my opinion of Germans and Germany—and certainly I have acquired no great predilection for either one or the other—it would be most unfair, or rather most unrighteous, in me not to bear a full testimony of gratitude to the Munich people. . . . . I have given away Trevy : first, because it was impossible to take him with us, and secondly, because he will be well taken care of where he is. *Mais cela m'a beaucoup coûté.*

On returning to England, where he remained during the rest of 1833 and the whole of 1834, Reeve lived for the most part with his mother at Hampstead, reading some law and dabbling in literature. He was introduced to Mr. Wentworth Beaumont, M.P. for South Northumberland, who had lately started the 'British and Foreign Review' and for this Reeve began to write regularly. He published also some translations in the 'Monthly Magazine,' and wrote a poem—'Laocoon'—which remained in manuscript. There are, naturally, very few letters of this date ; but it appears that in August 1833 he was visiting his uncle, John Taylor, in North Wales, and went on to Liverpool, where he was introduced to Roscoe, Mrs. Hemans, and some others, who then gave a certain literary reputation to that essentially commercial town. Afterwards, probably in October, he visited his friend Handley, who had married at Munich and was then at Cambridge, where Reeve made the acquaintance of Kemble, Whewell, Tennyson, and Christopher Wordsworth. He then settled down at Hampstead for the winter, reading, writing, philosophising, and smoking.

To Mr. E. H. Handley

Hampstead, December 3rd.

MY DEAR HANDLEY,—This letter is professedly and *ab initio* a troublesome one ; and to judge *a priori*, I should think it would rather excite your choler than your kindness. You hate shopping, I ask you to shop; you despise grocers, I crave grocery; you are married, and I smoke tobacco. In this lies, without more preface, the sum total of my prayer. I have already consumed the store of stout tobacco-coils with which I left Cambridge, partly in the elucidation of Dante's theosophical opinions, partly in a comparison of Odin, Fo, Buddha, and Hercules, and chiefly in the solace of my lonely and inactive hours. Now, if you have either affection or regard for any of my heroes, esteem for their characters or friendship for myself, I must beg you, when you come back to town, to bring me a pound of the Varinas tobacco which John Kemble smokes. He will tell you where it is to be gotten.[1]

After this indecent merriment on grave subjects, I have scarce any courage to enter upon loftier themes. I must not, however, fail to say that I hope you have gotten the portraits long ago, as I forwarded them to your father a week since.

I had an argument the other night with an Anglo-Saxon scholar on the derivation of the Saxon *Alderman* (quasi elder-man or chief) and of the Norwegio-Danish *Jarl*, which, after the Danish invasions, became *Earl* in English. I maintained—I know not with what truth—that these two words were strictly sisters, and that, as they both imply supremacy, so they must both be formed from a root signifying age, power, valour, or the like, by which supremacy

---

[1] We now consider this form as peculiarly American. It is, therefore, worth noting that in 1833 it was still familiarly used by a young literary student, presumably quite up to date.

may be acquired. I beg you to refer this matter to J. K., and to favour me with your own lights upon the subject. Camden seems to favour my opinion; but my antagonist maintains that they have no radical connexion.[1]

I am immersed in the 'Paradiso.' By the way, I have been delighted by a commentary which, perhaps, even you are not familiar with—I mean Dante's own essay on the 'Paradiso,' given in a Latin letter to the Can Grande della Scala di Verona, to whom the third part of the 'Divina Commedia' is dedicated. From this letter, turn it and pervert it as they will, the Allegorists have no appeal. Rossetti is to Dante what Dupuis is to all mythology and Scripture—a blasphemous heresiarch. By the same arguments, one might prove that Milton's 'Paradise Lost' is a satire on his times, Charles being represented by Lucifer, and Oliver Cromwell by God. All I can say is, in Dante's own words, 'Vivit Dominus, quique movit linguam in asinâ Balaam, Dominus est etiam modernorum brutorum.' What shall we say of a man who, whilst the hierarchies of angels and the hosts of Christ are passing before him, takes them for fat Guelphs and lean Ghibellines? Don Quixote's illusions were rational—aye, sublime—compared to this; inasmuch as it is better to take a wench for an angel than an angel for a wench. Good-bye, my dear fellow. Remember me kindly to all the Transcendentalists, and present my best regards to Mrs. and Miss Handley, to whom, as well as to yourself, my mother desires to be particularly commended and recalled.   Believe me, yours ever,

HENRY REEVE.

P.S.—Don't forget the pigtail, as the sailor said.

February 7th.—In the introduction to your translation, since Schelling is the object and positive substance of the work, I hope you will make due mention of Giordano Bruno, and especially of Hamann, whom Goethe styled the father of the German philosophy, and whom I have heard Schelling himself mention as the *Urquelle* of his system. Of the man and of his works I know nothing, except that he died in 1780; consequently a few years before Kant published his

---

[1] According to the N. E. D., ' the notion that *eorl* is a corruption of *ealdor* is wholly untenable.'

'Kritik.' I forgot to send you F. Schlegel's 'Philosophie des Lebens,' which you can have if you please ; but as there is nothing historical in it, I question if it will help you much. For the worst of our dogmatising friends is, that they all dogmatise at once, producing a rude chord which is anything but an accord.

CHAPTER II

EARLY MANHOOD

LITTLE as there is for the biographer to record of 1834, the year had a very singular influence on Reeve's life. It was then, whilst living in London, that, primarily through the Austins, he became acquainted with many of the best people in the literary world; among whom he names the Bullers, Romillys, Grotes, Seniors, Sterlings, Carlyles, Hayward, Prandi,[1] George Lewis, Bellenden Ker, and Mrs. Somerville. Through the Taylors he also made several acquaintances more or less distinguished in science; and his residence at Hampstead brought him into contact with the Longmans, Hodgsons, and Mrs. Joanna Baillie. It is difficult to over-estimate the importance of these acquaintances—many of which ripened into intimacies and life-long friendships—to a young man just entering on a literary career. Nor was it in London only that these openings presented themselves. His Journal tells how—

In January, 1835, I went to Paris and established myself in the Place de l'Odéon. Amédée Prévost introduced me to Lamartine, Alfred de Vigny, the Deschamps; and I knew Augustin Barbier. I soon found myself in excellent literary society. Thackeray was in Paris. I visited the prisons and wrote an account of them. This led to an intimacy with Léon Faucher, which only ended with his life.

Reeve's principal object in visiting Paris at this time was to obtain some insight into the practical working of French criminal law, the effect of the 'circonstances atténuantes,' and the management of French prisons; as to which he reported at length to his uncle, John Austin, then a member of the Criminal Law Commission, and which he afterwards made the subject of an article in the 'British

---

[1] Cf. *ante*, p. 21.

and Foreign Review.' [1]　His letters to his mother contain many notices of these studies, as well as of his social experiences of dinners and balls; but they, and still more his letters to Handley, which were at this time poured forth in great abundance and at great length, are chiefly interesting for the very frank opinions of the books he read, and of the men he met; men familiarly known to us in the full dress of society, but here introduced in dressing-gown and slippers. The judgements were, of course, immature; but it was with the immaturity of youthful conceit, founded on a singularly wide-extended reading and knowledge of society. Many years afterwards, in a review on the Papers of Lord Melbourne, he sanctioned, if he did not actually write, a criticism which might have passed for one on his own early letters. 'It should be borne in mind,' it ran, 'that the style of writing a hundred (or even fifty-five) years ago was far more stiff than at the present day; and also, that when a clever lad of twenty delivers an opinion upon literature or politics, it is apt, from its youthful superficiality, to appear more priggish than it is in reality. Moreover, the letters are written to his mother, to whom the lad naturally desired to show his literary knowledge and political attainments.' [2]　But, apart from these peculiarities incidental to twenty-one, there can be no doubt that in these familiar letters he was training himself, all unconsciously, to the quick insight and full criticism which he was afterwards to turn to such valuable account.

To Mrs. Reeve

Paris, January 14th.—Thackeray is flourishing, and after the opera we took tea, and had a long talk of the doings of French artists. He complains of the impurity of their ideas, and of the jargon of a corrupt life which they so unwisely admit into their painting-rooms. Thackeray's drawing—if I may judge by his note-book—is as pure and accurate as any I have seen. He is a man whom I would willingly set to copy a picture of Raphael's, as far at least as the drawing goes; but he does not seem likely to get into a system of massive colouring, if I may judge by what he said. Yesterday (Wednesday) was a busy day for me. I spent an hour in the morning with M. de Vigny, author of 'Stello,' to

---

[1] Vol. ii., Art. v. ' Moral Statistics—Prisons of Paris.'
[2] *Edinburgh Review*, April 1890, p. 309.

whom Prévost introduced me. I have long considered him as the most delicate and satisfactory writer of the new French school, and so I found him in conversation. I told him such was the opinion of my best English friends and myself. He is now bringing out a play founded on the death of Chatterton—that is to say, 'of Chatterton the marvellous boy;' for of Horace Walpole's correspondent, Beckford's assailant, and the booksellers' hireling, the French poet knows but little. Lamartine is convinced that party politics are his vocation, and a committee of the Chamber his Parnassus, so he has given up his verses and talks mighty things on the tobacco monopoly. Hugo has fallen rather low, and is so mad, so childish, and so black-guard that all his acquaintance have cut him, or he them. I saw him at the Bibliothèque du Roi, but did not care to renew our acquaintance.

To Mr. E. H. Handley

Paris, January 17th.—My business here is chiefly to report to Mr. Austin on the nature of the application of capital punishment in France, to visit the new normal schools, and to pursue my old scholastic lore in the libraries here. These several pursuits have contributed to bring me into closer connexion with Cousin, who is good enough to receive me into the cabinet of the philosopher, after he has terminated his misplaced daily toil in the Chambre des Pairs. I am happy to say that he still lingers in the groves, not of the Académie Française, but of the Academy he has himself planted in France. He is publishing a MS. of Abélard and a commentary of Olympiodorus, which will be of great value. We talked of Coleridge. Cousin, judging him from the 'Aids to Reflection,' observed that 'en traversant l'espace il a emprunté les rayons du soleil, sans arriver à son globe même.' This globe, this true and massive sun, existed no doubt in Coleridge's mind, and will perhaps be given to the world in his posthumous work; but I think Cousin is right. The abrupt and irregular style of Coleridge's philosophical essays is like the chequering and reflected play of rays and emanations from a great luminary, of which, as yet, we know but little.

January 18th.—At this point yesterday, Barbier entered and sat with me two hours. I could scarcely believe that eighteen solemn months have passed since we three were roaming together on Hampstead Heath; for this steady pause and seclusion have so checked the more rapid habits of my life that I watch the paces of Time and Man with great wonder. *Cras ingens iterabimus æquor.* And yet I know not why we should extend our mazes over the surface of the world, when every point of earth or water over which we linger for an hour has in its solid depths and pure heights enough to fill and rule our lives.

But to return to Barbier. He is but little changed, but that little is for the better. His spirit of rebuke is less rough, but more stern; his enmity to evil less rancorous, but more inexorable; his attachment clings less to the blandishments and more to the wisdom of art. In the workings which have thus far strengthened and secured his mind, I doubt not that some good work, or at least the materials for it, have been produced. But, as you know, I never ask for admittance behind the scenes of my friends' theatres, believing that, if I am ever to judge their works fairly and honestly, I must sit where the world sits, in front, in the pit.

I have been introduced to M. de Vigny, whom I like exceedingly. I told him what you and myself thought of his 'Stello,' at which he was much pleased. In the man I find the same delicacy and graceful anticipation of pleasant thoughts which characterise his book. I mean by this anticipation, that he penetrates and harmonises in conversation with the person whom he listens to or addresses—a rare quality when it is in presence and amalgamated with the insoluble salt of French wit. De Vigny is about to bring out a little drama in three acts, on the story of Chatterton, or rather on his version of that story; for I soon found out that his Chatterton was a mere abstraction founded on a succinct account of the lad in a prefix to his works. I am afraid that it will be too dreamy and bloodless a piece for the French to applaud, and too ludicrously un-English for me to approve.

To Mrs. Reeve

January 22nd.—Just as I was sitting down to write this morning the excellent Count Leo Thun came in, and we have been to the Criminal Courts of Assize together. I felt a pleasure in the company of one so good in a place where levity, severity, and vice were so strangely mingled. The more I read of criminal law, and the more I see of its practice, the more horror do I feel for these false and monstrous punishments, which tend to congeal the heart in its worst form, and to close the mind in its worst ignorance. The prisoner whom I saw tried to-day was condemned to seven years' *travaux forcés* for a robbery which he had committed on the very day that he was discharged from prison for a previous offence. They termed him incorrigible—and who in that horrible Bicêtre had attempted to correct or reform him? They taught him half his infamy, and they condemned him to bear the whole weight of it for ever. No observations I have made on the insane have given me half the pangs or recoil from human suffering that I endure in this study of criminal procedure. . . .

January 28th.—The most remarkable visit I have recently made was to M. de Balzac, and I am indeed embarrassed by the attempt to give you the faintest idea of this extraordinary man : such a singular contrast of profound philosophy—more of intuition than of analysis—combined with the variety and prodigality of an Eastern story-teller, expressed in a copious and brilliant language, frequently degenerating into the violence or rising into the ostentation of positive insanity, I have never met with. Balzac was seated in an elegant apartment, situated at the very extremity of this side of Paris, which he took because from some whim or strange reason the house is called ' La Fabrique de l'Absolu.' To this Fabrique we found our way, and at the end of a long low room, as it were between a study and a boudoir, we found the Magician himself, surrounded by proofs and manuscripts which he was correcting and composing with a rapidity that sets all the printers of Paris at naught. He talked chiefly of himself, with the most boisterous and fantastical self-acclamation, for it was more than

approbation ; above all, he drew out the lines and castrame-
tation of his great work [1] before us, to which all that he
has at present written belongs, and which will contain the
circumstances of human life in all their variety, the motives
and principles of human action in their irrevocable tendencies, and, thirdly, the causes of activity, and of thinking,
and willing, in their permanent unity—a work which will
reach at least to forty enormous volumes, and will in all
probability remain incomplete from the death or madness of
its author—the builder of a Babel which he intends to be a
mark to all nations, and to overshadow the earth. . . .

To Mr. E. H. Handley

Paris, February 2nd.—I was introduced to M. de Balzac
by Prévost about a week ago ; he resides near the Observa-
tory, in a house over which is inscribed 'La Fabrique de
l'Absolu.' This pertinent epigraph determined his choice of
an abode. In my conversation with him I tried to raise
him out of his detestable forms and his mendacious conceptions of human life into the region of those abstruse
contemplations where I think him supereminently great.
It is strange that a man, more conversant than any of his
contemporaries with the Romance of the Human Soul,
should so utterly degrade the activity of man by separating
it from all high principle. He has written in the godlessness
of a strong wit, saying, 'Let us form men and genii ; the
men of clay, the genii of smoke ; let us create ; let us people
the streets with a bad throng, for to-morrow we die.' But
the excess of his vanity prevented me from drawing any
distinct principle from him. He declaimed for an hour on
the extent of his labours, which, when terminated, will
consist of three parts : the first is to be the mirror of human
life, the vanities and vices and distinctions and sexes of
the world ; the second, of which the 'Physiologie du
Mariage' is a specimen, will exhibit by an elaborate analysis

---

[1] *La Comédie Humaine.* The history of the idea may be read in Mme
Surville's *Balzac, sa Vie et ses Œuvres,* p. 95. For a full prospectus of the
great work, drawn up in 1845, see Ch. de Lovenjoul's *Histoire des Œuvres de
Balzac,* p. 217. It was only about three-quarters done at the time of Balzac's
death, in 1850.

the principles (as Balzac calls them), the motives (as I term them) of social mankind ; lastly, the causes and the efficient generation of human ideas will be unfolded in a book of more abstruse doctrine. If Balzac wants a title for this great labour, which, he says, will reach to at least forty large octavos, I shall beg to suggest the parody of Dante's ' Divina Commedia '—for this modern ' Commedia ' is *tutta diabolica*—'La Diabolique Comédie du Sieur de Balzac.' Alas! my friend, I can scarce find courage to laugh at a theory which is dragging down hundreds of young souls into its pit with the impure claws of a ghoul. . . .

I have found a most efficient aid in Cousin in the study of my scholastic philosophies. I believe I told you that he is publishing a book of Magister Petrus [1] entitled ' Sic et Non,' which, however, I take to be more curious than valuable, and not worth Roger Bacon's little finger. If you can obtain a list of such MSS. of Abelardus as exist in the library at Munich, you will greatly oblige us. The MSS. of Occam are extremely rare ; there are none at Paris ; I believe only one of the ' Logic ' at Oxford, and I conclude that Munich must have the larger portion of them, since it was the place of his refuge and death. I should be obliged to you for a list of them if any exist. You should also visit his tomb, on which Cousin says there is a very grand inscription. Probably Schelling can furnish you with some of these details, and I beg you to present him with the united salutations of myself and my illustrious friend. You would smile to see me by the side of the great French transcendentalist, in the recesses of his study, the doors shut upon the whole world and the table covered with monkish penmanships and mountains of metaphysic. I reproach Cousin, however, for busying himself overmuch with the erudition of philosophy, when he is as competent to reap in the field as to thrash in the garner ; I reproach him still more for the part these absurd philosophists have induced him to take in politics.

I attend the Académie des Sciences Morales et Politiques every Saturday, where I see Mignet, of whom I judge most favourably as an historical thinker. Schelling

---

[1] *Sc.* Abelardus.

and my uncle, Mr. Austin, are corresponding members. With the exception of one or two strong heads, and a great many splendid reputations, the itching and scratching of all Academics is a disgusting spectacle. . . .

To Mrs. Reeve

February 12th.—Last Thursday, in the evening, Prévost accompanied me to the house of M. de Lamartine. The poet was nearly alone, but it was not the less difficult to discover the author of the 'Meditations' and the 'Harmonies' in the politician busy with his salt and tobacco monopolies and his savings banks. Now and then a swell of Parnassian enthusiasm reminds one 'of that large utterance of the earlier gods;' and the isolation in which his political creed has placed him becomes a poet and a thinker more than it assists a debater and a philanthropist. When you read 'Stello,' which I beg you to do, you will see all that is to be said on the fatal alliance of public power and the private energy of a pure and contemplative soul very admirably illustrated by M. de Vigny; when you visit Paris you will see an hundred victims of this new Juggernaut, who descend into the valley to fight instead of remaining on the mountain to pray. Mme. de Lamartine is an Englishwoman, devoted to her husband; that is to say, devoted to making him a political hero. Alas! for those false Pagans who leave the Hall of Apollo for the House of Mercury. . . .

February 19th.—When I last wrote I was on the eve of dining with Mr. Digby,[1] and going to M. de Vigny's 'Chatterton'—and so, indeed, I passed my Thursday evening, February 12th. Kemble's enthusiasm had shed such a glow of chivalrous distinction on the person of his friend, that I was almost surprised to see him without armour, or at least a *juste-au-corps* of chamois leather. Moreover, the table at which we dined was neither round nor knightly; but Digby himself is a man well worth knowing, and I derived much benefit from his stores of monastic lore. I left his party

---

[1] Kenelm Henry Digby, born in 1800, author of *The Broad-Stone of Honour* (first published in 1822), and—at a later period—of numerous other works. He died in 1880.

early to go to 'Chatterton,' which was received with triumphal honours. Some critics, indeed, have been malicious enough to publish an authentic biography of the boy, knave and poet, which contrasts monstrously with M. de Vigny's passionate and high-minded sufferer; and others have detected a defence of suicide in the language and actions of a youth who is thus presented to the attention of a nation of Chattertons. For my part, I found in the piece more sentiment than principle; and although the said sentiment is, by rare exception, pure and noble, all the soliloquies which ever rang round the garrets of Shoe Lane, and all the powers of M. de Vigny, will never make a healthy example or an honourable poet out of a man as weak and vain as Chatterton. The drama is therefore false. Had the character of the hero remained such as it really was, it would have been true to nature, and we should have bestowed upon him our natural contempt; but by changing the workings of his mind, by substituting external pressure for internal decay, M. de Vigny has failed in justifying his catastrophe. It is, however, a play of wonderful beauty, full of magical language, and hidden springs of passion and thought flowing under the surface of each character; the acting can scarcely be surpassed, particularly that of Mme. Dorval, who plays Kitty Bell, the hostess of Chatterton. . . .

February 25th.—M. de Tocqueville's book, 'De la Démocratie en Amérique,' is a work of first-rate order;[1] perhaps the most important treatise on the Science of States that has appeared since Montesquieu; and nothing can be more worthy of attention and of thought. I decline translating it, because I am determined never to write a sentence which I do not believe in my inmost heart; and I admire Tocqueville as a philosophical opponent, as a man in-

[1] Alexis, Comte de Tocqueville, born in 1805, having studied law at Paris, was, in 1827, appointed 'Juge Auditeur' at Versailles, where he contracted an intimate friendship with Gustave de Beaumont, one of his colleagues. During some years he and Beaumont made a careful study of the prisons and *bagnes* of France, and from April 1831 to March 1832 they travelled together in the United States. On their return they published *Du Système Pénitentiaire aux États-Unis, et de son application en France.* In May 1832 Beaumont was dismissed from his appointment, and Tocqueville resigned; and, thus free from the ties of office, devoted themselves at first solely to literature, though later on, as will be seen, they took an active part in politics. With Tocqueville Reeve became more especially intimate, though always on friendly terms with Beaumont.

finitely valuable to me, because he forces me to furbish all
my powers in the great debate which he propounds; but I
will not promulgate an erroneous doctrine, nor enter the
world with a list of articles in my hand which my hand
refuses to subscribe. . . .

The Lamartines are very kind to me. I go there every
Saturday evening, and the old harp-strings sometimes
vibrate for my sake. The impressions which the East has
made on M. de Lamartine are of a high and pure kind; he
tells his travels beautifully, but in a few weeks all the world
will know how he tells them, for his 'Notes de Voyage' will
be published. I thought of them for translation, but I find
that it would be a work of art, and to copy artfully is neither
an easy nor a gainful process.

To Mr. E. II. Handley

Paris, March 2nd.—You are mistaken in supposing that
MSS. of the 'Sic et Non' are rare; but not the less sincere
are our thanks to Schmeller and yourself for the communication of the Munich MS. It seems to be more extensive
and more ancient than those of Marmoutiers and the
Abbaye de St. Michel, from which Cousin publishes his text.
Yesterday Cousin read a splendid account of his scholastic
hero, and digressed into a copious improvisation on the
characters of those two philosophic bruisers of Brittany,.
Peter Abélard and René Descartes. You know that in all
questions of state and thought, of society and of man, I am
more prone to side with the bull which grazes than with the
bull which fights; with the mariner sounding the depths and
watching the stars than with the naked tar who launches
his broadside and boards his foe; with the sages who collect,
combine, and construct than with those who divide, repel,.
and deny. But, although the bump of philosophic combative-
ness is but partially developed on my skull, I am sensible
that tempests which were strong to purify monastic crypts
and to purge monastic miasmata in the twelfth century must
have been tempests pregnant with a divine and heaven-
clearing fire. Cousin's error consists, in my mind, in his
imperfect knowledge of that constructive philosophy of

which John Scotus Erigena was the faint representative, Thomas Aquinas the teacher, and Dante the master and the poet. . . .

Kemble gave me a letter to his friend Kenelm Digby, of whom you may know something. Digby is the true descendant of the great man whose name he bears, a Christian knight, a Catholic philosopher. At his house I made the acquaintance of M. Rio, a man whom I have long esteemed for his works, and who knows Schelling and Görres well. Another ward has been opened in the strange Panopticon of which I find myself the central point.

I have four windows to my cell. From the first I descry the populace of Paris, disguised in ribald masks, drunk with the lusts and follies of the closing carnival, laughing without mirth, swearing without a knowledge or a faith of that by which they swear, intemperate without enthusiasm, fickle without hope. . . .

From the second, I discover a more melancholy scene— the prisons of Paris, the death-beds of the poor, the idiot, and the maniac. I have descended into the dungeon of the assassin, into the cell of the galley-slave; and if the empty hearts and dead souls of the nation repelled me with dismay, the unmixed ferocity, the entire recklessness, of the criminals of France has overwhelmed me with horror. You know, my dear friend, that I am no vain philanthropist, and that the shapes I love are those of angels, not of men; but I will acknowledge that I had hitherto no conception or belief of sin and depravity as great as what I have witnessed here. By Heaven! '*Per me si va nella città dolente*'—I have seen Hell. I have gone down the subterranean staircase, and all that I had read or recorded before were things and passages belonging to the warmer surface of our earth.

The third aperture, if I may continue my metaphor, is the one from which I discover the groups of good and great men, who grow like plants rich in their own vegetation on the borders of the still glowing crater. With these men I mingle, with them I converse of the past and of the future, and by their backward intuitions and high prognostications I console myself for the hideous present. Amongst them I may quote some names and persons known to you, and others whom you are likely to hear of—De Vigny, with his quiet and elegant sensibility; Barbier, with his compassionate philosophy mixed with so rare a power of rebuke; De Wailly, his most intimate friend, the translator of 'Hamlet;' Antony Deschamps, the translator of Dante, whose only madness is to believe himself mad, and who actually lives in a madhouse under this conviction; the stately and benevolent Lamartine, whose madness is to believe himself a statesman, and who harangues me and the Chambers on the matters of salt and tobacco, and who is the poet in the man, instead of being what the true bard should be, a perfect man in a perfect poet; lastly, the excellent Ballanche, whom I see very frequently and whom I like better every time I see him. One of my greatest pleasures has been to find that all the opinions I had adopted or maintained in my discussion on Hercules are in accordance with his.　I hope that, by my mediation, a complete edition of Vico's works will appear before very long; Ballanche is most fit and most willing to co-operate in this good work.

My last look-out turns to the Catholic and untainted few who cherish, in their learned leisure, the traditions of aristocracy, monarchy, and Christianity.　To these Rio and Digby belong, and the English Catholics in Paris and a few of the most eloquent disciples of that congregation.　In this calm society I have found more reflection than I could have hoped to find in France; but I have seen little or nothing of the gaiety of the Court, where I will not, or the crowds where I cannot, go. . . . . I see a great deal of the Thuns, who are excellent.

To Mrs. Reeve

March 4th.—I have become acquainted with M. Rio, whose 'Histoire de l'Esprit Humain' I read at Geneva on Roget's recommendation, and I have seldom met with a person more bent on the same path and errands as myself. He has a book now in the press which will, I imagine, contain pretty nearly all that I had expressed in my Essays on the Christian Philosophy of the Middle Ages—as in Ballanche's works I now find the greater part of my views on the History of Religions; but if I hereby lose the credit which might have attached to the novelty of some of my lucubrations, I am amply compensated by the assurance that the road I have chosen is one trodden by a few good men. In a country which I believed myself to be exploring for the first time, I meet not only with a sign that the point I have reached is noted in the minds and charts of men, but I meet with the traveller himself, older and stronger than I am, whom I have been fortunate enough to overtake, and who may henceforth be my guide or my companion. The course of life and thought is not indeed to reach any point of repose, but to pass a perpetual line of starting-points, the furthest of which is only a beginning.

March 12th.—For the last week I have scarcely stirred out, having had a great inclination to labour, and no extraordinary enticements to draw me from my fireside. Moreover, I have so many near neighbours, that I never need to go far for amusement. Yesterday I called on my old and illustrious friend Mickiewicz, whom I found fattening in a neat and happy *ménage*; he has been married for some months, and with the exception of occasional fits of absence, such as forgetting his wife on the wedding day, &c., he thrives exceedingly. He gave me a translation of a new poem, which is admirably worthy of him.

March 21st.—On Sunday morning, after reading your letter, I started for Notre Dame with Léon Thun. We arrived at half-past eleven, and the service was only to begin at one o'clock; but the whole nave of that vast building was already filled; in a short time the aisles and the furthest chapels and confessionals were crowded by the audience. The nave was railed in, and reserved for the men; and here was gathered a motley group of poets, priests, philosophers, historians, scholars, young soldiers, *élèves de l'Ecole Polytechnique*, and every class of men capable of following an argument, or desirous of a pretext of reason for belief; in the side aisles the high ladies of the Faubourg St. Germain, the Duchess and the Chanoinesse of the Restauration, were heaped together promiscuously with the late comers. In the centre of the church sat the archbishop, simply dressed, with the clergy of Paris. In all, the building might contain five to six thousand souls. At one o'clock the Abbé Lacordaire entered the pulpit. He is a young man of mean appearance; his person is insignificant and his voice feeble. Nevertheless, for an hour and a half he sustained a discourse of remarkable logic and energy; never did words slacken to vent his ready thought, never did the elevation of his subject baffle his eloquence or his sincere philosophy. I, who am but a slender admirer of pulpit eloquence at any time, could not but acknowledge the solid arrangement of his subject, and the courage and propriety of his illustrations. I have rarely carried away a sermon, or rather discourse, so perfectly; indeed, on coming out, I repeated nearly the whole of it to Léon Thun, who from his deafness did not hear a word of it. To-morrow I hope to get a better place. . . .

On Monday evening I dined with M. de Tocqueville; he is a very agreeable man, and the more I see his book (which I have now nearly finished) the more I like it. My first impression as to its democratic tendency was entirely erroneous. He regards Democracy as the inevitable lot of Europe, and as an evil which we had best prepare to meet, since we cannot escape it. He will be in England in a month, and I shall hope to get him to Hampstead on my return.

March 29*th.*—The attack of sore-throat has made way for a very severe ordinary cold in my head, and before you get this epistle I shall be quite recovered. Barbier continues his amiable visits, and he and my doctor want to persuade me to go to Lyons and thence down the Rhone, to spend a few weeks in Provence. The truth is that I do not want much persuading, and if you see no objection I shall very likely devote a month to this excursion. Besides the pleasure of the climate and of seeing our colony at Marseilles, I want to stay a few days at Avignon and its neighbourhood, which has so long ' detained my predilection,' as Wm. Taylor says; and I want to see one of the Bagnes, to complete my studies on secondary punishments in France.

Last Wednesday was my friend Montalembert's first soirée. I arrived late, having dined with Thackeray and his grandmother at the other end of the Champs-Elysées; but the rooms were still filled with a notable company, though I met Ballanche on the stairs and Rio in the hall. The Abbé Lacordaire, whose preaching I described in my last, was there; as simple and unaffected in the world as he is *puissant* in the pulpit; Digby, with his large person, and quiet learned countenance; and others of all sects and schools and ranks. The rooms were simply decorated with several old Italian pictures, a copy of the portrait of the Virgin by 'Beatus Lucas,' vulgarly supposed to be St. Luke, and that same little German lithography in three compartments which we possess and admire. The library is a small room most richly filled with the learning and the poetry of the Middle Ages and the Church.

April 5th.—It is clear for several reasons that the sooner I return the better. My aunt's departure leaves you in a solitude which is neither expedient nor agreeable for you. The acquaintance of Lord Lansdowne is too important for me not to catch at it; and the intelligence you give about Tocqueville's book decides me to come over and join you in the translation of it. I was strangely mistaken in my appreciation of its democratic tendencies when first I read it; I now know the author, and sympathise with his views.

April 8th.—Yesterday, *par grand extraordinaire*, a circle of gentlemen who dine together once a fortnight thought fit to honour me by waiving their custom and admitting a stranger amongst them. The party consisted of Ballanche, Faucher, Tocqueville, Ste.-Beuve, Ampère, Vivien, a deputy, and another; and I never enjoyed a dinner more in my life. Tocqueville was incomparable with his stories of the Chicka-saws. After dinner, Ballanche and I sallied on to our friend Liszt's great concert. As we walked down the broad quay in the moonlight I was more than usually struck by the suavity of that old man's discourse, which is like the voice of his own mysteries, a sound revealing, in slight modulations and short lines of poetry, whole spheres and schemes of life and truth, warmed by the cheerfulness of an affectionate heart.

When we arrived at the concert room, it was very full, and I stood the greater part of the evening. I do not know whether I ever described to you my friend Liszt. His person is slight and tall, a delicate frame, not worn or wasted by weakness and malady, but perpetually strained by the flow of animated thoughts, by the violence of a musical soul, for which no sound affords an adequate expression. Liszt had already played a great Fantasia of his own, and Beethoven's 27th Sonata, in the former part of the concert. After this latter piece he gasped with emotion as I took his hand and thanked him for the divine energy he had shed forth. At last I had managed to pierce the crowd, and I sat in the orchestra before the Duchesse de Rauzan's box, talking to her Grace and Mme. de Circourt, who was there; my chair was on the same board as Liszt's piano when the final piece began. It was a duet for two instruments, beginning with Mendelssohn's 'Chants sans Paroles,' and proceeding to a work of Liszt's. We had already passed that delicious chime of the 'Song written in a Gondola' and the gay tendrils of sound in another lighter piece, which always reminded me of an Italian vine when Mrs. Handley played it to us. As the closing strains began, I saw Liszt's countenance assume that agony of expression, mingled with radiant smiles of joy, which I never saw in any other human face, except in the paintings of our Saviour by some of the early masters; his hands rushed over the keys, the floor on which I sat shook like a wire, and the whole audience were wrapped in sound, when the hand and frame of the artist gave way; he fainted in the arms of the friend who was turning over for him, and we bore him out in a strong fit of hysterics. The effect of this scene was really dreadful. The whole room sat breathless with fear, till Hiller came forward and announced that Liszt was already restored to consciousness, and was comparatively well again. As I handed Mme. de Circourt to her carriage, we both trembled like poplar leaves, and I tremble scarcely less as I write.

April 20*th*.—I have got several 'Protestants'[1] (oh! that I should be the bearer of the like! However, Protestants they are, safely lodged at the bottom of my trunk) for my uncle Richard. By the way, I never told you how the

[1] Presumably Tracts.

Paris City Missions have been visiting me, and how I fought the battle of the Faith with a good man who talked about Popish errors, and who did not know what I meant by the Council of Trent, nor what was the reason the sacramental cup was refused to the laity.   After all he was startled to find that, by his own showing, he was attempting the very task which the friars were ordained and empowered to perform.

It has been seen that in returning to England it was Reeve's intention to collaborate with his mother in the translation of Tocqueville's 'Democracy in America.' For some reason, the idea of collaboration was given up; and though written at Hampstead during the summer, the translation was Reeve's work throughout. We may, however, presume that he received some assistance, or rather advice, from Tocqueville himself, who came to England about the same time, and, falling ill in London, took lodgings at Hampstead, where the acquaintance between the two ripened into friendship. The book was published by Saunders & Otley, and was ' a great success.'

It may perhaps be thought, and it is certain that in after years Reeve himself thought, that of greater value to him than even the success of the work from the publisher's point of view was the thorough discipline and training in the opinions and methods of Tocqueville. In 1872 he wrote :[1] ' If there be any truth or merit in the opinions I have formed on the state of France and the history of her revolutions, their value is due, in great part, to the author of "Democracy in America." I had the good fortune to translate it into English when I was about one-and-twenty ; and from that time, till the date of his death in 1859, I lived in the intimacy of unbroken friendship with Alexis de Tocqueville. I was well acquainted with his opinions on many subjects which he never imparted to the world ; my own opinions were no doubt affected by the influence of that pure and subtle intellect ; and the highest merit I would venture to claim for them is their conformity with his principles.'

The labour of translating was relieved by writing occasional papers for different periodicals ; amongst others, one for the ' British and Foreign Review,' on the establishment of a consul at Cracow, in which Reeve was assisted by his friend Zamoyski. This attracted some notice, and it was

---

[1] *Royal and Republican France*, vol. ii. p. 79.

understood that Lord Palmerston intended to act on the suggestion. If so, he changed his mind, and nothing was done. At this time, too, Reeve was introduced by his aunt, Mrs. Austin, to Lord Lansdowne, then, and for the next six years, President of the Council. During the summer Lord Lansdowne showed him a good deal of attention, frequently inviting him to dinner, and in November to Bowood. Afterwards, on his return to Paris, Lord Lansdowne gave him also a letter to Lord Granville, the English ambassador. Of Reeve's mental activity at this period we have a good picture in his letters to Handley.

To Mr. E. H. Handley

July 8th.—As there is some pleasure in connecting a notion in topography with the position of one's friends, so your letter from Worcester was not entirely disagreeable to me. . . . 'Tis strange enough that the Fates should have thrown you upon the very tract of country which is the favourite and frequent haunt of my summer and autumn excursions; and that I shall drive past your door many times a year with the cheering hope of meeting you in the hop-market at Worcester, or at the shop of Mr. Deighton, who is beyond all compare the greatest literary celebrity of Worcester. Talking of Mr. Deighton, I conjure you to order through him No. II. of Cochrane's 'Foreign Quarterly Review,' which has just appeared. It contains a very able article of my aunt's upon the French Law of Education, with a few additions of my own, and an article of mine upon Quinet's 'Ahasuerus,' upon which I especially want your opinion. I have none to give away, or I would send you a copy.

Brougham's Bill on Education will soon be discussed. I have made sundry excursions to the House of Lords to hear the debate on it, which has, however, been deferred from day to day. I was dining last night at Lansdowne House, and Lord L. told me that it would assuredly pass without difficulty. By the way, my introduction at Lansdowne House is a novelty which affords me great enjoyment. I dine there about once a fortnight, to meet a party which has a thousand merits to compensate the solitary vice of Whiggism. In England I have never seen such purely æsthetic society before. It is a mansion replete with works of art, and with a good spirit of thought, fancy, and benevolence not unworthy of the ranks of Roman statues which fill the niches, the Canovas which sleep before you, or the Raphaels and Leonardos on the walls.

I have seen a good deal of Raumer, the historian, there and elsewhere ; a German of great penetration and singular merit in conversation. He brings me to Rotteck. I have read several portions of the volumes you lent me, and I confess I have rarely been pleased with the style, never with the stuff, of that author. A more godless denial of the supernatural, or rather of the natural raised to its highest power, in the flow of human history, I never met with ; he breaks the rod of Moses, he petrifies the Gods of Etruria ; and the whole range of theological and theistical tradition, which is and which alone is the record of early time, is evaporated to a whiff of delusion or condensed to a stone lie. I do not advert to his political opinions, because I only infer what they must be from such a commencement. Do you remember what that Italian madman said, whose deep wisdom struck us so much in Bedlam ?—'Les révolutions viennent de haut en bas, et non de bas en haut.' Such is and always was my creed ; the direct antipodes of Rotteck. I am not very deeply versed in history, and am incompetent to offer an opinion on his general accuracy, but I do not think that what he says of the Etruscan alphabet is correct. . . . I shall very soon have done my translation of the second volume of Tocqueville.

Coed Ddu House, September 13th.—It is clear that my parcel and your last letter crossed one another on the road, and I only hope that the former travelled as safely and was as cordially received as the latter. But here the parallel ceases ; for, if I hope you will find matter of meditation consonant to my own in the tomes I have sent you, I cannot the less frankly own that I dissent *in toto, immo etiam toto cælo,* from the conclusions at which you have arrived on the perusal of my second volume. As I have not got a copy of the work in my possession, I cannot refer to all your references, and point out others to you which make for my side of the argument. But I again repel your assertion that the work, either in foundation or construction, is a stronghold of democracy. In the passage which you quote, in which he says that no people has ever, by its voluntary activity, called an aristocracy into being, and that all aristocracies have been imposed or have imposed themselves by constraint, the fact results *ex natura rei*. A power emanating from the voluntary activity of the people is a democratic power ; but the very nature of the aristocratic principle is that it is self-generative. As to its being opposed to natural equity, I cannot admit that the necessary and constant results which arise from the collision and subsequently from the subordination of the weak to the strong, the foolish to the wise, is in any way opposed to the law of nature by which those very differences of strength and wisdom subsist. Tocqueville asserts, and with truth, that the American community will never, perhaps, constitute an aristocracy; but in what he says of the legal profession and the exclusive habits of the rich, you may trace the power-generating tendencies which are inseparable from the inequalities of technical skill, acquired knowledge, and possessed wealth.

As I have six young ladies laughing round me whilst I write, and as we are in a few minutes to sally forth on one of those shooting, fishing, riding, eating, sketching, and joking parties, which form the recreation of philosophers, and the occupation of the Celias and Rosalinds of our Ardennes, I herewith pitch democracy, ochlocracy, aristocracy, yea, and monarchy itself, to the devil, and wish you a very good morning.

I have, however, something to add which is of importance to us both. I have entered into a somewhat intimate connexion with the 'British and Foreign Review,' a journal whose object is to introduce and propagate European ideas of social and political amelioration in this island, whilst we hope that it will obtain some success on the Continent. I am about to undertake a journey, beginning with Paris, for the purpose of obtaining the assistance of all the distinguished men in Europe, who may be inclined to write, and to collect information for it. The proprietor is Mr. Wentworth Beaumont, a man of singular activity, boundless munificence, ample wealth, an ardent metaphysician, considerable talents, and views in politics which end in his hating the Radicals, repelling the old Tories, and despising the Whigs. Of course I am not responsible for all the political opinions put forth in this 'Review;' many of them will differ from my own; but the great questions of foreign policy and of general social amelioration on sound principles of rational philosophy will meet with my hearty co-operation, and I trust with yours. I have spoken to the parties about your article on Education in Bavaria, and I entreat you to review Comte Drechsel's books directly for our Christmas number. I have not the power to say that your article will be unconditionally accepted before it is written, but I have very little doubt that it will, and that both parties will be satisfied with each other. Beaumont pays a guinea a page, and adds a bounty when he is pleased. No article on German education has appeared in the 'Review' at present.

I shall be detained in England longer than I had expected, as I am going to stay at Bowood (Lord Lansdowne's) towards the end of October. All here desire to be kindly remembered to you.

Coed Ddu, September 23rd.—I have been reading Basil Montagu's 'Life of Bacon,' which I began some time ago. I was better pleased with it at first than I am in the end. It is Bacon larded. Montagu's mind and style are so grown into the shape and manner of Bacon's, without reaching a tenth part of his stature, or asserting the trace of a diversity of opinion or conclusion, that you arrive at nothing which a reader of Bacon does not know. It is my firm belief that Bacon was ignorant of the entire scheme of transcendental metaphysics, and that the denial or neglect of the supersensual which characterises his writings has had an evil influence on the real philosophy of the English. In saying this, I do not forget what Coleridge has upon the subject; but I doubt whether Bacon's own notions were ever raised to so high a significance as Coleridge's method has shown his principles to be capable of.

I do not think Montagu has satisfactorily defended Bacon from the charge of corruption, though he loses no opportunity of sinking the biographer in the advocate. My

Lord St. Albans was a man fond of purple and good living, and he never stirred without a fair train of the most gallant company. In short, he lived as the courtier of a foolish king and the friend of an unprincipled favourite; and he wrote like a sage who might have scorned James and rebuked Buckingham.

Bowood, November 4th.—Although I am just returned from a long canter with Lord Lansdowne, and have my feet to warm, my appetite to prepare, and my limbs to adorn before dinner, yet how can I forbear to offer you my hearty congratulations on the event which I have learned from your letter of Saturday, forwarded to me here this morning! You have made another step in the initiation of life. Your power to good and to evil is hereby increased; your reason has a new being to guide; your foresight, a new track to discern; your arm, a new bosom to protect. New things, before divined, but now known, are about you; and in this is the change greater than that of marriage; for there you were but joined to another in unity, here you are joined by another to infinity—a race of beings infinite, who will surely rise up to fulfil in their turns the purposes of God and man. I had no father; but the world has nursed me with extreme kindness in my orphanhood. Not the less do I look upon the laws and the course of human descent as the sacred stream which fills all cisterns with the waters of life; not the less do I look upon the father, the mother, and the child as three divine monitors teaching each other lasting truths in mutual harmony.

And now, may I hope, without offence, that at a moment when you and Mrs. Handley are naturally filled and animated by one sentiment of affection for one thing—a sentiment not only embracing each of you, but reaching still further to the being who is the child of both—may I hope that I may express even to her the pleasure and the hope with which I have learned this event?

We are going solemnly to drink the boy's health to-day at dinner. Lord Henry Fitzmaurice has heard so much about you—he having arrived at Munich just after your marriage—that I hope you will some day or other meet him at my house or elsewhere.

I return to town on Friday, and we shall sail for Boulogne about the 16th. Are you coming up to town? I would wait a day or two to see you. Write to me at Hampstead.

Shortly after the date of this last letter, Reeve returned to Paris, bearing—as has been said—a letter of introduction from the Marquis of Lansdowne to Lord Granville; and, what with his literary work and a good deal of society, he found himself fully occupied, as is outlined in the Journal:—

1836.—I spent the winter in Paris, where I had now a large acquaintance. M. and Mme. de Circourt I had known at Geneva. She had a capital salon, and that introduced me to another class of persons—the Duchesse de Rauzan, the Duchesse de Mailly, Marquise de la Grange, Marquise de Bellissen, in the Faubourg St.-Germain. I was intimate with Count Jenison-Walworth, the Bavarian Minister—saw at his house Dr. Koreffe, and a good many diplomats. Hiller had a good house for music—heard Nourrit, Ernst, and Chopin there; knew Henri Lehmann and other artists. The Czartoryskis were established at the Hôtel Lambert. Tocqueville, G. de Beaumont, C. Lucas, were in Paris. Faucher introduced me to M. Thiers. I also knew Dufaure, X. Marmier, Mme. d'Agoult,[1] whose house was delightful, Mme. Marliani, &c., and I spent a very brilliant winter. Lord and Lady Granville were very polite. Kenelm Digby must not be forgotten. At his house I met Rio, Montalembert, D'Eckstein and Lacordaire—the Catholic world.

I left Paris in March because Mr. Young ceased to edit the 'British and Foreign Review,' and I came back to take a more active part in it. I now wrote a good deal and largely increased my income.

All this is told more fully in his letters to his mother, some extracts of which are here given :—

Paris, December 6th, 1835.—This very evening I have been to dine with Meyerbeer. My aunt had seen Mme. Beer at Boulogne in the summer, and as they talked about

---

[1] The sister of Comte de Flavigny and, at this time, one of the leaders of Parisian society—rich, clever, enthusiastic, and, though past her first youth, still beautiful. She was afterwards known as a democratic, or even communistic, writer, under the pseudonym of 'Daniel Stern.'

me, I communicated my arrival at their hotel. Meyerbeer immediately wrote me a very proper and even affectionate note, inviting me to dinner; so to dinner I went. I confess that I suffered a little from the excess of their Judaism, which put me in mind of Monmouth Street [1] in gala; but Meyerbeer himself is less disagreeable than the rest of the family, and I sat next him. He is immersed in the rehearsals of his great opera,[2] which is positively coming out in January. The music is still a profound secret, but the singers themselves say that it is transcendent. . . .

This morning I had [Gustave] Beaumont sitting with me for a long time; Tocqueville is not yet returned from the country. I am happy to say that they are both very busy— Beaumont with his book on Ireland, which will, I think, be capital, and Tocqueville with a third volume, which is to treat more especially of the influence of democracy on the manners of the Anglo-Americans. Before I knew this I had attempted to do the same thing very cursorily in the article I have been writing. You remember that in his second volume he treats of the influence of manners in maintaining democratic institutions, and it is evident that the reciprocal influence is not less important. I shall probably translate both these works, and certainly Tocqueville's third volume ; but they will neither of them appear for many months. Beaumont talks of next January twelvemonth for his.

Paris, December 20th.—I am kept in hot water from the difficulty of sending my numerous packets. There are delays here, and delays in England; secretaries protesting, printer's devils waiting, and a thousand other miseries because there is no means of sending parcels from Paris to England, except by the Embassy. Even Galignani sends his bookseller's despatches by that conveyance. The upshot of all this is that I shall always write to you by post. Notwithstanding these delays, I am through the more active part of my contributions to the 'Review,' having written in all three long articles, which will all, I believe, appear. That on Tocqueville will be fathered upon Young, at my desire. I suppose they will add something about the trans-

---

[1] Then and for many years later the home of ' olc clo'' shops.
[2] *Les Huguenots.* See *post*, p. 64.

lation; I have of course said nothing. You may believe from this that I have still every reason to be satisfied with my connexion with the 'Review.' A further negotiation is, however, on foot, which may make my uncle Meadows's prognostications prove true in the end. I have consented to be put on the list for the Cracow appointment; [1] and though I do not expect to get it, and if I did get it, it would only be temporary, yet from the very strenuous manner in which they have advocated me at the Foreign Office, it cannot but do me good.

January 4th, 1836.—When I say that I have no excuse for not having written, I am afraid that I betray the real do-nothingness, laziness, and torpor in which I have been living ever since the cold began. Indeed, I am so ill-satisfied with the idle life I have been leading for the last fortnight that I am determined to come home much sooner than I otherwise intended, if I do not pick up something to occupy and stimulate my thoughts. I have been reading Michelet's 'Mémoires de Luther' with great interest, and I shall probably write something about the book; but I require my own papers and the British Museum in order to set to work. *Du reste*, I have not been reading, or writing, or hearing, or seeing anything: the dead blunt cold pursues one into the house.

I continue to see the Macaulays a good deal. The girls are dreadfully like Tom Babington, and very amusing from a mixture of saintship and politics, ignorance of the world and knowledge of Parliament. . . . I am now daily expecting that Mr. [Wentworth] Beaumont will arrive in Paris, and the arrangements which I may make with him will, in a great measure, determine my future movements.

January 16th.—Since the frost has disappeared, I have become a little more lively. I have even been writing with Faucher in the 'Courrier Français' a little article on the Municipal Elections, and I have laid out the trenches of a long poem about Giordano Bruno. I have more things in my head, and as it is now decided that Mr. and Mrs. Beaumont will be here next week, I shall soon know what I am going to do more precisely. . . . My present plan—you

---

[1] The proposed consulship. See *ante*, p. 50.

know I make one a week—is to come home about the end
of March, before I go to Germany, if I go there, in the
summer. One of the things which may disturb this arrangement is, I am sorry to say, the Handley business.[1] Matters
have arrived at the highest pitch of *inconvenance*, and a
public *exposé* may be dreaded. As for myself, I have made
up my mind to stand by Handley to the last, if I find
nothing to shake my present conviction that he has been the
victim of atrocious calumnies and intrigues ; and I have
written to him and to his father by the same post to that
effect. You need not be alarmed at anything which is likely to
happen, for I cannot yet believe those women to be so mad
as to draw down all the shame and expense upon their own
heads, when advantageous terms are offered them. With
these matters pending, I may be forced to come home at a
moment's notice ; but the present plan is for me to meet
Handley at Dieppe, or some port of France, which will I
hope do. My wish is—if you see nothing to the contrary—that you should call on the old Handleys and pay
them every attention, without alluding to anything you
may hear from me. They will probably be open-mouthed
enough. . . .

I have seen a good deal of Thackeray this last week.
That excellent and facetious being is at the present moment
editing an English paper here, in opposition to Galignani's.[2]
But what is more ominous, he has fallen in love, and talks
of being married in less than twenty years. What is there
so affecting as matrimony ! I dined yesterday with his
object, who is a nice, simple, girlish girl ; a niece of that old
Colonel Shawe whom one always meets at the Sterlings'. I
beg Simpson's[3] pardon, as well as yours, for not having said
more about him. His only subject of melancholy arises from
a lack of dancing exercise, and I cannot induce him to join
the 'Bals à 1 franc pour le Cavalier, avec 30 centimes en

---

[1] A matrimonial quarrel. See *post*, p. 66.

[2] This seems to be a mistake. There is no other record of anything of the
sort, and it is believed that Thackeray was at this time actually writing for
Galignani.

[3] John Palgrave Simpson, known to Mrs. Reeve as son of the town clerk of
Norwich. As he was six years older than Reeve, their acquaintance as boys
must have been slight ; but at Munich and during the past year in Paris they
had naturally become intimate friends.

consommation,' which abound at this season in every
street.   For my part, though I have bought a cocked hat
with a tassel on it, I have not been out more than last year.
To-night we are going to the Embassy to meet the Duke of
Devonshire, who is here; and I have been introduced into
one or two Chaussée d'Antin houses, which are warm, cheerful, nicely gilt and painted—one of them, at least—to imitate
the houses in Pompeii.

Saturday, January 16th.—The party at the Granvilles'
was horridly dull, and the only amusement I had was
treading on the D. of D.'s toe, in scrambling for a cup of
tea, and chatting a little foppery with Bulwer, to whom I
introduced myself as Mrs. Austin's nephew.   By the way,
what trash his last book about Rienzi is !

Paris, January 27th.—I am writing a little notice[1]
of a book of poems, accompanied by a long philosophical
preface, by a young Italian, Count Mamiani, a descendant
of Julius II.   By the way, the book is dedicated 'all' illus-
trissimo Signor Barbier, Clarissimo Poeta.'   That, however,
is not my reason for reviewing it; but I was glad to find so
good an opportunity of mentioning that school of thinking
and religious patriots of which Manzoni may be considered
the chief, Pellico the martyr, and Mamiani a disciple.   I
hope I shall be allowed to say in our ' Review ' what I think
of the Catholic and Christian spirit of these men, and of its
probable influence in a country where the question is not
between Peter and Paul, between Luther and Leo, but
between Christ and Voltaire.

Leo Thun has sent me from Prague a very interesting
and edifying book on the possible fusion of Protestant and
Catholic Christianity.   It is well worthy of notice from its
intrinsic merit; but its interest is heightened by the
circumstance of its being published anonymously by an
excellent and learned Catholic professor, who has for a
series of years drawn down unheard of persecutions upon
his head by the orthodoxy of his doctrine, joined to the
liberality of his views, which it seems did not suit the
fathers at Vienna, who had him deprived of his chair, and
even secluded him in an abbatial prison.

---

[1] 'Italy,' in *British and Forcign Review*, vol. ii., art. vii.

February 8th.—Fieschi's[1] trial has, as you know, long been announced for this month, and you have no doubt read reports of it in the 'Herald.' I have been twice, and nothing is more striking than the rude but forcible eloquence of Fieschi. His manner is not unlike that of Rossi, but somewhat less insinuating. His appearance is mean and ugly; his veracity, which is now his only remaining pride, is striking. By the way, how one observes, in all these great criminals, that the ruling passion in their defence and in their last moments is not revenge nor repentance, nor even regret, but a cold unmitigable pride. Christianity would be the wisest of all religions if it had said no more than that pride is the mother of all sins. Fieschi, however, is a man of warm feelings. I was present at the deposition of his friend and benefactor, M. Lavocat, during which he was exceedingly excited. It was at the beginning of the first *séance* which I witnessed, and I had not heard the prisoner speak before. When Lavocat had done, Fieschi rose and spoke with great force of the effect produced on him by the kindness of his old master. He afterwards resumed the discussion of circumstances concerning the event, and his accomplices, with the greatest coolness. Nina Lassave[2] is quite a heroine. I was not fortunate enough to hear her deposition, but Jeanie Deans was nothing to it, and that old musty, iron-cheeked House of Peers wept to hear her. The trial will last some days longer, and it is expected that at least three of the prisoners will be decapitated.[3]

February 18th.—Did you ever read that very mad clever book 'Vivian Grey'? I sometimes think that D'Israeli

[1] Fieschi, a Corsican, a discharged soldier, together with four other scoundrels, had constructed a machine by which twenty-five musket barrels, fitted in a frame, could all be fired simultaneously. These barrels, loaded to the muzzle with bullets and slugs, he fired from a window at the king, Louis Philippe, on July 28th, 1835, as he was returning from a ceremonial review. The king was uninjured: but of his staff and the bystanders more than forty were killed or wounded.

[2] Fieschi's mistress, 'a rather pretty young woman,' who, though quite ignorant of the plot, gave evidence which conclusively established the guilt of the accused. After the trial it was announced by the enterprising proprietor of a café that he had engaged her as a waitress; on which the girl wrote a denial in the papers. Offers, she said, had been made to her, but she had declined them, having no wish but to hide herself from public notice; the woman who was advertised as serving in her name was an impostor.

[3] Fieschi and two of his accomplices were guillotined; a third was condemned to twenty years' hard labour. The fourth was discharged.

has hit upon points of resemblance between his hero and
the life I lead. These points are however few, and God
forbid that they should be more numerous. But the natural
illusion of young men who rise from Plato to rush into
politics is the formation of an honourable and enlightened
party, till they find that the materials of which parties are
built are only mud and straw, like the bricks of Babylon;
or at best, the creation of their imagination and their efforts
shines and perishes in times as critical as ours, like the
Gironde.

Young has destroyed the peroration of my article on
Tocqueville; for which act I hate him with an author's
hatred; but he has taken an engagement to respect me
more for the future.

To Mr. E. H. Handley

Paris, February 27th.—Mr. Beaumont has been spending a fortnight with me in Paris, and we employed the time
very brilliantly. We were present at the great debate
which led to the astounding fall of the doctrinaires; we saw
Fieschi day after day haranguing the Court of Peers with
humorous familiarity from the pedestal of death and dis-
honour which his machine had made for him; we frequented
the salons of Lamartine, Dupin, and a crowd of deputies;
we penetrated into the haunts of Cousin, now installed in
the precincts of the Sorbonne, from which he has ejected the
Faculté de Théologie to make himself chambers; we dined
with that club of *beaux-esprits* projected by our kind and
meek Tiresias, Ballanche, to which I have so often alluded;
and, lastly, Beaumont gave a banquet at the Rocher de
Cancale to his Polish friends and many others, at which old
Niemiewicz, the friend of Kosciusko and aide-de-camp of
Washington, Odilon Barrot, and my friend Dufaure, the
Deputy of the Gironde, one worthy of the name, spoke with
amazing warmth and truth for Poland, for constitutional
liberty, and for mankind. These are things which have left
a lasting impression on my mind; and when I consider the
position in which I stand in Paris and even in London, I
tremble to think how I can remain worthy of such high
associates and live up to such great purposes.

Since Beaumont departed I have devoted myself wholly to the revisal and almost rewriting of the satire which I believe I mentioned to you two years ago. I sadly want a title : that of ' Laocoon ' is not sufficiently descriptive ; that of ' The Sorrows of a City ' not sufficiently striking. If Providence sends you a title, pray give it me. Bating this difficulty, I believe I shall publish the poem on my return to London, or at any rate after the dissolution which is positively announced for April.[1] I am in doubt whether I should take anybody's opinion on this matter. Have you any objection to read the MS. and give me yours unreservedly ? . . .

M. de Lamartine has just published his long-expected poem, entitled ' Jocelyn, Épisode trouvé chez un Curé de Village.' It is certainly the most complete poetic work that the modern French poets have produced. The delicacy of the language and of the details, as well as the noble simplicity of the theme, reminded me of Wordsworth ; but it is more full of human passion and less glowing with a divine, though sometimes cold, elevation than the works of our great poet. There is more of the South, more of the thrill of love, more of the corporal and tangible in Lamartine, in the place of that contemplative and spiritual love, expanding to universals, even in the smallest speciality, which characterises Wordsworth. But they agree in their common love of Nature, their common vindication of the law of duty, and their common purpose of beautifying life by ennobling man. Both write, as it were, in the presence of God and in the language of Providence ; the Frenchman, as an angle subtended by the abyss of infinite love and truth ; the Briton, as a sphere comprising and collecting within itself the attributes and the qualities of perfect humanity ; for to the perfection of humanity does the work of either tend, and the failings of the instrument do not so far fall short of their purpose as to render their labour vain.

The literary events of this month have been somewhat overlooked in the turmoil of political intrigue ;[2] and the

---

[1] See *ante*, p. 30. The poem was not published, nor is it again mentioned ; but the MS. has been preserved.

[2] The break-up of the French Ministry ; the retirement of Broglie and of Guizot ; and the nomination of Thiers to form a Government.

result of the recent change is one which affords a subject of very sad speculation to the reflecting European. To see a man like Thiers rise in five years from the dregs of educated society to his present lofty position, bringing with him to that position all the popular vices of excessive arrogance joined to excessive versatility; to see this man occupy by the excess of his unprinciple and the perfidy of his ability that station which belongs of right not only to the wisest but to the most honest—to see all this is to witness another and a shameful passage in the history of democratic States. I cannot describe to you the indignation with which this Ministry of able knaves and servile courtiers has been received by the French as well as by the representatives of foreign Powers in Paris. As to the line of policy to be pursued, that lies wholly with the King; the Ministry has been formed on the principle of everyone's abandoning the points to which he was individually most solemnly pledged; and as the dynasty has been termed 'La Restauration moins la Restauration,' so this Cabinet may be baptised 'Le Système moins les Doctrinaires.'

March 2nd.—As for Meyerbeer's opera 'Les Huguenots,' which was brought out last night, all I know is that stalls were selling from 80 to 200 francs; and that all who were fortunate enough to get in came out clamorous in their delight. As for the Salon, which opened yesterday at 12 o'clock, with more than 2,000 pictures, Thackeray and I breakfasted together, and then passed two hours there, till I was so tired with staring that I came home and went to sleep. There are about forty great battle-pieces, with heroes, and cannon-balls flying in all directions. These works have for the most part been ordered by the king for his national museum at Versailles; and some of them, particularly Horace Vernet's, are remarkably fine. In landscape there are as usual but few pictures, but some of them have great merit; what struck me most was that the best of them are in Constable's style; and if ever our friend quits his native fogs, he will find a very promising and sympathising school on this side the Channel. The portraits are not numerous, and the majority of them are of young ladies in white muslin.

About the middle of March Reeve returned to London, and, as his mother was then at Boulogne, he took lodgings in King Street, St. James's, to be near his aunt, Mrs. Austin, who was then living in Bury Street. A couple of letters from Tocqueville of this date are interesting as showing the footing the two men were on, rather than from any particular importance in themselves :—

From M. de Tocqueville

Cherbourg, April 17th.—I received your letter, my dear Reeve, a few days before my departure from Paris ; and not having been able to answer it at once, to thank you for the interesting details you send me, I do so now, taking advantage of the quiet of the country—if, that is to say, a miserable, little, badly paved, provincial town can be called country. . . . What you tell me about the London parishes is all the more interesting that it completely confirms the ideas I formed on the subject during my visit to England, and it is very satisfactory to find that my first impressions were correct. Your nation certainly presents a singular contrast to ours. Your social condition is much more aristocratic than ours, but part of your laws is more democratic ; you have only to extend and generalise what we must create.

Pardon me, my dear friend. Here I am, harping again on that damned democracy, which I've got on my nose like a pair of spectacles through which I see everything. One step further, and there will be nothing left for my family but to have me declared incapable, and remove me to Charenton. Let us talk of yourself, of whom you don't say one word in your otherwise charming letter. When are you coming to Paris ?—for it is not to be supposed that a man who speaks French as well as you do, and has so many friends among us, will abandon us for long. Why did you not save the fourth page to tell me this and speak of your present occupations ? How is Mr. Beaumont's Review getting on ? You see I ask many questions to oblige you to write again.

J'espère que vous avez bien parlé de moi à Madame Austin, et que vous avez dit à Madame Reeve tout le plaisir que j'aurais à la revoir. Je crois vous apercevoir d'ici, vous et elle, dans cette petite maison de Hampstead que j'ai visitée il y a précisément un an. Je vous découvre dans votre observatoire, dominant en philosophe les fumées de Londres ; et je vois plus bas dans le salon, Madame votre mère faisant bon visage à ses hôtes. Je n'oublierai jamais Hampstead ; il se rattache indirectement à une époque de ma vie dont je ne saurais jamais perdre le souvenir.[1]

Adieu, mon cher Reeve; parlez de moi à toutes les personnes de votre connaissance qui m'ont si bien reçu, et croyez à des sentiments d'une bien sincère amitié.

To Mr. E. H. Handley

May 4th.—You will by this time have seen the Review ; but I am sorry to say my article on Mamiani is so maimed and so squeezed of all juice of apostolic doctrine, that I disavow it as perverse and heretical. I am vastly annoyed at the absurd remarks on Sedgwick in the article on Universities ; and altogether I think it a very bad number.

Shortly after the date of this letter a long pending quarrel between Handley and his wife came to a head. Mrs. Handley does not appear to have been false, in the ordinary acceptation of the word, though grievously false in regard to the clauses of the marriage vow which bound her to love, honour, and obey her husband. She was insolent to Handley and his father, self-willed, greedy and unscrupulous, and her mother, who fostered and aggravated the quarrel, was worse. Mrs. Handley, leaving her husband and her baby, returned with her mother to Munich, where they were coldly received by society. Handley was for some time anxious to bring the matter to a public trial, but was eventually persuaded by Reeve and his other friends to let it rest. This forms the principal subject of Reeve's later letters, which it is unnecessary to repeat.

From M. de Tocqueville

May 22nd.—What you tell me of the tendency of our Cabinet to drift apart from yours appears to me only too likely, but I cannot share the satisfaction which you show. In my opinion, the union of the two people is essential to the maintenance of free institutions in Europe—a considera-

---

[1] Cf. *Notice sur Alexis de Tocqueville*, par G. de Beaumont, pp. 43-4.

tion which, in my eyes, surpasses all others. As to the desire which the aristocratic party in England is said to have to plunge their country into war, in order to occupy the minds of the people, I can understand it, but only by considering the desperate state to which that party seems to be reduced. In the position it is in, it may seem better to play double or quits than to keep on everlastingly losing petty stakes. But war is better fitted to prevent a revolution than to stop one when it has begun. Now it appears to me that among you revolution has been in full swing for the last five years; and I cannot believe that the disquiet necessarily attendant on a state of war—even supposing the issue of it to be fortunate, which must be doubtful—will not give fresh activity to the spirit of faction, and set free demagogic passions such as, at present, you have little idea of. Besides, you are not yet at war; and nowadays, it takes more than a wish to be so.

But enough of politics. What did our fathers talk about fifty years ago? I cannot imagine. Take politics from our conversation, and nothing is left but monosyllables and dumb show. Yet they talked as much as we do, and often better than we do; they found a hundred things to say where we do not find one to think; they had the gift of treating serious matters gaily; very different from us, who do our fooling so sadly.

Whilst in Paris, Reeve had made an engagement with the Thuns to visit them in their Bohemian home at Tetschen, and early in August he started for Germany. In the following summer he published some account of his tour in the ' Metropolitan Magazine; '[1] but his letters to his mother, though covering the same ground, have a personal interest which is wanting from the more finished narrative.

To Mrs. Reeve

4 *King Street, August 4th.*—I still adhere to my plan of starting on Saturday. . . . I look forward with much pleasure to a fortnight's repose at the good Thuns' at Tetschen, for I begin to find the life of an independent man a terribly

---

[1] ' Sketches of Bohemia and the Slavonian provinces of the Austrian Empire.'

busy one. I hope to get from Prague to the Carpathians before the season is too much advanced ; but if the autumn is a bad one, I must give up that part. You shall hear from me as often as I can [manage it], but do not be alarmed if I do not find post offices every week. Write to me at Prague for September 1st. I shall pass my birthday there, I dare say, and have my health drunk in imperial Tokay. . . .

Handley wants to know whether you will take him as a lodger for part of the time of my absence. You might write to him. The baby will stay with the old people ; but if you can be of any use to it, I am sure you will treat my little ward as you would my son.

Crossing over to Hamburg, he met on board the steamer Christopher Wordsworth, at that time head-master of Harrow, whose acquaintance he had made at Cambridge two years before, and Hymers, the tutor of St. John's College, whose name was long familiar to Cambridge men as the author of several mathematical text-books. With them he travelled to Berlin and Dresden.

To Mrs. Reeve

Dresden, August 16th.—[At Berlin] I was introduced to Count Raczynski, a very wealthy and agreeable connoisseur, who has a very fair gallery, and is publishing a splendid work on modern German art, of which I straightway forwarded a review to the 'Athenæum.' Ranke I did not see, as he was out, but his bookseller told me that no term is assigned to the length of the book, of which two volumes on the Popes have already appeared, exclusive of the first volumes. Tell this to my aunt. . . . We met in a beer garden at Berlin my very agreeable Worcestershire acquaintance, Mr. Galton, with his two boys,[1] and he proved to be a friend of Wordsworth's also ; so our caravan was at once increased by three members, and we are now all living together in the hotel here (Dresden), and lionising and laughing all day long. . . . To-morrow, however, this agreeable party will, I fear, be dispersed. The Galtons return to England, Wordsworth and Hymers go on to Prague, and I

---

[1] The younger of these boys was the present Sir Douglas Galton, K.C.B.

am waiting for further tidings from Franz Thun, who has written to say he shall come over to fetch me. The Tetschen plan fails, however, for the present, as (contrary to what Leo Thun had told me) the family are already gone to Prague, whither I shall consequently follow, either with Wordsworth or Franz Thun. . . .

The Gallery here is in confusion worse confused; and bad as was its arrangement when I was here before, the changes which have been made have in no wise improved it. Yet what an overpowering mass of pictures of the highest kind is here! The mind is stunned by the impressions which crowd upon the sense as by the sustained total music of some vast orchestra. It is not till the memory has relieved itself by subdivision that one is at ease to revert to the chief treasures of the collection.

Prague, August 25th.—Shortly after I had despatched my last letter from Dresden, our very pleasant party dispersed itself; the Galtons to Munich, Hymers and Wordsworth to Prague, and I into the Saxon Switzerland and the Bohemian mountains under the excellent care of Count Franz Thun, who came over to Dresden to fetch me. I cannot now describe at length all the beautiful scenery we wandered through on the wild and woody banks of the Elbe. . . . The first view of Prague is an epoch in one's life, only to be compared to the first view of Venice, or of Geneva from the Jura; as striking, indeed, though nowise resembling either. The thousand towers of the churches and convents and the whole character of the scene reminded me of what one hears of Eastern cities; and the swart beauty of the neighbouring peasants, the women with their thick white veils turned back over their brows, the fiery horses, and the animation of the people sufficiently indicated that I had left all traces of the German character at the frontier behind me. I cannot describe my delight as we drove across the bridge built by that Charles IV. who was the friend of Petrarch, and adorned at a more recent period with noble statues of the favourite saints of Bohemia, and in the middle with a huge altar surmounted by a splendid crucifix, at the foot of which, in the midst of the press and hurry of a metropolis, the afflicted and the devout were counting their rosaries and offering up their prayers. Although the preparations for the emperor's triumphal entry are already far advanced, as it will take place on September 1st, I found no difficulty in getting a room in a decent inn, and I shall probably remove in a day or two to a private lodging. I found my friend, Leo Thun, very busy with his judicial functions, and I have plenty of time to myself, which I am likely to employ very agreeably in reading up the history of the country, in visiting the endless wonders of a city where every house is a work of art, and in observing the manifold peculiarities of a people which interests me more every day.

Prague, September 7th.—I have delayed writing till I should think myself sure of catching you at Norwich, and till the ceremony which I have been so fortunate as to witness was terminated. I am this moment returned from the cathedral, where I have seen with these eyes the crown of Bohemia placed upon the head of the emperor. The scene was equal to the height of my conceptions of earthly grandeur; and whether I looked to the prince-archbishop on his throne at the altar, surrounded by the vast mitred clergy of the realm, or to the emperor kneeling opposite, in the midst of the ministers, nobles, and knights of the Golden Fleece, the feeling of the olden time stirred me in these living symbols. I beheld the junction of the two great potentates of Christendom, and I could not but delude myself into regarding them as the substance of that power of which they are now but the shadows—the Roman emperor and the Catholic pontiff. As this first impression subsided, however, the feeling of the national dignity of this noble Bohemia, here consecrated and recognised, came over me with a scarcely less elevating excitement; the whole pageant, the regalia which have been worn under such different and perilous circumstances by so many of the greatest of princes, the nobility still retaining their aristocratic bearing, and assisting the archbishop, in the person of their chief peer, to place the crown upon their sovereign's head, the herald of the kingdom with his tabard and two-tailed lion, and the solemnity of the Bohemian oath, with the enthusiasm of the people, made one forget the imperial character of the actors to admire the national splendour of the scene.

Nor was the religious impression the least profound effect of the ceremony; to me, at least, these things are not merely shows and plays, but acts of solemn worship, tenfold heightened by the gorgeous ornaments with which they are surrounded. The political character of the ceremony had, indeed, changed from the days of Charles IV. or of George of Podiebrad; but that religious truth, that blessed Christian rite, the divine melody of the service, the chorus of anthems, and the glorious initiatory character of the spiritual power, were still the same as they shall ever be under Him by whose grace all kings wear their diadems and all states exist. When, in the midst of the glitter of earthly regality, the Eucharist was raised and imparted in its mystical simplicity, and all the people, together with their new crowned king, dropped down in honour of the bloodless sacrifice, he could be no Christian man who did not feel himself moved by a tremor of devotion and of love.

I have not room to describe the details of the ceremony, or of all the spectacles which I have witnessed since the emperor made his triumphal entrance into Prague on September 1st. The city has been in one continual festivity; we have had the 'Crociato' at the Opera, attended by all the Court, where I saw for the first time those remarkable men whose names will live in the history of Austria and of our time—the Archdukes Charles and John and Prince Metternich.

On Sunday morning High Mass was performed on an immense plain near Prague, on which were met the court, the army, and the city, in all about 50,000 souls, kneeling round the same altar in the face of open day. To-night we are to have an illumination; on the 12th the empress is to be crowned; and the whole will conclude with a great national festival; the court will leave Prague on the 15th.

To descend to minor particulars, I must tell you that I am very well lodged, in one of the best streets; not far from the Thuns, who are unceasingly kind to me. If you hear anything about the cholera, I beg you not to be alarmed, as I am not. People here make a good deal of fuss about it because the Archbishop of Olmütz died of it the day before yesterday; but with a regular diet and tolerable precautions, I do not think it is more to be feared than the thousand and one events to which one is everywhere exposed.

Sir Frederick Lamb [1] is exceedingly polite to me. I dined with him yesterday to meet Lady Jersey, Prince Esterhazy, Prince Schwartzenberg, M. de Sainte-Aulaire, and the Prussian ambassador; and talked a great deal with Prince Esterhazy, who you know is half an Englishman. The Molesworths are here, and Sir William and I have interchanged visits. I expect the Milmans shortly. . . .

I am working very hard at Bohemian history and the present state of the country, and have already got nearly a volume of notes. My love of the Slavonians increases every half-hour; and I shall bring home a head full of Bohemian heroism, and a trunk full of Bohemian books and antiquities, to be elaborated this winter in the little room at Hampstead.

Prague, September 20th.—The festivities are over, and the court left Prague yesterday; but since my last letter I have assisted at a variety of scenes even more striking than the one I attempted to describe. The coronation of the queen was embellished with all the ladies of the court and all the diamonds of the empire. I was at an immense ball at court, where more than 3,000 persons were very pleasantly entertained in two rooms, with plenty of refreshments, and the divine Strauss in the orchestra. I have also been at sundry private parties, where we trod on archdukes and archduchesses, and had one's partners taken away from one by imperial command. I have seen Prague illuminated, with all its great amphitheatre of palaces glittering with lights, its broad river rolling between walls of Bengal fire, and its towers decked with vases of coloured light up to their very summits; and, to crown the whole, I was present at the Volksfest, or people's festival, where Bishop Blaise, and the Vignerons, and the Lord Mayor's show, and all the shows that ever existed since Noah's triumphal procession out of the Ark, were collected in one vast pageant, which took two hours to defile before the empress at a rapid pace. The peasants and the workmen,

---

[1] The English ambassador, created Lord Beauvale in 1839. He was the younger brother of Lord Melbourne, whom he succeeded in the title in 1848.

weavers, labourers, and miners, were collected in parties, one from each of the sixteen circles of Bohemia, headed by a bride and bridegroom from each circle, who were chosen for the occasion, with a train of twenty bridesmaids and bridesmen apiece, and followed by carriages very prettily adorned with all the various productions of the country—all which, I beg to state, I have described at great length in my notebook.

The festivities are over, but I am still so busied in Prague that I shall not leave it for ten days more. I have yet to go to Karlstein, an old palace of the Bohemian kings, and to the convent of St. Ivan near it; and I shall perhaps take a couple of days' shooting on one of the Thuns' estates in the Rakonitzer Kreis. But the Thuns are now gone back to Tetschen to receive the Archduchess Sophie, who went to stay there immediately after the ceremony. I expect them to start on the 30th inst. for Olmütz, Troppau, and Cracow. . . .

The Milmans arrived here the day after the fair, and only saw the peasants getting drunk after their rejoicings; but I had the pleasure of acting as their cicerone for two days; and they went away as convinced as I could wish them to be that Prague is the finest city in the world. We visited the city of the Jews together in great detail, where we found a synagogue which Rembrandt might have painted and filled with his own wrinkled and bearded Rabbins. I am sure they took Mr. M. for a foreign Rabbin of distinction, from the knowledge he showed of their language and customs; and they were very near giving him the Torah [1] to carry. For my part, I was very near destroying all the sorcery by crossing myself and pulling off my hat; and if the historian had not cautioned me in time, I should inevitably have shared the fate of St. William of Norwich.[2]

He adds in the Journal that whilst at Prague he became intimate with General Skrynecki, who had commanded the Polish armies in 1831, dined with him almost every day, and

---

[1] The Book of the Law—the Pentateuch.

[2] According to the hagiology, a child who was kidnapped by the Jews, tortured and crucified 'in derision,' anno 1144. His grave is in Norwich Cathedral. See Stanton's 'Menology,' p. 132.

received from him 'a course of military instruction,' which was afterwards useful.

Vienna, October 7th.—I can anticipate, my dear mother, a slight movement of surprise on your part when you read the date of this letter, and I am almost as much surprised at finding myself here as you can be. Circumstances, however, seemed to point out the expediency of this addition to my original plan, which only lengthens my tour by about two hundred miles, and I hastily decided to spend a few days in the imperial city. The last days of my stay in Prague were very agreeable, and I need not tell you with what regret I left a city which had awakened all my admiration, stimulated my inquiries by its inexhaustible treasures, and opened to my eyes an entirely new view of history and of Europe. I have sent off my trunk to Dresden, laden with spoils of various kinds, and with a collection of fine old Bohemian psalmody, which I flatter myself you will allow to surpass the unfortunate author of the 'Old Hundredth' himself. Thus disembarrassed of my luggage, I wrapped myself in my furs, which we are beginning to wear in these regions, and took my place in the mail—a vehicle which is really preferable to a private carriage—which speedily brought me to Vienna. . . .

I expected so little from Vienna, especially at a season of the year when it is as deserted as London, that I cannot say I have been disappointed. The Cathedral of St. Stephen, with its exquisite cone of Gothic architecture, is alone worth the journey; but it is a solitary exception, and of all the capitals of Europe, Vienna is that which I shall least care to revisit. My pleasures are not increased by the circumstance of my not finding a soul in the city I know, except the ambassador,[1] and an Austrian entomologist whom I met on the road, who shows me kindnesses for the pure love of Messrs. Kirby and Spence. *Me meâ virtute involvo*, and I shall leave Vienna as wise as I came into it, with the acquired right, however, of saying that I have been there. . .

I have not recovered from the emotion with which I have just learned the death of Malibran. I keep turning

---

[1] Sir Frederick Lamb.

over in my mind the various occasions and parts in which I saw her, just as one recalls every passage in the life of some dear departed friend; the whole array of her powers passes before me like a pageant; the wasting grief of her Desdemona, the passion of her Amina, the heroism of her Arsace, the truth of her Fidelio—it was in that part I saw her for the last time; and all these several shapes are like the vanities of a dream, having one soul to animate them. . .

Malibran was not made for age, and I never saw her without feeling that the light was wasting rapidly in proportion to the intensity of its splendour. She snapped like a spring, she is fallen like a bird from its perch; and I trust I am not wrong in thinking that, of all the blessings with which Providence gilds and enriches the children of genius, that of early death, in the glory of the bright sunshine of their lives, is not the least. Those whom the Gods love die young; and Malibran is gone to join the Raphaels, the Novalis, and those happy spirits who shared the gifts of the angels upon earth. We shall tell our children's children of her incomparable sweetness; and I trust that England will build a monument of pure silver over her grave.

Cracow, October 18*th.*—It is all true as I said in my last letter, my dearest mother, and I have the unspeakable satisfaction of addressing a letter to you from the ancient capital of old Poland! Whether I consider the beautiful antiquity of the city, the kind reception I have met with in a country where to me there are no strangers, or the manifold associations which hallow this spot in my mind, I cannot but consider this little sojourn in Cracow as the crown and flower of all my journeys, and as one of the most pleasing and remarkable passages in my life; and in a very few weeks, one may almost say days, I hope we shall talk it all over together.

My stay at Vienna displeased me mightily; but the last two days of it were rendered more agreeable by the very welcome company of John Murray fils, whom I found eating a sweet dish in the hotel where I lodged. I wish he had arrived sooner, for he is a very agreeable person, and the most thoroughgoing sightseer that ever trod the deck of a packet-boat. . . .

From Brünn to Olmütz we passed hard by Austerlitz, now a silent earth, seemingly unconscious of the great harvest of glory which it once bore. . . . At length we crossed the Galician frontier, and at dawn on the following day the magnificent valley of the Vistula lay at our feet, with the huge old walls of the royal castle, and the towers of the city, and the churches of Cracow glittering in the early beams of the sun. It was to me one of the most elevating and joyful sights that I ever remember to have witnessed. I was allowed to cross the Vistula without difficulty, and I was presently within the walls of the venerable, but, alas! the ruined city. I have no space to tell of half the admirable remains of architecture, connected with innumerable historic recollections, which I have found here—almost a second Prague—the same romantic character, the same Italian magnificence, the same ecclesiastical splendour, and the same deserted condition.

The Journal briefly mentions 'a dinner and four evening parties at Cracow;' but the letter gives an interesting account of a visit, on a Sunday, to Ruszcza, a neighbouring village, the country seat of a gentleman whose acquaintance he had made. It tells of the pleasant drive, of fantastic legends, of stalwart peasants—'tall, well-made, with strong marked features, and an air of heroism'—and of the house, the object of the visit.

To *Mrs. Reeve*

October 18th.—A more simple and elegant dwelling I have never entered. The furniture was made of a beautiful white wood of the country, and the rooms were scented from the rich perfumes of the flower beds under the large windows. We spent the morning in the contemplation of an excellent collection of prints from the early German masters, and in talking of art, of the countries which are so far off, and yet so near to the minds and hearts of this extraordinary people. Nothing is more astonishing than to find, at this distance from France and England, a whole circle of society better acquainted with the novelties in literature, with the remarkable men of the time, and all the changes and ideas of the world, than any of the departments of France, or than the ordinary run of society in the country in England. I could have imagined that Russia was not further from Paris than Montmorency, and at the same time as near London as Richmond. Our party was increased in the course of the day by some very delightful women, and we sat down to an excellent Polish dinner, accompanied with potent draughts of that celebrated wine 'Hungariâ natum, Cracoviâ educatum.' The evening was deliciously clear and still, and I stole away from the merry party to attend vespers in the village church close by.

The church of Ruszcza is one of the oldest in Poland, and under its simple roof it contains not a few monuments of good and great men, with a fine picture by a Polish artist of the beginning of the fifteenth century. The peasantry of the hamlet were assembled at their evening prayer : the priest, a worthy monk called Brother Florian, from a neighbouring abbey, was reciting the service of the close of the day, and the peasants (as is the custom in all the Slavonian countries) joined in the harmonious chant of the responses. The women, in their white dresses and peculiar white head-dresses falling back upon their shoulders, were devoutly kneeling side by side on the bare pavement ; and the men— those strong and brave Cracovian peasants of whom I spoke just now—were praying with equal devotion a little lower down the church. There was a serenity in their looks, and a fervour in their worship, which surpassed, to my mind, all the most splendid rites, and awakened the sweetest feelings which accompany that piety most acceptable to Heaven. The priest concluded the service, sprinkled the holy drops over the heads of his flock, and as we left the little church the peasants did homage to the lord, with a look of affectionate respect, kissing his hand as he passed, and touching his foot with the left hand. As we drove back to Cracow that night in the calm light of the horned moon, I could think of nothing but the patriarchal and holy scene which I had witnessed. . . .

I shall be at Dresden about this day week, and I count upon your letters. Who knows that I shall not find a whole bundle, if my correspondents have been faithful ? I expect to embark at Hamburg on November 12th, but perhaps I shall wait for the 'John Bull' on the 20th.   I have now only two more perils to escape—the one is from the fleas, which I find very hungry in Poland at this season, and the other is from a descent into Hades, four stories deep—i.e. into the salt mines of Wieliczka, which I project for to-morrow.   You know that the mines are so vast that you can scarcely walk round them in a fortnight; three hours, however, will suffice for me, who hate salt, and hold a salt cellar to be a world too big for my wants.

Dresden, October 28th.—I cannot get rid of the feeling that I am come back into Europe, after having set foot in some remote corner of the globe; yet when I remember the reception I found at Cracow—'The fathers in the old I met, and brothers in the young '—there is nothing to remind me that I was a stranger there.   And now that I am once more within call I already hear the signals of friendship and encouragement from you all—aye, and the good mother bird chirping upon her nest too.   God be thanked you are all well, and that in the midst of personal honours and enjoyments which are heaped upon me, like the jewels upon Aladdin in the cave, there is no sting to wound me in the persons of others not less dear, and no cloud visible at least above the horizon.   When shall I learn whether the springs which are well tempered for prosperity and pleasure are as strongly formed for evil times?   I strive daily to temper my long overflow of happiness by the thought of death, and changes for the worse; by sympathy with the sufferings of those about me, and by the contemplation of those immortal sufferings which saved the world.   But the devil who tempts by making rich is a wise devil, and it is no light task to be the spoiled child of the world and to live to some purpose in it.

The Journal winds up the story :—

Got back to Hampstead on November 9th.   I wrote a paper on the consulship at Cracow, which I gave in to William Strangways, then Under Secretary at the Foreign Office.   It was circulated to the Cabinet and made me known to Ministers.

I went to Bowood on December 29th, where I found

Senior and Miss Fox, and ended this Annus Mirabilis by drinking soda-water in the Oval room there. Tom Moore, Luttrell, Eastlake, and Spedding were also there.

To Mr. E. H. Handley

Bowood, December 30*th.*—It is a wonder that I have not been buried in the snow ; but in Wales the fall was very slight, and I was in no great danger till I entered the park here, which is a positive Mer de Glace . . . but the natives are sledging about gaily. In my way from Cheltenham, I made a pilgrim's visit to the venerable abbey of Malmesbury, and I expect that you will all honour me the more for having visited the tomb of King Athelstan. To me the place afforded food for melancholy reflection. . . . The abbey, or all the brutal Roundheads left of it, contains rich and rare wealth of arch and image, differing by their purely English character from the edifices I have mostly seen, and all the dearer to me on that account. . . .

I am here in clover, as you may suppose. To pass over the cookery in silence, I cannot conceive anything more exquisitely delightful than a dwelling in which the splendour of opulence is only the foil to the splendour of art, and in which one breakfasts with Titian, Rembrandt, and Michael Angelo. I roll on soft cushions, and see real visions. We are a small party, but Eastlake is coming to-day or to-morrow.

The first six months of 1837, ' spent in London, or at Hampstead, or in visits : a good deal in society,' call for no further notice.

To Mr. E. H. Handley

Parthenon, April 20*th.*—I dined last night at the Geological Club, with a very distinguished party, to meet the new Bishop of Norwich [Stanley], with whom I was much pleased. I talked with him with that warm interest which hangs about a man all his life touching the place and the recollections of one's earliest years. That old palace of Norwich was to me, a child, the seat of an august and amiable being [Bishop Bathurst], whom I regarded as the model of goodness and greatness. Our garden joined the palace grounds, and amongst those old ruins and quaint walks we were let to play our childhood away. When we left Norwich for Geneva, nine years ago, that venerable prelate gave me a blessing which I would fain believe to be still upon me, and he added, 'You are going, my dear boy, to the land which has been a world of visionary delight to me ever since I was a young man, and read Rousseau, and wept passionate tears under the fancied rocks of Meillerie; to you those delights and those scenes will be charming realities; to me, they still exist in imagination. You should take me with you as your chaplain. Take my blessing with you wherever you go, and my advice to love your good mother always; she is your best friend.' Was not this sweet counsel? Am I not right to cherish the memory of Dr. Henry Bathurst?

'I was at my uncle Thomas Reeve's, at Raydon,' he wrote in the Journal, 'when William IV. died and the Queen was proclaimed. On July 9th we started—my mother and I—for Geneva, by the Rhine.'

To Mr. E. H. Handley

Frankfort-a.-M., July 19th.—I met Dr. Bernays on board the steamer from Coblenz to Mainz, and we have been busy here together examining the public schools for the middle classes, which, you know, is an object of my peculiar attention. Is it possible that we have *no* public schools in England for the very class of the community which requires instruction most? The *Muster-schule* here is indeed a *muster* for us to follow. I was not aware to what an extent the system of public day schools for girls of the middle classes is carried in Germany. The school here contains two hundred girls from eight to seventeen years of age. I am inclined to think that this is a very bad thing. It is a Spartan education, though it does not make Spartans of the women. It may be well for the body and character of a young female child, to give her a large share of childish sports and school discipline; but from the age of thirteen, when the woman begins to exist, the hoop and ball of the playground ought surely to be given up for the more serious and tranquil education of domestic life.

I find all Germany in considerable agitation from the insane patent of the King of Hanover.[1] H.M. has undertaken a siege of Troy in this campaign against the institutions of Hanover, and he has begun it by burning the ship which might have brought him back to England. If I was in Parliament, I would support a Bill of Exclusion; for true Conservative principles consist in the maintenance of constitutional rights to all existing institutions, by warding off the aggressions of persons, and maintaining the fundamental principles of the realm—amongst which I place the elective character of the English monarchy, as sanctioned by the precedents from William the Conqueror to the present day.

In 1837 the unity of English history was but little understood, or Reeve would have carried his precedents back, not to William the Conqueror, but to the historic Egbert and the semi-mythical Cedric.

The autumn was passed, for the most part, at Geneva; and Reeve, with his mother, was still there when, on November 2nd, he received a letter from Lord Lansdowne offering him the Clerkship of Appeals. He immediately started for London, where he arrived on the 12th, and took up his old quarters in King Street. On the 14th he saw Lord Lansdowne, but hesitated about accepting the appointment, feeling some doubt of his competency, as he explained in his letters to his mother, who had remained at Geneva.

Parthenon Club, November 15th.

I saw Lord Lansdowne yesterday, who was as kind as possible, and I had the satisfaction to find that I was arrived in time at any rate. The place vacant is that of Clerk of the Appeals to the Queen in Council, or rather to the Judicial Committee of the Council. You may remember that I contemplated the offer of a legal post in the Council Office with extreme diffidence, amounting to a determination to refuse an appointment for which my studies have not fitted me. This clerkship is precisely the case I had foreseen and

[1] Ernest Augustus, Duke of Cumberland, eldest surviving brother of William IV., on announcing by letters patent, of July 8th, his accession to the throne of Hanover, declared also his intention of abolishing the existing constitution and representative government. The intention was carried into effect in the following November.

negatived in my own mind. It is very high in the office—
the second in rank. It is the head of the legal department
of the Privy Council, and it is, of course, very important,
very responsible, and very well paid. If it was an affair of
English law the thing would be settled directly. I told
Lord Lansdowne that I knew nothing of the practice of
English laws or English courts. But this ignorance is not so
misplaced in this case as I had anticipated. The Judicial
Committee of the Council is an anomalous court, which
hears none but colonial appeals, and appeals to be decided
by Indian law, Civil law, and French law, &c. My Roman
law consequently places me in a better position than half the
great English lawyers, who would find no use for their
knowledge of the law of real property, &c.; and after all,
whoever they appointed must have time to understand the
business of the office before much is expected of him.
Kemble, whom I have consulted, observes with truth that
in public affairs routine is everything, and that you have
only to allow yourself to float with the stream. I think,
therefore, that I shall accept. Lord Lansdowne evidently
urges it; and, after all, if he makes a bad appointment, I
am not to blame. . . . It is probable that if I accept the
place my functions will begin forthwith, and you must
wait for an opportunity to return *en poste*. I will send you
money enough. If I do not get the place, I shall probably
start for Paris about next Thursday—to-morrow week.

November 17th.—The whole affair is arranged and I am
now Clerk of Appeals to the Privy Council, with a handsome
salary and all sorts of consideration. I went down to the office
again yesterday, where all the people (i.e. the subordinates)
already receive me cap in hand, and saw Mr. Greville, the
senior Clerk of the Council, which corresponds in rank to an
Under-Secretary of State. He was as civil as Mr. Lennard
had been the day before, offered every kind of assistance,
said all kinds of flattering things to his new colleague, and
quite settled my determination. I saw Lord Lansdowne in
the evening, and I shall be entered on the books to-day.
I need not conceal from you, my dear motherly friend, that
I am satisfied with myself in this matter. I feel a pleasant
consciousness that I have not allowed myself to be elated or

made giddy by these events; that I have remained as I always try to be, the master of my boat across this rapid current of circumstances; and that I enter office with as much independence of spirit and discernment as I have in my nature. The only thing which has occurred to disturb my serene enjoyment in this singular elevation is the colossal joy of Handley, which bursts forth in grotesque symbologies, in bolts of poetry, in storms of metaphysics, and in hearty tugs of friendship which are better than all the rest. We dined together yesterday after it was all settled: drank the Queen in champagne, and the Lord-President in claret, and went to the Buffa Opera, which has just opened and is very charming.

Downing Street, November 27th.

MY DEAREST MOTHER,—Your letter of Wednesday last is this morning arrived, and very welcome it is to me. It had scarcely occurred to me that your joy would be of so great and intense a kind; because to myself these events, however flattering and prosperous, have appeared as a change from a state of known happiness, and liberal pursuits, to a condition of more worldly consideration certainly, but perhaps of less individual value. Therefore, upon the whole the balance appears to me to be nearly equal; and as I was never possessed with an overweening ambition to change my former manner of life, so now I should not feel it as a calamity if I had to return to it. Therefore my joy is moderate though deep, and I am most moved by it when I read the measure of this success in your letters or in my friends' faces.

The notices of all this in the Journal are very short, and add nothing beyond—

On Monday, December 4th, the Judicial Committee began to sit—Brougham, Parke, Bosanquet, and Erskine. Brougham was furious at my appointment and did all he could to oust me. But Greville and the other judges defended me.

This year decided the course of my life.

CHAPTER III

THE appointment of Henry Reeve to the clerkship in the
Council Office began a new chapter in his life; it marked
the end of preparation, the commencement of real work.
Hitherto he had been a student, acquiring and garnering
knowledge of different kinds, without any clear idea of
where or how it was to be used. And yet no prescription
could have better fitted him for the path he was destined to
tread. His education at Geneva, at Munich, and at Paris
had given him a mastery of French and German—of French
especially, which he spoke and wrote as a native; he had a
competent literary knowledge of Italian; he had been well
grounded and exercised in Latin, which he read with facility;
but his knowledge of Greek was limited, and probably did
not extend much beyond Porson's 'four plays' which he had
worked through as a schoolboy. In music and painting he
had a cultivated taste, though it does not appear that he
had any personal skill in either art; and the frequent
writing of very long letters on passing events—ordered, we
may suppose, by his mother—had given him a remarkable
ease and readiness in the use of the pen, which his literary
aspirations enabled him, at an early age, to turn to profitable
account. But more than these were the habit of society,
which had been cultivated almost from infancy, and the
chance which had everywhere made him acquainted with
men who either already were or in due time came to be
amongst the foremost in Europe, in politics, in literature, or
in art. It often occurred, even to himself, that there was
something unusual and extraordinary in a lad of eighteen or
twenty, or even twenty-four, with no particular advantage
of birth, associating familiarly with men of European reputation, ambassadors, ministers of state, poets, painters, or
musicians.

That he had made the most of his opportunities appears
in the story already related; and he owed his appointment

in the Council Office to no family interest, but to the favourable impression he made on the Marquis of Lansdowne, the President of the Council; an impression which a longer acquaintance confirmed and strengthened; so that we find him in future years not only a frequent visitor at Bowood, but selected by Lord Lansdowne and other presidents of the council as an agent trusted with the conduct of unofficial, but delicate and even critical, diplomacy.

During the first year of his service, however, we may assume that his time was fully occupied in learning the routine of the office, the work of which was of a most complex and varied description. The Judicial Committee of the Privy Council was called into being in 1833 by Lord Brougham's 'Act for the better Administration of Justice in His Majesty's Privy Council,' by which it was enacted that all appeals to the King in Council should be heard and tried, with full powers, by a committee presided over by the President of the Council, and consisting of all the high legal authorities of the realm, together with some few others named by the sovereign. Modifications in the constitution of the committee have been made from time to time, the most important of which was perhaps the introduction of bishops of the Established Church at first as judges, and afterwards as assessors and advisers in ecclesiastical cases; but in its essential features the committee remains the same as that ordered in 1833.[1]

It may be safely asserted that, not even excepting the Supreme Court of the United States, there is not and never has been any tribunal in the world which has been called on to administer laws of such variety, extending over so large a portion of the earth, or affecting such vast multitudes of people as does the Queen in Council through the Judicial Committee. In the United Kingdom the jurisdiction is not very large; it extends to the prolongation of patents and to ecclesiastical appeals, and, during some time of Reeve's service, it included appeals from the Admiralty Courts. But from every other part of the British Empire appeals lie to the Crown; and the laws applicable to the several dependencies are not only English Law as modified in each dependency by its own legislation, but French Law, Dutch Law, Roman Law, Canon and Civil Law, Hindoo Laws of various schools, Mohammedan Law and Buddhist Law. Besides this, the Crown may refer any question to the Judicial Committee for advice; and though such references are

---

[1] W. Macpherson's *Practice of the Judicial Committee*, pp. 10, 11.

not very frequent, when made they are usually of great importance.[1]

It was, of course, no part of Reeve's duty to form any opinion of the merits of the cases, nor to study them for that purpose; but it was necessary for him to understand their nature, in order to provide for their hearing by qualified men, and this demanded a clear intelligence as well as industry. He had to arrange the business of the Court in its minutest detail, and especially he had to ensure the attendance of a *quorum* of the committee, which was not always easy; for, though the number of members was large, they were all men who had their own specific work to do, or their holidays to take; and were often unwilling to put themselves out of the way to perform a duty which seemed to be somewhat unfairly laid upon them. All this involved a great deal of correspondence and a great deal of tact, and must at first have given the young clerk a good deal of trouble. It is thus not surprising that he had but little leisure for other work; and though he brought out (privately printed) 'Graphidæ, or Character- istics of Painters,' a small collection of poetical apostrophes, it appears from incidental references in his letters that at least some, probably most of them, were written at Munich in 1832-33, while the spirit of Italy and Venice was still on him. Very few letters of the year have been preserved, and the Journal speaks for itself.

1838.—I have no diary for this year and but a faint re- collection of it. But early in the year Henry Chorley[2] and I agreed to take lodgings in common, and established our- selves at No. 9, Chapel Street, Grosvenor Place. We set to work to make our house agreeable. He supplied the music and I part of the company. Through Chorley I became intimate with the Procters, Browning, Moscheles, and especially at Gore House.[3]

The coronation took place on June 28th. Faucher and his wife came over to stay with me in Chapel Street. I was one of the Earl Marshal's men in the abbey, and escorted the ambassadors &c. to their seats. Stood behind the throne during the ceremony with the maids of honour.

---

[1] For this note on the business of the Court the author is indebted to the kindness of Lord Hobhouse.

[2] Henry Fothergill Chorley, born in 1808, was by five years Reeve's senior. He was a writer of taste and refinement, but wanting the *verve* which could make his works acceptable to the public, and was perhaps best known in his connexion with the *Athcnæum*.

[3] The Countess of Blessington's. Cf. *The Greville Memoirs*, 2nd part, i. 167.

I first met the Richardsons in this year at a party at
Mrs. Martineau's in Fludyer Street. I afterwards saw them
at Mrs. Spottiswoode's ball and at Lansdowne House.

The following letter from M. de Tocqueville refers to the
concluding part of the ' Démocratie en Amérique,' which was
translated and published in 1840 :—

Baujy par Compiègne, March 2nd.—You ask when my
book will be finished. I can only repeat what I have already
told you, my dear translator, that I know nothing about it.
I am most anxious that it should be printed next winter ;
but, from past experience of such things, I feel quite unable
to say that this will be possible. Day after day I find
myself altogether wrong in my calculations—a thing you
will easily understand, as you know that I do not prepare
my work in advance, but that it is my custom only to
arrange the plan and principal ideas, and then to follow the
current of my thoughts, quickly or slowly, as they serve me.
So that I never know beforehand how much time or how much
paper will be needed for what remains to be done ; and I can
only say that I left Paris for the whole winter and came and
shut myself up here with Mme. de Tocqueville ; that I work
from morning till night ; that I am doing my best, and cannot
possibly go any quicker, except by turning out inferior work—
which is not to be thought of. For, naturally, I want to
succeed ; and if I must fail, will fail according to rule. So
I come back to where I started from, which is to tell you of
what I wish : and that is to finish my work by the end of
autumn, so that the printing may begin next December.
But I cannot answer for this till I have passed the first sheet
for ' press.'

Tocqueville, August 12th.—It is indeed treating you as a
friend to propose that you should come to us in the midst of
all the pulling down and building up again now going on in
this old hall, which was always ugly, and which half a
century of neglect has reduced to a ramshackle farmhouse. I
think I have already told you what to expect. On one side, a
heap of litter, tenanted by pigs, ducks, and geese ; on the other
side, some beds of peas ; and between the two, a dilapidated
old house re-echoing with the hammers of workmen. This

is the only shelter I can offer you; but I can assure you of a hearty welcome; you will share our present misery, and try, like us, to see this place, in imagination, as it will be in eighteen months' time.

Office work, reading, writing, and society—this last especially—occupied Reeve's time, and the months slipped away without any noteworthy occurrence. He was, in fact, strengthening the foundations of his future success. His Journal shows him as associating on friendly terms with artists and men of letters, and becoming known to members of the aristocracy of rank and intellect.

1839.—Our house in Chapel Street continued to be agreeable. January 31st we received Carlyle, Rio, Austin, the Grotes, the Melvilles, Von Glehns, Herbert (R.A.), Bell, Phillips, Thackeray, Sydney Smith, and Doyle. I was continually at Gore House, where I met the Duke of Beaufort, Brougham, Lyndhurst, Lord Stuart de Rothesay, Alfred Montgomery, Prince Louis Napoleon, Landseer, Countess Guiccioli, Maclise, John Forster, Lord Normanby, Lady Charlotte Bacon,[1] Landor.

On May 4th I was called to the Bar—Middle Temple; and took to reading law with Alfred Austin. May 22nd and 23rd I went to the Levee and the Drawing Room; but I had been presented by Lord Lansdowne in the preceding year. Saw the rehearsal for the Eglinton Tournament at St. John's Wood.

In August went to Scotland for the first time, with Charles Hamilton.[2]

With knapsack on back Reeve wandered from Callander to the Trossachs, where he stayed a couple of days, 'doing' the 'Lady of the Lake' country, then still comparatively unknown to Englishmen. His letters to his mother are filled with descriptions of it, which it is unnecessary to repeat. The short tour ended at Glasgow, whence he wrote :—

[1] Lady Charlotte Harley, daughter of the fifth Earl of Oxford, was, as a child of eleven, celebrated by Byron as Ianthe in the dedication to *Childe Harold*. In 1823 she married Major Anthony Bacon, and died in 1880. Her portrait by Westall is engraved in Finden's *Illustrations of the Life and Works of Lord Byron*.

[2] Charles Anthony Hamilton, born in 1809, a cadet of the family of Lord Belhaven, was Deputy-Clerk of the Privy Council. He died in 1860.

August 17th.—We passed Loch Katrine in a row-boat. The party from the inn was large, and we had a small boat to ourselves, rather more swift and secure than the Swiss lake boats we have been in under similar circumstances. When we arrived at the other end of Loch Katrine, we walked about five miles to Inversnaid, through a wild bleak pass, from which we took our leave of Benvenue. Amongst our party were two couples who soon excited our attention. The women, both handsome, and dressed alike in the Lennox plaid, were mounted on the Highland ponies which are kept to take people over that pass, and each one was attended by her most faithful and attentive squire, holding her bridle over the gullies and burns. They were sisters, we thought. Then we thought they were brides. At last, while we were waiting for the steamer at the foot of the Inversnaid waterfall on the bank of Loch Lomond, Charles Hamilton made a brilliant guess which explained the whole; and I then recognised them as the sister-brides, Sir S. Glynne's sisters, who were married the other day [July 25th], at the same hour, to W. Gladstone and Lord Lyttelton. A prettier or a happier party never journeyed across the heather. But this is not all. Before we could get from the shore to the steamer, I descried on board the other pretty bride, Thomasina Hankey, now Mrs. Maxwell, whom we were talking about at Richmond the other day. She only crossed and landed where we got on board; but I thought that it was a large sum of human happiness to have met in one day.

But, notwithstanding all the happiness, the wind was intensely cold, and I let the Hamiltons and the brides land at Tarbert and proceed to Inverary without me. I spent two or three hours more in taking a complete survey of Loch Lomond, which is exceedingly picturesque; then came from Balloch to Dumbarton, where I found a steamer which, for one shilling, brought me here to a late dinner. I never in my life met with anything like the cheapness of the Highlands. Since I left Edinburgh I have not spent 10*s.* a day, including conveyances. Accordingly I have spent the difference in divers stuffs of many colours and incredible cheapness—a magnificent plaid, a yard and a half wide and three yards and three-quarters long, for 17*s*. ; waistcoats, 3*s*. 6*d*. each ; trousers, 10*s*.—just what I give two guineas for in London.

He had intended prolonging his stay in the North for another week ; but an attack of gout—the first assault of a tyrant to whose sway he remained subject throughout his life—suggested that if he was to be ill, he might as well be so in his own rooms, with his home comforts and his books beside him. So as soon as he could move he took the steamer to Liverpool, and thence by train to London ; making this last journey in the amazingly short time of eleven hours, and reaching his lodgings on the 22nd.

The letters which follow were all written to his mother, and, whilst illustrating the almost child-like trust in her preserved by a man now of mature years—a trust and affection which lasted to the end—they afford also a singularly clear view of what he was doing, reading, hearing, saying—almost, indeed, of what he was thinking.

C. O., August 28*th*.—The Queen certainly was received yesterday with marvellous acclamations—a more numerous and respectable crowd than I ever saw before on the same occasion—a circumstance I can hardly account for, unless from the notion that she was to be unpopular, and so people went to shout with all their might. The provinces and the parsons all firmly believe that she can't go to church without being hooted.

I have got a decided attack of the Slave-trade frenzy, or Abolitionist fever ; and I think of Mr. Clarkson, who got off his horse to roll on the turf for sheer thinking of the horrors of the middle passage. I am now far advanced in my article, which will contain a vast quantity of fine parliamentary horrors, and a most hopeless view of the case, which I reduce to this dilemma :—either men will seek a profit by draining blacks out of Africa, which is the slave trade ; or they will seek a profit by exploring Africa, introducing whites into that continent, and probably extirpating the aborigines on their own soil.

A curious forecast of what is actually taking place now that the slave trade has been put an end to ; when the captive negro, no longer a marketable chattel, is converted into butcher meat or a sacrifice to a debased and foul superstition, and the nations of Europe are standing in arms, ready to fight for the heritage of the man and the brother.

C. O., September 3rd.—On Saturday I flew on the wings of fire, which is the Pindaric way of saying I went per railroad, to Slough, and was driven through a tornado to Burnham.[1] Poor Chorley sailed at three that morning for Hamburg; whereupon the Devil, who loves to subvert weak stomachs, brushed up the wind; and I expect to hear either that H. F. C. is Robinson Crusoing it at Heligoland, or that he died on the passage of retching. I have not heard such a gale for months. Happily it blew the right way for my poor mate.

The next day I went to church at Farnham Royal; and in the afternoon Mr. and Mrs. Grote and I took an immense ride. It is the sweetest sylvan spot in England—a vast range of tangled glades of beeches of immense size, all pollarded centuries ago, and now twisted in huge volutes with groves rising out of their heads, like antlers of trees. The whole ground is thick with fern and ling, which empurples the forest, and is intersected with the greenest paths winding under the big beeches; whilst, here and there, clumps of juniper trees, some of which are twelve feet high, give some break in the wood the air of a trim shrubbery. All this belongs to nobody but old Nature; though I would fain have thought that I saw the lord of the manor in a green baldric chasing a roe up the dargle, or some Jacques dreaming in this other Ardennes. . . . I need not add how much I enjoyed the exhilarating exercise, the fresh and active air, the witty and wise conversation of my hosts, with whom all topics were discussed, from Mehemet Ali to the propriety of wearing top-boots.

I walked over the fields yesterday with my gun, saw no game, the harvest being in the fields, and came to town to dine at Mr. Greville's—which, as you may suppose, I made rather a point of, from his perpetual kindness to me. The party consisted of Mr. Stephen, Henry Taylor,[2] Poulett

---

[1] Where Mr. Grote, the future historian of Greece, but already well known in the world of letters, was then residing.

[2] No relation. A clerk in the Colonial Office; K.C.M.G. in 1869; but already known as a rising man in the service, and as the author of *Philip van Artevelde.*

Thomson,[1] Tom Baring, and myself. We talked, of course, of Canada and colonies with all our might. I asked Pou. to send me a bear ham, which I am dying to taste; and that made everybody talk about wild beasts, from Lord Waterford's pet lions to Mrs. Stephen's cat. . . . To judge from appearances, P. T. means to set about his governor-generalship in just the contrary way to Lord Durham; and I was pleased by several little things which indicated in him a sense of what was kind and wise in the omission of that parade and ostentation which Lord Durham stuffed his empty embassy with.

Shortly after the date of this letter he visited his uncle at Dedham, joined his mother in Norfolk, attended the Norwich festival, and, after some more visits, was back in London by the beginning of October.

C. O., October 7th.—Nothing but my frequent changes of bed and abode, and the want of proper writing materials, prevented me from giving you the history of my adventures long ago; for, though the circuit was small, the scenery was pretty well varied. The horse and gig plan from Norwich answered capitally; it conveyed me rapidly, and it made me quite independent.

I left Norwich full of the strong impression which my visit to the Octagon gave me; a stronger one than I can well describe. The voices all haunted me . . . and the vulgarest drawl of the clerk, giving out a hymn, was mellowed by such old association that it melted into my heart. I disapproved the service and the sermon exceedingly; it chilled me; but there was infinite devotion, to my mind, in the re-awakened teachings of those early days. The marble slabs, too, over those who are dead, speak not in vain from the walls.

I drove to Buckenham through a storm of rain. However, since I was last in Norfolk, Mackintosh has apparelled the world, and society may face the deluge without getting wet. Nothing is so little changed as Buckenham, unless it be changed for the better. My aunt is rather weak, and

---

[1] Afterwards Lord Sydenham; at this time newly appointed Governor-General of Canada.

very deaf; but my uncle, quite unaltered. Emily in good
spirits, with pleasant neighbours, pleasant prospects, and a
very pleasant ally in Miss Brereton, who really has found
her mission in tending those old people. On Monday
Emily and I went to Quiddenham. I shot with Mr. Keppel[1]
on that day and the next, and though we found but little
game, I liked my host and my perambulation. Lady Maria,[1]
too, gains by being known; or, rather, one gains a great deal
by knowing her. She has the most strictly logical head I
ever met with in woman; this quality is, to be sure, dearly
purchased at the expense of all the imaginative and most of
the sensitive part of human nature; but it gives a high and
invigorated tone to the character. . . .

From Diss to Grafton (in Worcestershire), I went at
one bound; 272 miles in about twenty-six hours, allowing
time for afternoon service at Norwich Cathedral, and two
hours for breakfast at my own house in town. The chief
incident was the presence of Mr. Robberds[2] in the mail.
We talked a great deal, and he seemed to wish to insert Mr.
Taylor's discourse on my father's life in his works. I believe
I have the copy of it, which exists in your handwriting. I
shall have it copied for Mr. Robberds. At Grafton we found
that the partridge epidemic had not prevailed to the same
extent, and we shot a great many pheasants. William and
Tom Collett were there, whom I like very much. They have
quite as much talent as Ben ever had, with more polish and
knowledge of the world. I came home on Friday night, to
what Mrs. Smith declares to be the cleanest house in
London—I believe with entire truth. . . .

On Saturday I went over to neighbour Grote's, to chat
an hour. They are going to Belgium and Paris in a few
days, and I am to keep and ride the celebrated steed Nimrod
during their absence.

C. O., October 12*th.*—I presume that your visit to
Dedham will have closed with the week, and that you are,
by this time, either arrived at Lowestoft or on your

---

[1] The Hon. and Rev. Edward Keppel, rector of Quiddenham, married Lady
Maria Clements, second daughter of the second Earl of Leitrim.

[2] John W. Robberds, of Norwich; author of *A Memoir of William Taylor,*
who, though a Norwich man and a member of the Octagon congregation, was
not in any way related to the family of Mrs. Reeve.

way thither. . . . I have now got Mr. Grote's horse
Nimrod to ride for two months, whilst they are abroad;
and I am going to do wonders before anybody else in
London is up or awake. . . . I have reason to be
satisfied with the success of my Slave-trade article. Mr.
Stephen came here to talk about it, and Mr. Hamilton has
read and approved; so I have two under-secretaries to begin
with. I now turn my attention to the composition of a
practical article on Education, which I wish to make as
unpolemical and conciliatory as possible. It will appear in
the next number, if I can complete it to my mind. Emily's
'Schoolmistress' will appear in a month, and will furnish
me with some valuable practical extracts. I read the MS.
at Buckenham with great satisfaction. The Bishop of
Norwich and Lady Maria Keppel have also given it their
imprimatur.

My engagements have been few. I spent an evening at
Mrs. Jameson's with Ellen Tree and the Procters. I can't
conceive that Miss Tree is an actress of much grace or
ingenuity, but she is very handsome, and full of dignified
talent. Perhaps a woman of more solid parts than any
other now upon our stage. Young has been to force me to
go to assist at the *début* of a *protégée* of his—a Miss Austin
—at Covent Garden. This involves my sitting out the
opera of 'Artaxerxes,' which terrifies me unspeakably.
However, the old gentleman was so emphatic on the
occasion that I dared not refuse, and there are too few
people in London for a sociable being to quarrel with any of
them.

At Richmond, on Charlotte Austin's birthday, which was
Wednesday, we had all the Austins, Charles and Alfred to
boot. Alexander and Francis Thun and I slept at the Star
and Garter, which is perfect as a country house, for three
shillings a night—one can't be better anywhere. Mr. Austin
was in great force, as he generally is when there is somebody else to drive him to the right side by taking the wrong
one against him, and defeating his predilection for perverse
judgements and paradoxical opinions.

I am feeding my sympathies for Charles I., and Archbishop Laud by reading Clarendon, which enchants me ;

such ease of discernment, such wit in describing character, such a flow of words and feelings, that I don't know when I have flirted with the Muse of History in so agreeable a dress.

C. O., October 15th.—I have been a good deal at Gore House lately, attracted and amused by Mme. de Guiccioli, who is staying with my lady. Having recently made the acquaintance of Lady Byron, it is very curious to me to compare the manners and character of her celebrated rival. The Guiccioli is still exceedingly beautiful. She has sunbeams of hair, a fine person, and a milky complexion. Her spirits are wonderful, and her conversation brilliant even in the most witty house in London. Besides which, she alone of all Italian women knows some things. Besides a fine taste, which belongs to them by nature, she has a good share of literary attainments, which, as her beauty fails, will smooth a track from coquetry to pedantry, from the courted beauty to the courted blue.

On Sunday evening D'Orsay drew my likeness. They say it is capitally done. I smiled to think of the last time I sat. It was to Mlle. Mérienne ; Mme. Ivanowska, Mlle. Moultou, and poor dear Augusta Roguin sat with me for hours, to make me look pleasant, and to get you a nice drawing. Now, in the same position, there sat Lady Blessington, Mme. Guiccioli, and Miss Power, the same trio raised to a higher expression. This Miss Power has just arrived in England, and appeared on my horizon. She is Lady B.'s niece and god-daughter. Imagine a girl of seventeen, brought up in New Brunswick, in a small family circle in a small colony, of extremely cultivated mind, earnest sense, extreme serenity of manner, and very uncommon beauty ; imagine her transported at once from polar twilight to the tropics, launched at a bound in the vivacity and splendour of our painted artificial life, where everything is a contrast to her childhood and herself. I enjoy to see that security of simple hearts gazing, like deer in a glade, at what is going on about them. It is by such a demeanour that the Queen has learned to queen it. I accordingly watched my trio with uncommon interest, but perhaps there is more reflection than animation in the expression of the face which was transferred at that moment to paper. The person with whom Miss Power was most intimate in her colony was Mrs. Carter. I naturally mentioned the Judge, but I had soon said all I had to say about him. The other night Brougham was there, and of course very much struck by the newcomer. After sundry attempts at an introduction, he drew back, and said to my lady, 'I don't know what to say to these young things ; I should feel like the old Devil talking to an angel.'

C. O., October 18*th.*—I went on Wednesday to see a Miss Austin *débute* at Covent Garden as Mandane in 'Artaxerxes,' being thereunto moved by her patron and instructor, Mr. Young, and having likewise moved Mrs. Jameson to let me escort her. The whole thing was very successful. An opera without a chorus is a good deal like a picture without a background ; and the instrumental resources put me a little in mind of Giotto's perspective. But the recitative was very fine, and the airs very sweet. The English audience, who think airs are music, and music airs, began to applaud at the first notes of the symphony of 'In Infancy,' and 'The Soldier tired.' Miss Austin is really very good—a pupil of Welsh's, with a fine high soprano voice, with a good command of it, even in that old bravura which is so laborious—except when she sang out of tune for fright.

C. O., October 19*th.*—I dined yesterday at John Murray's the younger, with Charles Fellows and Paget. Both of them leave England on Tuesday ; the former returns to Asia Minor, to prosecute his researches in that forgotten land, backed by Government money and Queen's ships : the latter goes to Hungary.

The story which follows is not new, and is told in outline in the ' Greville Memoirs ; ' [1] but nowhere has it been related with the fulness of detail here given by Reeve.

C. O., October 22*nd.*—So rapid and so mysterious is the flight of all rumours which have grief in them, that I shall probably not be the first to announce to you the death of Lord Brougham ; but as few occurrences have ever made a more

[1] Second Part, i. 243.

forcible impression on my mind, have more suddenly and strongly arrested the current of daily circumstances, I sit down to express at length what fills me with so strange a mixture of grave thoughts on the occasion.

Yesterday morning Alfred Montgomery, Lord Wellesley's private secretary, a youth on whom Brougham doated, rushed over from Kingston Terrace to Gore House, before they had sat down to breakfast, with the letter in his hand. Poor Alfred was in a state of distraction. Their first impression at Gore House was that something had happened to Marquis Wellesley. The letter, however, told the whole truth. It was from Shafto, the only uninjured survivor of the party. Brougham, Leader,[1] and Shafto[2] hired a bad hack carriage to go from Brougham Hall to see a ruin in the neighbourhood. It was so like him to choose to go in a wheelbarrow instead of a coach and four. They had not gone far when the splinter-bar broke ; they were thrown out, and one of the horses kicked Brougham on the head, which made him insensible, so that he could not get out of the way of the carriage, which turned over on to him in the ditch, crushed his head, and killed him on the spot. Leader was so much hurt that his life is despaired of.

It seems that this letter from Shafto to Alfred Montgomery was the only one received in London. Leonard Edwards was at Brougham, but he was gone shooting in another direction. The 'womankind,' as he called them, were at Brighton. No sooner had Montgomery read his letter to D'Orsay and Lady Blessington than a post-chaise came to take him up at their door and convey him posthaste to Fern Hill, where the Marquis W. is staying. The consequence of this was that nobody knew anything about the event till the afternoon, when D'Orsay went out and told people. In an hour a rumour—distorted in a thousand ways—pervaded London. I heard, whilst I was dining at my club, that Brougham was dangerously ill. Upon this I went to Gore House, where I found them in possession of these details.

[1] John Temple Leader, born in 1810, and in 1839 M.P. for Westminster. He is still alive in 1898.
[2] Robert Duncombe Shafto of Whitworth Park, Durham.

It was the most melancholy evening I ever spent there. In no house was Brougham so entirely tamed ; in none, except his own, so much beloved. Only last Sunday week —not ten days ago—just six before his death—he dined there, and stayed very late, which he rarely did, leaving them dazzled with the brilliancy of his unflagging spirit. I was to have dined there too ; they very earnestly pressed me ; but I had promised to go to Richmond. They tried hard, too, to get Sir A. Paget ; but we both stayed away, and they sat down to table *thirteen*. I can only say that the deaths which have struck me most in my life have always been preceded by a dinner of thirteen, in spite of efforts to avoid it. Everybody will bear witness to the splendour of the genius which is now set and quenched. On that head I can add nothing to the general sense that England will be long before she nurses such a son again—a son, indeed, most prodigal of all his gifts, yet supplying from his own resources an unexhausted store.

October 23rd.—I suppose by this time you know it is all a hoax ; but I go on with my letter to give you an idea of the strange states of mind through which we had been passing. I had not half done my reflections on Brougham and his gifts, when I discovered that a letter had arrived at this office on Monday morning, dated from Brougham on Sunday. This was tolerable evidence that he did not die on Saturday. I galloped up to Gore House with this letter, and we instantly despatched an express to Alfred Montgomery, at Fern Hill, to recall him to town, without telling the Marquis, who is very weak and ill. Further evidence was soon received ; in the afternoon everybody learned it was a hoax, of which no one but Brougham himself was capable. So it proved. When the express returned from Fern Hill, he brought us word that Montgomery had received a letter from Lord B., saying that it was all a *thoughtless jest* of his own !

Just conceive the vapidity, the vanity, the contrasts of all the false emotions that everybody went through ; a very pretty piece of Devil's amusement, for I can call it no better. Sheil rushed from the Athenæum on Monday evening to pen a magniloquent obituary, which appeared in the next day's

' Chronicle.' Trelawny, hearing that there was still some life left in Leader, starts off for Westmorland to attend his last moments, and the chairman of the Westminster Election Committee does the same. Windsor Castle shook with glee, and Lord Holland began to think that he should venture to speak again in the Lords'. For the first time, for five years, all the world talked for a whole day about Brougham's virtues, and there was wondrous forgiveness of injuries in the whole metropolis. To the Continent the news was borne with signal rapidity, and the story, followed by a lagging contradiction, will take at least two months to be echoed from paper to paper round the globe. For my part, I contemplated the inquest sitting on the body, and I had selected the 12th and 13th verses of St. Jude's Epistle for the funeral sermon. D'Orsay drew a capital sketch of Brougham in his plaid trousers, from memory, which we thought invaluable; and nobody could look at his wild, uncouth handwriting without tears in his eyes. In short, so bad a joke was never played off on so large a scale before; but one can't look forward without a good deal of amusement to Brougham's telling the story, which he will infallibly do at all dinners, councils, and convocations for the next six months. H. B. will immortalise it by a sketch; and as we all cried on this occasion, the next time he dies we shall have the laugh all our own way.

Voilà l'histoire de vingt-quatre heures ! and I hope you will be as melancholy and as much annoyed and diverted as we have all been.

This curious hoax forms the subject of many succeeding letters, which trace the various scraps of evidence proving conclusively that Brougham was himself the author of it. Reeve seems to have fancied that the letter might have been actually written by Mrs. Shafto, but the weight of the evidence fixes it on Brougham. He tells, too, how, on November 23rd, after the Queen had withdrawn from the Council, ' the Duke of Cambridge ran round the room after Brougham, vociferating at the top of his voice, " By God, Brougham, you did it; by God, you wrote the letter yourself; " to which Brougham could not well reply. However '—he adds —' he had actually challenged his old friend Sir Arthur Paget the week before, for saying as much; probably well knowing

that Sir Arthur would never fight him. As I go about
everywhere, stating not only the fact, but giving perfect
legal proof of it, I wish he may challenge me.'

C. O., October 29th.—On Sunday, at Richmond, I found
the Austins recovering from the fatigue of putting out a fire.
Lucy's bed was wholly consumed, and it seems incredible
that the house escaped; but they (i.e. the women—mother
and daughter) exhibited their wonted energy and presence
of mind, to the astonishment of admiring ostlers from the
Star and Garter. My aunt pushed a man with a pail in his
hand into the thickest smoke, and then followed him with
another. Lucy signalised herself at the pump, and raised a
flood of water from the bowels of the earth. In short, they
got the fire under; Mr. A., of course, teeth chattering,
knees shaking, paralysed. And then, on the following day,
he had the face to use big adjectives, and talk of energy. . . .

Chorley came to town on Friday, but he is gone to
Liverpool for a few days. He is in great strength.

C. O., November 2nd.—Chorley comes home to-night, to
put an end to the very solitary life I have been leading for a
month—perhaps more solitary than any other month I
can remember, without seeing a single kinsman in town,
and with London like an exhausted receiver. Under these
circumstances I ought to have done more than I have done;
but I find the treatment of this matter of Public Instruction,
on which I am engaged, very uphill work, and what I have
been doing is not good. Last night I disinterred our old
article on Madame Necker's book,[1] which was never
published. I re-read it with pleasure and some astonishment; for with a strong tinge of those philosophical studies
which then filled my life, there is a freshness of pure thought
about it, which has been subsequently lost in the attempt to
square my style and habits to the business of the world.
However, one cannot always wear singing robes, and I am
content with the unadorned fustian of middling common
sense. By the way, I know not how that word fustian ever
came to be used to denote a pretentious style, since the
thing is only used for shooting-jackets and grooms' inex-

[1] Presumably Mme. Necker de Saussure's *L'Éducation progressive, ou
Étude du Cours de la Vie* (Paris, 1828–32).

pressibles. I suppose because it is a sort of synonym of *stuff*.

A good deal of both these commodities was to be heard in Bulwer's new play, which we attended last Thursday;[1] but it was finely acted by Macready and Mrs. Warner, and you shall have the 'Examiner' account of it, all *couleur de rose*. Bulwer, notwithstanding his deafness, could hear the solitary hiss which mingled with the thousand plaudits. The sweetest flowers prick him with a thorn, and the gayest insects sting him as they pass. He came into our box after having received a complete ovation, and the first words he uttered were : 'A great many enemies in the house to-night.' Poor fellow! who has so much talent with so little greatness; so much success, and so little happiness. That asp, his wife, sends over an abusive letter from Paris to the ' Morning Post,' just so that it may appear on the morning of the day fixed for bringing out his play.

C. O., November 6th.—At this moment I am very busy. Alfred Austin has kindly resumed our readings of English procedure, and I am now stringing together my article on Education with more difficulty and despondency than self-satisfaction.

November 11th.—Chorley's play is making a *furore* in the Green Room, and it is almost certain that Mathews will bring it out at Covent Garden. This is a great subject of rejoicing, and we won't let it be damned.[2]

November 18th.—I am just entering on a mighty series of businesses and negotiosities, as Cudworth called them. My educational paper is still in the hands of the compositors, and I am in warm water about it. My Council is going to sit, and I have my usual course of judge-hunting thrown on me, Greville being gone with D'Orsay to shoot; Brougham less manageable than usual; for, though he has had a resurrection, he may and must despair of an ascension; and Baron Parke, my sheet-anchor, going to hang some of the blackguards at Newport. In the midst of all this comes

---

[1] October 31st. The play was *The Sea Captain, or the Birthright*.

[2] It was not brought out, either at Covent Garden or elsewhere, and the editor of Chorley's *Autobiography* (vol. i. p. 132) says that he ' wisely abstained from giving it publication.' It does not appear that Reeve knew anything more about it than that it was written by his friend.

Tocqueville's letter to announce the completion of his labour, and the commencement of mine; and instead of living in a sober, pugilistic state of training for all this, my wits are wool-gathering and my pen song-writing all day long. However, I am never better than when I am worked to the full point of ebullition; and I hope nothing will suffer, not even my letters: and, thank God! the lengthy orations of our lawyers will leave me reasonable time to translate while they are quoting the Byabasthas[1] of pundits and the conditions of the Dayabhaga.[2]

C. O., November 20th.—Last night we summoned the whole Privy Council for Saturday, when the Queen is to make her declaration of marriage—a stranger position, I think, than any woman was ever placed in. They say she is excessively in love with Prince Albert, and that may help her; though, indeed, it makes it worse in some respects; and, though I am a man, I had rather marry without making a speech to my Council on the subject at all.

C. O., November 23rd.—Last night I dined at Gore House with Greville. Lady Charlotte [Bacon] and Mme. Guiccioli are both on the eve of their departure. After dinner we made Lady Charlotte read Lady Macbeth to us, Greville doing Macbeth with two paper-knives for daggers. It began in a joke; but such was the power of her art that it well-nigh ended in tears. I never heard finer touches of pathos. Then she healed this grisly tragic terror by the love of Juliet, and the naïve devotedness of Imogen; and we—band of bold talkers—sat listening as if we heard it all for the first time. . . .

Meadows Taylor writes to me of one of his Indian friends, who swallows his tongue from time to time, suspends respiration, and is buried for three months or so: in order, as he says, to meditate. I am going to do the same thing, only it is in order to translate; and as soon as I have got my first sheets of Tocqueville I shall renounce dinners, forswear theatres, eschew routs, and avoid mankind—with a reserve for the Austins and Gore House. . . .

The Queen has just made her declaration of marriage at the Council to-day. It was, I think, the largest Council

---

[1] Legal decisions, precedents.   [2] A law-book.

ever held—eighty-five present; amongst others, the two dead men, Brougham and the Duke,[1] whom the papers all but slew last Monday. I like what she said, though there is nothing about the Protestant line, and a good deal about her own feeling and her own happiness. You will see the speech in the paper. I am busy at this instant in correcting the proof of the ' Extraordinary Gazette,' and I hope to have some copies here before post time. The Queen read it in her usual clear, sonorous voice; but her hand trembled, and she could hardly hold the paper. She wore the bracelet with Prince Albert's portrait on her arm. Not the least interesting part of the scene was the Duke of Wellington, who is really very ill and weak; but the gallant old man *would* be there.

C. O., November 27*th.*—I have been busy with the household of Prince George of Denmark, which was enormous : a master of the horse, a master of the robes, six lords of the bedchamber, and eight grooms—all the first people of the time. I am afraid we shall not get anything so handsome for Queen Victoria's spouse.

C. O., November 30*th.*—Your spirits seem, I think, to be a little affected by the moist weather, and even the prospect of the black-satin robe does not entirely restore the *lumen siccum* which generally enlivens the correspondence. For my part, through fair weather and foul, I have been making a sort of carnival before my forty days in the wilderness ; and I shall almost be glad of a Lenten diet before we get to Christmas.

This week, all on a sudden, I have begun to know and got at home with our paulo-post-futurum connexions—the Gordons.[2] On Sunday I met Miss Gordon at Bayswater ; on Tuesday I dined there ; on Wednesday I went to see Mrs. Jameson, in their company ; and on Friday we all went to the play together. They are merry people, *le cœur sur la main*, and I dare say I shall find the house a pleasant encampment when they come back to town in the spring. For the present they are going to Herefordshire, carrying Lucy with them, to share the winter quarters.

---

[1] At this period ' the Duke ' always meant the Duke of Wellington.
[2] Sir Alexander Duff Gordon married Mrs. Austin's daughter Lucy, on May 16th, 1840.

On Thursday I dined at Tom Longman's, amid sheet lightning of wit. Sydney Smith, Forster of the 'Examiner,' McCulloch, Fraser Tytler, Miss Rogers, and self, composed the party, besides our host and hostess, dummies senior and dummies junior. Tom Longman made two puns, but, thank God, they were put down. We got Sydney on the overpowering topic of Macaulay. Macaulay is laying waste society with his waterspouts of talk; people in his company burst for want of an opportunity of dropping in a word; he confounds soliloquy and colloquy. Nothing could equal my diversion at seeing T. B. M. go to the Council the other day in a fine laced coat, neat green-bodied glass chariot, and a feather in his hat. Sydney S. had said to Lord Melbourne that Macaulay was a book in breeches. Lord M. told the Queen; so whenever she sees her new Secretary at War, she goes into fits of laughter. I said that the worst feature in Macaulay's character was his appalling memory; he has a weapon more than anyone else in the world's tournament. 'Aye, indeed,' said S. S.; 'why, he could repeat the whole History of the Virtuous Blue-Coat Boy, in 3 vols. post 8vo. without a slip. He should take two table-spoonfuls of the waters of Lethe every morning to correct his retentive powers.' . . .

Lady Gordon had Miss Coutts's box at Covent Garden, so we all went to see the 'Beggar's Opera.' A charming performance it was; the dress of our great-grandmammas so becoming, the language so pure, the dialogue so witty, the music so enchanting. When Polly had done her last song, we wished it all to begin over again, which is no joke, considering that we had previously undergone—I for the second time—the whole five acts of Knowles's 'Exposition of Love;' a loveless piece, indeed, it is, particularly the second time of hearing; and I have been abused on all hands for not having done what I could to damage it on its first appearance. But the 'Beggar's Opera!' May it live for ever!

C. O., December 2nd.—There never was a country like England. I enjoyed my skip into Hertfordshire very much, as one always does a foray from London, in whatever direction it may be. The floods had shaken the embankments of the road a little, and our huge train had to *wheedle* over the difficult place, at the cost of some delay; but by eight o'clock we sat down to dinner at Lockyer's house. It is the house in which all the Colletts were born, within hearing of the Hemel Hempstead chimes; and it is now occupied by Mr. and Mrs. Sanders and their quiverful of children— some almost grown up. She was the eldest Collett. They were very cheerful and hospitable, and some of the Longmans met me there. The next morning we went to the finest Saxon church I remember to have seen, and who but John Yelloby should read prayers. Mrs. Sanders laughed herself into fits to see me bowing to all the people of that ilk as I came out; but I was *en pays de connaissance*— Longmans, Dickinsons, and the curate to boot.

The object of my going down was to see a horse which I think of buying for Franz Thun—he having sent me 300*l.* to spend for him in horseflesh. Tom Collett and I rode in the afternoon to Ashridge Park, old Lady Bridgwater's place; I on this magnificent animal, for which I am to give 150*l.* if I buy him. It was like riding a large bird. We crossed the lovely soft lawns for miles, over park and common, till we got to Ashridge itself; a good, solid, modern castle, by Wyatt, as fit for a noble as Windsor is fit for a king. Then we came home, dined merrily, and I left them this morning, after breakfast, and got here in about as good time as I should have done from Hampstead.

December 3rd.—I have been breakfasting this morning very agreeably *tête-à-tête* with Lord Lansdowne, of whom I had seen little or nothing since his return from the Continent. Indeed, I had laboured under some apprehension that in these falling days of Whiggism he imputed to me a laxity of Whig views, which, Heaven knows! I felt and professed quite as strongly when they were at the height of Reform Bill power. The danger I now fear in politics is the too great reaction, over which Peel with his personal unpopularity, and the Duke with his failing health, cannot exercise a sufficient control. However, to return to Lord Lansdowne. I found him remarkably kind. His Continental journey appears to have succeeded in its chief object—that of meeting Prince Metternich, with whom he spent several days at Johannisberg—I presume between the cellar and the

cabinet, or in perpetual libations of what the Germans call
' Cabinets Wein.'   Nobody who ever heard Metternich converse was disappointed with him ; and Lord L. was
enchanted.   He (M.) was much interested about our great
Indian war, though the splendid completion of those British
achievements was then unknown in Europe.

If people would but care a little for Indian glories, that
war is the chiefest of them all.   It is barely fifteen months
since the Cabinet met at Windsor, and stayed there three
days to talk over the whole question of the Russian
aggression on India through Persia.   The result was a
despatch to Lord Auckland directing the course he was to
adopt to meet the emergency.   Before that despatch reached
Simla, Lord Auckland had adopted, on his own responsibility,
the very measures which were suggested to him from home.
Three armies moved over the vastest extent of territory ever
crossed by British troops ; swept central Asia ; united under
the walls of Ghuznee and Cabul ; restored a dynasty ; and,
having provided for the future security of the Empire,
returned almost unhurt within its frontiers.[1] . . . .

Mme. Guiccioli went back to France last night.   It
was Lady Charlotte Bacon who sailed for Spain on Saturday ;
I think I had mentioned her before more than once.   She
was Lord Byron's Ianthe.   One can't help loving the
Guiccioli for her *bonhomie* ; and though we have all been
hoaxing her for six weeks, I am sure she likes us all the
better for it, except that she never quite forgave Miss Power
for being three times as handsome as herself.   I am going to
dine at Lady Gordon's this day.   I have only seen the elder
daughter yet of the ladies of that family.

This morning we had M. de Schomburgk to breakfast ;
an agreeable little Dutchman, who has been exploring all
the creeks of the Orinoco and the sources of the Essequibo.
He has three real Indians with him, who, poor things, as
they happen to be of three different tribes of natives, neither
understand each other nor anyone else.   However, they are
going to be exhibited with other wonders from Guiana ; and

---

[1] The brilliance of this first Affghan campaign is an established fact,
though, in popular memory, it has been dimmed by the blunders and disasters
of the next two years.

that is, *è converso*, the same thing as exhibiting London to them.

C. O., December 7th.—I generally contrive, my dear mother, to salute you on Sunday morning ; nor will I omit so good a custom to-day, though I have to snatch an instant from a day full of business. For the last four days I have been worked to the utmost stretch—one day eighteen hours, without stoppage or rest, a quantity of private or semi-public matters coming in, of course, to interfere with my time while my court was sitting. . . .

My breakfast on Wednesday was very successful. Mr. Stephen charming ; but our Guiana guest made our blood run cold with mulatto horrors beyond all that was ever dreamt of for Paul Jones or Blue Beard. How strange it is to us who dwell between May-Fair and Kensington, that the earth should be so vast and so wild ; that there be rivers like the Orinoco ; and tribes of Amazons ; and savages and savannahs, and all that Adam found outside Eden ! . . .

My court began to sit on Thursday. Brougham had just buried his daughter,[1] on Wednesday afternoon, and the next morning came here as frisky as usual and most peculiarly civil to me. He and Dr. Lushington don't speak now, and between his peace with some of us, and his hostility to others, he is quite as droll as ever.

C. O., December 10th.—Since Brougham has been broken-hearted he is really so pleasant to mankind in general that one wishes he had a calamity two or three times at least in the course of the Session. We have now been sitting here nearly a week, and have had great diversion ; only that I have caught an insufferable cold from sitting in this mausoleum-like edifice without a wig. I declare I think I must wig it next winter ; and if so, I'll have a silk registrar's gown, though I am afraid it costs at least as much as a parson's.

C. O., December 13th.— . . . I have been weighing in my mind the evils of want of energy in woman, . . . and, captivating as is the notion of woman's reliance on man as

---

[1] She died on November 30th. In reality Brougham felt the loss deeply, but he was not the man to make any parade of his grief, and may, possibly enough, have overdone his affected stoicism.

the actor, that same bewitching languor is the nurse of ignorance and inaction, which mar all self-knowledge and all self-command. Women who have nothing else in them are sure to have a good deal of mischief; and all the demonstrations of a coquette, or the indiscretions of an energetic mind, are infinitely less dangerous than the simper of a weak, predestined victim. I once cured myself of a strongish liking for a person, which had resisted several other excellent remedies, by remarking that she was unpunctual; from thence I inferred a want of energy in things more important than time, and I traced this weak fibre through the whole character. After all, is not this habit of minute observation a very fatal one? After talking with Emily at Buckenham the other day, I felt almost ashamed of using so much selfish prudence in almost all the affairs of life; and I do so entirely repudiate and disavow all negative principles in my life that I am ashamed of that safe form of them which perpetuates a bachelor's peace. . . .

While my court sat I went out but little. Last night I met Bulwer and Fonblanque at Gore House—the former very deaf, the latter very droll. They related that when Sheridan Knowles was introduced to Bulwer, he said, 'Sir, you lead a very artificial life.' Bulwer, a bow, to own the soft impeachment. 'Shakespeare and I, sir,' added Mr. Knowles, 'are the children of Nature.'

Dr. Lushington talked to me for half an hour, the other day, about my Slave-trade article, and my strictures on the Portuguese Bill, which he mainly promoted. One can't argue with an author who is at the same time a legislator and a judge; but he did not convince me that I was wrong, and he was extremely kind in what he said. We are now intent on the reconstitution of my court. Fortunately, I am now strong enough to bear a hand in the operation, notwithstanding the anticipated resistance of the tongue fiend.[1] But the Chancellor and Dr. Lushington are extremely *bien disposés* to me.

C. O., December 16th.—Your letter of yesterday is very delightful. There certainly is something in the deliberate flow of written intercourse which gives it a satisfactory

[1] Lord Brougham.

completeness rarely attained in conversation. Somebody breaks in, or something breaks off, long before one has talked out a subject of interest, unless you have the happier chance of a long ramble in the fields. But I doubt whether either you or I ever speak to each other so thoroughly what we feel as when we are an hundred miles removed from speaking distance. I need not say how thoroughly I agree in what you enlarged on yesterday. But, as far as the observation can be generally applied, the thing most difficult to discern in a woman's character is the presence of strong, fixed principles; I mean before you have reached entire intimacy. There is so much in woman's manner of life which looks like principle, but is only a form of education; so much that is conventional instead of being fundamental, that it is hopeless to search for what no outward eye can with certainty detect. . . .

Lord Lansdowne seems to say that my visit to Bowood will be more opportune this week than at the end of the month: so I shall go down on Wednesday [18th], and probably come up on the following Tuesday in time for the Christmas dinner at Bedford Row.[1] We have a little theatrical scheme, too, on foot for the end of the week. Jack comes to town from Coed Ddu.

Your letters had better be sent here, as usual, and Mr. Greville will forward them. Lord John Russell is at Bowood this week, which is great additional inducement, for he requires the warm temperature of a circle in a country house to thaw his icy manners. I am sure, in writing to you, I may be pardoned for noticing my own position with *les personnages*: but it is strange that at twenty-six I should find myself on terms of acquaintance with the whole Cabinet, except Lord Melbourne and Baring. I rode down to the office with Lord Normanby this morning; he was very chatty and undignified—a word I use half in blame, half in praise.

Bowood, December 18*th.*—Lady Lansdowne is delighted with 'The Schoolmistress,' and has sent for a number of copies; but Darton seems to have made a mess of it, or the

---

[1] At the house of his uncle, John Taylor, a civil and mining engineer, also of Coed Ddu, in North Wales.

book has not been properly advertised, for Lady L.'s bookseller can't hear of it, and I can't get six copies I ordered a week ago. I think its success is, however, pretty secure. . . .[1]

C.O., December 26th.—We had great drollery at Bowood, with charades and Christmas pranks, the last evenings of my visit. Lord John's children grew more and more diverting every day, and though some of the days were dreary, there was always sunshine in the house. *Je me suis particulièrement rapproché des dames*, and the more I see of them the more I appreciate Lady Lansdowne's extreme good heart, Lady Louisa's good sense, and Lady Kerry's beauty.

Carlyle said of somebody the other day who shut himself up because he was out of humour, that ' it is well for a man to consume his own smoke.' . . . He is writing an *opusculum* on Chartism, and as his theory places omniscience in numbers, providential teaching in loud clamour, and political power in all gatherings of sturdy rustics or colliers on the hill-side, I apprehend it will be a book to do himself and the cause of rational government no good.

No news of Tocqueville's sheets, though I have got the Slave Abolition report, and have written a long article on it for the ' Athenæum.'

C. O., January 3rd, 1840.—My hermit life has begun, for I have declined almost all invitations; but I had Alfred Austin and Gordon to dinner the other day, and last night I went to the Austins to meet what the Canon Residentiary calls the pleasantest society in London—Milmans, Empsons, Seniors, &c. What, however, I found still pleasanter was Landor, who arrived yesterday on a visit to Gore House, where I dropped in after eleven o'clock, on my way home from Kensington. His face reminds me a little of Michael Angelo's. We were talking of that brilliant society of Leo X.'s Court, with its Bembo and its Mirandola, and I could not help thinking how truly Landor belongs to those scholarlike gentlemen in tastes and tone, and even in his whimsical faults. There is something of perpetual youth in his age; and he has that clear spirit of

---

[1] *Help to the Schoolmistress*, by Emily Taylor; published in 1839 by Harvey & Darton.

thought in him which shines like the eye of some large bird in the twilight.   I anticipate much pleasure from his visit.

I am going seriously to take up the musical instruction of one of the great metropolitan schools (a new one) : I helping with the powers, Chorley with writing, and Hullah the actual musical teaching, on which he seems much bent. I can't say that I am very zealous about sol-faing, and as I have not been able to get a capable teacher, that method must be given up, else I would try one plan against the other.   Kay has given us full power, and, *entre nous*, there is yet one field for us to work in, without any dread of inter-ference, and there the first stone even of a normal school is as good as laid.   But this is quite in confidence to you and Emily.

Nothing can equal the absurdity of Maule's blunder in managing the case against Frost,[1] which will very likely let the fellow escape.   The best opinion seems to be that it invalidates the whole proceeding, and that the prisoner might be arraigned again and convicted ; but the public feeling won't allow the Government to discharge two barrels at a man accused of treason.

C. O., January 7th.—We have just received a very ill-written, troublesome Treasury letter, by which it appears that each office is to pay its own public postage, and private letters are to be sent back, charged, and re-delivered.   The shortest way will be to write to me in future at my house.   I am having a hole and a box made to my hall door, and I think I shall not take in any but prepaid letters.   But you can have no conception of the immense quantity of trouble and embarrass-ment which the application of what is called a simple principle creates.   However, it will get right in time, and future generations will smile at our distress, when franks, double letters, and thick writing papers shall be as remote as the darker ages of the mythology or the origin of the alphabet.   Why, it will cost hundreds of thousands of pounds to provide the nation with letter-scales.   I have got

---

[1] John Frost, the Chartist.   He and two others with him were sentenced to death, but in view of the doubt held, by a minority of the judges, as to the validity of the trial, the sentence was commuted to one of transportation for life. In 1856 Frost received a free pardon and returned to England, where he died in 1877, at a very advanced age.

a balance at my office, which the Stationery Office supplied me with ; and at home I have established a neat bronze machine on the principle of a steelyard. My Uncle John has, of course, taken a line of his own, and invented something, with a mercurial column, which is cheap and convenient. . . .

C. O., January 9th.—There is something melancholy about the last of everything, and I enclose a sigh in this, the Last of the Franks. The privileged classes know how to be obliging to their neighbours. The great vehicles of correspondence are all to be stopped, and the penny level rises over them like a tide. It is the most democratic resolution we have had to sustain ; it affects more than our laws, our very manners. And such is the love of the English people for *tout ce qui tient du privilège*, that, instead of the ferocious triumph of French democrats over all exclusive rights and favours, there is a sort of reluctance to share a cheap benefit which rank and office have dignified while it was more confined.

Miss Edgeworth has been in the habit of sending all her correspondence here to be franked—for many years, far beyond the memory of clerks of the Council or anyone else. I believe it was some hereditary privilege inherent in the Edgeworth family ; for aught I know M. l'Abbé Edgeworth did the same. It had no beginning ; alas ! to-day it has its end ; or rather yesterday. A packet was received from Edgeworthstown of unusual dimensions, accompanied by a very pretty note to the clerks of the Council, thanking them for their unwearied politeness and industry, and begging them each to select and accept some one of Miss Edgeworth's books, as an acknowledgement of her sense of their kindness. I recommended the Memoirs of her father as the work most flattering to her family, and a letter has been despatched to ask for it.

I am amused to find Carlyle fairly brought before the world as a political writer, nay, even a political philosopher ; for his writings have convinced the ' Morning Post ' that such a thing as political philosophy exists. His little tractate on Chartism seems to have a great success. It is very genuine Carlylee.

C. O., January 10th.—*Le roi est mort ; vive le roi !* I wrote to everybody yesterday to bewail the Last of the Franks, and to-day I write to everybody for the sake of paying my penny. Man is such a pouting animal that he always quarrels with you for taking thorns out of his feet, and for services which would make wild beasts love you for ever. People have not sincerity enough even to tell themselves that their objections to improvement are lies. You would suppose, to hear them talk of postage, that the greatest pleasure in life had been the payment of ninepence per letter ; unless, indeed, the periodical visit of the tax-collector be, to some well-regulated minds, a source of higher and more lasting enjoyment. I have had a box and a slit fitted to my hall door, and intend soon to refuse all letters not prepaid.

Our dinner last night was very good fun, but we made rather too many puns. Landor rode several fine paradoxes with savage impetuosity ; particularly his theory that the Chinese are the only civilised people in the world. I am sure the Ching dynasty has not a firmer adherent than Landor within its own imperial capital. Landor, you know, is quite as vain of not being read, as Bulwer is of being the most popular writer of the day. Nothing can equal the contempt with which he treats anybody who has more than six readers and three admirers, unless it be that saying of Hegel's, when he declared that nobody understood his writings but himself, and that not always. Lady B. said the truest thing of Carlyle's productions that ever was uttered ; she called them 'spangled fustian'—a homely rough stuff, sparkling with genius in the seams.

The translation of the second part of Tocqueville's ' Democracy ' filled up Reeve's time during the early months of the year. It was published in April.

Both before undertaking it and during the progress of the work he must have written several letters to the author, but the following is the only one that has been preserved. As all his letters to Tocqueville, the original is in French.

C. O., February 22nd.—I have received the sheets up to and including No. 18, which arrived last Monday. Thursday's post brought me none. I suppose this simply means that none were ready, but I mention it for safety's sake. The little delay is not unwelcome to me ; I can breathe for a few days very much at my ease. The eighteen sheets are in the printer's hands.

I now venture to tell you of my great admiration for this work. I am honoured by being in a position to be the first to express to you a sentiment which will soon be shared by all the thinkers of the world. The chapters on the sources of poetry, the melancholy of democratic nations, and their public works, I find particularly striking ; it is perhaps the only modern book I have seen in which there is not a word to be cut out—that is, with very few exceptions. For instance, I regret that you should have said that Milton added six hundred words to the English language, because I do not think the statement is quite correct. I am very anxious to know where you got this idea. If it were not too late, I should venture to suggest your cutting the line out.

What will your democratic readers say of your book ? What will France say of it ? France so seldom named and so constantly portrayed ? Does the world contain a more melancholy picture than that which you draw of a people having all the elements of democratic decadence, without the spirit of order, association, and religion which has pre-served (will it always do so ?) the American Republics ? There is too much feeling in your words for it to be imagined that the picture is imaginary. It will be understood that you have written the book of the People for France, as Machiavelli wrote the book of the ' Prince ' for Cæsar Borgia. This expression may seem to you rather too strong, and I should perhaps have crossed it out, were it not for spoiling my page. But you will understand that I only compare you to Machiavelli as I compare France to the Duke of Valentinois—that is to say, two great writers and two great powers.

So the washing of the king's dirty linen is beginning again.[1] A humiliating spectacle for gods and men ! I

---

[1] ' Louis Philippe, more anxious to provide for his own children than to further French interests in the East, persuaded Soult to apply for a dotation of 500,000 francs a year for his second son, the Duc de Nemours. The French Chambers threw out the proposal, and Soult resigned.'—Walpole's *History of England*, iii. 646.

suppose a minister will be appointed *ad interim*—then there will be a two months' crisis, and the end of the Session. And with all this France expects to be included in the negotiations and arrangements of Europe ; although she never waits for the return of a courier sent by the Cabinet to Constantinople, and the reply to a despatch rarely finds the minister who sent it in office. Would to heaven we might see a ministry whose first policy would be to last ! it would be the first step towards doing much. We shall all be sorry if the fall of the ministry prevents M. Guizot from coming to London ; his presence would have been useful to both countries and agreeable to society.

To return to the book. I now see that I can just about keep pace with your printers, so that if you will give me some ten days between sending the last sheets and the French publication, the two books will appear together.

Later letters, subsequent to the date of publication, are referred to in the following from Tocqueville :—

Paris, May 23rd.—Thank you for all your enclosures. By sending me everything that appears on my book you do exactly what I wish. I am not afraid of criticism ; I am quite prepared for it. There is but one thing thoroughly annoying to an author—silence. I beg you therefore to continue as you have begun, and send me everything that is published. I should have written sooner, but I wanted to be able to speak about your translation. I have not yet seen the whole of it, but from what I have seen, I can honestly assure you that I am very much pleased with it. You have rendered my thoughts, in their most delicate shades, with a fidelity and clearness that seem to me perfect. As for the style, of which I am less able to judge, Mme. de Tocqueville assures me that it is excellent—clear, simple, and, in short, exactly what it ought to be for a book on political philosophy.

Meanwhile the current story of events is given by the Journal :—

On March 27th I dined with Prince Louis Napoleon in Carlton Gardens, with D'Orsay, Sir Robert Wilson, and Lord

Fitzharris.   M. Guizot arrived in April as ambassador, after the great coalition.   I knew him through Herbet, and dined at Hertford House on April 10th.   I translated his 'Washington,' and this contributed to our acquaintance, which soon ripened into friendship.

To Mrs. Reeve

C. O., April 13*th.*—On Friday I went to call on the Richardsons, in Fludyer Street.   My acquaintance with them has long been in growth at other people's houses, and I was determined to go at last to their own.   While I was there Mrs. Hudson Gurney came in, and I introduced myself, and she was *on ne peut plus aimable*.   These Richardsons lived at Hampstead whiles ago; then removed to Scotland, to be near Sir Walter Scott during the recess, he being a parliamentary attorney.   They are great friends of the Mintos, Mrs. J. Baillie, and all sorts of mutual acquaintances.   The young ladies—they have no mother—will suit you precisely, which is more than can be said of all young ladies.

That same day I dined with M. Guizot.   Nobody there but the people of the Embassy.   I cannot tell you how much I was flattered and pleased; nobody else has dined there at present, and to be asked in this easy manner, without any English people, was really charming.   I sat next him, and we talked a great deal about Rossi, Switzerland, Prévost, and a multitude of topics of common interest.   His conversation is certainly about the best I have heard; so full, so vigorous, yet not unpleasantly surcharged with learning or spirit.   You think I am at the end of my French felicities.   No such thing!   Tocqueville himself will be here in a few days, and we shall keep him as long as we can.   I have asked him to come to me if he is coming without his wife.   The book will be out in France and in England on the 20th—this day week.

Journal

Liszt was in London, and our musical parties were very brilliant.[1]   We had Liszt, the Battas, Ole Bull, Moscheles,

---

[1] Cf. Chorley's *Autobiography*, vol. i. pp. 268-9.

Benedict. On June 1st, M. Guizot and the Richardsons came. Liszt and Batta played the great Beethoven Sonata, *en doublant les passages.* I took Mme. d'Agoult to his recital on June 9th.

The translation of 'Washington' was finished while on a visit to Mrs. Austin at Richmond. Its publication in July brought Reeve the following note from its author :—

Londres, 7 juillet.—Je ne vous remercie pas, Monsieur ; je vous ai remercié en lisant vos épreuves. On est rarement, bien rarement content de son traducteur. Moi je suis heureux que vous ayez pris cette peine, et votre travail me cause une vraie satisfaction. Recevez, je vous prie, l'assurance de mes sentiments les plus distingués, et les plus affectueux. GUIZOT.

On August 6th Louis Napoleon made the abortive attempt at Boulogne which won for him and his companions the derisive nickname of *Les hommes de six sous.* Reeve noted in the Journal—

My servant, who knew the prince's servant, told us when we were dressing to go to the opera that the prince was going to France :[1] that seemed impossible, but it turned out to be true.

[1] Chorley's *Autobiography*, vol. i. pp. 271-2.

CHAPTER IV

EASTERN POLITICS

MEANTIME the threatening aspect of our relations with France, arising out of the perennial Eastern question, was finding Reeve a new and, for the time, an engrossing occupation. So far as it is possible to explain a very complicated matter in a few words, the case was this. The war between the Porte and its too powerful vassal, Mehemet Ali, which had raged intermittently for the last eight years, took a more active course during 1839. The Turkish army had been annihilated in the battle of Nezib on June 24th; the Sultan had been murdered on June 29th; and the Capitan-Pasha, fearing or pretending to fear the possibility of a Russian intervention at Constantinople, had taken the fleet to Alexandria and delivered it over to Mehemet Ali. On August 3rd Lord Palmerston, the then Foreign Secretary, wrote a despatch to Sir Robert Stopford, in command of the English fleet on the coast of Syria, giving him orders to demand, and, if necessary, to enforce, the restoration of the Turkish ships, and sent this by way of Paris, hoping and, in fact, believing that Marshal Soult, the president of the French ministry, would cordially agree with its purport, and would send identical instructions to the French admiral. Soult, however, refused, and the despatch to Stopford was not sent on.

In the negotiations which followed the difference between the English and French Cabinets widened. Mehemet Ali had been under the non-official protection of France, and his army was largely officered by Frenchmen. French feeling was in favour of establishing Mehemet Ali as an independent sovereign, with a territory extending to Mount Taurus. Palmerston understood this independence as involving a French suzerainty, if not sovereignty, in Egypt and the Euphrates valley, and was determined to maintain the integrity of the Sultan's dominions, with the assistance of the French if possible, without it if necessary. The matter was still unsettled when, in March 1840, Soult resigned office, and was succeeded by M. Thiers, in his day a politician of considerable weight if of doubtful honesty, but best known now as the writer of a voluminous, utterly untrustworthy and extremely chauvinistic history of the Revolutionary and Napoleonic wars. At the same time M. Guizot was sent to London as ambassador.

The policy of Thiers was still more antagonistic to Palmerston's than Soult's had been. Palmerston resolved to act independently of France; and on July 15th a 'quadrilateral' treaty was signed in London by himself for England, and by the representatives of Austria, Prussia, and Russia, pledging these four Powers to enforce the restoration of the Turkish ships and the withdrawal of the Egyptian troops from Syria. This treaty was signed without the concurrence or even the knowledge of France, and the indignation of the French was very great.

The danger was much increased by the weakness of the English fleet in the Levant. The ships had been commissioned on a system of false economy then known as 'the peace establishment,' with very reduced complements of men, and naval officers were doubtful if they could hold their own with credit against the French fleet, which was in the highest state of efficiency.[1] It has been said that it was suggested to the French admiral and to the French Government to seize the English ships as a basis for further negotiation, and there is no doubt that, at one time, some alarm was felt lest an attack of this kind should be made and the English fleet be found wanting. If there was any such suggestion, it was not entertained. The French admiral must have understood that the English fleet, even if under-manned, could not be seized without the French fleet being rendered unserviceable in the immediate future; and the French ministry recognised that the English fleet, such as it was, was but a detachment of England's naval power; a branch which, like the branch of gold—*primo avulso non deficit alter*—would, if torn off, be succeeded by another and stronger; whilst, on the contrary, the French fleet, however excellent, represented the whole available force of the French navy.

The familiar knowledge of this by the French ministers was a powerful incentive to peace, and had probably much more to do with its maintenance than all the efforts of all the

---

[1] In Jurien de la Gravière's *La Marine d'autrefois* (chaps. vi. and vii.) there is an interesting account of the French fleet in the Levant at this time.

diplomatists of Europe; but what really settled the matter was the prompt and decisive action of Stopford. In the middle of September Beyrout was forcibly occupied; on the 26th Sidon was stormed by a party landed under the command of Commodore Napier; and on November 3rd Acre was reduced after a few hours' bombardment. This was decisive. The possession of these three important points on the coast commanded the military route, and compelled the immediate evacuation of Syria by the Egyptian troops. But of greater weight than even the military advantage was the fame of the success. In France, at least, it was remembered that in 1799 this same Acre had baffled the French army under the command of Bonaparte himself; and it was still known that in 1831, when defended only by disorganised Turks, it had held out against the forces of Mehemet Ali for six months. That it should now fall to the English in three hours seemed to tell of a power whose existence they had not realised. The prestige of the victory put a very practical end to the war and the threat of war, with all the less strain as in the middle of October Louis Philippe, becoming thoroughly alarmed by the threatening appearance of the political horizon, dismissed Thiers and his colleagues, and recalled Soult to form a government in which Guizot was Ministre des Affaires étrangères.

Reeve, who had been introduced by Greville to Barnes, the editor of the 'Times,' on May 15th, began to write for that paper in the end of July. The treaty of July 15th became known on the 25th, and on the 31st he contributed an article on it. 'The views I supported,' he says in the Journal, 'were those of Lord Holland and Lord Clarendon, who thought that a success in Syria would be too dearly purchased by a quarrel with France.' Of a longer article, which appeared in the 'Times' of August 3rd, some sentences may properly be quoted as illustrating the position which, from the beginning, Reeve took up :—

'The details of the Eastern question are in themselves so contemptible, the rival Powers so similar in their badness, that this apple of discord is not even an apple of gold. The loss of one drop of Christian blood shed in war in the heart of Europe is followed by more calamities, and is more grievous to humanity than the massacre of a horde of Mussulman insurgents. The evils of war are exactly proportioned to the civilisation of the countries engaged in it. The nations which have made most progress in the arts of peace are most afflicted by the interruption of them; and if France and England stoop to share the violence they ought to moderate, the advantages even of victory will be shared or engrossed by Powers quite unable as yet to compete with either of them in benefiting mankind, though ready to surpass them in bloodshed; the burden and the ruin will rest upon themselves. But although it cannot be concealed that the utmost foresight cannot insure the avoidance of so fatal a rupture, is it too much to ask, and to hope, that a social and Christian spirit may yet command the elements of political strife? If we are separated from France on this question, that is no reason for severing the great and numerous interests by which we are now, and for the future, as much united to that nation as we were yesterday. If, on the other hand, we find ourselves strangely combined with Russia in this particular treaty, that is no reason for laying aside our long vigilance of her designs and our protestations against the spirit manifested by so many of her previous and her present actions. On the contrary, that vigilance requires to be redoubled, especially if we have to deal with her, either as friend or foe, single-handed. We have ere this contracted alliances with Russia, from which she has extracted all the benefit she sought; we have ere this fought battles, of which she has reaped the spoil. England is not more inclined now than she has ever been before to tolerate Russian dominion in Constantinople; and great as is the responsibility of those who have ventured on so bold a course for the attainment of its immediate object, that responsibility binds them under the heaviest and most solemn obligations to provide against the possibility of being deceived by its ultimate results.'

On August 30th Reeve started for France, and in company with his mother went by sea from Havre to Bordeaux. Thence through the south of France to Marseilles, where Mrs. Reeve remained, on a visit to her brother Philip, who, in 1836, had established some engineering works, which subsequently developed into the Société des Forges et Chantiers de la Méditerranée. Reeve himself went on to Toulon, where he wished to visit the dockyard, but was refused with scant courtesy, as—under the circumstances—was, perhaps, not to be wondered at. By October 2nd he was in Paris, and noted in the Journal—

The agitation in France was extreme. I dined at Auteuil, where Thiers was living, on October 6th. He made a grand appeal to me at dinner, and on the 10th gave me his Note, which I [afterwards] translated for the ' Times.' All this visit to Paris was very animated. Victor Cousin was Minister of Public Instruction. Dined with Lord Granville *père* on October 15th—Sebastiani, Duc de Broglie, &c. Back to London October 21st.

The story of this visit to Paris, important as it was to his future career, must be read in his correspondence. It is not directly stated, but we are permitted to infer that he had been asked, perhaps indirectly, by Lord Lansdowne, to write to him on the state of France, and some of his letters have thus an exceptional value.

To Mrs. Reeve at Marseilles

Toulon, September 23rd.—I found the Sous-Préfet very civil, but he has nothing of interest under his dominion. He took me to the Préfet Maritime, when the old Admiral very coldly informed me that he could not allow me to see the arsenal, bagne, or anything else, under existing circumstances; at which I am not a little disgusted. I have, therefore, ordered a carriage to take me to dine and sleep at Hyères, which I have always wished to see; and I shall return here to-morrow to sail round the port with the English Vice-Consul, who is very civil.

Paris, October 3rd.—Affairs are very gloomy. I suppose you know that Beyrout has been taken by the allies, after a bombardment of nine days.[1] Still, there will be no immediate declaration of war. The council sat late yesterday, but it seems the discussion was as to the convocation of the Chambers. Lord Palmerston is more buoyant than ever, and no concessions whatever will come from our side; hence the chances of peace are neither more nor less than the chances of a complete humiliation of France, equal, in my opinion, to zero. I write this because I feel that my uncle and all of you must be very anxious. If one was to live an hundred years one could never be witness to a more frightfully critical position—unhappily with very little hope of parrying the stroke.

To the Marquis of Lansdowne

Paris, October 5th.

My Lord,—I hope you will pardon me for troubling you with an account of what I see passing around me in Paris. My private relations give me, perhaps, a more complete insight into the views of the present French Administration than an official agent could obtain, and the importance of

---

[1] This, of course, was public gossip. Beyrout was certainly taken, but the details are imaginary.

the crisis, joined to my strong desire to furnish your lordship with correct information, must furnish me with an
excuse, if it be needed.

I arrived in Paris late on Friday night, just in time to
witness the effect of the news from Beyrout, the struggle
which is taking place in the Government here, and probably
its settlement. In my journey through the whole of the
South of France I have been very much struck by the
moderate and pacific views of all parties and classes, except
in towns like Marseilles and Toulon, which have direct
sympathies with Egypt, or direct interest in war. But
though no one is eager for war, and a war would not be
commenced with the enthusiasm which broke out in 1793,
and which was restrained in 1830, yet it would be supported
by public opinion, especially if that public opinion is to be
represented by the convocation of the Chambers in Paris,
where it would predominate over the influence of local or
individual interests. The convocation of the Chambers is,
therefore, the first grand point which M. Thiers is now
making a *sine qua non*. He consented to suspend it for
three days upon a strong representation from the British
Embassy, which gave him hopes that more pacific proposals
would be tendered to him in the interval. We are as yet
ignorant of the decision which, it is presumed, the Cabinet
adopted on Friday ; but the Government here have made up
their minds as to the course they intend to propose if that
decision is unfavourable, or if no fresh proposals are
tendered. It is feared that the last news of the complete
success at Beyrout, which has passed through Paris to-day,
may induce the Allies to be less inclined to an accommoda-
tion.

In the meantime the situation of the French Cabinet
with regard to the King has become extremely difficult.
Certain conditions and measures have been proposed, to
which Louis Philippe is most unwilling to accede. The
Government resign if they are not accepted. During the
greater part of yesterday this question was evenly balanced.
It is not yet decided. I know that the first of these proposals
is the convocation of the Chambers, to which, I apprehend,
no very great resistance is offered. Of the others I am

at present ignorant, but I have reason to suspect they go to the length of concentrating the French fleet at Alexandria, and even of landing 20,000 men in Egypt. This, however, I have learned from a doubtful source. On the other hand, the King is embarrassed. The Duke of Orleans is very decidedly with Thiers. The resignation of the Ministry would be looked upon in France as a complete triumph granted to Lord Palmerston. The army is said to be so excited and so impatient that the chance of a military revolt is an event of sufficient probability to weigh heavily in the calculation. The Chambers themselves would (I think) support Thiers, though some men of judgement and experience hold an opposite opinion. The ex-Administration would become enormously powerful and formidable in opposition; an hundred times more powerful and formidable than Thiers was when he went out on the Spanish question in 1836. Lastly, it is difficult to see who would consent to take office on such terms at such a time. No civilian will attempt it. Soult may possibly attempt it and succeed. The King will probably struggle for a time; but I doubt whether the Cabinet will give in, even on that head.

I do not believe that hostilities are inevitable if M. Thiers remains in power, or that they are certain to be avoided if he retires. So strong is the desire of the French Government to remain at peace with England, that I cannot conceive that the British operations in Syria will be met by decided measures of resistance. But the moment Russia assumes a more active part, either by her army or her fleet, M. Thiers will not, and Louis Philippe cannot, avoid making a positive demonstration; for the measures of England have no character of direct aggression on France, and England disclaims all such intentions; but the hostile feeling and purposes of Russia to France are avowed and undoubted. It is felt that the British Government have it now in their power to make a concession to which the recent success at Beyrout would give an air of magnanimity and forbearance; but if the operations are to be extended from Syria to Egypt itself, no Government in France can remain neutral.

Half-past Two.—Since the above lines were written two

accounts have reached me from England. By the one I am informed that you have decided to make immediate proposals of an amicable nature to M. Guizot; by the other (subsequently received) these hopes are not confirmed. I have, however, thought it best to act on the pacific supposition, and by that means I have elicited from my friends in the Cabinet (not including M. Thiers) the strongest and most vehement assurances of their desire for peace. I cannot convey to you, my lord, by my own language, any idea of the vehemence with which M. Cousin, speaking in his own name and in that of M. de Broglie, protested that he regarded the rupture of this alliance with the horror it must inspire in every enlightened statesman. But I am well assured that with a slight demonstration of amicable concession on the part of England, *no concessions* will be refused by France to restore a firm alliance against Russia. The King is for peace ; a portion of the Cabinet is for peace ; and though that portion does not include Thiers, it can control him. At the same time, that Cabinet—the whole Cabinet—man by man, have decided for war, as the cruel but inevitable necessity of the government of France, unless some overtures are made. The Conseil meets to-day at Auteuil (Thiers's house) at four, and it will sit late. We have spent the morning in trying to invigorate and encourage the pacific party. If the proposals arrive, or if there is any reasonable hope of their arriving, peace may yet be saved. If not, the convocation of the Chambers will probably be decided upon, and I know not what hope then remains ; for the concessions (even in Egypt) which France can make now, she will not be able to entertain when the Chambers are collected.

M. de Broglie's influence with the Cabinet is very great ; and as he belongs neither to the Government nor the Opposition, it might be most usefully employed in resuming the negotiations. The extreme *gauche* part of the Cabinet here are not very tractable, nor is the extreme anti-Egyptian party in Downing Street very easy of control; but I most fervently and humbly hope that between these two hostile elements, some voices of moderation, some counsels of concession, may yet be heard—and not only heard but brought into action ; and I trust I do not err in turning all my hopes upon your lordship's influence at such a juncture ; for in the contrary event, even those ministers who most abominate the accursed evils of war between our two countries have declared to me, upon their honour, before God, that before they witness the conflagration of the port of Alexandria, they must set their hands to a declaration of war, not for the sake of the Pasha, but for the sake of the balance of power in Europe.

I entreat your lordship, if possible, to do me the honour to answer this letter by a line to suggest to me the language which it may be most suitable for me to use here.

I remain always your most obedient and attached servant,

H. Reeve.

To this letter Lord Lansdowne replied on the 8th in a friendly note, to the effect that any fresh negotiation must be on a new base, which it was for the French to propose. The excitement about Beyrout seemed to him fictitious or factitious ; for what had been done there was strictly in accordance with the treaty, and the action of England rested on this : that 'We considered it unworthy of a Great Power to make promises to the Porte and hold out expectations, and then leave her at the mercy of events.' At present he did not see anything out of which France could make a *casus belli*, assuming that the French ministers and the French people were not eager to fight all Europe without any assignable provocation ; and that, as a plain fact, France had never declared that 'she sided with Mehemet Ali.'

Meanwhile, and before this was written, Reeve had sent off a second letter to Lord Lansdowne, sketching the situation as seen by him.

October 6th.—I spent the morning of yesterday with the Garde des Sceaux and the Minister of Public Instruction, the evening at Auteuil with the President of the Council. In the interval the Cabinet sat at Auteuil, not presided by the King. But since the Cabinet of the preceding day, the King had surrendered to the terms proposed by the Ministry, in the event of no proposals or inadequate proposals arriving from England. The Chambers will be convoked for November 1st ; but the ulterior measures may be regarded in abeyance as long as these hopes of adjustment can be maintained, and I was happy to find that Mr. Bulwer's [1] instructions and M. Guizot's despatches tallied precisely with my own information. Lord Palmerston's article in the ' Chronicle' was calculated to do a great deal of harm, and I believe it materially accelerated the hostile resolutions of the French Cabinet ; but I also believe that means have now been found to neutralise its effect here.

It will perhaps be satisfactory to your lordship to know exactly what passed between M. Thiers and myself, as he honoured me with a very long conversation. I shall therefore enter into some details. He began by a full statement of the course of negotiation on the Eastern question from March 1st to July 17th. He repeated all that was published in the ' Revue des deux Mondes ' six weeks ago ; but he most positively disclaimed any intention of negotiating a direct arrangement between the Pasha and the Sultan by the sole intervention of France ; he quoted a despatch of April 17th, in which he had plainly told the Pasha that if he did not accede to the terms which it was then supposed would be offered, the Four Powers would act without France and less favourable conditions would be imposed upon him. He denied having any previous knowledge of Sami Bey's mission, which emanated from the Pasha alone. He declared that he had repeatedly instructed M. de Pontois at Constantinople and M. Cochelet at Alexandria scrupulously to refrain from all attempts at direct or isolated negotiation, which might awaken the jealousy of England ; and he repeated—exactly what he said to me in April 1839—that he had always thought, and does still think, that the maintenance of the English alliance is a matter of immeasurably more importance than an allotment of land about the Lake of Tiberias. The conversation then turned on the intentions of the authors of the treaty. He expressed his convictions that Russia and Russia's policy were mainly bent on disturbing the relations between our two countries. He professed his readiness to meet half-way any clear, straightforward declaration of English

---

[1] Afterwards Sir Henry Bulwer and Lord Dalling. At this time Secretary of the Embassy at Paris and *Chargé d'Affaires*, in the temporary absence of Lord Granville.

views : he declared that he looked upon those views without jealousy and without apprehension. I am convinced from his language, and that of his colleagues, that provided Russia can be made to bear the burden which rightly belongs to her, provided the French nation can obtain from England a due admission of the value of the alliance, the Government will be ready enough to assume the defensive, and to direct its protestations in that direction, and in that alone, in which it believes hostile intentions to exist. The state of public feeling is hourly becoming more critical. Before many days elapse, the French Government will be forced to make a demonstration somewhere, either by the dismissal of the ambassadors and a diplomatic rupture, or by ordering the fleet to leave its quarters at Navarino ; but it is yet time to direct the brunt of this demonstration from England against Russia ; and if the Russian fleet approaches the west of Europe, that occurrence will perhaps be seized upon as the most favourable opportunity for decided resistance, without provoking a direct collision with England.

I may add what M. Thiers said to me as to his relations with the King. On the preceding day he said to the King in Council, 'If, Sire, you think that by my resignation peace can more easily be maintained, I shall most willingly resign ; and I give you my word of honour that I will not head a violent opposition to the course my successors may advise your Majesty to pursue. I must state my own opinion, but I will do it moderately ; and I readily admit that there is much to be said in favour of a more submissive policy, though I and my friends are not in a position to adopt it.' The King replied with great kindness, but he refused the offer, saying, ' We must not part now ; you must not abandon me, nor I you.' I should add that the King is still extremely irritated against Lord Palmerston, though there is no appearance that this irritation extends to the other members of the Administration. He says that all the mischief comes from ' that cursed expression calling the Mediterranean a French lake ; ' and that if he had never heard those words ' French lake,' we should never have heard of the treaty of July 15th.

And now, my lord, allow me to add one word as to my

own position. I am conscious that it is an anomalous and difficult one. I am not sure that your lordship, to whose judgement in these matters I shall always most respectfully and gratefully defer, will not think it a dangerous one. I cannot but feel, however, on the other hand, that I am honoured with the confidence of the most influential members of the French Cabinet ; that I am animated by no object on earth but the maintenance of peace, and that, as I am too insignificant a person to speak to them in anything but the language of private friendship, so my observations have a chance of doing some good here without compromising anyone in England. Nevertheless I await with some anxiety the receipt of a few lines from your lordship, which will decide whether it is better for me to remain here a few days longer, or to return immediately.

I dine with M. Thiers to-day.

Lord Lansdowne replied to this on the 9th, the day following his former letter, saying that 'he had communicated the substance of it where it would be useful ;' a remark which, meant as an encouragement to Reeve, shows also the value already placed on his services. For the rest, Lord Lansdowne said he had nothing to add to what he had written on the previous day ; except that, 'if he found it convenient to stay a little longer in Paris, he could do nothing but good by speaking strongly' of the wish in England to act in unison with France.

At the same time that Reeve was writing these letters to Lord Lansdowne, he was writing also to his mother. The subject was uppermost in his mind, so of course he spoke of it, with greater freedom, with greater self-assertion, as was only natural to a young man who felt himself, by a singular train of circumstances, suddenly placed in a position to sway the equilibrium of Europe.

To Mrs. Reeve, at Marseilles

Paris, October 6th. I thank God I did not take a day more holiday. I arrived in time, but only just in time, to play the last cards of this deal. When I wrote last they were on the brink of the most vehement resolutions. They have been checked for a few days. The news from Beyrout is received with tolerable calmness, and we are at present in rather a more hopeful condition, because we are expecting amiable overtures from England. They have received me with great kindness and friendship, and I have had long confidential conversations with Vivien, Cousin, and Thiers. The scene of Cousin shaving in his ministerial bedroom of purple and gold, vociferating as usual, and talking till he grew pale with excitement, I shall never forget. I was with him three hours, before the Cabinet met. He is pacific to the last degree.

I dined yesterday with Zamoyski and met Urquhart, a mad political dervish, who, I am sorry to say, has infected better minds than his own. But I listened to his fatidical harangues and was amused. In the evening I went to Auteuil, where Thiers received me with great *empressement*, and talked at great length. I met Cousin again there, Mignet, Léon de Malleville, &c. To-day I am to dine there. Cousin says, 'Mon cher Henri, vivez, vivez un peu avec Thiers et moi.' In fact, I may be said to have my board and lodging in the Cabinet. In the meantime, I have got Sir W. Follett here to act upon the Tory party at home ; and I write a long letter to Lord Lansdowne every morning.

Paris, October 8th.—I am over head and ears in the great business of this crisis. Here I meet with nothing but sense, moderation, and goodwill ; from England I receive nothing but fresh instances of desperate folly and violence. M. Thiers is everything I could wish, and I am in the most constant communication with him, as well as Cousin and Vivien. We shall fail, but not without a vigorous and honest struggle. Even the news from Beyrout has been received here with tolerable calmness. I arrived, fortunately, at the same instant, and I was able to check the *contre-coup* of that blow ; but the next will be fatal. If I had half the influence over the Cabinet at home which I have here, peace would be preserved ; but in Downing Street nobody has any influence but the devil. Mr. Greville has been excellent, and our party in the Cabinet has made a stout fight, but has utterly failed. Palmerston triumphs. I have rejoined Sir W. Follett here, and have flung myself into his arms, for nothing can exceed his good sense and good feeling. At such a time I have felt the full value of his support, and it has not failed me, for we are perfectly agreed on all the questions at stake.

Yet I have no hope of peace. The Ministry here has been all but out·; but the King has never decidedly given way, and I believe feels that the man who sits upon the throne of France has no more waverings to make. To-day it has been proposed that I should return instantly to England. This I shall discuss to-night with Thiers; but I am for staying, because Mr. Greville can do all I could do at home and more. . . .

The Ministre de la Marine has sent me a formal apology for the incivility of the Préfet Maritime at Toulon.

Paris, October 14th.—Without being over-sanguine, we have reason to believe that all the efforts of the peacemakers will be crowned with success. I don't know whether the Sermon on the Mount was intended to promise a beatitude to diplomatists, but in this cause I am sure that peacemakers are not unblest. . . .

I dined again at Auteuil last night. Thiers is everything that is obliging. I maintained most vigorously, on the strength of Stopford's despatches, that Beyrout (i.e. the town) has not been bombarded at all; and, in fact, the French Government have no real reason to suppose that all the violent accounts which reached Marseilles are not humbug. Stopford fired on the fort; Napier landed his men, and that is all. I met Lord Granville last night, and shall dine with them to-morrow. He was very civil, and this invitation relieves me from the unpleasant feeling of having been playing the busybody here without the knowledge of my own ambassador.

Paris, October 18th.—Who should arrive yesterday in this very hotel but Handley! I always predicted he would start as I got home; but, as it now turns out, we are spending three days together very pleasantly. He, Simpson, and I had not met for eight years. You will see him in about a week. I dined on Thursday at the Embassy. M. de Broglie and M. Sebastiani were there. Just before dinner the King had been shot at. The atrocity of this attempt at such a crisis is beyond all conception. Dear good Lady Granville, who is the most affectionate and motherly of women, was greatly affected, and especially for the Queen. What a position ! the Duchess of Orleans on the point of being confined after a very bad and dangerous pregnancy ; the Count de Paris in wretched health ; the Duchess de Nemours near her first confinement ; the King nearly murdered ; the throne tottering ; peace in danger. The King said, the moment the ministers arrived at St. Cloud, ' Messieurs, c'est la paix qu'on a voulu tuer en moi ! ' Alas ! it is so. I find on almost every side that the internal situation of the country excites even more dread than the chance of war. Between war and an anarchical revolution, the former is at least preferable. The winter will be troubled ; blood will be shed in the streets ; and we may have war under aggravating circumstances in the spring. At that point my sympathy with France ceases ; the day the revolution makes another stride I, for one, am ready to recommence the war policy of Pitt ; but our Whigs make war not on the French democracy, but on the power which alone controls it.

C. O., October 27th.—I hope you will have received a note from me, which I despatched to Paris per Embassy, and which will have assured you that I am neither blown up on a railroad nor sunk in the 'Phénix.' That fine vessel, with its incomparable cook, came into collision with the 'Britannia' off Dungeness, and went to the bottom. All on board were saved. You will see the details in the papers. M. Guizot had actually taken his places on board her, and was going to Havre in order to take his family with him to Paris, when he received [1] the news of Thiers's resignation, and the King's entreaties to go by the shortest road to Paris. But for this he must have been on board, and might have been drowned. When I got to London he was at Windsor, but he sent for me to breakfast on Saturday morning [October 24th], and I stayed full two hours. He communicated to me his whole views of the great external and internal questions—the greatest mark of confidence, as he said, which he could give me. And, indeed, I felt it so. So ended that short and eventful embassy ! He is gone, with the calm and devoted

---

[1] On October 24th the King had written, in his own hand : ' Je compte sur vous, mon cher ministre, pour m'aider dans ma lutte tenace contre l'anarchie.' —*Greville Memoirs*, II. i. 343.

courage which the posture of affairs demands, to take the King's government, or, at least, to assist him in forming it. It is hardly probable that he will return hither in any case. He will have a substitute; certainly no successor; and to me individually the loss is extreme.

Fancy what it is in one week to have M. Guizot and Lord Holland [1] taken away from us—the two greatest losses London society could possibly have sustained.   At no moment of Lord H.'s life was his political importance what it has become just now; but the burden of his championship was too heavy, and it killed him.   He died of that accursed treaty, and especially of the last vehement effort of the peace party, which had been attended with a hot altercation between Palmerston and himself.   In his last moments he began to wander, and talked of nothing but France and Syria; but the consciousness of his false position, in not having insisted on resigning before the mischief was perpetrated, hung about him with a killing weight.

I have had one of my worst colds, proceeding from the throat to the nose, which is only now upon the turn.   I have not for years felt such a *dégoût momentané* for England as I do at this moment.   The climate, the architecture, and the cookery are more than I can endure; add to which, I do not find *une âme de connaissance*, so that the contrast from Paris is rather more than is pleasant.

C. O., November 5th.—Lord Lansdowne is admirably disposed; I was with him a long time yesterday, and we may rely on him, Lord John, Lord Clarendon, Baring, and Labouchere; add to which, Prussia and Austria are very favourable to the arrangement—which is not yet proposed. But the unaccountable thing is that such mighty efforts should be needed to achieve such obvious and desirable objects; the right side seems to require a vast deal more shouldering and bolstering than the wrong.   However, I hope, in spite of Mr. Greville's gout, which is frightfully bad, that some energy will be infused into the mean-wells. Was there ever such an instance of meaning-well as what has occurred for the last three months?

---

[1] Died October 22nd.   Just before he died he said: 'These Syrian affairs will be too much for me.   Mehemet Ali will kill me.'—*Greville Memoirs*, II. i. 341.

A last letter to Lord Lansdowne at this time seems to have been intended rather as a record of opinions already offered *vivâ voce* a couple of days before, than as throwing new light on the situation.

November 6th.—As you have done me the honour to listen to some of the impressions I have received in various communications with some of the more able and prominent actors in public affairs in France, I venture to trouble you once more with a few rough notes which the importance of this juncture drives me to commit to paper.

The prospects of M. Guizot's Administration do not improve. I have written to Tocqueville to learn what side he is going to take, but the papers of to-day assert that he and his friends—that is, the most moderate and enlightened men of the *Gauche*, and indeed, in the country—have joined the Opposition. If this be so, I cannot conceive that the Government can long be carried on. If M. Guizot had been able to tell those members, that he brought with him or at least confidently expected, or had received an assurance of the goodwill of England and the natural termination of the treaty by its fulfilment, without doubt they would have listened to him. But could he give them any such assurance? Has the support afforded him been prompt? Has it been considerable?

The language of the French is this : ' We have reason to believe that Lord Palmerston's policy contemplates a rupture with France as an event which is neither to be dreaded nor avoided by England, if indeed it is not positively contemplated and intended. The British Cabinet, by adopting his measures, has of course adopted his views. We therefore assume a defensive position.' Is it wonderful that Frenchmen should entertain these notions when it is a matter of doubt and discussion among Englishmen, among English politicians, among the English ministers, whether Lord Palmerston does or does not entertain these projects of direct hostility to France? Part of the time during which it was possible to make a strenuous effort to deny the imputation of such a policy, if it be false, or to defeat it if it be true, is already gone. It may be doubted whether the hours, the minutes, that remain will suffice; for, as a great diplomatist said yesterday, ' Cette affaire doit se décider la montre à la main.'   The French Government is on the slope of revolution; the silence, the *morne* attitude of the populace yesterday at the opening of the Chambers, is the most frightful of all symptoms in France; it accompanied Louis XVI. from Versailles and from Varennes ; it followed Charles X. to Cherbourg.

Yet as far as the Eastern question is involved, the moment is most favourable to adjustment.   Syria is occupied, Ibrahim subdued, and the negotiation would of course re-open on a new basis.   The precautionary measures are consummated ; nothing but what is penal and vindictive remains to be performed.   No one can now assert that Ibrahim menaces Constantinople; and his moral defeat would seem to be more complete than his physical one.

If, then, the object of England in the Levant has been attained, is the object of the alliance attained?   I was glad to hear your lordship say it was ; but the acts of the Government must prove it to be so.   Suppose, for instance, that˙ you leave the viceroy in possession of Egypt, and give two Syrian pashaliks and perhaps Candia to various members of his family for their lives.   I merely put the case hypothetically.   Austria and Prussia would agree after the English Cabinet had acceded.   I believe I may venture to affirm (but quite confidentially to your lordship), that Russia will not resist, or at least not pertinaciously, and that M. de Brunnow requires no fresh instructions from St. Petersburg for that purpose.   The reason will at once strike your lordship.   If Russia were to resist as decidedly and on the same grounds as on the former occasion, she would show the cloven foot too openly.   She would openly and directly place obstacles in the way of an arrangement, which would disclose the darker side of her policy to her allies and perhaps hasten the very arrangement she deprecates.   She will probably yield in London, because by this time she may be provided with other means of defeating the combination for the readmission of France.   Those means are perhaps at Constantinople ; for there, under existing circumstances, she is certain of finding no British agent desirous of reinstating the pasha or of effecting a reconciliation with France.

If then the policy of peace is to prevail, if these measures are to be taken, they must not only be taken, but secured in their execution, in London and in Constantinople. It is not possible that Lord Ponsonby should represent the same policy as Lord Granville, nor indeed the policy of the Cabinet to which your lordship, Lord John Russell, Lord Clarendon, Mr. Baring, and others belong. As well make Lord Westmeath Lord-Lieutenant of Ireland while Lord Morpeth is Irish Secretary. And indeed, whatever proposals are made to the French Government from London, they will be received with infinite distrust if their execution is liable to be frustrated by an ambassador who openly declared to Admiral Roussin, more than a twelvemonth ago, that if instructions came to him to act in harmony with France, he should disobey them. With such a diplomatic representative the fullest measures must fall short of conciliation; without him the least may suffice. England may be tied up to her allies on questions of Eastern policy, but the recall of a minister is her own affair; the recall of a minister who has exceeded his instructions (at least his acknowledged ones, for I am not unacquainted with another channel of communication) twice at least in the last six weeks.

I trust, my lord, I have not allowed my pen to outrun my discretion; but I have not the courage to look with silent composure on the horrid aspect of the world if these things are not done; done, for the most part, before you rest to-morrow night; and if it come to the worst, I believe that those who are most warmly attached to the members of the present Government, and most jealous of their fame, would rather see the Cabinet broken up by a resolute defence of peace than exposed to future destruction by having sacrificed it.

To Mrs. Reeve

November 7th.—To-day the Cabinet meets, and we think ourselves certain either of carrying our conciliatory measures or of breaking up the Government. But if the plan of operations is steadily adhered to, I am pretty confident of success. However, our hopes are overcast by the storms which are lowering in France. I have very little confidence in the stability of M. Guizot's Government, especially if men of Tocqueville's opinion vote against him. It is not yet determined when our Parliament is to meet, but the Cabinet are at this instant sitting on the question ; this being—*nota bene*—the first time they have sat at all since I have been home !

November 13*th*.—The accounts from Paris are very encouraging. The Ministry may well gain strength and confidence in the presence of so disjointed an Opposition, and I think it is a great mistake for Tocqueville to have joined the latter. However, he is excessively frightened, and falls, I think, into the old Girondin error of joining a wrong party to set it right.

When Reeve wrote these letters he had not seen, and apparently had no knowledge of, Palmerston's despatch of November 2nd, which, in official language and bitter irony, had pointed out to the French Minister for Foreign Affairs that maintaining the independence of Egypt was not exactly the same thing as maintaining the independence of the Turkish Empire ; that Mehemet Ali was nothing but a subject of the Sultan, and that the Sultan's Government, which was better able to judge than any other, believed that the military power and hostile attitude of Mehemet Ali were 'incompatible with the internal peace and integrity of the Ottoman Empire. It rests,' it concluded, ' with the Sultan, as sovereign of the Turkish Empire, to decide which of his subjects shall be appointed by him to govern particular portions of his own dominions, and no foreign Power has a right to control the Sultan in the discretionary exercise of one of the inherent and essential attributes of independent sovereignty.' [1]

It was certainly not a conciliatory despatch, and drove the French Foreign Minister to despair. Turn it how he liked, he could get no comfort out of it. Lord Granville could give him none, but reported his views to Palmerston in very nearly the same words which Guizot wrote to Reeve.

Paris, 20 Novembre.

My dear Sir,—M. le baron Mounier, membre de la chambre des Pairs, l'un de mes amis particuliers et

---

[1] The whole despatch, which is well worth referring to, for the *manner*, more even than for the *matter*, will be found in the *Annual Register*, 1840, pp. 531-3.

l'un des hommes les plus distingués de notre pays, va passer quelques semaines en Angleterre. Il verra vos Ministres, vos hommes considérables. Il causera avec eux. Je désire beaucoup qu'il vous voie aussi et qu'il cause avec vous. Je vous le présente d'ici, et je vous demande pour lui vos bons avis. Personne ne peut l'éclairer mieux que vous ; et il vous comprendra parfaitement, et j'espère que son séjour à Londres ne sera pas inutile pour que la France et ses dispositions y soient comprises————un peu comprises.

The note of November 2nd has seriously injured my position and increased the difficulties which surround me. I do not know if there is any intention of repairing the evil ; if whilst repeating that the Porte is strongly advised to leave Egypt to the Pasha, it will be said or left to me to say that this is done out of consideration for France. Such a declaration would have a good effect. Indirectly and unofficially many fine words reach me, but nothing of any practical use ; no words of a public character, which I can turn to account. I am engaged in a great struggle for the cause of peace, of civilisation, of a straightforward and moderate policy. I am striving for the general good. Nothing shall discourage me. I do not know if I shall succeed, but if I do, I shall owe no gratitude to anyone ; at least I have the right to say so, at present. . .

Adieu.   Mille amitiés vraies.   GUIZOT.

To Granville's letter conveying Guizot's wish, Palmerston replied decidedly that he would not authorise him to make any such declaration : first, because it was not true; and secondly, because it was impossible to admit that France was, in any sense, the protector of Mehemet Ali—a rebellious subject of the Sultan.[1]   But meantime the news of the taking of Acre had arrived,[2] and the position was changed. Thiers might shriek hysterically for War ! but Guizot, as the responsible minister, recognised the necessity of accepting the *fait accompli.*

A little adventure of family interest, as related at this time by Reeve to his mother, lightens the strain of politics :—

---

[1] *Life of Lord Palmerston*, vol. ii. pp. 363-4.
[2] It reached Paris on the 23rd, and London on the 24th.

C. O., November 21st.—I intended to have written you an account of a most marvellous adventure which has occupied and diverted us for a couple of days. My uncle Edward Reeve, as Mrs. Merry's executor, had in his possession two cabinet-boxes and the cabinet key. The key being broken, he sent the box to a smith to have another made. The smith denounced him at the Foreign Office ; and when he went for his box he was arrested by a police inspector, and conveyed to Downing Street. The whole proceeding was totally illegal and unjustifiable ; and though they of course dismissed him as soon as it was known who he was, yet I have taken up the cudgels with some vigour in his behalf. The Foreign Office was thrown into consternation by the onslaught I made there. Colonel Rowan of the police is very civil, and he made every kind of apology, and it will be some time before these clumsy tyrants dare to offer another indignity to one of my family. Of course the story makes a good deal of sensation, for to drag an Englishman from his dinner, without a warrant, to a Secretary of State's office, is the most monstrous action in the eyes of this people that a minister can commit : and neither the police nor Lord Palmerston will soon hear the end of it.

To Mr. C. C. Greville

C. O., November 24th.—Certainly Lord Palmerston's position *se bonifie à vue d'œil*, and our friends, the French, are in the slough of despond, eating dirt, as the Orientals have it, in large quantities. You will see by the ' Chronicle ' of to-day that a new proposal is to be made to the pasha by Stopford, which I suppose he will accept, as it is to have even the moral support of France, if the ' Chronicle ' speaks the truth. On the other hand, the evidence that Thiers was playing a double game is more and more apparent ; but I cannot satisfactorily explain to myself how Guizot, as ambassador, held a language and defended a policy so entirely at variance with the principles of his speech. The speech is no doubt sound and right, but it cannot efface the impression of the effervescence of the autumn, in which I still believe Guizot was sincere.

You will see by the ' Courrier' the frantic state of the

Opposition. They write me word that they give up the Eastern question as utterly lost ; and as the debate will degenerate into personalities, they intend to muster their forces to begin the labour of opposition over again on home questions. With that we have nothing to do ; but a Sisyphean labour they will find it, if every time they get into office is to be followed by such a downfall as this has been. The despatches anterior to the treaty which appear in the 'Post' of to-day are very interesting, and would materially have elucidated the question if they had been laid before Parliament in August ; as they might have been.

From all that has now been said and published, it results that I, for one, have been in great part mistaken ; mistaken as to the danger of Russian interference, mistaken as to the result of the operations in Syria, and mistaken as to the real policy and feeling of France. Was I altogether wrong ? Have Palmerston's opinions been justified by an extraordinary good fortune or by superior knowledge ? It is difficult to decide ; but I still flatter myself with the notion that something was done, even by these unreal apprehensions, to prevent them from assuming a more serious and menacing shape. And whilst I cannot but applaud that success in the East which is due to Lord Palmerston's rare firmness, I am as fully convinced as ever that such hazards should not be incurred for the sake of such results.

The fact, of course, was that Palmerston had the 'superior knowledge.' Reeve had considered the dispute as one to be decided—whether for peace or war—by the diplomats of England and France ; for, ignorant of the effective force on which Palmerston relied, he accepted the belief of his French friends that the Egyptian army was, for the time being, master of the situation. It was a first lesson for him in the 'influence of sea-power ; ' and, after conning it for three days, he expounded it—imperfectly indeed, but with right understanding—in a leading article in the 'Times' of the 28th. To his mother he had previously written :—

November 25th.—After all, we are brought to confess that Lord Palmerston's star is in the ascendant ; that there will be no war ; that the question of the East will soon be settled, and that all the other Powers of Europe will shrink into the second rank beside the daring and overruling policy of England. As I have been all along among the warmest opponents of a scheme which, if it had not succeeded, would have consigned its authors to infamy and the world to misery, I am bound to acknowledge the superior knowledge or the superior luck of the Foreign Office. If it were to do over again, I do not know that I should think otherwise than I have done ; but as it is now well nigh accomplished, I cannot but rejoice in whatever chances have turned out so well for England.

M. Guizot's speech is certainly a great deal more philosophical and resigned than his conversation was in London three or four months ago ; and though I am very much obliged to him for preaching peace, I confess Montalembert's oration is more to my own taste. Lord Palmerston has now bowled everybody out ; and the consequence is that the earth can scarcely contain him. He is as proud of success as other men would be of deserving it. Wolsey himself was not more formidable, except that the Tower and the block are out of date.

However, to complete the story which I began in my note of the other day. I have extorted from the lower grades of the Foreign Office a full written apology to my uncle Edward for their offences towards him, and they are thought to have eaten large quantities of dirt at my hands. In which I mightily rejoice.

Bowood, Christmas Day.—My Court went on to sit with such vivacity ever since my last letter, that I hardly saw anybody or anything but judges, wigs, and Indian records. Indeed Lord Brougham threatened to sit till Christmas Eve ; but his colleagues relented, and I came down here yesterday with Lord Duncannon and Miss Ponsonby, whom I met in the railroad carriage. The line is now open to Wootton-Basset, which brought us to within fifteen miles of Bowood, and the journey is performed in five hours instead of nine or ten. Charles Austin and Senior came down a little before us, and as I lay in bed this morning I smiled to think of the whimsical contrast between two Suffolk millers [1] meeting in

---

[1] The Austins, John, Charles, and Alfred, were sons of Jonathan Austin, of Creeting Mill, in Suffolk.

Ipswich market and the meeting of their immediate descendants in this abode, which is more commodious and *orné* every time one comes. . . . I left London without much regret, for the party at Bedford Row is large enough without the collaterals. . . . John and Richard are both in the height of happiness,[1] and I rejoice to see my uncle and aunt at the head of so numerous a group of descendants, still united by as much love and confidence as if they had none of them left the nursery. . . .

Great *aigreur* prevails between France and the other Powers on the subject of her disarming, which I fancy M. Guizot is neither willing nor able to do. If we escape a conflagration, it will be because no spark falls on the train ; but politics are like a blacksmith's shop, where sparks are always spurting from the anvil, and I can scarcely conceive that some evil will not occur ; for it is certain that the evil dispositions on both sides tend rather to increase than to decline. However, the meeting of Parliament may do some good, by convincing even the French that the reluctance to go to war is universal.

I have been reading a good deal lately about Spanish history, especially during the War of Succession. M. Villemain has given me a copy of Mignet's collection of documents on that period, which are most interesting. I have likewise bought the ' Lettres édifiantes,' which revive my ancient veneration for the Jesuits.

You will be glad to hear that, in spite of our journey and divers other expenses, my budget for this year is a satisfactory one, and that I find myself a couple of hundred pounds within my income. To be sure I cannot hope for so profitable a literary year again. That reminds me of Tocqueville, whose speech and conduct in the recent debate have inflicted a most severe blow on his reputation here, and I deeply regret that he should have blundered into such a course.

1841.—The early part of the year in the usual routine of London society. I wrote a great deal in the ' Times ' to endeavour to make up the quarrel with France. In March I went to Paris, and first made acquaintance with Princess

---

[1] Reeve's cousins, recently married.

Lieven.[1] Dined with Montalembert and Mounier, and saw a great deal of Tocqueville.

So says the Journal, and so far as action is concerned there is little more to be said. The details are filled in by extracts from Reeve's letters to his mother :—

C. O., January 9th.—Louis Philippe says, as I am given to understand, that matters are rapidly subsiding, and improving in France ; but what I am sure of is, that in both countries a mass of petty plots and personal ambitions are *en jeu*, which will probably defeat all the precautions of honesty and virtue. Here people are not ashamed to avow that the object of keeping France down is a very praiseworthy end, in their opinion ; and the most peace-loving and prudent ministers in the world go on to sit side by side with the firebrands. I am disgusted to the last degree with everything in politics, and I read De Vere and revert with all my soul to a quiet study in a sunny country.

C. O., February 8th.—My first edition of ' Washington ' totally disappeared the other evening in the convivial enjoyments of John Murray's annual sale, and we are going to bring out another, cheap, and on a large scale.

My party the other night was a good deal agitated by tidings of the Duke of Wellington's illness. He had another touch of epilepsy in the House. The night before I heard him speak with unusual ease and distinctness on the Syrian operations. He had told Lord Aberdeen that he had not felt so well for months ; but whilst Brougham was speaking he observed a twist in the Duke's face, and a few minutes afterwards he was speechless. However, the attack is much slighter than the preceding one, and he has already nearly got over it.

You would laugh to see the agreeable terms I am on with my quondam foe, the Great B.[2] I receive a couple of

---

[1] Widow of the Russian Ambassador in England 1813-35. After her husband's death she settled in Paris, where, by the charm of her manner, her interest in politics, her ability and wit, she dominated society as she had previously done in London. She died in Paris in 1857. A *Portrait de Madame la Princesse de Lieven, à la manière du Duc de St.-Simon*, by Ralph Sneyd, was printed by the Philobiblon Society. See also *Greville Memoirs*, III. ii. 76-83 ; and *Edinburgh Review*, April 1890, p. 453.

[2] Lord Brougham.

little notes from him every morning, and we are as affectionate as turtle-doves, or, rather, as turtle-doves suspecting to see the hawk's beak every moment. The amnesty, however, has been general, and he has absolutely included in it all his oldest friends ; and though it is excellent sport to fight him, it is even better to be at peace.

C. O., March 4th.—By the time you receive this, Chorley and I shall be installed in a new dwelling. Mrs. Smith's altercations with our servants were so frequent, and her presumption that we should remain *à tout prix* was so unpleasant, that we summoned up our strength last Monday, and in the course of a few hours hired a house—No. 2, Wilton Street, Grosvenor Place—for a twelvemonth, with option to renew the occupation. Rent, 180 guineas ; which is what we pay now for part of a house. Furniture very good, handsome and abundant. Offices convenient. . . . I have brought down to my new room in the office a few shelvesful of the larger books ; and our removal will be completed next Monday, I visited your chattels at the Pantechnicon, and took the linen-chest, which, for the present, I shall venture to use—I trust with due care. We are very well pleased to be on the sunny side of the street, and we hope that the glories of the new temple will not be eclipsed by the recollection of our former success. When you come I shall be perfectly able to receive you, as we have five bedrooms, one of which I shall convert, for the present, into a summer study. Our landlady, Mrs. Morris, is very liberal, and will do, or allow to be done, whatever we please ; so that I may consider myself housed, I trust, for some time to come.

Paris, March 19th.—There is no chance of a war with France at present. The thing is now settled. You will have seen by the papers what a hornet's nest we brought down on Lord Ponsonby about the Hatti-Sheriff ; and I came here very sufficiently authorised to reprobate his conduct in the strongest terms. M. Guizot is very cordial. I dine or breakfast with him every day ; and I may confess to you how much I am gratified by his strong acknowledgements of my humble but unremitting exertions. I shall meet M. de Broglie and M. de Bresson at his table this evening.

Paris, March 26th.—Tout le monde m'a comblé de bontés; and nobody more than Lady Granville, who has made me call on her almost every day. Yesterday Baron Mounier gave me a great dinner of prodigious Dons. . . . Yet, upon the whole, my visit leaves a most melancholy impression. The dissolution of parties, the rancour of enmities, the absence of political convictions, or of courage to avow them, the excess of luxury, and the violence of a false excitement appear to me to augur nothing but the worst for the country. No man is respected. No government is permanent. And with all my liking for the people, there is an absence of truth and uprightness which convinces me that no serious or solid relation can ever unite the policy of England with that of France. The avenues to power are choked with adventurers struggling for the shattered prize. The accursed past throws its shame and terror over the future, and there is nothing great left in the nation but its splendid vices and defects. Tocqueville himself says that, as nothing remains to them but their national pride, that being shaken, they must fall below the average level of mankind.

C. O., April 27th.—I have seen a good deal of the Richardsons lately; for their children and the younger Elliots (Mintos) have been making a bazaar for the Poles at the Admiralty,[1] which produced 35*l.*, and Lady Fanny Elliot and Miss Richardson asked me to distribute the fund for them. I must say I like them more and more; and the only fault I find in them is that there are seven of them, and *multicity* is a heavy grievance in families; from which I esteem it the chief of all my blessings to have been exempted.

This is the first recorded mention of Miss Richardson, though, since first making their acquaintance, three years before, he had been gradually growing intimate with the family, and in the previous summer he would seem to have been thinking that here was the place to look for a wife. It is possible that he had mentioned this to his mother; but, in any case, we may be quite sure that she would understand the reference to 'seven of them.' To Reeve, on consideration, the objection did not seem fatal; and on May 15th,

---

[1] The Earl of Minto was at this time First Lord of the Admiralty.

acting on the suggestions of his foreign education, he wrote to Mr. Richardson, making his proposal in form.

Mr. Richardson was a most kind-hearted and estimable man, a parliamentary agent with a large practice, of literary tastes, a friend, a correspondent of Scott, of Campbell, of Jeffrey,[1] and devotedly attached to his eldest daughter—to such a degree that he considered her presence in the house as an absolute necessity. She, with a high standard of filial duty, put aside her own feelings, and acquiesced in a refusal of Reeve's offer. Reeve had, meantime, gone to Richmond, but returned on the Sunday evening to find Mr. Richardson's answer waiting for him. The disappointment was no doubt bitter, but he does not seem to have spoken of it. In his letters to his mother the subject is not alluded to, though we may perhaps think that we trace its effect in the moralising on the worthlessness of exalted position. But, in fact, the correspondence was broken for nearly a month by Mrs. Reeve's wanderings, and the first letter to her at Geneva is filled with no very important gossip.

C. O., Jnne 1st.—I don't complain of London this year for I have never been so much out of it. One week I persuaded the Taylors to spend at the Star and Garter, where I often joined them, to drive through my favourite park, or saunter to the meadows and the huge poplars by the brink of the river. For the last two days I have been riding over a part of Kent. Foot's Cray and Chiselhurst bewitch me, and I rejoice in cheese and cider at a country inn. As I am very well mounted this year, these excursions are easy to me, and they are the greatest pleasures I have. . . .

I have been concocting a performance for the Poles with Lord Dudley Stuart, and the Duke of Sutherland has very kindly lent us the great gallery of Stafford House for the occasion. Mlle. Rachel will declaim; Vieuxtemps and Liszt will play, and Adelaide Kemble will make her *début* in London. *C'est une grande affaire.* We have put the tickets at two guineas; and, as they are limited to four hundred, everybody is in fits to go. . . .

Nothing ever occurred in England so strange as the heat of the last ten days and nights. We sit abroad as late as you can do, eating ices in balconies; and in the middle of

---

[1] Cockburn's *Life of Lord Jeffrey*, i. 170.

the day one sees nobody walking about but a few lizards like myself. . . . I have now no doubt whatever that I shall join you at Geneva, and probably pass through Germany to get there—I hope before the end of September. . . .

Aldeburgh, July 19*th.*—I have been here three days, sitting on the sand in the sun, with nothing in life to perplex me and a free course for all my thoughts, rocked by the great waves of our coast. Yet repose on the sea-coast of Britain is not like repose on the margin of the Mediterranean ; the sea itself is more masculine, and there is a sort of energy in it which belongs to the island and the people. This life has a singular charm for me. In proportion as I have acquired and enjoyed most of the things in life which men court I have ceased to esteem or to desire them. I return, with more deliberate reflection, to earlier and more solitary tastes, which I encouraged years ago in the belief that I should have few opportunities of struggling for the world's pleasures and distinctions. That belief was erroneous. On few men have opportunities been more abundantly bestowed. I believe I have not neglected any ; and from most of them I have derived more power at twenty-seven than I ever dreamed of in visions at seventeen, and this without a serious conflict or one stunning reverse. But I remember in going up some lofty tower—as that church at Toulouse which we ascended last year—I remember that I have looked out from some belfry at mid-height, and, having ascertained that a few twisted streets and roofs of houses, with a vague horizon beyond, were all I should see from the very highest pinnacle, I have left the ball and cross to others, and sat waiting for them below in the grass of the churchyard. Thus it is with me in my present notion of life. The view which I can see by looking from any low belfry is not so different from that which men climb for to the highest spire, as entirely to mislead my judgement, nor certainly so encouraging as to embolden me to much more exertion.

With these thoughts in my mind, which have not been suggested by my present sea-side leisure, though it is only in such a retreat that one cares to put them into shape, I have taken little part in the ferment of the political world. Yet I have rejoiced in my heart to witness once again in

England the strenuous revival of those great principles of aristocratic government which constitute, as I believe, the solid framework of this commonwealth. The function of the Conservative party has ceased to be one of mere resistance and defence. Masters of the field of battle, they would ill deserve their victory if they could not spread their tents and raise their standard upon it. I confess that I had barely hoped ever to see a Tory government again strong enough to govern the country on its own fixed principles. But the thing is now almost assured; and the time invites me to put forward as much as I can those principles which I have thought of a good deal for many years, and which men engaged in active political life are apt to forget. In short, without going higher than my belfry I can ring the bells; and the best service I can render is, I think, by my influence over the press. The effect more than meets my hopes and wishes.

I came here to spend a few days with the Edward Reeves, instead of going to Dedham. They are remarkably well; my uncle in high spirits. Perhaps he is a good deal disappointed that his son should prove so blank a young gentleman—for he is a mere candidate for the humbler honours of squirearchy. But Edward James is a good fellow, and his father is not much surprised that he should follow in the track of most of his kinsfolk. The day I arrived here a Mr. and Mrs. Clarke came to call. Mr. C. said that, hearing my uncle was arrived, he could not forbear paying his respects to the brother of Dr. Reeve, to whose memory he bore the strongest regard. 'Why,' said my uncle, 'there sits his son, kicking his heels in the sun on the low garden wall near the beach.' With some difficulty the worthy man screwed up his courage to be introduced to me. I looked suddenly round, rather astonished at his address, for I knew nothing of what had passed. The poor man was quite overset. He shook my hand and burst into tears. They were obliged to support him, for a giddy fit came on; he was cupped that evening, and has kept his room ever since. You will recollect this Mr. Clarke, who was a lunatic patient of my father's; I believe you once stayed at his house near this place. He is, of course, a weak and excitable being ; and I was sorry this surprise came so suddenly upon him.

Brussels, August 25th.—Chorley and I sailed from London to Antwerp on Sunday [22nd]. Our vessel was good ; the weather propitious, and our party a good deal diversified, but vastly agreeable. . . I never started on a journey in more health and spirits ; and everything moves onwards as smoothly as usual. In ten days I shall be at Munich, and probably plunge into the Tyrol about September 5th, if the weather be not too cold. For here, already, there is a chill which reminds us we are on the confines of autumn. At any rate I hope to be at Geneva on the 20th.

Munich, September 9th.—I have now been installed for a few days in my old favourite city, where, in spite of the changes of nearly nine years, and the manifold and marvellous incidents which have arisen out of my first unpremeditated stay here, I find a great many old friends and a hearty welcome. . . It is very agreeable to me to find that Handley is everywhere very handsomely spoken of, and that she has her desert in her own country. *Du reste*, it is not very probable that we shall meet ; and if we do, *I* am not the crockery jar. I expect to start for Innsbruck on Saturday, and I shall travel onwards as straight as the Alps will allow me to do. I shall go through the Grisons if the weather is good, and pass from Dissentis to the St. Gothard, whence I must proceed northwards to get into a more beaten track and find more rapid conveyances than a mountain *char-à-banc*.

I am glad you will not have the bore of a double removal, and I shall find you at your *campagne*. I wish to leave Geneva not later than October 5th ; and if you have no objection, it will be a vast economy of time and money to go from Basle to Strasburg by the railroad, and from thence to descend the Rhine—stopping, if you please, to eat a few grapes at Johannisberg.

Adieu, my dear mother. In less than a fortnight I trust that I shall be with you, and I reckon the days very cheerfully from this my 28th birthday.

The itinerary of this tour is given in the Journal, which then passes on to speak with excessive brevity of the important step which Reeve was now taking :—

Left London with Chorley August 22nd, to Antwerp, Brussels, Trèves, the Moselle, Heidelberg, Augsburg, Munich, Tyrol, Ragaz, and so to Geneva, where my mother was. There I got Mr. Richardson's letter of recall.

The fact was that the strain on Miss Richardson's feelings had very seriously affected her health; and when the family, going down to Kirklands, Mr. Richardson's place in Roxburghshire, were joined there by their old friends, Sir Charles and Lady Bell, the physician's trained intelligence at once saw the necessity of immediate action. Lady Bell took on herself to represent this to Mr. Richardson, and the result was the letter which came to Reeve at Geneva; as to which he wrote in the Journal :—

Stayed at Geneva till October 4th. Had a bad journey home by Holland. Went down to Kirklands on October 22nd, and was engaged to Hope Richardson on the 26th. I returned to town on November 2nd.

Reeve's letters to his mother at this time have not been preserved : here is one to his friend Tocqueville :—

C. O., 8 *Novembre.*—Je vous aime trop, mon cher ami, pour ne pas vous dire moi-même une chose qui intéresse aussi profondément mon sort et ma vie que mon ménage.

Je crois avoir rencontré cet être que l'on cherche toujours et que l'on trouve si rarement, qui est le complément de l'existence individuelle ; et s'il y a foi dans les augures de ce monde, le bonheur qui m'attend est bien au-dessus de ce que je mérite.

Savez-vous le grand rôle dans les projets d'amoureux que jouent les élargissements des amitiés, et la satisfaction avec laquelle on espère un jour faire connaître ce qu'on aime à ce qu'on aime ? C'est un des plaisirs dont je jouis déjà, et le voyage de Normandie est un de ceux qui me sourient le plus en fait de course conjugale.

Plus d'une fois j'ai été frappé de certains petits détails de langage et de manière dans Mlle. Hope Richardson—c'est le nom de ma future—qui lui donnaient un air de famille avec vous-même ; et sans avoir tout à fait votre tête, elle a au moins votre cœur.

Faites, je vous prie, bien des amitiés de ma part à Madame de Tocqueville, et donnez-moi bientôt de vos nouvelles.

Tout à vous,   H. Reeve.

Je me marie à la fin de l'année, en Écosse.

It is unnecessary to refer more particularly to the many congratulatory letters which Reeve received at this time. We may, however, quote one from Lord Jeffrey to Mr. Richardson ; remarkable not only as showing Jeffrey's appreciation of the bride, as illustrating the relations between her and her father already spoken of, but also from the singular tone of the congratulations he offered.

November 1st.—MY DEAR RICHARDSON,—I really cannot wish you joy of your impending loss of such a daughter as my gentle, sensible, dutiful and cheerful Hopey, and I do not know that I can even wish her joy of such a separation. Yet I feel assured that there will be joy, lasting and growing for you all, and that in no long time we shall wonder that anybody thought of murmuring at so happy a dispensation. In the meantime, however, the only person I can candidly congratulate is Mr. Reeve, whom I think far better entitled to the name of ' the fortunate youth ' than any to whom it has ever been applied. I have scarcely the honour of his acquaintance (though if I live I hope to have), but I perfectly remember of meeting him at dinner at your house, and being struck with his vivacity and talent, and also of breaking in upon him in a morning call on Hopey and her sister, when certain vague suspicions and envyings did pass across my imagination. Do tell my dear Hopey how earnestly I wish and pray for her happiness, and that I hope she will not entirely cut me, now that she is to become the centre of a separate circle.   Ever affectionately yours.[1]

For the rest, the entry in the Journal tells the story with sufficient completeness and brevity :—

I went back to Kirklands on December 18th, and was married there on the 28th. Lord Minto lent us Minto for our honeymoon. We stayed there a few days, the Elliots coming to Kirklands.

Hope Richardson was born April 16th, 1815. She was the second, but eldest surviving, daughter of John Richardson

---

[1] Lord Cockburn's *Life of Lord Jeffrey*, vol. ii. p. 347.

of Kirklands, born May 9th, 1780, and of Elizabeth Hill, who died November 26th, 1836. Mr. Richardson's mother was Hope Gifford, a niece of Principal Robertson.[1] Hence the name of Hope came into the family.

The year opened on Hope and myself as we were travelling south. Our first visit was to the Taylors at Coed Ddu, and we reached London early in January. I had taken the house No. 16 Chester Square, and there we were installed on February 13th.

Society chiefly domestic; but on February 22nd we dined at the Sainte-Aulaires', then French ambassador, with the Clanricardes, Cannings, Stuart of Rothesays, Bunsens, Rehausens,[2] and Neukomm; and on March 3rd at Lansdowne House. We spent Easter at Waverley Abbey and Whitsuntide at Bracknell. Mendelssohn was in London and played the organ at Christ Church. We saw a good deal of Winterhalter. Went to stay at Edward Reeve's at Dedham in July. The summer of 1842 was one of singular beauty.

No family or private letters of this period have been preserved, with the exception of a few from his Aunt Sarah, Mrs. Austin, then living in Germany, and these are filled, for the most part, with her own literary projects or occupations. It was only occasionally that she wrote of personal matters, as in this, dated at Bonn on May 3rd, when, after a long list of articles or translations which she had in contemplation, she broke into raptures about her eldest grandchild, Janet Gordon, afterwards Mrs. Ross.

So much for business. At present it is all gone to the winds. The baby takes the place of all affairs and all pleasures, and is her little self the greatest. I never saw such a perfect little specimen of a Mensch. I hear, my dear Henry, you are in the way to possess one of these strange little creatures whose weakness and ignorance and imperfection is so infinitely engaging and interesting. May it bring blessings to you and your sweet wife, of whom I hear more and more praise, admiration, and love! It seems you have caught the phœnix. My best love to her.

---

[1] William Robertson, better known, perhaps, as the historian.
[2] Counsellor of the Swedish Embassy.

The sad conclusion of this story is told in the Journal. More words would be out of place.

On September 3rd we started for Scotland by sea, taking the carriage with us, and reached Kirklands on the 6th.   September 15th shot my first grouse at Todrig with John Elliot.   So passed the last six weeks.

On October 27th, at half-past 10 P.M., Hopie was born. All went right at first ; but bad symptoms came on about November 6th, and at half-past 11 A.M. on November 27th H. expired.   On December 3rd we laid her in Ancrum churchyard.   The pall-bearers were John Richardson, James Hill, Lord Melgund, Lord Polwarth, John Elliot, Gilbert Elliot, and Sir William Scott.   On December 7th I left Kirklands with baby in the carriage, and got home on the 9th.   How small is the record of so much happiness !

The disruption of the Scotch Kirk was impending, and interested me.   I deterred the minister of Ancrum from joining it.   The question of a Customs union between France and Belgium was also under discussion.   I remember that all through this period of deep anxiety I continued to write a great deal on public affairs.

It is unnecessary to dwell on the intensity with which Reeve felt this terrible blow, or to cite the long letter in which he poured forth his soul to his sympathetic friend, Handley.   Time alone brings the remedy ; and the only alleviation was suggested by Guizot—*travaillez.*

From M. Guizot

Paris, 13 Décembre.

MY DEAR SIR,—J'ai besoin de vous dire un mot, un seul mot.   Que j'ai pitié de vous !   Neuf ans se sont écoulés depuis que le même coup m'a frappé, exactement le même coup, deux mois après ses couches au lieu d'un mois. Depuis, ma vie a été bien active, bien pleine.   Des affections bien chères, bien douces sont sorties ou entrées dans mon cœur.   Le vide est toujours là.   Rien ne remplace le bonheur vrai et complet.   Que j'ai pitié de vous !   Je voudrais que cela pût vous faire quelque bien.   Soignez votre enfant et travaillez.   Ecrivez-moi si vous y prenez le moindre plaisir. Je vous écrirai.   Le temps ne me manquera jamais pour vous dire ce que je sens pour vous de pitié et d'amitié. Adieu. Adieu du fond du cœur.

GUIZOT.

The following, too, is noteworthy :—

From Lord Jeffrey to Mr. John Richardson

November 30th.—MY DEAR RICHARDSON,—A great sorrow has fallen upon you, and you must bear it ! And what more is there to say? I need not tell you that we mourn over you, and over the extinction of that young life, and the sudden vanishing of those opening prospects and innocent hopes that shed a cheering influence on our old hearts, and seemed yet to connect us, in sympathy and affection, with a futurity which we were not ourselves very likely to see. And all this is over, and she is gone ! and we are left to wonder and repine and yet to cling to what is left us of existence, and to feel that there are duties and affections that yet remain to us, and interests and sources of enjoyment too that will spring up anew when this blight and darkening have passed over. God help us ! . . .

God bless and support you, my dear and kind-hearted old friend.[1]

Life of Lord Jeffrey, vol. ii. p. 375.

CHAPTER V

ON THE 'TIMES'

So FAR we have followed Reeve's life in somewhat close detail. We have traced the unusual education and the extraordinary chances which fitted him in a very remarkable manner for the part he had to play; we have seen him appointed to an important and confidential post under Government, one which—though not prominent—brought him into familiar contact with many of the most powerful intellects in the country, and with many of the leaders of the people, men of high social rank and of political eminence; with many, too, of similar standing in other countries. The names of a few will emphasise the statement. They include the Marquis of Lansdowne, President of the Council; the Marquis of Normanby, Home Secretary; the Earl of Clarendon, Chancellor of the Duchy, but afterwards to be, for five eventful years, Lord-Lieutenant of Ireland, and for five more Foreign Secretary; M. de Tocqueville, known both as a writer and a politician; M. Guizot, Ambassador, and afterwards, in France, Foreign Secretary and President of the Council; Lord Brougham, ex-Lord Chancellor, a man of erratic, though singularly powerful, genius; Earl Granville, Ambassador at Paris, and his more distinguished son, so long Secretary for Foreign Affairs. We have been taught that 'as iron sharpeneth iron, so a man sharpeneth the countenance of his friend;' and the being thrown into familiar intercourse with men of this calibre necessarily sharpened the intellect of one whose early training had admirably tempered the metal.

Many others might be mentioned, and as years passed on the list was continually enlarged, till it included nearly every man of eminence in politics, in literature, or in society, whether in England, in France, or in Germany. And in himself the three elements were so mixed together that it would be difficult, if not impossible, to separate them. It may, however, be maintained that he was primarily and of freest choice a man of letters, but in a very practical form. Had fate gifted him, at the outset, with an independent income, it is conceivable that he would have devoted himself to works of history and philosophy similar to those of his friend Alexis de Tocqueville, for whom he always expressed and felt a profound admiration. We find a distinct evidence of such a tendency in his earlier writings—on education, on criminal procedure, and other similar essays—and it was probably the same impulse which, at a very early age, turned his attention to politics as the study of man, the proper study of mankind. But the necessities of life, which compelled him to undertake remunerative work, forced him into a more practical course; and his surroundings at the Council Office thrust him into the stream. It was thus that he was thrown into contact with and became a contributor to the ' Times '—not as a journalist working his way up from small beginnings, but taking the highest rank at once, as a leader writer on the most important topics of the day. Of the extent of his contributions it would be difficult to make any exact estimate; but after an experience of fifteen years, he noted in his Journal that he had frequently written four or five articles in the week, and that the payments made to him by the paper had averaged close on 1,000*l.* a year. It would be uninteresting, even if it were possible, to follow his proceedings in any detail. Extracts from his Journal will be a sufficient indication of them. But the life of a literary man is in his work, and the interesting part of this period of Reeve's career is the constant preparation for the exhaustive and exhausting articles which were so copiously poured forth to the ' Times ' in years when—to an extent which can now scarcely be understood—the ' Times ' was the guide of public opinion; when its voice was mighty in the Cabinet, not only of England, but of France and throughout Europe.

It is very clear that these articles could not have been produced without a great deal of study and of thought, supported by very unusual sources of information. No one better than Reeve knew and appreciated the tremendous power which the ' Times ' wielded; and he wrote with a full sense of the responsibility which attached to the service he performed. His judgements, as those of a fallible man, were not always correct; his information was sometimes inaccurate; but it is certain—not only from the esteem in which he was held by his wide circle of friends and acquaintances, but from his own intimate letters, that what he wrote was what he thought and what he believed. His criticisms and opinions came from his heart as much as from his head ; they were the best he had to dispose of, and their transparent honesty gave them weight and value.

The strain of continual preparation, of being always ready, liable to be called on at a moment's notice, added to the duties at the Council Office, which were frequently troublesome, left him little leisure for other work ; and for fifteen years his output, important as it was at the time, makes now no show, and is unknown except to those who, intent on working up the details of some incident in our foreign relations, turn to the files of the 'Times' and read his commentary, written with the *verve* of youth and the solid judgement of manhood—written, too, with extreme rapidity.   It was not unusual for him, coming home from the theatre or a dinner party, to find a messenger waiting for him with a note that an article was required at once.   On such occasions he would throw off his dress coat, pull off his dress boots, sit down to his desk and write.   When the messenger was dismissed with the MS. he could go to bed.   Now, a leading article in the 'Times' commonly runs between 1,500 and 2,000 words, an amount which—as we have been lately told by novelists of repute—is considered a good day's work, after weeks and months of preparation.   But neither fiction nor special forethought was permitted to Reeve.   The articles were put forth without stay, without hesitation, and with a truth and accuracy which he knew would be closely examined ; any flaw in which he knew would be loudly complained of.   Much of the information on which he wrote was, of course, furnished from the 'Times' Office, but much also from personal and private sources, a fact which gives a peculiar interest to his extensive correspondence, independent of and in addition to the interest which it has, as showing the inner working of the great political machine, and often as throwing new light on questions or incidents that still remain obscure.

It has already been said that Reeve's connexion with the 'Times' began in July 1840, under the editorial rule of Thomas Barnes ; but his visit to France followed shortly afterwards, so that he can scarcely have written much for the paper [1] during that year, and in the following May Barnes died ; 'a man,' Reeve noted on his last letter, 'who used the utmost power of the press without arrogance and

---

[1] One article, on Bonapartism, which appeared on December 18th, may be especially mentioned. The publication of such an article shows clearly enough the standing which Reeve had at once taken.

without bitterness to anyone   I deeply lamented his sudden andpremature death.'

Barnes was succeeded by John Thaddeus Delane, who had already been employed on the paper, and of whose ability Walter, the proprietor, had conceived a high opinion, which was, in fact, fully justified by the success of what appeared the dangerous experiment of appointing a young man, not yet twenty-four, to such an important and responsible position. With Reeve and Greville, Delane quickly became intimate, and, so far as the foreign policy of the paper was concerned, placed great confidence in them and in their sources of information. With Reeve he was more closely associated, and to a great extent entrusted him with the exposition of Continental affairs, the general line to be adopted being worked out in concert. When the two men were in London the more important discussions were naturally in the form of conversation. When one or other of them was out of town letters had to take its place, and the following from Delane has the peculiar interest of being written to Reeve whilst in Scotland by the death-bed of his wife. It is a curious commentary on Reeve's note that ' through this period of deep anxiety I continued to write a great deal on public affairs.'

November 18*th.*—I had a very long interview with Lord Aberdeen to-day, principally on the commercial treaty between France and Belgium, which I should wish you to make the subject of three or four more articles. He spoke very highly of those you have already written, but complains that the matter had never been regarded other than as it might affect commerce. It is, however, he says, of the very gravest political importance, being viewed by the Four Powers as, if carried, an infraction of the Protocol of 1831, by which the perpetual neutrality of Belgium was guaranteed. He hints, therefore, at an interference on their part, if necessary; but would, of course, greatly prefer that the progress of the treaty should be stayed definitively by the same causes which have now deferred its execution. That it will ultimately be concluded unless something is instantly done to bring these causes into more active and efficient operation, there is no doubt, as both kings, Louis Philippe and Leopold, are represented as fully determined to carry it through, if possible. One cannot blame the former, though from Leopold one has been accustomed to expect better things.

The best way to effect the object would, I think, be to have one article addressed principally to the Belgians, reminding them of their independence, and appealing to their nationality that they should not again permit their country to become a French province, as it would virtually be, and, in short, awakening all the vanity by which the *Braves* have always been distinguished. A second article might assist the fears of the French manufacturing interest, already somewhat strongly excited by the prospect of Belgian competition, and suggest the certainty that the Belgian factories would instantly acquire additional vigour from the importation of British enterprise and capital, for which France would afford a new field, and for which a means of employment is now so anxiously sought.

The remaining subject is one of such extreme delicacy and difficulty that I doubt whether it had not better be entirely passed over. I mean the political expediency of either nation venturing upon a treaty which, as contrary to that already existing, has so direct a tendency to disturb the peace of Europe. I am afraid that if this be suggested it will instantly be seized on as a reason not for stopping, but for going on, and that a plan which promises to secure to France, by peaceful conquest, all but the frontier of the Rhine, will become at once too popular for any commercial considerations to stay its progress. It will probably be argued that Belgium, though neutral, is independent, and therefore has a right to make what treaties she pleases; but the Government is prepared to answer that a Customs Union which binds her hand and foot to France—which would cover the country with French custom-houses—is not to be regarded in the light of a mere treaty; and that, therefore, they are called on to interfere. I doubt whether I have made myself intelligible, as I am writing in much haste to save the post; but there is, I dare say, enough of text for you.

Delane's letters were, of course, as guide-posts, indicators of what seemed the best line to take; but it was largely on his own judgement that Reeve had to depend, and from his private information that he had to draw his material. His correspondence during these years is thus very much of the nature of an old-fashioned panorama, or a modern kinematograph, in which the scene, always vivid, always life-like, is constantly changing.

At this period it is M. Guizot who holds the stage—M. Guizot, who, though nominally Minister for Foreign Affairs, was virtually the head of the French Ministry, Soult's advanced age and weak health preventing his taking any very active part in public business. His letters, always interesting, are thus important, as emanating from the premier; but it must be remembered that Guizot himself did not forget his position, and was quite alive to the advantage of obtaining the support of the 'Times,' and of making private friendship serve his official policy. The following is an instance more open than most :—

Auteuil, September 15th.—Here are the two volumes you want. I have only looked through them, but I think they are interesting. That was certainly a great diplomatic school. Together with this, you ought to read the Dutch diplomacy of the same period—of John de Witt and William III., two very great men, greater than their fame, for they upheld their cause, which was often the right cause, through its worst days, without doubting or faltering. You see I am a very impartial Frenchman.

Thanks for the details you give me of your internal policy ; they have greatly interested me, and I perfectly believe in them. When truth appears, it is recognised even from afar. I greatly desire the success of Sir Robert Peel ; it is as important to us as it is to you. I have passed through two very difficult years ; we had to pay the price of Lord Palmerston's policy. Up to the present I have only succeeded in preventing evil, a sad and unprofitable task. I hope that something better will be possible in future. Our last misfortune has given the public spirit a wholesome shock. Men will never learn to be wise of their own free-will and foresight; they must therefore content themselves with the wisdom which springs from necessity, in the hour of danger. I shall have great difficulties in the next Session, difficulties of jealousy, ambition, and intrigue. I shall walk among snares, surprises, and secret attacks. I shall do my best to turn all these into public contests, so as to compel those who are whispering conspiracy in the lobby to speak out before the whole Chamber. I hope I shall succeed. Help me still, 'my dear Sir,'[1] as you have often done before, and to such good purpose. . . .

Of the months immediately following the death of Reeve's wife, the little that is to be said is said in the fewest words in the Journal.

1843.—I lived of course in great retirement. Florence Nightingale came to stay with Helen. At Easter, Helen, Lizzie,[2] and I went to Paris, where I found Tocqueville, Guizot, Faucher, Cousin, and Thiers. This brought me back to society, and I resumed the current of my life. Lavergne came to stay with me in London.

On May 17th I got the news of Handley's death at Cadiz. Christopher Wordsworth and myself were the executors. The Bracebridges[3] soon after came to town. The Fauchers came to London. Winterhalter introduced me to Munro of Novar, who afterwards became a great friend.

Lady Smith[4] came more than once to stay in Chester Square. I shot at Beaumont's Moor at Allendale, with W. Longman, and then went on to Kirklands. Lord Cockburn came there. Shot at Todrig. Back to town. Went to see the Austins at Boulogne and met V. Cousin there. I bought a brougham—my first carriage—and jobbed a horse. An ugly attack in the head, for which I was cupped—the only time in my life.

The Duc de Bordeaux's visit to England in December and the great demonstration of the Legitimists amazed the French Government very much. I wrote an article in the 'Times' on the affair, which fell like a shell among them.

---

[1] The few words 'quoted' in Guizot's letters are in English in the original.

[2] Richardsons; Reeve's sisters-in-law.

[3] Mr. Charles Holte Bracebridge, of Atherstone Hall, Warwickshire, born in 1799, had travelled much, was a man of varied accomplishments, and was well known as a philanthropist and a philhellene. His wife shared his tastes. They were intimate friends of Florence Nightingale, accompanied her to Constantinople in the winter of 1854-5, and largely contributed to the success of her work.

[4] Widow of Sir James Smith, the botanist. She lived to an extreme old age, and died in 1877. Several of her letters will be found later on.

The French Government was more than amazed; it was indignant, and with good cause. The Duc de Bordeaux, afterwards better known as the Comte de Chambord, was at this time twenty-three, accepted as the representative of the elder branch of the Bourbons, and, as such, the hope of the Legitimists. On the abdication of Charles X., in 1830, he—then a mere child—had been proclaimed king as Henri V.; and though, at the time, this had been rightly regarded as a vain pretence, it seemed to have some significance now, if the young man was to be made the subject of popular display in England and to be received by the English Court. The demonstration thus drew from M. Guizot a strong letter to his personal friend, Lord Aberdeen, then Foreign Secretary; and to Reeve the following, which the recipient endorsed 'Communicated to Lord Aberdeen on December 5th. This very remarkable letter was the basis of the subsequent proceedings against the Carlists, both in the "Times" and in Guizot's speeches soon after.'

Paris, December 1st.

'MY DEAR SIR,'—I cannot bear to have any real disagreement with a friend without doing my best to put an end to it. Above everything, I wish to be understood and approved by those whom I esteem and love, and who esteem and love me. So I put on one side many things that call for my attention, in order to talk to you about the Duc de Bordeaux and the ideas which you entertain concerning him.

If the Duc de Bordeaux was simply an exiled and unfortunate prince travelling without any political object, we should think it very right and proper for you to pay all possible respect to his misfortunes and his rank. We should say nothing about it; we should not even notice it. But this is very far from being the case. Whether the Duc de Bordeaux wishes it or not, whether the step is conceived by him and his immediate advisers, or whether they are guided by his partisans in France, it is clear that he is, in fact, a Pretender, carrying out or preparing a policy of intrigue and conspiracy. Nothing can be more significant than this gathering round him of all the leaders of the faction—great and small, young and old, deputies, men of the world, journalists. Even the age and weakness of M. de Chateaubriand have not absolved him from the demands of his party.　The oath they swore to the King has not prevented MM. Berryer, de Valmy,[1] and the rest, from offering their homage, their allegiance, their devotion to the Duc de Bordeaux.　And not only have they thus assembled round him, but they take pains to noise it abroad in their newspapers.　Day after day they describe, they make capital of, the Duke's journey and their own also.　Every morning they cry—Henry V. is our King!

Here then, beyond any doubt, is a declared Pretender; here is a factious display, intended to stimulate and nourish the passions and the hopes of the party, and to prepare them for an attempt on some future day.　Consider too what, previous to the Duke's arrival in England, the Carlists have done on the Continent in order to give a political significance to his journey.　They summoned the Comte de St.-Priest to Berlin—the same who was minister under the Restoration. Before leaving Paris, M. de St.-Priest called on Count Arnim, the Prussian minister, and told him that the King of Prussia had invited the Duc de Bordeaux to Berlin— which the Prussian Government has formally denied.　They arranged for the Duke to arrive at Berlin while the Emperor of Russia and a number of other princes were assembled there.　They evidently wished to exhibit their Pretender in the company of foreign sovereigns, and to give him an appearance of being on terms of friendly intimacy with them.　These are facts, 'my dear Sir;' visible, palpable facts.　It is impossible not to take them into account. What would happen were your Queen to receive the Duc de Bordeaux, even if only privately, in a simple visit?　The Carlists would seize upon the visit, they would misrepresent it, they would multiply it in their letters and in their newspapers.　They would lie and deceive.　And in spite of every possible explanation and disavowal, their twofold purpose would be gained; abroad, they would have given their Pretender an air of importance; at home, they would have flattered and inspirited the hopes of their faction.　If, on the other hand, the Queen of England does not receive the Duc de Bordeaux at all, this fact alone will defeat the aims of the party both at home and abroad; it will show

---

[1] François de Kellerman, Duc de Valmy, grandson of Napoleon's Marshal.

the vanity of the rumours they have circulated ; it will make an end of the pretences they have put forward. Such a result, happy for us, will be happy also for the relations between our two countries. It will be a striking proof of the cordial friendship of the Queen of England for our royal family, of your Government for ours, of England for France. It will be the complement of the visit at the Château d'Eu ; [1] and from these two facts we shall deduce the most striking and convincing answer to loud-voiced invective and blind distrust.

But all these Carlist gatherings, these demonstrations, this factious agitation, afford the English Government—not a pretext, but—a positive reason for the Queen's refusing to receive the Duc de Bordeaux. Nowhere else has the party done so much. The prince, indeed, visited Vienna, Dresden, and Berlin ; but there was there no word of the party. In England it has shown itself openly and noisily. You may be quite sure that if, on the recent occasion at Berlin, the Carlists had attempted to make a quarter of the disturbance they are making in England, they would have been immediately requested to hold their tongues and to take themselves off. Because England is a free country where no one can be compelled to keep silence or depart, is the English Government obliged to allow a foreign faction to use English liberties for a political end without showing to them any mark of disapproval, to France any mark of friendship ?

On the 28th of last September, after the Duc de Bordéaux had left Berlin, M. de Humboldt wrote to me, by order of the King of Prussia, who read the letter :—' I do not think I go too far in saying that the young prince's visit would have been declined had not his uncle been still alive ; had he been dead,[2] the nephew's importance in the eyes of his party would have been greater, and he would have been regarded as a Pretender.' Does the Duc de Bordeaux pre-

---

[1] The visit of the Queen and Prince Albert to Louis Philippe at the Château d'Eu, September 1st–7th, 1843. An account of the *fêtes* &c. is in the *Annual Register*, 1843, Chronicle, 120–5.

[2] The Duc d'Angoulême—the elder son of Charles X. and the natural heir to the throne, though he had resigned his right in favour of his nephew—was still alive at the date of this letter. He died at Goritz in Illyria, on June 3rd, 1844.

sent himself to England as a Pretender? is he so presented by England to France and Europe? 'That is the question!' Have you any doubt about the answer?

But it is said that there is no danger to France, and that England is accustomed to show herself hospitable to misfortune. No; there is no danger to us, but there is scandal; and to that we neither can nor ought to show ourselves indifferent. The dignity of a government is part of its strength; and in this world, respect is due to other things besides misfortune. And, danger apart, excitement of this kind is embarrassing to a government; for the stirring up of passions on one side awakens opposing passions on the other. The Carlist spirit cannot show itself here without the revolutionary spirit reappearing to embitter discussions which would otherwise pass quietly and orderly.

I know and highly esteem the sentiment of generous interest, of free and noble hospitality, which prevails so strongly amongst you. But you also know what a king, what a royal family, what a government owe to their own dignity and the dignity of their country. You are accustomed to conduct your affairs soberly, to respect yourselves and to make others respect you. This is what we are doing; it is this which regulates our conduct on the present occasion.

I have written at great length, 'my dear Sir,' but I am anxious that you should know the truth and understand our attitude. I am also anxious that your Government's kind and friendly attitude towards us should not be to it a source of annoyance and vexation. I own that I shall be astonished if I have not convinced you; and if you are convinced, I beg you to employ yourself in convincing others. I count on your good judgement and your good friendship.

'Sincerely yours,'

GUIZOT.

The representations of Guizot were either unnecessary or effective. The Duc de Bordeaux was not received by the Queen, and he was warned by Lord Aberdeen that he could not be permitted to make England the base of his intrigues against a friendly Government. The affair, however, caused great excitement in Paris and in the Chamber, to which Reeve referred in his Journal :—

To Paris at Christmas. I was at the opening of the Chambers on December 27th. The Comte de Paris was there for the first time. On the 30th I was presented to Louis Philippe at the Tuileries [when the King personally thanked me for the article in the ' Times ' of the 7th].

1844.—The year opened brilliantly in Paris, M. Guizot was at the height of his power, and society very agreeable. The great debate on the Address took place on January 15th. I breakfasted with Guizot and went to the Chamber with him. It was on this occasion Berryer broke down. I was at Mme. d'Agoult's, Duchesse de Rauzan's, Mme. de Circourt's, the Embassy—then filled by Lord Cowley, the father; dined at the Harcourts'; saw the Marochettis, Wheatons, Austins, Vivien, Rémusat; heard Lacordaire preach. Came back to London on January 24th.

He does not mention having met Mignet at this time; but the following letter from Greville shows that he was at least in familiar communication with him. That the application which he made, or got Greville to make, on Mignet's behalf was not successful will not appear strange to any student of history who has had a similar experience, and has learnt how morbidly jealous the public or private possessors of such papers commonly are.

January 13th.—I have been with Sir George Murray to-day, but he turns a deaf ear to your proposal of allowing M. Mignet to inspect the Marlborough papers. There are twenty-nine large volumes, from 1702 to 1710–11—a correspondence both voluminous and miscellaneous. He has now nearly completed the perusal of them ; will not think of publishing anything till he has, but looks forward to doing so then, though he says there will be great difficulty in selection. He has, however, looked into the last books, and he assures me that they contain nothing which would be of any service to M. Mignet. I could not, of course, urge him very strongly ; but I did suggest that there must be much matter of a purely diplomatic character—e.g. the ineffectual attempts of Torcy and his negotiations with Buys and Vanderdussen, and all the political transactions which took place during the two last years of Marlborough's being in command of the army. He said, however, that it was impossible to open these sources of information to anybody till they had been examined throughout, and some determination come to as to their publication. He says they greatly exalt the character of Marlborough, who had difficulties and obstacles to overcome not less than those which beset the Duke of Wellington in Spain, and which he encountered with the same mixture of firmness, admirable sense and patience which so distinguish the great man of our time. You will assure M. Mignet that you and I have done all we can do. I long for some more of his work.

Sir George Murray's 'Letters and Despatches of the Duke of Marlborough' was published in the following year, but was edited with such extreme prudence as to leave it deprived of much of the value which the work might otherwise have had. The Journal continues :—

Pleasant expedition to Chenies at Easter. I subscribed to the Philharmonic this year.

June 6th.—I had the Grotes, Sartorises,[1] Mendelssohn, Gordons, and Galton to dinner; in the evening T. Carlyle and the Nightingales.

22nd.—The seven Taylors—John, Richard, Edward, Philip, Susan, Arthur, and Sarah—dined at Greenwich for the first and last time ; a curious meeting. The youngest of them was 50.[2] John Edward, myself, Nora Taylor, Arthur, Edgar, Chorley, and Rigby made up the party. John Taylor presided.

28th.—Mendelssohn's ' St. Paul ' was given. He conducted.

July 2nd.—Saw the launch of the ' Retribution ' frigate at Chatham.

August 10th.—Agreeable party at the Bracebridges', at Atherstone.

16th.—I went to Normandy on a visit to Tocqueville. Walked with him to Barfleur, Cherbourg, &c.

To Mrs. Reeve

Tocqueville, August 20th.—I never wished to draw more than to give you an idea of this place. In size it is about

---

[1] Mrs. Sartoris is better known by her maiden name—Adelaide Kemble.
[2] Sarah (Mrs. Austin), the youngest of the family, was born in 1793.

a match for Sir W. Scott's of Ancrum, and probably built
at a similar period and for similar purposes of defence ; for
the Cotentin, lying within eighteen leagues of the Isle of
Wight, may be considered as a border district in relation to
England ; and the manor houses, which are exceedingly
numerous, bore the same office of defence as the Peelhouses
of Teviotdale.   This château, however, has a more seigneur-
ial character.   It is a long irregular building, flanked on
the left by two large round towers with conical roofs, and
another tower behind contains the great staircase of colossal
granite steps.   The habitable part consists of a very good
suite of half a dozen rooms on two floors.   On the right are
the stables, and the remains of another tower, which was
the *colombier*, and lost its roof in the Revolution, so that the
whole place has an aspect of strength and dignity.   I found
Tocqueville very well, and we are all ready to talk for a
week without ceasing.

The story is continued in the Journal :—

From Tocqueville I went on to Paris, where there was
some excitement about the war with Morocco.   I saw M.
Guizot and Lord Cowley daily.   Went with Winterhalter
to see the castles of Touraine—Chambord, Blois, Loches.
Meanwhile the squabble about Pritchard and Tahiti was
arranged.

Politically speaking, this squabble was the event of the
year, and at one time threatened to cause a rupture between
the two countries.   In itself, and at first sight, the circumstance seemed to warrant a decided attitude.   Mr. Pritchard,
the British Consul at Tahiti, had been summarily arrested
by order of the French Resident, M. d'Aubigny, and been
released only on the condition that he would depart from
the island and never more return.   When he arrived in
England, the Government and the press denounced the
action of the French as a gross outrage, and demanded a
public apology, the recall and disgrace of D'Aubigny, and
substantial reparation to Pritchard.   All this the French
Government could not and would not concede.   Reeve had
several interviews with M. Guizot, and wrote to Lord
Wharncliffe, president of the Council, that Guizot would
resign sooner than yield ; that if he resigned, the question
of peace or war would mainly depend on whether he was

succeeded by Molé or Thiers, as to which Guizot said—
'Si Thiers me succède, il fera la guerre ; si c'est Molé, il fera
une lâcheté.' This Reeve thought an exaggeration, and
believed that even Thiers would do what he could to preserve peace ; at the same time he urged the advisability of
not forcing Guizot from office.

What probably had greater weight with the Cabinet was
the reflection, slowly forced on them, that though, as a
matter of form, D'Aubigny was quite in the wrong, as a
matter of common sense, Pritchard had got no more than he
deserved. He combined the office of consul with the duties
of missionary and Methodist preacher, and having both
political and religious objections to the French, who had
assumed the protectorate of the island, he was suspected,
and probably not without reason, of intriguing with the
natives against them. Delane's account of the final settlement is, of course, from the point of view of Printing House
Square.

From Mr. Delane

September 3rd.—The Cabinet met yesterday, but, as I
learn, no actual decision was come to, although there was
enough settled to warrant the article of to-day. My impression is that both Lord Aberdeen and Peel regretted the very
strong observations they had made in Parliament, and,
finding that the case scarcely justified them, were glad to
escape from the difficulty. The terms are—an apology for
D'Aubigny's conduct, a censure upon him, and a pecuniary
compensation for Pritchard. They take the two first as a
satisfaction as between the Governments, but require the
last as a salve for Pritchard's personal ill-usage. This, as
the most practical admission of error, would, of course, be
most offensive in France, and I have therefore blinked it
as much as possible with the public. As an excuse for not
granting more ample reparation, the French Government
allege against Pritchard a variety of overt acts, and a multitude of evidence to prove him the author of a plot for the
extermination of the French—all palliating D'Aubigny's
fault in seizing and imprisoning him, and reducing his
offence very much to a mere error in judgement, for which
the censure of Bruat,[1] renewed by the home Government, is,
they contend, a sufficient punishment.

[1] Then Governor of the Marquesas.

I confess that for the last week or two I have been coming round very much to this opinion, although it especially convicts me of having made a great deal too much of the 'outrages' in the first place. Of course we shall be well abused for accepting such slight reparation, but public opinion will, I think, be with us in deprecating war upon such a ridiculous squabble.

September 5th.—I am very much vexed and annoyed indeed about this so-called settlement of the Tahiti question. It is hard to say whether that or the reversal of the judgement in O'Connell's case is the more provoking. Personally, however, I think the latter rather a gain than a loss—i.e. I could see no good in keeping O'Connell in gaol. As to Tahiti, I can find no such grounds for consolation. We ['Times'] were put in the position either of quarrelling irreparably with the only department of the Government with which we have been able to keep on terms, or of drawing in our horns after a fashion I by no means approve. True it is that if we succumb, so do Sir R. Peel, the Duke, and Lord A. Their big words—'gross outrage, &c.'—bear no better proportion to the reparation they have obtained than our first article on D'Aubigny's misconduct to our last. The fact is, we were all wrong at both ends of the transaction. Both they and we said too much at first, and we have both assented to too little at last. Our only saving point is the compensation to Pritchard. Whatever else in the way of apology is shadowy and obscure, that, at least, is a tangible confession of wrong doing, and if to a tolerably handsome amount, it may salve all over. I am the more vexed at our Government having accepted shabby terms because I am convinced that better might have been had. Molé would have been much more conceding, and even Guizot, in spite of his protestations, would surely have rather advanced upon his offer than go out.

Reeve's personal interest in the affair had, however, ceased when he left Paris ; and from Touraine he went on to Avignon and Marseilles, which he reached on September 14th. His Journal gives an outline of the tour.

From Marseilles to Genoa and Leghorn by sea. Posted to Florence. Delightful evening at Fiesole, September 25th.

Thence to Bologna, Parma, Milan, and Vercelli, whence I went to visit the Abercrombys at Caluso.   He was minister at Turin, and married to Lady Mary Elliot.   Crossed the Mont Cenis, in the mail, and reached Geneva October 12th. Returned to England by the Rhine—absent 69 days.

Visit to Atherstone in October ; and in November, to Kirklands for a week.

November 30th, my first visit at the Grove.[1]   C. Greville, Senior, C. Villiers,[2] and F. Cadogan there.

From Lord Clarendon

The Grove, December 10th.—The state of things in Paris is certainly unexpected, absurd, shallow, and unreliable—as the Americans say.   It is really curious that a set of men like Thiers and his friends, at twenty-four hours' distance from London, and with every means of information at their command, should be gravely expecting by any manœuvre of theirs to influence—or determine, for aught I know—the fate of an administration here !   Guizot may perhaps profit by the delusion ; but it will be more by turning the tables upon his opponents than by giving effect to his dispositions uswards.

I have read the article on Greece with great interest, but I should like to know what Mr. Bracebridge now thinks of the constitutional prospects of Greece, and the working of representative government there.

Many thanks for what you say of your visit to the Grove. Lady C. and I are delighted that it was agreeable to you.   I assure you the pleasure was quite reciprocal, and we hope often to see you here again.

The personal items in the Journal for the spring of 1845 are few, but include the purchase of ' a phaeton and pair of horses ' early in the year, and—on April 11th—election to the Athenæum.   Politically, the question of the day was the Government bill for increasing the grant to Maynooth, which excited a very strong and general feeling of opposition, especially from the clergy of the Church of England and of all Protestant denominations.   The obloquy showered on

---

[1] Near Watford, the country seat of the Earl of Clarendon.

[2] Charles Pelham Villiers, Lord Clarendon's brother, who, after being M.P. for Wolverhampton for sixty-three consecutive years, died on January 16th, 1898, at the age of ninety-six.

Peel was outrageous. One popular preacher compared him to the 'young man void of understanding,' who was captured by 'a woman with the attire of a harlot,' as described in Proverbs vii. 7 *et seq.* The bill was none the less passed in both the Commons and the Lords by a large majority. It is to this popular opposition that M. Guizot referred in the following—

From M. Guizot

Paris, February 15th.—I am most grateful, my dear Sir, for your kindness. Thanks to you I realise your situation almost as clearly as if I was at Hertford House. As you say this morning, the only question is what will happen when once the bill is passed. And unless I am mistaken, this question as to the future depends on the personal wish and on the will of Sir Robert Peel. If he is determined to remain in power, and for that end to endure all the worries, the disagreeables, and the misunderstandings which a strong will despises, I am disposed to think he will succeed, and that no one is in a position to overthrow him. But is he so determined? I hope so, but I do not know ; I beg you to send me all the information, indications, and 'hints' you can collect upon this knotty point.

I have always supposed that if the Whigs returned to power Lord Palmerston would go back to the Foreign Office. . . . I have told you frankly my opinion of him, and my reasons for some uneasiness. The more I consider it, the more firmly I am convinced that his policy towards France, the King, and myself will be fair and friendly ; and I have no doubt that his colleagues, especially Lord John, will use all their influence for the same end. On our side, we should lend ourselves to it with absolute sincerity. Will all this good will and these united efforts be able to change the characters, inclinations, habits of thought, traditions and personal passions, which insensibly bias and complicate policy without the knowledge of those actually looking on, contrary even to the wish of the principal actor?

'That is the question.' If the attempt is made we shall see. Meanwhile I, on my part, am taking, and will continue to take, care neither to say nor do anything which may increase the difficulty, should the case arise. . . .

It is more than a little amusing to find—by the next letter from Lord Clarendon—Reeve in the position of an unsuccessful suitor to the 'Edinburgh Review,' over which he so long reigned supreme.

Grosvenor Crescent, May 31st.—You see you were quite right in supposing that your opinions upon the war policy of Mr. Pitt would be an obstacle to an article from you on Thiers being received by the 'Edinburgh Review;' and upon that point I think Napier[1] right, as he would have done himself irreparable injury with his old friends and supporters by departing from what is a sort of fundamental principle of the journal. However a communication is, I trust, opened with Napier, if you like to make use of it, and I am sure he will be glad if you do.

The Journal fills up the latter half of the year :—

June 21st.—Went to Portsmouth with the Lochs and saw the squadron—then all sailing vessels. On the 23rd the Queen reviewed the fleet.

I was laid up for some days with gout &c., and started on July 27th for Aix-la-Chapelle—my first visit there. Crossed to Antwerp.

The Queen came to Germany ; and I went with Chorley and Maude to Bonn, to the Beethoven Fest, conducted by Spohr, but mainly animated by Liszt. On August 11th the Queen arrived at Brühl. I went with the Rigbys and we heard the great 'Zapfenstreich.' The festival continued— 12th, 'Missa Solennis' of Beethoven ; 13th, Liszt's Cantata. Afterwards travelled with the Rigbys through the Eifel; went back to Aix, and returned to England on August 26th.

Spent September in and about London ; went to Kirklands on September 24th, and thence to Edinburgh.

November 15th.—Forster and Dickens acted in Ben Jonson's 'Every Man in his Humour.' I met Lucy Gordon there, with Lord Melbourne and Lady Charlemont. [Before the curtain rose, Lord Melbourne said that it was a dull play, 'with no μῦθος in it.' Between the acts he exclaimed in a stentorian voice, heard across the pit : 'I knew this play

---

[1] Macvey Napier, the editor of the *Edinburgh Review*.

would be dull, but that it would be so damnably dull as this
I did not suppose.'[1]]

From M. Guizot

Paris, November 20th.— . . . I shall be delighted to see
you again in January. You will find me in the midst of
battles. There will probably be all the more because fewer
are spoken of, and there is really less cause for them. Contrary to the expectation of my opponents, all important questions have been settled, and, I venture to say it, to the
advantage of the country. But a good many minor questions still remain—Texas, Albreda, Madagascar, La Plata,
Tahiti, and some others. The Opposition will bring them
all forward, and do what they can to exaggerate their importance. Quantity will make up for quality. It will be a
continuous series of skirmishes and surprises; of invective
and of criticism of details. In the beginning, at least, *le
parti conservateur* will not be stimulated by the apprehension of any great public danger; they will not at first see the
indirect importance of the questions raised. In democratic
and inexperienced societies, such as ours, political firmness
and foresight are developed only in the presence of a pressing
danger and an evident necessity.

For all these reasons, which are strong rather than good,
and in spite of the excellent position of the Cabinet, I expect
a very laborious and very 'intricate' session. I feel sure
that I shall surmount all obstacles and win the battles; for
I have confidence in the goodness of our cause, and in the
soundness of our arguments. Supported by this confidence
I have persevered through many trials and have succeeded.
I cling to it myself; I carefully nourish it in those around
me; and five years of success is a powerful argument.
But I continually repeat to myself and to my friends, that
in the present state of public morality, and under our
present form of government, neither a good cause, good
reasons, nor even success, will ever prevent attacks, intrigues or insults, and that the battle has always to
be begun again, as if no victory had been won. . . .

[1] *Greville Memoirs*, second part, ii. 302*n*.

The Journal notes that—

Early in December Peel announced to his colleagues his intention to repeal the Corn Laws. Lord Aberdeen told Delane on December 3rd, and on the 4th the 'Times' published it. The agitation was extreme, and Peel resigned on the 6th, but soon to come back again.

This announcement in the 'Times,' which, in point of fact, was a little premature—for at the time, the decision of the Cabinet had not been actually formed—was mainly, if not entirely, a piece of diplomatic strategy on the part of Lord Aberdeen, who, in the negotiations then pending, wished to soothe the Government of the United States by this indirect intimation of the market which was opening for their corn stuffs. The date was determined simply by the sailing of the American mail.[1] But this was, of course, not known then; and out of the many speculations as to how the 'Times' had obtained its very early information was born a scandalous story, to the effect that Delane bought the secret from Mrs. Norton, to whom it had been confided, in a moment of weakness, by one of her admirers; and when several years afterwards Mr. Meredith introduced such an incident into 'Diana of the Crossways,' the story was supposed to have received the highest possible confirmation. The falsehood of it had been repeatedly exposed; but as lately as 1894 it cropped up again, and drew from Lord Dufferin the following note to Reeve.

December 19th, 1894.—I wonder whether you could help me to solve a literary problem? In his autobiography Gregory has revived that scandalous story about Mrs. Norton having sold to the 'Times' the secret, supposed to have been confided to her by Sidney Herbert, of Sir Robert Peel's change of policy in regard to the Corn Laws. The whole story is an absolute myth, as I am, fortunately, able to prove; but what I want to find is, how the story originated. I cannot help suspecting that it was —— who set it going, he probably having heard some suggestion of the kind at a club where people were speculating as to how Delane got hold of the news.

It was presumably in consequence of this letter that, in an article on Meredith's Novels in the next number of the 'Edinburgh Review,' Reeve referred to the incident in

[1] Cf. *Greville Memoirs*, second part, ii. 311-15.

'Diana of the Crossways' as 'suggested, not by facts, but by calumnies which were exposed and refuted, though for a time they obtained circulation and a certain credence,' and added the following note : [1]—

We observe with regret that the late Sir William Gregory in his interesting autobiography has revived a calumnious and unfounded anecdote, to which Mr. Meredith had previously given circulation in this novel. We are enabled to state, and we do state, from our personal knowledge, that the story is absolutely false in every particular, and that the persons thus offensively referred to had nothing to do with the matter. The intention of the Government to propose the repeal of the Corn Laws was communicated openly by Lord Aberdeen to Mr. Delane, the editor of the 'Times;' there was no sort of intrigue or bribery in the transaction.

Lord Dufferin answered this with—

January 29th, 1895.—I have to thank you . . . for having written that most interesting and able article in the 'Edinburgh,' and more especially for the note which you have appended to it about Mrs. Norton. You have rendered us all a great service, for the contradiction coming from such a source will now be universally accepted as final.

Mr. Meredith has also added a note in the last edition of 'Diana of the Crossways,' to the effect that the story is fiction; but whether this any more than the authoritative contradiction by the 'Times' and the 'Edinburgh Review' will finally crush the scandal is very doubtful. A lie, once well started, has more lives than a legion of cats, and it may be confidently prognosticated that this lie will reappear, perhaps fifty years hence, as matter of certain fact. [2]

The Journal continues :—

December 8th.—I dined with Forster, Dickens, and Crowe

---

[1] *Edinburgh Review*, January 1895, p. 48.

[2] It is curious to note how persistently misrepresentation and inaccuracy have haunted the life and the memory of Mrs. Norton. Even in the *Quarterly Review* of July 1897 (p. 178) the story of *Diana of the Crossways* is referred to as ' Mrs. Norton's betrayal of the secret communication to Barnes,' who died more than four years before the supposed date: and in *Women Novelists of Queen Victoria's Reign* it is said (p. 289): ' She did not succeed in obtaining the relief of divorce until about 1853 : ' whereas, in fact, she not only never obtained, but never sought for, such relief. She wore the chain till Norton's death broke it in 1875.

about the 'Daily News' then starting; and started on the 11th for Paris. I saw a great deal of the Maberleys, the Cowleys, Guizot, Mrs. Austin, the Bracebridges, Princess Lieven, the Foxes, the Circourts, the Czartoryskis, Fanny Butler, Faucher, Lavergne, Lady Elgin, Rouher—all in Paris. The Lamartines were there. The Tocquevilles arrived a little later.

Lord Wharncliffe died, suddenly, on December 19th, partly from the excitement he had undergone on the Corn Law question. It was on December 5th he came into my room after the Cabinet to say we were all mistaken; and so, in truth, we were, as Peel resigned; but his return to office, on the failure of the Whigs, set things straight. The Duke of Buccleuch succeeded Lord Wharncliffe as Lord President.

1846.—The year opened in Paris. On January 6th, M. Guizot gave a great dinner to the Morocco ambassador, where I met Soult, Duc de Broglie, Delaport, Morny, Dwarkanath Tagore,[1] and Disraeli. I sat by Morny. Curious combination. The Conservatoire sang in the evening. I got the Maberleys invited. Brougham came to Paris, and brought Dr. Giffard[2] to Guizot. A brilliant and interesting time. Returned to England on January 28th.

January 31st.—Dined with Lord Clarendon, to meet Sainte-Aulaire, Lord Lansdowne, and Panizzi. My intimacy with Lord Clarendon dates from this time.

February 13th.—I had Wheaton, Lord Clarendon, Greville, Charles Fox, and Gordon to dinner.

March 4th.—Dined at the Foxes', with Lady Morley, Lord John Russell, Lord Glenelg, Panizzi, and Dedel.

Severe attack of gout in March. Took half a stall at the Opera this season. I dined several times with Sir Henry Webster at Putney, and met at one of these dinners Louis Napoleon, just escaped from Ham. His moustache, which he had shaved, was just beginning to reappear. He said,

---

[1] A Brahmin of noble family, great wealth, and enlightened views, who had crossed the 'black water,' settled in England, and was much consulted by the Government on questions relating to India. It was said to be in a great measure his advice that led to the abolition of Suttee. He died on August 1st, seven months after this dinner.

[2] Stanley Lees Giffard, LL.D., then editor of the *Standard*.

' What does a man in prison think of ? How to get out of it.'

June 2nd.—Baron Beust, Panizzi, Lord Dudley Stuart, and Zamoyski dined with me.

June 18th.—Dined at the Lewises' (Kent House), with Lord Clarendon and Cobden—the first time I met Cobden.

June 25th.—Peel was defeated by 73 majority, and his Ministry came to an end. Lord John Russell formed the new Cabinet, and Lord Palmerston returned to the Foreign Office. The result was a speedy quarrel with France about the Spanish Marriage, and a total change in the relations of the two countries. I did not approve Palmerston's conduct, but I could not defend M. Guizot.

From Lord Clarendon

Grosvenor Crescent, July 4th.—I don't think the ' Times ' is quite fair in altogether omitting my brother Charles in its *résumé* of the Corn Law battle. Charles, long before Cobden was heard of, persisted in bringing this question every year before the House, notwithstanding the sneers and the opposition of the Liberals; and as Peel at the beginning of the session said he could no longer resist the arguments of the member for Wolverhampton, it is not just to say that ' Cobden was bearing the brunt of the battle in the H. of C., and unconsciously convincing the Prime Minister.' The subject will probably again be reverted to in the ' Times,' and if you will mention Charles to Delane I have no doubt he will do him justice as a parliamentary leader, opponent of the Corn Laws; and Charles cannot, like the manufacturers, be supposed to have had the slightest interest in their abolition.

From M. Guizot

Paris, 24 Août.

MY DEAR SIR,—Je n'ai que le temps de vous envoyer la lettre que vous désirez pour M. de Flahault.[1] Je regrette que vous ne passiez pas par Paris. Nous aurions causé. Il y a de quoi. Bon voyage sur le Danube. L'Autriche

---

[1] The French ambassador at Vienna.

mérite bien d'être observée en ce moment. C'est évidem-
ment un Etat plus agité intérieurement qu'on ne le croyait,
et peut-être que vous ne trouverez vous-même en y regar-
dant, car les choses ne se voient là que lorsqu'elles éclatent.

Mille amitiés.   GUIZOT.

The outline of this Austrian tour is given in the Journal.

August 31st.—I started for Germany by Nuremberg and
Ratisbon, where I met Bonar. Thence down the Danube
to Linz and Vienna. Met Prince Esterhazy, Prince Hohen-
lohe (the miracle-worker), and Sir R. Gordon [1] on board the
steamer. After a day or two at Vienna, went on to stay
with Count Zichy Ferraris at Sandorf in Hungary—kind
reception. She was Charlotte Strahan. Thence by Babolna
(saw the stud) to Komorn and Pesth. I gave up going to
see John Richardson in Transylvania, and proceeded alone,
posting to Croatia, Warasdin, Agram, and Fiume; went to
Porto Rè and Buccari, and returned to Vienna on October
4th.

To Mrs. Reeve

Warasdin, September 26th.—I suppose I shall not write
many letters in my life from the wilds of Croatia, and therefore I sit down to give you this *indicium* of my progress, to
be put in the post at the first opportunity. . . .

Travelling alone, when one has the courage to undertake
it, has its peculiar pleasures and merits—to me especially,
who spend my whole life in company. I have an excellent
strong carriage which I hired in Vienna for only 5*l.* A
large basket contains the roast chickens and the ham, and
the remains of a bottle of sherry, for without these necessaries
you may be starved. I have books and plenty of things to
think about; and the changes of the country or the incidents
of the way afford sufficient variety. Do we not, after all,
travel though life alone, and for the most part in less easy
vehicles? Not often, indeed, on rougher roads. The roads
in Hungary are sometimes good, but just as you are
beginning to admire the progress of Macadam, the *chaussée*
stops, and you are up to your axles in sand, or threading
the mazes of an unhewn forest.

---

[1] Brother of the Earl of Aberdeen; at this time ambassador at Vienna.

The banks of the Platten See are not very striking ; but such an expanse of water (bigger than the Lake of Geneva) is always beautiful. The Monastery of Tihany, standing out in the middle of the lake on a promontory, which I thought must be like what they call ' Ireland's Eye ' (I only know that from your sketches), is a fine object.

South of the Platten See I entered immense forests of oaks, the largest and wildest I ever beheld. The forest seems untouched by man, for the old trees die where they stand, and the elder generation rear their bare or blasted arms high above the thick foliage of the grove. Night was coming on as I reached the banks of the Drave. The young moon stood high as the sun set. The postilion wound his bugle from the heights to warn the boatmen at the ferry of our approach. The boat was already nearly full of peasants and oxen and carts returning from the vintage. I lit the lamps as we were crossing the river, and the strong light fell on as beautiful a group as a painter could have chosen. Beside me, a young peasant mother of great beauty, with her infant at her breast, reclining in her cart ; beyond [at] the stern, long-haired husbandmen in their white draperies with crimson borders, the grey oxen, the rough boatmen. I fell asleep when we had crossed, and only woke at Kopremitz, where I stopped for the night. To-day I only came on here. To-morrow I hope to sleep at Carlstadt, and on Sunday at Fiume on the Adriatic. I expect to be in Vienna again on the 5th.

To continue the Journal :—

At Vienna I saw Count Kolowrat,[1] then Home Minister, and dined at the Embassy with Lord Jersey, Lord West-morland,[2] and Mr. Peel. October 11th went to Pottendorf (Prince Esterhazy's) to a shooting party, consisting of Sir R. Gordon, Magenis,[3] William Grey, Count Kolowrat (the son), M. de Flahault, Lord Jersey, Lord Westmor-

---

[1] Count Kolowrat-Liebsteinsky retired from public life in 1848, and died, at the age of 78, in 1861. His son had predeceased him, and this branch of the family then became extinct.

[2] Lord Westmorland was at this time ambassador at Berlin. Lord Jersey was his brother-in-law.

[3] Magenis was secretary of the Legation : Grey, an attaché.

land and Bourqueney—twelve guns. We shot on the 12th
at Eisenstadt, and killed 327 partridges, 58 pheasants,
and 91 hares. I returned by Prague to Dresden. At
Leipzig I went to a concert. Moscheles and Mendelssohn found me out, seized me and made me sup with them
—a pleasant evening—October 22nd. Then to Berlin,
where I saw Dr. Zinkeisen of the ' Staatszeitung,' and dined
with Lord Westmorland. Sailed from Hamburg to Hull,
and joined my mother and Hopie at Filey on October 30th.

November 7th.—Party at the Grove.

19*th* and 20*th.*— Shot at Sir James Flowers' at Eccles.

The following letter from M. Guizot refers to the very
bitter feeling which had been excited in England by the
marriage of the Duc de Montpensier, son of the French
King, to the Infanta Fernanda, sister of the Queen of Spain,
in shameless violation, it was generally believed, of the
distinct pledge of Louis Philippe and of Guizot. The
question of 'the Spanish marriages' had agitated the
statesmen of England and France for the last five years, but
had become more urgent as the girls approached the
marriageable age. It was clearly understood on the part of
the Queen of England and Prince Albert that a definite
agreement had been come to at Château d'Eu in 1845, that
Leopold of Saxe-Coburg—a cousin of Prince Albert and
brother of the King Consort of Portugal—should not marry
either of the princesses, and that the Duc de Montpensier
might marry Fernanda, but not till the Queen, her sister,
was married and had issue ; till, in fact, Fernanda was no
longer next in succession to the throne. When, however,
in July 1846, Lord Palmerston became Foreign Secretary,
Guizot, whose dislike and distrust of Palmerston amounted
to monomania, assumed that he was only waiting for an
opportunity to break the convention in the interest of
Leopold. He resolved to anticipate him, and pushed forward the marriage of the Duc de Montpensier and the
Infanta, which was celebrated on September 14th, at the
same time as the marriage of the Queen to her cousin, the
Duke of Cadiz. Under the circumstances, it is not surprising that public opinion in England took a very unfavourable view of Guizot's conduct in this matter. And this is
what Guizot said about it :—

Paris, November 19th.— . . . Your country, or I should
rather say some of your countrymen, are at present giving

one more example of the degree to which fickleness, blind
credulity, and ingratitude may be carried by passion and personal feeling.   For the last six years England has fully believed
in my sincere attachment to the *entente cordiale,* and in the
uprightness and integrity of my character. A question arises
in which I, a Frenchman, have thought and acted in a way
that does not happen to suit England, and in a moment I
am not only attacked, which is quite right and natural, but
I am no longer supposed to have any integrity, uprightness,
or sincerity.   All that has occurred during six years, all that
I have said and done, all the struggles I have maintained—
it all disappears like a puff of wind. In the twinkling of
an eye, your people forget all that they have thought,
believed, said, written, published ; and they think, say, and
write the exact opposite.

I have lived too long to be astonished at this ; but I
have too much esteem and real friendship for your country
not to be grieved and hurt by it.   I shall not be guilty of the
same fault.   I shall not change my feelings and language
towards England and my English friends because I find
myself at variance with them on some particular question.
I have still so much confidence in the sound judgement and
integrity of the English people, that I count upon finding
their opinion of me the same as it was, as soon as the
papers relating to the Spanish marriages have been issued,
and the facts—which, for the past three months, have been
ignored, misrepresented, and misunderstood, in so strange
and incredible a manner—have been publicly discussed. I
await that day with perfect tranquillity, and am now as
friendly to your country as ever I was. . . .

Endorsed—Lord Clarendon and Lord John Russell saw
this note.

Most quarrels arise out of a misunderstanding ; and in
this case a full knowledge of the correspondence and negotiations relating to this tangled affair does, to a great extent,
clear the French Minister from the charges of deceit and
duplicity which were hurled at him ; but not of having
acted hastily, unadvisedly, and in an unstatesmanlike manner,
on the promptings of personal dislike and ill-will. In Reeve's
biography, however, the affair has no further place, and

indeed is brought forward here mainly as an illustration of the very peculiar and confidential manner in which Guizot endeavoured to utilise his correspondence with Reeve—known to him, it must be remembered, as a leader-writer on the 'Times.'

The Journal for the concluding months of the year mentions a few matters of social interest :—

November 23*rd.*—Dined at Lord John Russell's. Duchess of Inverness, Pr. Löwenstein, Ashleys, &c.

December 4*th.*—Met Tennyson at the Procters'.

8*th.*—Dined with Thackeray to meet Tennyson.

Towards the close of this year I became more intimate with Bunsen, who recommended me to Prince Albert, to write a paper on our relations with Portugal.

December 26*th.*—Dined with Bunsen.

27*th.*—Went to the Grove, where I met the F. Elliots, Lady Macdonald, and the Lewises.

31*st.*—To Bowood, where I ended the year.

From Chevalier Bunsen

Carlton Terrace, January 1st, 1847.

MY DEAR MR. REEVE,—I have to thank you for your kind letter. I returned yesterday from Windsor, and hastened to communicate to you that the Prince, to whom I had occasion to communicate the tenour of your letter, will be very happy to confer with you personally on the subject. He finds your proposal perfectly just, and intends without delay to make the necessary communication to Lord John Russell. He is very desirous to see you. If you could be at Windsor, for instance, to-morrow, either very early, viz. about half-past nine or ten, or a little before two o'clock, you would probably have the best opportunity of seeing His Royal Highness quite at leisure. Baron Stockmar is the person after whom you will have to inquire when you arrive at the Castle. The Prince has spoken to him on the subject very fully, and Baron Stockmar will be happy to enter into communication with you on the same.

I shall probably go on Monday to Broadlands, and should be very happy to see you before ; for instance, on Sunday (by

2 o'clock) if you go to-morrow to the Castle, or on Monday morning, if that suits you better. This evening I have four German philologers and philosophers and one English (Donaldson, the Varrionianus) at dinner : it is too late to take the liberty of inviting you to dinner, but should, against all probability, you be quite alone this evening, we should think it a particular kindness if you would treat us as friends, and join our German party.

P.S.—The Prince sends me word this moment that there is a great hunting to-morrow ; but that he hopes you will be able to come on Sunday, either a little before 10 o'clock or a little before 1 o'clock.

This letter Reeve got as he came back from Bowood, and noted in the Journal :—

January 4th.—Returning to town, I found a summons to Windsor, and went down at once. I saw Baron Stockmar, lunched at the equerries' table, and then had a long political talk with Prince Albert. He asked me to examine the Portuguese treaties for him.

February 8th.—The Prussian Constitution arrived. Bunsen greatly excited.

12th.—I went to a Levee. The Queen very gracious. I had not been to Court for five years.

23rd.—Breakfast with Milnes. Sir Stratford Canning, Bancroft, Buller, Lord J. Manners.

27th.—The Prince was elected Chancellor of Cambridge. During all this time I saw him frequently.

Hunted a good deal with the Queen's hounds. Bought my horse Hazard for 70 guineas. Intimate with Prince Löwenstein, Prussian Secretary. Mendelssohn was in London.

From Lord Clarendon

April 1st.—I had some talk with Lord John about the expediency of rousing public opinion and informing the people of England that they are not the powerless, effete community which Foreign Powers delight in thinking them. I told him that this, although difficult, might be possible if the Government and the press acted together ; but that the latter would become ridiculous, and perhaps mischievous, if it blew up a great fire and the former had nothing to cook by it. He quite agreed, and was very glad to hear I thought the 'Times' would assist in this national work ; but he wished it to be postponed for a while, and until its absolute necessity was demonstrated. There is something like an *entente* proposed by France respecting Portugal and Spain, and it has been responded to in a becoming spirit. We shall see what ensues, but I do not expect that the divergent interests of England and France will ever run in the same line. As we have not, or ought not to have, anything to be ashamed of in our foreign policy, I believe that a frank avowal and steady pursuit of our intentions would be the best way to keep on good terms with France.

Grosvenor Crescent, April 20*th.*—I have spoken to Lord Lansdowne, who is as certain as I am that no such instructions have been given as those you mentioned to me this morning· Seymour has only been told that, in the event of our mediation being declined by either party, the three Powers— England, France, and Spain—would then take counsel together as to the course they should pursue. So Delane may be easy as to anything that has hitherto been published. I asked Lord Lansdowne what he thought of the articles in the 'Times' upon Portugal? He said they told the exact truth in the best possible tone, and that he thought, on reading them, there was not a word that he would wish to alter.

The Journal here notes :—

May 4*th.*—Jenny Lind's *début* in ' Robert le Diable : ' triumphant success. I was in Delane's box. On the 13th saw her in ' La Sonnambula.' That was her best part.

14*th.*—Prince Albert had me asked to the Queen's Ball.

19*th.*—Party at Mrs. Grote's to Jenny Lind.

29*th.*—The Prince held a Stannaries' Court in the Council Chamber.

At Holland House a good deal. Austrian Embassy Ball. Kirkman Hodgson had recently married Miss Butler. Went to see them at Kingston Hill.

July 30*th.*—To Norwich. Dined with Bishop Stanley.

Meantime Lord Clarendon had accepted the office of Lord Lieutenant of Ireland, vacant by the death of the Earl of Bessborough on May 16th; and his letters have thus a very singular interest in their relation to the history of Ireland during the troubled years which followed.

From Lord Clarendon

Vice-Regal Lodge, July 19th.—I ought long ago to have thanked you for your two interesting letters, but I have almost less time at my disposal here than in London. The whole day is taken up in talk, for my new acquaintances are garrulous, and nothing satisfies them but interviews. Then there is a great deal of general business, including the Poor Law, which latter is about to become the real government of the country; and with splendid hospitalities, as the lord mayor would say, and the long evenings they entail, my working hours are pretty well occupied. As yet I have no cause for complaint; men are civil and things are smooth; but the rub will be a month hence, when 3,000,000 persons now receiving daily rations are thrown upon the rates, which depend upon the resources of the country, which are *nil*! There will be work for all the Queen's horses and all the Queen's men to collect the rates, which they of course won't do; and then to keep the peace, in which, I have no doubt, they will equally fail.

The wounds inflicted by the articles in the 'Times' are by no means healed, and I have had to endure many jeremiads upon the injustice to Ireland that has been committed. It certainly would have done good if there had been more discrimination between the good and the bad landlords. The former do exist, though Delane may not believe it; and I have evidence of the zealous, self-sacrificing way in which they have performed their duty throughout the late period of suffering. Old and young Ireland have a quarrel, which may eventually be of public advantage, by breaking up the organised agitation which has so long been the curse of this country. In the meanwhile, moral persuasion always waylays physical force, and beats it within an inch of its life. The former—i.e. old Ireland—called in the navvies in support of their candidate, Mr. M'Tavish (a Yankee convert to

Repeal), and against Mr. Torrens M'Cullagh, a most respectable man, author of the 'Industrial History of Free Nations.' Upon this Dr. Cloyne, the R. C. parish priest, issued an address, which I enclose, for I think it excellent ; and if Delane would take notice of it, and make it the text of a short sermon to the priests, with words of encouragement upon the wide field of good now open to them, it would have a most beneficial effect throughout Ireland, and I should be very much obliged to him, as the young priests now are the quarter from which most mischief is to be apprehended. . . .

V.-R. L., August 2nd.—Judging by the spirit in which this new Parliament is being procreated, it will be a charming composition when it comes to maturity. The constituencies are like the witches in 'Macbeth,' each throwing some detestable condiment into the cauldron. 'How the Queen's Government is to be carried on ' I don't exactly see ; but I feel sure that neither Lord John nor any of his colleagues will attempt it discreditably ; and, if they have not an efficient support, and a fair prospect of doing the business of the country in a manner the very reverse of last session, they will make way for those who think they can do better. Unfortunately, however, this will not solve the difficulty ; for if conservative progress, which is the character of the present Administration, cannot form a strong government, I know not in what quarter that *desiderandum* is to be looked for ; and as I care nothing about party, and very much about the country, I confess I feel very uneasy about our prospects, with all the foreign and domestic troubles that are in store for us.

It is impossible to tell what will be the result of the elections here. We ought to have gained, and we shall probably lose, a few seats, entirely owing to the malevolence of the Repealers, who have just enough power left to do mischief. The physical force men, whenever they meet for spouting, have to be escorted home by two or three hundred police, or not one of them would escape alive from the moral persuasion party, who miss no opportunity of getting up a ferocious row. They very nearly killed Sir William Somerville, the other night, at Drogheda, the mob having been excited against him by Maurice O'Connell. . . . Everything is in a state of *gâchis* just now. Nevertheless, I believe that delusions are gradually becoming fainter, and that in time the people will understand their real friends and their true interests. The Repeal feeling is still strong throughout the country. It could not be otherwise after so many years' agitation; but the Repeal party is weak in talent, influence, and money. They are all jealous of each other, and quarrelling among themselves; and though the bubble may not actually burst, I look to its gradually disappearing. . . .

Normanby[1] says, in a letter I received yesterday: 'Here [Paris] the ministry may struggle on for a few months, but it is doomed. A government may recover a sudden fall, but this one has been gradually sinking deeper and deeper in the mud, and would have disappeared altogether but for the royal hand under their chins. Nothing can be more disaffected than public opinion throughout France; and, depend upon it, the dynasty of July never saw so sickly an anniversary.' I dare say this is true, and that a vast deal of smouldering discontent exists.

In August Reeve went for a six weeks' holiday, of which the Journal gives a very brief notice :—

August 16th.—To Scotland. Landed at Invergordon on the 19th. Drove by Tain to Meikle Ferry and Uppat. 25th.—Met G. Dempster. 27th.—First visit to Novar. Shooting there with Butler-Johnstone.[2] Stayed there till September 5th; then to Dunoon by the Caledonian Canal. Bad sprained ankle. Back to Kirklands on the 22nd, and to London on the 25th.

From Lord Clarendon

V.-R. L., September 18th.—I have hitherto had a tolerably prosperous time here. The relief committees have given food; the harvest has given work; and a glorious summer has checked fever among the people and disease in the potatoes. But *ces beaux jours sont passés*, or nearly so; for repudiating ratepayers are to take the place of undiscriminating committees; landlords and farmers declare they can't

---

[1] At this time ambassador at the French Court.

[2] The Hon. Henry Butler, younger son of Lord Dunboyne, took the name of Johnstone in 1834, on marrying Isabella Margaret, sister of Munro of Novar, and niece and heiress of General Johnstone of Corehead.

employ labourers ; doctors promise pestilence again ; and if the wet weather does not destroy the potatoes, their price will place them beyond the reach of the poor, for not above one-fourth of the usual amount were planted. So I look forward to a troublous winter, the difficulties of which will not be smoothed by England; for even if John Bull were willing to give, Charles Wood is unable.

The real difficulty, however, lies with the people themselves. They are always in the mud ; and when they have screamed out to Hercules, they have no doubt about having done everything necessary for extricating themselves. Their idleness and helplessness can hardly be believed. Still I cannot bring myself to despair. I can already detect germs of progress, which, if they can but be protected from their numerous assailants, may ripen into something good. A spirit of exertion and self-reliance, altogether new in Ireland, is manifesting itself ; landlords are beginning to bestir themselves, and to understand why hunting, drinking, and mortgaging bring their estates to auction, and themselves to jail.

After a short stay, Reeve again left London, as is told in the Journal :—

October 9th.—To Windsor to see the Prince. Visits to Hadzor (Galton's), and Crewe, where I met Sir Brooke Boothby. Thence to Dublin on the 30th, on a visit to Lord Clarendon, who was Lord-Lieutenant. Major Mahon murdered [1] [on the evening of November 2nd]. Home on November 7th.

Called on Lord John Russell in Richmond Park, by Clarendon's desire.

From Lord Clarendon

V.-R. L., November 12th.—Many thanks for your letters and for telling me that your visit here was agreeable. It was so, particularly so to us all, and its only fault was being much too short. I was glad on every account that you came here, for I know it is impossible to understand Irish

---

[1] Shot by two masked men as he was returning from a meeting of the Roscommon Board of Guardians.

difficulties without learning something about them *sur le lieu*; and they are so numerous and so odd, that I am sure you would have become immensely interested in them if you could have stayed a little longer. Things have so far improved since you went that no one has been murdered; but many have been threatened, and a terrible, though most natural, panic prevails. Even the Repealers are all in favour of restricting the indiscriminate possession of arms, and I am convinced that the suspension of the Habeas Corpus Act would not be unpopular, because people would have a certain sort of confidence that it would not be abused or made ancillary to landlord outrages, but that the prevention and punishment of crime would be the sole object of those to whom the extraordinary power was confided. If order can be restored without such power, and simply by an Act of Parliament, which partook more of a police regulation than a suspension of the law, it would, of course, be greatly preferable; and that is what I should like to try first. But, in one way or other, security to life and property must be given; and I certainly won't remain here for the purpose of not maintaining order or vindicating the law.

And so, according to the Journal—

Closed the year at the Duff Gordons', with Thackeray and Higgins.[1]

My diary ends: 'Remarkable depression in the last months of this year in society; general illness; great mortality; innumerable failures; funds down to 76; want of money; no society at all.' A curious presage of the impending storm!

---

[1] More generally known now as 'Jacob Omnium.'

CHAPTER VI

THE FRENCH REVOLUTION

THE storm was not long in following the presage of the old year. In February 1848 the Revolution broke out in Paris, and quickly spread through France and through Europe. Reeve was laid up at the time with a severe fit of gout, but during his illness he took the keenest interest in the current history, and wrote constantly in the 'Times' about it. 'My articles there,' he entered in the Journal, 'would be the best key to what I thought of those events.' They form, in fact, the only one ; for in the Journal itself they are barely even mentioned. But he was fortunate in his friend Simpson's being still in Paris, and from him he received very full accounts of what was going on. Simpson's letters were charming, and Reeve considered he was doing a good turn to his two friends—Simpson and Delane—by bringing them acquainted with each other. Simpson became the 'Times'' correspondent in Paris ; and continued so during the revolutionary frenzy. His letters to Reeve, the letters to the 'Times,' with some articles contributed to 'Blackwood's Magazine' and 'Bentley's Miscellany,' were afterwards recast and published under the title of 'Pictures from Revolutionary Paris,' perhaps the best account of the state of Paris and of the Revolution of 1848, as they appeared to an intelligent looker-on. On his return to England, Simpson settled in London, where he attained both reputation and profit as a dramatic writer. Living in South Kensington, and a member of the Athenæum Club, he continued on intimate terms with Reeve till his death, at the age of 80, in 1887 ; though the personal intercourse and his literary engagements put an end to the interesting correspondence.

Through 1848, however, the most valuable of Reeve's papers are the letters which he received from Lord Clarendon, or from Lord Clarendon's mother, Mrs. Villiers, who, in the pressure of business, frequently acted as her son's amanuensis. These letters have an extreme interest, not only with reference to the affairs of Ireland, which Lord Clarendon himself was conducting or studying at first hand, but also as to affairs on the Continent, which, though from a distance, he examined and discussed as a diplomat of the past, a foreign minister of the future.

From Lord Clarendon

Dublin Castle, January 21st.—I don't defend the line taken with regard to Greece ; [1] not because I think anything has been said that the Government of Greece does not deserve, but because things may be set forth in a manner to defeat the object in view, and to create sympathy with the offenders. Bad results must ensue from the use of language that diplomacy and society are alike interested in repudiating.   I cannot, however, agree with you that the exasperation of people abroad against Palmerston is perfectly boundless.   It is the policy of Guizot to proclaim that such is the case ; and through his many agents he has everywhere the means of exacerbating the jealousy that exists against England. We may be isolated at this moment ; but if Palmerston were the blandest of God's creatures, with what Power could we at this moment fraternise ?   With respect to Spain, Italy, and Switzerland, are we not compelled to oppose France and Austria ? and as regards the two latter, have we not done so successfully ? and must we not be prepared for all the phials of wrath that Metternich and Louis Philippe can pour upon us ?

Up to the time I left London there was little to object to in Palmerston's despatches, and such objections were gene- rally removed ; but for the last six months I know absolutely nothing of what he has done beyond what I have seen in the newspapers ; and unless you are certain of the fact, I am unwilling to believe that all he writes is now in the tone of the Greek despatch, and that Lord John has consequently ceased to exercise any control.

The tone taken by the 'Times' in the Hampden [2] con-

---

[1] The Greek dispute came more prominently before the public in 1850, when much of the correspondence relating to it was officially published (*Parlia-mentary Papers*, 1850, vol. lvi.).   See *post*, p. 218 *et seq.*

[2] 'Dr. Hampden, who was accused of heterodox opinions, and whose appoint-ment to a canonry at Oxford had already occasioned an explosion of bigotry

troversy has grieved me very much, not on account of the Government alone, and still less on Dr. H.'s account, about whom I know nothing, but upon public grounds; and I attach such immense importance to the tone taken by the 'Times' upon any great question, that it afflicts me when that tone is in my opinion leading to mischief. The contest is an open manifestation of a revival of [the struggle between] Protestant and Roman Catholic principles, within our own Church. The predominance of the latter would be quite fatal to all we are accustomed to regard as most precious. Yet that is what our High Church is now aiming at, in emancipation from the State. It intends to be all things to all men, not only in the next world but in this; to supersede virtually the actual governing powers, and to establish in their stead the worst of all despotisms-the theocratical. That at least is the tendency of its present movement; it soon will be its undisguised object; and I can't bear to see the 'Times' throwing its weight into the anti-social scale.

However, I won't embark on this subject, for it would carry me far beyond the time I can crib from other things, so I will conclude by saying, what I know you will be glad to hear, that the Commission and the new Bill [1] together have

---

and intolerance in the Church, was raised to the See of Hereford by Lord John Russell, chiefly, as it would seem, as an act of defiance to the clerical party. Hampden was a dull, heavy man, who made more noise in the world than he deserved, but he was not a bad bishop.'— *Greville Memoirs*, second part, iii. 109, note by Reeve. The objection at Oxford was to the appointment of Hampden as regius professor of divinity rather than as canon of Christ Church; but the controversy over this was now eleven years old, and Lord John possibly supposed that it was dead. As regius professor and rector of Ewelme, Hampden had been doing good work, and was popular; but, on the appointment to Hereford being made known, thirteen of the bishops presented an address of remonstrance, and the Dean of Hereford wrote to Lord John Russell, saying that he should vote against the election of Hampden. Lord John replied, 'I have had the honour to receive your letter of the 23rd [December], in which you intimate to me your intention of violating the law;' on which *Punch* neatly remarked—

> 'If brevity's indeed the soul of wit,
> Lord John has made a most tremendous hit.'

Hampden was elected in due course on December 28th, but the question was fought out at great length, and with much bitterness.

[1] The Coercion Bill, passed through Parliament in December 1847. On the state of public feeling at the time see *Greville Memoirs*, second part, iii. 103–6. For an outline of the condition of Ireland, Walpole's *History of England*, iv. 325–7.

far exceeded my most sanguine expectations. The convictions have put an end to the reign of terror, and the justice of the sentences has been so clearly established by the evidence that hardly any sympathy has been manifested for the guilty. All the firing at marks and carrying about arms have completely ceased; the guns are all stuffed into bogs and ditches; the farmers declare they can now sleep quiet in their beds, and the fear of having police quartered is manifested by resolutions to keep the peace and arrest evil-doers. Everything has been done in the manner and even at the hour that I intended; and from all quarters, even from people most confident that the Bill would fail, I learn that the people are completely cowed and admit that they must be quiet, for the law has got above them.

The 'Times' has written most admirably, and I wish you would tell Delane from me what great service he has done, and how particularly obliged to him I am for the articles on the Agricultural Instructor, which were really jewels of the first water. I am very glad he has taken up the Repeal rent paid by those who clamour the loudest for English money. That line will tell here, and if we could knock up the Association it would be a heavy blow and great discouragement to agitation. With little money in their till, and that vapouring fellow, J. O'Connell, for their champion, such an establishment ought not to exist much longer.

Many thanks for telling me what is thought in England of my goings on here. It is very agreeable to me, but always rather alarming to me, for fear of not coming up to the mark; and people who have bestowed an undue amount of confidence would consider themselves entitled to cast an unjust amount of censure; besides which, *las cosas de Irlanda*, like those *de España*, sometimes baffle all foresight or precaution; and the *vis inertiæ* and the great thwarting principle which animate ninety-nine out of every hundred Irishmen prevail over the best acts and intentions. It is a daily fight and one must never be caught sleeping at one's post. I should not despair of eventually doing some good by constantly making people do their duty, if it were not for the destitution. That increases daily, and threatens to swamp all men and things. Unless the social system is re-established upon

its potato basis, I don't see how we are to get on ; and yet
what a thing it is after the experience of the past to build
again upon rottenness !

From Chevalier Bunsen

March 7th.—I have Lamartine's manifesto and all
attaching to it, &c., &c., to our interview at Carlton Terrace
or the Council Office. What I have uppermost in my mind
to tell you is GERMANY. The English begin at last, and
slowly, to discover that there is such a country—yea, in
Europe ; yea, the land of their fathers—having now forty
millions, and those, by the law of Europe, and by the spirit
within them, as well as by mother-language, history of a thousand years, and literature of seven hundred, ONE nation. You
know the demands of Germany in 1813 and 1814 : you remember the (now incredible !) State Papers of Austria—not
only Prussian—in 1814 and 1815 respecting the erection of
a *Bundesstaat*, to all intents and purposes united towards the
Ausland. You know how Talleyrand and Count Münster
succeeded to blind and seduce Lord Castlereagh, and how the
whole ended in that *mauvaise plaisanterie* called *Bundesver-
fassung.* Klüber says much about it ; Stein will soon tell
his own story in his Memoirs, now about to be published by
Pertz. You know how we started from liberty of the press
as principle, and from unity of commerce and trade equally ;
how the ' Zollverein ' was the effort to do inorganically and
incompletely what the Pact had ordered the Diet to do
organically ; how the liberty of the press was abrogated by the
Carlsbader Beschlüsse—hypocritically called *provisorisch*—in
1820; how the twenty-two millions of good florins—two and a
quarter million sterling—taken from the French contribution
and consecrated for this purpose, were given feloniously, but
not inconsiderately—if that means ' without consideration '—
by Prince Metternich to Rothschild, first without interest
and then at 2 per cent. ; how the fortresses were not built,
because Austria held out against the whole of Germany that
the Rhine was to be covered by Ulm and not by Rastatt ;
how, even in 1840—twenty-five years after the Congress—
Frederick William IV. could not carry this point except by
giving 800,000*l.* sterling of his own to have both fortresses

built instead of one : how Austria then was obliged to regorge the money with the scanty interest, and how, in 1848, neither Rastatt nor Ulm is completed. What you cannot know, not being a German, is how, from 1820, there began a most systematic reaction, instigated by Metternich, executed by Prince Wittgenstein and Kampz, against all Liberal ideas, called *demagogische Umtriebe*, to find out the universal republican conspiracy directed by the Comité Directeur de Paris; how a whole generation was nipped in the bud by the orgies of police absolutism, from 1820 to 1840. Read Arndt's 'Erinnerungen,' as the faint, most loyal, and moderate expression of that feeling, and Vetter Michel—the most genial produce of that sort of the age—as the most extreme, and you have the never-yet-written history of German woe, and you can have a faint idea of what a German of the present generation feels. 1840, Vetter Michel began to breathe, and that breathing was a mild one. 'Er nahm sich vor die Geduld zu verlieren;' but he did not. Frederick William IV., 1847, had the immortal merit of showing the German mind in a sufficiently great fragment to give him a European voice. Let all Germans thank Frederick William IV. for having thus prevented Vetter Michel now appearing with the flaming sword of Archangel Michael, as in the last chapter of that popular prophet. But N.B., N.B., N.B., let the smaller princes 'bedenken zu dieser ihrer Zeit'—as the Gospel says, not to Jews only— that if they survive this present storm, instead of Ernest Augustus's brutal revolution and absolutism ; in spite of Brunswick pranks in 1830 and dulness since ; in spite of Hesse's atrocities, renewed in 1847, and all the *velléités* and open violations of charters, in Bavaria, Würtemburg, Baden, Darmstadt, Nassau, they may thank for it Vetter Michel's angelic patience and Frederick William IV.'s *chevaleresque* generosity and mediæval loyalty to Austria. Bassermann— a Baden Liberal, brother to the bookseller—spoke the word *before* the French Revolution, in the Chamber :—' Germany is defenceless and the German lawless—*rechtslos*—because there is no German parliament. We will have such a parliament ; besides the representatives of the thirty-eight princes, there must be in the Diet the representatives of the estates of the different German lands.'　This idea had been thrown out in 1814 ; had afterwards reappeared ; had been remembered by the comments upon our Zollcongresse and by the Prince of Leiningen's (the Queen's brother) remarkable Memoir of last year, which I enclose : but Bassermann spoke *the word*.　Welcker developed the idea of his colleague in the Chamber, in a beautiful speech.　Then the French Revolution came.　You see from the papers what has been done in Baden, Würtemburg, Nassau, and what is doing in these States and in Hessen-Cassel and Darmstadt.

Meanwhile Guizot and others of the late French ministry had come to London, the air of which, in time of revolution, they judged to be more salubrious than that of Paris.　The Journal notes :—

March 17*th*.—A long interview with Prince Albert on the conduct to be followed to Louis Philippe, whom Palmerston wanted to drive away.　The gout lasted till April 4th— nearly two months—but I attended old Mme. Guizot's funeral at Kensal Green on April 4th.　On the 10th we were all prepared to defend the office against the Chartists.

April 12*th*.—Dined at Bunsen's with the Prince of Prussia—afterwards Emperor William—Sir Robert Peel, Sir James Graham, Buckland, and Albert Pourtalès.

To Chevalier Bunsen

C. O., April 19th.

My dear Chevalier Bunsen,—Having been honoured in my life with the friendship of two of the most eminent statesmen of this time—yourself and M. Guizot—it has been my hard fate to differ from the authority of these illustrious names, and to go against the predilection of personal regard, in two important questions of contemporary politics.　However, as the Spanish marriages did not permanently dissolve the *entente cordiale* between the French minister and his very humble antagonist, H. R., so I hope that, though the Baltic ring with battle and the controversy extend even to these pacific shores, you will remain persuaded that no difference of opinion can operate the slightest diminution in my esteem and regard for yourself.　Though I confess I should plunge into the strife with far more alacrity if I did not know that Achilles is amongst the besiegers. What am I to say when the catapult which threatens Denmark bears no ram's head, but the honoured features of Bunsen?

I have read the pamphlet with great interest, for this subject has, for several years, attracted much of my attention, and I believe I am in possession of the leading German publications on the subject. You have given us the cream of them, and I am glad the question on the German side has been so ably stated. If it fails in your hands, in whose can it succeed?

But what a misfortune to Europe is this event! Instead of plunging into it, one would have expected that Prussia would have used every effort to avert it, for it has a strong tendency to leave Germany wholly unsupported in Europe. Russia has an undeniable *casus belli* under the Treaty of 1814, and you have deliberately thrown aside the support of this country to gratify a popular cry got up by Beseler and the 'Augsburg Gazette.' You may resort to the support of France; but when we see a French fleet in the Baltic it will be time for us to prick up our ears.

I have not the faintest idea of what Lord Palmerston and the Government think on this subject; but the public feeling is so vigorous and so universal against the German intervention that, even if the ministers were disposed to acquiesce in it, they would encounter a storm. This unhappy agitation has laid the basis of an Anglo-Russian alliance; and it is the triumph in Germany of the party who have for years been labouring to traduce the name of England and to destroy the independence of Denmark. Even you, who abhor these objects, are carried away by this crusade.

The Governments of Germany never would have originated or adopted this movement if it had rested with them. It rose from the people; it was fostered by popular agitation; and, though that be a recommendation in these times, I confess that, to my judgement, it is the severest condemnation. On a question of this nature the multitude errs; but it is evident that these discussions have served a remarkable purpose by virtually placing men like Dahlmann and Gervinus at the head of the German nation. Schleswig-Holstein has very materially contributed to the present political position of the sovereigns, ministers, professors, and people of Germany. If that be a good position, it has rendered you a great service; if bad, it has destroyed, or at least injured, you.

My pen runs on unconsciously, and I must have done. But although unconverted, and even convinced that the cause you have honoured by your defence is that of the Revolution, and not that of law and authority, I once more return you my sincere thanks. For my own part, all revolutions have the effect of throwing my sympathies into the opposite scale; and my only consolation is that my personal opinions in such matters are far too insignificant to have the slightest effect on the great changes of the world.

Ever yours very faithfully,

H. REEVE.

This was the beginning of a long and animated correspondence on the interminable Schleswig-Holstein affair. It is only introduced here to show clearly what were Reeve's views on the question—views which he stated fully and repeatedly in the columns of the 'Times,' to the annoyance of Bunsen and to the wrath of Germany, which—Bunsen wrote—'hates England more than it ever did Napoleon, for the Schleswig articles in the "Times;"' to the degree that a general vow has been taken in some southern provinces not to wear any article of English manufacture, in order to show the resentment of Germany against the insolent articles of the "Times."' Reeve's opinion, shared probably by most Englishmen, was that the attack of Prussia on Denmark in 1848 was iniquitous, and that her defeat was a thing to rejoice over; that the attack of Prussia and Austria combined, in 1864, was equally iniquitous, though it met with a lamentable success. One good has, however, resulted from it. The Schleswig-Holstein question, after being talked and written and fought about for nearly two centuries, has, for the present, been laid to rest. What the future may bring forth concerning it, for Denmark, for Prussia, and for the German Empire, it is impossible to say; but for us, in our time, there is peace. In 1848, however, the most serious question for England was the state of Ireland; as to which we are now fortunate in having Lord Clarendon's opinions at first hand :—

V.-R. L., May 10*th.*—Ireland has by no means checked my interest in foreign affairs, but they go at such a tremendous pace that it is difficult to keep up with them. Every country seems to jump twenty years in the night. Nothing has irritated me more than the ingratitude shown to the Pope, and the thought that his own people should adopt Brougham's views of him. I agree in every line of the article in the 'Times' of yesterday. If he is driven out, it will have an important effect upon the Catholic Church, which will set up for itself everywhere. Here, the loss of its head would make the tail even more dangerous than it now is; in France, probably it would be the instrument of the ruling power, whatever that might be, and think itself only fortunate if allowed to exist at all.

Our great *desiderandum* is peace. I don't say it should be maintained *à tout prix*, but our futurity depends upon it. If things keep quiet, trade and manufactures will revive, and the British belly—the seat of an Englishman's political opinions—being full, we shall hear less of wild reforms.

Here, the stream is going down wonderfully, and I have no reason to regret the course that has been taken, although Brougham and Stanley have clearly intimated they should have pursued a very different one. Nothing would have been so easy as to produce insurrection by too severe an application of the law; and, on the other hand, I needed only to hold up my finger to have had 50,000 Orangemen in arms, marching on the South, leaving everywhere traces of blood and sectarian hate that our grandchildren would not have seen effaced. Two hours' fighting in the streets of Dublin would have sufficed to cause a general rising in the country; and, looking at the strange and unexpected events on the Continent, and the Catholic composition of our army and constabulary, it would have been impossible to predict the issue. The great object, therefore, was to avoid collision anywhere, and that was best to be obtained by the imposing exhibition of force, and letting the evil-disposed see that we were thoroughly prepared for whatever they might attempt. This was really done without swagger and without fear, and the result has been that Dublin is almost the only capital of

Europe where during the last two months there has not
been a broken head or a broken window.

Young and old Ireland are covering themselves with
ridicule, and I have some means of keeping up dissension
among them, which you may be sure I do not neglect. I
need not say how glad I am that you have followed and
approved all that has been done.

V.-R. L., *June* 18*th*.—Whenever I can abstract my
thoughts from the Irish they turn to the Continent;
and as you know more than anyone about the latter,
I have been longing for the MS. which arrived yesterday.
Many thanks. It contained much that was entirely new to
me, and that gives rise to gloomy reflections. I had no idea
that the chances of peace with the Danes were complicated
by the popularity of the war with the Germans; I thought
they looked upon it as a *coup d'état manqué* of the King of
Prussia, and that he was desirous of retreating over any
decent bridge that England and Russia might make for him
by an Irish combination of moral and physical force. If,
however, he is coerced into proceeding, and the Danes are
encouraged by Sweden and Russia to resist, the question
becomes very serious. We have three months before us,
during which naval operations can be carried on to the great
damage and irritation of Germany; and it is next to impossible that all this should not lead to a general war ; an event
which might suit Continental anarchy, but which would be
most disastrous to England.

V.-R. L., *August* 17*th*.—Many thanks for your interesting letter. With the exception of hearing that the
people of Ireland were loyal and that the exchequer of
England was overflowing, nothing would give me greater
pleasure than the news of cordiality between the French and
ourselves. They could not have selected a better representative than Beaumont,[1] for he understands our faults and
our merits ; and if he is willing, he is quite able to *splice*
them with those of his own country. We cannot make a
more laudable commencement of harmony than co-operating
to keep the peace of Europe, and I think that our joint
mediation will nullify the effect of warlike clamour. I

---

[1] Gustave de Beaumont, the friend of Tocqueville ; see *ante*, p. 56.

confess, however, that I look upon the red republicans of Paris and the insolvency of France as better guarantees for peace than the new-born ambition to pull well with us; but, as the resources of the country are wonderfully elastic and will soon come into play again, I cannot reckon upon the international cordiality being very protracted. While it lasts, however, it is most useful, and should be turned to good account; but I should be sorry if, when catching at the shadow of French, we lost the substance of Russian alliance; and I think that Nicholas should be kept duly informed of the object and mode of our proceedings, and not be allowed to suppose that we are giving him the go-by.

The impossibility of union between the Italian States, their hatred and mistrust of each other, their boasting and their impotence, render it more difficult for the French to assist them than to refrain from it, while the conduct of Charles Albert has not been of a kind to inspire very lively sympathy or to justify any great sacrifice in his favour. The *labor et opus* will be to choke off old Radetsky; but if he will refrain from entering Piedmont, and the French can proclaim that he did so [in] consequence of their army of the Alps, things may yet come right. *Dieu veuille !*

Thanks for telling me that the mode of dealing with my little war here is approved of. The rebellion is scotched, but by no means killed, and would revive directly if the pressure of fear were removed. We have had a narrow escape. The organisation was nearly complete; and if the insurgents had been permitted to select their own time, instead of being forced to take ours,[1] we must have had a long and bloody struggle, the issue of which would, I hope, not have been doubtful, but there would have been a loss of life and property, and an amount of individual suffering, terrible to contemplate.

We are now about to enter on a fresh crisis—a famine, more extensive than in 1846 and incalculably more disas-

---

[1] By the suspension of the Habeas Corpus Act, which received the royal assent on July 25th. Smith O'Brien and his fellow-conspirators learned on the 22nd—the day the bill passed the Commons—that it was resolved on, and immediately took arms. On the 29th the 'rebellion' collapsed in Widow McCormack's cabbage garden.

trous, for the means of meeting it now are as nothing to what they were two years ago. A bad harvest here and an indifferent one in England must lead to another financial and commercial crisis—*et alors comme alors !* but I should like to go to sleep and not be called till August, 1849.

The Whigs are not *lucky* anyhow, and as an humble member of that body I think I shall have had a full share of fortune's favours—two famines, one period of agrarian murders and one rebellion, in little more than a twelvemonth. I shall probably be able to add another item or two to the list before Stanley, or G. Bentinck, or some other *Salvator Patriæ* comes to the rescue and takes us out of the pillory of office, never to return there, I hope, at least as far as I am concerned.

V.-R. L., August 21st.—Provided he doesn't mind wet, the Cholera will have *beau jeu* if he comes here and finds the whole population of the South and West dying of starvation ; for that I fear is the prospect now before them. They will be swept away like Hindoos by the cholera, and it will be almost a mercy that they should be spared more protracted suffering.

The Journal notes at this time—

Visits to the Longmans at Farnborough and to Woodham (with Delane) at Jesus College, Cambridge. Thence to Norwich and Cromer, where began my acquaintance with Mrs. Baring.[1] Shooting at Felbrigg, &c. The Norwich Festival took place in September. Met the Duke of Cambridge at the Palace. Mrs. Opie gave us a dinner. By Ely and York to Edinburgh on September 16th. Saw Lord Jeffrey at Craigcrook and Lord Cockburn at Bonaly. To Kirklands and then Novar, where I met Sir John Hippisley and Cornewall Legh on the 27th. Home on October 7th. Gustave de Beaumont had come to London as ambassador of the French Republic. Dined with him on October 10th. I think Tocqueville became foreign minister in the autumn.

October 27th.—At Windsor. Long interview with Prince Albert.

---

[1] Cecilia Anne, daughter of Vice-Admiral William (Lukin) Windham, second wife of Henry Baring ; a woman of cultivation and remarkable ability, which has been inherited by her sons.

November 15th.—Rossi was murdered in Rome. On the 23rd I gave a dinner to Lord Clarendon, M. Guizot, Charles Greville, Fred. Cadogan, John Lemoine, Woodham, and Dr. Southey. Hunted a good deal with the Surrey hounds. Dinner at Granville's on the 27th. On the 29th Charles Buller[1] died after an operation. Mrs. Buller came to my house.

The election of Prince Louis Napoleon as President took place in December.

From Lord Clarendon

V.-R. L., December 17th.—I should sooner have thanked you for your letter, but the many points reserved for my return, and the numerous palavers I have had to endure, make me worse off for time than ever. The French take care to provide the world with matter for wondering at them; and this result of universal suffrage is indeed marvellous. As they know nothing of L. N., they select him as their fittest governor; and as they have adopted a republic, they make the nearest available connexion of a fallen dynasty the president of it. But what next? I am surprised at the result of the poll. For some time past it has been clear that L. N. would win, but I did not expect that a French government, making unscrupulous use of its unlimited means, could ever be so dead beat.

Another curious thing is to observe how all men of note have laboured to place L. N. in his present position; and then, when they have put him there, all refuse to stand by him. They probably think to pull the strings and not be responsible for the way their puppet dances. This may be productive of mischief; and I am mistaken if Bugeaud, Changarnier, and one or two more don't cut out some work for Europe. They will all have an itch for Italian laurels, and I am glad that Austria has something to do at home and bears no goodwill to the Pope or she might give 'the Africans' a pretext for flying to the relief of they wouldn't know who, in Italy.

With respect to domestic affairs, I am convinced there is

---

[1] He was Reeve's next-door neighbour, in Chester Square.

not, nor has been, a particle of truth in all the rumours of changes that have been flying about, according to annual custom, a month or two before Parliament meets. Indeed, I have heard them discussed, in the best possible humour, by the parties immediately concerned; and since I left England I have heard from more than one person of Lord John's good spirits and improved health. He may of course break down when the active business of the session commences; and I am inclined to doubt if the Government could be carried on without him; for though, as a first minister, he may have defects, it cannot be denied that he has, and deserves to have, great weight in the H. of C. For recovering a rout and rallying his forces he is a Parliamentary Ney; and the whole machine would fall into disorder if he were absent for a month.

But if Lord John were compelled to resign from physical and not political causes, I really think that Sir George Grey would be the fittest man to succeed him. There is more stuff in him than the public are aware of, and I believe he would be found to rise with his difficulties, which is the best test of talent. Last session was in every respect a most trying one for a home secretary both in and out of Parliament; and, *consensu omnium*, he did admirably. His capacity for business is first-rate; no one speaks better, or is more ready in debate; his manners are conciliatory, his temper cannot be ruffled, he has the strictest sense of honour, and he is—what John Bull likes—a very religious man. We may go further and fare worse than him for first minister. I can tell you, too, that he takes the liveliest interest in foreign affairs, and that his views are as sound and wise as the best Englishman could desire, although he does not consider it within his province to meddle with subjects for which he is not immediately responsible. At present I see no prospect of his being placed at the head of affairs; but if, unfortunately for himself, he should be *dans cette galère*, he ought to have a fair trial, and no tocsin should be sounded till he gives ground for alarm.

We have awful work before us this winter, and I am dreading that in at least twenty unions we shall have deaths from starvation by wholesale. Delane has written some admirable articles, and I think the influence of the 'Times' is greater here than ever. There are some landlords doing their duty admirably, and working like heroes; and they are somewhat riled at being confounded with the bad ones, whom, however, they hate all the more for that. In time, I hope that England will create something like public opinion in Ireland.

The Journal winds up the year with :—

December 22nd.—Visit to Richard Taylor's in Cornwall. On the 31st to Bowood. Lady Davy there.

January 1st, 1849.—I hunted with the Duke of Beaufort's hounds on Lord Lansdowne's hack; but the party was overcast by news of Lord Auckland's death.

During the next four years the political interest, though occasionally diverted to other objects, was centred on the condition of France, which the Revolution had turned upside down, and where, as yet, there were no symptoms of a returning equilibrium. Prince Louis Napoleon had, indeed, been elected president of the republic; but no one in France supposed that to be finality. Patriotism, devotion, honesty even, seemed dead; the spoils of office seemed the aim of the political leaders; greed, selfishness, covetousness, were dominant; [1] and the fear was general that out of these and the attendant jealousy might spring civil war, anarchy, proscription —perhaps a new Terror. Everywhere there was uneasiness; everywhere there was alarm. Of this, however, the Journal makes no mention. It merely has :—

March 17th.—To Paris; first time since the Revolution. Léon Faucher was now minister of the interior. On the 22nd saw Rachel in 'Phèdre,' and went afterwards to the Elysée to see Louis Napoleon. Faucher presented me. The Prince was very civil. I never spoke to him again. Faucher gave a great concert and a great dinner; at the latter, on the 28th, I met Hugo, Berryer, and Horace Say. Returned to London on the 29th.

---

[1] Cf. the remarkable letter of M. Guizot, *post*, p. 343, in which he compares the state of things in France at this time with that in England under William III.

From Lord Clarendon

The Grove, April 20*th.*—I have seldom read letters more interesting than M. de Circourt's,[1] and I am much obliged to you for letting me see them. He collects accurate information from all quarters; his speculations upon it are always sagacious, and exhibit knowledge of different nationalities, and the unconstrained style of his English is really marvellous for a Frenchman.

The Austrians are in a sad hobble with their Hungarian war, and I am sorry for it, as the weakness of Austria is strength to German faction, and aid from Russia, although preferable to defeat, is little short of present disgrace, and may lead to future embarrassment. Bem appears to be a formidable fellow, and almost the only *homme d'action*, and organiser on a great scale, whom the revolutionary fermentation of the last fourteen months has anywhere brought to the surface. The Emperor of Russia cannot much longer remain inactive, and his own safety will justify him in not waiting till revolt breaks out at home. I should think his best course would be, if he really means conservation and not aggrandisement, to come to some amicable arrangement with the Turks about the occupation of the provinces while he keeps order in the neighbourhood.

If the French mean to restore the Pope and to secure for his subjects the blessings of liberty, they are likely to be detained long enough to learn what a particular fix they are putting themselves into. I hope they will be left alone in their glory, and that Austria will submit to their doing her work. Nothing but the jealousy of interference of other Powers can make them fraternise with the Romans; and if they don't do that, they must side with legitimate authority, as I suppose that dethronement of the head of the Church and the usurpation of his territory are not to be feared.

We start to-morrow morning for Ireland, and I do so with a heavy heart, for all is black and cheerless there.

---

[1] M. de Circourt was an old friend and frequent correspondent of Reeve's. Some of his letters of a later date are given in their place; but, however interesting, they are rather essays on the political situation, and were intended to be shown to a select few.

From the social point of view, the Journal here has—

Went the round of the studios with Novar.[1] Then followed the usual round of London engagements.

From Lord Clarendon

June 11th.—Many thanks for your interesting letter, which is full of undeniable and melancholy truths. A miraculous interposition seems necessary to save Europe from the abyss towards which it persists in marching; and as I am no believer in modern miracles, I expect an almighty smash before the summer is over, particularly if the weather happens to be hot, when the pulse of every man beats quicker, and he is more prone to excitement. When this occurs with millions of people already excited, it must tend to blind the judgement, and to favour wilfulness and folly.

Considering the difficulty of the task, I don't think the President's speech so bad. He has given the French people an inventory of their goods and chattels, and told them the state of their accounts; by promising nothing, he has not committed himself to what he can't perform; he has blinked all foreign questions except the one he was obliged to mention, and that one he has contrived to render unintelligible. I suppose the Austrians and Neapolitans and the Pope won't much care to contradict him; and if they do, he won't mind, as gaining time must be his object.

As for German affairs, I am afraid we shall wait long for a settlement of them, as so much depends on Austria. Her army is evidently demoralised, and I have great misgivings about the Russians. They have no good general, and their commissariat is sure to be bad, and their troops unable to endure much fatigue or bad climate; and I shall not be surprised if they are beaten by the Hungarians, who have certainly among them some men of dash and enterprise, quick in their measures, and well acquainted with the country; in short, just the qualities to bother such a slow cumbrous machine as a Russian army. I am glad the Prince of Prussia has got 100,000 men, but I hope he will know what to do with them.

---

[1] Munro of Novar, who formed a celebrated collection of pictures, which was broken up after his death. See vol. ii. p. 258.

Will you ask Delane if he wants a foreign correspondent, as I can recommend him a right good one, who is, moreover, very desirous to enlist into the service of the ' Times '?   It is M. de Marliani, who you may perhaps have met at Mrs. Grote's ; he is a great friend of mine, a Spaniard, and one of the most intelligent men and ablest writers I know.   He was at one time a senator in the Cortes, and tolerably well off, but is now poor, and would like to be employed in the way I have mentioned ; he cares not in what part of the world, as he is an excellent linguist, though I don't think he could write English letters correctly enough for publication.

When the session is near its close I think it would be very useful if Delane, when writing on Ireland, would recommend English M.P.s and the English public generally to visit this country, and to see for themselves what they hear and talk so much about.   There will probably not be much travelling on the Continent this year, and people might as well make a tour in Ireland as go to Scotland or Brighton.   It would tend to produce a better feeling between the two countries, and might lead to the investment of capital in land, which is the great desideratum here.

The outline of a six weeks' holiday is thus given in the Journal :—

August 17*th*.—Went to Crewe, where I found Lady Morley, Luttrell, the Henry Grevilles, and Brooke Greville. Thence, on the 28th, to Brougham.   Found B. making fire-balloons.   Stayed three days ; fell into the cellar and sprained ankle.   Thence to Edinburgh, Kirklands, and Novar.   There a fortnight in September, shooting.   Back to London with Lord Campbell on October 2nd.

The following letter from Lord Clarendon, which Reeve must have received during his holiday, calls attention to the facts that the Queen did not visit Ireland till after she had been twelve years on the throne, and that in the forty-nine succeeding years she has never repeated the experience.   We know that very good reasons for this apparent neglect have been alleged ; but all the same, the enthusiastic and warm-hearted people have naturally felt aggrieved by it ; and, in reality, the grievance is not merely sentimental ; for the absence of the Court, by making, or rather by leaving, Ireland unfashionable, has caused also the absence of summer visitors, of settlers, of capital, of material prosperity, and has perpetuated, amongst the English, a singular ignorance both of the people and the country. Lord Clarendon's letter goes far to strengthen the often expressed opinion that a second Balmoral amid the mountains of Kerry or of Donegal would have done much to prevent the chronic disaffection which has been the curse of Ireland ; an opinion which the welcome given to the Duke and Duchess of York in August 1897 seemed to justify and confirm.

V.-R. L., August 29th.—I am much obliged for your letter and kind congratulations upon the ' great fact ' of the Queen's visit. From various causes, this is the first year since she came to the throne that she could visit Ireland in comfort, and it would have been a mistake to miss the opportunity ; but when one considers how much might have gone wrong in bringing the sovereign and this excitable people into communion together for the first time, it is equally pleasant and strange that all went as if by clockwork, and as one could most desire the whole time her Majesty was in the country. She was enchanted with everything here, and she and the Prince really won all hearts by their tact and gracious kindness. I, of course, do not expect much permanent benefit from the momentary presence of the Queen ; and yet the people are so pleased at finding they were loyal and orderly, and so proud of having won the Queen's good opinion, that this may be a guarantee for future good behaviour. The guarantee would be strengthened if the Suspension [1] Act lasted a couple of years longer, in order that the people might be protected against themselves and their deceivers, and have time to be weaned from their bad habits ; and, strange to say, there would be no measure of protection so popular with all classes, excepting the professional agitators and a few editors. The latter are the monster nuisance of Ireland. We might defy them all if they had not destitution for an ally ; but until capital finds its way here, and land is properly owned and properly treated, and employment can, to a certain extent, be

[1] *Sc.* of the Habeas Corpus Act.

depended on by the peasantry, we must be exposed to political shindies.

The following is endorsed by Reeve :—' M. Guizot on the state of Europe.   Most remarkable.'

Val Richer, September 3rd.—If you were here, my dear Sir, you would quickly put on one side all fear that any active combinations or alliances would be formed by the great Powers of the Continent without England.   You may take it for certain that the French Republic does not think of such a thing, and would be very much afraid to think of it.   Should it appear to be absolutely necessary, she may possibly come to some agreement with Austria about Italy ; but even then in a half-hearted sort of way, and with a pretence of doing something quite different from the reality. There may be an exchange, and even a display, of courtesies between her and Russia : it is a little advance by the Emperor Nicholas, a little show of intimacy in return for there having been less noise in Paris than in London about Hungary.   In this there is nothing serious, nothing that really changes the situation, the base of which is that France, whether country or Government, is thinking of nothing but her own internal affairs ; and that unless some urgent and unavoidable case should arise, she has, at present, no foreign policy.   For what is left of it, she necessarily looks to you, because your friendship is the only one with which she can keep up a pretence of revolutionary policy while follow- ing a reactionary one ; a silly hypocrisy, which pleases the country, and which her Government—the Republican more especially—is neither strong enough nor bold enough to do without.   They may attempt, or feign to attempt, some- thing.   It is mere vain boasting.

In my opinion, the only good thing on which Lord Palmerston's policy can pride itself, is that by its revolu- tionary appearance, and by the friendly terms it is on with the French Republic, it exercises on it a soothing and restraining influence.   In this sense Lord Palmerston really contributes to the maintenance of the peace of Europe, which, in so many other ways, he disturbs and com- promises.

Austria, like France, is too much absorbed in her own internal affairs to turn her eyes abroad, except in case of necessity, for her own safety. Prussia is ambitious, and just now is very certainly in such a position that success abroad might help her in her difficulties at home. But by herself and her own unaided strength, she cannot obtain this success. She must have some strong, external support. Russia will not give it, for she could only do so at the expense of Austria and the Conservative policy. Nor do I think that you, notwithstanding your partiality for Prussia, will be disposed to give her this support, at the risk of initiating a bitter struggle, which must result in forcing France and Austria to unite. But without you, Prussia can neither originate nor carry out any scheme threatening to the *statu quo* of Europe. As to the Emperor Nicholas, I think I have already told you my opinion of him. Though a despot, he is but little ambitious, and though powerful, but little enterprising. He wishes to remain absolute in his own country, and to be the chief patron of absolutism in Europe. When the emergency arises, he will do what is needed to maintain himself in this position; but only when it arises. He will do nothing to anticipate it or to produce it; and I am disposed to think that he would rather it should not come too often to trouble him. He knows how to wait for what cannot be now; how to accept what is inevitable. He will steadfastly pursue the traditional policy of his empire, and will lose no self-offering opportunity of advancing it; but he will not meddle with nor devise new combinations. He has a sound judgement with a strong will, and is able to wield a despotic power or assume a chivalrous attitude; but he will weigh well the chances, and has no taste for adventures. You know as well as I do that in the present state of civilisation and of government in Russia, events depend entirely upon the judgement and character of the sovereign.

I therefore think that you in England may persevere in the evil courses in which Lord Palmerston is engaging you, without fearing any effective combination of the great Continental Powers, I do not say against you, but only without you. The internal condition of these Powers, or the dispositions of their Governments, will spare you the conse-

quences of the faults of your own. How long can this last ?
A long time, I think ; but not for ever. A man so narrow-
minded and so obstinate as Lord Palmerston can greatly
quicken the natural march of events.

I have amused myself in talking to you of Europe, and
have no time to return to France. Of great events, there is
none more important than the approach of the elections,
which, within the next two or three years, are to give us a
new President and Assembly ; and as to small events,
nothing but some slight changes in the cabinet when the
Assembly meets again in October. What seems to me most
probable is this. There is, at the present time, no one
strong enough to take the initiative in any important
measure, or bold enough to undertake the responsibility of one.
The Government will do what, from day to day, is necessary
to preserve the appearance of order—nothing more. The
ambition of honourable men goes no further. There are,
indeed, some few who propose to attempt something more
effective at the opening of the Assembly, and to seek deeper
for the root of the evil. I doubt it. We shall see.

In the meantime I stay quietly in my nest at Val Richer.
I receive a good many visits, which prevent me from working
as much as I should like. I do work, however, and hope, by
the end of the autumn, to publish a new edition of my
' Histoire du Règne de Charles I.,' with a new and somewhat
considerable addition, entitled ' Discours sur l'histoire de la
révolution d'Angleterre.' In a hundred or a hundred and
fifty pages I should like to recapitulate the history of your
revolution, and bring out its chief features, its alternations of
successes and reverses, and the true causes of its ultimate
success. I have not yet learned to believe that the great
experiences of a great people are of no use to others.

Adieu, mon cher monsieur. Mes respects, je vous prie,
à madame votre mère. Mes enfants vont très bien, et se
rappellent à son bon souvenir et au vôtre. Croyez-moi
toujours tout à vous.

GUIZOT.

From Lord Clarendon

V.-R. L., September 5th.—Many thanks for Circourt's
letter ; he is really a marvellous Frenchman to write such

English, and he has a talent for grouping together all possible contingencies into one melancholy *cadre* that is quite unique. The world would always be going from bad to worse, and running a gauntlet of catastrophes, if the Genius of Evil had it all his own way as completely as Circourt supposes ; but a counterbalancing power happily springs up in some quarter or another and limits the almighty smashes he predicts with so much reason and argument. Who would—e.g.—have expected the Hungarian problem to be solved, as it was, in a day? I understand that not a week before Görgey surrendered, Lord Ponsonby—all Austrian though his wishes were—could not conceal his apprehensions about the result of the war, and I doubt if anyone knows, except the high contracting parties, what led to the *dénouement*. The Russians have a very liberal mode of dealing with Gordian knots that they can neither untie nor cut, and the experiment that they found so successful at Varna in their Turkish campaign [1] may have been repeated in Hungary. Be that as it may, it is a right good job that such a conflict in the heart of Europe should be put an end to; and what an opening there is now for 'remedial measures,' as we Irish say! But I have more confidence in the moderation of Russia than of Austria.   There is something grand and generous in the nature of Nicholas that puts a check on his ambition and makes him value the good opinion of the world.

V.-R. L., October 4th.—This Turco-Russian affair is the most real danger that the peace of Europe has yet incurred, but it would seem passing strange that everybody went to war about the body of Bem.[2] A unanimous expression of opinion in England and France may still keep things straight ; but can we depend upon France? We may bark in concert

---

[1] In 1828. The story is told in Moltke's *Russians in Bulgaria and Rumelia* (English edition), p. 215.

[2] Why the body? It had a living soul in it ; a defect, however, which Austria would gladly have remedied. But not only Bem ; with him, Kossuth, Dembinski, and some five thousand others had taken refuge in Turkish territory. On the refusal of the Turks to deliver them up, Austria and Russia broke off diplomatic relations and prepared to enforce their claim, which was, in fact, authorised by existing treaties. On the other hand, public feeling, both in England and in France, ran strongly in favour of the Hungarians. Palmerston ordered the English fleet to the Dardanelles ; Tocqueville, then foreign minister in France, ordered the French fleet to Smyrna ; and before the implied threat the Eastern empires gave way.

with her, but will she be prepared to bite with us ?   I doubt
it.   Be that as it may, the article in the 'Times' of yesterday was excellent, and quite in the tone that England ought
to assume respecting this audacious assault upon the law and
usages of civilised nations.   There has been nothing like it
since the wolf ate up the lamb for troubling the water below
him ; and I can only suppose that Nicholas got into an
ungovernable passion, and sent off his messenger without
reflecting upon the possibility that the Sultan might not
eat dirt.   I am sorry for it, as it is the only great fault
he has committed during these two eventful years ; and,
having withdrawn his victorious army from Hungary and
made proof of moderation, his position was really a fine
one.

In the supposition, however—and it is a strong one—that
he admits his error, and that he has demanded what he
cannot get, how is he to back out ?   He will never proclaim
himself wrong, nor succumb to the opinion of that Western
Europe for which he professes such sovereign contempt.   If
he persists, are we really prepared for making, as well as
talking, war ?   Will the Hungarian sympathisers and Cossack
denouncers submit to be taxed 6d. in support of a principle
which involves neither cotton nor hardwares ?   It's rather
a fix, look at it as we will.   Much will depend on Austria,
who surely must care less about hanging Kossuth than
dealing with the 30,000 Frenchmen now in Rome and ready
to raise against her all the Carbonarism of the North of
Italy.   How often one has occasion to agree with Melbourne's dictum of 'Damn it ! why can't everybody be
quiet ? '

V.-R. L., October 14*th.*—I am really obliged for the two
articles in the ' Times,' which are admirable, and have had a
stunning effect here, where it is as well known as on the
Continent that the ' Times ' forms, or guides, or reflects—no
matter which—the public opinion of England.   It will, if anything can, put a curb on the mouths of these furious
Orangemen who, with their principles and their parsons, are
quite as subversive of law and order as the priests and Young
Irelandism. . .

Many thanks for the extract from M. de Circourt.   He

always alarms me, as he gives such good facts and good reasons for his opinions ; but something unforeseen happily prevents the fulfilment of his prophecies. It is clear, however, that to quarrel with Russia for a principle is *le cadet des soucis* of the President. I cannot but feel great anxiety till the answer comes from Petersburg, as Nicholas may possibly resent the disrespectful manner in which public opinion has been manifested towards him in England, and he must know that our naval hostilities would hurt him about as much as a gnat bite on his great toe.

The Journal notes visits in October to Bowood, and to Mr. Longman's at Farnborough.

From Lord Clarendon

V.-R. L., November 16th.—Pray let me have a line to say what you hear from Paris, and how Tocqueville has borne being dealt with so summarily. It will be very patriotic in him if he does not upset Rayneval. I know him—Rayneval —very well ; he is a hard-working, intelligent, worthy man, but not clever, or capable of dealing with great subjects ; he is an admirable subordinate, but not intended for a leader. I suppose that's what the President wants, if, indeed, his new cabinet is formed upon any system at all, and is not a haphazard result of his own wish for emancipation. As yet he has stuck firmer in the saddle than I expected ; but, to be sure, his animal has not kicked, but its ears are laid down, and it looks vicious, and as if it would not much care about being patted by him. The only thing I feel sure about in the *gâchis* is, that a republic without one single republican is an impossibility. How soon, or by whom, the *coup de baguette* is to be given that will transform it into something different depends, I suppose, on accident, or the more or less courage of L. B. to give effect to his own wishes.

The Journal has :—

December 18th.—The Gorham case was argued at the P. C. ; concluded by a ten hours' sitting.

19th.—Dinner at Procter's, with Harriet Martineau,

Carlyle and his wife, Thackeray, and Kinglake. Carlyle was so offensive I never made it up with him.

Visit to the Sartorises, in Northamptonshire ; took the horses, but the frost prevented hunting.

And the next year, 1850, began with a visit to Baron Parke, at Ampthill, whence, on January 4th, Reeve drove over to see the Duke of Bedford, at Woburn.

CHAPTER VII

THE 'COUP D'ÉTAT'

WHEN we now look back from a distance of nearly fifty years, it seems, at first glance, more than a little curious to find that the subject which was chiefly occupying the minds of Reeve and his correspondents in the early months of 1850 was not so much the state of France, still in the throes of revolution, but what we are now inclined to consider a mere trumpery quarrel with Greece. It is only by an effort that we realise that, uneasy as the state of France was, its uneasiness was mainly its own concern, and that England had neither intention nor desire to meddle with it. On the other hand, the quarrel with Greece, paltry in itself, appeared to rouse the sensibilities of France and Russia in a manner which threatened to become serious.

For some years past Greece, feeling itself strong in its very impotence, had committed outrages on British subjects, and had steadily refused all compensation or apology. A patch of land at Athens, belonging to Mr. Finlay, so well known as a Philhellene and the historian of Greece, had been seized for the king's garden, and a tardy payment of one-fifteenth of its estimated value had been offered. One Stumachi, an Ionian, and not improbably a thief, had been arrested in Greece, on suspicion, and tortured, in the hope of making him confess his crimes. A man-of-war's boat had been seized at Patras, and, though it was presently released, no apology had been given.

But these various grievances were brought to a head by the case of a certain Pacifico, commonly spoken of as Don Pacifico, the Portuguese consul-general at Athens, but a British subject, a native of Gibraltar. That he was a Jew had nothing to do with the matter as between Greece and England, though it was the first cause of the trouble. As part of the Easter celebration of 1847, the Athens mob broke into Pacifico's house, 'beat his wife and children, smashed his furniture, destroyed his papers, and carried off his money and jewels.' The minister at Athens was instructed to demand compensation; the several grievances were formulated; and when, after three years' negotiation, the affair seemed no nearer a settlement than it was at the beginning, the English fleet was ordered to Salamis Bay, Athens was blockaded, and a few Greek gunboats and small ships of war were seized. By the middle of February more than forty merchantmen had been detained.

The French offered their mediation; and, on this being accepted, sent Baron Gros to Athens to arbitrate between Mr. Wyse, the British minister, and the Greek Government. The blockade was temporarily relaxed; but, as Mr. Wyse and Baron Gros could not agree on the terms, the blockade was again enforced, and the Greeks, yielding to the pressure, paid the money demanded, and wrote the apologies which were insisted on. But the French were very angry at what they conceived to be the slight put on Baron Gros, and virtually recalled their ambassador; eventually, however, they were pleased to consider the vote of censure on the Government passed by the House of Lords on June 17th as sufficient reparation.

The letters of Lord Clarendon to M. Guizot show how the matter appeared at the time to two capable statesmen who were taking no part in the actual negotiations.

From Lord Clarendon

Dublin Castle, January 28th.—'Nothing of interest' is about the best news we can hope for from Paris. The President hates the Assembly, and the Assembly hates the President; but, as it won't provide the quarrel that Louis Napoleon is ready to pick with it, I have no doubt Guizot is right as to the rumbling on of the machine for a time; but the Red men would be almost capable of singing a Te Deum if Changarnier were deposed, for he is the cork that confines French effervescence. What can Louis Napoleon mean by making an enemy of the man who is loved by the army and feared by the National Guard?

Brougham writes to me from Paris 'qu'il a tout vu, tout entendu, et rien compris.' He gave me some curious statistical details of the minute subdivision and heavy taxation of land in France; and I wish he may furnish them to my lords, in answer to the fallacy of the untaxed foreigner against whom we cannot compete.

The Protection movement has altogether failed here, except in embittering the relations between landlord and tenant, and furnishing the demagogues with a cry of 'Low rents,' which is not a convenient one for the nominal owners of the soil. The Orangemen have likewise failed in a somewhat characteristic manœuvre of that party. There is no effort they have not made, by letters, personal canvas, threats and entreaties, to prevent people coming to the Levee and Drawing-room, forgetting, in the loyalty which they pretend to monopolise, that the attendance on such occasions is not upon the individual lord-lieutenant, but the representative of the sovereign. But everything here resolves itself into mean, vindictive personalities. The cabal did not succeed; for, though a few people were scared away, both Levee and Drawing-room were very full; and if they had not been, my night's rest would have been equally good.

If Croker has a vested interest in the 'Quarterly,' there is nothing to be said; otherwise such a long libel[1] is neither creditable nor advantageous to a respectable publisher. Rather a smart pamphlet has just been published here, called 'Calumny of Mr. Rigby against Lord Clarendon confuted and chastised,' which alludes to the transactions with Mrs. Clarke and with Lord Hertford in a manner which Croker will not much like.[2]

From M. Guizot

Paris, January 28th.—With this you will receive my 'Discours sur l'histoire de la révolution d'Angleterre,' which is just published here. It would be very kind if you would write a short notice of it for the 'Times.' I should

---

[1] 'Lord Clarendon and the Orange Institution,' in the *Quarterly Review* of December 1849.

[2] The publication of *Coningsby*, in 1844, had, for all time, saddled Croker with the name of Rigby. No one in political society had any doubt that he was the original of the not very flattering portrait. According to his biographers, indeed, he was 'a man of strict honour, of high principle, of upright life, of great courage, of untiring industry, devoted with singleness of heart to the interests of his country, a loyal friend, and in his domestic relations unexceptionable. No man was more thoroughly trusted by his friends or loved them more truly.' On the other hand, it may be said, with some certainty, that no man was more thoroughly hated and loathed by his enemies, according to whom there was no crime, in or out of the Decalogue, that he was not capable of committing; and the scandals to which Lord Clarendon refers—however false they may have been—were accepted as absolute truths.

like to be well understood in England, and no one can help
me in this so well as yourself.   I have sent copies to Mr.
Empson and to Mr. Woodham.   I hope Mr. Woodham will
undertake an article on it for the 'Edinburgh Review.'   I
have almost a right to expect it, and I shall be much pleased
if he will do it.   Is he still at Jesus College, Cambridge,
although married ?

From Lord Clarendon

Dublin Castle, February 6th.—Switzerland is going to be
a fresh embarrassment evidently, but I don't think Palmerston is responsible for that in any way; for, first, Switzerland always has been the refuge for revolutionists, and on
that account a source of uneasiness to *limitrophe* powers in
agitated times ; and second, the issue of events in 1847 was,
upon the whole, more proper and conducive to peace than
the one Guizot aimed at.   It was the policy of resistance and
nothing else, as he himself has avowed; and events have
proved that he miscalculated his power and misunderstood
the signs of the times.

On February 19 Count Nesselrode addressed to Baron
Brunnow, the Russian ambassador in London, a despatch
on the attitude of England in her dispute with Greece,
claiming that as the kingdom of Greece existed not by its
own strength, but by the guarantee of Russia and France
equally with England, these Powers ought to have been
informed of the intention to enforce the English claims.
This despatch arrived in Paris on March 2nd, with a copy to
the Russian ambassador there, who communicated it to
General Lahitte,[1] the minister of foreign affairs.   It arrived
in London probably on the same or the next day, and was,
in due course, presented to Lord Palmerston, by whom it
was laid before Parliament on May 17th.[2]   But long before
that time—on March 9th—thanks to Guizot, Reeve was able
to present the readers of the ' Times ' with a summary of it.
How Guizot obtained it does not appear; but this is the
substance of what he wrote about it.

Paris, March 7th.—There is no way of getting the actual
text of the despatch which you naturally wish to have, but

[1] Vicomte Ducos de Lahitte.
[2] This despatch and the whole story of the dispute with Greece are in
Parliamentary Papers, 1850, vol. lvi.

I send you a full and exact summary of it. I hope it will reach you in time. The passages in inverted commas are not exact quotations, but the differences are slight.

Je n'ai pas le temps ce matin de vous dire un mot de plus. On signe, ce soir, le contrat de mariage de ma fille. J'ai mille petits soins qui prennent le temps comme les grandes affaires.

At Easter, Reeve went for a few days to Paris, where he saw a good deal of the Princess Lieven, the high priestess of political and diplomatic gossip; and—as noted in the Journal—

March 31*st*.—Dined with the Lamartines, and went with them to see the 'Barbiere.' Returned to London on April 5th.

I saw a good deal of Drouyn de Lhuys, then French ambassador in London. He was recalled on May 15th.

I wrote the criticism in the 'Times' on the Exhibition of pictures (Royal Academy) this year. Saw Rachel in 'Polyeucte' and 'Adrienne Lecouvreur.'

From Lord Clarendon

V.-R. L., April 26*th.*—I have not time this morning, nor indeed have I sufficient information, for entering fully upon the Greek question—the most important of all at this moment; but I will mention one or two points upon which I am disposed to take a different view from yours. In the first place, although much that is improper may have taken place about sending and withholding instructions, and the protracted negotiation is evidence of misunderstanding, still I cannot think that Palmerston would venture to speak as positively as he does in his 'Morning Post' articles if he had not some reason to expect a satisfactory conclusion.

Second, it is to me quite evident that Russia is fanning the flame at Athens, and is the main cause of this wretched business not being settled. The advice of Nicholas is seen through and almost denounced by the 'Times' correspondent.

Third, as to breaking up the joint action of England and France in Greece, it has never existed; the policy of the two countries has been divergent, and their agents have lived like cat and dog for the last twenty years; in fact, it was almost coeval with the establishment of a monarchy in Greece. *Vide* what the ' Times ' correspondent says about Coletti; he was entirely upheld by France, and no country in Europe ever had such banditti for ministers as Greece; as such they have acted, and it has been impossible to treat them as men actuated by the commonest motives of honesty. To treat such people now as a succession of injured innocents creates erroneous impressions; and to argue that because a nation is weak it may offend against others with impunity is unjust and leads to dangerous consequences.

Fourth, I cannot admit that, because the independence of Greece has been guaranteed by three Powers, either of these three is bound to obtain permission of the other two before demanding reparation for injury; for this would imply the right of the two to withhold it, and the third must either quarrel with them or consent to go without redress.

Fifth, I am utterly at a loss to comprehend by what right, or according to what interpretation of the law of nations, the Emperor of Russia could justify an embargo upon British ships in the Baltic ports because he was offended with the policy of England at Athens; and I am sorry that you should view such a measure as little offensive to the people of England. For my part, I can conceive nothing more calculated to excite their indignation or to procure popularity and support for Palmerston.

Sixth, the Emperor [of Russia] might put himself at the head of a crusade against our Continental policy, and might find many governments, great and small, ready to back him; but governments are not everything nowadays, and the question is, how many nations would support him, even upon the supposition that they execrate us with all their hearts? The Austrians were not so delighted with his assistance in Hungary to make them eager to receive another Cossack on their territory. Throughout Germany, and more especially in Prussia, the approach of a Russian army, favoured by the governments, would be the signal for universal revolt. If he marches on Constantinople, would France approve or be a passive spectator?   If he attempts to bring out his fleet against us, how soon would it be demolished?

I don't say one word in defence of the whole or any part of our foreign policy. I say nothing of the nature of our claims upon Greece, still less of our manner of enforcing them ; and I simply affirm that the points I have indicated above should all be taken into consideration when viewing the past and present state of this unfortunate question and the future results to which it may lead. Palmerston may be all wrong, and I am quite ready to admit it ; but I am very certain that Nicholas is not all right ; and knowing as you do the exceeding interest I take in the 'Times,' and the exceeding importance I attach to whatever it promulgates, you will not be surprised at my regretting the warmth with which it occasionally takes up Russian views.

V.-R. L., May 24th.—I have not written lately because on the one engrossing topic, about which I should naturally write, I felt I had not sufficient data to form an opinion. Palmerston is very unpopular, and it is quite natural that the British public should sympathise with a weak State, and resent anything like oppression on the part of a powerful country ; but, on the other hand, it is not just to run a man down unheard, and the more I disapprove of his general conduct, the more inclined I am to distrust my own judgement upon any particular act of his, until I have the evidence on both sides before me.   I felt especially bound to put a check upon myself in this case, because I have a very bad opinion of King Otho.   I know also that no government in Europe, and least of all the French Government, having the power to assert its rights, would for an unlimited period allow those rights to be insolently disregarded ; but the mode of enforcing them, the real cause of their not being recognised by the Greek Government, and the manner in which the negotiation was conducted, both at Athens and London, were matters upon which reliable information was too scanty for any impartial person to form a conscientious opinion.

Even at this moment, and not knowing what passed last night in the H. of C., I cannot say that my mind is made up ; but I have read the papers laid before the National Assembly, and even from this French version of the case—which must be the worst view for England, and will probably improve when Palmerston's case makes the whole complete—I am bound to say that the unfavourable view I was disposed to take has been very materially modified. I have looked at it entirely as an A and B case, and have endeavoured to divest myself of all prejudices for or against individuals or countries ; and I declare I can find nothing on which to found a charge of bad faith, which, nationally speaking, is the most important point of all. There may have been delay, or haggling, or want of courtesy—those are matters that regard the individual ; and if there was no cause for them, they are to be regretted and censured, but they don't touch the national honour.

We have certain claims against Greece, and we have in vain endeavoured to obtain redress. There may be exaggeration in the claims, but Russia herself has long ago admitted their existence ; and as I think it was perfectly competent to us to enforce them without, in the slightest degree, compromising the independence of Greece, so I consider we were in no way called upon to announce our intentions to the other two guaranteeing Powers ; nor do I think they were called upon to interfere, nor entitled to resent what we did, except as concerned the territorial question of the two islands. They did so, however. Russia wrote an angry note, and France volunteered her good offices ; but I am by no means clear about the spirit and intentions with which that offer was made. That there was a desire to put an end to hostilities which would have produced disagreeable feelings in France I have no doubt ; but as Lahitte, and the Legitimist party of which he is the organ, must have felt towards Palmerston in February much about what they do now, and as the alliance of France with Russia was then very close, and the desire to render it closer very great, I am by no means sure that the main object of the mediation was not to humiliate England.

The letter which follows is endorsed in Reeve's hand :—
' M. Guizot on the recall of Drouyn de Lhuys and English foreign policy. I showed this to Lord Lansdowne and Lord Aberdeen.'

Paris, May 24th.—I do not know, my dear Sir, if the President wants to dismiss General Lahitte. I do not think he does; but I know very well that he cannot. Thanks to the articles in the ' Globe,' to the attitude of your Embassy, and to the tattle of your Foreign Office and its friends, and of Lady Palmerston herself—as we hear by letters from London—the affair is assuming great proportions here. The dismissal of General Lahitte would cause a rupture with the majority of the Assembly, the leaders and their followers; consequently the formation of a government of Cavaignac, Lamoricière, Lamartine, &c. &c., and therefore the, more or less direct, triumph of the *Montagne.* General Changarnier would also break with him. The President is not in a position to do, or support, such things. It is always wrong nowadays to assert anything whatever, but I think I may venture to assert that there will be no drawing back here, and I say without hesitation that, if there should be, the consequences would be so grave that even your Foreign Office, which nothing embarrasses, would find itself in a serious difficulty.

Personally, General Lahitte is quite determined to hold his own. He thinks himself in the right, and the only one offended. He is a man of honour; probably all, and certainly his principal, colleagues would follow him.

As a political question, the public strongly upholds Lahitte; and the unthinking populace gladly falls back on its old prejudices and antipathies against England. There is nothing so dangerous as to put the bad feelings of the multitude in the right for a moment. Lord Palmerston is bringing upon you and us this evil, which is very great, and might become immense. With us the foreign and the home questions are closely bound up together. The electoral law depends on the Greek business; the situation is greatly aggravated by it.

The reading of the despatches from M. Gros has carried conviction to the minds of those who were farthest from any ill will towards you, and most anxious to avoid coolness. It is now confidently believed that Mr. Wyse, on the instructions of Lord Palmerston, seized on the first pretext for brusquely and forcibly putting an end to an affair which

Lord Palmerston had no wish to have ended by the intervention of France. You may be quite sure that this is the universal feeling.

If you in England do not put an end to this thoughtless and obstinate presumption, England will come to be looked upon as an utter stranger, suspected by and antipathetical to the Continent. We shall suffer by it, and you will not gain.

May 26th.—I have nothing to add or change in what I wrote to you the day before yesterday. Here they are very determined to hold out, and they could not do otherwise.

Everything seems to show that the electoral law will pass without amendment. I do not know what its value in the way of elections will be two years hence, and I do not much care. It has a real political importance now; for on one side it marks and consolidates the agreement of the President with the majority, and on the other it places the leaders of the majority in the front, and at the head of their army. . . .

The political history of the season is summed up in the Journal in the fewest possible words :—

Lord Palmerston's proceedings against Greece in the Pacifico affair caused much excitement in and out of the Cabinet. I opposed them very strongly. They led eventually, though not ostensibly, to his fall. A vote of censure was carried in the Lords on June 17th by 37 majority. I stood all night at the bar to hear the debate. In the subsequent debate in the Commons, on June 28th, the Government had 46 majority. The following day, June 29th, Sir R. Peel fell from his horse on Constitution Hill, and died four days afterwards.

The Danish question assumed importance. I was intimate with Reventlow, the Danish minister in London, and stoutly defended the Danes. Cabinets were held to consider whether we should oppose the German intervention. Prince Albert took, of course, the German side. This led to a total loss of my favour with him, and gradually abated my intimacy with Bunsen.

From Lord Clarendon

V.-R. L., July 6th.—I have for a long time past regretted the apathy of Parliament with respect to foreign affairs, and that our foreign policy, whether wise or rash, whether too subservient or too vexatious for the interests of England, should always be beyond the control of public opinion. The difficulty of attracting attention to any foreign question, and the ease with which all discussion upon such subjects was evaded, seemed to me as injurious to the minister who presided over the foreign department as they were discreditable to the country ; and I rejoice, therefore, that this bad stimulus to the one and this stigma upon the other have now been effectually removed. I am not disposed to quarrel with the Lords for the result they arrived at ; [1] but I should have deplored a similar issue in the Commons, as I think it would have been an unseemly triumph to foreign governments, which would have rendered them arrogant and *exigeants* towards us ; and certain principles would have been laid down, or at least admitted, that must have hampered the action of the British Government, and invited the oppression of British subjects all over the world. I say nothing of all the domestic evils that would have ensued from a change of government, and an attempt to reverse the internal policy of the last five years ; but the confusion that must have been caused would have given unmixed pleasure to our Continental allies, whose hatred of England is of much older date than the Palmerston régime.

It is not only the division, but the general result of the debate, that will, I expect, produce important effects abroad ; and our foreign friends should carefully reflect upon what has occurred. They will learn that henceforward the acts of the Foreign Minister of England are within the control of Parliament, and that they can and will be discussed there, not only with knowledge and extreme ability, but in a spirit of severe and scrutinising criticism. This is a guarantee for the future to the world. They will also learn that the House of Lords does not constitute the legislature of England, and that its decision is neither recognised by the country nor

---

[1] In the Greek debate.

binding on the Government until it is confirmed by the House of Commons, whose decision, if adverse, will be considered as of greater weight both by the country and the Government.

From M. Guizot

Val Richer, July 9th.—I can think of nothing but the death of Sir Robert Peel. The loss is very great, and is felt in a becoming manner. The unanimous and respectful sorrow of England is a fine spectacle. England is right. I do not know if Sir Robert Peel foresaw revolutions in the distant future and took timely measures to prevent them, but he was well fitted to do so. He loved order, peace, a just and honourable policy, and enjoyed the confidence of the liberal country. It may well be that you will feel the want of him before long. I understand what you tell me of the new situation of Lord Palmerston. He defended himself well, and has been censured rather than attacked. His most serious adversaries had no real wish to overthrow him, and none of them understood what he was talking about so well as he did. I think England is strong against the republican spirit, and yet you should all be a little more careful. It is dangerous to keep on the downward slope, without mistrusting it ; and Lord Palmerston is one of those who have the twofold audacity to push forward upon it and to think they will be able to stop when they choose.

I share in your country's regret. Sir Robert was not a personal friend of mine, like Lord Aberdeen, but for five years we conducted in concord a policy which was really friendly for our two countries. This is a strong bond. It is a little thing to wish for peace : it needs much more than that to maintain it. Sir Robert took pleasure in the well-being and prosperity of France, as I took and always shall take pleasure in the well-being and prosperity of England. There is a great difference between this friendly though foreign equity, and the irritating and jealous though peaceful indifference of Lord Palmerston.

Val Richer, 22 juillet.—. . . Je regrette bien de ne pas me trouver à Paris quand vous y passerez. Si vous aviez, quand vous reviendrez de Suisse, quarante-huit heures à me donner

au Val Richer, ce serait bien aimable et nous causerions là
bien à notre aise.

The Journal here has :—

After the Greek fight, Fleming [1] made the peace between
the Palmerstons and me. I was introduced to Lady P. at
Lady Shelburne's concert on July 24th, and wènt to Lady
P.'s party on August 3rd for the first time.

August 14*th*.—Went to Boulogne with my mother and
the Scudamores, when Scudamore fell off the pier and broke
both his legs. [2] The railway was only open to Tonnerre,
whence we posted to Geneva.

From M. Guizot

Trouville, 21 *août*.—J'ai bien regretté, mon cher
monsieur, que vous eussiez retardé votre passage par Paris.
J'y ai été du 9 au 13, et je vous y attendais. Il faut que
vous m'en dédommagiez, à votre retour, en venant me voir
au Val Richer. J'y retourne mardi prochain, 28, avec ma
fille aîneé, pour n'en plus bouger jusqu'au mois de novembre.
La malle-poste vous mène de Paris à Lisieux en dix heures,
et de Lisieux au Val Richer il y a une heure, par un cabriolet
de place. Si vous m'avertissez du jour où vous viendrez, je
vous ferai prendre par ma petite voiture. . .

Je n'ai point de nouvelles à ajouter à celles que vous
donnent les journaux. La France et ses Prétendants sont
en visite mutuelle. Je ne sais trop lesquels avancent leurs
affaires. En attendant, le pays se calme et travaille. Je
n'ai jamais vu tant de tranquillité présente avec si peu de
sécurité future. Les hommes semblent avoir renoncé à
toute ambition et perdu toute prévoyance.

Adieu, mon cher monsieur, et au revoir bientôt, j'espère.
Mes respects à madame votre mère, et   Tout à vous,

GUIZOT.

---

[1] A clerk and afterwards secretary to the Poor Law Board, well known in
London society as a diner-out and political gossip. He was especially favoured
by Lady Palmerston, who made use of him to advertise any matters which she
or her husband wished to have noised abroad.

[2] This accident suggested the similar incident in *Paul Ferroll*, whose
author, Mrs. Archer Clive, was an intimate friend of the Scudamores.

Reeve, however, did not return in time to avail himself of this invitation to Val Richer. The Journal continues:—

Remained at Geneva till September 1st; then to Turin, Genoa, Leghorn, and Rome. Reached Rome on the 7th. Saw the Pope on the 8th. Went the round of churches and galleries.

September 17th.—To Frascati and Tusculum. Then to Albano, and so on to Naples. Reached Naples on the 21st. On the 22nd, sunset from Cape Misenum ; 24th, Pompeii and to Sorrento ; 25th, Amalfi ; 26th, Salerno ; 27th, Pæstum and back to Naples ; by sea to Cività Vecchia, Leghorn, and Genoa ; Philip Taylor there. At Turin, on October 3rd, saw Count Balbo, author of the ' Speranze d' Italia.' By Chambéry and Lyons to Paris.

October 10th.—Saw the great review at Satory, 14,000 men, 48 squadrons of cavalry. Cries of ' Vive l'Empereur! ' began to be heard. M. Guizot was in Paris. Got home on October 12th.

From M. Guizot

Paris, November 25th.—I wish I could send you clear and decisive news of France and Germany, but it is not possible. I may be nearer the scene than you, but I see no better. I do not yet believe in a war between Prussia and Austria ; still the question is no longer in the hands of the Governments ; it has passed into those of the assemblies, regiments, and streets. How deplorable is the state of those countries where absolute power is dead and liberty still unborn ! If war breaks out, we shall have a good deal of trouble here. The Élysée wants to be mixed up in it, in hopes of territorial aggrandisement, out of which may come the empire. The Assembly will have nothing to do with it, and is preparing to paralyse the President. They delay the report on the subsidies which he has asked for. They propose to form a commission of all the diplomatic big-wigs of the Assembly—MM. Molé, Thiers, Broglie, Montebello, &c. They know that these gentlemen are all against any intervention in this war, and they count upon the authority of their advice. On his side, if he cannot intervene in the war, the President promises himself at least the formation of an army of observation, which will furnish him with a decent pretext for ridding himself of the presence of General Changarnier in Paris. And General Changarnier gone, he would see his way to many other things, which will probably never be done. Two things are certain : the country would like war, but wants peace, the Élysée would like the empire, but will not risk the presidency. On both sides prudence is stronger than desire. But once again in Germany the decision escapes from the hands of the prudent, and there is no knowing how far the madmen may go. If the war is quickly ended by a decisive blow, the result will be the absolute preponderance of one great power in Germany which will be very displeasing to us, whichever power it may be ; but we will not go beyond displeasure. If the war is prolonged, it will necessarily end by being revolutionary and European, and we shall be dragged into it. In any case, war is an act of folly, and we all—France, England, and Russia—ought to do our very utmost to prevent it. But the wisdom of the wise, in our days, does not go far ; they are content with not being mad.

You want to know whether there was a conspiracy to overthrow the President three weeks ago. I do not believe it, and I am sure that none of those around me can say that I ever said I did. I believe that this is what happened. The President has a wish to be something different from what he is. The Assembly fears that his wish may be too strong. The permanent commission, charged to keep watch on him in the absence of the Assembly, was afraid of not watching closely enough, and that its precautions might be taken too late. At the Élysée, the Palais Bourbon, the État-major, and the Prefecture of Police, they were all spying on each other, and putting themselves upon their guard, so as not to be taken unawares. The President did not want to be kidnapped ;[1] General Changarnier did not want to be deprived of his office ; M. Dupin did not want

---

[1] Such a possibility was in the air. In the summer of 1851, wrote Odilon Barrot, ' sur la demande que je lui ai carrément adressée s'il était en mesure d'arrêter le Président, le général Changarnier m'a répondu que quand je lui en donnerais l'ordre il le mettrait dans un panier à salade, et le conduirait sans plus de cérémonie à Vincennes.'—*Mémoires Posthumes* d'Odilon Barrot, iv. 61.

to be assassinated; in presence of all these chances, sensible people who want a different régime from that which exists kept themselves ready to profit by whatever might happen. Nothing could be less like a conspiracy than the play of secret hopes and ambitions. We are destined to live long in the midst of such a conspiracy as this. For the moment the President is the cock of the walk. His message has succeeded very well. It is a retreat; but a very clever retreat, made in a triumphal chariot. . . .

Endorsed—This letter was greatly admired by Lord Lansdowne and Lord Clarendon, to whom I sent it.

The Journal notes :—

December 12*th*.—Green's lecture at the Royal Academy; very striking. Radowitz came to England; I met him at Bunsen's. Caught cold and was laid up at the close of the year.

1851. *January* 14*th*.—I went to Paris. Saw Faucher, Guizot, Circourts, Duchesse de Luynes, Duchesse de Rauzan. Heard debates in the National Assembly; Berryer's great speech on the 16th; Cavaignac's speech, Thiers, and Baroche. The Assembly was violently hostile to Louis Napoleon, and the ministers were defeated.

17*th*.—Dined with Drouyn de Lhuys; evening at Lamartine's and Flavigny's. Returned to London on the 21st.

24*th*.—Dined at Delane's, with Walter, Lowe, Roebuck, and Byng.

From Lord Clarendon

Dublin Castle, January 26*th*.—I envy you your visit to the headquarters of the Impracticables, and am much obliged to you for your interesting account of it. There could be nothing more like a *Plaza de Toros* than the Assembly last week; and the excitement both of the performers and spectators must have been of the same kind as when the *corrida* is known to be of the best bred, and therefore the most reckless, bulls. Thiers 'has done it all,' and certainly he served up an *olla* in which every condiment likely to

damage the Government found its place. There's no use
speculating upon French fears and hopes and whims, but I
should think he had overshot his mark this time, and that
the Assembly won't always *tirer les marrons du feu* for a
man who will accept no responsibility beyond rendering
government impossible, and injuring the cause of order. I
remember the time when he was just as violent against
Louis Philippe as he is now against Louis Napoleon, and
his telling me one night at Lord Granville's that he had his
foot upon his—Louis Philippe's—neck, and there he would
keep it ; the very thought of which so excited him that he
began stamping and digging his heel into the ambassadorial
carpet as if it was the actual cervix of royalty, till I was
horrified that others should hear the treason I was listening
to. Yet he could do nothing, and I expect now that *il se
brisera* against the not undignified *vis inertiæ* of the President, backed by the country.

If he, Louis Napoleon, had not been dreaming of empire
and meditating *coups d'état*, his position would have been
more *nette* ; but as he appears now to have abandoned these
notions and to wish only to keep his present place as long
as possible, I think he will be looked upon as *l'homme
indispensable*, and his enemies as those of the public. I
hope it may be so, as the state of things most favourable to
peace and to friendly relations with England. But how
strangely the latent hatred and suspicion of us developes
itself upon every occasion, even among men who, one would
think, must know better. They seem, however, to have
learnt nothing better since the days of Mr. Pitt, when *l'or
anglais* was the only cause of their intestine commotions
and foreign disasters. The whole press of England bribed
by the Government to defend the President against the
Assembly, in return for an expected reduction of duty on
coals ! ! !

On February 21st Lord John Russell resigned somewhat
unexpectedly, owing—it was announced in the 'Times' of
the 22nd—'to the loss of Parliamentary confidence,' which
meant, 'to the Government majority having sunk to fourteen on a hostile motion of Disraeli's.' The 22nd was a
Saturday, and it was thus not till the 24th that Russell

made the announcement to the House, and then said that
Lord Stanley (shortly to become Lord Derby), who had been
sent for, was not prepared to form a ministry, and that he
had, therefore, been desired by the Queen to undertake the
task of reconstructing one. This, however, proved difficult.
For several days the crisis was acute; and it was not till
March 3rd that it was announced that the former ministers
had resumed their places.

In France the state of things was bad, and was rapidly
getting worse. In view of the result, it is well to follow
carefully M. Guizot's *résumé* of the situation :—

Paris, March 24th.—I have been long in answering you,
'my dear Sir.' My only excuse is that it vexes me to speak
of what I see. I do not despair either of my time or of my
country. I do not believe France has gone mad for ever.
All nations, your own included, have passed through periods
of weakness. You yourselves are not in a very glorious
phase just now. But all my faith in the future cannot
console me for the present. I am sad ; and when I am sad
I am silent, even to my friends.

The public is sad also, though in the departments, as in
Paris, there has been much merriment and dancing during
the winter. Anxiety is coming back; affairs advance but
slowly. The crisis of 1852 is still far off, but its approach is
felt. It will begin in May with the question of the revision
of the constitution. Then, perforce, the battle will break
out between the two parties which for the last year have
been struggling in silence—the party of the *impatients* and
that of the *prévoyants.* The *impatients* wish to overthrow
the President at any price, at all risks ; before 1852 or in
1852 ; without knowing what will come after him, careless
of what may be the power to succeed him. Among the
impatients there are all kinds of people—*montagnards,*
legitimists, some Orleanists—all promising themselves victory after chaos. The *montagnards* form the largest portion
of the party. M. Thiers is at their head. He has a small,
a very small staff, with which he turns now to right, now to
left, alternately caressing M. de Saint-Priest and M. Charras,
seeking everywhere for forces to overthrow the President, in
the hopes that on the ruins of the President, of the Right and
of the Left, he will be able to form a government of his

own—monarchical regency or republican directory. I do not quite know which; he does not quite know himself; but a regency more probably than any other.

In the party of the *prévoyants* there are also all sorts of elements; no *montagnards*, but moderate republicans, *Élyséens*, Orleanists, and legitimists. These are not anxious to overthrow the President; they do not even wish him to fall in 1852, unless they are assured that he will be replaced by the government they want. This is more especially the view of the Orleanists and legitimists, partisans of fusion. The *Élyséens* would like the empire, but they no longer hope for it, and would content themselves with a prolongation of their power. The moderate republicans would like another President and constitution, but they do not flatter themselves that they will get it, and would be resigned to a new lease for Louis Napoleon, so long as they are not called upon to sign it themselves, unconstitutionally. The *prévoyants*, as different and disunited in their aims as the *impatients*, have not, like them, the factitious and momentary union which results from the same passion for attack; but they rely on the very decided instinct of the country which upholds the President, without enthusiasm, without confidence, as the only means of preserving order, of escaping a violent crisis, and after it—chaos.

The President seeks the support of the *prévoyants*. He feels himself, truly enough, weakened by the attacks made upon him by the Assembly, though they have gained nothing by them—far from it; still, they have beaten the President, and no one was ever the better for being beaten. The President would like, with the help of the *prévoyants*, to form a cabinet strong enough to enable him to turn the crisis of 1852 against the *impatients*. In this the *prévoyants* are disposed to assist him; they feel that they have need of the President, as he has need of them. Meantime the vital question is who will win in the next elections, whether they take place soon, consequent on the revision of the constitution, or not until 1852. It is also very clear that if the *prévoyants* and the President do not act in unison, the victory in the elections of the future Assembly will fall, not to all the *impatients* promiscuously, but to the *mon-*

tagnards in particular. The presentiment of this weighs upon everyone, even now, and is the cause of all the attempts made by the President and the *prévoyants* to reconstruct a majority and a cabinet in concert. As yet their success has been small. M. O. Barrot is too weak; M. Léon Faucher is unbearable. The President wants two of his own men— M. Fould and M. Baroche; the party will only let him have M. Fould, but offer him a second on condition that it is not M. Baroche. There must be one or two legitimists in the cabinet; but which? M. de Falloux is absent and ill; M. de Kerdnel is unknown. I bore even myself in telling you all these miserable petty pretensions and narrow views. I think that, ultimately, the *prévoyants* and the President, seeing the imminence of the danger, will unite and form a cabinet. But will they do this in time? will they form one equal to its task? I doubt it. My country is able to resist and to survive the unknown trials which the future has in store for her; she is not able to prevent them.

I am curious to see the issue of the much less important trial which your country is undergoing. I cannot feel seriously anxious for you. I even persist in thinking that the outcome of your present difficulties, and of your fit of religious fanaticism and political impotence, will be to the honour of England; and that in the end religious equity and political good sense will triumph. What will the Peelites do when the present Cabinet falls? Will they join the Protectionists and form a stable government at once; or will they join the Opposition and do so later on? This seems to me the whole question. Am I wrong? It would be very kind of you to keep me informed. I live both in France and England.

Adieu, 'my dear Sir.' My respects to your mother. It is a long time since I had news of Mrs. Austin; I believe it is my fault; but I love her as much as if I wrote often. I hope soon to get away from Paris. When not actively employed, I must have quiet and freedom of thought, and these I can only get at Val Richer. In a few days I will send you a new volume of 'Études Biographiques' on the history of your revolution—Holles, Ludlow, Fairfax, Mistress Hutchinson, Lilburne, Burnet—a series of portraits, a

Madame Tussaud's of the time, though I hope the figures will not look like wax. The work amuses me, and will, I hope, amuse others also. Here it is of some use. Constant repetition is the only way of making one's self understood.

The Journal notes :—

April 5th.—I had Count Reventlow, Mareschalchi, Marochetti, Strzelecki, Lord Wodehouse, Raikes Currie, H. Merivale, and Mr. Richardson to dinner.

May 1st.—The Great Exhibition opened. Lady Granville, Lady Palmerston, and Lady Molesworth had numerous parties. On the 16th Bulwer's play 'Not so Bad as we Seem,' acted by Dickens and others at Devonshire House. Munro lit up his pictures on the 22nd.

At a party at Lady Palmerston's met Countess Teba, afterwards the Empress Eugénie; Narvaes, too, was there. He called on my mother next day. The Binets came to stay with me, May 31st. Took Binet to Ascot.

It was during this spring that, at one of Lady Molesworth's 'numerous parties,' Reeve met Miss Gollop, the daughter of Mr. Gollop, of Strode Manor, in Dorset, where the family had been settled since the time of Henry VII. Reeve spoke to Lady Molesworth of the pleasure he found in Miss Gollop's society, and Lady Molesworth gave him opportunities of improving the acquaintance. The Exhibition gave him others, and, after a very brief courtship, he proposed and was accepted. It appears in the Journal in the fewest possible words :—

June 9th.—My engagement to Christine G.
June 11th.—Binets and Christine to Hampton Court.

The announcement of the engagement to his friends brought him the following, amongst other congratulations :—

From Lord Clarendon

V.-R. L., June 17th.—The S.-W. gale, or some other cause, made the packet three hours later than usual, so I have little time; but I won't let a post go without thanking you for your communication, and congratulating you sincerely on Lady C.'s part, as well as my own, upon an event

·so important to yourself, and therefore, believe me, very interesting to us. We feel sure that you have reflected maturely and chosen wisely for your own happiness and that of your child; and we look forward with pleasure to making the acquaintance of your lady. Pray tell her that we must start at once on the footing of old friends.

From M. Guizot

Paris, 2 juillet.—C'est un rare privilège, mon cher monsieur, que de retrouver le bonheur perdu. Dieu vous le garde! Vous le méritez, car vous le sentez vivement. Serez-vous bientôt marié? Il n'est pas impossible que j'aille passer quelques jours à Londres vers la fin d'août. J'aurais un vrai plaisir à vous voir heureux, et à revoir réellement Lucy Hutchinson.[1] Je la connais bien, et je l'honore, et je l'aime beaucoup dans l'histoire. Je suis sûr que vivante elle me plaira bien davantage encore. Parlez-lui, je vous prie, un peu de moi d'avance, et assurez-moi de sa part quelque bonté. . . .

The engagement was but little longer than the courtship. Its conclusion is told in the Journal :—

To Strode. Married at Netherbury Church on August 21st by E. J. Reeve and Mr. Pulteney. To Southampton and then Sparrow's Herne, lent us by Hodgson, where we stayed till September 5th, and then started by sea for Edinburgh. Thence to Glasgow, Loch Lomond, Dunoon, Oban, Caledonian Canal, Drumnadrochit, and Novar. Left Novar October 16th.

Back to town. Visit to Farnborough in November. Hunting ; Christine rode pony.

This was the first of the many visits which Mrs. Reeve paid to Farnborough Hill, where Mr. Longman at that time rented a place which he afterwards bought, and where he built, on top of the hill, the house now the property of the Empress Eugénie. He kept a small pack of harriers—writes Mrs. Reeve—and 'we had many a pleasant run over heath

---

[1] There is no known portrait of Lucy Hutchinson, but Guizot had just published a character-sketch of her in his *Études Biographiques sur la Révolution d'Angleterre* (8vo. 1851), p. 219, to which Reeve had evidently referred.

and fern, of a morning, before going up to town. For many successive years we spent Christmas and Easter with the Longmans, besides frequent visits at other times.'

From Lord Clarendon

V.-R. L., November 22nd.—I have had a long conversation with Count Nugent, who is an intelligent old gentleman. He certainly defends the Government he serves *con amore*, and can find no speck in Austrian policy. He was delighted that no respectable persons had figured in the Kossuth ovations, and very grateful for the service which the ' Times ' has rendered to the cause of order abroad and common-sense at home. It must have been a difficult task to stem the tide of ignorant enthusiasm ; but it was done with consummate skill and tact, and the ' Times ' will be all the more powerful for risking momentary unpopularity, and showing that it knew what public opinion ought, and, in fact, what it has turned out to be. . . .

Lady C. desires to be kindly remembered to you. We both look forward with pleasure to making Mrs. Reeve's acquaintance. I wish I knew when we had a prospect of doing so. My ambition is modest, for it consists in permanent promotion to the Grove ; but even that seems not to be easy when once one has the misfortune to be in official harness.

With December came the solution of the problem over which Guizot had been pondering. The Journal tells that—

Louis Napoleon's *coup d'état* against the Assembly took place on December 2nd, when most of my political friends in France were arrested, and many of them banished. I guessed while at Novar that the blow was coming when I saw that Faucher left office, and hastened south accordingly. At Carlisle I met Count Flahault on the platform, going to Paris from Tullyallan.[1] Morny was his son. This confirmed my suspicions.

---

[1] The seat of the Baroness Keith and Nairne (daughter of Admiral Viscount Keith), whom Flahault married in 1817. She died in Paris, at the age of eighty, in 1867 ; Flahault, at the age of eighty-five, in 1870. On the mother's side Morny was half-brother of Louis Napoleon.

On the first news of the arrest of the deputies, Reeve wrote to Lord Clarendon, giving 'all that was known of the strange, eventful story at Paris,' the story, that is, of the *coup d'état.* It was necessarily imperfect; for, though the monster was born on December 2nd, its baptism (with blood) was not till the 4th, the very day on which Clarendon wrote his answer, in which he was able to say that, if the *coup d'état* was to be, he was 'glad that it came off quickly and completely, and without occasion for red or white men to support their respective politics in the streets.' His comments were all on the understanding that the revolution had been effected without bloodshed; and he continued—

December 4th.—It is lucky that the 'Great Hungarian '[1] is now on the other side of the water, as he would otherwise find his way into France and do some mischief. I wish he was not coming back to us in February, but he will be no longer a lion then. I should like to know the speculations of *les experts* upon the consequences to ourselves of this French melodrama. Will the sacred flame of liberty burn brighter for it, and excite John Bull to demand a large measure of reform? or will it inspire a wholesome fear of organic changes, and a desire to leave well alone as far as is consistent with keeping the promise held out of some reform? The more *plebs* can be encouraged to take the latter view, the better, I think.

On the 10th, however, he wrote again with fuller knowledge of what had taken place :—

December 10th.—It is rather a humiliating confession, but the fact is I have not yet been able to make up my mind as to what I should think, or rather wish, respecting the French events. As to the methods by which L. N. has established himself, there can be no difference of opinion ; but I am not so clear that a *coup d'état quelconque* had not almost become necessary, as the only way out of the deadlock to which things had been brought by the misconduct of the Assembly and the selfish, reckless intrigues of parties. For some time past it has been evident that a legal and constitutional solution of difficulties was impossible; that the Gordian knot would have to be cut, and that violence of some

[1] *Sc.* Kossuth.

kind would be resorted to by one or other of the contending parties ; and it seems best therefore that the attempt should be made by the one in which there was the greatest concentration of force, in order that the contest should be as short as possible ; and with that end, it is impossible not to rejoice that the arrangements were complete and every precaution taken ; for even in the presence of 100,000 soldiers, unembarrassed by the National Guards, and without the faubourgs and the working classes taking an active part, the disposition to resist was very great—very natural too, of course ; and partial success must have entailed even more serious consequences both in Paris and the departments than those which are now to be lamented. Some deputies have been horribly maltreated (though Changarnier, Cavaignac, and Thiers were all ready for their own *coup d'état* and for locking up L. N. if they could), and many innocent persons have been massacred ; but I doubt if, beyond a narrow circle, that will excite much horror or produce a lasting bad impression. . . .

I entirely agree with you as to the possible results of the army becoming bored with the rôle of gendarmes and wanting some foreign pastime ; in which case our Continental friends would assuredly like to divert attack from themselves by directing it towards us. Against such a calamity it is almost impossible to provide ; but if my advice be of any avail, no practicable precaution will be neglected. It would never do for the ' Times ' to sound any alarm ; for the French would then think we were afraid.

V.-R. L., December 17th.—I have not differed with you in your estimate of the President's acts ; but his *coup d'état* once made, I wished him success, simply because failure would have brought with it horrors of a worse kind. I thought also that we should not measure his acts by an English standard, or ask ourselves how we should have liked to see our Parliament shut up, the press abolished, and everybody imprisoned at pleasure ; for we must remember that the French are more or less accustomed to such proceedings, and that L. N. put an end to a system that everybody knew was a fraud, and could not last. . . .

I thought therefore that the press (and when I say press

I mean the ' Times,' for nothing else signifies abroad) went too far in denouncing that which would soon be popular in France. . . . I thought also that we ought not uselessly to irritate L. N., or give him the pretext that his uncle always seized upon for hostility—that public opinion in England was insulting to him and injurious to the cause of order in France. . . .

It was for the French people to decide what they would endure or reject; and as the working classes took no part, the National Guard was delighted not to be called on to do so. The upper classes were passive, and the popular leaders in prison; the issue after the first eight and forty hours was not doubtful in Paris, while in the departments it was clear that the generals and préfets either thought the movement would succeed, or that opinion was in its favour. . . . Remember, too, that things had come to a deadlock, and that a *coup d'état* or *de main* by *somebody* was almost inevitable. Remember that some time before December 2nd Guizot prophesied what must happen, and conjured his friends and the Assembly to take warning and not lead the way to a *dictature*; so that it can hardly be said to have taken us by surprise.

I shall be very curious to hear more about the spirit of the French army. Much will depend on that, both as regards Louis Napoleon and ourselves; but I expect that he will keep all his military apparatus in good humour and readiness.

Both in England and in France the excitement was intense. Except amongst his immediate followers, few could be found to approve of the action of Louis Napoleon; but the general belief in France was that his unscrupulous conduct had saved the country from something much worse. 'L'Anarchie,' said the Duc de Broglie, ' est accouchée de la Dictature. La mère et l'enfant se portent bien;' but Madame de Lieven, with a neatness peculiarly her own, described the new constitution as ' d'une habilité extrême. Il se résume ainsi : Je prend tout, je garde tout, vous aurez le reste. Voilà la constitution.' In England, on the other hand, where the fear of anarchy and the Terror had not been felt, the crime appeared in its naked enormity, and toleration of it, and still more approval, was looked on as an outrage of decency.

For more than two years the relations between Lord Palmerston and his colleagues in the Government had been excessively strained, and latterly almost to breaking point. The Foreign Secretary's conduct of the Greek negotiations had deeply offended the Court, and had drawn from the Queen the celebrated memorandum of August 12th, 1850, to the effect that, in any given case, a distinct statement of what it was intended to do should be put before her, and that after she had approved of any measure, no alteration should be made in it. He had again run counter to the views of the Queen and Prince Albert, as well as of the members of the Cabinet, by receiving a deputation which attended to congratulate him on the liberation of Kossuth, and to refer, incidentally, to the Emperors of Russia and Austria as despots, tyrants, and odious assassins. For such an outrage on the feelings of the Queen, the Ministry, and the friendly potentates, Palmerston would very certainly have been dismissed from office, had not Lord John Russell realised that the cause which he was championing was the one supported by a vast preponderance of public opinion, and that to take action on these grounds would imperil the existence of the Ministry, and excite a strong feeling against what was supposed to be the German influence at the Court.

Under the soothing influence of time and of Sir Theodore Martin's very able Biography, the memory of Prince Albert now lives only as that of the trusted and generous adviser of the Queen ; a view which is not exactly that held fifty years ago by the general public and the man in the street.[1] The humanitarian sentiment which was roused by the story of Hungary's wrongs was none the less popular because it conveyed a fancied snub to German sympathies. No such feeling complicated our relations with France ; and when, after the *coup d'état*, Palmerston—who, as Foreign Secretary, wrote officially to the Marquis of Normanby, the English ambassador in Paris, 'to do nothing that could wear the appearance of interference in the internal affairs of France '—was convicted of personally expressing to Count Walewski, the French ambassador in London, ' a strong opinion on the necessity and advantage for France of the bold and decisive step taken by the President,' the cup of his iniquities was held to be full and running over, and he was promptly dismissed, December 22nd.[2]

---

[1] Cf. *Memoirs of Baron Stockmar* (English edition), ii. 481 ; and *Greville Memoirs*, III. i. 126–130.

[2] *Greville Memoirs*, II. iii. 426–7 and 446.

From M. Guizot

Paris, December 25th.—Your few lines were very welcome, my dear Sir; they brought to Paris the first news of the London *coup d'état.*[1] If I am rightly informed, neither Lord Normanby nor the President was aware of it when your letter arrived. It is excellent. You have less reason to fear isolation than any nation in Europe; but it is not good even for you; you were falling into it, but this has saved you. If I found any pleasure in revenge, I should be fully satisfied. Where is the republic? Where is M. Thiers? Where is Lord Palmerston? But the downfall of my personal adversaries is nothing to me compared to the downfall of my unhappy country. This is the cause of my not having written to you for so long. I cannot bear to speak of her wounds. If I followed my inclination, I would shut myself up at Val Richer and see and hear nothing; but I stay on here, a sad spectator of this wretched spectacle. Public feeling is much divided. The great bulk of the people, those to whom their private interest is the sole consideration, are satisfied. The expectation of the crisis of 1852 weighed upon these interests like a nightmare. The President has delivered them from it; he is fighting against socialism and demagogism. By his triumph, manufacturers, merchants, honest artisans and peasants may look for some security in their work and business for some time to come. They ask nothing more of him. Among the higher classes, interested in politics—legitimists, Orleanists, or republicans—there is great irritation. They have lost their share, and all near chances, of power; they have seen all rights brutally violated, the most honourable men treated like malefactors. They feel oppressed and injured.

This is the President's honeymoon. By means of the soldiers he has succeeded against the Assembly, and in the streets; by means of the peasants he has won the elections. But now his difficulties will begin. He must govern; and he cannot govern with soldiers and peasants; he will need the support of the higher classes, and that he will not have

---

[1] Lord Palmerston's dismissal. It has already been seen that M. Guizot did not love Palmerston. It was a way foreign statesmen had.

except in an incomplete and uncertain fashion. They will
not oppose him at present in spite of their irritation ; for
they are afraid of socialism and the Jacquerie. But this fear
will die out, and then remembrance of the affronts they have
received, regret for lost liberty, ill-will, disdain, party spirit,
and all that makes the higher classes ungovernable and
dangerous, will return.   For a time, longer or shorter, they
will bear with the government of Louis Napoleon ; I doubt
if they will ever uphold it.

The President's ideas on political economy and finance
are very false, almost socialistic. He would do away with
almost all the indirect taxes, and lay nearly the whole burden
of taxation on landed and moveable property and on the rich.
It is mainly by such a step that he hopes to achieve popularity ; and though his councillors oppose it and will continue
to oppose it, he will some day succeed in crushing their
opposition, and will cause in the finances of France such
confusion as would compromise and shake the most firmly
established governments.

Many people think that his foreign policy will be warlike.   I doubt it ; for some time at least. He is an indolent,
pleasure-loving man ; he will not make war himself ; and
neither the country nor even the army wishes for it. Nowadays, every war must become revolutionary, and he is out of
favour with the makers of revolutions. But as the difficulty
of his situation in the country increases, it is very possible
that, with his visionary and imaginative turn of mind, he
may dream of and seek territorial aggrandisement in order
to recover his popularity. Perhaps even now he dreams
that, thanks to his anti-demagogic and military policy, he
may gain sufficient favour with the great Continental Powers
to induce them to lend themselves to the necessities of his
situation.   An expedition to Switzerland next summer, to
drive out the refugees, is already talked of, and later on the
occupation of Savoy, if the Austrians enter Piedmont to put
an end to the refugees of Lombardy and the constitutional
Piedmontese.   This is where the revolution of February will
probably lead the Italian liberals.

Amid these doubtful chances of the European future, it
is an enormous advantage that the revolutionists of all

countries have no longer a patron in England. It would be very kind of you to let me know how and why he fell. I should like to understand the play of which you only tell me the *dénouement*.

What is the 'Morning Chronicle' thinking of to say that the fusionists, especially M. Guizot and his friends, are giving their full support to the Élysée? We are exactly what we were, conservatives and monarchists; and are absolutely independent of all existing parties, either of the Government or the Opposition. I hold to my past; I await the future; and I am not hostile, but entirely apart from the present.

Adieu, my dear Sir. It pleases me to think that I am writing to a happy man. I hope I shall some day have the honour of being presented to Mrs. Reeve. Those around me are well, and I have good news of my eldest daughter, who is spending the winter in Rome. Remember me to your mother and believe me, tout à vous,

GUIZOT.

On Palmerston's dismissal, the post of foreign secretary was offered to Clarendon, who refused it, and thus commented on the position :—

V.-R. L., January 2nd.—Eviction from office must have been a rude shock to Palmerston, and if the 'Morning Post' is any index to his feelings, he seems to resent it bitterly and to meditate an onslaught on Lord John, quite as much as a defence of himself. In the meanwhile, every variety of lie will be circulated to the prejudice of Lord John for a month; but we have often seen how a debate will dispel the mist in which men's minds get enveloped just before the meeting of Parliament, and I hope this may occur in the present case. . . Abroad the Government will gain by his loss, but at home I expect they will feel it, for Palmerston is deservedly liked; his good-nature, courtesy, and hospitality made him many friends, and he was able to turn away the wrath of opponents as no other member of the Government can do. How Lord John is to go on without more strength, or where that strength is to come from, are problems that I don't pretend to solve.

Eventually the vacancy was accepted by Lord Granville, but the loss and the enmity of Palmerston were fatal to the administration.　Parliament was opened on February 3rd. On the 16th Russell brought in a Militia Bill, to which Palmerston moved an amendment and carried it, against the Government, by a majority of nine.　On the 23rd Russell formally resigned, and was succeeded by Lord Derby, in whose ministry Palmerston had, of course, no place.

CHAPTER VIII

THE SECOND EMPIRE

THE agitation—Reeve wrote in his Journal—produced by the *coup d'état* and Palmerston's fall was great. I wrote with great vehemence against Louis Napoleon and published Tocqueville's narrative in the ' Times.'

These vehement articles gave rise to the following correspondence, especially interesting as showing Reeve's views of journalistic responsibility at a time which he very well knew to be critical. The opening was given by a letter from Reeve on his news from France :—

To Lord Granville

Chester Square, Saturday, January 17th.

DEAR LORD GRANVILLE,—I receive from M. de Circourt a few more particulars of interest. There is certainly a strong conflict between the more violent and the more moderate advisers of the President. Persigny heads the former, Morny the latter. In Paris they believe that the post of foreign minister is reserved for Persigny, not for M. de Flahault. Even St.-Arnaud refuses to assent to the decree for sequestrating the Orleans property ; yet I am assured this measure has been resolved upon, and the decree is only suspended. Persigny is supposed to be the most influential adviser, and his schemes for remodelling Europe are of the wildest character. L. N. has got some high-sounding names for his senate, but they are very empty persons. The Duc de Luynes refused, and is now threatened with having his house—the old and magnificent Hôtel de Luynes—pulled down to make a useless street. The elections are not expected before April, and in the meantime this *régime* is to continue. I will not detain you longer. I go out of town on Monday, but shall be back the latter part of next week.

Believe me, most faithfully yours,

H. REEVE.

My impression is that we shall see Morny and Rouher retire from the Government.

From Lord Granville [1]

London, January 17th.

MY DEAR REEVE,—A thousand thanks. I am inclined to believe that you are right in supposing that *one* mind has been made up to confiscate the Orleans property. It is impossible, even with the assistance of Talleyrand's epigrammatic saying as to faults and crimes, sufficiently to describe such an act of folly and wickedness.

I hear that Louis Napoleon is irritated and annoyed beyond measure by the language of the 'Times.' However deserved such castigation may be, it will be a serious responsibility to goad him on to acts of violence which may be seriously inconvenient to us. Ever yours,   G.

To Lord Granville

16 Chester Square, January 18th.

DEAR LORD GRANVILLE,—Many thanks for your kind note, which I have shown to Delane. Allow me to say a few words in reply. I should agree with you in deprecating the censure of the 'Times' on the French Government if I thought that it had been incited by any foolish desire to goad on Louis Napoleon to acts of violence, or that it had been carried beyond the bounds of a just commentary on the events of the day. But with the exception of two or three letters of which I disapprove, I am not aware that such is the case. M. de Flahault called on me, to remonstrate on those letters, but he said not a word on the tone of the principal articles in the paper, and even admitted that less could hardly be said by Englishmen on such a subject.

---

[1] At this time Foreign Secretary.

The responsibility of journalists is in proportion to the liberty they enjoy. No moral obligation can be graver. But their duties are not the same, I think, as those of statesmen. To find out the true state of facts, to report them with fidelity, to apply to them strict and fixed principles of justice, humanity, and law, to inform, as far as possible, the very conscience of nations and to call down the judgement of the world on what is false, or base, or tyrannical, appear to me to be the first duties of those who write. Those upon whom the greater part of political action devolves are necessarily governed by other rules.

In this particular case, I further see advantage from the course of a fair and independent judgement on these affairs. It will not perhaps be forgotten by France, when her press recovers its voice, and her real leaders their power, that the public opinion of England protested with indignation against the violence done to her neighbour ; and as I believe this eclipse of liberty in France to be ephemeral as it is violent, it would be a permanent source of resentment abroad if this country had not expressed what every free people must feel on such an occasion.

Nor is it in my opinion useless or unnecessary to keep alive in England a strong feeling on this subject. This nation is a good deal enervated by a long peace, by easy habits of intercourse, by peace societies and false economy. To surmount the dangerous consequences of such a state, the Government will require the support of public opinion, and that can only be obtained by convincing our countrymen of the truth that we have now a dangerous and faithless neighbour. Happen what may, there is nothing so important as to sustain a tone of moral independence and a clear judgement among the people of England, who will grudge no sacrifices if they are convinced that the principles they cherish are even indirectly threatened from abroad.

I will only add that after the election of December 20th, there was, I believe, no disposition in the ' Times ' to revert to the iniquities of the *coup d'état*. But fresh events are daily occurring. The expulsion of M. de Rémusat and his friends, this absurd constitution, and the threatened decree on the Orleans property, which last has not been publicly

alluded to, show what we have to expect. These and any
other incidents for evil or for good must needs excite the
criticism of public opinion in this country as they arise.
The irritation of Louis Napoleon is merely the vulgar disappointment of a tyrannical power, which finds that, strained
as all its forces may be, there is still an appeal, beyond its
reach, to that which anticipates the judgement of posterity.

I beg your pardon for this long epistle, and I will conclude in assuring you that, as far as my limited influence
extends, there shall be no wanton provocation.

Believe me, most faithfully yours,

H. REEVE.

Lord Granville to Mr. Delane

January 18th.—I send you a very good letter of Reeve's
and my reply. Pray direct the letter to him in the country.

From Lord Granville

January 19th.—I will, as Lord Overstone in examining
a witness, suppose a case. I am the servant of an old
bachelor. My master likes to have everything well conducted
about his own house and those of his neighbours, but he
abhors expense, or any disturbance of his ease and comfort.
He desires me to take charge of his house, which, like other
houses in our square, is surrounded by inflammable materials.
A strong energetic schoolboy—vain, irritable, without
principle, and latterly much spoilt—walks about the square,
with a lighted candle which has been given to him by those
in authority over him, and which I have no right and am not
strong enough to take away from him, until after he has made
a bad use of it. A fellow-servant of mine, very influential
with my master and the household, in mild and dignified
language, in every word of which I agree, explains every
morning to the schoolboy that he is an unmitigated little
scamp, who deserves to be well whipt. I, who have no right
to quarrel with my fellow-servant for holding language which
I know to be true, and which may moreover have, as he says, a
salutary effect on the teaboys [1] of our own and our neighbours'
establishments, cannot help fearing that the schoolboy in

---

[1] A bit of family slang. A 'teaboy' meant a 'steward's-room boy.'

his anger may set fire to some of my neighbours' houses, and
that I shall have, to the infinite annoyance of my master, to
put it out.

Your letter is able and unanswerable. I have no doubt
that what the 'Times' says is right, and that it is justified
in saying it ; but I cannot help rejoicing that you will do
what you can to soften the tone of it.

From Mr. Delane

Monday [January 19th].—You did not tell me of the
correspondence enclosed, but I like your letter so much that
I am glad it was sent without any consultation with me.
Our earl's reply is not very felicitous. It comes to no more
than this : that his duty is not identical with ours. He has
no necessary concern in the French people and its institutions, except as they directly affect England. If the old
Reign of Terror were revived, and five hundred heads a day
falling in the Place de la Concorde, it would be no business
of his so long as the heads were those of Frenchmen ;
though he would then scarcely affect to blame us for expressing the indignation of all humanity. Except that our feelings
are not shocked by the actual effusion of blood, the deporta-
tion to Cayenne is as cruel a measure as the decrees of the
Revolutionary Tribunal, and we are as much bound, in the
cause of justice and humanity, to exclaim against it. But
though this is our business, and our duty too, he is under
no such obligation ; whatever he may feel as a private
person, he, in his dealings with the French Government, is
as much bound to suppress as we are to publish our opinions.
We may have the same object in view, but our means are
necessarily different—my own estimate of them being that
ours are the most efficient.

However, we can neither change our respective courses.
He need not substitute leading articles for civil despatches,
nor can we bore and perplex our readers with materials for a
blue book. So let us each keep our own line.

After all, what Reeve said, what the 'Times' said, was
very much what everybody who knew anything of the circumstances was saying in public or in private. In France,
as was natural, feeling ran very high ; and intelligent men,

who were free to have an opinion, condemned the action of
the Prince President still more bitterly than in England.
Even Guizot, who endeavoured to take a view of the situation becoming an historian and a philosopher, wrote as
follows :—

Paris, 26 janvier.—Votre lettre du 24, que j'ai reçue
hier, me désole.   J'ai pour votre tante une vraie et profonde
amitié.   Elle serait ma sœur que je ne l'aimerais pas d'avan-
tage.   Vos dernières lignes me rassurent un peu.   Dans ces
maladies là, c'est quelque chose qu'un commencement de
mieux, et Madame Austin a beaucoup de force et de vitalité
naturelle.[1]   J'espère que vous aurez eu la bonté de m'écrire
deux lignes tous les jours.   Malheureusement rien n'arrive de
Londres aujourd'hui.   J'attendrai bien impatiemment tous
les matins.   Ne m'oubliez pas un seul matin, je vous prie,
tant qu'il y aura le moindre danger.

The public illness here has got much worse.   The consequences of the President's personal character and political
situation are developing rapidly.   In himself he is a small
chaos : imperialist and revolutionist, absolutist and socialist,
with aristocratic tastes and democratic ideas, with a reverence
for tradition and a passion for enterprise, the desire of order
and a contempt for equity, in action most rash, yet cold,
taciturn, and obstinate.   Until now these inconsistent traits
have been bridled by the obstacles which he met with, and
the struggles he had to maintain with rival powers.   But
now there are no more obstacles, no more rivals ; he stands
alone, absolutely alone, absolutely master.   In outward
appearance he is the same as before—cold, silent, quiet, and
gentle ; but inwardly he is intoxicated by his triumph, the
7,500,000 votes that elected him, and the 400,000 bayonets
which surround him.   He considers these unanswerable as
arguments, irresistible as force ; he is thus led to believe that
he may and can do what he pleases, and plunges headlong
into the frenzies and fancies of absolute power, with the
pride of an old despot and the blind confidence of a young
mystic.

[1] Mrs. Austin, who, in 1850, had translated Guizot's *Discours sur l'histoire
de la Révolution d'Angleterre* under the title of *On the Causes of the Success of
the English Revolution*, recovered from this illness, and lived for fifteen years
longer.   She died in 1867.

And all around him tends to force on the rapid developement of his character. He is still a favourite of the masses who raised him to power. For the present they are satisfied as to their civil interests, which are all they care about; the factories are at work, the price of wheat and agricultural produce is rising; order reigns everywhere; in every locality, great or small, the Democrats and Socialists have been defeated; the spectre of anarchy, relentless, inevitable, no longer exists. In most of the departments, town or country, the people—that is, the honest and industrious part of them—are content, and, in a few weeks, will probably elect for the legislative body the men pointed out by 'the President's agents.

Among the better classes, on the other hand, old or new, noble or *bourgeoises*, there is much and increasing discontent. In the bottom of their hearts they regret the free institutions and the importance and amusement they drew from them, more than they say, or than is generally supposed. Having once tasted liberty, it is easier to traduce it than to do without it. They may speak evil of the parliamentary system, but they bear despotic and arbitrary power very impatiently; they spy out its faults, and denounce them bitterly; they foretell and await the consequences of them. The lists of exiles and the decrees of confiscation have excited a lively indignation. Resignations of office and refusals to accept it are multiplying. The honest and industrious among the working classes are just as much for the President as the more distinguished, honourable and estimable men among the upper classes are every day more and more opposed to him. This want of agreement may last for a long time. Amongst us, at present, there is an immense distance, almost an abyss, between the classes accustomed to take an interest in public affairs and the rural or urban masses, who know nothing about them but what they are taught by their instincts, good or bad. Ideas and impressions scarcely ever pass from one of these worlds to the other. They live side by side without knowing each other, almost without communication. Thanks to universal suffrage and the tendencies of the Government itself, political power is now wholly in the hands of the masses; and the upper classes, who alone take an interest in politics, and are accustomed to the discussion of public affairs, are almost powerless. But this is an abnormal state of things, which cannot possibly last, and when it comes to an end, when the upper classes resume their proper place and their natural influence in the affairs of the country, the President will find it hard to bear the weight of their discontent.

When he sees that day approaching, it is very possible that he will seek some great adventure abroad to escape the difficulty of his position at home; and that war may be the last resource of his worn-out power, just as, fifty years ago, his uncle used it as a means of expelling revolution from France. I do not at all believe that he will enter this perilous path soon, and of his own free will; but it is commonly said that the unknown men who surround him are urging him to it, wishing, at any cost, to gain a little glory abroad in order to strengthen the absolute power at home. It would be rash to say, at present, that France will not let them go to any length, but I do not think that her lassitude or blindness will be so great as to let her plunge into such danger.

To Lord Granville.

C. O., January 28th.—I hear an interesting account of the Duc de Bordeaux's instructions to his friends. He orders them to abstain from all connexion with the Government and to refuse all salaried places, but to take whatever they can get by election, and to hold their commissions in the army and navy. Louis Napoleon told M. d'Audiffret that he had no intention of touching the property of the elder branch. As for the Comte de Chambord, he said, we fight *avec des armes courtoises.* However, he had given old Pasquier[1] a similar assurance that the Orleans property would not be taken, a few days before the decrees came out, which gave the Orleanists a false security. Pasquier also remonstrated against the oath of allegiance; but L. N. said he could not do less in that way than his predecessors, if his reign was to

---

[1] President of the Upper Chamber and Chancellor during the reign of Louis Philippe. He retired from public life at the revolution of 1848, and died—aged 95—in 1862. The Duc d'Audiffret-Pasquier was his grand-nephew.

be thought serious. The refusals to serve on the senate were infinite.

From Lord Clarendon

Dublin Castle, February 1st.—A casual despotism founded on a popular delusion is the most accurate description that can be given of the present state of things in France; and, though I agree with you that such power can take no permanent root, yet I fear it may last long enough to do irreparable mischief. . . . The attitude of society may be dignified now, but I expect there will soon be deserters enough to save Louis Napoleon from isolation; and the taste for grouping round the man who strikes and pays will increase. . . .

I have no doubt the 'Times' has had good and sufficient reasons for the course taken with respect to him, but I own that to me they are not apparent. To denounce in the strongest terms such acts as Louis Napoleon committed, at first was a duty on the part of the English press. Occasionally to do the same at subsequent periods of his two months' career was likewise perhaps necessary; but to go on battering at him every day[1] was more, I think, than was required, either by public opinion at home or by English interests abroad. How far the 'Times' is now read or permitted to circulate in France I don't know; but I do know that Louis Napoleon reads it. . . .

If we were invulnerable, and had an army, and navy, and rock-defended shores, we might thunder away to any extent; but, in our present helpless state,[2] it seems to me that to persist in irritating France is a luxury for which we may pay dearly; every newspaper, at the same time, overflowing with proofs of national panic, and the most *naïf* indications

---

[1] See, among many others, the articles in the *Times* of January 14th, 15th, 16th, and 17th. It has been seen (*ante*, p. 249) that Reeve acknowledges them as his.

[2] This helpless state of the country is a subject to which Clarendon frequently refers. After visiting at the Grove in the following October, Mrs. Reeve wrote to her father: 'Nothing can exceed the alarm expressed on the subject of invasion and the absence of preparations for defending our coasts. A French general is reported to have said: "The decree for the annexation of Belgium will be dated from London;"' but no one at the Grove seems to have asked how they were to cross the Channel.

of where we can be best attacked and how most easily
conquered.

In reply to this, Reeve forwarded to Lord Clarendon a
copy of his correspondence with Lord Granville, and received
the following answer :—

Dublin Castle, February 9th.—I return your very able
and excellent letter to Granville, with many thanks for
letting me see it.

I never dreamt of denying or questioning the right of the
press to denounce in the strongest terms the acts of the
President; but I entirely agree with you when you say,
'there is of course a limit to be observed in all this,' and
I think the limit has been overstepped. It was sound policy
to put England on her guard; it was absolutely necessary
to rouse our countrymen from the apathetic habits and
utilitarian selfishness engendered by a long peace, and to
stimulate public opinion in favour of the principles we hold
dear, and which, at no distant day, we may be called upon to
defend. Now all this has been done, but I think it has been
overdone. The same effect might have been produced with
a much less expenditure of ammunition. We might have
secured all our objects at home and not have given so much
offence abroad. The press either does or does not express
the public opinion of England. If the latter, it should not
assume to speak as if it was so backed; if the former, then
England voluntarily steps forward to exasperate the man
who had, and still retains, power enough to keep thirty-two
millions of Frenchmen in hand, and who can at any moment
detach from his army of 400,000 men a force sufficient to
avenge the insults offered to him by the English nation.

I am no advocate of truckling, as I need hardly say, and
still less of any exhibition of cowardice, though every newspaper that thundered against Louis Napoleon swarmed with
proofs of the national panic; but I simply want to keep the
peace, and to give a neighbour no pretext for war; and I
think that the press, after performing its proper functions,
has been unnecessarily provocative.

Nor can I altogether admit the grounds upon which this
seems to be justified; for you say 'It is the business of a

newspaper to say what it thinks, every day, on all the topics of public interest, both at home and abroad.' If this is to be, irrespective of the harm it may do, it is irresponsibility as great as Louis Napoleon's; and such power as the press now possesses, if irresponsible, will become an intolerable despotism. You refer to the cases of Gladstone and Palmerston as having more outstepped their duty than any newspaper; and I fully admit it as regards Palmerston, whose circulation of the pamphlet was unprecedented and unwarrantable; but I think that Gladstone, an independent gentleman, after a lengthened residence at Naples, was quite within the line of duty to make known the result of his observations. The cause of humanity and justice required that they should not be kept secret; but if he had continued a series of pamphlets, or if he had daily published some fresh atrocities of the Neapolitan Government, and heaped fresh odium on the king, I should then have thought he went beyond his duty, that he had lost sight of what were supposed to be his original objects, and that he would injure the victims he meant to save, by making it a point of honour in the king not to yield to foreign dictation.

The reign of Louis Napoleon may be ephemeral; but if it lasts a few months longer, rely upon it there will be desertions enough—even from the Salons, whose attitude is now so dignified—to rescue him from his state of present isolation; and every man who deserts will make common cause with him against those who denounce his system. You have some reliance upon the grateful feeling of France, for the manner in which the cause of liberty and truth has been upheld by us. I confess I have none; nor indeed can it fairly be expected in this case; for while we have placed Louis Napoleon's acts in their true light, we have necessarily shown also the position which the French people occupy in the eyes of the world.

The injured and outraged exiles now in England and Belgium applaud and thank us for what we are doing; and if their gratitude on being restored to their country differs from that of the *émigrés* in 1814, I shall be equally surprised and pleased. You are a better judge than I can pretend to be of how truly the press has represented public opinion on

this subject ; but, as far as my experience goes, I should say
that the onslaught has been considered too violent and too
long continued.

The Journal here has :—

Thiers had arrived in England on January 16th. I
dined with him at Edward Ellice's in Arlington Street. On
February 1st I took him and Jules de Lasteyrie to Novar's
pictures ; and on the 9th he dined with us, to meet the
Molesworths, Lord Lovelace, Lord Wodehouse, Baron
Bentinck, F. Cadogan.

Constant dinners in February with the Grotes, Senior,
Thiers, Morier, Molesworths, Duke of Newcastle, Lord
Crewe, Prince Nicholas of Nassau, Van de Weyers, Lord
Normanby. Luncheon at Lady Alice Peel's. Rémusat
was in town.

On February 16th, the Government, as has been said,
was defeated ; and on the 20th Lord John Russell announced
their intention of resigning : as to which Lord Clarendon
wrote :—

The Liberals who were doing everything to thwart the
Government are now probably blaspheming against Lord
John for his precipitation, but I think he did quite right to
take the first unmistakeable hint and not wait to be kicked
out. . . . I am curious to know who will be my successor.

The Journal continues :—

April 1st.—Christine was presented at the Drawing-room
by Lady Clarendon.

Went to Paris at Easter with Christine.

April 11th.—At Princess Lieven's met M. Guizot, Prince
Nicholas of Nassau, Molé, Lahitte, and Morny.

14th.—Morning with music in Ary Scheffer's atelier.
Cavaignac there with his bride. Home on April 20th.
This visit to Paris was very interesting.

Mrs. Reeve thought so too, and wrote to her father on
April 15th :—

'I don't believe any Englishwoman ever came here
under such auspices as I have. Henry knows every inch of

Paris and all the distinguished people. We have engagements till the day we start (Monday), and might have many more, and he does take the greatest pleasure in showing me everything. The weather is lovely—clear, bright, and warm. I do not write praises of buildings, galleries, and museums, or of views, &c., because, as you must have seen them, you can take for granted my astonishment and admiration.'

May 15th.—Expedition to Gosport with Christine and John Richardson to see Granville Loch's ship the ' Winchester ' [a 50-gun frigate, going out to the East Indies as the flag-ship of Rear-Admiral Charles Austen].

May 19th.—Queen's ball. To Bracknell for the Ascot week.

To M. de Tocqueville

16 Chester Square, May 23rd.

MY DEAR FRIEND,—I have just read, with great interest, a letter you wrote lately to Mrs. Grote, and as I must renounce the pleasure of conversing with you for the present, I obey an impulse which leads me to answer you in writing.

I am doubtless less inclined than most of my fellow-countrymen to admit that we can isolate ourselves from matters which affect the liberty of other nations and the general good of humanity, nor am I one of those who take off their hats to a man because he has succeeded in founding an inconceivable despotism. Yet neither can I hide from myself that for fifty years all our efforts in favour of constitutional liberty on the Continent have had very little result. In one place, the soil has refused the good seed, as in the Gospel ; in another, men have uprooted it; everywhere the harvest is bad. Between mixed politics and mixed breeding there is so much similarity ; when the cross is too different, it is barren.

Happily for England, this is neither her principal mission nor her first duty. If she has not succeeded in founding anything durable on the Continent of Europe, the same cannot be said of the rest of the globe ; and whilst we see the fires we have kindled among European nations, dying out because they do not know how to keep them alight, we are invincibly attracted to America and Australia, which are the awakening of a world. Never was England less disposed to shut herself up in her isle, and devote herself exclusively to manufacturing cottons, and rearing fine oxen. On the contrary, the greatest questions rise before her. Our fraternal relations with the United States, the Government of Canada so sensitive, the exodus of the Catholic people of Ireland, who seek a happier destiny elsewhere, leaving at our doors an island they have never known how to cultivate, the astonishing developement of the Australian continent, the rapid march of civilisation in the Eastern islands, and the government of India, with its marvellous problems—these are the first duties of the English statesman, and if it be selfishness, the self is a very large one. For note that I do not say we ought to govern this empire according to English views, or for the benefit of England. That would be a very cramped way of considering it. But we ought to found free states wherever we have the power and right ; and these, I am persuaded, will one day justify the somewhat fantastic saying of Canning, who boasted of having raised up a new world to restore the balance of the old. Whatever may be the fate of Europe, if these efforts are successful, the general cause of liberty and civilisation will not suffer.

It is true that the complete fall of constitutional government in France has profoundly grieved and astonished all those who had a sure and rational belief in the system which France has practised so brilliantly for thirty-three years. But it is said that, of all countries in the world, France is, and rightly so, the one least likely to endure the influence of foreign ideas ; and thus her actual condition places us in this dilemma—either she is tamely submitting to a power she dislikes, or she does not really dislike it. On this point I am without any clear or fixed ideas. All the intelligence, the aristocracy of birth or education, is doubtless very hostile to the empire. But there was a wish for democracy, a demand for the sovereignty of the people ; things identical with absolute power and empire. This is what seems to me to separate the rule of L. N. from an ordinary despotism, and, taking the facts as they are, it is the condition of the country which should be found fault with, rather than the man who turns it to his profit in a manner which is without parallel.

I will only add a word on our fears and warlike preparations. I agree with you that, so far as one can judge, war is by no means imminent, and that the wish is to avoid it at all costs. I will even say that I doubt the warlike disposition of France, to the extent of thinking that other nations are readier to fight. But what guided our policy in this matter was that we found ourselves face to face with an immense force, whose movements could not be depended upon ; and nearly all the French statesmen whom we were able to consult warned us to be on our guard ; many of them believed that some foreign *coup* was imminent. As a matter of fact we fear nothing on that score at present ; but it has taken some months of vigorous preparation to enable us to say so. . .

The Journal notes here :—

July 13*th.*—Dined at M. de Bille's (Danish Minister) to meet Lavradio. . . .

14*th.*—Dined at Senior's with M. de Cavour, Lord Lansdowne, and the Twisletons.

28*th.*—Evening at the Royal Academy. The Duke of Wellington was there. It was the last time I saw him. I had the proof of my memoir[1] of him in my pocket. He died on September 14th.

Fit of gout in August. Started for Aix with Christine and Hopie on the 8th.

To M. de Tocqueville

Aix-la-Chapelle, August 11*th.*—See the result of human plans ! To-day, when I should have been with you, listening to your conversation and breathing the air of your cliffs, here I am, by the doctor's orders, on the banks of a stream which is none the less wearisome because Charlemagne delighted in it. Still, it is a considerable improvement for a man who could not walk a few days ago, to be able to figure among the maimed of the place, and I hope that a short stay will complete my cure.

---

[1] *Times*, September 15th, 16th.

I should have liked to see how France looked when power put on a newer and gentler aspect. When someone has taken everything from you, a vast deal of gratitude is of course due for whatever his highness deigns to give back. The wonder is not that Thiers and M. de Rémusat should be recalled to their country, but that they should ever have been sent out of it. But we are made thus ; we allow ourselves to be thrashed, and when the executioner stops, are overcome with gratitude. Never was so good a prince seen ! In spite of all Thiers's vehement language against his persecutor, I should not be greatly surprised to see him reconciled with the Élysée. It is only vanity which prevents him. He often said in London, 'It is not possible that I who have treated great affairs with men like Prince Metternich and Sir R. Peel should consent to put myself at the head of these adventurers.' But successful adventurers are sometimes emperors ; and if Thiers thought he could give full play to his shameless political imagination at the expense of France, he would be more at his ease as minister of a despotic than of a constitutional state.

I cannot close this letter without again expressing my own and my wife's regret at the mishap which has upset our journey ; but we will try to end it where we had meant to begin.

The Journal continues :—

From Aix-la-Chapelle we went by the Rhine to Geneva. Visit to Binet. To Chamonix, with the Binets, on August 30th. Went with Christine round Mont Blanc by the Col du Bonhomme, and so to Aosta and the St. Bernhard. Went to see the Duc de Broglie at Coppet. Home by Paris.

October 12*th.*—To Newmarket with Mrs. Grote, to see the Cesarewitch. Visits to Stondon and Atherstone, and to the Grove, October 30th.

November 5*th.*—Farnborough ; hunting. Run with Assheton Smith on the 11th ; got the head of the fox.

18*th.*—The Duke of Wellington's funeral at St. Paul's. On the 28th, dined at Bath House with Thiers.

December 2*nd.*—The French Empire was proclaimed. I dined that day at Lansdowne House with Thiers, Lord

Aberdeen, Macready, Senior, Ed. Ellice, Vernon Smith, Lord Mahon, Lord de Mauley, and West.

The Cosmopolitan Club was founded, meeting first at Morier's. Morier, Layard, and myself were the first members.

From M. Guizot

Paris, December 2nd.—I have laughed at the reports you mention of my supposed approval of what is happening here. Similar rumours reach me from Germany ; they have evidently been carefully circulated. I do not worry myself about it, for experience has strengthened my instinctive confidence that, in respect of those who have the honour of being known to the public, the truth is always recognised in the end. It is well known here that, of all men in France, I am the furthest from approving of what has passed in France since 1848. . . For thirty-eight years I have been devoted to the cause of constitutional monarchy, which I have always regarded as the wisest and noblest form of government. But it is to true and truly constitutional monarchy that I belong ; falsehood decked out as royalty or liberty I cannot endure. Please say this from me to all those you may hear speak of my adhesion to the ridiculous and shameful comedy in whose honour I hear the cannon at this moment. After what happened in 1848 it was inevitable and deserved, which is all I can say in its favour.

He goes on speak at great length of the general coldness, the want of enthusiasm with which the Emperor had been received. The masses of the people have voted for the Empire to get rid of the republic which they mistrusted, to guard against the anarchy which they feared ; but they have no confidence in the future, and are full of apprehensions of financial confusion and war. The attitude of the upper classes remains much the same as it was. They did not like the President ; they like the Emperor still less. They would not support the President ; they certainly will not support the Emperor, but they will not make any active opposition to his government ; the masses cannot or dare not ; any attempt would certainly be severely repressed ; and the army is pledged to the Empire—which can now only be overthrown by its own act and fault. And he continues in language which reads like the outpourings of a prophet :—

Will these faults be soon committed ? I very much doubt it. This man is a strange mixture of rashness and patience, of fatalism and prudent calculation ; he believes in his star ; he follows it, and in his inmost soul is resolved to follow it to the end ; but at the same time he fights against it, and does not blindly rush to that end. Of late he has advanced rapidly ; more rapidly, in my opinion, than was to his advantage, but he is able to check himself and to wait. He has not, like his uncle, an inexhaustible fertility of genius, and an insatiable ardour of character ; on the contrary, he is slow and indolent ; he loves pleasure and leisure. He will get what enjoyment he can out of his position ; he will do and say whatever is necessary to prevent Europe from disquieting herself about him, and will postpone as long as possible the taking of any compromising step towards realising his ambitious dreams.

But the moment will come ; I am convinced of it. A fatalist may struggle for a time against the destiny to which he believes himself called ; but sooner or later he will yield and throw himself into it. Besides, something must be done to amuse and occupy France. Our country is a prey to two contradictory cravings ; a craving for repose, and a craving for new and violent emotions. She wishes to have her interests assured, but also to have her imagination satisfied at the same time. It was for this that Napoleon I. gave her war, and that we instituted the tribune. I think the new Emperor would like to follow the policy of Louis Philippe, without the tribune, under the name of Napoleon, without the war ; but he will not succeed ; and when he finds this out, he will return, either as conqueror or conspirator, to the traditions of the Empire whose flag he is now raising. Whether he wishes it or not, this is his future ; I am convinced that he does wish it, but he will endeavour rather to retard than to hasten it. Those in his confidence already show themselves eager to find some means of filling the stage and amusing the spectators without seeking great adventures. M. Fould said the other day : 'We shall have the marriage in the spring, the coronation in the summer, the heir in March 1854, and then we shall see.'

The Journal notes :—

December 17th.—Lord Derby resigned, and negotiations began for a coalition of Peelites and Whigs : Lord Aberdeen premier.

And the year 1852 ended with the accustomed visit to Mr. Longman at Farnborough, and afterwards to Ventnor, where Mrs. Austin was then living.

The year 1853, so notable from the diplomatic point of view as the date of the growing quarrel with Russia, which in the following year culminated in war, is, from the biographer's point of view, notable as the date of Reeve's beginning a journal of current events in addition to the curt entries in his diary. Sometimes written continuously and in considerable detail, sometimes very briefly and with long gaps intervening, it reaches down to 1877, and for these years forms the staple material to elucidate and connect the voluminous correspondence.

January 1st.—It was at the close of the year 1852 that Lord Derby's administration was suddenly terminated by a vote of the House of Commons on Mr. Disraeli's budget. This cabinet had existed about ten months upon false pretences and without a policy. The bubble broke on the first shock of serious debate; and on the first disputed vote, the Government was beaten by 19 in the fullest House ever known. I think all the members except twenty-five took part in the vote. Upon this occurrence the Queen at once sent for Lord Aberdeen and Lord Lansdowne together (December 18th). But Her Majesty's real intention had long been to place Lord Aberdeen at the head of the administration, for I think no man at this time possesses to an equal degree her confidence and her regard. I had myself observed, for at least six months, that Lord Aberdeen was preparing to take office. The Whigs cherished the notion that Lord Lansdowne would be sent for, and would accept the task of reconstituting the Liberal party. I thought otherwise. He was summoned, however, to lend his sanction to the combination; but having taken colchicum the night before, he could not undertake the journey to the Isle of Wight, and Lord Aberdeen ultimately went alone.

Lord Lansdowne distinctly declined to undertake the

formation of the Cabinet; but though Lord Aberdeen contested the point with him, I know he (Lord Aberdeen) had long made up his mind that no one could unite the elements of a strong government but himself.

Two important obstacles were to be overcome in this negotiation. The one, the pretensions of Lord John Russell; the other, the ambiguous position of Lord Palmerston, who had staked all his hopes on the prospect of a Lansdowne Ministry. In the preceding week a party had met at Woburn, consisting of Lord Aberdeen, Lord Clarendon, the Duke of Newcastle, Lord John, and Graham—Lord Lansdowne being too ill to attend it—and here no doubt the preliminaries were laid. But after Lord Derby was out and the formation of the new Cabinet begun, the truth is that at least three days elapsed before Lord John definitively consented to join it, though that was a condition *sine qua non*. Lord Clarendon exerted himself with great activity and effect to counteract his objections; but everything was kept in suspense by this hesitation; and even on Christmas Day Clarendon left his family and guests at the Grove, to endeavour to smooth matters in London. Lord John would have preferred, I think, for his own dignity's sake, to have had no office, but only a seat in the Cabinet with the lead of the House. But that might have been regarded as an insincere arrangement, and, as far as he was concerned, an arrogant one. He ended by taking the Foreign Office, upon Clarendon's promise that he would relieve him of it whenever the business of the Session began. The Whig party were already sufficiently disposed to grumble at an arrangement which placed so large a portion of the highest offices and the premiership in the hands of their new allies, and if Lord John had not done what he was at last persuaded and compelled to do, the combination must have failed, and we must have surrendered at discretion to Lord Derby.

The case of Lord Palmerston was an unexpected good fortune. Lord Aberdeen had gone to him in person to propose office. Palmerston received him not only with politeness, but with cordiality; reminded him that they had been acquainted for over sixty years—for they were playmates at Harrow—and declared that in all their political differences he had borne him no ill-will. But, he added, the country would never understand his notions in joining an Aberdeen administration. The Earl intended to have offered him the Admiralty, but would have consented to anything else, except the Foreign Office ; but upon his refusal he said nothing of the office, and relinquished the task. This was another great danger ; for had Palmerston remained out of the Government, he would probably have joined Lord Derby and led the Opposition. On the other hand, his health was beginning to fail ; a mere attack of cold and gout had just transformed him suddenly into an old man ; he was pressed for money, and immediate office had its charms not only for himself, but for Lady P. I saw, even at the moment of his refusal, an indication of her relenting, and I was not surprised to learn that on the more pressing solicitation of his old friends, and especially of Lord Lansdowne, he had consented to take the Home Office, which is what he wished for.

The Cabinet was wisely completed by the admission of Sir William Molesworth as a representative of advanced Liberal opinions. The place first offered to him was the War Office without the Cabinet, but he resolutely declined it. I endeavoured to persuade him to accept, but he gave some valid reasons for that resolution ; and we endeavoured (with Delane) to persuade Lord Aberdeen to put him in the Cabinet, which at last he consented to do, even though Cardwell, the President of the Board of Trade, was still excluded. I have very little doubt that Molesworth will prove a more tractable colleague than many of the Whigs, though I feel less certain of his administrative capacity. It was wise to give office to Bernal Osborne, C. Villiers, and some members of the Irish brigade ; for these appointments have silenced the complaints already raised by many of the Liberal party.

Under these circumstances, at the commencement of a new year, and of a new government composed almost entirely of my personal friends, and to some extent of my own contemporaries, I propose to begin some record of passing events, of which it is commonly my fate to be a very near spectator, and I hope I may have time and perseverance to continue it.

January 5th.—The Cabinet was no sooner formed than most of the ministers left town, for the Christmas holidays had been sacrificed to the crisis.   The peers went to their country houses, and the commoners to their elections, which passed off well, and almost entirely without opposition. There is no doubt that the formation of this Government is well received by the country.   The only danger is that they will be expected to perform miracles, which, as C. Villiers said at Wolverhampton, is what their predecessors promised, but did not perform.   Some anxiety is felt about Gladstone's election at Oxford, where they have at last set up a candidate in the person of Dudley Perceval, son of the minister, a very low Churchman, a very high Tory, and a madman to boot.   It is, however, true that Gladstone's opinions are widely different from those predominating in the Ministry, and it will probably be advantageous to him to have the connexion dissolved by the bigotry of his adversaries.

Amongst other novelties of this new year, I may record that George Lewis succeeds Mr. Empson as editor of the ' Edinburgh,' having made up his mind that this or any other task is preferable to the drudgery of subordinate office.

Abroad, the principal affair of the moment is the recognition of the Emperor Napoleon III., which has been somewhat needlessly retarded by the Northern Powers, and conceded at last in rather an uncivil form.[1]   I have read the Prussian despatches to Count Hatzfeld, in Paris, on the subject, and they imply that Louis Napoleon is only recognised by way of acknowledging that a government exists and of preserving the peace of Europe.   The French cannot be satisfied, but it seems to be their policy to *faire bonne mine à mauvais jeu.*   M. Guizot says truly enough that the Empire has no honeymoon.   The funds fall, the marriage is broken off; the Senate resists, and the Northern Powers growl; and even now perhaps the Imperial authority is less secure than that of the President was.   In the composition of his household he has not obtained a single name of rank, and the

---

[1] 'I hear,' wrote Lord Clarendon to Reeve on January 4th, 'that *les lenteurs des Cours du Nord* have irritated H.I. Majesty; and I must say that their *coups d'épingles* are undignified. When people dare not say No, they had better say Yes with a good grace.'

three first places are given to Vaillant, Magnan, and St.-Arnaud, three marshals of his own making.

I saw Lockhart to-day at the Athenæum, and was struck by the moderation of his language about the Government. He said they were entitled to great forbearance, and that he had great confidence in Lord Aberdeen and Lord Lansdowne, and that, at any rate, the last Cabinet had only been bidding for the support of the mob, and had produced a ridiculous budget. How far will the next 'Quarterly' support this strain? Unhappily Croker's influence still condemns us to several sheets of his scourings, which he has an indefeasible right to put in, by an ancient and deplorable compact with old John Murray. Meanwhile he goes on to write articles, as St. Buonaventura did his memoirs, after death; for he has already taken leave of all the world several times and positively announced his final exit, though he has not been as good as his word.

January 7th.—Our new Lord President, Lord Granville, broke his collar-bone yesterday by his horse falling while he was hunting with Rothschild near Woburn, but the accident is not serious. It is an amusing trait in Lord Palmerston that upon his arrival at the Home Office, where he has transacted business twice, he ordered a clerk to go to the Foreign Office to see how they folded their despatches, and likewise ordered that blue instead of green riband should be used to tie up papers.

I dined at Lady Flower's. The Verschoyles and Blacketts there—in all sixteen people—and I between Lady Talbot de Malahide and Fanny Blackett. They relate incredible things of the 'charades en action' at Compiègne. A sort of *curée des dames* was celebrated, which consisted of the women scrambling for jewellery on all fours, and the Emperor acting as *piqueur de la meute*, the lights having been extinguished![1] Such are the Imperial dignities of France. Even the Duc de Guiche refused a place in the household, as too low for him.

January 8th.—The Cabinet meet to-day for the first time since the completion of the new administration. I saw,

---

[1] This was afterwards contradicted (see *post*, 286), but it was very generally believed at the time.

however, none of the ministers, for Lord Granville was at home suffering pain from the results of his accident, and Lord Clarendon, who was to have called on me, sat with the patient. The post of master of the horse has, I hear, been offered to the Duke of Wellington II., and accepted by him in a very good spirit. He has also had the good sense to let the public see Apsley House and the relics of the Great Duke for three days a week during this present month.

Lord Cranworth is stoutly resolved on prosecuting the reform of the Ecclesiastical Courts, in which labour he will, of course, be mainly guided by his brother-in-law and friend, Dr. Lushington. In truth, however, the main evil of those courts are the sinecures which encumber them by Act of Parliament. For 20,000 wills and administrations proved in a year, probably not 300 are litigated : but the issue of probate in common form must remain in the hands of certain confidential public officers. Another important measure which, I hear from Shuttleworth, the Government have in contemplation, is some more expeditious mode of reaching and utilising charitable endowments for the purposes of national education. He has a book in preparation on the subject, and suggests, I believe, that powers should be given to another committee of council to exercise the necessary control over these charities.

January 10*th.*—The recognition of Louis Napoleon by the Northern Powers has taken place, but not without a hitch which threatened at any moment to break off all relations. The credentials of Kisseleff did not contain the *formule consacrée* of ' My good brother ; ' he was instructed to leave Paris if they were not received, and all the German ministers were instructed to do what the Russians did. Under these circumstances it was decided by the Emperor and the French Cabinet not to receive what they considered a slight, and an intentional one. Drouyn de Lhuys formally told Lord Cowley that such were their intentions—at the same time he asked Lord Cowley's opinion. Lord Cowley replied that, in his judgement, the nobler and more polite course was to overlook the affront, and receive the credentials, and Drouyn was authorised to repeat this to the Emperor.

The next morning early Fould came to Lord Cowley and

told him that the Emperor had slept on his advice and had resolved to take it, but had told no one but himself, not even Drouyn de Lhuys, of his intention. Soon afterwards Kisseleff came in, as if to take leave; said it was all up, and that he should be gone in twenty-four hours. Cowley held his tongue. But in the afternoon the Cabinet met; Louis Napoleon declared he should receive the credentials; and at 4 P.M. the Court carriages were sent to fetch the minister. I apprehend the determining motive, however, was the state of the Bourse; for the departure of the ministers would have been followed by a heavy *baisse*, and a perfect *débâcle* on the Exchange.

January 12*th.*—Comte d'Haussonville, the Duc de Broglie's son-in-law, called on me to-day and confirmed this last observation in a striking manner; he said the Emperor's resolution to accept the credentials was due in part to Lord Cowley's opinion, but much more to the appalled and appalling aspect of Rothschild, who told his Majesty that if Kisseleff went away it would be a *baisse*—not of one or two francs, but a sinking of the funds to perdition and a catastrophe on the Bourse. M. d'Haussonville says that the attitude of society in Paris continues good, that Louis Napoleon is even less the fashion than he was a year ago; that—les salons boudent et exécutent ceux qui se valèrent; and that the change in the tone of the foreign diplomats at Paris, especially since the Emperor of Austria's last visit to Berlin, is very curious and remarkable. Princess Lieven believed for forty-eight hours that she should have to leave Paris after Kisseleff, and her despair was extremely burlesque. She has contrived to attach Fould to her court in the Rue St.-Florentin, as completely as other and greater men had been before. He goes there once or twice a day, and the Princesse des Ursins,[1] in all her state, was not more powerful. The *bourgeoisie*, Haussonville said, are still blind and infatuated; they talk of the stability of a government whose next heirs are a man of seventy and after him a *Rouge*; and they will believe in peace till they are on the brink of war,

---

[1] The dominant favourite of Louise of Savoy, the first Queen of Philip V. of Spain. For the way in which she was bundled out of the country by Philip's second wife, see Armstrong's *Elisabeth Farnese*, chap. ii.

when it will be too late to avoid it, though dangerous enough to encounter it. Ce sera un mauvais moment à passer.

I sat some time both yesterday and to-day with Lord Granville, who is better, and had to-day got his coat on. Everybody wonders at M. de Flahault's accepting the senatorship, which he is obliged to conceal in this country, pretty much as Cardinal Wiseman hides his red robe under his great coat. Lord John says that the late Government has done little in foreign affairs, but that little not ill; and he was satisfied with the hour's conversation he had with Malmesbury on his going out. They all seem of opinion now that the secret memorandum signed at the Foreign Office by the four Powers on December 3rd last ought not to be made public.

January 13th.—Having recently been elected a Fellow of the Antiquarian Society, I took my seat this evening for the first time, and was received by Mr. Payne Collier. Nothing was more ancient than the aspect of the apartment in Somerset House. A few Holbeins on the walls; a few mummies and Babylonish birds in the cases; some old books; and very old men were the company. A paper was read on some Roman limekilns in the New Forest.

January 14th.—They say there are symptoms in Paris of the near approach of the crash in financial affairs we have long foreseen. French houses borrowing all they can, even in London. Sat some time with Lord Granville, who was well enough to go to the Cabinet yesterday. He told me that the Cabinet sits round the room, with a small table in the middle, and not, as I had always supposed, round a large table.

I forgot to record yesterday the 'poultry show' to which I went, and where Pepys would have lost himself in amazement at the sight of the new cocks and hens—Cochin China fowls, just introduced. They are big creatures, and people give fifty guineas a pair for them to get the breed. It was droll enough to hear such cock-concert.[1]

---

[1] These brutes, more like young ostriches than domestic fowls, though now practically extinct, remained in vogue for ten or twelve years. Not the least remarkable thing about them was the voice of the male, which resembled the roar of an angry bull rather than the clarion of chanticleer. The present writer

January 16th.—I took a pew in Harness's church,[1] which led to my removing to Rutland Gate.

January 18th.—I am confined to the house by gout. John Walter and Delane called, somewhat disturbed by a long and direct attack in the 'Moniteur' of the preceding day on the 'Times,' 'Chronicle,' and 'Morning Advertiser.' But, as far as the 'Times' is concerned, the inculpated passage is a palpable forgery. No such expressions have been used in the 'Times' at all, and the date given is absurd, for they attribute this article to the 2nd inst., which was a Sunday! They probably had in view the survey of external affairs which appeared on the 3rd inst.; but even in that there is hardly a vestige of what they complain of. I wrote a strong reply, saying that Louis Napoleon had more reason to dread our facts than our invention.

January 19th.—Sat with Lord Granville in the morning. He acknowledged that the Cowleys had not made the embassy in Paris what it used to be—a centre for all parties; and observed that, if it had become so, it would have had more influence with Louis Napoleon himself. Nobody ever possessed that art in a higher degree than Granville's own father and mother, as I remember in 1840 and earlier. However, by all accounts, parties never ran so fiercely in society as at present. M. de la Rochejaquelin and M. de Pastoret have been cut and insulted in the most deliberate manner. People have left P.P.C. cards at their doors, and when old Mme. de la Rochejaquelin—the widow of two Vendéan chiefs, and a matron of eighty—was told that M. Pastoret had done the same thing as her son, she replied: 'Oui, monsieur, mais au moins il a attendu la mort de sa mère.' After such taunts they will wear their senatorial robes uneasily. Every sort of song and sarcasm is poured out on the official world, and, by way of distinction, the men who are not of it desist from wearing their decorations.

M. de Bille, Danish minister, came to tell me the Danish

knew one, in a small provincial town, which drew down on its owner a request from the neighbours to shut up his new dog at night, as his baying was an intolerable nuisance.

[1] All Saints', Knightsbridge, built in 1849 by the exertions of Mr. Harness, who was incumbent of it till his death, in 1869. Besides his clerical work, of which Reeve formed a high estimate, he was known as an editor and student of Shakespeare.

Parliament is dissolved, because they have rejected the ministerial proposal to include Holstein in the Danish commercial frontier, by moving the custom-house from the line of the Eyder; and what is most strange is, that this is done by the ultra-Danish party, who hate the Germans as much as the Germans hate them, and would sacrifice the German parts of the monarchy altogether to be joined to the Scandinavian kingdom. Holstein, however, must be commercially united to Denmark, if not to the Zollverein. The interests and wishes of the population must decide it. And probably they are in favour of the Danish tariff, which is lower than the German. The Ministry are resolved to stand or fall on this question.

Called on Bunsen, who related with great drollery an Egyptian romance, said to be written about four years after the exodus of the Jews, which M. de Rougé has deciphered. Sir James Graham expressed to him at Windsor the other day considerable uneasiness on the French navy, and said that in all their dockyards they had taken on many additional hands—in one 500 workmen. Yet the French Government declare they have reduced their naval estimates this year by forty million francs. Bunsen and other ministers are annoyed that the present English Cabinet has resolved not to communicate the secret quadruple memorandum of December 3rd to France. Of course it leads the Continental Courts to say there is no acting with so changeable a Government, and it will surely be worse if Louis Napoleon discovers the existence of the memorandum by other means.

We dined at the Worsleys, with Justice Crompton and Lady C., and went in the evening to the tail of an academic repast at the Eastlakes'—Mrs. Jameson, Mrs. R. Boyle, Milman, Sir R. Inglis, Landseer. Some wonderful calotypes of Venetian palaces, far beyond anything of the kind I have seen; but then they are painted by the Italian sun. Eastlake said the prices now given by the Birmingham and Manchester manufacturers for modern paintings were beyond all limit, and the largest any painters had been able to get for their own works. One of his pieces had sold lately for 1,400*l.*, for which he had 500*l.*; and he is offered 200*l.* for any single head he may paint. The Orleans Scheffers were sold yesterday in Paris. The Francesca di Rimini, 43,000 fr.; the Christus Consolator, 52,000 fr.; the Giaour and Medora, about 1,000*l.* each. Delaroche's Death of the Duc de Guise, 52,000 fr.; all immense prices.

January 20th.—Hopie's party took place to-night with the dissolving views, which amused a host of pretty children.

January 21st.—The Imperial marriage still uppermost. We dined at T. Longman's; a family party with Count Strzelecki[1] and Sir T. Mitchell, the inventor of the boomerang propeller, with which he unmercifully boomerang-ed us. Strzelecki has been everywhere and is excellent company.

January 22nd.—Hunting with Longman and Delane at Farnborough.

January 23rd.—People talk of nothing but the Montijo marriage, which was formally announced yesterday, and is to be solemnised this day week. We called on Mrs. Eric Smith, and found she was 'Eugénie's' intimate friend—i.e. the future empress; had known her from a child at Clifton and in Paris. She describes her as amiable, affable, captivating, but bold, independent, unbending, wilful, and indifferent alike to the opinion of others and to danger. Yet the romantic vein in the English character is rather touched by this marriage, and I have no doubt it is more popular in England than in France.

January 25th.—Two dinners a day is severe work, but I went through it to-day, and both were agreeable. Lady Alice Peel had asked me to meet the Duc d'Aumale at Marble Hill, Twickenham, and I rode over with Lord Ribblesdale, so as to get there at two. The house is old and picturesque, built by Lady Suffolk, and very much à la Louis XV. The Altons were there; soon came Lady John Russell (whom I had not met for some time, and who was very cordial), the Colloredos,[2] Prince Carini, young Reventlow and the Duc et Duchesse d'Aumale. He evidently desired that

[1] The Australian explorer and author of *Physical Description of New South Wales* (8vo. 1843). He spoke English fluently and well, though with a slight foreign accent, and was much liked in London society. He died at the age of 77, in 1873.

[2] The Austrian ambassador.

I should be presented to him, and immediately began to talk very agreeably. He is spare in figure, thoughtful in face, easy in manner, but his eye is eager, restless, and penetrating. Much of what he said was of our common friends—Haussonville, Thomas, Thiers, &c.—but he spoke, without constraint and without bitterness, of the present state of things in France ; considered war the great danger, as that would force all parties to take the national cause ; but added that he saw in this marriage an additional proof that Louis Napoleon is far more addicted to self-indulgence than to the laborious efforts of military life ; that a man must make war with his whole mind and body, drinking water, living hardly, shunning excess ; and that neither Louis Napoleon's habits nor age nor health were very well fitted to such privations. I mentioned that Napoleon himself said in 1806, soon after Austerlitz, that he was only fit for war for five years more—which proved true.

The Duke talked of General Canrobert, who seems likely to succeed St.-Arnaud, and said he was a good colonel. He expressed an opinion that no one had any hold on the troops after he had ceased to command them, especially in the French army, which changes so rapidly. Except sergeants and petty officers, there is no one now in the army who knew either himself or the African generals [of] five years ago. Even at Ham Lamoricière found this, for the garrison was composed of a regiment which had been with him some years before in Algeria, but that had no effect. The Duke told an anecdote of the great Condé's arrest, when he appealed to the musketeers who had fought with him a short time before at the Plaine de Larne, but quite in vain.

During luncheon the Duke talked incessantly, and spoke with enthusiasm of the pleasure of buying a pennyworth of hot chestnuts or galette on the boulevards by the Gymnase, as if he had often done it. He told a good thing of M. Beugnot. It was proposed under the Restoration to put up a crucifix in the Chamber of Deputies. 'By all means,' cried B., 'but I hope you will put over it the sublime words, *Pardonnez leur, mon Père, car ils ne savent ce qu'ils font.*' Upon the whole, the impression produced on me by this prince is very agreeable. He is fond of historical reading, has got his library at Osborne House, and is busy with the Condé papers.[1]

I got back in time to dress and go to dine at Lord Mahon's, where I found old Lord Stanhope, looking like old Dowton[2] the actor *en père noble*, Lady Dalmeny, Hallam, Goulburn, M.P. for Cambridge University, and Hayward. Nothing could exceed old Lord Stanhope's vehemence about Louis Napoleon; he said he could kill him with his own hands. He told some anecdotes of Lord Chesterfield, not however very remarkable; and Lord Mahon showed me the originals of the letters to his son, written in a very fair hand. The Elector of Saxony said that Mr. Stanhope was the best-informed Englishman he had ever seen at the Court.

January 28th.—I had an interview with Sir James Graham at the Admiralty to ask him to review the court-martial by which Godfrey Taylor was reprimanded and placed at the bottom of the lieutenants on December 4th, for sleeping on his watch, when at Woolwich, the day before the ship was paid off. Graham received me very cordially and promised to speak to Admiral Parker about it, as he could not interfere himself in a matter of naval discipline. He afterwards let me know that Parker was of opinion that the sentence could not be reversed immediately.[3]

January 29th.—Hunted with Longman at Farnborough.

January 30th.—Louis Napoleon's marriage was solemnised at Notre Dame with great pomp. Delane went over to the ceremony.

February 1st.—Delane returned from Paris, where he had been to see the marriage, and reported that it had been the most splendid and the most ungenial ceremony in the world—all trappings and gold without; all smothered contempt within. Nobody even took off his hat to the Emperor and Empress as they were going to St. Cloud. Lady

---

[1] The result of which study has been given to the world in the *Histoire des Princes de Condé pendant les XVIe et XVIIe siècles* (7 vols. 8vo. 1869–96). The first two volumes were, in fact, printed in 1863; but as they were on the point of being published, they were sequestrated by the Government, and the stop was not taken off till 1869.

[2] William Dowton, died in 1851 at the age of 87.

[3] In the spring of 1855 Lieutenant Taylor was restored to his original seniority, January 15th, 1850.

Molesworth brought in the same account. Indeed as she was going to Notre Dame with Lady Cowley, the aspect of the crowd was so sinister and ill-humoured as to frighten them.

February 2nd.—The Judicial Committee sat the rest of the week—Saturday not inclusive.

CHAPTER IX

THE EASTERN QUESTION

IT is just at this time that, like the servant of Elias, we catch the first glimpse of the little cloud rising out of the sea which was presently to cover the heavens and usher in a great European storm. In the previous year Montenegro had broken out into more active and aggressive rebellion than usual, and Omar Pasha had been ordered to quiet the disturbance. Austria took alarm, and, in January 1853, sent Count Leiningen to Constantinople with a peremptory demand for Omar Pasha's recall.[1] From the very first, the matter appeared to the Government to forebode mischief, and was thus spoken of by Lord Clarendon :—[2]

The Grove, February 2nd.—I saw Lord John yesterday and found that he by no means considered the Montenegro affair an unimportant struggle, and said that it may become more serious from the eagerness of the Emperor of Russia to pick a quarrel with his *bon ami* of France, and the readiness of the latter to oblige him. I am sorry to say the former is not acting with quite the same magnanimity that he has displayed upon all serious questions during the last five years, but Lord John is doing what he can to smoothe differences. It appears that we remonstrated strongly against any Turkish troops being sent to Montenegro, but without success. As far as Turkey alone is concerned, there can be no valid reason for upholding her *à tout prix*, particularly now that the old fanatical régime is restored, except the fear of worse things.

The Journal mentions :—

February 3rd.—A pleasant dinner at Twiss's rooms at the Albany; Count Colloredo, Bille, Cardwell, now President of

---

[1] Kinglake's *History of the Crimean War*, i. 76 *et seq.*
[2] Not in office at this time, though he became Foreign Secretary a few days later.

the Board of Trade, Judge Erle, Strzelecki, young Reventlow, and myself. Cardwell, however, talked gloomily enough of railway accidents, of which he seems to have witnessed as many as a man can do without being killed. He said the increase in our exports is inconceivably rapid—one million sterling in the last month only.

February 4th.—We had to dinner, at home, the Billes, Sir Charles and Lady Eastlake, William Hamilton[1] and wife, Marochetti, Hayward, who made himself very agreeable, and Munro. In the evening, the Bunsens and a good many people.

February 5th.—Hunted at Farnborough with Longman and Bonamy Price, an acute man enough. I bought poor Bailey's mare Polly for 40*l.*

February 6th.—An interesting conversation with young Philip Taylor of Marseilles on the French steam navy, which it is the fashion here greatly to overrate. He says that they have no steamships really fit for war except the 'Napoleon' and the 'Charlemagne;' that there are no important vessels or marine engines building in France; that their stores are low and bad, in so much that the sails of the fleet were blown to pieces last time they went out of Toulon, and no new tenders are advertised for; that the transatlantic steamers of 1840 are all paddle, and unfit to carry great guns, though useful as transports; that the 'Isly' is a failure, and even the 'Napoleon' cannot carry ten days' coal; that he firmly believes no considerable naval constructions are taking place in any part of France, and that there are no *marchés d'urgence*; that besides his own house, which Louis Napoleon has christened *Forges et Chantiers de la Méditerranée*, there are but two private establishments in France capable of turning out powerful engines, and neither of these is fully employed; that Ducos[2] is an old merchant of Bordeaux, known to have committed bigamy, who is anything but a lion; and that there is, in short, nothing to warrant the apprehensions en-

---

[1] William Richard Hamilton, diplomatist and antiquarian; father of Charles Hamilton already noticed (*ante*, p. 88). By a curious coincidence he was for some years (1822–5) minister at the Court of Naples.

[2] Ministre de la Marine; nephew of Roger Ducos, Bonaparte's colleague in the Consulate. Whatever his matrimonial relations may have been, he was a man of some ability, and had had twenty years' experience as a deputy. He was only 54 at his death in 1855.

tertained here. I wrote on the spot to Sir J. Graham to tell him he ought to see P. Taylor.

February 7th.—We saw Graham, but he was more anxious to defend his own opinions and proceedings than to listen to P. Taylor's facts. He talked of twenty line-of-battle ships to be fitted with screws in France, and appeared to be struck with an excessive veneration for the power of the French people. One takes a different impression from P. Taylor's account of his own workshops, in which he has, at Marseilles and at Toulon, some 1,500 men, all bitterly hostile to the Emperor, and for the most part socialists. In fact, the only sort of education they seem to have received is that of socialist doctrines and seditious pamphlets, and they confidently await the realisation of their dreams. None of them voted for the Emperor.

We went to Bille's in the evening; pleasant enough. I saw Mr. Fergusson, author of a pamphlet,[1] which makes some noise, on the fortifications of Portsmouth.

February 8th.—The Judicial Committee closed its sittings, and seemed disposed to think that a remedy for some of its delays is to make me registrar. I had a crowd of people all day. Lord Clarendon sat with me a long time; said John Russell was anxious about the Montenegrin question, and that, though he blamed the Turks, he thought the Austrians had gone too far in Leiningen's mission, which may very likely end in a declaration of war, especially as he was first to exact an apology about the Hungarian refugees, which he will not get. Lord Stratford is to go back.

Louis Napoleon is charmed with the civility of the English press about his marriage, and has sent Baudin to Lord John to tell him so. At the same time, he is uneasy about the tone of society and of the army, and this is what will lead him into war, which will finish him or make him master of Europe.

---

[1] *The Perils of Portsmouth; or, French Fleets and English Forts.* An ingenious pamphlet, based on an entire misconception of the conditions of the problem, but which, falling in with the spirit of the day, attained considerable popularity, ran through many editions, and was largely responsible for the wasteful expenditure of millions on the fortifications of Portsmouth and Plymouth. Fergusson, who died in 1886, is now better and more favourably known as the author of several standard works on the history of architecture.

February 10th.—Parliament re-opened to-day after nearly two months' recess, without the slightest excitement or formality. I went to the House of Lords. Lord John Russell is to give up the Foreign Office to Clarendon on the 19th, and wanted to have rooms at the Council Office, which we told him was quite impossible; so he is to return to his first *gite* at the Pay Office. Lady Granville had her first assembly, which was, as usual, very pleasant. There is certainly a greater air of ease and of refinement in her house than anywhere else—I mean of *salons politiques*. Colloredo treated the Montenegrin affair lightly, Bunsen more seriously. Lord Wodehouse said he believed there was a strong party for Illyrian independence, neither Russian nor Austrian. I think (and so, I hear, does Lord Aberdeen) that Russia and Austria are not acting together on this matter, but rather in opposition. The French are strong for the Turks, and their right to put the Montenegrins down, but that is probably from hostility to the North.

February 11th.—A good deal of discussion has taken place of late about the mode of proroguing Convocation. Twiss and I found by the Council Register of 1708 that a writ of exoneration was the form used in the contests of that time, and recommended the Government to employ it. Lord Aberdeen, however, accepted the Bishop of Oxford's assurance that all should pass off quietly, and added, 'One must give some of them credit for being gentlemen.' Accordingly, Convocation being prorogued to the 16th to go up with the address, the Queen fixed one o'clock to receive it, thinking the Houses would meet at noon. Upon this the Bishop of London and the Bishop of Oxford came to the archbishop, and persuaded him to meet at ten. These sort of tricks are very characteristic of churchmen.

February 12th.—I saw Lord Clarendon in the morning, and found that, in consequence of a conference he had had with Lord Stratford, he was more disposed to support the Turks than the Montenegrins. In point of strict law, the district is part of Turkey; but it has practically enjoyed privileges which it is impolitic to attack, and I still think the Russians cannot suffer them to be crushed with indifference. Dined at Dasent's, to meet M. de Bille, Twiss, the Lowes, Delane, and a young Indian officer. Dinner rather overdone with turtle soup, but uncommon good Tinto.

Bunsen had a reception in the evening, to which we went, after a dinner he had given to Lord and Lady John. Nothing can exceed the beauty of the Prussian Embassy, which is now the best house of the kind in London, and has just been decorated under Grüner's direction.

A letter from Lord Clarendon marks the Government's growing uneasiness about the trouble in Montenegro:—

Grosvenor Crescent, February 14*th.*—I have had great pleasure in reading the Montenegrin article—many thanks for it. . . . The Turk is not a gentleman who takes lessons from experience, otherwise he could have spared himself an expedition he can ill afford in support of rights so feeble and valueless. I earnestly pray for the *status quo*, but don't expect my prayers to be heard. Colloredo, I understand, does the same; but he is as profoundly ignorant of the real intentions of his Court as we ourselves.

The Journal continues :—

February 16*th.*—Convocation this day went up to the Queen with its address in great state, and was prorogued, after some hours' palaver, by the archbishop. The proceedings lasted from half-past 10 A.M. to half-past 5 P.M. Twiss and I were strongly of opinion that the Crown should have sent down a writ of exoneration, and we got a precedent from the Council Book of 1708, and a writ from the Crown Office of 1712. But Lord Aberdeen was coaxed by the Bishop of Oxford into letting the thing take its course; so that, in a few months hence, we shall have the whole question over again.

We dined at James Loch's, with the Kennedys, Joseph Denmans, and Sir Baldwin Walker. The latter gave us some most curious details about the Turkish fleet in 1840, when he commanded it as Walker Bey. They were lying in the harbour of Alexandria,[1] the 'Mahmoudieh' with scarce water to float her, for she was then the biggest ship in the world, and Mehemet Ali refused to let them quit the

---

[1] See *ante*, p. 118.

port until the French steamer arrived from Constantinople with the news of the acceptance of Charley Napier's treaty. Anxious to be gone, Walker summoned his Turkish captains to a council of war, at which he proposed to them to land in the night with the boats, surround the palace (which is on the water's edge), and carry off Mehemet Ali himself on board ship, whence he might have him sent by a steamer to Constantinople. The captains readily agreed, and probably the plan would have been executed, but Mehemet Ali consented to let the fleet sail. They started, met the French steamer at the mouth of the harbour, and she brought the rejection of the treaty. But the ships were gone.

February 17th.—Millais' in the evening; pleasant party, with a sprinkling of artists and literature.

February 18th.—Heard Disraeli's speech in the House of Commons on our relations with France—in reality, his first attack on the new Government; as bitter as distilled gall. Theatrical in manner and undignified in substance; mischievous abroad. His own people certainly did not approve or applaud. Dined afterwards at Lord Lansdowne's.

February 19th.—Dined at Munro's; Sir R. Murchison, Verekers, Eastlakes, ourselves. The laird gave us a capital dinner, and we lit up the pictures with great effect.

Lord Clarendon sat some time in my room, but the talk was of Irish affairs, and scarce worth recording. By the way, Lord Cowley, who is come over, utterly denies the truth of the story about the *curée des dames* at Compiègne.

February 20th.—Rode with Delane to Mortlake, the frost being still very hard, but the mare carries me well.[1] Meeting at Phillips' studio in the evening to settle the rules of our club for evening meetings.

February 21st.—The Longmans and Whieldons dined here. For some days past a discussion has been going on as to the propriety of raising me to the functions of registrar of the Privy Council under the provisions of the 3rd and 4th William IV., cap. 41. All the members of the Judicial Committee are in favour of it, and it is, of course, an advantage to have Lord Granville at the Office. Dr. Lushington

---

[1] See February 5th, *ante*, p. 282.

has written to the chancellor for his consent, and then I suppose it will be done.

February 22nd.—We dined at the Granvilles with a large party of the *Nots* in office—Lord Carlisle, Sir G. Grey, Labouchere, and Layard. The Duchess of Sutherland was immensely grand, and an interview between her and Mrs. Grote very diverting. In our time there has been nobody who continues to surround herself with a sort of fictitious dignity like the Duchess of Sutherland. She is not clever; and in anyone else, her affectations might be laughed at. But she is neither worldly nor ambitious; is very good-natured and has a thoroughly kindly heart; all which, added to her beauty and high character, gives her an influence in society far beyond what wealth and rank could claim for her.

We went afterwards to Mrs. Stephenson's,[1] where there was music. Dr. Weber and his brother sang the duet in 'Otello' with great effect—a music we have, alas! almost ceased to hear; yet, besides its beauty, it has all my early associations in it—Rubini, Donzelli, Pasta, Malibran, and I know not who besides—voices which seem to have passed from the world.

February 23rd.—Countess Colloredo's evening. A good many people to congratulate on the Emperor of Austria's recent escape from assassination; but it is astonishing how a dislike of the Austrians has filtered into every class of society, and at Vienna they are perfectly rabid against us.

February 25th.—Dined at the Richardsons'. Macqueen[2] there. He said the Divorce Commission proposes the creation of a distinct court, and not to send the divorce cases to the judicial courts. Meanwhile my affair of the registrarship goes on. Lord Truro, Dr. Lushington, Lord Justice Knight Bruce, Lord Justice Turner, Sir E. Ryan, Sir John Jervis,

---

[1] Sister of Charles Hamilton (*ante*, p. 88) and wife of Mr. W. H. Stephenson, a clerk in the Treasury, nominated a K.C.B. in 1871. Lady Stephenson died in 1883.

[2] John Fraser Macqueen, a barrister, frequently engaged in Scottish appeals and in proceedings for divorce; afterwards Q.C., a bencher of Lincoln's Inn and official reporter of Scottish and divorce appeals in the House of Lords; author of—among many other law books—*A Practical Treatise on the Appellate Jurisdiction of the House of Lords and Privy Council* (1842). He died at the age of 78, in 1881.

and Sir John Patteson have signed or will sign the representation in my favour.

February 26th.—Dined at Longman's; nobody there but Twiss. We went afterwards to Lady Molesworth's, who was in all the glory of dukes and Cabinet ministers. A coalition is an odd thing to see, and one laughed at Lord Aberdeen and Sidney Herbert talking to Cobden and Milner Gibson. The Radicals, however, are enthusiastic about Lord Aberdeen, who certainly has a fund of liberalism in him which no one would have suspected. Clarendon warm about refugees.

February 27th (Sunday).—Harness admirable. Rode in the afternoon, with Christine on the new mare, Delane, and Longman, and spent an evening at home for the first time for a fortnight. Finished my review of 'Marcellus'[1] for the 'Edinburgh.'

February 28th.—Delane called after a long chat he had with the premier. Found him very strong against the Turks, whom he calls 'crapulous barbarians;' he entirely agrees with a recent article in the 'Times' against Turkey, which makes a great noise. There must, however, be a great divergency in the Cabinet on this subject, though Palmerston studiously avoids saying anything on foreign affairs.

Evening at home again, and wrote up my week's journal.

March 3rd.—A list of evening parties. First to Fred. Elliot's, then to Lady Molesworth's, then to the Attorney-General's. Molesworth's dinner had been made to bring Lord Aberdeen into contact with Bright. The topic of the day was the choice of Jackson, of St. James, to be bishop of Lincoln. Bright said to the earl that he could not be expected to rejoice in the creation of bishops; but, as long as such evils existed, he hoped the appointments would be as good as that just made—of which, indeed, everybody speaks most highly. What a lottery is life! Jackson is a man of little more than forty; sometime curate of a church at Muswell Hill; then rector of St. James; preached a few

---

[1] *Marcellus: Memoirs of the Restoration,* in the *Edinburgh Review* of April 1853.

sermons to prime ministers, and is now a bishop, more likely than most men, perhaps, to be the primate.[1]

March 4th.—Went to the House of Lords to hear Lord Lyndhurst speak on the refugee question, which has thrown Germany and diplomacy into a paroxysm of irritation. Nothing could be better; clear, precise, and statesmanlike, especially in laying down, for the information of foreign governments, the limitations of English jurisprudence, which are not in the law, but in the proof of the facts charged. Lord Aberdeen said the Government are resolved to prosecute if a case arises. Brougham had a fine burst afterwards —his voice and style as grand as ever.

From Lord Clarendon[2]

Grosvenor Crescent, March 4th.—In the article you are about to write[3] (which I heard of with extreme satisfaction), pray take care to condemn thoroughly the abuse of hospitality by the refugees. It will give much greater weight to the arguments against the demands of the arbitrary governments, and it would never do to afford them a pretext for saying that revolution or assassination found countenance from *the* organ of public opinion in England. Aberdeen's answer to Lyndhurst this evening will supply you with the opinions of the Government.

March 4th [later].—I have just received a most satisfactory letter from Cowley, telling me that the French Government will not stir in the refugee question, and that the Emperor feels, in the first place, how much he owes to England as an asylum in the days of his misfortune, and, next, that on the question of his recognition we took our own line without waiting for the Northern Courts.

---

[1] Jackson was, however, a much better known man than this remark seems to imply. He had graduated at Oxford as one of that brilliant first class which contained the names of Liddell, Scott, and Robert Lowe; had been incumbent —not curate—of St. James', Muswell Hill, for eleven years, and in 1847 had been appointed chaplain in ordinary to the Queen. In 1853 it was commonly said, in clerical circles, that his nomination to Lincoln was strictly the Queen's own; but in any case, he had a considerable repute both as a preacher and as —which is apparently a higher qualification—the successful master of the Islington proprietary school. He was translated to London in 1868, and died in 1885.

[2] At this time Foreign Secretary.

[3] The article appeared in the *Times*, March 5th. See next page.

AT THE LEVEE

Under these circumstances Cowley is most anxious that a line should be put in the ' Times ' acknowledging the fair dealing of the Emperor, though, of course, it must be alluded to as an *on dit*. I think this might come well into your article, and I shall be much obliged for it, as it will help to check the combined remonstrance with which we are threatened. I had satisfactory assurances from Bunsen on this subject—he says Prussia won't join in any league, though she will be sorely pressed.

To continue the Journal :—

Tuesday, March 8th.—Lady Clarendon held her first reception in the rooms of the Foreign Office, which have just been gilt and carpeted by Lord Malmesbury—' Sic vos non vobis ;' but this case is not so bad as Disraeli's, who paid for his upholstery and then left it to the Gladstones.

Of course all the foreign ministers were there, or ought to have been, but oddly enough I did not see the Walewskis. Bunsen protested to me that Prussia would take no part against us in the refugee question.

Wednesday, March 9th.—I went to the levee, which was very full. I stopped in the throne room till the end, having something to say to Lord Granville. Prince Albert held the levee for the Queen, as she is near her confinement. Lord Clarendon walked out with me, and expressed great delight at an article in the ' Times ' of the 5th, on the refugees.

Dined at Longman's—an ' Edinburgh Review ' dinner, in honour of Lewis's inauguration. Macaulay could not come, but we had Sir J. Stephen, Senior, Bonamy Price, Mrs. Jameson, and Milnes—not, to say the truth, a very exhilarating assembly. Lady Molesworth had her second assembly in the evening ; amusing to see a host of new grandees there.

March 11th.—We had to dinner at home the Fords,[1] Walters, James Booths,[2] Danby Seymour, K. Hodgson,

---

[1] Richard Ford, an amateur artist of distinguished merit, and a frequent contributor to the *Quarterly Review*, but best known as the author of the *Handbook to Spain*. He married, in 1851, the sister of Sir William Molesworth, and died, at the age of 62, in 1858.

[2] Secretary to the Board of Trade.

Phillips, and Simpson—a party which turned out uncommonly pleasant.

Saturday, March 12th.—Christine and I rode to Sydenham to see the Crystal Palace, which begins to throw its spires and domes over the hill; a wonderful creation, like some Belshazzar's palace in one of Martin's pictures; the vastest building on the earth and the most fragile; one can hardly conceive its durability, much less permanence.[1]

From M. Guizot

Paris, March 12th.—Is the readiness you are showing to accept the fall of the Ottoman Empire quite serious? or is it a *ruse de guerre* to divert those who may wish it, by showing them that you will not be taken unawares? But take care! Predicting an event is very apt to bring it to pass; touching fruit to see if it is ripe often makes it fall. There is no question purely Eastern; as soon as one is started, it will become the Western question; and as soon as a serious question is raised in the West, it will become the revolutionary question, the question of social change, of territorial readjustment throughout Europe—the question of chaos. . . .

I do not, however, think that this Eastern question is likely to come upon us just now. Empires sometimes remain in a moribund state for centuries. The Greek Empire has given us one example of it; Turkey, in the same place, may perhaps give us another.

In writing this, Guizot seems to have missed the very obvious consideration that the Byzantine Empire was surrounded by people far lower in the scale of civilisation than herself, and that her power of cohesion was much greater than that of her neighbouring enemies. The same can scarcely be said of the empire which now sits at Constantinople, though it is quite possible that a very different cause—the mutual jealousy and distrust of the Great Powers—may produce the same effect. But after this Guizot goes on to argue that at that time there was no disposition to bring about the end. The policy of the Great Powers was necessarily pacific. Austria had her hands full with Hungary and Lombardy,

---

[1] Forty-five years ago, and it's there still.

and the Emperor of Russia, though absolute and powerful, was *peu ambitieux*, and—not being a soldier himself—had no wish to see his generals winning distinctions in which he could have no share.   In France, too, there was a general apprehension that war would bring on revolution; and the Emperor, governed by *idées fixes*, 'never pursues more than one hare at a time.   At present the Pope is the hare. He wants to catch him and bring him to Paris so that he may be crowned by him.   To this *idée* all his policy is sub-ordinated, and he will make any concession to Austria and Russia to prevent their opposing it.'   In England alone there seemed no guiding principle, and the articles in the ' Times ' might become mischievous by their impression on public opinion, which again, in England, had more weight on the Government than it ought to have.

Lord Clarendon's letters, several of which are here given, show how mistaken was Guizot's estimate of his conduct, and the history of the next three years shows that his estimate of Nicholas was equally erroneous.   In this there is no dis-paragement to Guizot, who was looking on indeed, but without seeing the cards; and the general consent of Euro-pean statesmen may be held to establish the fact that Nicholas's conduct in 1853–4 gave the lie to the reputation which he previously held.   The Duke of Wellington alone, is reported to have ' had a bad opinion of Nicholas's character for sincerity, and to have said " there was much in him of the Greek of the Lower Empire." '[1]   But the great Duke was dead, and his wisdom was buried with him.

Continuing the Journal :—

Sunday, March 13*th.*—We went to the Temple Church. The musical service by Hall and Hine in B flat, and not very good.   The day was lovely, and all London turned into the parks for the first time.

Dined at Sir William Molesworth's in great state, my lady having brought over a new chef from Paris, who how-ever is not quite a *cordon bleu.*   The dinner was large, and consequently I saw and heard nobody but the Fords, near whom I sat.   One prefers a leg of mutton and conversation to a feast without it.

March 15*th.*—Sat some time this morning with Lord Clarendon while he breakfasted, never having been near him

---

[1] Lord Malmesbury's *Memoirs of an Ex-Minister*, i. 318.

before since he took office. He said the Government were doing all they could to support the Turks, and hoped they would go on ; but he admitted that Nicholas believes in a fatal necessity impelling him to Constantinople ; that he never would assent to the creation of any intermediate independent State, and that, secretly, he would be very happy to treat with us for a partition. I observed that it might well happen that when Nicholas is gone we shall have a less powerful and energetic man to deal with, but also a less upright one ; for, as Lord Clarendon himself observed, his chief ambition is to be treated like an English gentleman.

There seems no likelihood of any improvement in our relations with Austria, for they are as mad as ever about the refugees. Lord Clarendon had anticipated any application on the subject by writing a despatch which was shown to Buol, and in fact Lord Aberdeen repeated the substance of it in the House of Lords on the 4th. It was to the effect that, even if we had an Alien Bill, the application of it would be an endless source of dispute with other Powers, who are much more apt to make charges than to substantiate them.

March 19th.—As Easter approaches the gaieties of London cease, but I dined to-day at Twickenham with the Duc et Duchesse d'Aumale, who had kindly sent de Mussy to invite me to dinner *en famille*. The Duke, who has realised all he could out of the wreck of the Condé property by sales under the decree of January 22nd, 1852, has bought the house at Twickenham in which his father spent his years of exile. There he has brought a splendid library, a rich collection of furniture and clocks, trophies of arms from the Algerian wars, and all the souvenirs of his family and his life. Over the chimney-piece in the library was Abd-el-Kader's sabre, taken at the Prise de la Smala, and his telescope, surrendered by the emir to the Duke on his final capture. On my arrival I found the Duchess with a lady of honour in a small drawing-room. The Duke soon entered, and dinner was announced. All the household, down to the groom and gardener, are French. We proceeded through some immense conservatories to a sort of octagon tower, which is the dining-room. It was horribly cold, ill-warmed, large windows, and frost out of doors. The little Prince de Condé dined with us, but in a cap and great-coat, and I wished I had been him or Rogers, to do the same. The conversation turned a good deal on Church affairs in France. The Prince said he was a stout Gallican, which is in truth the only form of opposition nowadays, and he showed great knowledge of the personal character of the French prelates. He said Thiers had made M. Affre archbishop of Paris, because he was the first prelate who had ever filled that see *sans être gentilhomme*—an odd distinction to make in the Church and in France, which we certainly have never made here. He said the great error of the Revolution of 1848 is that it has for a time destroyed liberalism, and proscribed liberal opinions; and then talked of Italy, and quizzed Naples, till the Duchess told him to hold his tongue. They both said their grandfather (the old King of Naples, for they are first cousins) was much more beloved than the present king, but deserved it much less. Unhappily the present man has not a man of ability and uprightness in his service, except Filangieri, and he is half a Muratist. The Prince stood before the fire after dinner for more than an hour, till I was ready to drop, which the Duchess perceived and made me sit down. He laughed, and said it was the bad habit of princes *de se dandiner sur les deux jambes*, and very prevalent in the whole House of Bourbon, even at Naples and in the younger branch. He asked me to come again frequently.

This was the commencement of an intimacy which endured till Reeve's death. The Duke himself, though some eight years younger than Reeve, did not long survive him. He died at Palermo on May 7th, 1897,[1] consequent on the shock he received from the news of the terrible death of his niece, the Duchesse d'Alençon, in the fire at the Bazar de la Charité, on May 4th. The Journal goes on :—

Sunday, March 20th.—To-day as I was starting to ride

[1] Among the many obituary notices in the newspapers and magazines, may be mentioned one, by M. Laugel, in the *Revue de Paris* of October 1st, 1897, and a short article, *in memoriam*, by Mrs. Reeve, in *Longman's Magazine* for July 1897. Memoirs have also been published under the titles *Le Duc d'Aumale : le Prince, le Soldat, l'Historien*, par le Commandant Grandin, avec introduction de son Eminence le Cardinal Perraud (1897), and *Le Duc d'Aumale*, 1822–1897, par Ernest Daudet (1898).

with Delane he told me that the French Government had ordered their fleet to the East, in consequence of the imperious tone of Prince Menschikoff's mission to Constantinople. Rose had sent to Malta for our fleet, but very properly Dundas refused to stir. The messenger arrived with these despatches in the night, and a sort of small Cabinet was held at the Admiralty, at which Lord Aberdeen, Clarendon, Lord John, Graham, and Palmerston alone were present. They approved Dundas for not sailing, and I think ordered a reinforcement to be got ready. I at once saw, before I knew all this, that the French had got into a scrape, in which we should not follow them, and wrote an article accordingly, which turned out to be quite correct. Indeed the 'Times' of the 20th, 21st, and 22nd illustrates my view of the whole question. Windsor Castle took fire last night, but it was not very serious.

March 22nd.—I heard from Delane that Lord Aberdeen entirely concurs in the article of the 'Times.' They are all angry at the French sending off their fleet without consulting us at all. The consequence has been a *rapprochement* with Russia. Lord Clarendon went to Brunnow and said that he had entire confidence in the Emperor's word of honour, and accepted his assurance that Menschikoff's mission was confined to the question of the Sanctuaries, in which the French have brought a palpable defeat upon themselves.

March 24th.—Dined at Longman's with Delane, Sir Emerson Tennent, Count Strzelecki, Mr. Caird, and George Lewis. The India question very much talked of; it revives the identical controversy of 1783.

Good Friday, March 25th.—After church went to Slough, to see Ward's new pictures for the Exhibition; one, the executioner tying Wishart's book on to the breast of Montrose before he was hung; the other Josephine signing the divorce; both very powerful. Ward is now by far our most vigorous and original historical painter, and is *not* an Academician. We had a pleasant afternoon with him and his pretty wife, who paints also with great truth and good style.

Easter Sunday, March 27th.—Attended with Christine at Harness' church and took the Sacrament, unhappily from the hands of a young curate, who whined and grimaced like a bonze, and disturbed one's religious feeling. Saw Lord Clarendon for a few minutes after church, and Graham. He said he was quite satisfied with the course we had pursued, though there had been some ferment here and more in Paris. But that he continued to place implicit confidence in the declarations of the Emperor of Russia as a man of honour, touching the mission of Menschikoff. Brunnow had said, I dare say truly, that nothing was so likely to affect the Emperor favourably to the new Foreign Minister as this sort of confidence among gentlemen. The French, however, are angry at having got into a scrape without us, and invent every sort of lie to explain their case. However, considering this irritation, Lord Clarendon entreated me not to fall upon them, and I wrote an article for the next day—the 28th—which I afterwards heard had (oddly enough) delighted both Russia and France.

From Lord Clarendon

G. C., March 27th.[1]—I did not finish half of what I wished to say, so must add a line to beg of you not to allow the insertion in the ' Times ' of anything irritating to France. They are at this moment in such a state of self-dissatisfaction, and so afraid of the ridicule they may incur for the haste with which they have acted, that they are looking for a cause of quarrel somewhere, if only to *détourner* public attention. They explain that they wished to make no fanfaronnade, but meant to be ready for any eventuality ; and that by sending the fleet to Salamis and no further, they merely wished to be in the same position as us at Malta.

In speaking in general terms of the confidence that the Emperor of Russia deserves, it should be said that he can have no reason for wishing a quarrel with France, and that events will probably show that, even with respect to the Holy Places, notwithstanding his ground for complaint there, his conduct towards France will be marked by good faith as well as friendly feeling.

Kisseleff's communications on Monday last fully bear out

---

[1] This and the two following notes were all written in sequence to the hurried interview after church, mentioned in the Journal.

this. France will have a double satisfaction—first, that of showing to Europe how quickly her fleet can be under way ; and, secondly, that of finding there was no occupation for it.

F. O., Sunday.—The despatches only arrived at 12 last night—there is every reason to believe (i.e. it is quite certain) that our fleet has not left Malta. Menschikoff arrived with great pomp and circumstance, called on the grand vizier, but not on Fuad Effendi, minister for foreign affairs, who accordingly resigned. The Sultan would not accept his resignation ; he insisted, and the Sultan yielded, with a firman saying he did so in compliance with the wish of his minister—a great compliment, and a great novelty, as in questions of that sort nothing but the Sultan's will is ever heard of. This has broken Fuad's fall. Menschikoff had not had his interview with the Sultan, nor were all the objects of his mission precisely known ; supposed to have reference only to the Holy Places, and with respect to them the only difficulty of course is France. If there is not discretion and moderation on both sides, the whole affair may be complicated and dangerous, but there ought not to be any real difficulty ; a European war over the tomb of our Saviour would be too monstrous in the nineteenth century.

Sunday.—I wrote to you from the F. O. this evening, but forget whether I mentioned the French fleet. All we know is that a telegraphic despatch at 5 yesterday said ' the fleet will sail for the Greek waters.' Walewski has nothing from his Government, owing to their having stupidly sent their despatch by the English post ; *ergo* it passes this day at Calais.

I hardly think the French fleet can have sailed, or can have done more than get ready for sea, without first communicating with us, or at least knowing whether our fleet had really sailed ; and they would know from me this morning that I thought it highly improbable.

It would be a great object, if possible, to calm the susceptibilities of France, and to say that, although the Holy Places, and indeed anything connected with his religious supremacy, were objects not only of ecclesiastical, but of political, importance to the Emperor of Russia, yet that we won't believe, without better evidence, that he means to offend France or to risk a European war upon such a question.

Since writing the above I have seen a private letter saying that Menschikoff and all his suite had been received by the Sultan, and that the messages he delivered were of a very friendly character.

Returning to the Journal :—

March 29th.—Arrived a telegraph despatch *via* Trieste with the heavy news that poor Granville Loch was killed[1] in an attack on a place called Donabew, on the Rangoon River. I communicated the bad news to Willie, who was dreadfully overpowered, and so was Mr. Loch when he got to town, as well he might be. By the last letter from Granville he was just starting to renew an attack in boats—one attack having already been repulsed—upon the hold of a formidable robber who had got possession of Donabew and stockaded the creek up to it. Some men had already been lost in this first attack, though, according to G.'s expression, they could not see the flashes of the muskets that killed them. In this same place he probably perished. We shall soon know more, but I am afraid there is a defeat to boot, for the expedition is said to have lost two guns. In all 88 persons were killed or wounded—an enormous proportion. Poor Granville Loch was a brilliant officer; small or rather *grêle*, putting one in mind of Nelson's appearance, but refined in conversation, with infinite gaiety and spirit. Yet, with all this gloss on the surface, he was a most resolute officer, strict on board his ship, and bold enough to undertake anything· In one of his last letters he relates how with 22 men and a corporal he chased 300 Burmese soldiers for a couple of miles across country, with the bayonet. Had he lived, I have always felt he would have been at the top of his profession, and it is most sad to think of such a man dying such a death.

April 6th.—The subsequent accounts have confirmed all this melancholy story, and in the 'Times' of to-day there is a narrative of the occurrence which I compiled from the despatches. The feeling of regret is deep and universal, and

[1] He was shot through the body on February 4th, and died on the 6th.

Mr. Loch has received marks of sympathy from everyone, from the Queen downwards. I asked Captain Denman to join with me in setting on foot a subscription for a monument,[1] and we have got Lord Adolphus Fitzclarence to take the chair at a meeting next Monday.

The Queen signed yesterday the warrant appointing me to the office of Registrar of the P.C., with 1,000*l.* a year; a pleasant and permanent change in my position, but I have to pay a stamp of 75*l.* We dined with Bonamy Price to meet William Greg—a great contributor to reviews—Francis Newman, Sir James and Lady Stephen, and a Mr. Lord, an American. Conversation interesting on slavery, Stephen oddly enough taking the anti-emancipation view, and saying that in Mauritius, for instance, the negroes had already relapsed into beggary and fetichism, and would disappear in fifty years wherever they were set free. So that slavery alone perpetuates the black race out of Africa. Queer doctrine this for Clapham! F. Newman said, in his keen bitter way, that he thought it more wicked and abominable to keep men in bondage than to make them into butcher's meat!

The Cosmopolitan afterwards was very brilliant. Tennyson there, Higgins, Milnes, Spedding, Stirling, Hodgson, &c. I don't know any other room in London which could contain such a force of men.

April 14th.—The Judicial Committee was sitting to-day and the Attorney-General just going to open a case, when he was suddenly summoned to attend the Home Secretary. I found from Chief Justice Jervis, whom Cockburn consulted, that a seizure of ammunition and arms had been made, which were supposed to belong to Kossuth, and that proceedings were to be taken against him. Upon this news I repaired to the Foreign Office, where I saw Lord Clarendon, who had just got a letter from Palmerston, saying that they had made a *razzia* the night before on Kossuth's rocket manufactory, and had seized forty chests of rockets of war, packed for exportation, and ready to start, it seems, for Rostock, besides some gunpowder. The law officers were consulted as to the grounds of indicting Kossuth for levying

---

[1] Now in St. Paul's. See *post*, p. 301.

war against a foreign State. Lord Palmerston was uncommonly eager in the pursuit.

April 15th.—This story appeared next day in the ' Times,' and when the House met, the Radicals tried hard to exculpate Kossuth, and to get Palmerston to say he was wrongly accused ; which, however, he would not do. It seems there were 70 chests of rockets, 2,000 shells (empty), and 500 lbs. of gunpowder in a factory at Rotherhithe, belonging, not to Kossuth, but to a Mr. Hale. This Mr. Hale succeeded Warner, and in the schedule of the latter there was an item of 200*l.* for rockets supplied to the Hungarians during the war. The mere fact of the existence of such enormous stores of war in Rotherhithe is evidently a serious public danger. It remains to be seen what case there is against Kossuth personally.

Saturday, April 16th.—I have forgotten to record the gaieties of the week. On Wednesday we dined at the Butts' [1] with a party of Tories, including Whiteside, the Irish lawyer, who is agreeable but not brilliant. Then we went to the Chancellor of the Exchequer's, where there was a House of Commons squeeze. On Thursday we dined with Higgins ; Friday, parties at Lady Talbot de Malahide's and the sempiternal Lady Morgan ; and Saturday, a small choice party at the Clarendons'.

I rode over to-day to call on the Duc d'Aumale, and sat an hour with him. His home, as he calls it, is full of pictures and relics after the great shipwreck. He showed me the first thing his sister, Princess Mary, had modelled— a Joan of Arc on horseback, at the moment she has first struck down a man-at-arms. Unnerved by her own triumph, the woman and the enthusiast once more throb in her heart, and she pauses in the battle—a fine and original conception. The King was touched by it, and said in consequence, ' Tu devrais me faire une grande Jeanne d'Arc pour Versailles.' The Duc also showed me a wax head of Henry IV., moulded in a cast from his face, and no doubt perfectly like. De la Roche's picture of the Duc de Guise's death—uncommonly grand both in composition and expression, rather dark in colour. Fine Napolitaine of Léopold Robert.

[1] George Medd Butt, M.P. for Weymouth.

We talked chiefly of English affairs, but also of Belgium, where the heir-apparent of Leopold is just coming of age, and great rejoicings have taken place; even the clergy behaving well. But these are strange times to rejoice over the prospects of heirs-apparent, when half the governments of the world are distributed by lot.   The Prince said Leopold is the shrewdest man he had ever seen—reserved, retired, an immense reader, sleeping hardly at all, a great observer of mankind.

An impression begins to exist somewhat unfavourable to the prospects of the Government, which has sustained two small defeats.   I have always thought they would have to dissolve the present House of Commons before they got an effective majority and this I suspect they have decided to do, when the necessity is more strongly felt.   At present, much depends on the reception of the budget, which will be announced on Monday.

April 18*th*.—Christine and I went by water this morning to St. Paul's, to go with Dean Milman into the church to select a site for Loch's monument, or rather to see what could be selected.   The practice of placing monuments against the walls with light behind them is, however, fatal to their effect.   I believe we shall have about 400*l*. to spend on the monument.   St. Paul's really looks very grand, especially with the great doors open looking on to Ludgate Hill.   They are refreshing the paintings in the cupola, which are said to deserve it, but, independent of the smoke, the oils have turned black.

Being in the City, we went to the 'Times' office to see the second edition printed.   Applegath's machine is certainly a marvellous invention.   The huge drum whirls off 200 printed copies of the paper per minute, and to stand in the gallery above these two machines, which throw off these winged sheets with such power and rapidity, gave me a strange and almost exciting sensation, for by this instrument my own thoughts and opinions are propagated and diffused over the habitable earth, with a power that seems at times irresistible.   Without the engine, however, the same thoughts and opinions would perhaps not keep a Grub Street author from starvation.

April 20*th*.—A great reception of Lady Clarendon's at

the Foreign Office. Cobden and, I believe, Bright were there, though they affect to hold off from the relaxing society of the aristocracy.

April 22nd.—I had a long conversation with Lord Clarendon previous to going to Paris. Lord Stratford writes from Constantinople that there is considerable excitement there, but apparently no real political danger. The prospect of a rising of the Christian population is, however, precisely the circumstance I have looked to all along as the direct cause of a change in Turkey.

Lord Clarendon said there was no doubt that proof would be given by a Hungarian witness, and by written evidence, at Bow Street to-morrow, of Kossuth's participation in the gunpowder plot at Rotherhithe.

Lord Mahon lent me to read a curious note by the late Lord Chesterfield on the mistresses of George I. and II. ; gross enough, yet related with exquisite continuity of style. After all, it seems Mrs. Bellenden and Mrs. Howard were not really the King's mistresses at all, for he had the greatest dread of illegitimate progeny.

Very pleasant dinner at Kirkman Hodgson's. B. Beaumont, a promising young man, and far saner than his poor father, Strzelecki, Glyn, Danby Seymour, Currie, and Phillips. How odd it is that men's parties are so much the most agreeable, when women cannot sit an hour in a hen-roost without ennui.

Gladstone's budget, which is the great affair of the week, promises to be most successful, and was introduced by a speech of unexampled power.

The Notebook here breaks off for several months, during which its place is rather meagrely supplied by the Chronology :—

To Paris on April 24th. Dinner and breakfast with Guizot, Lavergne, Faucher, Circourt, Tocqueville, Princess Lieven, Duchesse de Rauzan. We were at the height of the *entente cordiale.*

May 5th.—Lord Hatherton and I set to work to raise money for casting Marochetti's Richard Cœur de Lion.

Saw a good deal of Lockhart, and wrote in the ' Quarterly.'

From Lord Clarendon

G. C., Sunday [May 22nd].—On the 10th the Porte rejected the proposed convention. Prince Menschikoff then, *proprio motu*, adjourned his departure to the 14th, 'en exprimant l'espoir qu'on ne fermerait pas la porte à tout accommodements.'

On the 13th the Ministry was modified, and Reschid Pasha has now the foreign affairs, instead of Rifaat. What led to this we don't know.

G. C., June 4th.—I wished much to have a talk with you to-day, as many things are better and more quickly said than written ; but both before and after the Cabinet my visitors were legion, and I could not send to you.

We have intelligence from Constantinople to the 22nd ; unsatisfactory as regards Menschikoff, but satisfactory as to Turkish conduct and foreign influence. The Porte has shown the utmost desire to meet every claim that Russia had a shadow of a title to make ; but Sultan, ministers, and divan were unanimous as to not conferring on the Emperor a right by treaty to the protectorate over the Greek Church, or, in other words, the indirect (which would soon be direct) government of the rayahs. The representatives of the four Powers were equally unanimous in considering the decision of the Porte a right one ; but they appear not to have interfered unduly, and to have left no means untried to bring about an amicable solution. Even at the last moment they sent M. Kletzl, the Austrian *chargé d'affaires*, to express their regret at the rupture, and to offer their services, but in vain ; which is not much to be wondered at, because *the* thing which, with Prince Menschikoff, was a *sine qua non*— viz. the treaty—the Turks were determined to refuse, and nobody could advise them to accept.

By our latest date from St. Petersburg, the news of Prince Menschikoff's departure had not arrived, but the rejection of his ultimatum was known, and the language about it was indignant, but as yet no announcement of measures. The Russians everywhere talk of war ; but we know nothing except from our consul at Warsaw, who says that the 4th corps d'armée had, according to general belief, been ordered to proceed by forced marches, so as to be on the frontier of Moldavia by the 9th.

As peace must be the object of everybody, it is of great importance at this moment to adopt a conciliatory tone, or at least to avoid any just cause of irritation. A disbelief in war would be the best tone, founded not alone upon the declared intentions of the Emperor to uphold the Turkish empire, but upon the pacific principles which he has adopted throughout his reign, and which have been of most essential service to Europe on more than one critical occasion. He cannot go to war without considering what his real *casus belli* against Turkey is, or knowing that all mankind are as capable as himself of forming a correct judgement upon that question; and it will be found that Turkey has given him no just cause of offence, except as regards the Holy Places, which, by the admission of Prince M. himself, has been satisfactorily settled; that there has been no violation of treaty, no maltreatment of Russian subjects, no outstanding claims unsettled, no complaint from the Greek Church which required redress; but, *à propos de bottes*, he proposed to share the Sultan's throne, and the latter declined; saying, however, at the same time, 'I will give you all you want, but not in the way you want.' If Turkey is to be chawed up for this, there will have been nothing like it in history since the wolf performed that office for the lamb. It is impossible to believe that Europe is to be plunged in war for such a cause, and that all the revolutionary elements are to be let loose that the Powers of Europe live in dread of, and have such difficulty in restraining. This last point will have more weight than any other in a pacific appeal.

F. O., June 6th.—You were gone when I was able to send to C. O. Excellent article in ' Times.' No further news to-day, except a letter, of 2nd inst., from Westmorland, who had just seen young Nesselrode, and it is clear that the whole onus of Russian failure is to be laid upon us alone, or rather upon Stratford, who no more deserves it than you do, and it is an unworthy dodge.

Austria is more strong in reprobation of Prince Menschikoff's mission and its results than I expected; Prussia quite energetic, and France holding rather strong language, but without flourish, and anxious to act with us in any way we please.

Young Nesselrode is come (so Lord Aberdeen, who is just gone out of the room, says), and I shall probably see him to-morrow. If you come up on Wednesday morning you will perhaps call in Grosvenor Crescent.

The difficulty is to find a decent mode of backing out for the Emperor.

G. C., June 16*th*.—Many thanks for the article of to-day, which is excellent in tone, and quite sufficient for the purpose. I am particularly glad it has appeared, because Aberdeen and Graham, who I consulted, begged of me not to make a statement in the House of Lords, which I wished to do to-day. They said, and with some truth, that a public answer would merely invite fresh attacks, and that the proper time for refuting them would be when the whole subject came under discussion ; moreover, that as we had deprecated debate in both Houses, it would be unfair to those who are bursting with Eastern lore and anti-Russian anathemas to state just what suited ourselves, and still to require that, even upon that statement, they should hold their tongues.

No news to-day, except a report from Paris that the Emperor was about to issue a manifesto to the ' Russian nation,' which I hope is not true.

F. O., June 29*th*.—I know nothing about Woronzow beyond what is in the newspapers, nor does Sidney Herbert, his first cousin. There was a telegraphic despatch just now from Cowley, announcing that Lord Stratford's despatches of the 15th had arrived; but he makes no allusion to the passage of the Pruth. We had a distinct assurance from Nesselrode (as had also Austria and Prussia) that no final resolution respecting the occupation of the Principalities would be taken by the Emperor until the arrival at St. Petersburg of the answer from the Porte. That answer could not arrive there till the 24th ; and I have despatches of the 21st from Seymour to-day, but no allusion is made to any change of determination. I think, therefore, it cannot be true, though I have little doubt that the act will be perpetrated. The Emperor seems to have excited a good deal of fanatical feeling in Russia, and it will augment the difficulties of the position into which he has got himself.

G. C. [*July 3rd*].—Not a particle of news since I saw you on Friday, except one or two facts and *obiter dicta* showing the determination of the Emperor to proceed, and to disregard even *les vives instances* of his brother of Austria. I am more afraid of the manifesto he is about to publish than of the occupation of the Principalities, as it will be harder to retreat from the first than the latter. Brunnow is in despair, and says the excitement of the Russian nation increases rapidly, and that the Imperial wrath will be frightful when the language of the English press gets known at St. Petersburg.

Sunday evening [*July 3rd*].—I have just got a telegraphic despatch from Berlin, dated to-day, with news from St. Petersburg of the 30th, saying that the Emperor insists on the immediate and unconditional acceptance by the Turkish Government of the *projet de note* which was delivered to them by Prince Menschikoff.

G. C., July 5th.—I am sorry I can't send you the manifesto, as I haven't it here. Bad it certainly is, but not worse than I expected, and I think I detect a loophole through which negotiation might enter. Brunnow says it will be considered ' quite mild ' by the Russians ; but the Emperor is evidently exciting the fanaticism of his people, which is a very dangerous game and may cost him dear. In the meanwhile I believe he would much rather repass the Pruth upon a bridge built for him by us than cross the Danube on a bridge of his own.

The discussion of Friday won't do much good, I am afraid, i.e. towards peaceful solution ; for Dizzy, I am told, means to make political capital out of it, by identifying himself with the war cry, or, in other words, with the party that wants confusion *à tout prix*.

Tom Baring told me yesterday that the notion of war was anything but popular in the City, and that men of intelligence and property would require a wonderfully good case to be made for it before such a nuisance would be tolerated.

There was a report in Paris this afternoon that Austria is preparing to occupy Bosnia and Servia, but I have no news of it. I conclude it would not be in a Russian sense, and that self-preservation would be pleaded. It would be another ingredient cast into the war caldron.

The Journal here notes :—

July 5th.—To the military operations at Virginia Water, with Edward James Reeve. The Queen there.

15th.—To Portsmouth with George Loch and William Peel. The Queen reviewed the fleet; saw the 'Agamemnon.'[1]

From Lord Clarendon

G.C., July 17*th.*—One is compelled now to doubt everything but *faits accomplis.* I should otherwise feel certain that there is an anxiety at St. Petersburg to be helped out of the scrape, and a disposition to complain that friends are backward in proposing something. Nesselrode was quite pleased with a French attempt, in the shape of a note, to split the difference between Menschikoff's and Reschid's last notes, and seemed to think it might do. I hope it may. Austria has strongly advised its adoption.

The Journal continues :—

July 18*th.*—Circourt came to Chester Square.

27th.—Christine and I to the military operations at Cooper's Hill. Sent horses down and rode when there. Dinner afterwards at Lord Clarendon's, with the Truros, Howard de Walden, Tricoupi, and Lavradio.

August 11*th.*—Great naval review at Spithead. I went with the corps diplomatique in the 'Vivid.' Twenty-one line-of-battle ships, seven great war steamers. Bunsen said as we sailed down the line of ships, 'This is the guarantee of peace.'

---

[1] The 'Agamemnon,' of 91 guns on two decks, was the first screw line-of-battle ship designed and built as such. She was thus naturally a good deal talked about as a ' show ship.'

CHAPTER X

THE RUSSIAN WAR

THE remark of Bunsen's, with which the last chapter terminated, was by no means the general feeling either in the navy or in the country at large. War was in the air. It was believed that the review of August 11th was very much in the nature of a preliminary demonstration; and the popular idea was, on the whole, fairly well represented by the cartoon in 'Punch' of 'The Sham Fight at Spithead,' representing a burly bluejacket saying to his disarmed and prostrate foe, 'It's all werry well; but O Jack, if you had been a Rooshian!'

In political and diplomatic circles the interest of the year was concentrated on the Eastern question, and little else is mentioned in either the Journal or the correspondence of this date.

From Lord Clarendon

G. C., August 24th.—I have no news and am much provoked thereat, for *the* note arrived at Constantinople on the 9th, and with it of course the information that it was approved by the four Powers. Instructions more direct and explicit were sent to Lord Stratford by the 'Caradoc,' which ought to have arrived on the 13th at latest. I cannot but fear therefore that Turkish independence is going to play us some trick.

From M. Guizot

Val Richer, September 1st.—I am sorry not to see you at Val Richer, my dear Sir, but you are right to go to Constantinople. The effects of the crisis which is just over [1] are worth seeing on the spot. It is one of the accesses of a

---

[1] 'Qui vient de finir.' Guizot's forecasts of affairs in the East were not particularly happy.

mortal illness, which I think will be long. In any case your Cabinet has rendered Europe two considerable services; it has maintained peace and prevented the Emperor Nicholas from doing *all* he wanted. It is good policy, and for the sake of my friends I am glad that it has succeeded. I hope there will be no Turkish affair next summer, and that Val Richer will profit by it. This year you are doing well to go in search of the sun; here we have quite got out of the way of seeing it.

From Lord Clarendon

G. C., September 9th.—No news from St. Petersburg. There are letters and despatches from Stratford of the 25th —very warlike, and rejoicing in the state of *preparedness* to which the Porte has brought itself. He has evidently caught some of the martial ardour with which his friends are inspired. Nevertheless I believe he honourably endeavoured to get the note accepted, and that we have no cause to complain about that. He is again riled about the 'Times' not being complimentary.

By way of combining business with pleasure and forming an opinion on the actual state of things in the East at first hand, Reeve had determined to go to Constantinople as soon as he could leave London. Accordingly, on the evening of September 13th, he and Mrs. Reeve started for Paris. The entries in the diary during this very interesting tour are more than usually scanty, possibly because Reeve knew that his wife was keeping a detailed journal. In fact, writing from day to day, Mrs. Reeve noted down not only what they did and what they saw, but also the heads of such conversations as she either took part in or were repeated to her by her husband. Her journal is thus, in a manner, his also, so far as the substance is concerned, and is here considered as such; extracts from it being, however, distinguished by square brackets.

September 14th.—[We reached Paris soon after 9 A.M. After dressing and dejeuning, Henry went to pay visits. The only person he found was Mme. de Lieven, who received him in spite of the early hour. Presently M. Guizot came in, and an interesting conversation on the *Question d'Orient* ensued. The Tsar has rejected the Turkish alteration of the Note. Mme. de Lieven pronounced Menschikoff 'par-faitement mal élevé,' and lamented he should have been chosen for the mission which required so much delicate tact. Mr. F. Elliot [1] called the while on me and mentioned that he and his wife were starting for Marseilles in the evening. This induced us to alter our plans and profit by their society, at least part of the way. . . . We left Paris at 8.5 P.M.] and on to Châlons, Valence (St. Péray), Avignon, and Marseilles.

21st.—Embarked on board the ' Caire ' for Constantinople. Met Xavier Raymond and wife on board—[Xavier Raymond [2] of the ' Revue des deux Mondes ' and the ' Débats,' never weary of talking, and doing it pleasantly too, with reminis-cences of China as well as politics and literature, and a little wife very good-natured, pleased and astonished at everything. . . . Our captain, M. Garberon, was shy and at first very silent, but he was gentlemanly and well informed, as we found afterwards].

24th.—Malta. *27th.*—Passed Cape Matapan and entered Greek Archipelago. [Henry is struck by our captain, a lieutenant in the navy, calling the Emperor a serpent, and using strong language about the *coup d'état* ; and, expressing this astonishment to Raymond, was told ' There is not a mess in which similar language is not held.' [3] ' Above all,' said Garberon, ' Louis Napoleon is not a Frenchman.'] *28th.*—Syra. *October 1st.*—Smyrna. First view of the East.

October 2nd.—We stopped some hours in Besika Bay, and I went to see Admiral Dundas on board the ' Britannia.' Found Lady Emily Dundas there.

October 3rd.—Arrived at Golden Horn. Went up to Therapia with Captain Glyn to see Lord Stratford. Turkey had declared war against Russia the day before we arrived.

---

[1] Thomas Frederick Elliot, first cousin of the then (the second) Earl of Minto, and Under-Secretary for the Colonies.

[2] In 1845 he had made a voyage to China as *Historiographe* to the French Embassy. For a French landsman he had paid much attention to naval affairs, and afterwards wrote, among many other works, *Lettres sur la Marine Militaire* (1856) and *Les Marines de la France et de l'Angleterre* (1863), both in a tone of warm admiration of England.

[3] In the summer of 1855 it happened to the present writer to be on terms of friendly intimacy in the ward-room of a French line-of-battle ship, and he can say that in that mess, at any rate, neither Emperor nor Empress was ever referred to except in terms of disparagement or contempt.

[The Elchi received Henry most kindly, in spite of the reports so absurdly invented by the French papers[1]: and when Henry protested that he had no political position or influence, his Lordship said, ' There are various kinds of influence ; one may meet Junius at a *table d'hôte* now-a-days '—not a bad bit of flattery.]

4th and 5th.—Shopping and sightseeing in Constantinople.

6th.—Rode round the walls of Constantinople.

7th.—Moved to Therapia. Dined with Lord Stratford every day while there.

8th.—[With Mrs. Marsh, the wife of the American Minister, visited the harems of Reschid and Fuad Pasha. . . . Henry had visitors nearly the whole day ; three hours of Slade Pasha[2] ; he called, too, on the Elchi, and had a confidential talk with him. The present complication seems inexplicable without war, for the Tsar and the Ulemas are alike intractable. What will be the chances of the war, and will France and England be compelled to interfere to prevent Russia from taking Constantinople ? With whoever you talk on the subject, from whatever point of view you start, all opinions agree that Moslem rule over Turkey in Europe cannot last many years. An intelligent Turk, speaking of the Ulemas, said lately to Slade, ' They are anxious for this war ; the best plan would be to distribute them, three or four to each ship and regiment, and let them taste its pleasures.']

Sunday, 9th.—[Captain Drummond[3] sent off a boat, and we went on board the ' Retribution ' for church. The chaplain was taken ill in the middle of the service, and Captain Drummond had to read the other part, which he did remarkably well. The boys sang, and there was a violoncello and flute. Strange and touching the service was.] Went to call on Slade Pasha on board ' Mahmoudieh.' Then to th-

---

[1] See *post*, p. 315.

[2] Captain, afterwards Vice-Admiral, Sir Adolphus Slade, K.C.B. At the time of the demonstration against Austria and Russia in 1849 (see *ante*, p. 214 *n*.) he had been lent to the Turks to re-organise their navy, and had remained with them. He continued in their service till he had attained his flag in the English, when he retired. He died in London in 1877.

[3] Afterwards Admiral Sir James Drummond, for many years Gentleman Usher of the Black Rod to the House of Lords. He died in 1895.

Embassy. Lord Stratford in great agitation about calling up the fleet. Kept me there half the night.

10th.—Embarked on board the 'Egitto' for Athens.

14th.—Sun rose behind Hymettus. Piræus. Moonlight walk to the Temple of Olympian Jove and round the Acropolis. Evening at Mr. Hill's, American chaplain.

15th.—Acropolis, Parthenon, Pnyx, Mars Hill.

16th.—Drove and dined with the Wyses; saw General Church and Mr. Finlay.

17th.—To Mount Pentelicus with Captain Marceau.[1] [The view of Marathon and Eubœa was very fine, and the sea, the mountains, and the islands made a grand panorama, which, with the lights and shades of a bright sun, would have been still grander; but I was grateful for the clouds during the ascent, and, as we gained the top, felt invigorated by the delightful change of temperature; but it grew warmer as we descended, and the heat was stifling in the plain. . . . Dinner at the Embassy. The minister and attaché were dining at the French Legation, but General Church, M. Boudouris (whom Henry had known as a student at Geneva) and the ladies made a pleasant little circle. General Church thinks more highly of the Turkish army than anyone we have met, and says the Russians dare not attempt to march on Constantinople, without taking Varna and Schumla, as before.]

18th.—[Decided for a quiet day. The conspirator[2] came into our room to smoke and talk. He is one of the twelve who, after assembling in church and hearing divine service, have sworn a solemn oath to devote themselves, lives, and property to obtaining the independence of the Greek population in Turkey. He lamented the policy of England . . . which has placed at Constantinople a minister who, believing in the Turks, ignores the existence of that element which must supersede the Moslem, and which should have been encouraged to look to England, and rely on her support,

---

[1] A French cavalry officer in the Turkish service, who had been a passenger in the 'Egitto.'

[2] M. Manos, a lawyer from Bucharest, 'ready to quarrel at the least word of disparagement of the Greek cause,' who had come from Constantinople in the 'Egitto.' The similarity of name suggests a relationship with another 'conspirator,' who organised the insurrection in Crete in February 1897.

instead of on that of Russia—for they do look to Russia as a means to enable them to throw off the hated yoke of Turkey, though they will never consent to become a province of Russia. . . .   Dinner at the Embassy.]

19*th*.—Rode to Eleusis. [Again we dined with the most hospitable of ministers. . . .   Mr. Wyse was very agreeable. He possesses wonderful stores of information and erudition, and is most moderate (for a Roman Catholic) towards the Greek and Anglican Churches ; but he is a Roman Catholic, and does not, therefore, represent Protestant England ; and the unfortunate squabble with the Court, and the grudge about the Pacifico affair, altogether prevent his having the position and influence which would be so desirable for Greece and England. He has been reading to the Government here a despatch from ours, to the effect that ' we should view with great displeasure any attempt of territorial aggrandisement on the part of Greece, or any attempt to incite the Christian subjects of Turkey to acts of rebellion.' It is well known that they are moving troops to the frontier, that Otho's health has been given as ' Emperor of Constantinople,' and that the Queen has declared that if he won't go when the signal is given, she will drag him by the hair of his head across the frontier.]

20*th*.—Rode to Phyle, up a defile in Mount Parnes. [On our way back to Athens we met the King and Queen and *cortège* riding. She had on a white hat and feathers, and a light-coloured riding habit, and looked stout and red-faced, though not uncomely. I did not notice him, for, as the person who called out to us said ' The Queen is coming,' it was only afterwards we were told she was accompanied by him. She is far more popular than he is, because she identifies herself with the nation more ; on festivals, she attends the Greek service in a Greek costume. Otho can't stand the climate of Greece, and is constantly laid up with fever. She never knows a day's illness. At 4 A.M. she drives down in a close carriage to the Phalerum, takes her sea bath, returns to bed, breakfasts at half-past ten, receives visitors or does business till half-past three, then eats a huge dinner, after which she takes—and makes all around her take—a long ride ; the evening is finished with billiards ; and each day's routine is the same. In the winter there are balls every week or alternate week, and in the cotillon she will dance with anyone who takes her out.]

21*st*.—Sailed by the 'Australia,' Austrian steamer, for Trieste. Osman Bey on board, with his wives, going to Avlona.

23*rd*.—[We anchored at Corfu at 2 A.M., and one's night's rest was of course ruined by the detestable row. Sir Henry Ward [1] sent for Henry. The heat was intolerable, so I hurried my toilette and rushed on deck. . . . At last Henry returned to take me on shore. We looked at Sir F. Adam's [2] statue, and lounged along the walks he planted, and then— it was only nine—went to the palace, a very handsome building . . . and after the sour bread, milkless and medicinal tea, tough sodden cutlets we have undergone, the dainty *déjeuner* of the L. H. C. was truly welcome. . . . We were amused to hear the quondam radical, now regal, Ward expatiate on the advantages of 'High Police.' 'I have sent off half a dozen of the worst men, and since then have had two blank reports from Zante'—i.e. no more murders or attempts. 'But we have been told you cannot obtain convictions.' 'Oh, we send off the scoundrels without troubling ourselves about convictions.' His Excellency was very pleasant, hospitable and conservative, gave us the last 'Times' and 'Galignani,' and sent us in his boat to our steamer at noon. At five minutes past we were off.]

25*th*.—Landed at Trieste. Thence to Laibach and Vienna.

28*th*.—[We dined at the Embassy, the party consisting of Lord and Lady Westmorland, Lady Rose and Lord Burghersh, and a number of attachés and gentlemen. . . . A very different tone from that of Therapia and Athens prevails here; no dread of Russia, or Russian influence or pretensions. The Earl told us to go to his opera box, and we heard Flotow's pretty opera 'Marta' charmingly given.]

29*th*.—[Henry paid various visits . . . and returned much pleased with Count Buol, and greatly gratified by a long

---

[1] The Lord High Commissioner since 1849. In 1856 he was made Governor of Ceylon, and in 1860 was transferred to Madras, where he died a few days after landing.

[2] Lord High Commissioner, 1824-31.

conversation with Prince Metternich, who, at eighty-one, is the most extraordinary of living personages.]

31*st.*—Left Vienna. Home by Dresden and Cologne. Arrived November 5th. Saw Greville and Lord Clarendon the same day.

On passing through Paris on September 14th I called on Princess Lieven, and M. Guizot came in while I was there. I saw no other acquaintance in Paris at all. Four days afterwards, however [on the 18th], the 'Journal des Débats' inserted the annexed paragraph :

M. Reeves, l'un des secrétaires du conseil des ministres de la reine d'Angleterre, est parti de Londres mardi soir 13 Septembre, pour se rendre à Constantinople, afin de remettre à lord Stratford de Redcliffe les nouvelles instructions de son gouvernement. Ces instructions sont de la nature la plus pressante et des plus catégoriques ; elles ont été délibérées d'urgence dans un conseil tenu par le comte d'Aberdeen, lord Clarendon, lord John Russell et lord Palmerston, seuls ministres présens, à Londres. Les résolutions ont été prises à l'unanimité, dit-on. On a remarqué que les quatre ministres qui ont participé à cette délibération remplissent ou ont rempli la charge de premier secrétaire d'Etat, ministre des affaires étrangères.

M. Reeves est arrivé à Paris le 14 au matin ; il en est reparti le même jour dans la soirée. On assure qu'il a communiqué au cabinet français les instructions dont il était porteur.

And a few days later—

Il est aussi fort question du voyage de M. Reeves, quoique l'on conteste beaucoup la version du 'Journal des Débats,' en Angleterre surtout. On affirme, en particulier, que M. Reeves, en traversant Paris, n'a pas vu l'empereur. C'est une erreur, du moins si je suis bien informé. M. Reeves a été à Saint-Cloud, et il y est resté assez longtemps. On ajoute que M. Reeves n'est pas le secrétaire du conseil des ministres : en cela, on a raison ; il n'est, je crois, que secrétaire du conseil privé de la reine ; mais on prétend qu'il est le rédacteur en chef du 'Times,' ce qui est, je crois, une nouvelle erreur. M. Reeves est un des rédacteurs du 'Times,' qui en a plusieurs, mais il n'y travaille pas avec régularité, quoique ce soit à lui que l'on doive les principaux articles qui ont paru dans le journal anglais sur la question turco-russe. Du reste, M. Reeves connaît très-bien l'Orient, où il a été plusieurs fois.

This gave rise to infinite comments about my journey, all over Europe, and proved very disagreeable. On my return to England it very nearly led to a rupture between myself and Walter and Delane. There was not one syllable of truth in the story of my mission.

It must not, however, be supposed that the journey was a mere holiday trip. Although bearing no mission, the man known to be on terms of confidential intercourse with several members of the Government could not, at such a time, visit our ambassadors at Constantinople and Vienna on the footing of the average 'globe-trotter;' and the curt entry of October 9th tells its own tale. Lord Stratford de Redcliffe did not discuss the advisability of calling up the fleet, through half the night, with a casual acquaintance. It was that he considered Reeve a living commentary on Lord Clarendon's celebrated despatch of September 23rd. That on his return Reeve had much to tell, Clarendon much to hear, is evident from the following :—

From Lord Clarendon

G. C., November 7th.—Pray tell me whether it was from Buol that you got the suggestion about the Porte addressing the note to the four representatives or to the conference. Do you think this can be relied on as a mode of proceeding that—to the knowledge of the Austrian Government—would be accepted by the Emperor of Russia?

I am so overwhelmed with appointments—Cabinet, three messengers to send, and Lord Mayor's dinner—that I don't venture to ask you to call upon me to-morrow or next day; but the little I heard from you makes me long exceedingly for more.

Endorsed—Just after my return from the East and Vienna.

The next letter refers to what has been often called 'The Massacre of Sinope.' Except that it was done cruelly, with much unnecessary slaughter, it was the perfectly legitimate destruction of an enemy's squadron, caught, in very inferior force, in an open roadstead. The Russians had, indeed,

given the Western Powers to understand that they would
not commence hostilities by sea, and the attack was consequently denounced as treacherous.   From the Russian point
of view, it was not so : it was the Turks who began.   The
Porte had learned that a Russian squadron had been at sea,
and felt it a point of honour for a Turkish squadron to be
out also.   A squadron of frigates was accordingly ordered to
go for a cruise ; but, on the remonstrance of Slade Pasha,
several ships of two decks were added to it.   As they were
on the point of sailing Lord Stratford de Redcliffe intervened,
and prohibited the ships of the line.   He was acting, he said
afterwards, on the advice of the English and French admirals.
What the English and French admirals had said to give him
this impression was never known ; but it is highly probable
that it was nothing more than that the Black Sea was no
place for line-of-battle ships—Turkish line-of-battle ships
especially—to be cruising in in the winter : that they advised
the sending of a frigate squadron to lie in an open roadstead,
within easy reach of the whole Russian fleet, is quite impossible.   The blame must be divided between the Porte itself,
for ordering the squadron to go, Lord Stratford de Redcliffe,
for interfering in a matter beyond his competence, and the
Capitan Pasha, for allowing and acting on such interference.
The squadron put to sea, was scattered in a gale, put into
Sinope, and was there destroyed, on November 30th, by a
Russian squadron which included three three-deckers and
three two-deckers.   The Russians supposed that the frigates
were carrying stores and reinforcements to Batum and the
other stations on the coast—a most natural idea, as nothing
else could have excused the sending such a squadron to such
a place at such a time.[1]   In reality, they were only attempting
a meaningless piece of swagger.

From Lord Clarendon

G. C., December 13th.—I have a telegraphic despatch of
the 3rd (we hear as quickly sometimes by Marseilles) con-
firming the news. A French and English steam frigate have
been sent to Sinope, and two others to Varna, to procure
precise information, and, on their return, it is probable that
the combined fleets will enter the Black Sea to prevent any
fresh disasters.

[1] For the full story of this commonly misrepresented affair, see Slade's
Turkey and the Crimean War, pp. 127-144.

I have seen a copy of Menschikoff's despatch to Gortschakoff, saying that the Turkish squadron was conveying forces to attack Sukhum Kale, and that it was pursued to Sinope by the Russian fleet. If this should be true, it would certainly give a different character to the attack, though it would throw great blame on the Turkish Government for having undertaken such an operation without more support or a better look-out for the enemy. The probability is that they were sending reinforcements and provisions to Batum.

Our *chargé d'affaires* at Teheran is reported to have suspended his diplomatic relations with the Persian Government, which, it is said, was on the point of taking part against the Porte, and sending two armies to the frontiers.

In Thessaly, Macedonia, Epirus, &c., the anti-Mohammedan spirit is rising every day, so that things in general don't look over well for the Turks; and what I have never ceased telling Stratford may come to pass—that, while we are contending for the integrity &c. of the Ottoman empire, the empire itself may slip through our fingers.

The Journal notes :—

1854.—Several dinners at home in January. On the 5th, Lord Granville, the Lavradios, Sir Baldwin Walker, Charles Villiers, Reventlow, and Baudin.

January 30th.—Shot at Claremont with the Ducs de Nemours and Aumale.

February 13th.—Dinner at Pemberton Leigh's—all lawyers.

A good deal of society, as usual.

From Lord Clarendon

F. O., February 20th.—I have despatches from Seymour of the 11th, but he had not yet received his recall. Extraordinary activity in every department, and preparations for war on the most extensive scale. The Emperor unapproachable. He has been suffering from erysipelas. Louis Napoleon does not intend to publish the answer from Nicholas.

F. O., March 18th.—The 'Secret and Confidential'

papers were not ready last night. They are rather a mare's nest, and will grievously disappoint the blunderers who are firmly convinced that Nicholas made a clean breast to us about the objects of Menschikoff's mission ; whereas he did nothing but develope the same idea that he has held since 1829, about the dissolution of the Ottoman Empire being inevitable, and the desirableness of avoiding a scramble by being prepared for the event. With the exception of suggesting a portion of spoil to us if Turkey did fall to pieces, there is nothing in his conversation with Seymour beyond what is to be found in the memorandum of 1844. He certainly, however, had no monopoly of the notion that Turkey couldn't last. It was largely shared and boldly expressed by the 'Times,' which, as the 'organ of the Government!' stated its own opinions, although it must have known how unpalatable such opinions were to a Government engaged in upholding that empire.

Pray remark the last memorandum of the Emperor, which is as satisfactory a termination to a correspondence as I ever remember ; for he adopts all the opinions we had been urging, and agrees to the course of policy we recommended, adding assurances that fully justified the confidence we expressed in his intentions. Note also that he says he had not moved a man or a ship ; and I verily believe it to have been the case ; for the immense publicity given to the movements of this and that *corps d'armée* was proof that little or nothing was doing. Now, when we want to know about military movements, not a word upon which reliance can be placed escapes.

M. Guizot's occasional letters on literary or personal matters break the monotony of a uniform course of politics.

Paris, 19 *mars.*—Mon cher Monsieur, vous recevrez, presque en même temps que cette lettre, mon *Histoire de la République d'Angleterre et de Cromwell* qui vient de paraître. Je désire beaucoup qu'elle soit un peu approuvée et goûtée

---

¹ *Eastern Papers, Part V.*, being 'Communications respecting Turkey made to Her Majesty's Government by the Emperor of Russia, with the answers returned to them,' laid before Parliament on March 17th, and delivered to members a few days later.

dans votre pays, car je l'ai écrite autant pour l'Angleterre que pour la France. Si mon expérience des révolutions m'a servi à comprendre et à peindre avec vérité la vôtre, cela me consolera un peu de ce qu'elle m'a coûté.

J'aurais bien envie que vos grands journaux, le ' Times ' entre autres, disent un peu ce qu'ils pensent de mon travail, si tant est que la guerre leur laisse le temps d'y faire attention. Vous seriez bien aimable d'en prendre un peu de soin. . .

Paris, 30 *mars*.—Deux mots seulement, mon cher Monsieur ; je pars demain pour une petite course de campagne ; mais je ne veux pas partir sans vous dire, d'abord, que j'accepte très volontiers votre dédicace de la nouvelle édition de Whitelocke's ' Swedish Embassy ' ; ensuite que j'espère bien que nous aurons le plaisir de vous voir cet été au Val Richer, avec Madame Reeve. J'y serai établi du 15 mai au 15 novembre, et n'en sortirai que pour aller, au commencement de l'automne, en octobre probablement, passer quinze jours chez le duc de Broglie. Je crois fort aux grands évènements de l'été prochain ; mais je me promets qu'ils vous laisseront assez de loisir pour une si petite, si courte et si prochaine course.

Pourquoi Mr. Longman ne publie-t-il pas en même temps une nouvelle et bonne édition de Whitelocke's ' Memorials of English affairs ' ? Les deux éditions in-fol° qui en existent sont très incorrectes, confuses et incommodes. . .

But the Journal has :—

March 28*th*.—War was declared against Russia. I took an active part in the proceedings of the Council Office on the subject, and attended the Courts. Wrote the papers opposing licence system, and defended liberality of trade and to neutrals.

April 11*th*.—Important deliberations as to trade with the enemy. On October 30th, Wilson [1] proposed restrictions, but was beaten.

Lord Clarendon had a very strong feeling that the policy of Prussia at this period was unworthy of a great nation. The ' Times ' took the same view of it, and, in most uncom-

---

[1] James Wilson, founder and editor of the *Economist*, and at this time Financial Secretary to the Treasury.

promising language, had described Prussia as thrall to Russian influence.   The Tsar was portrayed as the suzerain of Prussia in the present, to be sovereign of Prussia in the near future; the King, as himself honest and well-meaning, but the dupe of ministers, bound body and soul to Russia, and working in Russian interests.   These ministers were thus naturally irritated against the 'Times,' and had no friendly feelings towards the Government which they believed to have inspired the offensive articles.   Between them and Bunsen, too, there were many points of difference, and it suited them to represent him as denationalised :—he had married an Englishwoman ; he had resided for many years in London ; he had imbibed English ideas, and was subject to English influences.   His recall is referred to in many letters of this period, and was spoken of very freely by Bunsen himself.   The King of Prussia was unwilling to recall him, but suggested that he should absent himself from London for a while, so that the King might say that 'just now Bunsen was not the organ of his policy.'   Bunsen refused to do anything of the kind, and demanded his recall, which was eventually ordered.

From Lord Clarendon

G. C., April 11*th.*—I have written a line to Granville concurring in the resolution of to-day, but saying that we ought to show it to the French Government before it is acted upon.   Will you have the goodness to bring before My Lords (as I have no chance of attending the P. C.) the enclosed set of queries from Baron Bentinck?[1]   All our neutral friends are making the same inquiries, and it is time they were answered.

I shall be very sorry if Bunsen is victimised.   He has his faults, of course ; but he understands this country and has served his master here faithfully.   He may perhaps be succeeded by such a man as Groeben, who came here in the firm belief that H.M.'s ministers were distinguished by their dirty shirts, and passed their nights with Mazzini and Kossuth, plotting against the good Governments of Europe.

G. C., April 14*th.*—I think Bunsen will do quite right in demanding his dismissal, for if he submitted to the disgrace of absenting himself, the moment for reinstating him would

------

[1] The Dutch Ambassador.

never arrive. As for my having insisted on his removal, it is only one of the many lies in circulation at Berlin. I have not mentioned his name since Groeben's mission till the other day; and I am perfectly certain that Lord Aberdeen has never said a word to anyone respecting Bunsen.

I am glad the 'Kreuz Zeitung' is attacking the 'Times.' It is a proof that the Russian party feels the necessity of defending itself. The greatest care should be taken to say nothing offensive to the Prussian people; nor will it do to abuse the King personally, for the monarch is a point of national honour.

Here the Journal has :—

Bracknell for the Ascot week. It was on the cup day at Ascot that an article by me appeared, announcing the Crimean expedition.

June 27th.—Manin, the dictator of Venice, breakfasted with us. The same day I went to the French Embassy for the first time since the *coup d'état*. We had previously met Walewski at Lady Granville's.

July 18th.—Chorley's dinner to Mrs. Kemble, the Viardots, Edward Devrient,[1] and the Hallés.

The next day, July 19th, Reeve wrote to his wife, who was then in the country :—

Chorley's dinner was wonderfully brilliant. The Amphitryon sat between Juliet and Desdemona—Fanny Kemble and Pauline Viardot. The Cushman did not appear, but Edward Devrient came, and the Hallés. Conversation on the decline of the drama in England, Mrs. Kemble declaring Society had outgrown the Theatre, and Devrient maintaining this was impossible in the country of Shakespeare. It ended in my challenging Fanny K. to read a French play; in Hallé's playing a magnificent sonata; in Devrient's reading the *Oster-tag* scene from 'Faust;' in Viardot's singing, and in Fanny K.'s reading 'Antony and Cleopatra' compressed. However, before we reached the later portions of this splendid programme, I was obliged to go home to do some work.

---

[1] A distinguished actor, and author of *Geschichte der deutschen Schauspielkunst*. Cf. *Memoirs of Bunsen*, ii. 284-5.

Two days later Reeve started for Aix-la-Chapelle, feeling
a good deal knocked up by the fatigue of the year, and
desirous of warding off the premonitory symptoms of an
attack of gout. Tocqueville was then at Bonn, and there,
or at Aix, the two were a good deal together during the next
fortnight. On his return to London, Reeve, for another
three weeks, established himself at Richmond, not caring
to go far from town and the office of the 'Times' at this
critical stage of the war.

From Lord Clarendon

The Grove, August 23rd.—Many thanks for the excellent
article of yesterday.

We have news from Vienna as to the points at which the
Austrian army is about to enter the Principalities. There
is every reason to believe that this is in entire concert
with the Porte and Omar Pasha ; and such being the case,
Austria engaging to keep the Russians out and to evacuate
the Principalities the moment peace is signed between the
Porte and Russia, the occupation cannot but be useful, by
relieving Omar Pasha of much of his work, and setting a
portion of his army free. In exactly a year from the time
the *gage matériel* was taken, it has been relinquished, not
only without the object of Russia being attained, but [with]
the ally, upon whom Russia counted so much as not even to
consider her wishes or interests, having pronounced against
her and having declared she should never attain that
object.

Why shouldn't you and Mrs. Reeve come here on Friday,
if you have no other engagement? I mean, if possible, not
to go to London on Saturday. If Miss Reeve would accompany you, our girls would be delighted.

Lady C. is not downstairs yet, or she would have written
to Mrs. R., and I avail myself of a messenger just going to
send this.

The invitation was accepted, and the Journal has :—

At the Grove, August 26th [Saturday].

Visit to the Essingtons at Ribbesford in September.
Shot there. Thence to Teddesley. Then in town for some
weeks. Battle of the Alma on September 20th.

October 3rd.—When I was coming up from Farnborough false news came of the taking of Sebastopol.

November 2nd.—Went to Novar. Shot there for a fortnight. I was at Novar when the news of the battle of Inkerman arrived. The whole year was one of excitement from the war.

To M. de Tocqueville

London, December 7th.—We live in a time when we must learn to bear suffering and the sight of suffering. The sword of war pierces to the very marrow of our bones. But what a powerful influence the struggle exercises over the political and social body! What union of feeling and effort, what an awakening of the forces which, after all, make the grandeur of nations! I willingly accept all the pangs, all the evils, of war for what it brings us in the moral more than in the political sense.

I think I never believed so strongly as you did that aristocratic institutions were stricken with certain death, and that the whole world is being democratised without appeal. It is true of many countries, but it has been given to the English aristocracy to march with the times, and even to take the lead. Nothing could be more aristocratic than our army, yet nothing is more national. What it has just accomplished in the Crimea, the chivalrous devotion, the unshaken firmness before the enemy, the ardour which turned its advantage in position to account, at the price of its blood, is a new pledge of its life, and will win for it a new existence engrafted on all the traditions of the past. I am also delighted with the effect of the struggle on the alliance of our two countries, which, at this price, will perhaps become popular.

We have no anxiety about the fate of the army, though the task is greater than was expected. The engineers and the artillery of both armies thought themselves sure of success, but they were mistaken; they did not know the surprising strength of the Russian artillery. It is no longer a siege; but the place will be taken as the result of the field operations which it is intended to undertake.

The treaty signed at Vienna on December 2nd is the

best answer to your question concerning the conduct of
Austria.   This preliminary treaty engages Austria to
conclude the treaty of alliance, offensive and defensive, with
us, if peace is not made, before the end of the year, on the
basis laid down by the three Powers.   The explanations
which brought about this treaty were very satisfactory, and,
according to all appearances, Austria will declare war within
two months.   If she has any success, this campaign will
probably be the last.

I hope that we shall have the pleasure of seeing you in
Paris in the course of a few months, and that you will have
a pleasant winter. . . .

The following letter from Lord Clarendon was addressed
to Mr., afterwards Sir George Cornewall, Lewis, at this time
editor of the ' Edinburgh Review,' as a commentary on the
proof slips of ' The War in the Crimea ' written by Reeve
for the forthcoming number of the ' Review '—January 1855.
A reference to the article will show that many of Clarendon's
suggestions were adopted.

The Grove, December 29th.

MY DEAR LEWIS,—I thought it best to read the whole
article at once, or it might have been indefinitely delayed.
I like it much ; the public requires to have its judgement on
the conduct of the war guided by reference to facts taken in
their chronological order, and to be reminded that the events
of one month were not and could not have been anticipated
in the month before.   This has been done succinctly, with
moderation and with unimpeachable truth.   The fault is too
great brevity and not bringing out certain salient points prominently enough—e.g. the earnest entreaties of Omar Pasha
to St.-Arnaud and Lord Raglan to come with a large portion
of their forces to Varna ; his declaration that the *morale* of
his troops required this support, even if it was not given
more effectively ; the intense anxiety felt here about Silistria,
and the utter disgrace that would have assailed the allies if
they had been deaf to the prayer of Omar Pasha, and the
place had in consequence fallen.

Then, enough is not made of the cholera—its ravages, so
much greater than any we know of in England—the impossibility of active exertion under its demoralising influence.

People here thought they settled that matter when they said the expedition should have been undertaken sooner; change of air and scene with excitement would soon have driven cholera away; or let the troops take a trip to sea. But the ships that put out to sea had the cholera break out on board worse than in the regiments on shore, and there was no possibility of undertaking the expedition without the French, who suffered more than ourselves from cholera.

To proceed actively with the vast preparations for such an expedition until it was certain to be undertaken would have been absurd; but not a moment was lost; much of the craft, such as flat-bottomed boats, having had to be constructed in the arsenal at Constantinople.

The expedition is not done justice to. Let anyone bear in mind the numbers at Chobham,[1] and think that nearly six times that number had to be conveyed across the sea at the same moment; let him bear in mind the space occupied by the ships at Portsmouth naval review, and think that more than 600 vessels of different descriptions all were laden and proceeding to their destination at the same moment, while the British men-of-war were still in fighting trim and ready to engage the whole Russian fleet if it had ventured to come out; let him also bear in mind that the embarkment and disembarkment of these troops, horses, guns, ammunition, stores, &c., were effected without a casualty, and that the armies were ready almost in a few hours afterwards to fight and win the battle of Alma, and any impartial man will admit that the operation was quite without parallel in ancient or modern history.

The reasons why it was thought that Sebastopol could be taken with comparative ease should be more insisted upon. The only certain information we had (and it has been confirmed by subsequent Russian despatches) was that Menschikoff had but 50,000 men; and the force with which we landed was considered quite equal to cope with that. The first event seemed to prove it; for we carried in three hours the position that Menschikoff had promised the Emperor to hold for three weeks; but we could not tell that there were deep ravines on the south-east side of Sebastopol, or that the

---

[1] The precursor of Aldershot.

ground was all solid rock and that every atom of earth to make the trenches had to be brought from a distance. But these obstacles gave the enemy time to make works of his own, and to impede ours, and to delay the siege, till by incredible exertions nearly 50,000 fresh troops were added to Menschikoff's army.

It would be useful also to get from Graham the total number of ships sent to sea (Baltic and Black Sea); the number of transports employed; the assistance we gave to the French; and to take some of Sidney Herbert's returns as to supplies of ammunition, guns, stores, &c. This would occupy little space, but would give a great idea of the energy of the Government working upon a pared-down peace establishment.

When speaking of the Militia and Foreign Enlistment Bills, I think it essential to allude to the factious spirit displayed in Parliament. Something of the kind is required to check this when Parliament meets again, and as a counterpoise to Layard in the 'Quarterly.'

I am afraid I can suggest nothing more pacific, as in fact I think the latter part of the article tame, and hardly up to public opinion mark. The part about revolution is very good —our eschewing it at present, but possibly being obliged to consent to it.

The explanation of the four bases in the last paragraph is much below the mark, and might cause dissatisfaction. I should put nothing of this kind; there is no question at present of curtailing the territory of Russia; there is no question of humiliating her, unless she chooses to regard as humiliation the intention of Europe to be safe from her aggression. England, Austria, and France are agreed about the guarantees upon which that safety will depend: they consider that Russia must no longer have the right, which she now possesses by treaties, to enter the Principalities, and to deal with that portion of the Sultan's territory as her own; they consider that the navigation of the Danube must be secured, not by treaty, as now, which only secures the accumulation of obstacles to it, but by an independent authority at the mouths of that stream; they consider that Russian preponderance in the Black Sea is incompatible with the maintenance of the Ottoman empire, and consequently with the equilibrium of Europe ; they consider that it would be monstrous to renew that part of the treaty of Kainardji,[1] by the misinterpretation of which the Emperor of Russia claims to interfere between the Sultan and twelve millions of his subjects, and virtually to obtain on land the preponderance he has acquired in the Black Sea ; in fact, to displace the Sultan and become the virtual, until he constituted himself the actual and inexpugnable, possessor of the Ottoman dominions.

Is there anything unreasonable in these conditions ? In demanding them, do England, Austria, and France exhibit ambition or selfishness ? Do they, in behalf of Europe, ask too much ? Can they, in behalf of Europe, be content with less ? Will England and France, after pouring forth their best blood and expending vast treasure, leave things as they were, and thus expose not themselves alone but all Europe to a recurrence of the same dangers within a few years, but under circumstances far less favourable for proceeding against them ?

I have written these few hints in a great hurry, as you will see ; but if you think them of any importance, you will best know how to turn them to account.

Ever yours truly,

C.

The year, as usual, was ended by a visit to Farnborough. But, meantime, the war excitement was turned into indignation by the daily reports of the sufferings of the army. People did not and could not understand that officers and departments, without either theory or experience to guide them, must necessarily make egregious blunders. They would not see that the blame lay on the nation for not having insisted, years before, that the army should be maintained in a state of efficiency, and they cried aloud for vengeance on the Government at home, and on the commander-in-chief abroad. In the House of Commons a commission of inquiry was appointed. Lord John Russell, the President of the Council, disclaiming responsibility, resigned on January 23rd,

---

[1] By this treaty, concluded in 1774, the city of Azof and the fortresses of Kertch, Yenikale and Kilburn were ceded to Russia ; so also was a protectorate of Moldavia and Wallachia ; and Turkey pledged herself to protect her Christian subjects, a clause easily stretched in the direction indicated by Clarendon.

1855, and on the 29th was followed by Lord Aberdeen. The ministry was reconstituted, with Lord Palmerston as first Lord of the Treasury, Clarendon remaining Foreign Secretary. It was rumoured that Lord Raglan was to be superseded. The 'Times' had taken a very prominent part in the agitation condemning the conduct of the war, and thus Reeve had a personal as well as a general interest in the measures now adopted. He had, doubtless, made inquiries, to which the following was the answer :—

From Lord Clarendon

G. C., February 15th.—Lord Raglan is not recalled, and we should not know who to put in his place ; and with all his defects I believe he is the best man out there. One thing he has done which no one else could have done ; he has kept on perfectly good terms with the French under circumstances more trying than the public here have the least notion of.

Captain Mahan has taught us to recognise the ' flabby ' nature of coalitions, as affecting the operations of fleets and the conduct of naval war. Lord Clarendon's letter may be taken as illustrating one form of weakness on shore. The commander-in-chief of either contingent must be chosen not so much for his ability as a soldier as for the sweetness of his disposition and his readiness to maintain the *entente cordiale*. In the spring of 1855 it was commonly said that, but for this necessity, the command of the army in the Crimea would have been given to Sir Colin Campbell.

From Lord Clarendon

G. C., February 19th.—Nothing is settled about the Emperor [of the French] going to the Crimea, but there is too much reason to fear that he meditates this act. The matter must be most delicately handled, for he has already taken great offence at the remonstrances addressed to him. The absolute necessity of his presence for the welfare of France, as indicated by the fall of the funds and the panic throughout all classes at the rumour of his temporary absence will be the best argument. He can have no better or more flattering manifestation of public opinion, founded, as it is, upon a feeling of self-preservation, and to that he might properly defer.

The article in the 'Times' is far better to-day. All attacks on the Government are perfectly legitimate; but the country, the institutions, the upper classes, all have been run down by the 'Times' latterly, and the feeling thereby created abroad—at home, too, I believe—is that we are in a state of helpless confusion, and drifting to revolution.

It was not long before a further reconstruction of the Ministry was found necessary. Three members of the Cabinet, whether unwilling to serve under Palmerston or to meet the public wrath, resigned. Cardwell, President of the Board of Trade, was invited to take the office of Chancellor of the Exchequer, which had become vacant. He refused it, wrongly thought Clarendon, who wrote :—

February 22nd.—His acceptance would have given general satisfaction, and I hear that the growlers at Brookes's were unanimous yesterday in thinking him the man for the place. But everybody seems afraid of danger now, and gets away from it under the shelter of a quirk or a sentiment.

Failing Cardwell, the office was accepted by Sir George Cornewall Lewis, and Reeve undertook to edit the 'Edinburgh Review,' at first as a mere temporary arrangement, but afterwards as a permanency. From the biographical point of view, this and—to some extent springing out of it—his severing his connexion with the 'Times,' were the most important events of the year, and Reeve noted them in his Journal with some interesting particulars, which must, however, be postponed for the present. He noted also :—

March 2nd.—The Emperor Nicholas died.

From M. Guizot

Paris, March 26th.

. . . I should like the two great English Reviews, the 'Edinburgh' and the 'Quarterly,' to notice my History of Cromwell. I ordered a copy to be sent to Sir George Lewis. I know he was looking for some one whom he could ask to write this article. Now he is a minister, who will be Editor of the 'Edinburgh Review,' and who will be charged to write on my 'Cromwell'? It would be very kind of you if you would look after this little matter. Does Mr. Woodham no longer write for the 'Edinburgh Review'?

As to public affairs, I have nothing to tell you which you

do not know already. Here, the country is more desirous
of peace than ever, and I think the Government begin
to resign themselves to it. The difficulties outweigh the
pleasure of the dreams. Some day when these things are
recorded in history, it will be said, unless I am mistaken—
' Guerre faite sans raison suffisante de part ni d'autre ; paix
faite sans raison suffisante de part ni d'autre.' But if peace
is made, it will be necessary to give the people here some
peace-pageant instead of the war-spectacle of which they
will be deprived ; and the Industrial Exhibition and your
Queen will be asked to re-place the expedition to the
Crimea and the taking of Sebastopol.

The Journal indicates the external circumstances of
Reeve's life at this time. His interest in this particular and
very sensational Derby was his personal acquaintance with
the owner of Wild Dayrell.[1]

April 16*th.*—Louis Napoleon entered London in state.

26*th.*—Went to Paris. Met Christine there, who had
been to Tours. On May 3rd we dined at the Hôtel de
Luynes, with the Circourts and the Duchesse de Chevreuse.
Home on the 5th.

Popham's horse, Wild Dayrell, won the Derby. Dined
with him next day at Twiss's.

May 26*th.*—Hopie appeared at Countess Bernstorff's
child's ball. Montalembert was in London.

Long attack of gout in June. I purchased the site of
Rutland Gate, and the building began.

From Lord Clarendon

G. C., June 3*rd.*—A despatch to the Foreign Office is just
arrived from Varna, which is, of course, the same as the one
to the Admiralty ; but it says that six millions of rations of
corn and flour destined for the Russian army at Sebastopol
have been destroyed, as well as 240 vessels. I send you
this because I believe that the actual number of rations cannot
have been given in the despatch to the Admiralty ; at least,
in the copy sent to me it was left in blank ; and the point is
very important on account of the deficiency of food it must
soon create.

[1] See *post*, p. 361.

This bloodless success in the Sea of Azof will have greater results than Alma or Inkerman, and I think it is highly creditable to Lyons (who, I suppose, commanded) to have destroyed everything at once, instead of thinking about prizes, by which a great deal of time would have been lost, and many vessels might have escaped. It all was done in four days.

G. C., June 24th.—It has been constantly occurring to me how much I wished to see you and talk over some events as they happened, as they must be taken flying, as they are stale in four-and-twenty hours. I thought you were out of town, and am very sorry to hear you have been confined with the gout.

We have not a word of news from the Crimea since the 18th, and we don't know that the telegraph, which was reported to be utterly useless, has been repaired. The damage was in the Austrian territory, and despatches had to be carried by the post from the broken to the sound station. If anything arrives before 12 to-night you shall have it.

I think just as you do about the reverse, and hope that a low tone will not be taken. It will only stimulate our troops, but I am not so sure about its effect on the French.

G. C., July 7th.—Have you seen—and if not, pray read—a remarkable diplomatic correspondence in the ' Moniteurs ' of June 30th and July 1st ? It has been published in order to meet the present cry in France that the war is for English objects, and that no French interests are involved in it.

These despatches, however, show that France clearly foresaw seventy years ago what were the dangers to be apprehended from Russian aggression, and what were the means of averting those dangers, while England, on the other hand, declined to unite herself with France for a European object, and tacitly abetted Russia. The proposal of France to limit the naval force of Russia in the Black Sea is curious at the present moment ; and, indeed, much of the correspondence seems as if it was written within the last six months, instead of in 1783. We learn from it, too, what was the policy of Catharine at that time, and how steadily it is adhered to still.

The Journal here shortly notes :—

July 13*th*. I definitely accepted the editorship of the
' Review.'

August 2*nd*.—Started for Luchon in the Pyrenees, by
Poictiers, Bordeaux, Bayonne, and Pau. Met the Boothbys
going there too. Stayed at Luchon till August 28th. Home
by Paris on September 7th.

The siege of Sebastopol lasted all the summer. The
final attack was made on September 8th.

From M. Guizot

Val Richer, September 8*th*.— . . . I am glad that it is Mr.
John Forster who is reviewing my ' Cromwell.' No one is
better acquainted with those times than he is. We do not
always agree in our judgements of men and events, but I
value his work, have learnt much from it, and took pleasure
in proving it by quoting him.

From Lord Clarendon

F. O., September 10*th*.—I have been at the Cabinet from
the moment that I received your note, and am now returning to the Grove; but at 12.30 or 1 on Wednesday I should
be delighted to see you. Sebastopol is now in our hands :
all the ships sunk, all the steamers burnt, the town in conflagration, the Russians asking for an armistice, and scuttling
away as hard as they can.

And as it was in the days of Noë, so also was it in this year
of bombardments and sieges ; men feasted and men married ;
as also women. The Journal records :—

September 17*th*.—Breakfasted at Twickenham with the
whole royal family of France. Queen Amélie, Nemours and
wife, Joinville and wife, Montpensier and wife and three
infantas, Duchess of Orleans, Comte de Paris. I was the
only stranger there, and sat with the Queen.

October 3*rd*.—Emma Hawkins married to Edward James
Reeve from my house.

From Lord Clarendon

The Grove, October 3*rd*.—Immediate demolition would be
[equivalent to a] public announcement that Sebastopol, and

with it the Crimea, will be ultimately restored to Russia ;
and whatever the future determination may be, such an
announcement at the present moment would be highly
impolitic. We have come into a property ; and having paid
very dearly for it, it would be unwise to order its destruction
before we even know of what it consists, or to what uses it
may be turned. Demolition, moreover, would not be consistent with occupation ; and no where can the allied armies
and fleets pass the winter more conveniently and economi-
cally than at Sebastopol. It is the best harbour in the
Black Sea, far better placed for such operations as the winter
will permit than the Bosphorus ; detachments can be sent
to occupy Perikop, Kertch, &c., after Anapa and other
fortified places are taken ; provisions are more abundant in
the Crimea than in Turkey, and the climate is quite as good
or better.

In short, there are abundant reasons for not leaving
the Crimea at present. It is our *gage matériel*, and may be
made useful in a variety of ways. However, we don't know
that the reports upon the *terra incognita* of Sebastopol and
the Crimea may not lead to some modification of our views.
We might hear, for example, though I don't expect it, that
Sebastopol is hopelessly unhealthy.

I think the public may wait for the details of possession before disposal is decided upon, and that it will
be sufficient to assume that what has been so hardly gained
will not be lightly parted with.

The Journal notes :—

October 11*th.*—Thackeray's friends gave him a dinner at
the London Tavern. Dickens in the chair.

This was a farewell dinner on the eve of Thackeray's
departure for the United States. To readers of the present
day, accustomed to the full reports with which they are
furnished when even the lesser lights in the sky of literature
meet to celebrate the temporary extinction or the refulgence
of one of their companions, this bare mention of a dinner
at which Dickens proposed the toast of the evening and
Thackeray replied to it will seem almost irritating. It was
the custom of the age. The dinner was reported in the
'Times,' but at scarcely greater length than in Reeve's

Journal; and Forster, in his 'Life of Dickens,' only says that the chairman ' gave happy expression to the spirit that animated all, telling Thackeray not only how much his friendship was prized by those present and how proud they were of his genius, but offering him, in the name of the tens of thousands absent, who had never touched his hand or seen his face, life-long thanks for the treasures of mirth, wit, and wisdom within the yellow-covered numbers of " Pendennis " and " Vanity Fair." '

13th.—Went to Kirklands for a fortnight.   Shooting with Sir William Scott and Sir George Douglas.

From M. Guizot

Val Richer, October 5th.—I have just written to my translator, Mr. Andrew Scoble, to send immediately to Mr. John Forster the MS. of the three volumes of my ' Histoire du Protectorat de Richard Cromwell et du rétablissement des Stuarts,' which is in his hands.   The work will be in four volumes, so that Mr. Forster will have seen the greater part before it appears.   I shall be very glad if he will speak of it beforehand.   I have given Mr. Forster's address to Mr. Scoble, telling him the matter was urgent. Should he delay, Mr. Forster might ask him for the MS.

I am sorry you should have been obliged to leave the ' Times,' but delighted that you have done so.   I am no longer familiar with the course of thought in England, but I cannot believe that the stupid violence of the ' Times ' (to say no more) can be a necessary means of success.   If that were so, England would be in a bad way, and I am confident that she is not.

I am just finishing the fourth and last volume of my ' Histoire du rétablissement des Stuarts.'   It will appear in the course of the winter.

Paris, 19 *Novembre.*— . . . Je vous donnerai volontiers, quand j'aurais un peu de loisir, quelques articles pour ' l'Edinburgh Review.'   Je suis sûr que vous la ferez prospérer et briller.

CHAPTER XI

THE 'EDINBURGH REVIEW'

THE very important and indeed decisive change in Reeve's literary career, which occurred in the course of 1855, has been already referred to. It is, however, necessary to speak of it in greater detail, and this can happily be done in Reeve's own words, as recorded in his Journal :—

January 1856.—The year 1855 led to some changes in my own position and pursuits, but I was so occupied during the whole of it that I found it impossible to resume this Journal. Indeed I believe that to write a journal of any value a man must do nothing else, as Horace Walpole and M. de Circourt exhale their souls in letters, and I have done in newspaper articles.

In February 1855, Sir George Cornewall Lewis, who had just succeeded to his baronetcy, his father's seat, and 4,000*l.* a year, became Chancellor of the Exchequer on Gladstone's quitting the Cabinet. The post was first offered to Cardwell, who consulted me about it when it was too late. He declined, chiefly from sentimental motives, and displayed a signal want of energy in grasping a great opportunity. However, on his refusal, Lewis took it, and as he was then editor of the 'Edinburgh Review,' a substitute was wanted in that capacity. I was asked to perform this duty for two numbers, leaving Lewis at liberty to resume the editorship in July, or to resign altogether.[1] On these terms I accepted it, more from personal friendship for Longman and Lewis than from any other motive, for I foresaw that I could not permanently retain all my avocations together, some of which

---

[1] At the time, it was thought highly probable that, after the many resignations, the Ministry would collapse, so that Lewis's tenure of the office of Chancellor of the Exchequer appeared very uncertain.

were more lucrative and influential than the 'Edinburgh Review.' Moreover, I found the 'Review' encumbered with a mass of onerous engagements which I was obliged to repudiate. However, I was then installed, and edited the April number for 1855 (No. 206)—very nearly the commencement of the third century of numbers, and the second half-century of the existence of the journal. Probably I was the only contributor to the present 'Review' whose father had been a contributor to the first numbers. On this occasion, Lord Brougham, now the only surviving original contributor, behaved very civilly about me, and I called to thank him. The appointment was wholly unsolicited by me (as everything I have ever held is and has been), and indeed I was much solicited to take it.

When July arrived, Lewis found that the Ministry was not so precarious as he had at first supposed it to be, and he then definitively retired from the editorship. Longman then offered me the permanent editorship in the name of his firm. It was done verbally, without any agreement or even letter to that effect. Some correspondence, however, had previously taken place, as to my assenting to a condition that I should cease to contribute to the 'Times.' I refused to bind myself by any conditions whatever not to publish my opinions in the manner which I might deem most suitable, and said in writing that I should decline the editorship on such terms. Longman behaved very handsomely, and said he should not insist on any conditions which might be thought to fetter me.

I told Delane what had passed, and said that my chief reason for this conduct was that I felt it would be unhandsome to my old friends at the 'Times' to retire from the journal in the present state of affairs ; but I added that I certainly did not intend to hold permanently these two literary offices, besides my duties at the Privy Council. So the thing went on, and from February to October 1855 I did hold them all—contributed largely to the paper, edited the 'Review,' and worked the Judicial Committee. Yet I can't say I felt worked to excess, though perhaps it was this which brought on a long fit of gout in June and July. As soon as I could get away, we went to Bagnères de Luchon for the waters, rode about the Pyrenees, and stayed a few days in Paris to see the Exposition Universelle in our way home. Early in September I resumed the triple oar in London, and Delane went abroad for recreation, leaving his brother-in-law, Dasent, in charge of the paper, and expecting me to control the foreign policy and the war articles.

As so often happens under similar circumstances, the arrangement did not work smoothly; and when the acting editor claimed the right to discuss foreign questions in accordance with his own opinions rather than in accordance with those of his powerful contributor, Reeve felt that it was time for him to withdraw; and he did so. The Journal continues :—

This terminated my long connexion with the paper, which began in June 1840 and ended in October 1855—fifteen years and four months. I believe I wrote in that time about 2,482 full-paid articles, and received upwards of 13,000*l.* for them. Reckoning each article at three common pages of print, I must have written about fifteen octavo vols. of 500 pages each. Longman was, of course, delighted at this occurrence, and Delane extremely annoyed when he returned to England. Our friendship, however, suffered no interruption; and he expressed to my wife, even more strongly than to me, his regret at my secession.

Probably no one had ever written as much as I have done in the English press with equal opportunities of acquiring information on the subjects I professed to treat. During a great portion of these fifteen years, I lived on terms of confidential correspondence and intercourse with several of the leading ministers of England and of France—more especially with M. Guizot and Lord Clarendon; whilst Delane acted as a means of communication with Lord Aberdeen. Through Mr. Greville, my own chief and afterwards colleague, who had originally introduced me to Barnes in 1840, and sanctioned my writing for the paper, I could always ascertain what was going on; and I question whether there was any person out of the Cabinet more correctly acquainted with the course of affairs; indeed, sometimes things reached me which the bulk of the Cabinet did not know. The consequence of this information was that, although I am not conscious of ever having published to the world what it was desirable to conceal, the 'Times' became a Power in Europe, more dreaded by kings and more read by statesmen than the most elaborate despatches.

Its circulation rose in fifteen years, from about 13,000 when I joined it, to 62,000 when I left it; and although I do not take to myself any peculiar share in this result, for many other contributors wrote as well as I did, and the editor was usually judicious and always active, yet I doubt whether any other writer had occasion to do as much. My articles were almost always printed first, at the head of the paper, and averaged latterly four or even five out of six days. They were the expression of a great system of foreign policy, such as I should have acted upon if I had been born to the position of a minister. They were never dictated or even influenced by any authority but my own free will—very seldom even suggested to me, either by the editor or by any minister or other person; and though they were often regarded as expressions of the opinion of the Cabinet, or of Lord Aberdeen, or of this country, they never in reality expressed anything but my own convictions. If they did, as was often the case, express the opinions of Sir Robert Peel, or Lord Aberdeen, or Lord Clarendon, it is because I commonly found that I took the same view they had formed on public affairs. As for the managers of the 'Times,' they never interfered at all with foreign subjects, except that I may have had some half-dozen conversations with John Walter on the subject in the course of my life. Had this state of things continued I should probably have stuck to the 'Times' in preference to any other literary or official occupation; for I enjoyed the power it conferred of governing public opinion. But the moment an attempt was made to interfere with me and to garble my articles, I resigned, and fell back on the 'Edinburgh Review,' which is a sort of peerage as compared with the tumult of the Lower House.

This being the case, I have more leisure, and I shall endeavour to acquire the habit of keeping up this Journal.

1856.—*January 1st.*—We went in the evening to the French Embassy in honour of the New Year. Mme. de Persigny receives three times a week, without inviting people. She is a granddaughter of Marshal Ney and Jacques

Lafitte ; young, handsome, and with a degree of energy rare among young Frenchwomen, passionately fond of horsemanship, and reading ' Jorrocks ' and ' Pickwick.' Almost all the diplomats were there, except Bernstorff the Prussian ; only three or four English. A lottery was drawn, and the evening was pleasant enough. Young Borthwick of the ' Morning Post ' was there, and very much in Persigny's confidence.

A few days ago a furious article appeared in the ' Morning Post ' threatening Prussia with the supreme vengeance of the allies if she persisted in maintaining her very dubious system of neutrality. The article was so violent that it annoyed the Government, Lord Palmerston's relations with the ' Post ' being no secret. Bernstorff remonstrated ; but the truth is our ministers had nothing to do with it. It was no doubt inspired by Persigny, who represents the war party among the advisers of Louis Napoleon.

My impression of the present state of affairs is that Louis Napoleon would now, upon the whole, prefer to make peace on the terms which have last been offered to Russia ; but that if these terms are rejected, as they probably will be, he will say ' I cannot ask the French people for the money and men required to carry on this war, without offering to France something for her efforts ; and so will come an attack on the Rhenish provinces, that Prussia may be made to pay the bill.

The other day when the King of Sardinia was at Windsor he asked Lord Clarendon a similar question. ' What am I to get for my services ? How am I to justify another loan ? ' and fairly added that he expected a slice of territory—an embarrassing communication to an English minister.

Persigny and Walewski (now foreign minister at Paris) are on the worst of terms. But I think the Emperor likes to have two opposite systems of policy represented by his agents, that he may at last choose which he prefers. He is slow even to vacillation in making up his mind, but very tenacious when his resolution is taken.

The other day M. de Seebach, Nesselrode's son-in-law and Saxon minister at Paris, who is in great favour at the Tuileries, had a long interview with the Emperor before he started for St. Petersburg. This audience made Lord Cowley horribly jealous; but the Emperor related to Persigny what had passed, and so it was reported here. Louis Napoleon begged M. de Seebach to inform the Emperor of Russia from himself how matters stood; that there had been some slight difference of opinion between the allies as to the terms to be offered—that is between France and England, for Turkey was, oddly enough, never consulted in the matter; but that, this being settled, France and England would act as one man; that both Governments were prepared to do all they could out of consideration to the other; and that, although Louis Napoleon desired peace much, he desired the maintenance of the British alliance much more.

January 3rd.—I called on Count Bernstorff and had a long talk with him. I had not seen much of him before, but I told him that I hoped the extreme gravity of the state of our relations with Germany would be my best introduction. He went back to the old story of our opposition to the policy of Prussia in the Danish and German questions of 1849, which he said had weakened Northern Germany and alienated her from us; to which I replied that I had predicted at that time to Prince Löwenstein that such would be the inevitable consequence of Prussia's conduct on those questions. He admitted the danger of the Rhenish provinces, and the manifest advantage to France of widening the difference between Germany and England. It is a notable fact that now, as I believe, for the first time in history, there is reason to think that an extension of France to the Rhine would be even popular in this country, provided Belgium were respected. Bernstorff complained with great bitterness of the exclusion of Prussia from the conference, which is the result of her own negative acts. He is a heavy man, quite unfit to deal with so critical a situation, for his political isolation here is complete.

January 5th.—We had to dinner at home the Fords, Lady Flower, S. Lucas,[1] Wm. Donne,[2] Wm. Harness, the Butts, Forster. Very pleasant dinner.

[1] An Oxford man, a barrister and a writer on the *Times.*

[2] A Norwich man. In 1852 he had declined the editorship of the *Edinburgh Review,* on the ground that he was not in the current of public opinion. He was afterwards examiner of plays.

8th.—Sat some time with Lord Clarendon, whom I had not seen for some weeks. He said that, from accounts from prisoners, he believed the Russians to be very severely pressed to raise men; that the reserves about Nicholaieff consist of militia, who have been embodied under false pretences by the Russian Government: 250,000 animals are said to have been used up in transporting stores last year.

No expectation is entertained here that the Russians will accept the terms, nor, to say the truth, is their acceptance desired. The real desire of the Government and people of England is to accomplish more than they have hitherto done in this war, especially by sea; and the belief is that the enormous force now in preparation for the Baltic will command that success. They say the gunboats and mortar batteries will be light enough to float over the spits and banks which form the deep channel of Cronstadt. Captain Denman told me this some days ago.

January 9th.—A child's ball at the Stephensons'. Old William Hamilton's 79th birthday. Hopie went and looked well. I proceeded to the Cosmopolitan, where I found Milnes, Higgins, Mansfield, Harcourt, &c.

10th.—Attended a meeting of the Nightingale Fund Committee. It seems difficult to satisfy people what the money is to be used for. I had said from the first that the public would give money not from sheer enthusiasm, but for a purpose. However, about 12,000*l.* is raised already.

The great talk of the day is Macaulay's Vols. III. and IV. of his History, which has upon the whole disappointed people. Expectation had been raised too high; 25,000 copies were sold the first day, weighing 61 tons, and all the world set to work to read the book. But it wearies by the sustained effort of the style; and having looked into some of the authorities I am astonished at its inaccuracies. There is a capital article in the 'Times' of to-day on the book by S. Lucas. The blunder about Schomberg [1] was discovered by myself, on a hint from Panizzi. I wrote to Macaulay on it, and he

---

[1] The picturesque account of his burial in Westminster Abbey, whereas, in fact, he was buried in St. Patrick's. The error, which was corrected in subsequent editions, is referred to, with a curious detail, in the review of Macaulay's 'Life and Letters' in the *E. R.* of April 1876.

admitted it to be ' a blemish.'   Sir J. Stephen said to me that it was ' the most valuable and inimitable of books ; ' but with all its brilliancy, there is a want of temper, of truth, and of taste about it which makes me feel I had rather not have written it.

January 13*th, Sunday.*—In the morning, on my way to church, meeting Bonamy Price, I assured him that there was nothing in the rumours of peace which began to be current. In the afternoon I met Lord Granville in Grosvenor Place, who said the Russian answer had arrived, but that he did not know what it was, though no one expected it to be in the affirmative.   It turned out, however, that it went considerably further than anyone had imagined to be possible, and that the Russians acceded to all the terms, except the cession of part of Bessarabia and the fifth proposition, which is indistinct.

From M. Guizot

Paris, January 14*th.*—It was very kind of you to send me Mr. Forster's article a little in advance.   I have read it with great interest and pleasure.   I persist in thinking my ' Cromwell ' truer than his, and I am glad that you are of my opinion.   The longer I live the more I am convinced that to understand revolutions and revolutionists, one must have lived in the midst of them.   Seen from afar, they are rearranged and recast at will, to suit or confirm our preconceived ideas of history or art.   I have often reproached our French republicans and revolutionists with loving the republic better than liberty, and revolution better than the republic.   I might almost say the same of Mr. Forster.   He pardons everything—even actions the most illiberal and iniquitous—in the leaders of the Rump, because they were republicans ; and in Cromwell, even the destruction of the republic, because he was the great leader of the Revolution. I wish to be more liberal and more consistent.

M. Guizot then called attention to two or three slight inaccuracies in the article, and suggested one or two verbal alterations, regretting, however, that it was too late for them to be corrected.   After which, he continued :—

With these exceptions I find Mr. Forster's article full of wit, vivacity, talent, ingenious views and subtle appreciations. It is an excellent exposition and defence of his general idea of the times and men whose history we have both narrated ; and I should feel almost as much pleasure in discussing the questions with him, when I am not of his opinion, as in receiving his approbation when he is of mine. . . .

I am reading 'Philip II.' It is inferior to Mr. Prescott's previous histories, and, above all, is much below the grandeur of the subject. Philip II. and William III. are the leaders and the types of the two different policies which have divided Europe since the sixteenth century. I should take pleasure in illustrating the men by what they believed and what they did, but I cannot undertake it till I go to Val Richer in the summer. Of Macaulay I will say nothing, though I might say much. In a few words, his work is a brilliant embroidery on strong material. Great qualities are so rare that when I find them I forget the faults.

Reeve considered the concluding paragraph of this letter as equivalent to an offer to write on the subject named, for the 'Edinburgh Review.' As he had already asked Guizot to contribute, he gladly accepted the offer, making himself responsible for the translation of the article, which appeared in January 1857.[1] Returning to the Journal :—

January 15th.—The Chancellor of the Exchequer [2] sent for me this morning to say that the reason the Russians made these objections was that Kars had fallen since the proposal was framed, and must now be taken into the account ; and, secondly, that France and Austria had not put the minor conditions, which make up the fifth point, in the clear and precise form which had been adopted here. The Cabinet met, however, in the afternoon, and the result of their deliberations was that Russia had conceded enough for us to enter upon further negotiations. Louis Napoleon had intimated the same opinion, though he said he should give no answer to Vienna until he had received the opinion of the English ministers. Russia had intimated that she thought the question of territorial compensation might be

[1] See post, p. 375.   [2] Sir G. C. Lewis.

left to negotiation : so that she admits the principle. In fact, the allies hold not only part of Sebastopol and the southern part of the Crimea, but Kinburn, Kertch, Eupatoria, Taman, Anapa, Redut-Kale, the coast of Mingrelia, and St. Nicholas.

Austria has ordered her legation to leave St. Petersburg on the 18th ; but she has intimated at the same time to the Western Powers that she is not prepared to go at once to war with Russia. This circumstance is so far fortunate that it relieves us from the necessity of supporting *à outrance* the Austrian part of the demands.

January 17th.—Thus matters stood yesterday, and I went in the evening to see Delane, who is ill, and urge him to publish an article in favour of the conclusion of peace ; which, however, he did not do. By eleven o'clock, however, telegraphic despatches arrived stating that Russia had accepted the whole of the terms unconditionally. This was afterwards modified by the addition of the words ' as a basis of negotiation.' But of the fact of the acceptance there is no doubt. The funds instantly rose about four per cent., and the satisfaction is universal—far greater than could have been imagined from the very warlike tone which prevailed till within the last few hours.

Glehn had called on me the day before to say that his letters from Petersburg assured him that the desire for peace was intense and universal there; in fact, everything seems to indicate that the resources of the Russian Empire have collapsed ; that they feel the contest cannot be carried on, and look forward to the future with increasing dread.

We went in the evening to the French Embassy. The Palmerstons and Wodehouses were there. Palmerston in great spirits, and proud of the success of the firm and consistent language his Government has held. Persigny assured me that it was the energy and prevision of the British Cabinet which had mainly, if not solely, brought about this result; for that Walewski and most of the Emperor's advisers in Paris would have given in half a dozen times over, and continued to send the most inaccurate reports to Vienna and Petersburg. The Emperor and Persigny himself alone stood firm to the English policy ; and at last

Louis Napoleon asked Seebach to go to his father-in-law, Nesselrode, and tell him that France was peremptorily resolved to adhere to the English claims and the English policy. Probably this was one of the causes which led the Russians to give in. Another was the vehement remonstrances and entreaties of the German Powers, who represented to Russia that, if the war continued, nothing could save them from being compelled to take part in it, and that the whole of Europe would be set on fire.

It is now certain that negotiations will be opened—probably in Belgium or at Frankfort ; and I should not be surprised if Lord Clarendon goes to them himself.

January 21st.—Down to Twickenham early in the morning in the brougham, with a pair of horses (having just bought a second carriage-horse) ; breakfasted at Orleans House at half-past eight ; Prince de Joinville then joined us, and we went over to Claremont to shoot. The Duchess made her appearance at this early breakfast. We killed seventeen pheasants, twelve hares, and ten rabbits.

The conversation was as usual curious and animated. Bocher[1] spoke of M. de Persigny's career as the most extraordinary event imaginable. There still exists a petition, ill-spelt, from him to Louis Philippe's private domain, soliciting a place of *garde-chasse* at 80*l.* a year. The other day, when he set up for a count and wanted a coat of arms, he just took the ancient coat of the kingdom of Arles. Yet everybody agrees that Persigny is about the least dishonest of the Emperor's adherents.

Prince de Joinville said he thought that peace would now be made, but that it would not last above two years. By that time France will have recovered from her sacrifices, the army will want employment, the nation will want amusement, and Russia will direct all her arts to establish an alliance with France which may enable her to wreak her vengeance on Germany and her hatred on England. He said he thought the chief cause which had brought Russia to terms was the naval armament for the Baltic, which would, he thought, have destroyed Cronstadt by successive

---

[1] The legal adviser and agent of the French princes. He lived in Paris, but was often in this country.

bombardments. The small steam gunboats—*la poussière navale*—are a part of his old theory, and he maintains that they will change the tactics of naval warfare, and bring us back to the galleys of the ancients, manœuvring in squadrons and probably to be armed with *rostra.*[1]

When we came home from shooting I dressed, and at six went into the picture gallery, where I walked for an hour with the Duchess. She and her lady of honour had been to Richmond on foot, got caught in the rain, and half drowned in the mud. There is something grotesque in the picture of a Neapolitan princess, who at Naples never set foot to the ground, paddling through the mud of the Middlesex road. However, after her marriage, both the Duchess and Princess Joinville used to walk about Paris with their husbands, draggled to their waists, and thought it vastly amusing. At dinner the Duke talked a great deal of his campaigns. At the Smala[2] he had been three days and nights on horseback, with no interval but to feed. The Chasseurs à pieds and Zouaves were less exhausted than the horses. Once in Africa he lost eleven men in a night encampment in the mountains from the severity of the cold. The place has since been called *le camp de la mort.* All the men were severely depressed and alarmed; but they made them sing the ' Marseillaise,' and as they descended the next morning into the warm atmosphere of the plains, the change was most striking. On one occasion, when Baraguay d'Hilliers was threatened by a troop of Arabs, he wound the reins of his bridle round the stump of his lost arm and drew his sword with the other hand. This action had a great effect on the men, who instantly repulsed the enemy.

The Duke talked a good deal of his family ; spoke highly of the military talents of the Regent, who was kept in the shade by Louis XIV. from jealousy on behalf of the Duc de

---

[1] The general truth of this forecast is noteworthy. The peace lasted barely three years, and the army got employment ; later on, more than it wanted ; the Russo-French alliance has been established; *rostra* have been a familiar arm of our ships for many years ; and the theory of *la poussière navale*, after being long preached in France by Admiral Aube and other less responsible writers, has recently, in a modified form, won for itself an advocate in this country, in the person of Admiral Colomb.

[2] The capture of the Smala of Abd-el-Kader, May 16th, 1843. The Duke's official account was published in the same year, and ran through several editions. The story is told in a lively manner by M. Grandin.

Maine. It was the Regent who collected the Orleans gallery of pictures. His son was an ascetic, and wanted to burn all the nudities. At last Égalité (whom the Duke always calls *mon grandpère*) sold them, but not to the English purchasers—to some middleman—I think a connexion of the present Delesserts, though of a different name. Louis Philippe was very fond of talking to his sons of the traditions of the Orleans branch. They have the most minute knowledge of their own history, and the history of all the titles and estates. The third title of the Orleans branch was Duc de Valois, because some of the appanage was in the Valois. The King wanted to give one of his sons that title, but was afraid, as it was supposed to be unpopular. Yet I remember in 1830, when the Revolution occurred, an attempt was made to persuade the people that Louis Philippe himself was not a Bourbon but a Valois. The Duc d'Aumale said that the Valois princes had their merits, but that they had never produced two such sovereigns as the Bourbon kings, Henry IV. and Louis XIV. Nothing can be more animated and instructive than the Duc d'Aumale's conversation. I had a most pleasant day.

January 22nd.—Confidence in the prospect of peace has very rapidly succeeded the rage for war. The only hitch visible at present is that Walewski very unfairly took upon himself not to forward to Vienna the English explanation of the fifth point of the preliminaries. This has now been done, but in the meantime the terms had been presented to and accepted by Russia. Count Buol positively declines to forward the amended terms to St. Petersburg.

Moreover, it is not quite clear what the Russians mean by having 'no arsenals' on the Black Sea. We meant no fortified places. Baudin, who was in Paris, has been sent back here to settle these points. He sat with me some time to-day, and said the feeling for peace was absolutely universal in France. It is quite clear they will not continue the war.

January 23rd.—We dined at Lord Stanhope's to meet the Milmans, Jim Wortleys, E. Ellice, Smirke the architect, and Mr. Barrington. It was one of the first dinners Lord Stanhope had given since he succeeded to the paternal honours and the paternal fortune, and he has removed into one of the large Grosvenor Place houses on the strength of it. From his taste and literary attainments, and her extreme grace and good nature, it is likely to become one of the pleasantest houses in London. Ellice talked, as usual, for everybody. He said Lord Brougham's illusions about the part he took in the affairs of Lord Grey's Government are extraordinary. Lord Grey seldom took him into his close confidence at that time. Brougham at one moment wanted to have the Mastership of the Rolls and to stay (as was then the custom) in the House of Commons ; but of course Lord Grey would not hear of that, and Brougham now seems to have forgotten the story. Ellice has been much opposed to Palmerston all his life, yet he said he thought he would stand in history above all contemporary statesmen ; for in two years he had beaten the Court, beaten Lord Aberdeen, beaten Lord John Russell, beaten the Russians, and made a peace.

January 24th.—Dined with Mowbray Morris.[1] It was the first time I had seen him since I withdrew from the ' Times.'

25th. Dined in Henry Phillips' studio with Layard, Fergusson, and Scott Russell. Phillips has re-broken the kneepan of his leg, and is quite laid up. It is a severe trial of patience. We talked chiefly of art and a little of Ruskin's new volume. Fergusson criticised the Houses of Parliament, and said the front greatly wanted shadow and effect. The great tower is injured by being divided into three stories, each 100 feet high. Barry's plan was originally to have six stories and more windows, on a smaller scale. Barry's first conceptions are usually better than his complete works. It is remarked that Paxton, who invented the iron and glass architecture of this age, got no distinction at Paris.

26th.—Dinner at home. The Joseph Denmans, Greville, the Longmans, Higgins, Colonel Rawlinson, and Dr. Sandwith, who is the lion of the day, because he is just arrived from Kars. Joanna Richardson said he had been inkarscerated.

---

[1] Manager of the *Times*.

From Lord Clarendon

The Grove, January 26th.—I was so busy all day that I did not read the 'Times' till this evening, and I saw in it a semi-announcement that I was to go to the negotiations which were to be held at Frankfort. Will you have the goodness to let Delane know that I am to go, but that the negotiations will take place at Paris?

I never consented to do anything with greater reluctance in my life, but I felt I ought not to shrink from it, having, of course, gained some experience about the different questions that must come under discussion; but I make no illusion to myself as to what will be my fate—no peace that is within attainable limits can satisfy the excited people of this country. John Bull will be glad enough to put an end to the war, but he will be without mercy for the terms on which peace is made; so that the negotiations must be the grave of the negotiator's reputation.

These reflections are, of course, *entre nous*, but I think you will agree with me.

Continuing the Journal :—

January 28th.—Breakfasted at Lord Stanhope's, with Macaulay, Gladstone and his wife, and Lord Stanley. A breakfast party of that size and that quality is certainly as perfect an occasion of table talk as ever existed, but it is exhausting from the brilliancy of the performance. Macaulay coughed a great deal and looked ill, but talked as usual. He began with art. It was a reproach to connoisseurship that such an inordinate value attached to originals and such indifference to copies, even though one might be hardly distinguished from the other. Painting had fortunately escaped from the traditions of antiquity, which to this day imposed their yoke on sculpture, and caused Canova to represent Washington in Roman armour. M. thought all sculpture unsatisfactory, especially monumental sculpture which goes beyond the effigy of the person.

A good deal was said of the duration and emoluments of office. M. thought the salary of a minister at 5,000*l.* a year under the Georges equal to 20,000*l.* a year now. The revenues of the See of Canterbury doubled between the Reformation and the Revolution of 1688, and have more than doubled since. The old Duke of Newcastle and Lord Lansdowne have been ministers longer than anybody else; at intervals, for nearly half a century. Lord Stanley talked very little. Nothing was said of current politics or of Macaulay's book.

This was a strange day of society, for I dined at Hayward's in the Temple, and met Gladstone again, Mr. Ellice, Greville, Landseer, Rawlinson, and Strzelecki—rather too many plums in so small a pudding.

The feeling about the peace is that the French have got all they want by the war, but that England has not; hence much discontent here. Tocqueville remarked in a letter that it would be far more easy to engage France in another war than to make her persevere in this war, which had never been popular. I quoted this opinion at the dinner, and Gladstone seemed much struck by it. Ellice maintained that as soon as peace is made the country would cease to care for the army, and would cut down the establishments. But that I denied. The country is roused, not exhausted by war; and the prospects of peace are not very durable. Gladstone said it was a great thing to have shown that we do not want a force in the Colonies or in Ireland, and that the army may henceforth be far more concentrated. The dinner was good and a little whimsical—boiled pheasants and marrowbones.

We agreed to take the old supper-room at Crockford's for the Cosmopolitan, from March 13th, at 150*l.* a year.

January 29*th.*—Conferred with Mrs. Grote on the publication of a new book by Tocqueville, on the state of France before the Revolution, and the causes of that event. Then went to the Spottiswoodes', where I saw Dr. Barth, the African traveller—a younger man than I supposed. Then to the Persignys', where we found most of the Corps Diplomatique. Persigny told me it was determined to exclude Prussia from the conferences which are to be held in Paris. It seems there has been a good deal of squabbling about trifles on these preliminaries between Paris and London, principally by the fault of Walewski. However, they have ended by Persigny's making a direct report to the Emperor, who has generally agreed with England and settled the point. It is curious to remark that at a moment when France stands so uncommonly high in Europe, her sovereign is much more influenced by his English friends than by his French advisers.

I talked with Count Colloredo about the Austrian Concordat, on which I am writing a paper. He admitted that it had been chiefly framed by the Cardinal Archbishop of Vienna, who signed it on behalf of the Emperor. The surrender of the *placitum regium* was, he said, a great concession in form, but he—Colloredo—doubted whether it was of much value. I merely answered that it had been highly prized by all the most Catholic princes of the House of Austria. Colloredo said the Concordat gave more liberty to the Church in Austria. To Rome, perhaps; but not, I think, to the Austrian Church. After all, the only defence I hear made for the Concordat is that, if Rome or the bishops go too far, the police will put them down.

Persigny said the Emperor of the French had not attended much to the religious disputes; that upon the whole the clergy had been useful to him, and were still so to a certain extent; but that when they became troublesome, the Emperor would kick them over like an ant-hill.

By the way, it is related that the Empress says the life of her baby is not safe among the French doctors, and she wants Locock to go over to her confinement, which Queen Victoria tries to persuade him to do.

30th.—We went this morning to see Sam Rogers's house in St. James's Place, before the pictures are dispersed.[1] I had no recollection of their number or their excellence, for it is long since I had been in the house, as Rogers detested me. Macaulay said the other day he thought one of the most interesting things there was the terra-cotta sketch for the Duke Lorenzo, probably modelled by the thumbs of Michael Angelo. Another striking thing is a bust of Pope, modelled from the life by Roubiliac. We went into the old man's bedroom where he died. Nothing could be more simple. He

---

[1] Rogers died on December 18th, 1855. His art collections and library, sold at Christie's, realised 50,000*l.*

lived in St. James's Place about fifty-one years. Hereafter, men will be curious to mark the house ; not from any love of Rogers or any admiration of his writings—for he well-nigh outlived both those sentiments—but from the place he fills in literary history. It would be difficult to name a spot more frequented by those whose names and haunts society will not forget. William Sharpe said Rogers never kept any regular or complete journal of his life.

We dined at John Murray's, to meet Mr. Whitwell Elwin, now editor of the 'Quarterly Review.' It is odd that the editors of the two reviews should both be Norfolk men, and, indeed, distantly connected through the Bracondale Martineaus. Nothing, however, can be more unlike than this editor and myself. He is a Norfolk parson of immense reading, great knowledge of books, and great ignorance of the world ; evidently unversed in politics and in society. However, he called on me next day, and nothing could be more friendly. The other people at Murray's were the Milmans, Fords, Panizzi, Rawlinson, Kinglake, and Lady Eastlake.

In the evening Lady Granville had her first reception— on the eve of the meeting of Parliament. It was extremely brilliant, and people met again with prodigious cordiality. After the party a good many men adjourned to the Cosmo-politan ; Lowe and Wilson in uniform, which amused the factious. Willes, too, was there—the new judge.

To M. de Tocqueville

16 *Chester Square, January 30th.*—I learned with great pleasure from Mrs. Grote, as well as from yourself, that you are on the eve of publication. I shall be glad if I can be of any use to you about it. When you have given me exact details as to the size, character, and title of your work, I shall be better able to enter into negotiations with Longman or Murray. With the former of these, who is the proprietor of the ' Edinburgh Review,' I am on intimate terms.

The present law—new since 1834 and 1840—secures you the right of translation by a simple declaration ; and this right you have, therefore, the power of selling. In this way M. Guizot has made a considerable profit by his last works. But this is the result. The publisher can only give a certain price for a book, calculated according to the chances of sale and the interest of the subject. This price must cover the author's rights and the cost of translation—as one increases the other diminishes. It is thus, in fact, the translator who pays the author's rights, as these are deducted from the price of his work; and if this remains inadequate, a competent man will not undertake it.

I suppose that the value of an English translation of your volume might be about 100*l.*—everything included. How much of this would you think proper to take for yourself? What share would remain to the translator? My present occupations prevent me from undertaking the task, as I did, with great pleasure, in the case of the 'Democracy.' But the interest I shall always take in all that concerns you is such that I cannot make up my mind to let you fall into the hands of someone who may do you less than justice. I will, therefore, propose to Longman, if agreeable to you, to make myself responsible for the translation, and to revise it with the greatest care, even though it may be partly done by someone else.

But before getting Longman to make an offer, I must be able to explain the nature of the work more clearly. Is it a book in the style of Mme. de Staël's 'Considérations sur la République Française;' or of M. de Maistre; or of M. de Thierry's book on the *Tiers Etat*; or is it more in the character of a narrative?

Your opinions on the peace are mine. It is not impossible that I may come to Paris during the conferences. It would be interesting to attend them.

Returning to the Journal :—

January 31st.—Parliament opened under circumstances of unusual interest, but which had the still more unusual effect of imposing silence on the debaters. The Queen's Speech was remarkably ill written, which surprised people, and more especially those who knew that Lord Palmerston wrote the whole of it himself. I went to the House of Lords and heard Lord Derby and Lord Clarendon : the former gave us a brilliant flourish with his foils, and a burst of eloquence on the fall of Kars; the minister traced out very judiciously his future position in the negotiations. Upon the whole, the result of this first night was very favourable to the Government. Disraeli made a remarkably temperate speech.

February 1st.—The Judicial Committee began to sit. The lawyers greatly excited about the life-peerage just granted to Baron Parke. They are to a man opposed to it, but I question if they can make out a case against the legality of the patent.

Dined at Lansdowne House. Lord Hatherton, Wodehouse,[1] W. Strangways,[2] Alexander Gordon[3] were there ; and though Lord Lansdowne called it a bachelors' party, we had Lady Somers and Lucy Gordon;[3] but I suppose they are bachelors too. Wodehouse said he thought the withdrawal of the ministers between us and the United States was imminent.[4] I found Lord Lansdowne strongly in favour of the life-peerages. I have no doubt of the power of the Crown to grant them. I think it may be advantageous to the House of Lords to introduce a certain number of men of eminence without the encumbrance of an hereditary peerage; but I think the practice might become a powerful means of influence and corruption, and that the exercise of it should be recognised and limited by Act of Parliament. Lord Stanhope agrees, I think, with this opinion.

February 2nd.—Went to Lady Palmerston's evening for the first time this year. It was not very full. Lord Palmerston said he was extremely pleased at the dignified and discreet conduct of Parliament, which would do them great honour in Europe. Sir Edmund Lyons was there—I had never seen him before ; a thorough sailor, but with a look of intelligence, as well as firmness.

To-day, in my Court, there was some discussion about giving costs in an appeal. Maule observed, drolly enough, ' I wonder what Bob Richards would say, if he were alive ? '

---

[1] Lord Wodehouse, created Earl of Kimberley in 1866.
[2] Succeeded, in 1858, as 4th Earl of Ilchester.
[3] Sir Alexander and Lady Duff Gordon.
[4] The States' Government considered themselves aggrieved by the alleged illegal enlistment of Americans for the British army, and, after a dispute extending over the best part of a year, ordered Mr. Crampton to quit Washington, May 28th. It was believed in England that Crampton had acted injudiciously, and, after a short interval, diplomatic relations were resumed.

'Oh!' said Pemberton Leigh, 'it was always said that Richards would not mind being damned, if it were without costs.'

Sunday, February 3rd.—Afternoon a little frosty. I rode over to Twickenham to call on the Duc d'Aumale, and sat half an hour there. He said he heard the French army in the Crimea was now in a bad sanitary condition.[1]

At the Cosmopolitan in the evening, Rawlinson said he believed the generals had committed an enormous blunder in not attacking the north side of Sebastopol at once after September 8th, and that an expedition might have been sent with ease to land at the mouth of the Salghir, and advance in the rear of the Russians. Had any such demonstration been made they would have been compelled to evacuate the lines of the Crimea. After the Alma, and after the fall of Sebastopol, the allies did not rely enough on the moral results of their victory.

4th.—Dined at Chorley's with the Eastlakes and Miss Cushman, the American actress. Chorley says she has made 50,000*l.* in twelve years. In spite of all that is said of the decline of the drama, I doubt whether dramatic talent was ever more remunerative both to actors and authors.

In the evening to Mrs. Stephenson's. Weber sang.

February 7th.—To the House of Lords to hear the debate on the peerage granted to Lord Wensleydale for life. Lord Lyndhurst moved its reference to a committee of privileges, in a speech which had all the characteristics of his eloquence —an exquisite propriety of language, an inimitable perspicuity of arrangement, learning without effort and wisdom without heaviness, relieved by a sparkle of playfulness or a touch of satire. He spoke for upwards of an hour—an unparalleled feat for a man of eighty-four. I have heard him say that he was born in the North American Colonies before the Declaration of Independence.

Lord Granville defended the legality and expediency of the measure with great spirit and force. None of the peers, except Lord St. Leonards, have ventured positively to deny

---

[1] This was not commonly known in England then, and still less is it known now; but it was a ghastly fact which caused the death of between eighty and ninety thousand Frenchmen. Cf. Rousset, *Histoire de la Guerre de Crimée*, tom. ii. pp. 458–63.

the legality of peerages for life; but very few of them will admit that such creations are constitutional or expedient. The reference to a committee of privilege was carried by a majority of 33.   Upon the whole, it is much to be regretted that this measure was inconsiderately taken.   The result of the defeat will be that the enemies of the House of Lords will accuse it of exclusiveness and incapacity, and that it will be more than ever difficult to make life-peerages either by the prerogative or by law.

February 10th.—Went to hear Dr. Guthrie preach at a Scotch Presbyterian chapel near the Edgware Road.   I had recently read with interest his sermons, entitled 'The Gospel in Ezekiel'—characteristic enough of a people who find the Gospel itself in the denunciations of the Hebrew prophets.   Guthrie's faith seems to be a lurid Calvinism, refined by that poetic fervour and love of nature which is so intense among the Scotch.   His sermons are *Noctes Ambrosianæ* in the pulpit; there is the exuberance of Wilson over a punch bowl, and sometimes the pathos of the Shepherd.   The Scotch have almost repudiated the theatre, but they are more theatrical than the English.   Jeffrey, Cockburn, and Rutherfurd always talked and behaved like men acting a part.   Guthrie's preaching was a finished performance—tones, gesture, diction highly spirited and sometimes highly effective—but I could hardly trace an idea.   He passed from one topic to another, as if he were exhibiting dissolving views of the perdition of man.

February 13th.—Dined at Serjeant Kinglake's.   The Attorney-General [Sir Alexander Cockburn], Phinn, Keating, Montague Smith, Milner Gibson.

Gibson, in the usual strain of the Manchester men, threw all the blame on this country, and gave all the credit to the Yankees in the disputes now pending.   I think this passion for depreciating the policy and resources of England is peculiar to Englishmen.   They do it to affect an unbounded ingenuousness, and are unjust to no [one] but their country. Gibson said it was very difficult to prevent filibustering expeditions; that Louis Napoleon's expedition to Boulogne was filibustering.   'No,' said the Attorney-General, 'it was a Louis-Philibustering expedition.'

The Judicial Committee finished its list of causes to-day : fourteen causes—eight reversed, two varied, and four affirmed. The opinion gains ground that they ought to transfer the Scotch appellate jurisdiction to the P.C.; but I doubt if the Lords will ever consent.

To M. de Tocqueville

C. O., February 19*th.*—I have to apologise for my silence. I duly received your letter of the 6th, but the sittings of the Council were prolonged to the 15th, and it was not till then that I was able to attend to your business. I have entered into negotiations with Messrs. Longman, and I shall shortly have their answer, which I shall at once communicate to you. I find the résumé of the work extremely interesting ; but the subject is not so fresh as the American Democracy.

The Journal goes on :—

February 21*st.*—Evening at the Van de Weyers', the first time they have received for two or three years. Not many people. Considering that we are in the prime of the session, the town is dull. People have nothing to talk of but the Wensleydale peerage, the observance of the Sabbath, and the administration of the army.

Mrs. Villiers [1] said, a little time before she died—at the age of eighty—that no change had taken place in her time more remarkable than the change in the observance of the Sabbath. Queen Charlotte used to have drawing-rooms after church, and women went in full dress to the Chapel Royal. Everybody had dinners, and some people played cards. Now we are Judaised, and the whole idea of the Sabbath is brought back from the Christian holyday to the Mosaic observance. A motion to open the galleries &c. on Sunday after church has been defeated in the H. of C. by 376 to 48.

February 22*nd.*—Two questions were debated to-night in the House of Lords. First, whether the Wensleydale peerage should be referred to the judges ; second, whether the patent for life conferred a right of sitting in Parliament. The Government were beaten on the first by a majority of 31,

---

[1] Lord Clarendon's mother. She died on January 12th, 1856.

and on the second by 35.   I heard the beginning and the end of the debate, having gone away in the middle to dine at Merivale's.

Though Lord Granville takes a very warm interest in this life-peerage question, and I should be disposed to agree with him if I could, I find it impossible to do so.   The absurdity of modifying the present constitution of the British Legislature, upon the questionable authority of precedents not later than the Plantagenets and the Tudors, is so palpable that it admits of no justification.   As for consulting the judges, I told Lord Granville from the first that they would not carry it, and that if they did carry it, the judges would in all probability decline to answer a question which is exclusively one of prerogative and privilege, as regulated by the law of Parliament.   Moreover, it would have indefinitely protracted the settlement of the question.   As for the validity of the patent for life, it has certainly lost ground in the course of the debate; and as the thing has never been done before, even under the strongest pressure, it is obvious the whole onus of proof rests on those who seek to do it now.   The best thing for the Government to do would be for the Crown to make Baron Wensleydale a viscount, with remainder to the heirs male of his body.[1]   Lady Ashburton said drolly enough that he had better be made a peer with remainder to David Dundas, who has been toadying Parke all his life.

February 23rd.—Meeting Sir Henry Bulwer in the Green Park this morning, we talked of the Anglo-French alliance, which he said the French always used as a stepping-stone to some better connexion in Europe.   I said : 'The French find themselves with us in the position of a man who marries a woman with a great fortune, all in strict settlement, and cannot make away with a penny of it ; an alliance with Russia, on the contrary, would be like running off with a girl who has plundered the till, and is ready to spend half of it with her lover.'

February 27th.—Dined at Procter's, now almost the *doyen* of literature.   Milnes there.   Lord Palmerston has

---

[1] The Committee of Privileges reported that the Crown had lost, by disuse, the power of creating life-peerages, and a new patent was drawn.   As Lord Wensleydale's sons all died in infancy, it came to the same thing.

just offered his father a peerage, which he has declined.
Milnes said he had never been into a church till he was
twenty, his family being strict Unitarian Dissenters. It is
very remarkable how great a part the Unitarian families or
their descendants have played in literature, law, and society;
yet at the present day there are no eminent Unitarians.

February 28*th*.—Dined at Longman's. Bulwer, and
some African travellers—Barth and Burton—but they might
as well have been at Timbuctoo. Bulwer said Persigny had
made considerable contributions to his book on France twenty
years ago—the part about the army.

To M. de Tocqueville

16 *Chester Square, March* 4*th*.—I propose coming to
Paris next Sunday, and shall stay at No. 11 Rue Richepanse.
I shall try to force your door on Monday morning, if I have
arrived by then. The wish to talk to you has a great deal to
do with this little trip.

Would it not be possible and useful to indicate by the
title of your work the characteristic which distinguishes it
from the other innumerable works on the French Revolution?—I mean its dealing specially with the state of France
and Europe at an epoch previous to the actual Revolution.

If I have caught your idea, you deal with facts and causes
which are, so to speak, the sources of the Revolution, rather
than with the events which have occurred since 1789, and
this is what makes the originality of the work; but I submit
these considerations to you in all humility, as you are the
most competent judge of the matter. Besides, we can talk
it over.

The Journal continues :—

Sunday, March 9*th*.—Christine and I went to Paris by
Boulogne, starting at 8 A.M., and getting to the Rue
Richepanse at half-past 10. Christine went on next day to
Tours. I breakfasted with Tocqueville; went to Ary Scheffer's
studio.

The interest of this visit was heightened by the negotiations for peace which were going on, and by the birth of the
Imperial heir, which took place on March 16th. I saw,

however, but little of Lord Clarendon, who was extremely engaged ; and my French friends know nothing of the official world. Paris is more splendid and costly than ever, supported, as it is, by the Imperial budget ; but neither success in war, nor the return of peace, nor the Imperial heir can excite any enthusiasm among the people.

In society I frequented the Duc and Duchesse de Luynes, the Duc and Duchesse de Rauzan, Mme. Blaise de Bury, where I dined, on March 17th, with Villemain, Cousin, Rémusat and Gounod, the Circourts and Raymonds. Dined one day with Admiral Rigault de Genouilly and a party of Crimean officers, who were very courteous and pleasant.

We came home with Charles Greville on the 19th, and read the Duchesse de Gontaut's MS. Memoirs [1] on the way.

March 22nd.—Went to Littlecote House, near Hungerford, to see F. Popham. We found there Twiss, the Oxholms, and Sir F. Doyle, and had a very pleasant visit till the 25th. The house is the most perfect specimen of a mediæval mansion I know in England—with the armour, the buff jackets, the arquebuses, the ghost-chamber, and the fish-ponds of the seventeenth century, all in complete preservation. It was here that William III. slept on his march from Exeter ; and here that Captain Popham, that famous companion of Cromwell and Blake, ended his career.[2] Of all these memorials, what most interested me was the family papers. They contain some of the correspondence between Charles I. and Henrietta Maria, four letters of Cromwell, the papers of Clarke [3] (who was Monck's private secretary), a narrative of the Restoration by another Mr. Clarke, and a life of Dr. Clarke [4] who was secretary to William III.

One effect of Reeve's position as editor of the 'Edinburgh Review' was to bring him into entirely new relations to

---

[1] *Mémoire de Madame la Duchesse de Gontaut, Gouvernante des Enfants de France pendant la Restauration*, 1773–1836. Written by the Duchess in 1853 ; published 1891.

[2] Alexander Popham, died in 1669. His younger brother Edward, whose career was more intimately mixed up with Blake's, died at Dover in 1651.

[3] Sir William Clarke, for twelve years Monck's secretary, and, after the Restoration, secretary at war, was slain in fight with the Dutch on June 2nd, 1666. His diary is now in the British Museum (Addl. MS. 14,286).

[4] George Clarke, son of Sir William, was secretary at war from 1692 to 1704, and afterwards secretary to Prince George of Denmark. He died in 1736, leaving large legacies to Worcester and All Souls' Colleges, in Oxford.

Lord Brougham, who had always considered himself as a constituent proprietor. It will be remembered that, many years before, Macaulay had been frequently irritated by the way in which he pressed his fancied and admitted claims, and his intercourse with Reeve on his first coming to the Council Office, had not been altogether such as to bode well for future harmony. There was, however, a marked change.

> That which moulders hemp and steel
> Mortal arm and nerve must feel;

and the old pugnacity was calmed, the violent self-assertion restrained. His correspondence with Reeve, which his interest in the 'Review' rendered frequent, was friendly, often even affectionate; and during these later years a very kindly feeling sprang up between the two. The following letter refers to the discussion of February 28th in the House of Lords, on its 'Appellate Jurisdiction,' and the appointment of a Select Committee to inquire into the matter. This had, to some extent, a personal interest both to Brougham and Reeve, and almost of necessity called for an interchange of views. Reeve would seem to have consulted the old Chancellor as to the terms of an article on this debate and the forthcoming report of this Committee, and received the following reply :—

Cannes, March 28th.—I fear if you wait for the Committee's Report, and for the measures to be grounded thereon, it will be too late for this number,[1] because there are so many things to be inquired into that a considerable delay is certain to take place. But there will be very great advantage to the discussion, and to the measures which shall arise out of it, in having the matter fully and calmly, and without party bias, considered. I don't, however, at all mean that there should be an exclusion of the topics connected with the strange conduct of some of the party leaders, and especially the Conservatives, who in the most unexpected manner joined the cry out of doors against the House of Lords. As an instance of the effect produced by Derby's declaration that the judicial business in the Lords was 'most unsatisfactory' to the people, and especially the courts in Scotland, I may mention (of course this is for yourself) that I had

---

[1] The article on 'Supreme Courts of Appeal' was published in the July number of the *Review.*

letters immediately after, from judges there, especially from the [Lord] Justice Clerk [the Right Hon. John Hope] (the Hopes, as you are aware, having always been at the head of the Conservative party in Edinburgh), expressing astonishment at the attack coming from such a quarter, and declaring readiness to bear testimony to the entire satisfaction of Scotland for a hundred and fifty years. The President, whom Derby most indiscreetly cited, has since informed him that he was mistaken, and did not wish to be examined on the subject.[1]

I mentioned to you in my letter two days ago that this extraordinary movement of the Conservatives has given rise to the belief in this country (I believe I referred to the ' Revue des deux Mondes ' [March 15th], where there is an article on the subject) that the House of Lords is found unfit for judicial duties, and is condemned to immediate reform ; and this is given by friends of constitutional government as proof that our institutions are changed as soon as they are found to fail. It appears to me quite necessary that the attention of the country should be called to this proceeding of the Conservatives, and to the false position into which they have chosen to place themselves. I need not add that Lyndhurst and the reflecting portion of their leaders had no hand in it ; and both Campbell and myself felt with Lyndhurst that it was most unfortunate that the subject should be taken out of his safe hands by persons wholly ignorant of the subject, and who had the gross imprudence to state that the House of Lords did not depend on its judicial functions for its weight in the constitution.

You mention Langdale. I have no recollection of ever seeing him at the Judicial Committee, but he may have been there in 1836, when I was absent till November. When I came back to it I found Parke, Erskine, &c., there as before. When you say I was the *regenerator* of the Judicial Committee, pray take care not to fall into the error

---

[1] Lord Derby's words were : ' As regards Scotland, I am bound to say that the present state of things is most unsatisfactory, and that opinion is shared by persons who are very distinguished members of the Scotch Bar ; and, in point of fact, it was only this morning that I received a letter from the Lord Justice General, saying that he was desirous of stating the cause of Scotland before a Committee, if one was appointed.'

of supposing it had any existence at all before 1832-3. Till my bills transferred from the abolished delegates one year and created the Committee the next, the jurisdiction was in the P. C. at large.   I have always regarded the chief excellence of the Court to be the rule of practice, in which Shadwell mainly helped me, taking cases in turn and giving written judgements, and no debate.

To this, the first of Lord Brougham's letters here printed, it is well to add that his writing, always hurried and careless, was at this time, when he was approaching his eightieth year, almost illegible—not only from its exceeding badness, but from his habit of cutting short the words, omitting letters, and sometimes beginning one word and ending another. It forms an especially difficult cryptogram, which only time and patience can decipher.   It recently happened to the present writer to be speaking of this to Miss Courtenay, herself, in past years, on terms of familiar friendship with Lord Brougham.   'Oh, yes,' she answered, 'I know that difficulty very well.   I was one day dining at a house where Mrs. Austin was on a visit, and a small party had been invited to meet her.   She called on me to help her in deciphering a note from Lord Brougham which she had vainly tried to make out.   Looking over her shoulder, I spelt it out aloud, word by word ; and there was a general laugh when we came to the last sentence—"Of course all this is only for your private eye." '

It may be noticed, also, as one of his many eccentricities, that, though a peer of many years' standing, he continued to sign his friendly letters 'H. B.' or 'H. Brougham,' though latterly the name became more like Brogm.

The Journal has :—

April 15th.—Xavier Raymond and his wife came to Chester Square on a visit.   Raymond and I went down to Portsmouth to see the great naval review on April 23rd, after the war.[1]   We were on board the 'Vivid,' with the Corps Diplomatique.

To M. de Tocqueville

16 *Chester Square, April 18th.*—I have received the first sheets of your work with great pleasure, and shall set to work at once.

---

[1] It was on this magnificent spectacle that Raymond based his *Lettres sur la Marine Militaire.*

Murray (the publisher) says that it is decidedly impossible to make use of the expression *ancien régime* in the title of a translated work. I therefore propose 'On the State of France before the Revolution of 1789,' which is equivalent to the *ancien régime.*

You must be careful to announce on the first page that the author reserves the right of translation. The book must then be deposited at one of the Government offices—I do not know which. We will do everything on our part to protect your rights.

The Mr. Merivale I recommended to you is the brother of the man who is writing the history of Imperial Rome. The book is a little too Cæsarean for my taste, but much less so than is reported in France. On the whole, it is a very good book.

I am anxious to know your opinion of the last number of the 'Edinburgh Review.' Rémusat could lend it to you. . . . .

April 27th.—I am extremely flattered at the opinion you express of the 'Review.' It is the height of my ambition to make it the organ of liberal and moderate opinions, and to find some support abroad as well as in England. The first article you read is by Lewis; that on the Concordat is mine.

The more closely I study your work in the chapters already received, the more I am impressed and delighted by it. Everything in it is striking as a work of art, and I find in it the grace and truth of Greek sculpture.

My cousin, Lady Duff Gordon, is helping me with the translation, which she does admirably.

From Lord Clarendon

G. C., April 29th.—Many and sincere thanks for your letter. I am gratified beyond what I can express that you, who are so thoroughly acquainted with all the bearings of the question, should think that nothing has been neglected, and that all has been obtained that we had a fair right to demand.

On public even more than on personal grounds, I regret that the people of England cannot have the benefit of an explanation from you of the treaty and the protocols, for they will not be understood, nor will the true bearing of what has been arranged be appreciated unless it is all suggested. I suppose that the ingenuity of party patriotism will pick holes enough in the treaty, and on Monday be able to prove that we were in a position to have made Hungary independent, to have reconstituted Poland and un-Austrianised Italy, and that not to have accomplished these trifles is deserving of censure.

To M. de Tocqueville

16 *Chester Square, May 1st.*—I have finished the first six sheets. The further I get, the more it pleases me, and I am so taken up with it that I give all my time to the work. What pleases me most is that I find myself so entirely in agreement with you. You say many things which I have often thought before, but with less clearness and force. Twenty years ago, when you were writing your apology for American Democracy, I was not always of your opinion; I had less faith than you in those institutions; and to-day I have still less. But as to the great lesson of the past which you now lay before us, I heartily agree with you. Here are a few slight printer's errors. . . .

The peace and protocols are a great success here. Above all, Lord Clarendon is overwhelmed with praise, to which he is every way entitled.

May 15th.—The quotation from Arthur Young's book, page 152, puzzles me a little. I have found in the original the visit of Arthur Young to the Duke of Liancourt. But what he says is the exact contrary of what you attribute to him. M. de Liancourt took him to the Assemblée de Clermont. He dined with the leading agriculturists of the country; he was pleased with everything, but thought it very remarkable that two ladies should be present at a dinner of twenty-five men ; a thing which, he says, would never have happened in England. This is very different from your quotation. Perhaps I have made a mistake, but it does not seem that he went to Liancourt twice. Please let me know *the date* of the visit you quote ; then I shall be able to verify it without difficulty. The work progresses, and always with increased pleasure. . .

May 20*th*.—I have verified the quotation from Arthur Young, and this is the mistake. It was when he was with M. de la Rochefoucauld at La Roche Guyon, and not at Liancourt, that the circumstance occurred ; and he mentions in a note that at Liancourt, out of Anglomania, they took him to dine with farmers. The thing is of no importance in itself, but one likes to be exact.

June 8*th*.—The last sheets have arrived. We have already translated about nineteen, and now the printing will go on rapidly. I am spending these days in the country for the Ascot races, where I shall finish the text. My address is still London. . . . I told you that we proposed coming to Normandy in October, and you kindly invited us to Tocqueville at that date. We now find that, for several reasons, August would suit us better, and I think I may say with some certainty that we could come on August 15th if you were disposed to receive us then. Would this suit you as well as October ? Please answer with as much frankness as I show in asking you. I am delighted that you should have the idea of choosing a person out of English literature as a rest from the Revolution. I will find out whatever can be useful to you ; but while waiting for something better, let me recommend a book entitled ' The Life and Times of Oliver Goldsmith,' by John Forster—last edition, two vols. 8vo. It is an excellent work, in which Dr. Johnson is a prominent figure. Forster has a very exact knowledge of English society at that period. . . .

June 16*th*.—Mon cher ami, j'apprends avec la plus grande peine la perte douloureuse qui vient de vous atteindre.[1] Il suffrait d'avoir entrevu M. votre père pour reconnaître en lui un des plus dignes et respectables représentants d'un temps et d'une race d'hommes qui n'est plus ; et en lisant le livre qui vient de vous occuper, il me semblait voir à chaque page l'empreinte noble et honorable d'un caractère qui avait conservé les belles qualités de l'Ancien Régime à travers soixante-cinq ans de révolution. Je connais d'ailleurs la profonde affection qui unit tous les membres de votre famille à son digne chef, et, pour tout dire, à son père. Je comprends combien cette blessure est profonde. Votre conso-

---

[1] Tocqueville's father had died on June 9th.

lation c'est que pendant tant d'années vous avez fait le bonheur et la gloire de celui que vous regrettez à tant de titres.

I imagine that this sad event, and the completion of your work, will hasten your departure for Normandy. It will be a real pleasure to me to catch sight of your turrets at the end of two busy months. My wife and daughter are eagerly looking forward to the journey. As the latter can almost be looked upon as grown up, I hope she will be no trouble to anyone. Our plan is to arrive at Tocqueville about August 15th. I do not know whether you will think your guests are abusing your Norman hospitality if we stay a fortnight. On leaving you we mean to go on to Jersey. In coming, we shall take Havre on the way, for I have long owed M. Guizot a visit at Val Richer.

The Journal notes here :—

June 17*th*.—Queen's ball ; first time the new ball-room was used. Dinner at Milnes' on July 1st, to meet Ristori ; Lord Lansdowne and Duchess of Somerset there. Ristori was splendid in ' Medea.'

July 5*th*.—Higgins and Stirling[1] gave a dinner to the Philobiblon at the Crystal Palace.

To M. de Tocqueville

July 15*th*.—I did not write because I felt sure that you had left Paris, but did not know that you were at Tocqueville ; besides, I have been very busy ; for, in addition to my literary occupation, this is the thirtieth day that the Council has been sitting without an interval, and I am chained to my bench. However, I finished my work for you a fortnight since. Everything was in the printers' hands by the first of July ; it is now all corrected, and it is only the delay of these good people which prevents the flight of your thoughts and my style.

I cannot flatter myself that I have completely come up to your expectations ; the less so as both time and leisure have been greatly wanting. But one thing is certain, that in translating you, I write with as much dash as if I were putting my own thoughts on paper. I will send you by post the first

---

[1] Afterwards Sir William Stirling-Maxwell, K.T.

copy that I get.   To-day I send you a notice in the ' Saturday Review.'

At present all our plans are turned towards Normandy. We hope to embark for Havre on August 4th ; from Havre to Val Richer, where we shall spend a few days ; then to Caen, and then on to Tocqueville.   Where should we leave the diligence?   At Valognes?   I think the public conveyances do not go as far as the village.   Let me know.

Everyone who has read your book is enchanted with it, but this is not a good time for serious reading, so that it will be a few months before the effects of the book are felt in this country.

I cannot admit the rusticity of Tocqueville, and I am sure we shall not perceive it ; what we shall really find there, worthy of the days of Homer, will be your hospitality and friendship.

And then the Journal :—

July 30*th.*—Went to Farnborough.   Grand review at Aldershot—about 23,000 men, chiefly from the Crimea.   The French princes were there.   [We started from Farnborough Hill—wrote Mrs. Reeve—a large party, including our host (Mr. T. Longman) and his daughter, Delane and two or three officers.   We rode a little distance behind the Queen and Prince.   It was a lovely day, and a most interesting occasion.]

CHAPTER XII

CONDUCT OF THE 'REVIEW'

IT is probably unnecessary in itself to say that the 'Edinburgh Review' is published quarterly, about the middle of January, April, July, and October; but, as affecting Reeve's future life, it must be remembered that these dates, or rather some ten days earlier, marked the editor's temporary release from his duties. As the weeks slipped away, the shadow of the next number gradually deepened, till, as a rule, for a fortnight or three weeks from the middle of the months before publication, his presence was required in or near London, he himself, without an assistant, superintending all the details of the arrangement and the printing. He not only read the articles to approve of them, very commonly in the MS., but in all cases he revised the proof slips, a work involving enormous labour, which, it was sometimes suggested, might be safely entrusted to a deputy. Reeve did not think so; and thus every article that appeared in the 'Review' bore, to some extent, the impress of his own mind. But, far more than this, he seldom decided on publishing the review of a book which he had not himself read. To arrive at subjects of interest and importance, and to select contributors who could do justice to them, were his never-ending care. In this he was, of course, often many months ahead of the requirements of the 'Review,' though it frequently happened that the publication of a particular book called for immediate attention, and an article was demanded in relatively as much haste as a leader for the 'Times.' The political articles, too, were almost always written, or at any rate finished, at the very latest moment, to allow for changing conditions, though Reeve was ever careful to discriminate between the functions of a daily newspaper and of a quarterly review.

For these political articles he was scrupulously careful to select some one combining a knowledge and a correct judgement of the facts with a literary and artistic power of setting them forth, and such a writer was not always easy to find. There was less difficulty in meeting with capable contributors for the more purely literary, historical, or scientific articles, though Reeve limited his choice by certain rules which admitted of no relaxation, the chief of which were to entrust a review to no one whose relations—of blood, of friendship, or of enmity—to the author of the work in question might be supposed to give his opinions a personal bias ; nor yet to anyone who had already reviewed the work in any other periodical. His letters make frequent mention of his being disappointed of the assistance of some contributor whom he had considered particularly suitable, by learning that he had already written in the ' Athenæum,' ' Academy,' or other journal. As the years passed on, he naturally got together a body of contributors on whom he could rely, and who, without being formally recognised as ' on the staff' of the ' Review,' were practically so by mutual understanding and, to a large extent, by personal acquaintance and friendship.

We have seen that, as early as the beginning of June, Reeve had laid his plans for a visit to Normandy in August, and these he now carried out. His Journal records :—

August 4th.—Went to Normandy with Christine, Hopie, and Munro. We stopped at Rouen to see Jumièges. Then to Val Richer, on a visit to M. Guizot, August 7th. Then to Caen and Cherbourg, and to Tocqueville, on a visit there.

A few details of a very interesting visit may be taken from Mrs. Reeve's letter to her father.

Château de Tocqueville, August 15th.—. . . Our stay with M. Guizot was full of interest. He is most amiable in his relations with his family, and to hear so great a statesman and historian speak on books and politics is indeed a privilege. We left early on Monday (the 11th), and took the rail from Lisieux to Caen. The afternoon was devoted to the churches &c. of that town. . . . The next day we took a carriage and went to Falaise, the birthplace of William the Conqueror. . . . The annual horse fair was taking place, and we looked at the horses and listened to the jargon of French dealers after we had ' done ' the antiquities. On Wednesday we had a long diligence journey to Cherbourg, and yesterday morning took a carriage and drove here. Pray take the map and look at the peculiar position of the Cotentin, surrounded on three sides by the sea. This château is only about two and a half miles from the sea, but the wisdom of three hundred years ago placed it in the valley instead of on the height, and one has five miles to walk for the views. The neighbourhood is thickly peopled, and each cottage seems surrounded by woods which reach to the water's edge, apparently; I believe there is a bare half-mile, quite on the level of the sea; but the charm of the view, wood and water, is indescribable. Monsieur de T. is a great walker, and we are to make excursions every day. This morning we all went to the grand mass in honour of the Fête of the Virgin, of France, and of the Emperor—a very pretty sight; for the population here have been little affected by chances and changes, and retain their picturesque dresses and primitive habits.

The Journal adds :—

Stayed at Tocqueville till August 23rd. Then to Avranches, Dol, St. Malo, and Jersey. Home on September 3rd.

To M. de Tocqueville

September 10*th.*—I send to-day the second part of the 'Times' article, which is just out. Of all I have read on your book, these articles seem to me incontestably the best. It is impossible to have a more brilliant success. It seems that the effect of all these newspaper articles has been to sell a large number of copies of the original work, rather than of the translation.

The Journal interrupts the correspondence to note :—

October 5*th.*—Sailed for Aberdeen; crossed from Burgh Head to Little Ferry, and thence to Skibo. Shooting there.

To M. de Tocqueville

October 13*th.*—I do a splendid stroke of business in sending you some sheets of my review, as you are good enough to study them so conscientiously, and to let me know what you think of them. I set a high value on your criticism, and hope you will continue it, when you find anything worthy of remark.

It may be said that the state of the Church in Austria before the Concordat, and under the Josephine legislation, came into the category of subjection, and was for seventy-five years rather too much of an instrument in the hands of a despotic State.   True; but, taking it all in all, the greatest drawback in my eyes is that the Church should be above the laws of the country; and note that so long as the principle of ecclesiastical enfranchisement is sacred, the Church is willing, and all the more willing, to accept the subjection of everything else; whereas the Church, when reduced to the same level as other political and social institutions, lends powerful assistance to the liberty of countries.

I saw Lord Clarendon for a moment, when he was passing through London.   He who has read nothing but despatches for three years had read your book, and was enchanted with it.   When he was leaving Balmoral, Prince Albert insisted on his taking his own copy to read 'en route,' which he did.

Here is another flattering anecdote for your satisfaction as an author.   Mrs. Basil Hall had just lost a daughter whom she adored.   She could find no distraction or amusement in reading.   One of my friends sent her 'L'Ancien Régime.'   She read your work, and it was her first calm and happy moment since her loss.

I am writing from an old Highland castle, surrounded by sea and mountains, and the splendid weather is allowing the poor Highlanders to gather in the little oats which they wring from the rude and stubborn soil.

For myself I find an inexpressible pleasure in this wild scenery, and I shoot a good deal.   We shall stay here till the end of the month, and on our return to London shall take up our quarters in my new house, No. 62 Rutland Gate, where please address me in future.

In a few days you will receive the new number of the 'Edinburgh Review.'   There is nothing of mine in it, but I especially commend to you the article on the affairs of the United States.   The review of the novel 'Perversion' is by our friend Milnes.

I am quite of your opinion about this abominable business at Naples, and have said so to Lord Clarendon.   I am disposed to think that this ridiculous intervention will come to nothing in the end.[1] . . .

---

[1] For many years the internal government of Naples had been a scandal to European civilisation.   England and France attempted to interfere, and were

The Journal here has :—

October 16th.—To Uppat. Started with George Loch for the town of Sutherland. Two days at Loch Inver—west coast very fine. Scowin, and back to Uppat by the Reay Forest. Then went south, by Dundee, to Keir; Westquarter (in Lanarkshire), where Moncreiff was, and Kirklands, where I found Sir E. Colebrooke, who soon after [on November 12th] married Lizzie Richardson.

Returned to London on November 4th, and took possession of my new house, 62 Rutland Gate.

The visit to Skibo in Sutherlandshire, the country seat of Mr. George Dempster, whose acquaintance he had made some years before, at Uppat, led to an intimate friendship, and a correspondence which continued to the end. Dempster was much interested in agriculture, the fisheries, the state of the country, and the condition of the peasantry—points on which Reeve frequently consulted him : and though not literary, in the narrow sense of the word, he had a large circle of literary acquaintance, and was himself a lover of books and of literature. So also were his nieces, one of whom was in after years a frequent contributor to the 'Review,'[1] and the author of—among other works—'The Maritime Alps,' published in 1884, of which Reeve wrote :—

To Miss C. Dempster

November 21st, 1884.

MY DEAR CHARLOTTE,—Longman has just sent me a copy of the 'Maritime Alps,'[2] and I really must offer you my congratulations on the birth of so beautiful and interesting a work, which far surpasses my expectations. I think it is quite your *capo d' opera*, and full of most curious and original research. The Comtesse de Paris will be delighted with the dedication.

It was just after his return to London in November that Reeve wrote to his late host :—

---

told—in diplomatic language—to mind their own business. This led to the recall of the ambassadors in November 1856, and a cessation of diplomatic intercourse, which was not renewed till June 1859; and in the following year Garibaldi's adventure effected a radical change.

[1] Many of her contributions were collected in 1872, under the title of *Essays*, by the author of *Vera*.

[2] It was reviewed in the *Edinburgh Review*, April 1885.

To Mr. G. Dempster

62 Rutland Gate, November 12th.

MY DEAR DEMPSTER,—I conclude that by this time, as everybody is shaking down into winter quarters, you have accomplished your movement to the South; that Mrs. Dempster is within easy reach of Arniston; that the young ladies have made a *razzia* on the music-shops and circulating libraries of Edinburgh, and are in a world of new songs and new books; and that the young laird has found two horses to carry him gallantly in the field. In my eyes all this is very inferior to the autumnal sunshine upon the woods and water of Skibo, for I know of no place which leaves a more delightful impression on the memory. But autumnal sunshine, you will say, cannot last for ever, though, indeed, it still lingers over the fogs of London, and the recollection of your Highland hospitality will very long outlive it.

I made out my tour in Sutherland with very great success—had delightful weather, and saw more of the people on the west coast than often falls to the lot of us Saxons. Much that I saw confirmed what you had told me, but I hope there is now some disposition to increase the number of moderate-sized farms. The condition of the men I thought wonderfully good; that of the women much more to be deplored, and, if possible, amended. In my way back I visited Stack and the forester's lodge—the house that Loch built—on Loch Stack; the country wonderfully wild and fine, but for my own tastes I prefer grouse moors.

When I know whether this reaches you, I propose, with your permission, to send down a small parcel of German books which I said I would look out for Miss Dempster and Miss Charlotte, if they will do me the favour to look over them; but at this moment I am not quite sure of your address.

We find our house very comfortable, and I hope before long it will be quite habitable; but it takes a few months to make a home of a new dwelling. . . . Most faithfully yours,

H. REEVE.

From M. Guizot

Val Richer, 6 novembre.—Voici l'article que je vous ai promis sur Philippe II. Il vous arrivera bien à temps, je pense, pour votre numéro de janvier.

L'ouvrage de Mr. Motley a plus d'importance et de mérite que vous ne le présumiez. C'est un mélange, assez rare aujourd'hui, de passion sincère et d'érudition solide.

Il conviendrait, ce me semble, de mettre, au haut des pages de l'article dans l'Edinburgh Review, ce titre courant (est-ce ainsi que vous dites en anglais ?) ' Prescott and Motley—Philip II. and his Times.'

Faite par vous, je suis parfaitement tranquille sur la traduction. . . .

To M. de Tocqueville

62 *Rutland Gate, November* 18*th.—* . . . The victory of Mr. Buchanan does not surprise me, though all my sympathy was with his antagonist. But the Southern party has the advantage over the Northern, both in daring and organisation—the two great conditions of success. By dint of being conquered, the North will learn to conquer, and the struggle which is commencing is not of a nature to end amicably. Everyone who returns from the United States this year is struck by the profound alteration in the institutions of that country. Democracy is sweeping over it like a torrent.

I understand, too, that in France during the last three months there has been a marked change in men's minds, and that the horizon of the Government has been overcast. It is true that several accidental circumstances, joined to the fundamental nature of things, have contributed to cause uneasiness since the end of the war. The alliance has sunk into what may be called friendly relations, and public opinion in England is becoming freed from the constraint under which it was placed by the war. The remarkable prosperity and steadiness of trade on this side has greatly strengthened the English Cabinet, both within and without. Our friend Lewis is truly astounded at the readiness with which money comes to him.—he is the luckiest of ministers of finance. . . .

To Mr. Dempster

December 3*rd.*—The little box of German books for the amusement of the young ladies was despatched on Monday per goods train, and I hope it will have arrived in safety. It so happens that I am personally acquainted with Mr. E.

Hornby, the gentleman who has edited James Boswell's letters; and to him I have forwarded your kind contribution. I hope it may not be too late for the volume already advertised.[1]

December 24th.—Your letter from Boswell was in time, and it figures at the end of the volume. You will probably have no difficulty in procuring the book at any circulating library, but I will tell Hornby he owes you a copy. The collection of letters is, however, the greatest farrago of vanity, absurdity, and indecency it is possible to conceive; Boswell *tout nu*; and I can't recommend it for the young ladies' reading. One allusion they have settled on the head of your uncle which it is by no means clear belongs to him. With all this, the volume is amusing enough, and I believe it would have gratified Boswell to know that mankind are laughing at him near a century after he flourished.

The Journal mentions :—

A good deal of pleasant society in London. On December 19th I breakfasted with Macaulay at Campden Hill. Lord Carlisle, Dundas, Hibbert, F. Ellis, and Ryan there. We spent Christmas with the Clarendons at the Grove.

My diary is scanty for 1857.

It is singular that I have made no note with reference to the Indian Mutiny, which was the great and terrible event of the year. I remember Rawlinson saying to me as we rode in the Park that at this moment we held no land in India except that occupied by our armies. But this was an exaggeration. My cousin, Meadows Taylor, was in India during the Mutiny, and I corresponded with him regularly during the whole time of his service there.

January 3rd.—Christine and I started for Paris, and crossed in a tremendous gale of wind. Our chief object was to buy furniture &c. for the new house. We dined at M. Guizot's on the 8th, with St.-Marc Girardin, Ampère, Prince de Broglie, and Lavergne. On the 12th we returned to London. Before I started, I sat an hour with Princess Lieven. She died on the 19th.

January 19th.—We had a dance and housewarming at

---

[1] *Letters of James Boswell addressed to the Rev. W. J. Temple.*

Rutland Gate.   About 250 people.   The French, Turkish, Swedish, Danish, Greek, and Prussian ministers were there.

29th.—Shooting with the Duc de Nemours at Claremont.

A General Election took place in March.   I neglected my diary during the season.

In undertaking the editorship of the ' Edinburgh Review,' Reeve had of course fully understood that it was to be conducted on Whig principles, and as the organ of the Whig party.   These principles he had always advocated, and, though in no way bound to the party, had been on terms of familiar intercourse and friendship with several of the party's leaders, and especially with Lord Clarendon.   Now, however, that he was formally attached to it, he conceived it his duty— and in the spring of 1857 it was certainly his inclination —to denounce those members or associates of it who had made common cause with the Opposition in the endeavour to harass and defeat the Government, and especially Mr. Gladstone and Lord John Russell, who had not only voted against the Government, but had spoken in unmeasured language against its policy.   He believed that these men had acted treacherously, and in April 1857 published in the ' Review ' an article on ' The past Session and the new Parliament,' in which their conduct was unsparingly exposed by Mr. Lowe, the vice-president of the Board of Trade— afterwards Viscount Sherbrooke—a man of remarkable ability, and though—it has been said—erratic as a politician, a singularly brilliant, and occasionally vitriolic, writer.   In the present instance he felt warmly the defection, or, as he considered it, the treason of which he, with his colleagues in the Government, had so nearly been a victim, and he laid on the punishment with a cool and relentless vigour which may even now be studied as a model of vituperation.   The publication of this article raised a storm which must, for the moment, have forced Reeve to doubt the accuracy of his comparison of the editorship of the ' Review ' with the honourable retirement of the House of Lords ;[1] and though the excitement gave the number a brisk sale, which promised to send it quickly into a second edition, the very strong letters which he received convinced Mr. Longman that the attack on Lord John Russell was a mistake, which might do harm both to the ' Review ' and to the party.   Reeve thought otherwise ; he believed that the chastisement of the culprits was loudly

---

[1] See *ante*, p. 339.

called for, and that the plain speaking put life into the 'Review.' When such a question was raised between two men in the very delicate relation of proprietor and editor, it was perhaps fortunate for both that each had confidence in the other. The point at issue was discussed without heat, without any interruption to the friendship, then more than twenty years old, which continued for twenty-two years more, when it was ended by death. Eventually, Reeve gave way, the more readily as it appeared to be the general opinion of the party that Lord John's past services gave him a certain claim on the forbearance of all Whigs; and the matter was finally settled by a promise to him that the offensive number should not be republished. As, however, he had written to Longman in terms strongly condemning the present conduct of the 'Review,' as tending to plunge the party in a swamp of political immorality, Reeve wrote :—

To Mr. T. Longman

May 8th.—It has occurred to me to inquire of myself who are my accomplices in this atrocious design. I have just put on paper the names of the present contributors to the 'Review,' all of whom have written in the last two years, at my request. We may not be so fortunate as to possess a Jeffrey for an editor, or a Sydney Smith, a Macintosh, a Horner, and a Macaulay for contributors; but I think I may say without conceit that this list of contributors contains names of the highest honour and the most consistent adherence to Liberal principles, and I will add that it contains nothing else.

All the contributions I have inserted are by one or other of these men, except three or four casual contributions of secondary importance. I have not inserted any contributions of my own of any political interest, except the article on the war in October 1855, and that on the Austrian Concordat.

I should be glad if it were practicable to submit this short statement to Lord John Russell, and I think it due to myself and to the 'Review' that he should be in possession of it.

The following is the list referred to, which, independent of its reference to this controversy, has now considerable literary interest :—

The present Bishop of London (Dr. Tait, afterwards Archbishop of Canterbury).
George Grote.
Edward H. Bunbury.
John Forster.
Monsieur Guizot.
The present Lord Advocate (James, afterward Lord, Moncreiff).
The present Chancellor of the Exchequer (Sir G. C. Lewis).
The present V. P. of the Board of Trade (Robert Lowe).
The Duke of Argyll.
A. Hayward.
Charles Greville.
Rev. Canon Moseley.

Ross Mangles, Chairman of the E. I. Co.
John W. Kaye.
Rev. Wm. Harness.
Professor Baden Powell.
W. R. Greg.
W. B. Donne.
George S. Venables.
Sir Henry Holland.
Samuel Laing.
Fitzjames Stephen.
R. Monckton Milnes.
Henry Rogers.
Sir Henry Lytton Bulwer.
Herman Merivale.
E. Beckett Denison.
Sir E. Perry.
James Fergusson.

A list which surely bears out what Reeve claimed for it.

To Mr. Dempster

62 Rutland Gate, June 19th.—I dare say this flying leaf may follow you to the wild banks of the Laxford, where I judge . . . that you are likely to be staying.   I heartily wish I were now breathing Highland air in your pleasant company, instead of hearing long-winded speeches, or eating elaborate dinners, or fighting my way through crowded assemblies.   But my day of freedom is not yet, and when it does come, I very much fear we may not be able to reach your extreme northern Highlands this year.   But I heartily congratulate your nephew on his occupation of Stack.   He is the only man I ever saw with energy enough to run up those hills, and I have no doubt the deer will soon learn they have a mighty hunter among them.

My object in writing at this moment is to say that I contemplate the publication in the 'Edinburgh,' next autumn, of an article, by a competent person, entitled 'Men, Sheep, and Deer,' in which we shall discuss the subject of deer forests, clearances, lots, sheep farms, &c.   You would render us a real service if you are disposed to put on paper any of the facts which are familiar to you on these subjects—such as increased rent of forests, head of deer, head of sheep, price of sheep, state of population in the Highlands, &c. ; and I am sure your opinion on the subject would have very great weight, though—if you prefer it—the communication should be considered quite confidential.

London is prodigiously brilliant and animated; people seem extremely resolved to amuse themselves, but there is a want of interest, and the severity of the times is becoming rather oppressive. I think I prefer the clouds and the breezes.

Clouds and breezes! whirlwinds and hurricanes, rather. When these lines were being written the massacres of Meerut and Delhi had passed into history; the tragedy of Cawnpore was close at hand. But of all this, of course, Reeve was ignorant, and he continued :—

We shall remain here till August, and then probably go to Appleby Castle, in Westmorland, taking Manchester in our way. Then, in October, we talk of making a little expedition to Dresden. What has become of your Continental projects? I hope, at any rate, you do not intend to deprive us of your society, and of all your party, for another whole season; and I hope the young ladies will not allow you to persuade them that Haddingtonshire and the Lothians are as civilised as Middlesex. We really very much regret their and your absence.

June 27*th.*—We are going in August and September as far north as Westmorland and Lanarkshire, and I do not feel confident that we shall not be tempted to strike onward to the Highlands; but I do not clearly see that I can bring out an 'Edinburgh Review' without coming up to town. I am greatly obliged to you for your intended notes on 'Men, Deer, and Sheep,' which I am sure will be of great value, since you are the most dispassionate Highland proprietor I have ever known.

July 11*th.*—My best thanks are due to you, and are most heartily offered, for the admirable paper you have sent me on the subject of Highland estates. It will be of the greatest use to us. I should be very much influenced by an opinion as judicious and well founded as yours, even though I had been previously disposed to differ from it. But such is not the case. In the course of my tour in Sutherland last autumn, I was forcibly struck by the policy and propriety of increasing the number of holdings, and especially of 40-acre and 200-acre farms, wherever tillage is practicable. And I have no doubt I should have been even more convinced of this if I had visited the parish of Farr. Is not your estimate of 20,000*l.* a year rental of deer forests below the mark? The value of the lands devoted to this purpose by their own proprietors—as the Duke of Athole, Lord Fife, Lord Lovat, and others—must, of course, be added to the sum paid by strangers; but I should have thought even this latter sum exceeded 20,000*l.* a year.

I begin to think there is rather more chance of our reaching the Highlands this year than I had supposed. We have resolved to start for Dresden on August 8th, instead of going there in October. Hence the latter month will be more at our disposal for Scotland, though I cannot yet say whether we shall reach your northern latitudes; but nothing in life is more tempting to me than that region. *A propos* of the North, pray tell the young ladies I recommend them to get Lord Dufferin's 'Letters from High Latitudes,' a book which some people laugh at, but which I think vastly amusing.

An interesting visit to Johannisberg in the autumn is described in the Journal :—

August 8th.—We started, with Miss Alpe, Hopie's governess, for Hamburg. Thence we made a tour through Lübeck, Berlin, Dresden, Prague, Carlsbad, and Frankfort, and arrived on September 9th—my forty-fourth birthday— at Rüdesheim, on the Rhine. There I learned that Prince Metternich was staying at his Castle of Johannisberg hard by, as he is wont to do in the autumn; and as he had received me with great kindness at Vienna, in 1853, on my return from Constantinople, I thought it proper to pay my respects to him.

On driving up to the castle, by rather a rough and narrow road through the vineyards, a servant in livery told me the prince was just gone to walk in the 'weingarten,' and was but a few yards ahead. I had chosen the hour after his dinner, when I thought him most likely to be disengaged;

and so it proved. The servant ran after the walking party
with my card. I followed, and soon came up with them—
the prince, with a lady on his arm, whom I found to be
Marion Ellice, the same who lived so long with Princess
Lieven, one of Metternich's daughters in a garden chair, and
I think one of his younger sons. They were throwing an
india-rubber ball for a spaniel to run after, and down it went,
bounding along the steep conical side of the vineyard, which
sheds drops of gold. The prince said : 'First you must
admire my vines and the exquisite skill with which they are
dressed.' Nothing could be more perfect. Every stock
looked like a greenhouse plant—not·a weed was to be seen
or a tendril out of place, and each individual vine was as
symmetrical as a soldier under arms. At my delight the
prince smiled and said, ' If I were as flourishing as my vines,
it would be well.' 'Nay,' said I, 'you have both a splendid
autumn, and your vines are drawn up like files of soldiers.'
' Would, indeed, they were soldiers,' rejoined he, 'that I
might send them to your assistance in India ! '

The conversation then took a more serious turn, and he
expressed his unbounded interest in the great and melancholy
events which had just overshadowed the horizon of the
British Empire, which he called an ' incident effroyable dans
l'histoire des nations.'

' Cependant mon expérience me dit que souvent les choses
que l'on redoute le plus finissent par être un vrai sou-
lagement lorsqu'elles sont passées. Le gouvernement de
l'Inde est pour vous une immense charge. Le commerce
que vous y faites pourrait également se maintenir par
quelques stations restreintes, et je ne sais si l'administration
entière du pays pourra valoir ce qu'elle va vous coûter. Je
fais des romans, sans doute ; et je tiens le gouvernement
anglais pour un gouvernement sage, sachant bien ce qu'il
fait ; toutes fois je doute qu'il sache beaucoup mieux que vous
et moi, ici sur ce coteau de Johannisberg, jusqu'où cette
catastrophe pourra aller. J'aimerais mieux laisser ces Indiens
se tirer d'affaires eux-mêmes. Ce n'est pas que je craigne
fort le jacobinisme indien—le socialisme indien—c'est leur
affaire ; mais je redoute une perturbation qui pourra amener
de nouvelles difficultés dans la situation financière du con-

tinent et qui affaiblisse l'Angleterre. D'ailleurs vous ne
pouvez pas gouverner l'Inde par la force seulement. Je ne
vois pas que vous ayez la matière humaine pour cela, et que
sans la conscription vous puissiez maintenir dans l'Inde des
armées anglaises de 100,000 hommes.'

He then proceeded to speak of the prevailing financial
insecurity of the Continent—that France had set the example
which Germany was always ready to follow, and that the
most pestilent delusions were propagated on the subject of
credit ; that it was like a farmer who undertook to sell his
milk to the public through a company, such as he had heard
of in Glasgow and elsewhere, and that the company kept the
cream for itself and sold the residue for pure milk.

Nothing could be more friendly or amiable than his
manner, and as he more than once put his hand on my knee
in conversation, the remembrance of his celebrated conversations with Napoleon and all the great men of this age crossed
my mind. We walked some time on the terrace, watching
that magnificent view which extends from Biberich to Bingen,
along the richest part of the Rheingau. On the opposite
bank, at Ingelheim, once stood the old palace of Charlemagne,
and down the broad valley the great border stream rolled its
waters at our feet. In one of the pavilions a crowd of
tourists were come to see the view ; but when they beheld
the old prince pacing up and down in front of his castle, their
eyes turned from the Rhine, and were riveted on him as if
Charlemagne himself had stood before them.

September 18*th.*—Home by Holland.

In the course of the following weeks Reeve wrote a
remarkable article on the 'Prospects of our Indian Empire,'
which appeared in the 'Review' of January 1858. It was
shown in proof-slips to Lord Clarendon, who wrote :—

The Grove, December 6th.—I have read your article with
the greatest interest, and think it quite excellent. You have
collected and brought together an immense mass of valuable
information, and you have stated the truths upon which
men's minds must be fixed with great vigour and energy.
The catalogue you have given of the appalling difficulties
against which we shall have to contend in restoring and

maintaining our supremacy will, I think, be very useful in checking the hasty legislation of Parliament, as well as the muck which people are disposed to run against the Company. Whether the Company is to be retained, modified, or abolished, you have said nothing about it which can embarrass the Government, or that you can wish not to have said. In that I congratulate you upon having done the right thing in the right way at the right moment.

From Lord Brougham

Cannes, December 26th.—I am very much obliged to you for your letter, even when I cannot avoid differing with you. But it gives me great gratification, because it proves your feelings towards me to be entirely right, as, indeed, I ought to have assumed even without your assurances. In truth, I had much experience of the Edinburgh clique—or, rather, cliques, for both the little exclusive sets of the Parliament House are exactly the same, the Tories as well as the Whigs ; indeed, they used to be much the worse, and the Whigs being now in power may possibly have succeeded to the bad eminence ; and this experience had made me erroneously suppose that you had got into their hands. I know they never will forgive me any more than O'Connell did, and for the same reason. I set my face against their jobs, and I assure you that at one time Cockburn was exposed to risk from the same clique feeling. He had come over from the Tories, and the Whigs grudged him, and anyone else who came over, any share of the spoil. I joined with Jeffrey and Murray in making head for Cockburn.

That the 'Edinburgh Review,' under your predecessors, was very much affected by the same influences is undeniable. That clique never forgave a minister who was out of office. Accordingly, as soon as Lord Grey was out, the ' E. R.' discovered how much better Lord Melbourne was ; and actually charged upon Grey, and, by implication, on myself also, the Irish coercive measures, of which it said Melbourne was incapable, though they came from his own department, as Home—that is Irish—Secretary. Empson never discovered any fault in Grey while he remained in power, any more than he did in Denman, whom he almost worshipped both as leader of his circuit and as chief justice, until he retired; and then Campbell was set up in a manner so offensive to Denman that he never could speak with patience of Empson, though before his (Empson's) death, he, in a fashion, forgave him the gross and even personal offence. Perhaps I might add the silence of the 'Review' on my publications. . . . Altogether I laboured under the impression, which, as far as you are concerned, is entirely groundless, that the 'E. R.' lent itself to the little exclusive party I have alluded to.

As to poor Cockburn, I cannot at all agree with you in holding the attacks upon him to go beyond an undervaluing, perhaps an unjust undervaluing, of his judgement. That he has shown this defect in both his books is undeniable; but I only think, and think with great pain, of his 'Life of Jeffrey.' I assure you Murray and myself and others of Jeffrey's friends have been beyond measure distressed by his most injudicious publication of letters, and we have been doing our best to counteract this, and I hope we may still succeed. I must mention, in passing, that you suppose Cockburn to have been much more connected with the 'Review' and with our set—I mean Jeffrey, Murray, Smith, Horner, and Allen—than he really was. He became intimate with them many years after the 'Review' began, and I don't believe he ever wrote a line in it for the first fifteen years, and very little at any time. I greatly blame his family for the publication of some things. Certainly I have personally not the least right to complain, for the anecdotes, which are not only untrue, but impossible respecting me, are all, from Cockburn's great personal kindness, intended to do me honour. But the pain which has been given to others (also without any intention on C.'s part) has been very great. I mean to the families of Horner, Murray, &c. &c. When I have the pleasure of seeing you I will explain this and other matters.

As to Normanby, if he really has attacked the fallen Royal Family, nothing can be more blamable. Respecting Guizot, no one can more than myself value his great and good qualities. But I regard him as the Necker of 1848; and besides, though no man's hands can be more clean than his, he had—what Necker had not—an *entourage* as corrupt as possible. He and I were at issue on one of them—his minister of justice, Hébert; but he had worse men and much more near him. However, I dare say he will defend himself, and I believe you do a right and a kind thing in letting Normanby's book alone.

The Journal for 1858 notes:—

We began the year at Farnborough Hill.

January 23rd.—Breakfasted with Lord Macaulay at his own house, Holly Lodge, Campden Hill. Nobody there but the Trevelyans and Frederic, commonly called Poodle, Byng. As the marriage of the Princess Royal was to take place two days later, it naturally became the subject of conversation. I related that I had had a call from the Sub-Dean of the Chapel Royal, to settle the form of the Royal declaration of consent, which is inserted in the register of the Chapel Royal. This register, which was produced at the Council Office, is a most curious volume, containing the entries of all the Royal marriages from 1757 to this day, with the signatures of the personages married and the persons present. The sub-dean, who used till lately to be called the 'deputy-confessor,' has the custody of this precious volume. At the marriage of the Queen it chanced to be mislaid for a quarter of an hour—an event of so terrible a nature, that the sub-dean of that day died of the shock a few days afterwards.

This subject being uppermost, Poodle Byng astonished us by declaring that he had been present at the marriage [1] of George IV. and Caroline in the capacity of page to the prince, and that he perfectly remembered every detail of that luckless ceremony. The prince kept the whole cortège waiting for more than an hour, while he was conversing with a party of men at Carlton House; and when at last he made his appearance, his high colour and talk showed that he was extremely drunk; though, as the fashion of those days was, he carried his liquor like a gentleman. Out he came in a coat shot with gold, and his splendid legs in irreproachable silk stockings. The page Byng stood behind the prince at the altar, marvelling at the grandeur of the royal calves,

[1] April 8th, 1795.

while the prince looked in all directions except at his bride.
I remarked that perhaps this demeanour was as much as
could be expected from a man in the act of committing
bigamy, and who had heard the marriage service read
between himself and Mrs. Fitzherbert.

Byng kissed hands as page of the prince in 1790—just
sixty-eight years ago, and he is now as fresh and vigorous as anybody.[1]   His father said he ought to be presented to his royal
master.   George received the boy in his dressing-room and
in his dressing gown, bare legs, and bare altogether under
this loose garment.   He took the child up in his arms, kissed
him, and then said, ' Now, sir, you are to kiss my hand.'

Once launched on these times, Byng is inexhaustible.
He said he had twice met Lord Nelson and Lady Hamilton
at dinner—she, after dinner, singing songs to Lord Nelson
in praise of himself, and Nelson rapturously applauding her.[2]
Macaulay said the first thing he could recollect was the
battle of Trafalgar, when he was six years old.[3]   He sat on
the rug in his mother's room spelling out the ' Gazette,' with
a plan of the action, the ' Royal Sovereign ' leading a column
into action.

It is a curious thing what first hits a young memory and
sticks there.   My own first impression was the death of the
Princess Charlotte in November 1817.   I was just four.   We
were staying with the Pontignys, in a gloomy house on Tower
Hill.   It was a yellow November morning.   Pale with
emotion, somebody, I think Mrs. John Martineau, announced
the fatal event of the preceding night.   I never forgot her
look.   But I also remember Mrs. Barbauld, who taught me
to read in the same year, when we stayed with her at Newington Green, and read me the story of Midas' ears.

Everything indicates a dangerous and stormy session.
The Government have irritated and defied public opinion
by appointing Clanricarde lord privy seal, and by giving
some small legal appointments to aristocratic hangers-on of

---

[1] He died in June 1871.

[2] This is quite independent of Mrs. St. George's testimony to the same
effect, for Mrs. St. George's Journal was not printed till 1861, and then only
privately.

[3] Macaulay's wonderful memory misled him. He was not five when the
battle was fought, and was just twelve days over five when the news reached
England.

Lord Palmerston. But with a very inadequate force on the treasury bench, and a formidable, though scattered, array against them, they mean to propose and carry two organic measures—an India bill and a Reform bill. My own belief is they will carry neither. The Liberal party are generally by no means favourable to the transfer of the favour and patronage of the Company to a secretary of state, and they think that no case has been made out against the Company. In fact, all the most questionable measures of Indian policy have been adopted by the Board of Control against the will of the Company. We dined yesterday at the Grotes', with J. Parkes, F. Elliot, &c.; and there, as everywhere else, the current of opinion runs rather in favour of the Company than against it. This has been considerably assisted by a very able petition of the Company to Parliament, showing the danger of a change at this moment. Possibly Lord Palmerston may evade the danger by consenting to refer this bill to a committee for inquiry, which is, of course, to postpone it for at least a year.

January 25th.—The Princess Royal was married. There was a party at the Prussian Embassy for the princes, and a drawing-room for the bride on the 30th.

From Lord Brougham

Paris, March 28th.—Your letter was delivered safely to M. Guizot yesterday, and I had a long conversation with him to-day on the whole state of matters here. I assure you it gives me very great comfort to find that there has been so much exaggeration both as to the conduct of the Government and as to the sufferings of our friends. He more than confirmed all he had written to Aberdeen as to the perfect freedom of society. He won't allow that anyone feels the least alarm as to the *arrestations*, of which I hear opposite accounts from those connected with the Government and from their adversaries, especially the Legitimist party; the former deny there have been more than three or four hundred in all France, of which sixty or seventy at Paris; the latter affirm that at Paris there have been 1,300, which I take to be a gross exaggeration. The numbers of the *graciés* are admitted by even the Legitimists not to exceed four or five thousand. I believe they are little above three thousand. But the violent enemies of the Government, not only Legitimists, but Orleanists, are bawling that the number of these not among the *graciés*, but who, having been *expulsés* or otherwise subject to the new law, are two or three hundred thousand, which is as gross exaggeration as possible ; and such people forget the maxim often in Romilly's mouth : ' On diminue tout ce qu'on exagère.'

The army is believed to be quite staunch to the Government, and Guizot believes it is by no means desirous of war. Certainly the country is not ; quite the contrary.

Cannes, April 7th.—What I mentioned in my letter from Paris has been confirmed by all I have seen, both there and in the provinces. There is gross exaggeration, but some considerable foundation for the account of both the means taken and their effect in creating apprehension. For instance, I found in several places that the greatest relief had been offered to the quiet and well-disposed, those who only desired tranquil times and cared not for the state of parties, by the banishment of the most troublous pests in the world—those who, ever since 1848, have been the plague of their neighbourhood, with their extravagant doctrines and their perpetual plottings and agitations. But then, whoever had been rashly talking, even though not of the Rouge party, are alarmed because their towns may come under a police not always very scrupulous, and never accurately informed. The persons arrested have been, with few exceptions, utterly insignificant, and only had influence over persons a little more insignificant than themselves.

The feeblest of all governments among us seems likely to be kept in place (power is out of the question) by the driving of the Opposition. But on any stage of any bill, e.g. of the India bill, they may be left in a minority.

Their removing Howden [1] at such a crisis in Spain, and professedly because he belongs to the Opposition, is a marvellous act of folly. Then sending Chelsea to Paris, where, if Cowley is absent, he must be *chargé d'affaires*, is inconceivable, and all because he spent his money at an election. Nobody could be more astounded by it than his near

---

[1] Lord Howden had been minister at Madrid from 1850. He retired on account of ill health—so it was announced—in March 1858.

kinsman, both by blood and marriage, Cowley himself.[1] Crampton's appointment makes the Russians stare ; I believe Loftus' will be as astonishing to the other diplomats.

Cannes, April 22nd.—I now know from Howden himself the ground of his recall, and it exceeds belief. It is distinctly put upon his belonging to the Opposition party, although five years ago, when the same men were in office, he tendered his resignation on the ground of differing entirely with them, and he was told that party and political opinions had nothing to do with it, but his services were wanted ; and now, when they are wanted a thousand times more in the Spanish crisis, he is recalled because his politics are not those of the Government ! The feeling of all parties in Madrid, even of the Carlists, is that of astonishment, though the latter are too glad of his removal. Howden supposes it is a sacrifice to the Tuileries, whose Carlist intrigues he has been successful in counteracting. I much doubt this, because I know that the same reason was given to Normanby—namely, that the Government owed it to their supporters, who could not stand retaining adversaries in missions.

Chelsea's appointment to Paris exceeds all other jobs. He was, twenty-four years ago, unpaid attaché for twelve months at Petersburg ; and that is his whole diplomatic service ; but he spent money in a contested election, and this is his compensation. At Paris he may any day be obliged to act as *chargé d'affaires*. His near kinsman, Cowley, I will venture to say, is more annoyed at it than anybody.

The article on 'Canning's Literary Remains' in the Review of July 1858 roused the hypercritical spirit in Lord Brougham, and in a succession of letters, none of which are dated, he sent Reeve his comments. Of these, many are of little or no value—such as, ' Extravagant praise of T. Moore,' ' Too much importance given to Gifford and P. Pindar ; ' but this is interesting as the opinion—though fifty years after date—of a not incompetent contemporary : ' Canning never could by any possibility be ranked as "an orator of the first class long prior to 1808," in the days of Pitt and Fox, Burke and Windham ; ' and the following

---

[1] Chelsea's father, Lord Cadogan, was Lord Cowley's first cousin, and Lord Chelsea had also married Lord Cowley's niece.

seems really noteworthy, especially now when Darwin's poetry—Erasmus Darwin's—is almost forgotten :—

Nothing can be more absurd than the running down of Darwin's poetry by the Cannings and Frere. There are things of the very highest merit in it. ' Cambyses' March ' stands so high that I recollect T. Campbell going so far as to pronounce it the finest passage in all English poetry.[1] I see I am charged in the 'Saturday Review' with always quoting Darwin, which I believe I never did but once, in my inaugural discourse, in reference to the steam engine. But as a philosophic poem, I certainly rate it high; and the prediction of steam navigation and gun-cotton in 1787 (I rather think electro-type, too) is one of the most marvellous instances of sagacity—almost equal to Sir I. Newton and the diamond. So much delighted was Professor Playfair with the magnificent lines in Canto IV., on the fate of the solar system, that he cites them entire in his review of Laplace, ' Ed. Rev.' vol. xv. [p. 411]. I believe it will be found that Canning and Co. were really great admirers of Darwin ; that they freely stole from him is certain.

He goes on to say that ' Jeffrey estimated Stoddart's parody as of higher merit than the " Anti-Jacobin," ' chiefly because it was on a more nonsensical and unsubstantial subject—the old children's rhyme of

> Ziggory, Diggory, Dock,
> The mouse ran up the clock ;
> The clock struck one,
> Down the mouse ran,
> Ziggory, Diggory, Dock.

Stoddart's verses run thus :—

> Gnomes ! ye who sing of Diggory and Dock,
> Tell how the mouse adventurer clomb the clock ;
> Viewed the round dial plate with wondering eyes,
> Traced the revolving wheel in mute surprise,
> With tiny fore-paw touched the organic spring,
> And marked the pendulum's oscillating swing.

---

[1] Whatever Campbell may have said, or Brougham, in his old age, fancied he had said, his published judgement, prefixed to this very piece in his *Specimens of British Poets*, amounts to no more than this: ' If Darwin was not a good poet, it may be owned that he is frequently a bold personifier, and that some of his insulated passages are musical and picturesque.' Certainly, few readers at the present day will be inclined to go farther than this.

> The clock struck one ; by that resistless roar
> Deafened, he dropt deciduous on the floor :
> Such, Science, thy hallucinative shock—
> So ends the tale of Diggory and Dock.

A certain recrudescence of the Slave-trade, especially to Cuba, had led the inhabitants of Jamaica to represent that this was in violation of the treaty with Spain and of great injury to the Jamaica planters, and to pray that the Spanish Government might be compelled to redeem their pledges. The presentation of this petition to the House of Lords by the Bishop of Oxford on June 17th led to some conversation —rather than discussion—in the course of which Lord Malmesbury, then Foreign Secretary, spoke of the great difficulties in the way of our cruisers so long as foreign nations, and especially the United States, refused to allow the right of 'search' or even of 'visit.' Lord Brougham had said that, whilst the right of search was a purely belligerent right, the right of visit could not be so considered ; and that, although we have no right to search, we have a right to visit in order to carry out the police of the ocean. But, said Lord Malmesbury—

'The United States have constantly and categorically refused to admit that distinction. They say that on no account, for no purpose, and on no suspicion, shall a ship carrying the American flag be boarded except by an American ship, unless at the risk of the officer boarding or detaining her ;[1] and the doctrine laid down by the United States has been adopted by other countries. . . . I need hardly tell the House that I have admitted the international law as laid down by the American Minister for Foreign Affairs ; but I have not done so until that statement had been approved and fortified by the opinions of the law officers of the Crown. But, having admitted that, I have put it as strongly as possible to the American Government that, if it is known that the American flag covers every iniquity, every pirate and slaver on earth will carry it, and no other.'

It has been seen that, from boyhood, Reeve had been deeply impressed by the horrors of the Slave-trade, and that one of his earliest essays was a denunciation of it.[2] The debate of June 17th suggested an article on the subject in the 'Edinburgh Review,' and this he had mentioned to Lord Clarendon, who wrote :—

---

[1] In May 1862, the English and the United States Governments mutually conceded to each other's men-of-war the right of searching suspected ships within thirty leagues of the coasts of Africa and Cuba.

[2] See *ante*, p. 90.

The Grove, August 8th.—I am glad you mean to have an article upon the Slave-trade, and I hope it will be mainly addressed *ad verecundiam* of the Americans ; for, unless some check is imposed upon them, they will re-establish the trade upon a broader and more permanent basis than it has been since we withdrew from it. The Southern States have hitherto been breeders of slaves, and were naturally opposed to the competition of the African slave-trade ; but their supply is now not equal to the demand, as is evidenced by the enormous increase in the price of slaves. Their old plantations are exhausted, they want to break up fresh ground, and they must have more hands. The question, therefore, of re-establishing the slave-trade is now freely discussed ; and, as soon as public opinion in South Carolina and Virginia pronounces in its favour, we may expect to see it carried on with all the energy and contempt for law which characterise the Southerns.

Looking, therefore, at what is oncoming, and the certainty that France will make common cause with the U.S. respecting the immunity of the flag, I think that the concessions made by Malmesbury are unfortunate, and may lead to increased difficulties hereafter. It is desirable that the right of ascertaining whether a ship is entitled to the flag she flies should be settled and conceded by agreement between different maritime powers ; but the best way of effecting this would have been to make no change in our instructions and arrangements until the question had been settled. Everything is now suspended until the negotiations are concluded, and the U.S. will have an interest in protracting them. It must be remembered, too, that we cannot have one practice for the strong and another for the weak ; and that, if we are not to stop a Spanish ship full of slaves merely because she hoists the U.S. flag, we shall be bound to respect the flag of Monaco used for the same purpose ; so that, until an understanding is come to, every flag will give complete immunity, not for the Slave-trade alone, but for piracy and any other offence against the law of nations that a vessel may have committed.

I admit, however, that the subject is beset with difficulties ; because, although every nation pretends aversion to the Slave-trade, we are the only one in earnest, and sincere about suppressing it, and we shall find that none will give us the facilities which we are ready to concede to them for ascertaining facts.

The article was published in the October number of the 'Review,' and assuredly did not err on the side of lenity. Reeve had given his contributor a free hand, and the result was remarkable. It described the internal condition of the United States as already showing that rift between the South and North which was to open, three years later, into a yawning chasm; and, externally, the moral responsibility of the Slave-trade and the onus of suppressing it were alike thrown on the U.S. Government. And nothing in the article was more powerful than the exposure of Liberia, instituted and maintained as a settlement of free negroes, which the writer asserted was itself a sink of iniquity, in which the Governor and the other officials were slave-dealers and agents of slave-dealers. He referred to the experiences and the narrative of Dr. Bacon, whom zeal for the cause had carried to Liberia, where, and in the neighbourhood, he had spent three years :—

'He found Roberts, now known as the late President of the Republic of Liberia, acting as the agent and factor of the great slave-trader, Pedro Blanco. He found John N. Lewis, secretary of the colony, also an agent of Blanco's. He found Payne, known as the Missionary Payne, a regular workman at the slave factory of New Sesters. Roberts was employed in purchasing condemned vessels at Sierra Leone for Blanco's use as slavers; and Lewis stored the goods and merchandise which were to be bartered for slaves. . . . Thousands of dollars were received by these three agents from the slave-traders; and from 1835 to 1840 the colony was one of the chief auxiliaries of the traffic which it pretended to supersede.'

And much more to the same effect. The charges were so detailed, so categorical, that the accused parties were bound to take notice of them. And they did. This, however, was later. The article was not published till October; and meantime, according to the Journal—

August 11*th*.—Went to the Colebrookes', at Abington, for the first time, and shot there with Charles Manners Lushington. Thence to Auchin, and on a visit to the Duke of Argyll at Inveraray. The Kildares and Lord E. Cavendish were there. The Duke and I afterwards posted to Glasgow, and I went up to Bywell on a visit to the Beaumonts there.

Then to Appleby Castle and to Brougham. Crossed by Ulleswater to Ambleside to see Harriet Martineau. Back to London on September 8th.

On October 2nd we started for Paris; reached Geneva on the 5th. Saw the Binets and De Roches. To Turin on the 10th; then to Genoa, and sailed from Leghorn to Civita Vecchia, 14th. Reached Rome on the 15th. Met the Eastlakes there, and drove with E. E. to the Colosseum by moonlight. We remained at Rome till November 6th, and went the round of the sights. At the Colloredos' (Austrian Embassy) we met a good deal of society—Antonelli, Mérode, Talbot, &c. Cardinal Wiseman had given me a letter to Cavaliere Rossi, who showed us the Catacombs.

The Motleys, Storeys, and Westons were at Rome, and very hospitable. Saw Mr. Hawthorne at the Westons'. Ampère, too, was there, and Lady Granville. Went to vespers in the Sistine Chapel on Sunday, October 31st, when the Pope officiated; and on November 4th saw the Pope go in semi-state to San Carlo Borromeo. We left Rome on November 6th, after a delightful visit of three weeks, and reached Marseilles in thirty-two hours; dined with the P. Taylors, and returned by Paris to London on November 15th.

This was one of the most delightful journeys I ever made, and I fear I shall never see Rome again. At that time no one thought of catching fevers, which are now so common and so fatal.

From M. Guizot

Val Richer, 4 novembre.

MON CHER MONSIEUR,—Si j'avais su où vous prendre Rome, je vous aurais écrit tout de suite pour vous dire avec quel plaisir j'ai lu votre excellent article; excellent pour moi, excellent en soi. Je serais charmé de croire que tout ce que vous dites de moi est vrai, et je suis sûr que tout ce que vous dites de ma politique est utile pour ma cause, qui est la bonne cause, la vôtre comme la mienne, comme celle de tous les hommes de sens et d'esprit en Europe. Si nous causions, je discuterais quelques points; spécialement vos observations sur l'extension du droit de suffrage. Un seul mot à ce sujet pour vous indiquer mon idée fondamentale.

We were forced by necessity to make or accept the Revolution of 1830.   We wished to found the constitutional system.   Before us were the Legitimist party, which would not accept the monarchy of 1830, and the masses of the people, of both town and country, who neither cared nor understood anything about the constitutional system.   They proved this clearly in 1848, and again at the present time. We had no support but the middle classes; they alone were really with us in wishing to restore the younger branch of the Bourbons and free institutions.   It was necessary for us to keep in line with our only true and intelligent friends. The moment we advanced beyond it we got in amongst the revolutionary longings, Bonapartist memories, or the constitutional ignorance and indifference.   In this lay the real difficulty.   I should not have had the least objection to extending the suffrage, if it had been likely to strengthen our cause; but it promised us nothing but danger or embarrassment.   I hope that some day we shall be able to talk over all this. . . .

To Lord Brougham

November 15th.—On my return to England I find two notes from you on my table, and when I inquire where you are, I learn with sorrow that you have been recalled to Brougham by illness in the family.   I trust it may not be serious. . . .

This expedition of Palmerston and Clarendon to Compiègne, just when they are trying Montalembert for having written a eulogy on England, is most untimely, and will cost them much here.   As for France, they never were better pleased with their *tyran* than at this moment, and the public seem disposed to applaud even his outrages.   They did, however, blush a little—in secret—for the affair of the ‘Charles Georges.’

They might well blush.   The ‘affair’ was as impudent and bullying a violation of international law and international courtesy as any recorded in civilised history.   In November 1857, the bark ‘Charles et Georges,’ of Saint Malo, lying at Conducia, in the Mozambique, embarking negroes for Réunion, and with one hundred and ten actually on board, was seized by a Portuguese brig of war and taken to Mozambique, where she was tried and—on proof that the negroes were slaves—was condemned as a slaver. The French, however, continued to assert that the so-called slaves were hired labourers, and that the condemnation of the ' Charles et Georges ' was illegal. They refused to submit the case to arbitration ; and, when the bark was brought to Lisbon, in August 1858, they sent a powerful squadron of ships of war to the Tagus to demand her release. The Portuguese Government was offered the pretext of admitting some informalities in the trial ; but the King openly said that they gave up the bark because they ' were obliged to yield to the peremptory exaction.' [1]

The trial of Montalembert, emphatically the *cause célèbre* of the time, began on the 25th November. He was charged, on different counts, with libelling and insulting the French Emperor and the French constitution in a pamphlet entitled ' Un Débat sur l'Inde au Parlement Anglais,' by comparing the state of things in France with those in England, very much to the disadvantage of the former. The whole pamphlet will repay reading ; but, here, one sentence must serve for an illustration :—

' When I feel the pestilential influence rising higher and higher around me, when my ears ache with the buzzing of ante-room gossip or the babble of fanatics who think themselves our masters, or of hypocrites who believe us to be their dupes—when I feel smothered under the weight of an atmosphere loaded with servile and corrupting vapours—I rush to breathe for a time a pure medium, and to take a life-bath in the free air of England.'

Montalembert was defended by M. Berryer, who seems— to our English judgement—to have sought rather to bring himself into prominence than to obtain the acquittal of his client ; so that it does not appear surprising that Montalembert was found guilty, and sentenced to pay a fine of 6,000 francs and to undergo six months' imprisonment. Montalembert appealed, but, before the appeal came on, the Emperor cancelled the sentence. Montalembert insisted on his right to appeal, so the appeal was tried, and he was again condemned ; but finally, the sentence was annulled, by act of grace, on December 21st.

From Lord Brougham

Brougham, November 19th.—Your letter of the 15th came here this morning. I had been told by our friend at

---

[1] *Parliamentary Papers*, 1859, vol. xxvii.

Harpton [1] that you were to return the beginning of next month, and I had not expected to be still in London, so I sent him all the particulars of what had passed between me and the Liberian consul and others in the threatened proceedings against the ' E. R.' on account of the Slave-trade article in last number—whether by action or prosecution had not been determined. I think I put a stop to them, and Ralston (the consul) came round entirely to my opinion. But among other arguments used by me was this—that I should fully make known to you how grossly the author of the article had been deceived, probably by Yankee statements, and that justice would be done. I sent the consul's statement to Harpton five days ago, but I retain the copy of the ' Review,' annotated, which I will give you when I am in town, which I hope and trust will be this day week. . . .

Alas for France! What you say of their contentment is as bad a symptom as possible. I remonstrated by letter both with Pam. and Clarn. P.'s answer is enclosed, and Clar.'s—to the same effect. . . . There is much in what they both say of the difficulty of refusing, and my objection to the visit is not so much the effect it has in this country against themselves, as its evil tendency in France and its lessening Mont.'s chance of escape. I had written very strongly to Fould and others on that insane prosecution, as I had on the Portuguese business. My recommendation of L. N. getting out of the scrape by at once abandoning the Free Emigration scheme had been anticipated, as Fould wrote. I hope I may be so now as to Mont.

To Lord Brougham

November 21st.—I am much obliged to you for your good offices in the matter of the threatened prosecution ; but, as far as I know, no communication has been addressed to the publisher—none, certainly, to me—on the subject. Whether all the statements in the article are correct is more than I can affirm of my own knowledge, though I took some pains to satisfy myself they had not been made without authority, inasmuch as they had all been previously published in America, and were uncontradicted. But I certainly do not

[1] Sir George C. Lewis.

think that the article contains anything to justify legal proceedings, or that any such course can be persisted in. On arriving in Paris I was assured, by persons likely to know, that the Emperor had read the article, and that it had contributed to induce him to write the letter in which he throws over the emigrant scheme. I am firmly convinced that in the affair of the 'Charles Georges,' the French Government have no legal ground whatever to stand on ; indeed, the only pretence they put forward—that of the presence of the imperial commissary on board the vessel—is absurd ; but I have reason to fear the Foreign Office has not been well advised on this point. I am obliged to you for Lord Palmerston's letter, which I return. But the truth is that, if Louis Napoleon were the only man in France favourable to the English alliance, peace would not be of long duration. I hold, on the contrary, that the bulk of the French nation are extremely averse to war with us or any other Power.

My friend Tocqueville is at Cannes—condemned to spend the winter there by the physicians—having had some alarming symptoms of bronchitis. He is forbidden to speak ; so that, when you get there, I fear he will not be equal to much conversation ; but if you will give him access to your library there, you would confer a very great favour upon him.

From Lord Brougham

Brougham, November 21st.—There could be no communication either to Longman or to you after what passed with Ralston, unless his principal differed with him and disavowed him. But I undertook to make his complaint known to you, and I sent his statement to Harpton at the time that I had no hope of seeing you before I go to the South. There is a feud between the Liberian Government and the Yankees, evidently.

I am sorry to see the account you give of Tocqueville's health. Our little library will be entirely at his service, I need not say.

P.S. —The first complaints I received of the article came from the Anti-Slavery Society. But before I could see the parties I had a letter from the consul, and I made him call in Grafton Street, which he did twice, and gave me his statements.   The Liberian Government complain of Louis Napoleon as having broken faith with them, and he was quite certain to take part with their Yankee adversaries.

Grafton Street [*December*].—I saw the consul again yesterday, and he remains in the best possible disposition. But the delays arising from the new regulations as to the mail will make it late in January before he can receive the governor's (Roberts) answer and statement.   He sees clearly that no statement by anyone else than Roberts can be available.   Meanwhile he left the paper which I enclose.   I have no doubt that the statement of Roberts will either be sufficient to satisfy you, or, at all events, that if not long you can give it insertion.   However, that must depend on what it proves to be.

Roberts's statement, here referred to, being, in fact, a positive denial of the charges, was published in the April number of the ' Review,' and so the matter terminated.

But meantime the political excitement in England was about Parliamentary Reform, on which, it was understood, Lord Derby's Government intended to introduce a bill early next session.   No one seemed really to want it, except, perhaps, Lord John Russell, the apostle of Reform ; but among Reeve's political friends there was a widespread feeling of anxiety lest a Radical, or even a revolutionary measure, introduced by the Tories in order to ' dish the Whigs,' might be supported by the Whigs for fear that the Tories might point the finger of scorn at them as the enemies of Reform.   It was thus that Reeve invited Sir George Lewis to write the political article for the forthcoming number of the ' Review '—January 1859—and which, in fact, Lewis did write, notwithstanding the opposition of Lord John Russell, who may have thought the time inopportune for a declaration of Whig opinions, but who may possibly have been actuated, to some extent at least, by pique at the attitude of Reeve during the previous year.   It is to this that the following letters from Lord Clarendon refer :—

The Grove, December 18*th*.—I was in London all day yesterday, and could not answer your letter.   At the same time that Lewis received your proposal he got a letter from me, strongly urging him to accept it, and his answers to us both are most satisfactory.   I have since written to him my notions as to how far it would be safe to go in sketching a measure. He is quite right in thinking that the article would be a Whig manifesto, but it is quite unnecessary to give it the air of a Whig ultimatum.

He could not write an article, which sooner or later will be known to be his, without consulting Palmerston and Lord John; but their replies may hamper him. The former for various reasons—personal, party, and conservative—may wish nothing to be said until the Government produce their measure; and Lord John may think himself forestalled when he sees some of his own plums in Lewis's programme; but when they both learn that an article there will be in the 'Edinburgh,' they will probably like its being handled by Lewis better than by anybody else.

Miladi and I are delighted that you liked your visit here. The feeling is cordially reciprocated. Our girls were very happy with Miss Reeve, and I hope they will continue to see much of each other. Pray remember us very kindly to Mrs. Reeve.

December 21st.—I had already heard from Lewis of Lord John's opposition to the article, which is greater than I expected. It would have been impossible, however, for Lewis not to consult him; they have been in constant correspondence the whole year upon Reform, and Lewis is in possession of Lord John's views, as far as they are formed; and it would have been a kind of *lèse-amitié* and *lèse-confiance* to publish anything upon it without his previous knowledge.

I have no doubt, and I said so to Lewis in my first letter, that a telling review of Tory illiberality and hindrance-spirit for the last thirty years, and of Radical rashness, would have brought the public by induction to look to the Whig party for protection from the extremes, and that this might have spliced together the mangled remains of the party, and galvanised them into life again; but if this is not to be, and if Lord John, and perhaps Palmerston, are to repudiate the article, and the former is to be angry when Parliament meets, I think it will be better to have none at all, although I am sure you would write an excellent one. It is so important for the 'Review' not to be silent on such an occasion that I would regret your determination not to write an article, if you had not told me that you had no knowledge of those statistical and other intricate details which are indispensable for dealing safely with the question.

We were all, young and old, delighted with Loch. He has seen much, and observed accurately, and contributes his information most agreeably. His experience and judgement would, I am sure, be useful to Bruce, and he deserves to be promoted; instead of which he is eliminated; [1] which is a bad compliment to Elgin, and a disservice to Bruce.

From Lord Brougham

Cannes, December 18th.—All through the country and everywhere hereabouts I find the same unhappy feeling of utter indifference to whatever the Government does that is most wrong, whether foolhardy or tyrannical. No one feels any kind of interest in Montalembert, and after his conduct in 1851 it is not to be wondered at; besides the exaggeration of his merits of all kinds sets people rather unjustly against him. With his own shouting partisans his low tone at the trial did him infinite harm, and I believe almost everyone disapproved the refusal of the pardon. That refusal has done the Emperor, as I find in all quarters, great service. The epigram that runs round in the salons at Paris is rather good—' flétri par le coup d'état, fini par le coup de grâce.' The result of it all is that even those reflecting persons whom I converse with say, 'We formerly had too much freedom and abused it; now we have none, and must content ourselves with quiet and peace.'

No one but himself can make the Emperor's position dangerous. If he meddles in Italy and intrigues with Russia towards the Sardinian plan of getting Lombardy from Austria, and indemnifying her on the Danube—which means also giving Russia something in Turkey—he will inevitably lead to general war, and he never could stand that. The people are for peace; even the lower orders are in the greatest terror of

---

[1] Henry Brougham Loch, now Lord Loch (brother of Granville Loch, *ante*, p. 298), had been attached to Lord Elgin's mission to China in 1857-8, and had brought home the Treaty of Tien-tsin. He had no appointment in Mr. Frederick Bruce's abortive mission in 1859, but was again with Lord Elgin in his second mission, in 1860.

the conscription, and the state of the finances will not help him much. He is exceedingly vexed at the attacks upon him in England, but he would make a bad exchange for our alliance if he thought to throw himself on his army, a very small part of which alone is for war. My chief uneasiness is from the want of firmness which he shows in resisting the bad advice of those about him. In this respect he is a good deal changed since the assassination plot; also he allows precautions of an oppressive nature to be taken, which are more likely to increase his risks than to lessen them. Thus, all Italians being assumed to be assassins, they are not only in great numbers stopped at the frontiers, but a considerable number are, without any process, seized and sent away to Algeria or even Cayenne. This, at least, is most confidently asserted, and its being believed by Italians may be dangerous to him.

I have not seen Tocqueville. I called as soon as I could, and left a letter and the catalogue of the library here; but he had the night before such an increase of his spitting of blood that the doctor, whom I saw, said he was quite exhausted, although the day before he was a good deal better. The doctor (who used to attend me before Dr. Whiteley settled here) says he has good hopes of him, as Garnier-Pagès[1] recovered here. But he says the lungs are seriously affected, which G.-P.'s were not. His brother, who called here two days ago, says he is better than when he came, but I don't think they are aware of his danger. The doctor has sent for a *sœur de charité* to him.

[1] He lived twenty years longer, and died November 1st, 1878.

END OF THE FIRST VOLUME

PRINTED BY
SPOTTISWOODE AND CO., NEW-STREET SQUARE
LONDON

A Classified Catalogue

OF WORKS IN

GENERAL LITERATURE

PUBLISHED BY

LONGMANS, GREEN, & CO.

39 PATERNOSTER ROW, LONDON, E.C.

91 AND 93 FIFTH AVENUE NEW YORK. AND 32 HORNBY ROAD, BOMBAY.

CONTENTS.

INDEX OF AUTHORS AND EDITORS.

History, Politics, Polity, Political Memoirs, &c.

Abbott.—*A History of Greece.* By Evelyn Abbott, M.A., LL.D.
Part I.—From the Earliest Times to the Ionian Revolt. Crown 8vo., 10s. 6d.
Part II.—500-445 B.C. Crown 8vo., 10s. 6d.

Acland and Ransome.—*A Handbook in Outline of the Political History of England to 1896.* Chronologically Arranged. By the Right Hon. A. H. Dyke Acland, M.P., and Cyril Ransome, M.A. Crown 8vo., 6s.

ANNUAL REGISTER (THE). A Review of Public Events at Home and Abroad, for the year 1897. 8vo., 18s.
Volumes of the *Annual Register* for the years 1863-1896 can still be had. 18s. each.

Arnold.—*Introductory Lectures on Modern History.* By Thomas Arnold, D.D., formerly Head Master of Rugby School. 8vo., 7s. 6d.

Baden-Powell.—*The Indian Village Community.* Examined with Reference to the Physical, Ethnographic, and Historical Conditions of the Provinces; chiefly on the Basis of the Revenue-Settlement Records and District Manuals. By B. H. Baden-Powell, M.A., C.I.E. With Map. 8vo., 16s.

Bagwell.—*Ireland under the Tudors.* By Richard Bagwell, LL.D. (3 vols.) Vols. I. and II. From the first invasion of the Northmen to the year 1578. 8vo., 32s. Vol. III. 1578-1603. 8vo., 18s.

Ball.—*Historical Review of the Legislative Systems operative in Ireland,* from the Invasion of Henry the Second to the Union (1172-1800). By the Rt. Hon. J. T. Ball. 8vo., 6s.

Besant.—*The History of London.* By Sir Walter Besant. With 74 Illustrations. Crown 8vo., 1s. 9d. Or bound as a School Prize Book, 2s. 6d.

Brassey (Lord).—*Papers and Addresses.*
Naval and Maritime. 1872-1893. 2 vols. Crown 8vo., 10s.
Mercantile Marine and Navigation, from 1871-1894. Crown 8vo., 5s.
Imperial Federation and Colonisation from 1880-1894. Cr. 8vo., 5s.

Brassey (Lord) Papers and Addresses—*continued.*
Political and Miscellaneous. 1861-1894. Crown 8vo., 5s

Bright.—*A History of England.* By the Rev. J. Franck Bright, D.D.
Period I. *Mediæval Monarchy*: A.D. 449-1485. Crown 8vo., 4s. 6d.
Period II. *Personal Monarchy.* 1485-1688. Crown 8vo., 5s.
Period III. *Constitutional Monarchy.* 1689-1837. Crown 8vo., 7s. 6d.
Period IV. *The Growth of Democracy.* 1837-1880. Crown 8vo., 6s.

Buckle.—*History of Civilisation in England and France, Spain and Scotland.* By Henry Thomas Buckle. 3 vols. Crown 8vo., 24s.

Burke.—*A History of Spain* from the Earliest Times to the Death of Ferdinand the Catholic. By Ulick Ralph Burke, M.A. 2 vols. 8vo., 32s.

Chesney.—*Indian Polity*: a View of the System of Administration in India. By General Sir George Chesney, K.C.B. With Map showing all the Administrative Divisions of British India. 8vo., 21s.

Corbett.—*Drake and the Tudor Navy,* with a History of the Rise of England as a Maritime Power. By Julian S. Corbett. With Portraits, Illustrations and Maps. 2 vols. 8vo., 36s.

Creighton.—*A History of the Papacy from the Great Schism to the Sack of Rome,* 1378-1527. By M. Creighton, D.D., Lord Bishop of London. 6 vols. Crown 8vo., 6s. each.

Cuningham.—*A Scheme for Imperial Federation*: a Senate for the Empire. By Granville C. Cuningham, of Montreal, Canada. With an Introduction by Sir Frederick Young, K.C.M.G. Crown 8vo., 3s. 6d.

Curzon.—*Persia and the Persian Question.* By the Right Hon. George N. Curzon, M.P. With 9 Maps, 96 Illustrations, Appendices, and an Index. 2 vols. 8vo., 42s.

De Tocqueville.—*Democracy in America.* By Alexis de Tocqueville. 2 vols. Crown 8vo., 16s.

History, Politics, Polity, Political Memoirs, &c —*continued.*

Dickinson.—*The Development of Parliament during the Nineteenth Century.* By G. Lowes Dickinson, M.A. 8vo., 7s. 6d.

Eggleston.—*The Beginners of a Nation:* a History of the Source and Rise of the Earliest English Settlements in America, with Special Reference to the Life and Character of the People. By Edward Eggleston. With 8 Maps. Cr. 8vo., 7s. 6d.

Froude (James A.).

The History of England, from the Fall of Wolsey to the Defeat of the Spanish Armada.

Popular Edition. 12 vols. Crown 8vo., 3s. 6d. each.

'*Silver Library*' *Edition.* 12 vols. Crown 8vo., 3s. 6d. each.

The Divorce of Catherine of Aragon. Crown 8vo., 3s. 6d.

The Spanish Story of the Armada, and other Essays. Cr. 8vo., 3s. 6d.

The English in Ireland in the Eighteenth Century. 3 vols. Cr. 8vo., 10s. 6d.

English Seamen in the Sixteenth Century. Cr. 8vo., 6s.

The Council of Trent. Crown 8vo., 3s. 6d.

Short Studies on Great Subjects. 4 vols. Cr. 8vo., 3s. 6d. each.

Cæsar: a Sketch. Cr. 8vo, 3s. 6d.

Gardiner (Samuel Rawson, D.C.L., LL.D.).

History of England, from the Accession of James I. to the Outbreak of the Civil War, 1603-1642. 10 vols. Crown 8vo., 6s. each.

A History of the Great Civil War, 1642-1649. 4 vols. Cr. 8vo., 6s. each.

A History of the Commonwealth and the Protectorate. 1649-1660. Vol. I. 1649-1651. With 14 Maps. 8vo., 21s. Vol. II. 1651-1654. With 7 Maps. 8vo., 21s.

What Gunpowder Plot Was. With 8 Illustrations. Crown 8vo., 5s.

Gardiner (Samuel Rawson, D.C.L., LL.D.)—*continued.*

Cromwell's Place in History. Founded on Six Lectures delivered in the University of Oxford. Cr. 8vo., 3s. 6d.

The Student's History of England. With 378 Illustrations. Crown 8vo., 12s.

Also in Three Volumes, price 4s. each. Vol. I. b.c. 55—a.d. 1509. 173 Illustrations. Vol. II. 1509-1689. 96 Illustrations. Vol. III. 1689-1885. 109 Illustrations.

Greville.—*A Journal of the Reigns of King George IV., King William IV., and Queen Victoria.* By Charles C. F. Greville, formerly Clerk of the Council. 8 vols. Crown 8vo., 3s. 6d. each.

HARVARD HISTORICAL STUDIES.

The Suppression of the African Slave Trade to the United States of America, 1638-1870. By W. E. B. Du Bois, Ph.D. 8vo., 7s. 6d.

The Contest over the Ratificaton of the Federal Constitution in Massachusetts. By S. B. Harding, A.M. 8vo., 6s.

A Critical Study of Nullification in South Carolina. By D. F. Houston, A.M. 8vo., 6s.

Nominations for Elective Office in the United States. By Frederick W. Dallinger, A.M. 8vo., 7s. 6d.

A Bibliography of British Municipal History, including Gilds and Parliamentary Representation. By Charles Gross, Ph.D. 8vo., 12s.

The Liberty and Free Soil Parties in the North West. By Theodore C. Smith, Ph.D. 8vo, 7s. 6d.

*** Other Volumes are in preparation.*

Hammond.—*A Woman's Part in a Revolution.* By Mrs. John Hays Hammond. Crown 8vo., 2s. 6d.

Historic Towns.—Edited by E. A. Freeman, D.C.L., and Rev. William Hunt, M.A. With Maps and Plans. Crown 8vo., 3s. 6d. each.

Bristol. By Rev. W. Hunt.	Oxford. By Rev. C. W. Boase.
Carlisle. By Mandell Creighton, D.D.	
Cinque Ports. By Montague Burrows.	Winchester. By G. W. Kitchin, D.D.
Colchester. By Rev. E. L. Cutts.	York. By Rev. James Raine.
Exeter. By E. A. Freeman.	New York. By Theodore Roosevelt.
London. By Rev. W. J.	Boston (U.S.) By Henry Cabot Lodge.

History, Politics, Polity, Political Memoirs, &c.—*continued.*

Joyce (P. W., LL.D.).

A SHORT HISTORY OF IRELAND, from the Earliest Times to 1603. Crown 8vo., 10s. 6d.

A CHILD'S HISTORY OF IRELAND. From the Earliest Times to the Death of O'Connell. With specially constructed Map and 160 Illustrations, including Facsimile in full colours of an illuminated page of the Gospel Book of Mac-Durnan, A.D. 850. Fcp. 8vo., 3s. 6d.

Kaye and Malleson.—*HISTORY OF THE INDIAN MUTINY*, 1857-1858. By Sir JOHN W. KAYE and Colonel G. B. MALLESON. With Analytical Index and Maps and Plans. 6 vols. Crown 8vo., 3s. 6d. each.

Lang (ANDREW).

PICKLE THE SPY: or, The Incognito of Prince Charles. With 6 Portraits. 8vo., 18s.

ST. ANDREWS. With 8 Plates and 24 Illustrations in the Text by T. HODGE. 8vo., 15s. net.

Laurie.—*HISTORICAL SURVEY OF PRE-CHRISTIAN EDUCATION.* By S. S. LAURIE, A.M., LL.D. 8vo., 12s.

Lecky (The Rt. Hon. WILLIAM E. H.)

HISTORY OF ENGLAND IN THE EIGHTEENTH CENTURY.

Library Edition. 8 vols. 8vo. Vols. I. and II., 36s.; Vols. III. and IV., 36s.; Vols. V. and VI., 36s.; Vols. VII. and VIII., 36s.

Cabinet Edition. ENGLAND. 7 vols. Crown 8vo., 6s. each. IRELAND. 5 vols. Crown 8vo., 6s. each.

HISTORY OF EUROPEAN MORALS FROM AUGUSTUS TO CHARLEMAGNE. 2 vols. Crown 8vo., 16s.

HISTORY OF THE RISE AND INFLUENCE OF THE SPIRIT OF RATIONALISM IN EUROPE. 2 vols. Crown 8vo., 16s.

DEMOCRACY AND LIBERTY. 2 vols. 8vo., 36s.

Macaulay (LORD).

THE LIFE AND WORKS OF LORD MACAULAY. 'Edinburgh' Edition. 10 vols. 8vo., 6s. each.

Vols. I.-IV. *HISTORY OF ENGLAND.*
Vols. V.-VII. *ESSAYS; BIOGRAPHIES; INDIAN PENAL CODE; CONTRIBUTIONS TO KNIGHT'S 'QUARTERLY MAGAZINE'.*
Vol. VIII. *SPEECHES; LAYS OF ANCIENT ROME; MISCELLANEOUS POEMS.*
Vols. IX. and X. *THE LIFE AND LETTERS OF LORD MACAULAY.* By the Right Hon. Sir G. O. TREVELYAN, Bart.

This Edition is a cheaper reprint of the Library Edition of LORD MACAULAY'S *Life and Works.*

COMPLETE WORKS.
Cabinet Edition. 16 vols. Post 8vo. £4 16s.
Library Edition. 8 vols. 8vo., £5 5s.
'Edinburgh' Edition. 8 vols. 8vo., 6s. each.

HISTORY OF ENGLAND FROM THE ACCESSION OF JAMES THE SECOND.
Popular Edition. 2 vols. Cr. 8vo., 5s.
Student's Edition. 2 vols. Cr. 8vo., 12s.
People's Edition. 4 vols. Cr. 8vo., 16s.
Cabinet Edition. 8 vols. Post 8vo., 48s.
'Edinburgh' Edition. 4 vols. 8vo., 6s. each.
Library Edition. 5 vols. 8vo., £4.

CRITICAL AND HISTORICAL ESSAYS, WITH LAYS OF ANCIENT ROME, etc., in 1 volume.
Popular Edition. Crown 8vo., 2s. 6d.
Authorised Edition. Crown 8vo., 2s. 6d., or gilt edges, 3s. 6d.
'Silver Library' Edition. With Portrait and 4 Illustrations to the 'Lays'. Cr. 8vo., 3s. 6d.

CRITICAL AND HISTORICAL ESSAYS.
Student's Edition. 1 vol. Cr. 8vo., 6s.
People's Edition. 2 vols. Cr. 8vo., 8s.
'Trevelyan' Edition. 2 vols. Cr. 8vo., 9s.
Cabinet Edition. 4 vols. Post 8vo., 24s.
'Edinburgh' Edition. 3 vols. 8vo., 6s. each.
Library Edition. 3 vols. 8vo., 36s.

ESSAYS, which may be had separately, sewed, 6d. each; cloth, 1s. each.

Addison and Walpole.	Ranke and Gladstone.
Croker's Boswell's Johnson.	Milton and Machiavelli.
Hallam's Constitutional History.	Lord Byron.
Warren Hastings.	Lord Clive.
The Earl of Chatham (Two Essays).	Lord Byron, and The Comic Dramatists of the Restoration.
Frederick the Great.	

MISCELLANEOUS WRITINGS
People's Edition. 1 vol. Cr. 8vo., 4s. 6d.
Library Edition. 2 vols. 8vo., 21s.

History, Politics, Polity, Political Memoirs, &c.—*continued.*

Macaulay (LORD)—*continued.*

MISCELLANEOUS WRITINGS, SPEECHES AND POEMS.
Popular Edition. Crown 8vo., 2s. 6d.
Cabinet Edition. 4 vols. Post 8vo., 24s.

SELECTIONS FROM THE WRITINGS OF LORD MACAULAY. Edited, with Occasional Notes, by the Right Hon. Sir G. O. Trevelyan, Bart. Crown 8vo., 6s.

MacColl.—*THE SULTAN AND THE POWERS.* By the Rev. MALCOLM MacCOLL, M.A., Canon of Ripon. 8vo., 10s. 6d.

Mackinnon.—*THE UNION OF ENGLAND AND SCOTLAND: A STUDY OF INTERNATIONAL HISTORY.* By JAMES MACKINNON. Ph.D. Examiner in History to the University of Edinburgh. 8vo., 16s.

May.—*THE CONSTITUTIONAL HISTORY OF ENGLAND* since the Accession of George III. 1760-1870. By Sir THOMAS ERSKINE MAY, K.C.B. (Lord Farnborough). 3 vols. Cr. 8vo., 18s.

Merivale (CHARLES, D.D.), sometime Dean of Ely.

HISTORY OF THE ROMANS UNDER THE EMPIRE. 8 vols. Crown 8vo., 3s. 6d. each.

THE FALL OF THE ROMAN REPUBLIC: a Short History of the Last Century of the Commonwealth. 12mo., 7s. 6d.

GENERAL HISTORY OF ROME, from the Foundation of the City to the Fall of Augustulus, B.C. 753-A.D. 476. With 5 Maps. Crown 8vo, 7s. 6d.

Montague.—*THE ELEMENTS OF ENGLISH CONSTITUTIONAL HISTORY.* By F. C. MONTAGUE, M.A. Crown 8vo., 3s. 6d.

Richman.—*APPENZELL: PURE DEMOCRACY AND PASTORAL LIFE IN INNER-RHODEN.* A Swiss Study. By IRVING B. RICHMAN, Consul-General of the United States to Switzerland. With Maps. Crown 8vo., 5s.

Seebohm (FREDERIC).

THE ENGLISH VILLAGE COMMUNITY Examined in its Relations to the Manorial and Tribal Systems, etc. With 13 Maps and Plates. 8vo., 16s.

THE TRIBAL SYSTEM IN WALES: Being Part of an Inquiry into the Structure and Methods of Tribal Society. With 3 Maps. 8vo., 12s.

Sharpe.—*LONDON AND THE KINGDOM:* a History derived mainly from the Archives at Guildhall in the custody of the Corporation of the City of London. By REGINALD R. SHARPE, D.C.L., Records Clerk in the Office of the Town Clerk of the City of London. 3 vols. 8vo. 10s. 6d. each.

Smith.—*CARTHAGE AND THE CARTHAGINIANS.* By R. BOSWORTH SMITH, M.A., With Maps, Plans, etc. Cr. 8vo., 3s. 6d.

Stephens.—*A HISTORY OF THE FRENCH REVOLUTION.* By H. MORSE STEPHENS. 8vo. Vols. I. and II. 18s. each.

Stubbs.—*HISTORY OF THE UNIVERSITY OF DUBLIN*, from its Foundation to the End of the Eighteenth Century. By J. W. STUBBS. 8vo., 12s. 6d.

Sutherland.—*THE HISTORY OF AUSTRALIA AND NEW ZEALAND*, from 1606-1890. By ALEXANDER SUTHERLAND, M.A., and GEORGE SUTHERLAND, M.A. Crown 8vo., 2s. 6d.

Taylor.—*A STUDENT'S MANUAL OF THE HISTORY OF INDIA.* By Colonel MEADOWS TAYLOR, C.S.I., etc. Cr. 8vo., 7s. 6d.

Todd.—*PARLIAMENTARY GOVERNMENT IN THE BRITISH COLONIES.* By ALPHEUS TODD, LL.D. 8vo., 30s. net.

Wakeman and Hassall.—*ESSAYS INTRODUCTORY TO THE STUDY OF ENGLISH CONSTITUTIONAL HISTORY.* By Resident Members of the University of Oxford. Edited by HENRY OFFLEY WAKEMAN, M.A., and ARTHUR HASSALL, M.A. Crown 8vo., 6s.

Walpole.—*HISTORY OF ENGLAND FROM THE CONCLUSION OF THE GREAT WAR IN 1815 TO 1858.* By Sir SPENCER WALPOLE, K.C.B. 6 vols. Crown 8vo., 6s. each.

Wood-Martin.—*PAGAN IRELAND: AN ARCHÆOLOGICAL SKETCH.* A Handbook of Irish Pre-Christian Antiquities. By W. G. WOOD-MARTIN, M.R.I.A. With 512 Illustrations. Crown 8vo., 15s.

Wylie.—*HISTORY OF ENGLAND UNDER HENRY IV.* By JAMES HAMILTON WYLIE, M.A., one of H.M. Inspectors of Schools. 4 vols. Crown 8vo. Vol. I., 1399-1404, 10s. 6d. Vol. II., 1405-1406, 15s. Vol. III., 1407-1411, 15s. Vol. IV., 1411-1413, 21s.

Biography, Personal Memoirs, &c.

Armstrong.—*THE LIFE AND LETTERS OF EDMUND J. ARMSTRONG.* Edited by G. F. Savage Armstrong. Fcp. 8vo., 7s. 6d.

Bacon.—*THE LETTERS AND LIFE OF FRANCIS BACON, INCLUDING ALL HIS OCCASIONAL WORKS.* Edited by James Spedding. 7 vols. 8vo., £4 4s.

Bagehot.—*BIOGRAPHICAL STUDIES.* By Walter Bagehot. Crown 8vo., 3s. 6d.

Blackwell. — *PIONEER WORK IN OPENING THE MEDICAL PROFESSION TO WOMEN:* Autobiographical Sketches. By Dr. Elizabeth Blackwell. Cr. 8vo., 6s.

Brown.—*FORD MADOX BROWN:* A Record of his Life and Works. By Ford M. Hueffer. With 45 Full-page Plates (22 Autotypes) and 7 Illustrations in the Text. 8vo., 42s.

Buss.—*FRANCES MARY BUSS AND HER WORK FOR EDUCATION.* By Annie E. Ridley. With 5 Portraits and 4 Illustrations. Crown 8vo, 7s. 6d.

Carlyle.—*THOMAS CARLYLE:* A History of his Life. By James Anthony Froude.
1795-1835. 2 vols. Crown 8vo., 7s.
1834-1881. 2 vols. Crown 8vo., 7s.

Digby.—*THE LIFE OF SIR KENELM DIGBY, by one of his Descendants,* the Author of 'Falklands,' etc. With 7 Illustrations. 8vo., 16s.

Duncan.—*ADMIRAL DUNCAN.* By The Earl of Camperdown. With 3 Portraits. 8vo., 16s.

Erasmus.—*LIFE AND LETTERS OF ERASMUS.* By James Anthony Froude. Crown 8vo., 6s.

FALKLANDS. By the Author of 'The Life of Sir Kenelm Digby,' etc. With 6 Portraits and 2 other Illustrations. 8vo., 10s. 6d.

Faraday.—*FARADAY AS A DISCOVERER.* By John Tyndall. Crown 8vo, 3s. 6d.

Fox.—*THE EARLY HISTORY OF CHARLES JAMES FOX.* By the Right Hon. Sir G. O. Trevelyan, Bart.
Library Edition. 8vo., 18s.
Cabinet Edition. Crown 8vo., 6s.

Halifax.—*THE LIFE AND LETTERS OF SIR GEORGE SAVILE, BARONET, FIRST MARQUIS OF HALIFAX.* With a New Edition of his Works, now for the first time collected and revised. By H. C. Foxcroft. 2 vols. 8vo., 32s.

Halford.—*THE LIFE OF SIR HENRY HALFORD, BART., G.C.H., M.D., F.R.S.* By William Munk, M.D., F.S.A. 8vo., 12s. 6d.

Hamilton.—*LIFE OF SIR WILLIAM HAMILTON.* By R. P. Graves. 8vo. 3 vols. 15s. each. ADDENDUM. 8vo., 6d. sewed.

Harper. — *A MEMOIR OF HUGO DANIEL HARPER, D.D.,* late Principal of Jesus College, Oxford, and for many years Head Master of Sherborne School. By L. V. Lester, M.A. Crown 8vo., 5s.

Havelock.—*MEMOIRS OF SIR HENRY HAVELOCK, K.C.B.* By John Clark Marshman. Crown 8vo., 3s. 6d.

Haweis.—*MY MUSICAL LIFE.* By the Rev. H. R. Haweis. With Portrait of Richard Wagner and 3 Illustrations. Crown 8vo., 7s. 6d.

Holroyd.—*THE GIRLHOOD OF MARIA JOSEPHA HOLROYD (Lady Stanley of Alderley).* Recorded in Letters of a Hundred Years Ago, from 1776-1796. Edited by J. H. Adeane. With 6 Portraits. 8vo., 18s.

Jackson. — *STONEWALL JACKSON.* By Lieut.-Col. G. F. Henderson, York and Lancaster Regiment. With Portrait, Maps and Plans. 2 vols. 8vo., 42s.

Lejeune.—*MEMOIRS OF BARON LEJEUNE,* Aide-de-Camp to Marshals Berthier, Davout, and Oudinot. Translated and Edited from the Original French by Mrs. Arthur Bell (N. D'Anvers). With a Preface by Major-General Maurice, C.B. 2 vols. 8vo., 24s.

Luther. — *LIFE OF LUTHER.* By Julius Köstlin. With 62 Illustrations and 4 Facsimiles of MSS. Translated from the German. Crown 8vo., 3s. 6d.

Macaulay.—*THE LIFE AND LETTERS OF LORD MACAULAY.* By the Right Hon. Sir G. O. Trevelyan, Bart.
Popular Edition. 1 vol. Cr. 8vo., 2s. 6d.
Student's Edition. 1 vol. Cr. 8vo., 6s.
Cabinet Edition. 2 vols. Post 8vo., 12s.
'Edinburgh' Edition. 2 vols. 8vo., 6s. each.
Library Edition. 2 vols. 8vo., 36s.

Marbot. — *THE MEMOIRS OF THE BARON DE MARBOT.* Translated from the French. 2 vols. Crown 8vo., 7s.

Max Müller.—*AULD LANG SYNE.* By the Right Hon. F. Max Müller. With Portrait. 8vo, 10s. 6d.
Contents.—Musical Recollections—Literary Recollections—Recollections of Royalties—Beggars.

Biography, Personal Memoirs, &c.—*continued*.

Meade.—*GENERAL SIR RICHARD MEADE AND THE FEUDATORY STATES OF CENTRAL AND SOUTHERN INDIA*: a Record of Forty-three Years' Service as Soldier, Political Officer and Administrator. By THOMAS HENRY THORNTON, C.S.I., D.C.L., sometime Foreign Secretary to the Government of India, Author of 'The Life and Work of Colonel Sir Robert Sandeman'. With Portrait, Map and Illustrations. 8vo., 10s. 6d. net.

Nansen.—*FRIDTJOF NANSEN*, 1861-1893. By W. C. BRÖGGER and NORDAHL ROLFSEN. Translated by WILLIAM ARCHER. With 8 Plates, 48 Illustrations in the Text, and 3 Maps. 8vo., 12s. 6d.

Newdegate.—*THE CHEVERELS OF CHEVEREL MANOR*. By Lady NEWDIGATE-NEWDEGATE, Author of 'Gossip from a Muniment Room'. With 6 Illustrations from Family Portraits. 8vo., 10s. 6d.

Place.—*THE LIFE OF FRANCIS PLACE*, 1771-1854. By GRAHAM WALLAS, M.A. With 2 Portraits. 8vo., 12s.

Rawlinson.—*A MEMOIR OF MAJOR-GENERAL SIR HENRY CRESWICKE RAWLINSON, BART., K.C.B., F.R.S., D.C.L., F.R.G.S., ETC.* By GEORGE RAWLINSON, M.A., F.R.G.S., Canon of Canterbury. With 3 Portraits and a Map, and a Preface by Field-Marshal Lord ROBERTS of Kandahar, V.C. 8vo., 16s.

Reeve.—*THE LIFE AND LETTERS OF HENRY REEVE, C.B.*, late Editor of the 'Edinburgh Review,' and Registrar of the Privy Council. By J. K. LAUGHTON, M.A.

Romanes.—*THE LIFE AND LETTERS OF GEORGE JOHN ROMANES, M.A., LL.D., F.R.S.* Written and Edited by his WIFE. With Portrait and 2 Illustrations. Crown 8vo., 6s.

Seebohm.—*THE OXFORD REFORMERS—JOHN COLET, ERASMUS AND THOMAS MORE*: a History of their Fellow-Work. By FREDERIC SEEBOHM. 8vo., 14s.

Shakespeare. — *OUTLINES OF THE LIFE OF SHAKESPEARE*. By J. O. HALLIWELL-PHILLIPPS. With Illustrations and Fac-similes. 2 vols. Royal 8vo., £1 1s.

Shakespeare's *TRUE LIFE*. By JAMES WALTER. With 500 Illustrations by GERALD E. MOIRA. Imp. 8vo., 21s.

Verney. —*MEMOIRS OF THE VERNEY FAMILY.*
Vols. I. & II., *DURING THE CIVIL WAR*. By FRANCES PARTHENOPE VERNEY. With 38 Portraits, Woodcuts and Fac-simile. Royal 8vo., 42s.
Vol. III., *DURING THE COMMONWEALTH*. 1650-1660. By MARGARET M. VERNEY. With 10 Portraits, etc. Royal 8vo., 21s.

Wakley.—*THE LIFE AND TIMES OF THOMAS WAKLEY*, Founder and First Editor of the 'Lancet,' Member of Parliament for Finsbury, and Coroner for West Middlesex. By S. SQUIRE SPRIGGE, M.B. Cantab. With 2 Portraits. 8vo., 18s.

Wellington.—*LIFE OF THE DUKE OF WELLINGTON*. By the Rev. G. R. GLEIG, M.A. Crown 8vo., 3s. 6d.

Wills. —*W. G. WILLS, DRAMATIST AND PAINTER*. By FREEMAN WILLS. With Photogravure Portrait. 8vo., 10s. 6d.

Travel and Adventure, the Colonies, &c.

Arnold.—*SEAS AND LANDS*. By Sir EDWIN ARNOLD. With 71 Illustrations. Crown 8vo., 3s. 6d.

Baker (SIR S. W.).
EIGHT YEARS IN CEYLON. With 6 Illustrations. Crown 8vo., 3s. 6d.
THE RIFLE AND THE HOUND IN CEYLON. With 6 Illustrations. Crown 8vo., 3s. 6d.

Ball.—*THE ALPINE GUIDE*. By the late JOHN BALL, F.R.S., etc. A New Edition, Reconstructed and Revised on behalf of the Alpine Club, by W. A. B. COOLIDGE.
Vol. I., *THE WESTERN ALPS*: the Alpine Region, South of the Rhone Valley, from the Col de Tenda to the Simplon Pass. With 9 New and Revised Maps. Crown 8vo., 12s. net.
Vol. II., *THE CENTRAL ALPS, NORTH OF THE RHONE VALLEY, FROM THE SIMPLON PASS TO THE ADIGE VALLEY*. [In prep.

Bent.—*THE RUINED CITIES OF MASHONALAND*: being a Record of Excavation and Exploration in 1891. By J. THEODORE BENT. With 117 Illustrations. Crown 8vo., 3s. 6d.

Bicknell.—*TRAVEL AND ADVENTURE IN NORTHERN QUEENSLAND*. By ARTHUR C. BICKNELL. With 24 Plates and 22 Illustrations in the Text. 8vo., 15s.

Brassey.—*VOYAGES AND TRAVELS OF LORD BRASSEY, K.C.B., D.C.L.,* 1862-1894. Arranged and Edited by Captain S. EARDLEY-WILMOT. 2 vols. Cr. 8vo., 10s.

Travel and Adventure, the Colonies, &c.—*continued.*

Brassey (THE LATE LADY).

A VOYAGE IN THE 'SUNBEAM'; OUR HOME ON THE OCEAN FOR ELEVEN MONTHS.

Cabinet Edition. With Map and 66 Illustrations. Crown 8vo., 7s. 6d.

'Silver Library' Edition. With 66 Illustrations. Crown 8vo., 3s. 6d.

Popular Edition. With 60 Illustrations. 4to., 6d. sewed, 1s. cloth.

School Edition. With 37 Illustrations. Fcp., 2s. cloth, or 3s. white parchment.

SUNSHINE AND STORM IN THE EAST.

Cabinet Edition. With 2 Maps and 114 Illustrations. Crown 8vo., 7s. 6d.

Popular Edition. With 103 Illustrations. 4to., 6d. sewed, 1s. cloth.

IN THE TRADES, THE TROPICS, AND THE 'ROARING FORTIES'.

Cabinet Edition. With Map and 220 Illustrations. Crown 8vo., 7s. 6d.

Popular Edition. With 183 Illustrations. 4to., 6d. sewed, 1s. cloth.

THREE VOYAGES IN THE 'SUNBEAM'.

Popular Ed. With 346 Illust. 4to., 2s. 6d.

Browning.—*A GIRL'S WANDERINGS IN HUNGARY.* By H. ELLEN BROWNING. With Map and 20 Illustrations. Crown 8vo., 3s. 6d.

Churchill.—*THE STORY OF THE MALAKAND FIELD FORCE,* 1897. By WINSTON SPENCER CHURCHILL, Lieut., 4th Queen's Own Hussars. With 6 Maps and Plans. Crown 8vo., 7s. 6d.

Froude (JAMES A.).

OCEANA : or England and her Colonies. With 9 Illustrations. Crown 8vo., 2s. boards, 2s. 6d. cloth.

'Silver Library' Edition. Crown 8vo., 3s. 6d.

THE ENGLISH IN THE WEST INDIES : or, the Bow of Ulysses. With 9 Illustrations. Crown 8vo., 2s. boards, 2s. 6d. cloth.

Howitt.—*VISITS TO REMARKABLE PLACES.* Old Halls, Battle-Fields, Scenes, illustrative of Striking Passages in English History and Poetry. By WILLIAM HOWITT. With 80 Illustrations. Crown 8vo., 3s. 6d.

Knight (E. F.).

THE CRUISE OF THE 'ALERTE' : the Narrative of a Search for Treasure on the Desert Island of Trinidad. With 2 Maps and 23 Illustrations. Crown 8vo., 3s. 6d.

WHERE THREE EMPIRES MEET : a Narrative of Recent Travel in Kashmir, Western Tibet, Baltistan, Ladak, Gilgit, and the adjoining Countries. With a Map and 54 Illustrations. Cr. 8vo., 3s. 6d.

Knight (E. F.)—*continued.*

THE 'FALCON' ON THE BALTIC : a Voyage from London to Copenhagen in a Three-Tonner. With 10 Full-page Illustrations. Crown 8vo., 3s. 6d.

Lees and Clutterbuck.—B.C. 1887 : *A RAMBLE IN BRITISH COLUMBIA.* By J. A. LEES and W. J. CLUTTERBUCK. With Map and 75 Illustrations. Crown 8vo., 3s. 6d.

Macdonald.—*THE GOLD COAST : PAST AND PRESENT.* By GEORGE MACDONALD, Director of Education and H.M. Inspector of Schools for the Gold Coast Colony and the Protectorate. With Illustrations.

Max Müller.—*LETTERS FROM CONSTANTINOPLE.* By Mrs. MAX MÜLLER. With 12 Views of Constantinople and the neighbourhood. Crown 8vo., 6s.

Nansen (FRIDTJOF).

THE FIRST CROSSING OF GREENLAND. With 143 Illustrations and a Map. Crown 8vo., 3s. 6d.

ESKIMO LIFE. With 31 Illustrations. 8vo., 16s.

Oliver.—*CRAGS AND CRATERS :* Rambles in the Island of Réunion. By WILLIAM DUDLEY OLIVER, M.A. With 27 Illustrations and a Map. Cr. 8vo., 6s.

Smith.—*CLIMBING IN THE BRITISH ISLES.* By W. P. HASKETT SMITH. With Illustrations by ELLIS CARR, and Numerous Plans.

Part I. *ENGLAND.* 16mo., 3s. 6d.

Part II. *WALES AND IRELAND.* 16mo., 3s. 6d.

Part III. *SCOTLAND.* [*In preparation.*

Stephen. — *THE PLAY-GROUND OF EUROPE* (The Alps). By LESLIE STEPHEN. With 4 Illustrations. Crown 8vo., 6s. net.

THREE IN NORWAY. By Two of Them. With a Map and 59 Illustrations. Crown 8vo., 2s. boards, 2s. 6d. cloth.

Tyndall.—*THE GLACIERS OF THE ALPS :* being a Narrative of Excursions and Ascents. An Account of the Origin and Phenomena of Glaciers, and an Exposition of the Physical Principles to which they are related. By JOHN TYNDALL, F.R.S. With 6 Illustrations. Crown 8vo., 6s. 6d. net.

Vivian.—*SERVIA :* the Poor Man's Paradise. By HERBERT VIVIAN, M.A., Officer of the Royal Order of Takovo. With Map and Portrait of King Alexander. 8vo., 15s.

Veterinary Medicine, &c.

Steel (JOHN HENRY, F.R.C.V.S., F.Z.S., A.V.D.), late Professor of Veterinary Science and Principal of Bombay Veterinary College.

A TREATISE ON THE DISEASES OF THE DOG; being a Manual of Canine Pathology. Especially adapted for the use of Veterinary Practitioners and Students. With 88 Illustrations. 8vo., 10s. 6d.

A TREATISE ON THE DISEASES OF THE OX; being a Manual of Bovine Pathology. Especially adapted for the use of Veterinary Practitioners and Students. With 2 Plates and 117 Woodcuts. 8vo., 15s.

A TREATISE ON THE DISEASES OF THE SHEEP; being a Manual of Ovine Pathology for the use of Veterinary Practitioners and Students. With Coloured Plate and 99 Woodcuts. 8vo., 12s.

OUTLINES OF EQUINE ANATOMY; a Manual for the use of Veterinary Students in the Dissecting Room. Cr. 8vo., 7s. 6d.

Fitzwygram. — *HORSES AND STABLES.* By Major-General Sir F. FITZWYGRAM, Bart. With 56 pages of Illustrations. 8vo., 2s. 6d. net.

Schreiner. — *THE ANGORA GOAT* (published under the auspices of the South African Angora Goat Breeders' Association), and a Paper on the Ostrich (reprinted from the *Zoologist* for March, 1897). With 26 Illustrations. By S. C. CRONWRIGHT SCHREINER. 8vo., 10s. 6d.

'Stonehenge.' — *THE DOG IN HEALTH AND DISEASE.* By 'STONEHENGE'. With 78 Wood Engravings. 8vo., 7s. 6d.

Youatt (WILLIAM).

THE HORSE. Revised and Enlarged by W. WATSON, M.R.C.V.S. With 52 Wood Engravings. 8vo., 7s. 6d.

THE DOG. Revised and Enlarged. With 33 Wood Engravings. 8vo., 6s.

Sport and Pastime.
THE BADMINTON LIBRARY.
Edited by HIS GRACE THE DUKE OF BEAUFORT, K.G., and A. E. T. WATSON.

Complete in 28 Volumes.   Crown 8vo., Price 10s. 6d. each Volume, Cloth.

*** *The Volumes are also issued half-bound in Leather, with gilt top.   The price can be had from all Booksellers.*

ARCHERY. By C. J. LONGMAN and Col. H. WALROND. With Contributions by Miss LEGH, Viscount DILLON, etc. With 2 Maps, 23 Plates and 172 Illustrations in the Text. Crown 8vo., 10s. 6d.

ATHLETICS. By MONTAGUE SHEARMAN. With Plates and Illustrations in the Text. Crown 8vo., 10s. 6d.

BIG GAME SHOOTING. By CLIVE PHILLIPPS-WOLLEY.

Vol. I. AFRICA AND AMERICA. With Contributions by Sir SAMUEL W. BAKER, W. C. OSWELL, F. C. SELOUS, etc. With 20 Plates and 57 Illustrations in the Text. Crown 8vo., 10s. 6d.

Vol. II. EUROPE, ASIA, AND THE ARCTIC REGIONS. With Contributions by Lieut.-Colonel R. HEBER PERCY, Major ALGERNON C. HEBER PERCY, etc. With 17 Plates and 56 Illustrations in the Text. Cr. 8vo., 10s. 6d.

BILLIARDS. By Major W. BROADFOOT, R.E. With Contributions by A. H. BOYD, SYDENHAM DIXON, W. J. FORD, etc. With 11 Plates, 19 Illustrations in the Text, and numerous Diagrams. Cr. 8vo., 10s. 6d.

COURSING AND FALCONRY. By HARDING COX and the Hon. GERALD LASCELLES. With 20 Plates and 56 Illustrations in the Text. Crown 8vo., 10s. 6d.

CRICKET. By A. G. STEEL and the Hon. R. H. LYTTELTON. With Contributions by ANDREW LANG, W. G. GRACE, F. GALE, etc. With 13 Plates and 52 Illustrations in the Text. Crown 8vo., 10s. 6d.

CYCLING. By the EARL OF ALBEMARLE and G. LACY HILLIER. With 19 Plates and 44 Illustrations in the Text. Crown 8vo., 10s. 6d.

DANCING. By Mrs. LILLY GROVE, F.R.G.S. With Contributions by Miss MIDDLETON, The Hon. Mrs. ARMYTAGE, etc. With Musical Examples, and 38 Full-page Plates and 93 Illustrations in the Text. Crown 8vo., 10s. 6d.

DRIVING. By His Grace the DUKE of BEAUFORT, K.G. With Contributions by A. E. T. WATSON the EARL OF ONSLOW, etc. With 12 Plates and 54 Illustrations in the Text. Crown 8vo., 10s. 6d.

Sport and Pastime—*continued.*
THE BADMINTON LIBRARY—*continued.*

FENCING, BOXING, AND WRESTLING. By Walter H. Pollock, F. C. Grove, C. Prevost, E. B. Mitchell, and Walter Armstrong. With 18 Plates and 24 Illust. in the Text. Cr. 8vo., 10s. 6d.

FISHING. By H. Cholmondeley-Pennell.

Vol. I. SALMON AND TROUT. With Contributions by H. R. Francis, Major John P. Traherne, etc. With 9 Plates and numerous Illustrations of Tackle, etc. Crown 8vo., 10s. 6d.

Vol. II. PIKE AND OTHER COARSE FISH. With Contributions by the Marquis of Exeter, William Senior, G. Christopher Davis, etc. With 7 Plates and numerous Illustrations of Tackle, etc. Crown 8vo., 10s. 6d.

FOOTBALL. By Montague Shearman. [*In preparation.*

GOLF. By Horace G. Hutchinson. With Contributions by the Rt. Hon. A. J. Balfour, M.P., Sir Walter Simpson, Bart., Andrew Lang, etc. With 32 Plates and 57 Illustrations in the Text. Cr. 8vo., 10s. 6d.

HUNTING. By His Grace the Duke of Beaufort, K.G., and Mowbray Morris. With Contributions by the Earl of Suffolk and Berkshire, Rev. E. W. L. Davies, G. H. Longman, etc. With 5 Plates and 54 Illustrations in the Text. Cr. 8vo., 10s. 6d.

MOUNTAINEERING. By C. T. Dent. With Contributions by Sir W. M. Conway, D. W. Freshfield, C. E. Matthews, etc. With 13 Plates and 95 Illustrations in the Text. Cr. 8vo., 10s. 6d.

POETRY OF SPORT (THE).— Selected by Hedley Peek. With a Chapter on Classical Allusions to Sport by Andrew Lang, and a Special Preface to the BADMINTON LIBRARY by A. E. T. Watson. With 32 Plates and 74 Illustrations in the Text. Crown 8vo., 10s. 6d.

RACING AND STEEPLE-CHASING. By the Earl of Suffolk and Berkshire, W. G. Craven, the Hon. F. Lawley, Arthur Coventry, and A. E. T. Watson. With Frontispiece and 56 Illustrations in the Text. Crown 8vo., 10s. 6d.

RIDING AND POLO. By Captain Robert Weir, The Duke of Beaufort, The Earl of Suffolk and Berkshire, The Earl of Onslow, etc. With 18 Plates and 41 Illustrations in the Text. Crown 8vo., 10s. 6d.

ROWING. By R. P. P. Rowe and C. M. Pitman. With Chapters on Steering by C. P. Serocold and F. C. Begg; Metropolitan Rowing by S. Le Blanc Smith: and on PUNTING by P. W. Squire. With 75 Illustrations. Crown 8vo., 10s. 6d.

SEA FISHING. By John Bickerdyke, Sir H. W. Gore-Booth, Alfred C. Harmsworth, and W. Senior. With 22 Full-page Plates and 175 Illustrations in the Text. Crown 8vo., 10s. 6d.

SHOOTING.

Vol. I. FIELD AND COVERT. By Lord Walsingham and Sir Ralph Payne-Gallwey, Bart. With Contributions by the Hon. Gerald Lascelles and A. J. Stuart-Wortley. With 11 Plates and 94 Illusts. in the Text. Cr. 8vo., 10s. 6d.

Vol. II. MOOR AND MARSH. By Lord Walsingham and Sir Ralph Payne-Gallwey, Bart. With Contributions by Lord Lovat and Lord Charles Lennox Kerr. With 8 Plates and 57 Illustrations in the Text. Crown 8vo., 10s. 6d.

SKATING, CURLING, TOBOGGANING. By J. M. Heathcote, C. G. Tebbutt, T. Maxwell Witham, Rev. John Kerr, Ormond Hake, Henry A. Buck, etc. With 12 Plates and 272 Illustrations in the Text. Crown 8vo., 10s. 6d.

SWIMMING. By Archibald Sinclair and William Henry, Hon. Secs. of the Life-Saving Society. With 13 Plates and 106 Illustrations in the Text. Cr. 8vo., 10s. 6d.

TENNIS, LAWN TENNIS, RACKETS AND FIVES. By J. M. and C. G. Heathcote, E. O. Pleydell-Bouverie, and A. C. Ainger. With Contributions by the Hon. A. Lyttelton, W. C. Marshall, Miss L. Dod, etc. With 12 Plates and 67 Illustrations in the Text. Cr. 8vo., 10s. 6d.

YACHTING.

Vol. I. CRUISING, CONSTRUCTION OF YACHTS, YACHT RACING RULES, FITTING-OUT, etc. By Sir Edward Sullivan, Bart., The Earl of Pembroke, Lord Brassey, K.C.B., C. E. Seth-Smith, C.B., G. L. Watson, R. T. Pritchett, E. F. Knight, etc. With 21 Plates and 93 Illustrations in the Text. Crown 8vo., 10s. 6d.

Vol. II. YACHT CLUBS, YACHTING IN AMERICA AND THE COLONIES, YACHT RACING, etc. By R. T. Pritchett, The Marquis of Dufferin and Ava, K.P., The Earl of Onslow, James McFerran, etc. With 35 Plates and 160 Illustrations in the Text. Crown 8vo., 10s. 6d.

Sport and Pastime—*continued.*
FUR, FEATHER, AND FIN SERIES.

Edited by A. E. T. WATSON.

Crown 8vo., price 5s. each Volume, cloth.

*** *The Volumes are also issued half-bound in Leather, with gilt top. The price can be had from all Booksellers.*

THE PARTRIDGE. Natural History, by the Rev. H. A. MACPHERSON; Shooting, by A. J. STUART-WORTLEY; Cookery, by GEORGE SAINTSBURY. With 11 Illustrations and various Diagrams in the Text. Crown 8vo., 5s.

THE GROUSE. Natural History, by the Rev. H. A. MACPHERSON; Shooting, by A. J. STUART-WORTLEY; Cookery, by GEORGE SAINTSBURY. With 13 Illustrations and various Diagrams in the Text. Crown 8vo., 5s.

THE PHEASANT. Natural History, by the Rev. H. A. MACPHERSON; Shooting, by A. J. STUART-WORTLEY; Cookery, by ALEXANDER INNES SHAND. With 10 Illustrations and various Diagrams. Crown 8vo., 5s.

THE HARE. Natural History, by the Rev. H. A. MACPHERSON; Shooting, by the Hon. GERALD LASCELLES; Coursing, by CHARLES RICHARDSON; Hunting, by J. S. GIBBONS and G. H. LONGMAN; Cookery, by Col. KENNEY HERBERT. With 9 Illustrations. Crown 8vo, 5s.

RED DEER.—Natural History, by the Rev. H. A. MACPHERSON; Deer Stalking, by CAMERON OF LOCHIEL; Stag Hunting, by Viscount EBRINGTON; Cookery, by ALEXANDER INNES SHAND. With 10 Illustrations. Crown 8vo., 5s.

THE SALMON. By the Hon. A. E. GATHORNE-HARDY. With Chapters on the Law of Salmon Fishing by CLAUD DOUGLAS PENNANT; Cookery, by ALEXANDER INNES SHAND. With 8 Illustrations. Cr. 8vo., 5s.

THE TROUT. By the MARQUESS OF GRANBY. With Chapters on the Breeding of Trout by Col. H. CUSTANCE; and Cookery, by ALEXANDER INNES SHAND. With 12 Illustrations. Crown 8vo., 5s.

THE RABBIT. By J. E. HARTING, etc. With Illustrations. [*In preparation.*

WILDFOWL. By the Hon. JOHN SCOTT MONTAGU, etc. With Illustrations, etc. [*In preparation.*

André.—*COLONEL BOGEY'S SKETCH-BOOK.* Comprising an Eccentric Collection of Scribbles and Scratches found in disused Lockers and swept up in the Pavilion, together with sundry After-Dinner Sayings of the Colonel. By R. ANDRÉ, West Herts Golf Club. Oblong 4to., 2s. 6d.

BADMINTON MAGAZINE (*THE*) *OF SPORTS AND PASTIMES.* Edited by ALFRED E. T. WATSON ("Rapier"). With numerous Illustrations. Price 1s. monthly.

Vols. I.-VI. 6s. each.

DEAD SHOT (*THE*): or, Sportsman's Complete Guide. Being a Treatise on the Use of the Gun, with Rudimentary and Finishing Lessons in the Art of Shooting Game of all kinds. Also Game-driving, Wildfowl and Pigeon-shooting, Dog-breaking, etc. By MARKSMAN. With numerous Illustrations. Crown 8vo., 10s. 6d.

Ellis.—*CHESS SPARKS;* or, Short and Bright Games of Chess. Collected and Arranged by J. H. ELLIS, M.A. 8vo., 4s. 6d.

Folkard.—*THE WILD-FOWLER:* A Treatise on Fowling, Ancient and Modern, descriptive also of Decoys and Flight-ponds, Wild-fowl Shooting, Gunning-punts, Shooting-yachts, etc. Also Fowling in the Fens and in Foreign Countries, Rock-fowling, etc., etc., by H. C. FOLKARD. With 13 Engravings on Steel, and several Woodcuts. 8vo., 12s. 6d.

Ford.—*THE THEORY AND PRACTICE OF ARCHERY.* By HORACE FORD. New Edition, thoroughly Revised and Re-written by W. BUTT, M.A. With a Preface by C. J. LONGMAN, M.A. 8vo., 14s.

Francis.—*A BOOK ON ANGLING:* or, Treatise on the Art of Fishing in every Branch; including full Illustrated List of Salmon Flies. By FRANCIS FRANCIS. With Portrait and Coloured Plates. Crown 8vo., 15s.

Sport and Pastime—*continued.*

Gibson.—*TOBOGGANING ON CROOKED RUNS.* By the Hon. HARRY GIBSON. With Contributions by F. DE B. STRICKLAND and 'LADY-TOBOGANNER'. With 40 Illustrations. Crown 8vo., 6s.

Graham.—*COUNTRY PASTIMES FOR BOYS.* By P. ANDERSON GRAHAM. With 252 Illustrations from Drawings and Photographs. Crown 8vo., 3s. 6d.

Lang.—*ANGLING SKETCHES.* By ANDREW LANG. With 20 Illustrations. Crown 8vo., 3s. 6d.

Lillie.—*CROQUET :* its History, Rules and Secrets. By ARTHUR LILLIE, Champion, Grand National Croquet Club, 1872; Winner of the 'All-Comers' Championship,' Maidstone, 1896. With 4 Full-page Illustrations by LUCIEN DAVIS, 15 Illustrations in the Text, and 27 Diagrams. Crown 8vo., 6s.

Longman.—*CHESS OPENINGS.* By FREDERICK W. LONGMAN. Fcp. 8vo., 2s. 6d.

Madden.—*THE DIARY OF MASTER WILLIAM SILENCE :* a Study of Shakespeare and of Elizabethan Sport. By the Right Hon. D. H. MADDEN, Vice-Chancellor of the University of Dublin. 8vo., 16s.

Maskelyne.—*SHARPS AND FLATS :* a Complete Revelation of the Secrets of Cheating at Games of Chance and Skill. By JOHN NEVIL MASKELYNE, of the Egyptian Hall. With 62 Illustrations. Crown 8vo., 6s.

Moffat.—*CRICKETY CRICKET:* Rhymes and Parodies. By DOUGLAS MOFFAT, with Frontispiece by Sir FRANK LOCKWOOD, Q.C., M.P., and 53 Illustrations by the Author. Crown 8vo, 2s. 6d.

Park.—*THE GAME OF GOLF.* By WILLIAM PARK, Jun., Champion Golfer, 1887-89. With 17 Plates and 26 Illustrations in the Text. Crown 8vo., 7s. 6d.

Payne-Gallwey (Sir RALPH, Bart.).

LETTERS TO YOUNG SHOOTERS (First Series). On the Choice and use of a Gun. With 41 Illustrations. Crown 8vo., 7s. 6d.

LETTERS TO YOUNG SHOOTERS (Second Series). On the Production, Preservation, and Killing of Game. With Directions in Shooting Wood-Pigeons and Breaking-in Retrievers. With Portrait and 103 Illustrations. Crown 8vo., 12s. 6d.

Payne-Gallwey (Sir RALPH, Bart.) —*continued.*

LETTERS TO YOUNG SHOOTERS. (Third Series.) Comprising a Short Natural History of the Wildfowl that are Rare or Common to the British Islands, with complete directions in Shooting Wildfowl on the Coast and Inland. With 200 Illustrations. Crown 8vo., 18s.

Pole (WILLIAM).

THE THEORY OF THE MODERN SCIENTIFIC GAME OF WHIST. Fcp. 8vo., 2s. 6d.

THE EVOLUTION OF WHIST: a Study of the Progressive Changes which the Game has undergone. Cr. 8vo., 2s. 6d.

Proctor.—*HOW TO PLAY WHIST : WITH THE LAWS AND ETIQUETTE OF WHIST.* By RICHARD A. PROCTOR. Crown 8vo., 3s. 6d.

Ribblesdale.—*THE QUEEN'S HOUNDS AND STAG-HUNTING RECOLLECTIONS.* By LORD RIBBLESDALE, Master of the Buckhounds, 1892-95. With Introductory Chapter on the Hereditary Mastership by E. BURROWS. With 24 Plates and 35 Illustrations in the Text. 8vo., 25s.

Ronalds.—*THE FLY-FISHER'S ENTOMOLOGY.* By ALFRED RONALDS. With 20 coloured Plates. 8vo., 14s.

Thompson and Cannan. *HAND-IN-HAND FIGURE SKATING.* By NORCLIFFE G. THOMPSON and F. LAURA CANNAN, Members of the Skating Club. With an Introduction by Captain J. H. THOMSON, R.A. With Illustrations and Diagrams. 16mo., 6s.

Watson.—*RACING AND 'CHASING :* a Collection of Sporting Stories. By ALFRED E. T. WATSON, Editor of the 'Badminton Magazine'. With 16 Plates and 36 Illustrations in the Text. Crown 8vo, 7s. 6d.

Wilcocks.—*THE SEA FISHERMAN :* Comprising the Chief Methods of Hook and Line Fishing in the British and other Seas, and Remarks on Nets, Boats, and Boating. By J. C. WILCOCKS. Illustrated. Cr. 8vo., 6s.

Mental, Moral, and Political Philosophy.

LOGIC, RHETORIC, PSYCHOLOGY, &C.

Abbott.—*THE ELEMENTS OF LOGIC.* By T. K. ABBOTT, B.D. 12mo., 3s.

Aristotle.

THE ETHICS: Greek Text, Illustrated with Essay and Notes. By Sir ALEXANDER GRANT, Bart. 2 vols. 8vo., 32s.

AN INTRODUCTION TO ARISTOTLE'S ETHICS. Books I.-IV. (Book X. c. vi.-ix. in an Appendix). With a continuous Analysis and Notes. By the Rev. E. MOORE, D.D. Crown 8vo. 10s. 6d.

Bacon (FRANCIS).

COMPLETE WORKS. Edited by R. L. ELLIS, JAMES SPEDDING and D. D. HEATH. 7 vols. 8vo., £3 13s. 6d.

LETTERS AND LIFE, including all his occasional Works. Edited by JAMES SPEDDING. 7 vols. 8vo., £4 4s.

THE ESSAYS: with Annotations. By RICHARD WHATELY, D.D. 8vo., 10s. 6d.

THE ESSAYS : with Notes. By F. STORR and C. H. GIBSON. Cr. 8vo, 3s. 6d.

THE ESSAYS : with Introduction, Notes, and Index. By E. A. ABBOTT, D.D. 2 Vols. Fcp. 8vo., 6s. The Text and Index only, without Introduction and Notes, in One Volume. Fcp. 8vo., 2s. 6d.

Bain (ALEXANDER).

MENTAL SCIENCE. Cr. 8vo., 6s. 6d.

MORAL SCIENCE. Cr. 8vo., 4s. 6d.

The two works as above can be had in one volume, price 10s. 6d.

SENSES AND THE INTELLECT. 8vo., 15s.

EMOTIONS AND THE WILL. 8vo., 15s.

LOGIC, DEDUCTIVE AND INDUCTIVE. Part I. 4s. Part II. 6s. 6d.

PRACTICAL ESSAYS. Cr. 8vo., 2s.

Baldwin.—*THE ELEMENTS OF EXPOSITORY CONSTRUCTION.* By Dr. CHARLES SEARS BALDWIN, Instructor in Rhetoric in Yale University.

Bray.—*THE PHILOSOPHY OF NECESSITY:* or, Law in Mind as in Matter. By CHARLES BRAY. Crown 8vo., 5s.

Crozier (JOHN BEATTIE).

CIVILISATION AND PROGRESS: being the Outlines of a New System of Political, Religious and Social Philosophy. 8vo., 14s.

HISTORY OF INTELLECTUAL DEVELOPMENT: on the Lines of Modern Evolution.

Vol. I. Greek and Hindoo Thought; Græco-Roman Paganism; Judaism; and Christianity down to the Closing of the Schools of Athens by Justinian, 529 A.D. 8vo., 14s.

Davidson.—*THE LOGIC OF DEFINITION,* Explained and Applied. By WILLIAM L. DAVIDSON, M.A. Crown 8vo., 6s.

Green (THOMAS HILL).—THE WORKS OF. Edited by R. L. NETTLESHIP.

Vols. I. and II. Philosophical Works. 8vo., 16s. each.

Vol. III. Miscellanies. With Index to the three Volumes, and Memoir. 8vo., 21s.

LECTURES ON THE PRINCIPLES OF POLITICAL OBLIGATION. With Preface by BERNARD BOSANQUET. 8vo., 5s.

Hodgson (SHADWORTH H.).

TIME AND SPACE : A Metaphysical Essay. 8vo., 16s.

THE THEORY OF PRACTICE : an Ethical Inquiry. 2 vols. 8vo., 24s.

THE PHILOSOPHY OF REFLECTION. 2 vols. 8vo., 21s.

THE METAPHYSIC OF EXPERIENCE. Book I. General Analysis of Experience ; Book II. Positive Science ; Book III. Analysis of Conscious Action ; Book IV. The Real Universe. 4 vols. 8vo.

Hume.—*THE PHILOSOPHICAL WORKS OF DAVID HUME.* Edited by T. H. GREEN and T. H. GROSE. 4 vols. 8vo., 56s. Or separately, Essays. 2 vols. 28s. Treatise of Human Nature. 2 vols. 28s.

James.—*THE WILL TO BELIEVE,* and Other Essays in Popular Philosophy. By WILLIAM JAMES, M.D., LL.D., etc. Crown 8vo., 7s. 6d.

Justinian.—*THE INSTITUTES OF JUSTINIAN :* Latin Text, chiefly that of Huschke, with English Introduction, Translation, Notes, and Summary. By THOMAS C. SANDARS, M.A. 8vo., 18s.

Kant (IMMANUEL).

CRITIQUE OF PRACTICAL REASON, AND OTHER WORKS ON THE THEORY OF ETHICS. Translated by T. K. ABBOTT, B.D. With Memoir. 8vo., 12s. 6d.

FUNDAMENTAL PRINCIPLES OF THE METAPHYSIC OF ETHICS. Translated by T. K. ABBOTT, B.D. Crown 8vo, 3s.

INTRODUCTION TO LOGIC, AND HIS ESSAY ON THE MISTAKEN SUBTILTY OF THE FOUR FIGURES.. Translated by T. K. ABBOTT. 8vo., 6s.

Killick.—*HANDBOOK TO MILL'S SYSTEM OF LOGIC.* By Rev. A. H. KILLICK, M.A. Crown 8vo., 3s. 6d.

Mental, Moral and Political Philosophy—*continued*.

LOGIC, RHETORIC, PSYCHOLOGY, &C.

Ladd (GEORGE TRUMBULL).

PHILOSOPHY OF KNOWLEDGE: an Inquiry into the Nature, Limits and Validity of Human Cognitive Faculty. 8vo., 18s.

PHILOSOPHY OF MIND: An Essay on the Metaphysics of Psychology. 8vo., 16s.

ELEMENTS OF PHYSIOLOGICAL PSYCHOLOGY. 8vo., 21s.

OUTLINES OF DESCRIPTIVE PSYCHOLOGY: a Text-Book of Mental Science for Colleges and Normal Schools. 8vo., 12s.

OUTLINES OF PHYSIOLOGICAL PSYCHOLOGY. 8vo., 12s.

PSYCHOLOGY, DESCRIPTIVE AND EXPLANATORY. 8vo., 21s.

PRIMER OF PSYCHOLOGY. Cr. 8vo., 5s. 6d.

Lewes.—*THE HISTORY OF PHILOSOPHY,* from Thales to Comte. By GEORGE HENRY LEWES. 2 vols. 8vo., 32s.

Lutoslawski.—*THE ORIGIN AND GROWTH OF PLATO'S LOGIC.* With an Account of Plato's Style and of the Chronology of his Writings. By WINCENTY LUTOSLAWSKI. 8vo., 21s.

Max Müller (F.).

THE SCIENCE OF THOUGHT. 8vo., 21s.

THREE INTRODUCTORY LECTURES ON THE SCIENCE OF THOUGHT. 8vo., 2s. 6d. net.

Mill.—*ANALYSIS OF THE PHENOMENA* OF THE HUMAN MIND. By JAMES MILL. 2 vols. 8vo., 28s.

Mill (JOHN STUART).

A SYSTEM OF LOGIC. Cr. 8vo., 3s. 6d.

ON LIBERTY. Crown 8vo., 1s. 4d.

CONSIDERATIONS ON REPRESENTATIVE GOVERNMENT. Crown 8vo., 2s.

UTILITARIANISM. 8vo., 2s. 6d.

EXAMINATION OF SIR WILLIAM HAMILTON'S PHILOSOPHY. 8vo., 16s.

NATURE, THE UTILITY OF RELIGION, AND THEISM. Three Essays. 8vo., 5s.

Monck.—*AN INTRODUCTION TO LOGIC.* By WILLIAM HENRY S. MONCK, M.A. Crown 8vo., 5s.

Romanes.—*MIND AND MOTION AND MONISM.* By GEORGE JOHN ROMANES, LL.D., F.R.S. Cr. 8vo., 4s. 6d.

Stock (ST. GEORGE).

DEDUCTIVE LOGIC. Fcp. 8vo., 3s. 6d.

LECTURES IN THE LYCEUM; or, Aristotle's Ethics for English Readers. Edited by ST. GEORGE STOCK. Crown 8vo., 7s. 6d.

Sully (JAMES).

THE HUMAN MIND: a Text-book of Psychology. 2 vols. 8vo., 21s.

OUTLINES OF PSYCHOLOGY. Crown 8vo., 9s.

THE TEACHER'S HANDBOOK OF PSYCHOLOGY. Crown 8vo., 6s. 6d.

STUDIES OF CHILDHOOD. 8vo., 10s. 6d.

CHILDREN'S WAYS: being Selections from the Author's ' Studies of Childhood '. With 25 Illustrations. Crown 8vo., 4s. 6d.

Sutherland. — *THE ORIGIN AND GROWTH OF THE MORAL INSTINCT.* By ALEXANDER SUTHERLAND, M.A. 2 vols. 8vo, 28s.

Swinburne. — *PICTURE LOGIC:* an Attempt to Popularise the Science of Reasoning. By ALFRED JAMES SWINBURNE, M.A. With 23 Woodcuts. Crown 8vo., 5s.

Webb.—*THE VEIL OF ISIS:* a Series of Essays on Idealism. By THOMAS E. WEBB, LL.D., Q.C. 8vo., 10s. 6d.

Weber.—*HISTORY OF PHILOSOPHY.* By ALFRED WEBER, Professor in the University of Strasburg. Translated by FRANK THILLY, Ph.D. 8vo., 16s.

Whately (ARCHBISHOP).

BACON'S ESSAYS. With Annotations. 8vo., 10s. 6d.

ELEMENTS OF LOGIC. Cr. 8vo., 4s. 6d.

ELEMENTS OF RHETORIC. Cr. 8vo., 4s. 6d.

LESSONS ON REASONING. Fcp. 8vo., 1s. 6d.

Zeller (Dr. EDWARD).

THE STOICS, EPICUREANS, AND SCEPTICS. Translated by the Rev. O. J. REICHEL, M.A. Crown 8vo., 15s.

OUTLINES OF THE HISTORY OF GREEK PHILOSOPHY. Translated by SARAH F. ALLEYNE and EVELYN ABBOTT, M.A., LL.D. Crown 8vo., 10s. 6d.

PLATO AND THE OLDER ACADEMY. Translated by SARAH F. ALLEYNE and ALFRED GOODWIN, B.A. Crown 8vo., 18s.

SOCRATES AND THE SOCRATIC SCHOOLS. Translated by the Rev. O. J. REICHEL, M.A. Crown 8vo., 10s. 6d.

ARISTOTLE AND THE EARLIER PERIPATETICS. Translated by B. F. C. COSTELLOE, M.A., and J. H. MUIRHEAD, M.A. 2 vols. Crown 8vo., 24s.

Mental, Moral, and Political Philosophy—*continued*.
MANUALS OF CATHOLIC PHILOSOPHY.
(Stonyhurst Series.)

A MANUAL OF POLITICAL ECONOMY. By C. S. DEVAS, M.A. Crown 8vo., 6s. 6d.

FIRST PRINCIPLES OF KNOWLEDGE. By JOHN RICKABY, S.J. Crown 8vo., 5s.

GENERAL METAPHYSICS. By JOHN RICKABY, S.J. Crown 8vo., 5s.

LOGIC. By RICHARD F. CLARKE, S.J. Crown 8vo., 5s.

MORAL PHILOSOPHY (ETHICS AND NATURAL LAW). By JOSEPH RICKABY, S.J. Crown 8vo., 5s.

NATURAL THEOLOGY. By BERNARD BOEDDER, S.J. Crown 8vo., 6s. 6d.

PSYCHOLOGY. By MICHAEL MAHER, S.J. Crown 8vo., 6s. 6d.

History and Science of Language, &c.

Davidson.—*LEADING AND IMPORTANT ENGLISH WORDS*: Explained and Exemplified. By WILLIAM L. DAVIDSON, M.A. Fcp. 8vo., 3s. 6d.

Farrar.—*LANGUAGE AND LANGUAGES:* By F. W. FARRAR, D.D., Dean of Canterbury. Crown 8vo., 6s.

Graham. — *ENGLISH SYNONYMS*, Classified and Explained: with Practical Exercises. By G. F. GRAHAM. Fcp. 8vo., 6s.

Max Müller (F.).

THE SCIENCE OF LANGUAGE.—Founded on Lectures delivered at the Royal Institution in 1861 and 1863. 2 vols. Crown 8vo., 21s.

Max Müller (F.)—*continued.*

BIOGRAPHIES OF WORDS, AND THE HOME OF THE ARYAS. Crown 8vo., 7s. 6d.

THREE LECTURES ON THE SCIENCE OF LANGUAGE, AND ITS PLACE IN GENERAL EDUCATION, delivered at Oxford, 1889. Crown 8vo., 3s. net.

Roget.—*THESAURUS OF ENGLISH WORDS AND PHRASES.* Classified and Arranged so as to Facilitate the Expression of Ideas and assist in Literary Composition. By PETER MARK ROGET, M.D., F.R.S. With full Index. Crown 8vo., 10s. 6d.

Whately.—*ENGLISH SYNONYMS.* By E. JANE WHATELY. Fcp. 8vo., 3s.

Political Economy and Economics.

Ashley.—*ENGLISH ECONOMIC HISTORY AND THEORY.* By W. J. ASHLEY, M.A. Crown 8vo., Part I., 5s. Part II., 10s. 6d.

Bagehot.—*ECONOMIC STUDIES.* By WALTER BAGEHOT. Crown 8vo., 3s. 6d.

Barnett.—*PRACTICABLE SOCIALISM.* Essays on Social Reform. By the Rev. S. A. BARNETT, M.A., Canon of Bristol, and Mrs. BARNETT. Crown 8vo., 6s.

Brassey.—*PAPERS AND ADDRESSES ON WORK AND WAGES.* By Lord BRASSEY. Edited by J. POTTER, and with Introduction by GEORGE HOWELL, M.P. Crown 8vo., 5s.

Channing.—*THE TRUTH ABOUT AGRICULTURAL DEPRESSION*: an Economic Study of the Evidence of the Royal Commission. By FRANCIS ALLSTON CHANNING, M.P., one of the Commission. Crown 8vo., 6s.

Devas.—*A MANUAL OF POLITICAL ECONOMY.* By C. S. DEVAS, M.A. Cr. 8vo., 6s. 6d. (*Manuals of Catholic Philosophy.*)

Dowell.—*A HISTORY OF TAXATION AND TAXES IN ENGLAND*, from the Earliest Times to the Year 1885. By STEPHEN DOWELL, (4 vols. 8vo). Vols. I. and II. The History of Taxation, 21s. Vols. III. and IV. The History of Taxes, 21s.

Jordan.—*THE STANDARD OF VALUE.* By WILLIAM LEIGHTON JORDAN. Cr. 8vo., 6s.

Leslie.—*ESSAYS ON POLITICAL ECONOMY.* By T. E. CLIFFE LESLIE, Hon. LL.D., Dubl. 8vo, 10s. 6d.

Macleod (HENRY DUNNING).

BIMETALISM. 8vo., 5s. net.

THE ELEMENTS OF BANKING. Cr. 8vo., 3s. 6d.

THE THEORY AND PRACTICE OF BANKING. Vol. I. 8vo., 12s. Vol. II. 14s.

THE THEORY OF CREDIT. 8vo. In 1 Vol., 30s. net; or separately, Vol. I., 10s. net. Vol. II., Part I., 10s. net. Vol. II., Part II., 10s. net.

A DIGEST OF THE LAW OF BILLS OF EXCHANGE, BANK-NOTES, &c. 8vo., 5s. net.

THE BANKING SYSTEM OF ENGLAND. [*In preparation.*

Political Economy and Economics—*continued.*

Mill.—*POLITICAL ECONOMY.* By JOHN STUART MILL.
Popular Edition. Crown 8vo., 3s. 6d.
Library Edition. 2 vols. 8vo., 30s.

Mulhall.—*INDUSTRIES AND WEALTH OF NATIONS.* By MICHAEL G. MULHALL, F.S.S. With 32 full-page Diagrams. Crown 8vo., 8s. 6d.

Soderini.—*SOCIALISM AND CATHOLICISM.* From the Italian of Count EDWARD SODERINI. By RICHARD JENERY-SHEE. With a Preface by Cardinal VAUGHAN. Crown 8vo., 6s.

Symes.—*POLITICAL ECONOMY*: a Short Text-book of Political Economy. With Problems for Solution, and Hints for Supplementary Reading; also a Supplementary Chapter on Socialism. By Professor J. E. SYMES, M.A., of University College, Nottingham. Crown 8vo., 2s. 6d.

Toynbee.—*LECTURES ON THE INDUSTRIAL REVOLUTION OF THE 18TH CENTURY IN ENGLAND*: Popular Addresses, Notes and other Fragments. By ARNOLD TOYNBEE. With a Memoir of the Author by BENJAMIN JOWETT, D.D. 8vo., 10s. 6d.

Webb (SIDNEY and BEATRICE).

THE HISTORY OF TRADE UNIONISM. With Map and full Bibliography of the Subject. 8vo., 18s.

INDUSTRIAL DEMOCRACY: a Study in Trade Unionism. 2 vols. 8vo., 25s. net.

PROBLEMS OF MODERN INDUSTRY: Essays.

STUDIES IN ECONOMICS AND POLITICAL SCIENCE.

Issued under the auspices of the London School of Economics and Political Science.

THE HISTORY OF LOCAL RATES IN ENGLAND: Five Lectures. By EDWIN CANNAN, M.A. Crown 8vo., 2s. 6d.

GERMAN SOCIAL DEMOCRACY. By BERTRAND RUSSELL, B.A. With an Appendix on Social Democracy and the Woman Question in Germany by ALYS RUSSELL, B.A. Crown 8vo., 3s. 6d.

SELECT DOCUMENTS ILLUSTRATING THE HISTORY OF TRADE UNIONISM.
  1. The Tailoring Trade. Edited by W. F. GALTON. With a Preface by SIDNEY WEBB, LL.B. Crown 8vo., 5s.

DEPLOIGE'S REFERENDUM EN SUISSE. Translated, with Introduction and Notes, by C. P. TREVELYAN, M.A. [*In preparation.*

SELECT DOCUMENTS ILLUSTRATING THE STATE REGULATION OF WAGES. Edited, with Introduction and Notes, by W. A. S. HEWINS, M.A. [*In preparation.*

HUNGARIAN GILD RECORDS. Edited by Dr. JULIUS MANDELLO, of Budapest. [*In preparation.*

THE RELATIONS BETWEEN ENGLAND AND THE HANSEATIC LEAGUE. By Miss E. A. MacARTHUR. [*In preparation.*

Evolution, Anthropology, &c.

Clodd (EDWARD).

THE STORY OF CREATION: a Plain Account of Evolution. With 77 Illustrations. Crown 8vo., 3s. 6d.

A PRIMER OF EVOLUTION: being a Popular Abridged Edition of 'The Story of Creation'. With Illustrations. Fcp. 8vo., 1s. 6d.

Lang.—*CUSTOM AND MYTH*: Studies of Early Usage and Belief. By ANDREW LANG. With 15 Illustrations. Crown 8vo., 3s. 6d.

Lubbock.—*THE ORIGIN OF CIVILISATION*, and the Primitive Condition of Man. By Sir J. LUBBOCK, Bart., M.P. With 5 Plates and 20 Illustrations in the Text. 8vo., 18s.

Romanes (GEORGE JOHN).

DARWIN, AND AFTER DARWIN: an Exposition of the Darwinian Theory, and a Discussion on Post-Darwinian Questions.
  Part I. THE DARWINIAN THEORY. With Portrait of Darwin and 125 Illustrations. Crown 8vo., 10s. 6d.
  Part II. POST-DARWINIAN QUESTIONS: Heredity and Utility. With Portrait of the Author and 5 Illustrations. Cr. 8vo., 10s. 6d.
  Part III. Post-Darwinian Questions: Isolation and Physiological Selection. Crown 8vo., 5s.

AN EXAMINATION OF WEISMANNISM. Crown 8vo., 6s.

ESSAYS. Edited by C. LLOYD MORGAN, Principal of University College, Bristol. Crown 8vo., 6s.

Classical Literature, Translations, &c.

Abbott.—*HELLENICA.* A Collection of Essays on Greek Poetry, Philosophy, History, and Religion. Edited by EVELYN ABBOTT, M.A., LL.D. Crown 8vo., 7s. 6d.

Æschylus.—*EUMENIDES OF ÆSCHYLUS.* With Metrical English Translation. By J. F. DAVIES. 8vo., 7s.

Aristophanes. — *THE ACHARNIANS OF ARISTOPHANES,* translated into English Verse. By R. Y. TYRRELL. Crown 8vo., 1s.

Aristotle.—*YOUTH AND OLD AGE, LIFE AND DEATH, AND RESPIRATION.* Translated, with Introduction and Notes, by W. OGLE, M.A., M.D. 8vo., 7s. 6d.

Becker (W. A.), Translated by the Rev. F. METCALFE, B.D.

GALLUS : or, Roman Scenes in the Time of Augustus. With Notes and Excursuses. With 26 Illustrations. Post 8vo., 3s. 6d.

CHARICLES : or, Illustrations of the Private Life of the Ancient Greeks. With Notes and Excursuses. With 26 Illustrations. Post 8vo., 3s. 6d.

Butler.—*THE AUTHORESS OF THE ODYSSEY, WHERE AND WHEN SHE WROTE, WHO SHE WAS, THE USE SHE MADE OF THE ILIAD, AND HOW THE POEM GREW UNDER HER HANDS.* By SAMUEL BUTLER, Author of ' Erewhon,' etc. With Illustrations and 4 Maps. 8vo., 10s. 6d.

Cicero.—*CICERO'S CORRESPONDENCE.* By R. Y. TYRRELL. Vols. I., II., III., 8vo., each 12s. Vol. IV., 15s. Vol. V., 14s.

Egbert.—*INTRODUCTION TO THE STUDY OF LATIN INSCRIPTIONS.* By JAMES C. EGBERT, Junr., Ph.D. With numerous Illustrations and Facsimiles. Square crown 8vo., 16s.

Horace.—*THE WORKS OF HORACE, RENDERED INTO ENGLISH PROSE.* With Life, Introduction and Notes. By WILLIAM COUTTS, M.A. Crown 8vo., 5s. net.

Lang.—*HOMER AND THE EPIC.* By ANDREW LANG. Crown 8vo., 9s. net.

Lucan.—*THE PHARSALIA OF LUCAN.* Translated into Blank Verse. By Sir EDWARD RIDLEY. 8vo., 14s.

Mackail.—*SELECT EPIGRAMS FROM THE GREEK ANTHOLOGY.* By J. W. MACKAIL. Edited with a Revised Text, Introduction, Translation, and Notes. 8vo., 16s.

Rich.—*A DICTIONARY OF ROMAN AND GREEK ANTIQUITIES.* By A. RICH, B.A. With 2000 Woodcuts. Crown 8vo., 7s. 6d.

Sophocles.—Translated into English Verse. By ROBERT WHITELAW, M.A., Assistant Master in Rugby School. Cr. 8vo., 8s. 6d.

Tacitus. — *THE HISTORY OF P. CORNELIUS TACITUS.* Translated into English, with an Introduction and Notes, Critical and Explanatory, by ALBERT WILLIAM QUILL, M.A., T.C.D. 2 vols. Vol. I. 8vo., 7s. 6d. Vol. II. 8vo., 12s. 6d.

Tyrrell. — *DUBLIN TRANSLATIONS INTO GREEK AND LATIN VERSE.* Edited by R. Y. TYRRELL. 8vo., 6s.

Virgil.

THE ÆNEID OF VIRGIL. Translated into English Verse by JOHN CONINGTON. Crown 8vo., 6s.

THE POEMS OF VIRGIL. Translated into English Prose by JOHN CONINGTON. Crown 8vo., 6s.

THE ÆNEID OF VIRGIL, freely translated into English Blank Verse. By W. J. THORNHILL. Crown 8vo., 7s. 6d.

THE ÆNEID OF VIRGIL. Translated into English Verse by JAMES RHOADES. Books I.-VI. Crown 8vo., 5s. Books VII.-XII. Crown 8vo., 5s.

Wilkins.—*THE GROWTH OF THE HOMERIC POEMS.* By G. WILKINS. 8vo., 6s.

Poetry and the Drama.

Allingham (WILLIAM).

IRISH SONGS AND POEMS. With Frontispiece of the Waterfall of Asaroe. Fcp. 8vo., 6s.

LAURENCE BLOOMFIELD. With Portrait of the Author. Fcp. 8vo., 3s. 6d.

FLOWER PIECES ; DAY AND NIGHT SONGS ; BALLADS. With 2 Designs by D. G. ROSSETTI. Fcp. 8vo., 6s. large paper edition, 12s.

Allingham (WILLIAM)—*continued.*

LIFE AND PHANTASY : with Frontispiece by Sir J. E. MILLAIS, Bart., and Design by ARTHUR HUGHES. Fcp. 8vo., 6s. ; large paper edition, 12s.

THOUGHT AND WORD, AND ASHBY MANOR : a Play. Fcp. 8vo., 6s. ; large paper edition, 12s.

BLACKBERRIES. Imperial 16mo., 6s.

Sets of the above 6 vols. may be had in uniform Half-parchment binding, price 30s.

Poetry and the Drama—*continued.*

Armstrong (G. F. Savage).

Poems : Lyrical and Dramatic. Fcp. 8vo., 6s.

King Saul. (The Tragedy of Israel, Part I.) Fcp. 8vo., 5s.

King David. (The Tragedy of Israel, Part II.) Fcp. 8vo., 6s.

King Solomon. (The Tragedy of Israel, Part III.) Fcp. 8vo., 6s.

Ugone : a Tragedy. Fcp. 8vo., 6s.

A Garland from Greece : Poems. Fcp. 8vo., 7s. 6d.

Stories of Wicklow : Poems. Fcp. 8vo., 7s. 6d.

Mephistopheles in Broadcloth : a Satire. Fcp. 8vo., 4s.

One in the Infinite : a Poem. Crown 8vo., 7s. 6d.

Armstrong.—*The Poetical Works of Edmund J. Armstrong.* Fcp. 8vo., 5s.

Arnold.—*The Light of the World:* or, The Great Consummation. By Sir Edwin Arnold. With 14 Illustrations after Holman Hunt. Crown 8vo., 6s.

Beesly (A. H.).

Ballads and other Verse. Fcp. 8vo., 5s.

Danton, and other Verse. Fcp. 8vo., 4s. 6d.

Bell (Mrs. Hugh).

Chamber Comedies : a Collection of Plays and Monologues for the Drawing Room. Crown 8vo., 6s.

Fairy Tale Plays, and How to Act Them. With 91 Diagrams and 52 Illustrations. Crown 8vo., 6s.

Cochrane (Alfred).

The Kestrel's Nest, and other Verses. Fcp. 8vo., 3s. 6d.

Leviore Plectro : Occasional Verses. Fcap. 8vo., 3s. 6d.

Douglas.—*Poems of a Country Gentleman.* By Sir George Douglas, Bart., Author of 'The Fireside Tragedy'. Crown 8vo., 3s. 6d.

Goethe.

Faust, Part I., the German Text, with Introduction and Notes. By Albert M. Selss, Ph.D., M.A. Crown 8vo., 5s.

The First Part of the Tragedy of Faust in English. By Thos. E. Webb, LL.D., sometime Fellow of Trinity College ; Professor of Moral Philosophy in the University of Dublin, etc. New and Cheaper Edition, with *The Death of Faust,* from the Second Part. Crown 8vo., 6s.

Gurney (Rev. Alfred, M.A.).

Day-Dreams : Poems. Crown 8vo., 3s. 6d.

Love's Fruition, and other Poems. Fcp. 8vo., 2s. 6d.

Ingelow (Jean).

Poetical Works. Complete in One Volume. Crown 8vo., 7s. 6d.

Poetical Works. 2 vols. Fcp. 8vo., 12s.

Lyrical and other Poems. Selected from the Writings of Jean Ingelow. Fcp. 8vo., 2s. 6d. cloth plain, 3s. cloth gilt.

Lang (Andrew).

Grass of Parnassus. Fcp. 8vo., 2s. 6d. net.

The Blue Poetry Book. Edited by Andrew Lang. With 100 Illustrations. Crown 8vo., 6s.

Layard and Corder.—*Songs in Many Moods.* By Nina F. Layard ; *The Wandering Albatross,* etc. By Annie Corder. In One Volume. Crown 8vo., 5s.

Lecky.—*Poems.* By the Right Hon. W. E. H. Lecky. Fcp. 8vo., 5s.

Lytton (The Earl of), (Owen Meredith).

Marah. Fcp. 8vo., 6s. 6d.

King Poppy : a Fantasia. With 1 Plate and Design on Title-Page by Sir Edward Burne-Jones, Bart. Crown 8vo., 10s. 6d.

The Wanderer. Cr. 8vo., 10s. 6d.

Lucile. Crown 8vo., 10s. 6d.

Selected Poems. Cr. 8vo., 10s. 6d.

Poetry and the Drama—*continued*.

Macaulay.—*Lays of Ancient Rome, with 'Ivry' and 'The Armada'.* By Lord Macaulay.

Illustrated by G. Scharf. Fcp. 4to., 10s. 6d.

———————— Bijou Edition. 18mo., 2s. 6d. gilt top.

———————— Popular Edition. Fcp. 4to., 6d. sewed, 1s. cloth.

Illustrated by J. R. Weguelin. Crown 8vo., 3s. 6d.

Annotated Edition. Fcp. 8vo., 1s. sewed, 1s. 6d. cloth.

MacDonald (George, LL.D.).

A Book of Strife, in the Form of the Diary of an Old Soul : Poems. 18mo., 6s.

Rampolli : Growths from a Long-Planted Root : being Translations, New and Old (mainly in verse), chiefly from the German ; along with 'A Year's Diary of an Old Soul '. Crown 8vo., 6s.

Moffat.—*Crickety Cricket:* Rhymes and Parodies. By Douglas Moffat. With Frontispiece by Sir Frank Lockwood, Q.C., M.P., and 53 Illustrations by the Author. Crown 8vo, 2s. 6d.

Morris (William).

Poetical Works—Library Edition. Complete in Ten Volumes. Crown 8vo., price 6s. each.

The Earthly Paradise. 4 vols. 6s. each.

The Life and Death of Jason. 6s.

The Defence of Guenevere, and other Poems. 6s.

The Story of Sigurd the Volsung, and The Fall of the Niblungs. 6s.

Love is Enough ; or, the Freeing of Pharamond : A Morality ; and *Poems by the Way.* 6s.

The Odyssey of Homer. Done into English Verse. 6s.

The Æneids of Virgil. Done into English Verse. 6s.

———

Certain of the Poetical Works may also be had in the following Editions :—

The Earthly Paradise.
Popular Edition. 5 vols. 12mo., 25s. ; or 5s. each, sold separately.
The same in Ten Parts, 25s.; or 2s. 6d. each, sold separately.
Cheap Edition, in 1 vol. Crown 8vo., 7s. 6d.

Morris (William)—*continued.*

Poems by the Way. Square crown 8vo., 6s.

**** For Mr. William Morris's Prose Works, see pp. 22 and 31.

Nesbit.—*Lays and Legends.* By E. Nesbit (Mrs. Hubert Bland). First Series. Crown 8vo., 3s. 6d. Second Series. With Portrait. Crown 8vo., 5s.

Riley (James Whitcomb).

Old Fashioned Roses : Poems. 12mo., 5s.

A Child-World : Poems. Fcp. 8vo., 5s.

Poems : Here at Home. 16mo, 6s. net.

Rubáiyát of Doc Sifers. With 43 Illustrations by C. M Relyea. Crown 8vo.

Romanes.—*A Selection from the Poems of George John Romanes, M.A., LL.D., F.R.S.* With an Introduction by T. Herbert Warren, President of Magdalen College, Oxford. Crown 8vo., 4s. 6d.

Russell.—*Sonnets on the Sonnet :* an Anthology. Compiled by the Rev. Matthew Russell, S.J. Crown 8vo., 3s. 6d.

Shakespeare.—*Bowdler's Family Shakespeare.* With 36 Woodcuts. 1 vol. 8vo., 14s. Or in 6 vols. Fcp. 8vo., 21s.

The Shakespeare Birthday Book. By Mary F. Dunbar. 32mo., 1s. 6d.

Tupper.—*Poems.* By John Lucas Tupper. Selected and Edited by William Michael Rossetti. Crown 8vo., 5s.

Wordsworth. — *Selected Poems.* By Andrew Lang. With Photogravure Frontispiece of Rydal Mount. With 16 Illustrations and numerous Initial Letters. By Alfred Parsons, A.R.A. Crown 8vo., gilt edges, 3s. 6d.

Wordsworth and Coleridge.—*A Description of the Wordsworth and Coleridge Manuscripts in the Possession of Mr. T. Norton Longman.* Edited, with Notes, by W. Hale White. With 3 Facsimile Reproductions. 4to., 10s. 6d.

Fiction, Humour, &c.

Allingham.—*CROOKED PATHS.* By FRANCIS ALLINGHAM. Crown 8vo., 6s

Anstey.—*VOCES POPULI.* Reprinted from 'Punch'. By F. ANSTEY, Author of 'Vice Versâ'. First Series. With 20 Illustrations by J. BERNARD PARTRIDGE. Crown 8vo., 3s. 6d.

Beaconsfield (THE EARL OF).

NOVELS AND TALES. Complete in 11 vols. Crown 8vo., 1s. 6d. each.

Vivian Grey.	Sybil.
The Young Duke, etc.	Henrietta Temple.
Alroy, Ixion, etc.	Venetia.
Contarini Fleming, etc.	Coningsby.
	Lothair.
Tancred.	Endymion.

NOVELS AND TALES. The Hughenden Edition. With 2 Portraits and 11 Vignettes. 11 vols. Crown 8vo., 42s.

Deland (MARGARET).

PHILIP AND HIS WIFE. Crown 8vo., 2s. 6d.

THE WISDOM OF FOOLS. Stories. Crown 8vo., 5s.

Diderot. — *RAMEAU'S NEPHEW:* a Translation from Diderot's Autographic Text. By SYLVIA MARGARET HILL. Crown 8vo., 3s. 6d.

Dougall.—*BEGGARS ALL.* By L. DOUGALL. Crown 8vo., 3s. 6d.

Doyle (A. CONAN).

MICAH CLARKE: A Tale of Monmouth's Rebellion. With 10 Illustrations. Cr. 8vo., 3s. 6d.

THE CAPTAIN OF THE POLESTAR, and other Tales. Cr. 8vo., 3s. 6d.

THE REFUGEES: A Tale of the Huguenots. With 25 Illustrations. Cr. 8vo., 3s. 6d.

THE STARK MUNRO LETTERS. Cr. 8vo, 3s. 6d.

Farrar (F. W., DEAN OF CANTERBURY).

DARKNESS AND DAWN: or, Scenes in the Days of Nero. An Historic Tale. Cr. 8vo., 7s. 6d.

GATHERING CLOUDS: a Tale of the Days of St. Chrysostom. Cr. 8vo., 7s. 6d.

Fowler (EDITH H.).

THE YOUNG PRETENDERS. A Story of Child Life. With 12 Illustrations by PHILIP BURNE-JONES. Crown 8vo., 6s.

THE PROFESSOR'S CHILDREN. With 24 Illustrations by ETHEL KATE BURGESS. Crown 8vo., 6s.

Froude.—*THE TWO CHIEFS OF DUNBOY:* an Irish Romance of the Last Century. By JAMES A. FROUDE. Cr. 8vo., 3s. 6d.

Gilkes.—*KALLISTRATUS:* an Autobiography. A Story of Hannibal and the Second Punic War. By A. H. GILKES, M.A., Master of Dulwich College. With 3 Illustrations by MAURICE GREIFFENHAGEN. Crown 8vo., 6s.

Graham.—*THE RED SCAUR:* A Story of the North Country. By P. ANDERSON GRAHAM. Crown 8vo., 6s.

Gurdon.—*MEMORIES AND FANCIES:* Suffolk Tales and other Stories; Fairy Legends; Poems; Miscellaneous Articles. By the late LADY CAMILLA GURDON, Author of 'Suffolk Folk-Lore'. Crown 8vo., 5s.

Haggard (H. RIDER).

HEART OF THE WORLD. With 15 Illustrations. Crown 8vo., 3s. 6d.

JOAN HASTE. With 20 Illustrations. Crown 8vo., 3s. 6d.

THE PEOPLE OF THE MIST. With 16 Illustrations. Crown 8vo., 3s. 6d.

MONTEZUMA'S DAUGHTER. With 24 Illustrations. Crown 8vo., 3s. 6d.

SHE. With 32 Illustrations. Crown 8vo., 3s. 6d.

ALLAN QUATERMAIN. With 31 Illustrations. Crown 8vo., 3s. 6d.

MAIWA'S REVENGE: Cr. 8vo., 1s. 6d.

COLONEL QUARITCH, V.C. With Frontispiece and Vignette. Cr. 8vo., 3s. 6d.

CLEOPATRA. With 29 Illustrations. Crown 8vo., 3s. 6d.

Fiction, Humour, &c.—*continued.*

Haggard (H. RIDER)—*continued.*

BEATRICE. With Frontispiece and Vignette. Cr. 8vo., 3s. 6d.

ERIC BRIGHTEYES. With 51 Illustrations. Crown 8vo., 3s. 6d.

NADA THE LILY. With 23 Illustrations. Crown 8vo., 3s. 6d.

ALLAN'S WIFE. With 34 Illustrations. Crown 8vo., 3s. 6d.

THE WITCH'S HEAD. With 16 Illustrations. Crown 8vo., 3s. 6d.

MR. MEESON'S WILL. With 16 Illustrations. Crown 8vo., 3s. 6d.

DAWN. With 16 Illustrations. Cr. 8vo., 3s. 6d.

Harte.—*IN THE CARQUINEZ WOODS* and other stories. By BRET HARTE. Cr. 8vo., 3s. 6d.

Hope.—*THE HEART OF PRINCESS OSRA.* By ANTHONY HOPE. With 9 Illustrations by JOHN WILLIAMSON. Crown 8vo., 6s.

Hornung.—*THE UNBIDDEN GUEST.* By E. W. HORNUNG. Crown 8vo., 3s. 6d.

Jerome.—*SKETCHES IN LAVENDER: BLUE AND GREEN.* By JEROME K. JEROME, Author of 'Three Men in a Boat,' etc. Crown 8vo., 6s.

Joyce.—*OLD CELTIC ROMANCES.* Twelve of the most beautiful of the Ancient Irish Romantic Tales. Translated from the Gaelic. By P. W. JOYCE, LL.D. Crown 8vo., 3s. 6d.

Lang.—*A MONK OF FIFE;* a Story of the Days of Joan of Arc. By ANDREW LANG. With 13 Illustrations by SELWYN IMAGE. Crown 8vo., 3s. 6d.

Levett-Yeats (S.).

THE CHEVALIER D'AURIAC. Crown 8vo., 6s.

A GALAHAD OF THE CREEKS, and other Stories. Crown 8vo., 6s.

Lyall (EDNA).

THE AUTOBIOGRAPHY OF A SLANDER. Fcp. 8vo., 1s., sewed.

Presentation Edition. With 20 Illustrations by LANCELOT SPEED. Crown 8vo., 2s. 6d. net.

THE AUTOBIOGRAPHY OF A TRUTH. Fcp. 8vo., 1s., sewed; 1s. 6d., cloth.

DOREEN. The Story of a Singer. Crown 8vo., 6s.

WAYFARING MEN. Crown 8vo., 6s.

Melville (G. J. WHYTE).

The Gladiators.	Holmby House.
The Interpreter.	Kate Coventry.
Good for Nothing.	Digby Grand.
The Queen's Maries.	General Bounce.

Crown 8vo., 1s. 6d. each.

Merriman.—*FLOTSAM:* A Story of the Indian Mutiny. By HENRY SETON MERRIMAN. With Frontispiece and Vignette by H. G. MASSEY, A.R.E. Crown 8vo., 3s. 6d.

Morris (WILLIAM).

THE SUNDERING FLOOD. Cr. 8vo., 7s. 6d.

THE WATER OF THE WONDROUS ISLES. Crown 8vo., 7s. 6d.

THE WELL AT THE WORLD'S END. 2 vols. 8vo., 28s.

THE STORY OF THE GLITTERING PLAIN, which has been also called The Land of the Living Men, or The Acre of the Undying. Square post 8vo., 5s. net.

THE ROOTS OF THE MOUNTAINS, wherein is told somewhat of the Lives of the Men of Burgdale, their Friends, their Neighbours, their Foemen, and their Fellows-in-Arms. Written in Prose and Verse. Square crown 8vo., 8s.

A TALE OF THE HOUSE OF THE WOLFINGS, and all the Kindreds of the Mark. Written in Prose and Verse. Square crown 8vo., 6s.

A DREAM OF JOHN BALL, AND A KING'S LESSON. 12mo., 1s. 6d.

NEWS FROM NOWHERE; or, An Epoch of Rest. Being some Chapters from an Utopian Romance. Post 8vo., 1s. 6d.

** For Mr. William Morris's Poetical Works, see p. 20.

Newman (CARDINAL).

LOSS AND GAIN: The Story of a Convert. Crown 8vo. Cabinet Edition, 6s.; Popular Edition, 3s. 6d.

CALLISTA: A Tale of the Third Century. Crown 8vo. Cabinet Edition, 6s.; Popular Edition, 3s. 6d.

Oliphant.—*OLD MR. TREDGOLD.* By Mrs. OLIPHANT. Crown 8vo., 2s. 6d.

Phillipps-Wolley.—*SNAP:* a Legend of the Lone Mountain. By C. PHILLIPPS-WOLLEY. With 13 Illustrations. Crown 8vo., 3s. 6d.

Quintana.—*THE CID CAMPEADOR:* an Historical Romance. By D. ANTONIO DE TRUEBA Y LA QUINTANA. Translated from the Spanish by HENRY J. GILL, M.A., T.C.D. Crown 8vo., 6s.

Fiction, Humour, &c.—*continued.*

Rhoscomyl (OWEN).

THE JEWEL OF YNYS GALON: being a hitherto unprinted Chapter in the History of the Sea Rovers. With 12 Illustrations by LANCELOT SPEED. Cr. 8vo., 3s. 6d.

BATTLEMENT AND TOWER: a Romance. With Frontispiece by R. CATON WOODVILLE. Crown 8vo., 6s.

FOR THE WHITE ROSE OF ARNO: a Story of the Jacobite Rising of 1745. Crown 8vo., 6s.

Sewell (ELIZABETH M.).

A Glimpse of the World	Amy Herbert
Laneton Parsonage.	Cleve Hall.
Margaret Percival.	Gertrude.
Katharine Ashton.	Home Life.
The Earl's Daughter.	After Life.
The Experience of Life.	Ursula. Ivors.

Cr. 8vo., 1s. 6d. each cloth plain. 2s. 6d. each cloth extra, gilt edges.

Stevenson (ROBERT LOUIS).

THE STRANGE CASE OF DR. JEKYLL AND MR. HYDE. Fcp. 8vo., 1s. sewed. 1s. 6d. cloth.

THE STRANGE CASE OF DR. JEKYLL AND MR. HYDE; WITH OTHER FABLES. Crown 8vo., 3s. 6d.

MORE NEW ARABIAN NIGHTS—THE DYNAMITER. By ROBERT LOUIS STEVENSON and FANNY VAN DE GRIFT STEVENSON. Crown 8vo., 3s. 6d.

THE WRONG BOX. By ROBERT LOUIS STEVENSON and LLOYD OSBOURNE. Crown 8vo., 3s. 6d.

Suttner.—*LAY DOWN YOUR ARMS* (*Die Waffen Nieder*): The Autobiography of Martha von Tilling. By BERTHA VON SUTTNER. Translated by T. HOLMES. Cr. 8vo., 1s. 6d.

Taylor. — *EARLY ITALIAN LOVE-STORIES.* Edited and Retold by UNA TAYLOR. With 12 Illustrations by H. J. FORD.

Trollope (ANTHONY).

THE WARDEN. Cr. 8vo., 1s. 6d.

BARCHESTER TOWERS. Cr. 8vo., 1s. 6d.

Walford (L. B.).

LEDDY MARGET. Crown 8vo., 6s.

IVA KILDARE: a Matrimonial Problem. Crown 8vo., 6s.

Walford (L. B.)—*continued.*

MR. SMITH: a Part of his Life. Crown 8vo., 2s. 6d.

THE BABY'S GRANDMOTHER. Cr. 8vo., 2s. 6d.

COUSINS. Crown 8vo., 2s. 6d.

TROUBLESOME DAUGHTERS. Cr 8vo., 2s. 6d.

PAULINE. Crown 8vo., 2s. 6d.

DICK NETHERBY. Cr. 8vo., 2s. 6d.

THE HISTORY OF A WEEK. Cr. 8vo. 2s. 6d.

A STIFF-NECKED GENERATION. Cr. 8vo. 2s. 6d.

NAN, and other Stories. Cr. 8vo., 2s. 6d.

THE MISCHIEF OF MONICA. Cr. 8vo., 2s. 6d.

THE ONE GOOD GUEST. Cr. 8vo. 2s. 6d.

'PLOUGHED,' and other Stories. Crown 8vo., 2s. 6d.

THE MATCHMAKER. Cr. 8vo., 2s. 6d.

Watson.—*RACING AND 'CHASING:* a Collection of Sporting Stories. By ALFRED E. T. WATSON, Editor of the 'Badminton Magazine'. With 16 Plates and 36 Illustrations in the Text. Crown 8vo., 7s. 6d.

Weyman (STANLEY).

THE HOUSE OF THE WOLF. With Frontispiece and Vignette. Crown 8vo., 3s. 6d.

A GENTLEMAN OF FRANCE. With Frontispiece and Vignette. Cr. 8vo., 6s.

THE RED COCKADE. With Frontispiece and Vignette. Crown 8vo., 6s.

SHREWSBURY. With 24 Illustrations by CLAUDE A. SHEPPERSON. Cr. 8vo., 6s.

Whishaw (FRED.).

A BOYAR OF THE TERRIBLE: a Romance of the Court of Ivan the Cruel, First Tzar of Russia. With 12 Illustrations by H. G. MASSEY, A.R.E. Crown 8vo., 6s.

A TSAR'S GRATITUDE: A Story of Modern Russia. Crown 8vo., 6s.

Woods.—*WEEPING FERRY,* and other Stories. By MARGARET L. WOODS, Author of 'A Village Tragedy'. Crown 8vo., 6s.

Popular Science (Natural History, &c.).

Butler.—*OUR HOUSEHOLD INSECTS.* An Account of the Insect-Pests found in Dwelling-Houses. By EDWARD A. BUTLER, B.A., B.Sc. (Lond.). With 113 Illustrations. Crown 8vo., 3s. 6d.

Furneaux (W.).

THE OUTDOOR WORLD; or The Young Collector's Handbook. With 18 Plates (16 of which are coloured), and 549 Illustrations in the Text. Crown 8vo., 7s. 6d.

BUTTERFLIES AND MOTHS (British). With 12 coloured Plates and 241 Illustrations in the Text. Crown 8vo., 7s. 6d.

LIFE IN PONDS AND STREAMS. With 8 coloured Plates and 331 Illustrations in the Text. Crown 8vo., 7s. 6d.

Hartwig (DR. GEORGE).

THE SEA AND ITS LIVING WONDERS. With 12 Plates and 303 Woodcuts. 8vo., 7s. net.

THE TROPICAL WORLD. With 8 Plates and 172 Woodcuts. 8vo., 7s. net.

THE POLAR WORLD. With 3 Maps, 8 Plates and 85 Woodcuts. 8vo., 7s. net.

THE SUBTERRANEAN WORLD. With 3 Maps and 80 Woodcuts. 8vo., 7s. net.

THE AERIAL WORLD. With Map, 8 Plates and 60 Woodcuts. 8vo., 7s. net.

HEROES OF THE POLAR WORLD. With 19 Illustrations. Cr. 8vo., 2s.

WONDERS OF THE TROPICAL FORESTS. With 40 Illustrations. Cr. 8vo., 2s.

WORKERS UNDER THE GROUND. With 29 Illustrations. Cr. 8vo., 2s.

MARVELS OVER OUR HEADS. With 29 Illustrations. Cr. 8vo., 2s.

SEA MONSTERS AND SEA BIRDS. With 75 Illustrations. Cr. 8vo., 2s. 6d.

DENIZENS OF THE DEEP. With 117 Illustrations. Cr. 8vo., 2s. 6d.

Hartwig (DR. GEORGE)—*continued.*

VOLCANOES AND EARTHQUAKES. With 30 Illustrations. Cr. 8vo., 2s. 6d.

WILD ANIMALS OF THE TROPICS. With 66 Illustrations. Cr. 8vo., 3s. 6d.

Helmholtz.—*POPULAR LECTURES ON SCIENTIFIC SUBJECTS.* By HERMANN VON HELMHOLTZ. With 68 Woodcuts. 2 vols. Cr. 8vo., 3s. 6d. each.

Hudson (W. H.).

BRITISH BIRDS. With a Chapter on Structure and Classification by FRANK E. BEDDARD, F.R.S. With 16 Plates (8 of which are Coloured), and over 100 Illustrations in the Text. Cr. 8vo., 7s. 6d.

BIRDS IN LONDON. With 17 Plates and 15 Illustrations in the Text, by BRYAN HOOK, A. D. McCORMICK, and from Photographs from Nature, by R. B. LODGE. 8vo., 12s.

Proctor (RICHARD A.).

LIGHT SCIENCE FOR LEISURE HOURS. Familiar Essays on Scientific Subjects. 3 vols. Cr. 8vo., 5s. each.

ROUGH WAYS MADE SMOOTH. Familiar Essays on Scientific Subjects. Crown 8vo., 3s. 6d.

PLEASANT WAYS IN SCIENCE. Crown 8vo., 3s. 6d.

NATURE STUDIES. By R. A. PROCTOR, GRANT ALLEN, A. WILSON, T. FOSTER and E. CLODD. Crown 8vo., 3s. 6d.

LEISURE READINGS. By R. A. PROCTOR, E. CLODD, A. WILSON, T. FOSTER and A. C. RANYARD. Cr. 8vo., 3s. 6d.

*** *For Mr. Proctor's other books see pp. 13, 28 and 31, and Messrs. Longmans & Co.'s Catalogue of Scientific Works.*

Stanley.—*A FAMILIAR HISTORY OF BIRDS.* By E. STANLEY, D.D., formerly Bishop of Norwich. With 160 Illustrations. Cr. 8vo., 3s. 6d.

Popular Science (Natural History, &c.)—*continued.*

Wood (REV. J. G.).

HOMES WITHOUT HANDS: A Description of the Habitations of Animals, classed according to the Principle of Construction. With 140 Illustrations. 8vo., 7s. net.

INSECTS AT HOME : A Popular Account of British Insects, their Structure, Habits and Transformations. With 700 Illustrations. 8vo., 7s. net.

INSECTS ABROAD : a Popular Account of Foreign Insects, their Structure, Habits and Transformations. With 600 Illustrations. 8vo., 7s. net.

BIBLE ANIMALS : a Description of every Living Creature mentioned in the Scriptures. With 112 Illustrations. 8vo., 7s. net.

PETLAND REVISITED. With 33 Illustrations. Cr. 8vo., 3s. 6d.

OUT OF DOORS ; a Selection of Original Articles on Practical Natural History. With 11 Illustrations. Cr. 8vo., 3s. 6d.

Wood (REV. J. G.)—*continued.*

STRANGE DWELLINGS : a Description of the Habitations of Animals, abridged from ' Homes without Hands '. With 60 Illustrations. Cr. 8vo., 3s. 6d.

BIRD LIFE OF THE BIBLE. With 32 Illustrations. Cr. 8vo., 3s. 6d.

WONDERFUL NESTS. With 30 Illustrations. Cr. 8vo., 3s. 6d.

HOMES UNDER THE GROUND. With 28 Illustrations. Cr. 8vo., 3s. 6d.

WILD ANIMALS OF THE BIBLE. With 29 Illustrations. Cr. 8vo., 3s. 6d.

DOMESTIC ANIMALS OF THE BIBLE. With 23 Illustrations. Cr. 8vo., 3s. 6d.

THE BRANCH BUILDERS. With 28 Illustrations. Cr. 8vo., 2s. 6d.

SOCIAL HABITATIONS AND PARASITIC NESTS. With 18 Illustrations. Crown 8vo., 2s.

Works of Reference.

Gwilt.—*AN ENCYCLOPÆDIA OF ARCHITECTURE.* By JOSEPH GWILT, F.S.A. Illustrated with more than 1100 Engravings on Wood. Revised (1888), with Alterations and Considerable Additions by WYATT PAPWORTH. 8vo, £2 12s. 6d.

Longmans' *GAZETTEER OF THE WORLD.* Edited by GEORGE G. CHISHOLM, M.A., B.Sc. Imp. 8vo., £2 2s. cloth, £2 12s. 6d. half-morocco.

Maunder (Samuel).

BIOGRAPHICAL TREASURY. With Supplement brought down to 1889. By Rev. JAMES WOOD. Fcp. 8vo., 6s.

TREASURY OF GEOGRAPHY, Physical, Historical, Descriptive, and Political. With 7 Maps and 16 Plates. Fcp. 8vo., 6s.

THE TREASURY OF BIBLE KNOWLEDGE. By the Rev. J. AYRE, M.A. With 5 Maps, 15 Plates, and 300 Woodcuts. Fcp. 8vo., 6s.

TREASURY OF KNOWLEDGE AND LIBRARY OF REFERENCE. Fcp. 8vo., 6s.

HISTORICAL TREASURY. Fcp. 8vo., 6s.

Maunder (Samuel)—*continued.*

SCIENTIFIC AND LITERARY TREASURY. Fcp. 8vo., 6s.

THE TREASURY OF BOTANY. Edited by J. LINDLEY, F.R.S., and T. MOORE, F.L.S. With 274 Woodcuts and 20 Steel Plates. 2 vols. Fcp. 8vo., 12s.

Roget. — *THESAURUS OF ENGLISH WORDS AND PHRASES.* Classified and Arranged so as to Facilitate the Expression of Ideas and assist in Literary Composition. By PETER MARK ROGET, M.D., F.R.S. Recomposed throughout, enlarged and improved, partly from the Author's Notes, and with a full Index, by the Author's Son, JOHN LEWIS ROGET. Crown 8vo., 10s. 6d.

Willich.--*POPULAR TABLES* for giving information for ascertaining the value of Lifehold, Leasehold, and Church Property, the Public Funds, etc. By CHARLES M. WILLICH. Edited by H. BENCE JONES. Crown 8vo., 10s. 6d.

Children's Books.

Crake (Rev. A. D.).

EDWY THE FAIR; or, The First Chronicle of Æscendune. Cr. 8vo., 2s. 6d.

ALFGAR THE DANE; or, The Second Chronicle of Æscendune. Cr. 8vo. 2s. 6d.

THE RIVAL HEIRS: being the Third and Last Chronicle of Æscendune. Cr. 8vo., 2s. 6d.

THE HOUSE OF WALDERNE. A Tale of the Cloister and the Forest in the Days of the Barons' Wars. Crown 8vo., 2s. 6d.

BRIAN FITZ-COUNT. A Story of Wallingford Castle and Dorchester Abbey. Cr. 8vo., 2s. 6d.

Lang (ANDREW).—EDITED BY.

THE BLUE FAIRY BOOK. With 138 Illustrations. Crown 8vo., 5s.

THE RED FAIRY BOOK. With 100 Illustrations. Crown 8vo., 6s.

THE GREEN FAIRY BOOK. With 99 Illustrations. Crown 8vo., 6s.

THE YELLOW FAIRY BOOK. With 104 Illustrations. Crown 8vo., 6s.

THE PINK FAIRY BOOK. With 67 Illustrations. Crown 8vo., 6s.

THE BLUE POETRY BOOK. With 100 Illustrations. Crown 8vo., 6s.

THE BLUE POETRY BOOK. School Edition, without Illustrations. Fcp. 8vo., 2s. 6d.

THE TRUE STORY BOOK. With 66 Illustrations. Crown 8vo., 6s.

THE RED TRUE STORY BOOK. With 100 Illustrations. Crown 8vo., 6s.

THE ANIMAL STORY BOOK. With 67 Illustrations. Crown 8vo., 6s.

Molesworth—*SILVERTHORNS.* By Mrs. MOLESWORTH. With 4 Illustrations. Cr. 8vo., 5s.

Meade (L. T.).

DADDY'S BOY. With 8 Illustrations. Crown 8vo., 3s. 6d.

DEB AND THE DUCHESS. With 7 Illustrations. Crown 8vo., 3s. 6d.

THE BERESFORD PRIZE. With 7 Illustrations. Crown 8vo., 3s. 6d.

THE HOUSE OF SURPRISES. With 6 Illustrations. Crown 8vo. 3s. 6d.

Praeger.—*THE ADVENTURES OF THE THREE BOLD BABES: HECTOR, HONORIA AND ALISANDER.* A Story in Pictures. By S. ROSAMOND PRAEGER. With 24 Coloured Plates and 24 Outline Pictures. Oblong 4to., 3s. 6d.

Stevenson.—*A CHILD'S GARDEN OF VERSES.* By ROBERT LOUIS STEVENSON. Fcp. 8vo., 5s.

Sullivan.—*HERE THEY ARE!* More Stories. Written and Illustrated by JAS. F. SULLIVAN. Crown 8vo., 6s.

Upton (FLORENCE K. AND BERTHA).

THE ADVENTURES OF TWO DUTCH DOLLS AND A 'GOLLIWOGG'. With 31 Coloured Plates and numerous Illustrations in the Text. Oblong 4to., 6s.

THE GOLLIWOGG'S BICYCLE CLUB. With 31 Coloured Plates and numerous Illustrations in the Text. Oblong 4to., 6s.

THE VEGE-MEN'S REVENGE. With 31 Coloured Plates and numerous Illustrations in the Text. Oblong 4to., 6s.

Wordsworth.—*THE SNOW GARDEN, AND OTHER FAIRY TALES FOR CHILDREN.* By ELIZABETH WORDSWORTH. With 10 Illustrations by TREVOR HADDON. Crown 8vo., 3s. 6d.

Longmans' Series of Books for Girls.

Price 2s. 6d. each.

ATELIER (THE) DU LYS: or, an Art Student in the Reign of Terror.

BY THE SAME AUTHOR.

MADEMOISELLE MORI: a Tale of Modern Rome.

IN THE OLDEN TIME: a Tale of the Peasant War in Germany.

A YOUNGER SISTER.

THAT CHILD.

UNDER A CLOUD.

HESTER'S VENTURE

THE FIDDLER OF LUGAU.

A CHILD OF THE REVOLUTION.

ATHERSTONE PRIORY. By L. N. COMYN.

THE STORY OF A SPRING MORNING, etc. By Mr. MOLESWORTH. Illustrated.

THE PALACE IN THE GARDEN. By Mrs. MOLESWORTH. Illustrated.

NEIGHBOURS. By Mrs. MOLESWORTH.

THE THIRD MISS ST. QUENTIN. By Mrs. MOLESWORTH.

VERY YOUNG; AND QUITE ANOTHER STORY. Two Stories. By JEAN INGELOW.

CAN THIS BE LOVE? By LOUISA PARR.

KEITH DERAMORE. By the Author of 'Miss Molly'.

SIDNEY. By MARGARET DELAND.

AN ARRANGED MARRIAGE. By DOROTHEA GERARD.

LAST WORDS TO GIRLS ON LIFE AT SCHOOL AND AFTER SCHOOL. By MARIA GREY.

STRAY THOUGHTS FOR GIRLS. By LUCY H. M. SOULSBY. 16mo., 1s. 6d. net.

The Silver Library.

CROWN 8VO.   3s. 6d.   EACH VOLUME.

Arnold's (Sir Edwin) Seas and Lands. With 71 Illustrations. 3s. 6d.

Bagehot's (W.) Biographical Studies. 3s. 6d.

Bagehot's (W.) Economic Studies. 3s. 6d.

Bagehot's (W.) Literary Studies. With Portrait. 3 vols. 3s. 6d. each.

Baker's (Sir S. W.) Eight Years in Ceylon. With 6 Illustrations. 3s. 6d.

Baker's (Sir S. W.) Rifle and Hound in Ceylon. With 6 Illustrations. 3s. 6d.

Baring-Gould's (Rev. S.) Curious Myths of the Middle Ages. 3s. 6d.

Baring-Gould's (Rev. S.) Origin and Development of Religious Belief. 2 vols. 3s. 6d. each.

Becker's (W. A.) Gallus: or, Roman Scenes in the Time of Augustus. With 26 Illus. 3s. 6d.

Becker's (W. A.) Charicles: or, Illustrations of the Private Life of the Ancient Greeks. With 26 Illustrations. 3s. 6d.

Bent's (J. T.) The Ruined Cities of Mashonaland. With 117 Illustrations. 3s. 6d.

Brassey's (Lady) A Voyage in the 'Sunbeam'. With 66 Illustrations. 3s. 6d.

Clodd's (E.) Story of Creation: a Plain Account of Evolution. With 77 Illustrations. 3s. 6d.

Conybeare (Rev. W. J.) and Howson's (Very Rev. J. S.) Life and Epistles of St. Paul. With 46 Illustrations. 3s. 6d.

Dougall's (L.) Beggars All: a Novel. 3s. 6d.

Doyle's (A. Conan) Micah Clarke. A Tale of Monmouth's Rebellion. With 10 Illusts. 3s. 6d.

Doyle's (A. Conan) The Captain of the Polestar, and other Tales. 3s. 6d.

Doyle's (A. Conan) The Refugees: A Tale of the Huguenots. With 25 Illustrations. 3s 6d.

Doyle's (A. Conan) The Stark Munro Letters. 3s. 6d.

Froude's (J. A.) The History of England, from the Fall of Wolsey to the Defeat of the Spanish Armada. 12 vols. 3s. 6d. each.

Froude's (J. A.) The English in Ireland. 3 vols. 10s. 6d.

Froude's (J. A.) The Divorce of Catherine of Aragon. 3s. 6d.

Froude's (J. A.) The Spanish Story of the Armada, and other Essays. 3s. 6d.

Froude's (J. A.) Short Studies on Great Subjects. 4 vols. 3s. 6d. each.

Froude's (J. A.) Oceana, or England and Her Colonies. With 9 Illustrations. 3s. 6d.

Froude's (J. A.) The Council of Trent. 3s. 6d.

Froude's (J. A.) Thomas Carlyle: a History of his Life.
1795-1835. 2 vols. 7s.
1834-1881. 2 vols. 7s.

Froude's (J. A.) Cæsar: a Sketch. 3s. 6d.

Froude's (J. A.) The Two Chiefs of Dunboy: an Irish Romance of the Last Century. 3s. 6d.

Gleig's (Rev. G. R.) Life of the Duke of Wellington. With Portrait. 3s. 6d.

Greville's (C. C. F.) Journal of the Reigns of King George IV., King William IV., and Queen Victoria. 8 vols., 3s. 6d. each.

Haggard's (H. R.) She: A History of Adventure. With 32 Illustrations. 3s. 6d.

Haggard's (H. R.) Allan Quatermain. With 20 Illustrations. 3s. 6d.

Haggard's (H. R.) Colonel Quaritch, V.C.: a Tale of Country Life. With Frontispiece and Vignette. 3s. 6d.

Haggard's (H. R.) Cleopatra. With 29 Illustrations. 3s. 6d.

Haggard's (H. R.) Eric Brighteyes. With 51 Illustrations. 3s. 6d.

Haggard's (H. R.) Beatrice. With Frontispiece and Vignette. 3s. 6d.

Haggard's (H. R.) Allan's Wife. With 34 Illustrations. 3s. 6d.

Haggard (H. R.) Heart of the World. With 15 Illustrations. 3s. 6d.

Haggard's (H. R.) Montezuma's Daughter. With 25 Illustrations. 3s. 6d.

Haggard's (H. R.) The Witch's Head. With 16 Illustrations. 3s. 6d.

Haggard's (H. R.) Mr. Meeson's Will. With 16 Illustrations. 3s. 6d.

Haggard's (H. R.) Nada the Lily. With 23 Illustrations. 3s. 6d.

Haggard's (H. R.) Dawn. With 16 Illusts. 3s. 6d.

Haggard's (H. R.) The People of the Mist. With 16 Illustrations. 3s. 6d.

Haggard's (H. R.) Joan Haste. With 20 Illustrations. 3s. 6d.

Haggard (H. R.) and Lang's (A.) The World's Desire. With 27 Illustrations. 3s. 6d.

Harte's (Bret) In the Carquinez Woods and other Stories. 3s. 6d.

Helmholtz's (Hermann von) Popular Lectures on Scientific Subjects. With 68 Illustrations. 2 vols. 3s. 6d. each.

Hornung's (E. W.) The Unbidden Guest. 3s. 6d.

Howitt's (W.) Visits to Remarkable Places. With 80 Illustrations. 3s. 6d.

Jefferies' (R.) The Story of My Heart: My Autobiography. With Portrait. 3s. 6d.

Jefferies' (R.) Field and Hedgerow. With Portrait. 3s. 6d.

Jefferies' (R.) Red Deer. With 17 Illusts. 3s. 6d.

Jefferies' (R.) Wood Magic: a Fable. With Frontispiece and Vignette by E. V. B. 3s. 6d.

Jefferies (R.) The Toilers of the Field. With Portrait from the Bust in Salisbury Cathedral. 3s. 6d.

Kaye (Sir J.) and Malleson's (Colonel) History of the Indian Mutiny of 1857-8. 6 vols. 3s. 6d. each.

Knight's (E. F.) The Cruise of the 'Alerte': the Narrative of a Search for Treasure on the Desert Island of Trinidad. With 2 Maps and 23 Illustrations. 3s. 6d.

Knight's (E. F.) Where Three Empires Meet: a Narrative of Recent Travel in Kashmir, Western Tibet, Baltistan, Gilgit. With a Map and 54 Illustrations. 3s. 6d.

Knight's (E. F.) The 'Falcon' on the Baltic: a Coasting Voyage from Hammersmith to Copenhagen in a Three-Ton Yacht. With Map and 11 Illustrations. 3s. 6d.

Köstlin's (J.) Life of Luther. With 62 Illustrations and 4 Facsimiles of MSS. 3s. 6d.

Lang's (A.) Angling Sketches. With 20 Illustrations. 3s. 6d.

Lang's (A.) Custom and Myth: Studies of Early Usage and Belief. 3s. 6d.

The Silver Library—*continued.*

Lang's (A.) Cock Lane and Common-Sense. 3*s.* 6*d.*

Lang's (A.) The Monk of Fife: a Story of the Days of Joan of Arc. With 13 Illusts. 3*s.* 6*d.*

Lees (J. A.) and Clutterbuck's (W. J.) B. C. 1887, A Ramble in British Columbia. With Maps and 75 Illustrations. 3*s.* 6*d.*

Macaulay's (Lord) Essays and Lays of Ancient Rome, etc. With Portrait and 4 Illustrations to the 'Lays'. 3*s.* 6*d.*

Macleod's (H. D.) Elements of Banking. 3*s.* 6*d.*

Marbot's (Baron de) Memoirs. Translated. 2 vols. 7*s.*

Marshman's (J. C.) Memoirs of Sir Henry Havelock. 3*s.* 6*d.*

Merivale's (Dean) History of the Romans under the Empire. 8 vols. 3*s.* 6*d.* each.

Merriman's (H. S.) Flotsam: A Tale of the Indian Mutiny. 3*s.* 6*d.*

Mill's (J. S.) Political Economy. 3*s.* 6*d.*

Mill's (J. S.) System of Logic. 3*s.* 6*d.*

Milner's (Geo.) Country Pleasures: the Chronicle of a Year chiefly in a Garden. 3*s.* 6*d.*

Nansen's (F.) The First Crossing of Greenland. With 142 Illustrations and a Map. 3*s.* 6*d.*

Phillipps-Wolley's (C.) Snap: a Legend of the Lone Mountain With 13 Illustrations. 3*s.* 6*d.*

Proctor's (R. A.) The Orbs Around Us. 3*s.* 6*d.*

Proctor's (R. A.) The Expanse of Heaven. 3*s.* 6*d.*

Proctor's (R. A.) Light Science for Leisure Hours. First Series. 3*s.* 6*d.*

Proctor's (R. A.) The Moon. 3*s.* 6*d.*

Proctor's (R. A.) Other Worlds than Ours. 3*s.* 6*d.*

Proctor's (R. A.) Our Place among Infinities: a Series of Essays contrasting our Little Abode in Space and Time with the Infinities around us. 3*s.* 6*d.*

Proctor's (R. A.) Other Suns than Ours. 3*s.* 6*d.*

Proctor's (R. A.) Rough Ways made Smooth. 3*s.* 6*d.*

Proctor's (R. A.) Pleasant Ways in Science. 3*s.* 6*d.*

Proctor's (R. A.) Myths and Marvels of Astronomy. 3*s.* 6*d.*

Proctor's (R. A.) Nature Studies. 3*s.* 6*d.*

Proctor's (R. A.) Leisure Readings. By R. A. PROCTOR, EDWARD CLODD, ANDREW WILSON, THOMAS FOSTER, and A. C. RANYARD. With Illustrations. 3*s.* 6*d.*

Rhoscomyl's (Owen) The Jewel of Ynys Galon. With 12 Illustrations. 3*s.* 6*d.*

Rossetti's (Maria F.) A Shadow of Dante. 3*s.* 6*d.*

Smith's (R. Bosworth) Carthage and the Carthaginians. With Maps, Plans, etc. 3*s.* 6*d.*

Stanley's (Bishop) Familiar History of Birds. With 160 Illustrations. 3*s.* 6*d.*

Stevenson's (R. L.) The Strange Case of Dr. Jekyll and Mr. Hyde; with other Fables. 3*s.* 6*d.*

Stevenson (R. L.) and Osbourne's (Ll.) The Wrong Box. 3*s.* 6*d.*

Stevenson (Robert Louis) and Stevenson's (Fanny van de Grift) More New Arabian Nights.—The Dynamiter. 3*s.* 6*d.*

Weyman's (Stanley J.) The House of the Wolf: a Romance. 3*s.* 6*d.*

Wood's (Rev. J. G.) Petland Revisited. With 33 Illustrations. 3*s.* 6*d.*

Wood's (Rev. J. G.) Strange Dwellings. With 60 Illustrations. 3*s.* 6*d.*

Wood's (Rev. J. G.) Out of Doors. With 11 Illustrations. 3*s.* 6*d.*

Cookery, Domestic Management, &c.

Acton. — *MODERN COOKERY.* By ELIZA ACTON. With 150 Woodcuts. Fcp. 8vo., 4*s.* 6*d.*

Buckton.—*COMFORT AND CLEANLINESS:* The Servant and Mistress Question. By Mrs. CATHERINE M. BUCKTON, late Member of the Leeds School Board. With 14 Illustrations. Crown 8vo., 2*s.*

Bull (THOMAS, M.D.).

HINTS TO MOTHERS ON THE MANAGEMENT OF THEIR HEALTH DURING THE PERIOD OF PREGNANCY. Fcp. 8vo., 1*s.* 6*d.*

THE MATERNAL MANAGEMENT OF CHILDREN IN HEALTH AND DISEASE. Fcp. 8vo., 1*s.* 6*d.*

De Salis (MRS.).

CAKES AND CONFECTIONS À LA MODE. Fcp. 8vo., 1*s.* 6*d.*

DOGS: A Manual for Amateurs. Fcp. 8vo., 1*s.* 6*d.*

DRESSED GAME AND POULTRY À LA MODE. Fcp. 8vo., 1*s.* 6*d.*

De Salis (MRS.).—*continued.*

DRESSED VEGETABLES À LA MODE. Fcp. 8vo., 1*s.* 6*d.*

DRINKS À LA MODE. Fcp. 8vo., 1*s.* 6*d.*

ENTRÉES À LA MODE. Fcp. 8vo., 1*s.* 6*d.*

FLORAL DECORATIONS. Fcp. 8vo., 1*s.* 6*d.*

GARDENING À LA MODE. Fcp. 8vo. Part I., Vegetables, 1*s.* 6*d.* Part II., Fruits, 1*s.* 6*d.*

NATIONAL VIANDS À LA MODE. Fcp. 8vo., 1*s.* 6*d.*

NEW-LAID EGGS. Fcp. 8vo., 1*s.* 6*d.*

OYSTERS À LA MODE. Fcp. 8vo., 1*s.* 6*d.*

PUDDINGS AND PASTRY À LA MODE. Fcp. 8vo., 1*s.* 6*d.*

SAVOURIES À LA MODE. Fcp. 8vo., 1*s.* 6*d.*

SOUPS AND DRESSED FISH À LA MODE. Fcp. 8vo., 1*s.* 6*d.*

Cookery, Domestic Management, &c.—*continued.*

De Salis (MRS.)—*continued.*

SWEETS AND SUPPER DISHES à LA MODE. Fcp. 8vo., 1s. 6d.

TEMPTING DISHES FOR SMALL INCOMES. Fcp. 8vo., 1s. 6d.

WRINKLES AND NOTIONS FOR EVERY HOUSEHOLD. Crown 8vo., 1s. 6d.

Lear.—MAIGRE COOKERY. By H. L. SIDNEY LEAR. 16mo., 2s.

Poole.—COOKERY FOR THE DIABETIC. By W. H. and Mrs. POOLE. With Preface by Dr. PAVY. Fcp. 8vo., 2s. 6d.

Walker (JANE H.).

A BOOK FOR EVERY WOMAN. Part I., The Management of Children in Health and out of Health. Crown 8vo., 2s. 6d.

Part II. Woman in Health and out of Health. Crown 8vo., 2s. 6d.

A HANDBOOK FOR MOTHERS: being Simple Hints to Women on the Management of their Health during Pregnancy and Confinement, together with Plain Directions as to the Care of Infants. Crown 8vo., 2s. 6d.

Miscellaneous and Critical Works.

Allingham.—VARIETIES IN PROSE. By WILLIAM ALLINGHAM. 3 vols. Cr. 8vo., 18s. (Vols. 1 and 2, Rambles, by PATRICIUS WALKER. Vol. 3, Irish Sketches, etc.)

Armstrong.—ESSAYS AND SKETCHES. By EDMUND J. ARMSTRONG. Fcp. 8vo., 5s.

Bagehot.—LITERARY STUDIES. By WALTER BAGEHOT. With Portrait. 3 vols. Crown 8vo., 3s. 6d. each.

Baring-Gould.—CURIOUS MYTHS OF THE MIDDLE AGES. By Rev. S. BARING-GOULD. Crown 8vo., 3s. 6d.

Baynes. — SHAKESPEARE STUDIES, and other Essays. By the late THOMAS SPENCER BAYNES, LL.B., LL.D. With a Biographical Preface by Professor LEWIS CAMPBELL. Crown 8vo., 7s. 6d.

Boyd (A. K. H.) ('**A.K.H.B.**').

And see MISCELLANEOUS THEOLOGICAL WORKS, p. 32.

AUTUMN HOLIDAYS OF A COUNTRY PARSON. Crown 8vo., 3s. 6d.

COMMONPLACE PHILOSOPHER. Cr. 8vo., 3s. 6d.

CRITICAL ESSAYS OF A COUNTRY PARSON. Crown. 8vo., 3s. 6d.

EAST COAST DAYS AND MEMORIES. Crown 8vo., 3s. 6d.

LANDSCAPES, CHURCHES, AND MORALITIES. Crown 8vo., 3s. 6d.

LEISURE HOURS IN TOWN. Crown 8vo., 3s. 6d.

LESSONS OF MIDDLE AGE. Crown 8vo., 3s. 6d.

OUR LITTLE LIFE. Two Series. Crown 8vo., 3s. 6d. each.

OUR HOMELY COMEDY: AND TRAGEDY. Crown 8vo., 3s. 6d.

RECREATIONS OF A COUNTRY PARSON. Three Series. Crown 8vo., 3s. 6d. each.

Brookings and Ringwalt.—BRIEFS AND DEBATE ON CURRENT, POLITICAL, ECONOMIC AND SOCIAL TOPICS. Edited by W. DU BOIS BROOKINGS, A.B. of the Harvard Law School, and RALPH CURTIS RINGWALT, A.B. Assistant in Rhetoric in Columbia University, New York. With an Introduction on 'The Art of Debate' by ALBERT BUSHNELL HART, Ph.D. of Harvard University. With full Index. Crown 8vo., 6s.

Butler (SAMUEL).

EREWHON. Crown 8vo., 5s.

THE FAIR HAVEN. A Work in Defence of the Miraculous Element in our Lord's Ministry. Cr. 8vo., 7s. 6d.

LIFE AND HABIT. An Essay after a Completer View of Evolution. Cr. 8vo., 7s. 6d.

EVOLUTION, OLD AND NEW. Cr. 8vo., 10s. 6d.

ALPS AND SANCTUARIES OF PIEDMONT AND CANTON TICINO. Illustrated. Pott 4to., 10s. 6d.

LUCK, OR CUNNING, AS THE MAIN MEANS OF ORGANIC MODIFICATION? Cr. 8vo., 7s. 6d.

EX VOTO. An Account of the Sacro Monte or New Jerusalem at Varallo-Sesia. Crown 8vo., 10s. 6d.

SELECTIONS FROM WORKS, with Remarks on Mr. G. J. Romanes' 'Mental Evolution in Animals,' and a Psalm of Montreal. Crown 8vo., 7s. 6d.

THE AUTHORESS OF THE ODYSSEY, WHERE AND WHEN SHE WROTE, WHO SHE WAS, THE USE SHE MADE OF THE ILIAD, AND HOW THE POEM GREW UNDER HER HANDS. With 14 Illustrations. 8vo., 10s. 6d.

Miscellaneous and Critical Works—*continued*.

CHARITIES REGISTER, THE ANNUAL, AND DIGEST: being a Classified Register of Charities in or available in the Metropolis, together with a Digest of Information respecting the Legal, Voluntary, and other Means for the Prevention and Relief of Distress, and the Improvement of the Condition of the Poor, and an Elaborate Index. With an Introduction by C. S. LOCH, Secretary to the Council of the Charity Organisation Society, London. 8vo., 4s.

Dowell.—*THOUGHTS AND WORDS.* By STEPHEN DOWELL. 3 vols. Crown 8vo., 31s. 6d.

*** This is a selection of passages in prose and verse from authors, ancient and modern, arranged according to the subject.*

Dreyfus.—*LECTURES ON FRENCH LITERATURE.* Delivered in Melbourne by IRMA DREYFUS. With Portrait of the Author. Large crown 8vo., 12s. 6d.

Evans.—*THE ANCIENT STONE IMPLEMENTS, WEAPONS AND ORNAMENTS OF GREAT BRITAIN.* By Sir JOHN EVANS, K.C.B., D.C.L., LL.D., F.R.S., etc. With 537 Illustrations. Medium 8vo., 28s.

Hamlin.—*A TEXT-BOOK OF THE HISTORY OF ARCHITECTURE.* By A. D. F. HAMLIN, A.M. With 229 Illustrations. Crown 8vo., 7s. 6d.

Haweis.—*MUSIC AND MORALS.* By the Rev. H. R. HAWEIS. With Portrait of the Author, and numerous Illustrations, Facsimiles, and Diagrams. Cr. 8vo., 7s. 6d.

Hime.—*STRAY MILITARY PAPERS.* By Lieut.-Colonel H. W. L. HIME (late Royal Artillery). 8vo, 7s. 6d.

CONTENTS.— Infantry Fire Formations— On Marking at Rifle Matches—The Progress of Field Artillery—The Reconnoitering Duties of Cavalry.

Hullah.—*THE HISTORY OF MODERN MUSIC;* a Course of Lectures. By JOHN HULLAH, LL.D. 8vo., 8s. 6d.

Jefferies (RICHARD).

FIELD AND HEDGEROW: With Portrait. Crown 8vo., 3s. 6d.

THE STORY OF MY HEART: my Autobiography. With Portrait and New Preface by C. J. LONGMAN. Cr. 8vo., 3s. 6d.

RED DEER. With 17 Illustrations by J. CHARLTON and H. TUNALY. Crown 8vo., 3s. 6d.

THE TOILERS OF THE FIELD. With Portrait from the Bust in Salisbury Cathedral. Crown 8vo., 3s. 6d.

Jefferies (RICHARD)—*continued*.

WOOD MAGIC: a Fable. With Frontispiece and Vignette by E. V. B. Crown 8vo., 3s. 6d.

THOUGHTS FROM THE WRITINGS OF RICHARD JEFFERIES. Selected by H. S. HOOLE WAYLEN. 16mo., 3s. 6d.

Johnson.—*THE PATENTEE'S MANUAL:* a Treatise on the Law and Practice of Letters Patent. By J. & J. H. JOHNSON, Patent Agents, etc. 8vo., 10s. 6d.

Joyce.—*THE ORIGIN AND HISTORY OF IRISH NAMES OF PLACES.* By P. W. JOICE, LL.D. 2 vols. Crown 8vo., 5s. each.

Lang (ANDREW).

THE MAKING OF RELIGION. 8vo.

MODERN MYTHOLOGY: a Reply to Professor Max Müller. 8vo., 9s.

LETTERS TO DEAD AUTHORS. Fcp. 8vo., 2s. 6d. net.

BOOKS AND BOOKMEN. With 2 Coloured Plates and 17 Illustrations. Fcp. 8vo., 2s. 6d. net.

OLD FRIENDS. Fcp. 8vo., 2s. 6d. net.

LETTERS ON LITERATURE. Fcp. 8vo., 2s. 6d. net.

ESSAYS IN LITTLE. With Portrait of the Author. Crown 8vo., 2s. 6d.

COCK LANE AND COMMON-SENSE. Crown 8vo., 3s. 6d.

THE BOOK OF DREAMS AND GHOSTS. Crown 8vo., 6s.

Macfarren. — *LECTURES ON HARMONY.* By Sir GEORGE A. MACFARREN. 8vo., 12s.

Madden.—*THE DIARY OF MASTER WILLIAM SILENCE:* a Study of Shakespeare and Elizabethan Sport. By the Right Hon. D. H. MADDEN, Vice-Chancellor of the University of Dublin. 8vo., 16s.

Max Müller (The Right Hon. F.).

INDIA: WHAT CAN IT TEACH US? Crown 8vo., 3s. 6d.

CHIPS FROM A GERMAN WORKSHOP.
Vol. I. Recent Essays and Addresses. Crown 8vo., 5s.
Vol. II. Biographical Essays. Crown 8vo., 5s.
Vol. III. Essays on Language and Literature. Crown 8vo., 5s.
Vol. IV. Essays on Mythology and Folk Lore. Crown 8vo., 5s.

CONTRIBUTIONS TO THE SCIENCE OF MYTHOLOGY. 2 vols. 8vo., 32s.

Miscellaneous and Critical Works—*continued.*

Milner.—*COUNTRY PLEASURES :* the Chronicle of a Year chiefly in a Garden. By GEORGE MILNER. Crown 8vo., 3*s.* 6*d.*

Morris (WILLIAM).

SIGNS OF CHANGE. Seven Lectures delivered on various Occasions. Post 8vo., 4*s.* 6*d.*

HOPES AND FEARS FOR ART. Five Lectures delivered in Birmingham, London, etc., in 1878-1881. Crown 8vo., 4*s.* 6*d.*

AN ADDRESS DELIVERED AT THE DISTRIBUTION OF PRIZES TO STUDENTS OF THE BIRMINGHAM MUNICIPAL SCHOOL OF ART ON 21ST FEBRUARY, 1894. 8vo., 2*s.* 6*d.* net.

Orchard.—*THE ASTRONOMY OF 'MILTON'S PARADISE LOST'.* By THOMAS N. ORCHARD, M.D., Member of the British Astronomical Association. With 13 Illustrations. 8vo., 6*s.* net.

Poore (GEORGE VIVIAN), M.D., F.R.C.P.

ESSAYS ON RURAL HYGIENE. With 13 Illustrations. Crown 8vo., 6*s.* 6*d.*

THE DWELLING HOUSE. With 36 Illustrations. Crown 8vo., 3*s.* 6*d.*

Proctor.—*STRENGTH :* How to get Strong and keep Strong, with Chapters on Rowing and Swimming, Fat, Age, and the Waist. By R. A. PROCTOR. With 9 Illustrations. Crown 8vo., 2*s.*

Richmond.—*BOYHOOD :* a Plea for Continuity in Education. By ENNIS RICHMOND. Crown 8vo., 2*s.* 6*d.*

Rossetti. --*A SHADOW OF DANTE :* being an Essay towards studying Himself, his World and his Pilgrimage. By MARIA FRANCESCA ROSSETTI. With Frontispiece by DANTE GABRIEL ROSSETTI. Crown 8vo., 3*s.* 6*d.*

Solovyoff.—*A MODERN PRIESTESS OF ISIS* (*MADAME BLAVATSKY*). Abridged and Translated on Behalf of the Society for Psychical Research from the Russian of VSEVOLOD SERGYEEVICH SOLOVYOFF. By WALTER LEAF, Litt. D. With Appendices. Crown 8vo., 6*s.*

Soulsby (LUCY H. M.).

STRAY THOUGHTS ON READING. Small 8vo., 2*s.* 6*d.* net.

STRAY THOUGHTS FOR GIRLS. 16mo., 1*s.* 6*d.* net.

STRAY THOUGHTS FOR MOTHERS AND TEACHERS. Fcp. 8vo., 2*s.* 6*d.* net.

STRAY THOUGHTS FOR INVALIDS. 16mo., 2*s.* net.

Southey.—*THE CORRESPONDENCE OF ROBERT SOUTHEY WITH CAROLINE BOWLES.* Edited, with an Introduction, by EDWARD DOWDEN, LL.D. 8vo., 14*s.*

Stevens.—*ON THE STOWAGE OF SHIPS AND THEIR CARGOES.* With Information regarding Freights, Charter-Parties, etc. By ROBERT WHITE STEVENS, Associate-Member of the Institute of Naval Architects. 8vo., 21*s.*

Turner and Sutherland.—*THE DEVELOPMENT OF AUSTRALIAN LITERATURE.* By HENRY GYLES TURNER and ALEXANDER SUTHERLAND. With Portraits and Illustrations. Crown 8vo., 5*s.*

Warwick.—*PROGRESS IN WOMEN'S EDUCATION IN THE BRITISH EMPIRE :* being the Report of Conferences and a Congress held in connection with the Educational Section, Victorian Era Exhibition. Edited by the COUNTESS OF WARWICK. Crown 8vo., 6*s.*

White.—*AN EXAMINATION OF THE CHARGE OF APOSTACY AGAINST WORDSWORTH.* By W. HALE WHITE, Editor of the 'Description of the Wordsworth and Coleridge MSS. in the Possession of Mr. T. Norton Longman '.

Miscellaneous Theological Works.

•₊• *For Church of England and Roman Catholic Works see* MESSRS. LONGMANS & CO.'S *Special Catalogues.*

Balfour. — *THE FOUNDATIONS OF BELIEF :* being Notes Introductory to the Study of Theology. By the Right Hon. ARTHUR J. BALFOUR, M.P. 8vo., 12*s.* 6*d.*

Bird (ROBERT).

A CHILD'S RELIGION. Cr. 8vo., 2*s.*

JOSEPH, THE DREAMER. Crown 8vo., 5*s.*

Bird (ROBERT)—*continued.*

JESUS, THE CARPENTER OF NAZARETH. Crown 8vo., 5*s.*

To be had also in Two Parts, price 2*s.* 6*d.* each.

    Part I. GALILEE AND THE LAKE OF GENNESARET.

    Part II. JERUSALEM AND THE PERÆA.

Miscellaneous Theological Works—*continued*.

Boyd (A. K. H.) ('**A.K.H.B.**').

OCCASIONAL AND IMMEMORIAL DAYS: Discourses. Crown 8vo., 7s. 6d.

COUNSEL AND COMFORT FROM A CITY PULPIT. Crown 8vo., 3s. 6d.

SUNDAY AFTERNOONS IN THE PARISH CHURCH OF A SCOTTISH UNIVERSITY CITY. Crown 8vo., 3s. 6d.

CHANGED ASPECTS OF UNCHANGED TRUTHS. Crown 8vo., 3s. 6d.

GRAVER THOUGHTS OF A COUNTRY PARSON. Three Series. Crown 8vo., 3s. 6d. each.

PRESENT DAY THOUGHTS. Crown 8vo., 3s. 6d.

SEASIDE MUSINGS. Cr. 8vo., 3s. 6d.

' *TO MEET THE DAY* ' through the Christian Year : being a Text of Scripture, with an Original Meditation and a Short Selection in Verse for Every Day. Crown 8vo., 4s. 6d.

Davidson.—*THEISM*, as Grounded in Human Nature, Historically and Critically Handled. Being the Burnett Lectures for 1892 and 1893, delivered at Aberdeen. By WILLIAM L. DAVIDSON, M.A., LL.D. 8vo., 15s.

Gibson.—*THE ABBÉ DE LAMENNAIS. AND THE LIBERAL CATHOLIC MOVEMENT IN FRANCE.* By the Hon. W. GIBSON. With Portrait. 8vo., 12s. 6d.

Kalisch (M. M., Ph.D.).

BIBLE STUDIES. Part I. Prophecies of Balaam. 8vo., 10s. 6d. Part II. The Book of Jonah. 8vo., 10s. 6d.

COMMENTARY ON THE OLD TESTAMENT: with a New Translation. Vol. I. Genesis. 8vo., 18s. Or adapted for the General Reader. 12s. Vol. II. Exodus. 15s. Or adapted for the General Reader. 12s. Vol. III. Leviticus, Part I. 15s. Or adapted for the General Reader. 8s. Vol. IV. Leviticus, Part II. 15s. Or adapted for the General Reader. 8s.

Lang.—*THE MAKING OF RELIGION.* By ANDREW LANG. 8vo., 12s.

MacDonald (GEORGE).

UNSPOKEN SERMONS. Three Series. Crown 8vo., 3s. 6d. each.

THE MIRACLES OF OUR LORD. Crown 8vo., 3s. 6d.

Martineau (JAMES).

HOURS OF THOUGHT ON SACRED THINGS : Sermons, 2 vols. Crown 8vo., 3s. 6d. each.

ENDEAVOURS AFTER THE CHRISTIAN LIFE. Discourses. Crown 8vo., 7s. 6d.

THE SEAT OF AUTHORITY IN RELIGION. 8vo., 14s.

ESSAYS, REVIEWS, AND ADDRESSES. 4 Vols. Crown 8vo., 7s. 6d. each.

I. Personal; Political. II. Ecclesiastical; Historical. III. Theological; Philosophical. IV. Academical; Religious.

HOME PRAYERS, with *TWO SERVICES* for Public Worship. Crown 8vo., 3s. 6d.

Max Müller (F.).

THE ORIGIN AND GROWTH OF RELIGION, as illustrated by the Religions of India. The Hibbert Lectures, delivered at the Chapter House, Westminster Abbey, in 1878. Crown 8vo., 7s. 6d.

INTRODUCTION TO THE SCIENCE OF RELIGION : Four Lectures delivered at the Royal Institution. Crown 8vo., 3s. 6d.

NATURAL RELIGION. The Gifford Lectures, delivered before the University of Glasgow in 1888. Crown 8vo., 5s.

PHYSICAL RELIGION. The Gifford Lectures, delivered before the University of Glasgow in 1890. Crown 8vo., 5s.

ANTHROPOLOGICAL RELIGION. The Gifford Lectures, delivered before the University of Glasgow in 1891. Cr. 8vo., 5s.

THEOSOPHY, OR PSYCHOLOGICAL RELIGION. The Gifford Lectures, delivered before the University of Glasgow in 1892. Crown 8vo., 5s.

THREE LECTURES ON THE VEDÂNTA PHILOSOPHY, delivered at the Royal Institution in March, 1894. 8vo., 5s.

Romanes.—*THOUGHTS ON RELIGION.* By GEORGE J. ROMANES, LL.D., F.R.S. Crown 8vo., 4s. 6d.

Vivekananda.—*YOGA PHILOSOPHY :* Lectures delivered in New York, Winter of 1895-96, by the SWAMI VIVEKANANDA, on Raja Yoga ; or, Conquering the Internal Nature ; also Patanjali's Yoga Aphorisms, with Commentaries. Crown 8vo, 3s. 6d.

www.ingramcontent.com/pod-product-compliance
Lightning Source LLC
Chambersburg PA
CBHW031054110726
47900CB00003B/923